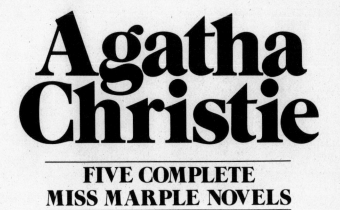

Agatha Christie

FIVE COMPLETE
MISS MARPLE NOVELS

Agatha Christie

FIVE COMPLETE
MISS MARPLE NOVELS

The Mirror Crack'd

A Caribbean Mystery

Nemesis

What Mrs. McGillicuddy Saw!

The Body in the Library

AVENEL BOOKS · NEW YORK

Copyright © 1980 by Agatha Christie Ltd.
Nemesis Copyright © Agatha Christie Limited, MCMLXXI.
A Caribbean Mystery Copyright © MCMLXIV by Agatha Christie Ltd.
The Mirror Crack'd © Agatha Christie Ltd., MCMLXII. (Published in England as *The Mirror Crack'd from Side to Side*)
What Mrs. McGillicuddy Saw! © MCMLVII by Agatha Christie Ltd. (Published in England as *The 4:50 from Paddington*)
The Body in the Library Copyright MCMXLI, MCMXLII by Agatha Christie Mallowan. Copyright renewed MCMLXVIII, MCMLXX by Agatha Christie Mallowan.
All rights reserved.

This 1980 edition is published by Avenel Books,
distributed by Crown Publishers, Inc., 225 Park Avenue South, New York, New York 10003,
by arrangement with Dodd, Mead & Company.

Manufactured in the United States of America

Library of Congress Cataloging in Publication Data

Christie, Agatha Miller, Dame, 1891-1976.
    Five complete Miss Marple novels.

    CONTENTS: Nemesis.—A Caribbean mystery.—The mirror crack'd.—[etc.]
    1. Detective and mystery stories, English.
I. Title.
PZ3.C4637Fh [PR60005.H66] 823'.912 80-23686
ISBN 0-517-321777 (jacketed edition)
ISBN 0-517-321769 (library edition)

aa z y x

CONTENTS

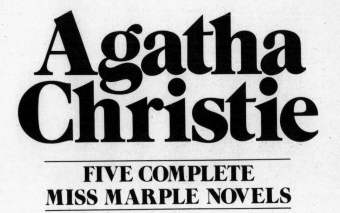

Agatha Christie

FIVE COMPLETE
MISS MARPLE NOVELS

The Mirror Crack'd

To
Margaret Rutherford
in admiration

Out flew the web and floated wide;
   The mirror crack'd from side to side;
"The curse is come upon me," cried
   The Lady of Shalott.

—ALFRED TENNYSON

CAST OF CHARACTERS

CHAPTER ONE

I

MISS JANE MARPLE was sitting by her window. The window looked over her garden, once a source of pride to her. That was no longer so. Nowadays she looked out of the window and winced. Active gardening had been forbidden her for some time now. No stooping, no digging, no planting—at most a little light pruning. Old Laycock, who came three times a week, did his best, no doubt. But his best, such as it was (which was not much), was only the best according to his lights, and not according to those of his employer. Miss Marple knew exactly what she wanted done, and when she wanted it done, and instructed him duly. Old Laycock then displayed his particular genius which was that of enthusiastic agreement and subsequent lack of performance.

"That's right, missus. We'll have them mecosoapies there and the Canterburys along the wall and as you say, it ought to be got on with first thing next week."

Laycock's excuses were always reasonable, and strongly resembled those of Captain George's in *Three Men in a Boat* for avoiding going to sea. In the captain's case the wind was always wrong, either blowing offshore or inshore, or coming from the unreliable west, or the even more treacherous east. Laycock's was the weather. Too dry—too wet—waterlogged—a nip of frost in the air. Or else something of great importance had to come first (usually to do with cabbages or Brussels sprouts, of which he liked to grow inordinate quantities). Laycock's own principles of gardening were simple, and no employer, however knowledgeable, could wean him from them.

They consisted of a great many cups of tea, sweet and strong, as an encouragement to effort, a good deal of sweeping up of leaves in the autumn, and a certain amount of bedding out of his own favorite plants, mainly asters and salvias—to "make a nice show," as he put it, in summer. He was all in favor of syringing roses for green-fly, but was slow to get around to it, and a demand for deep trenching for sweet peas was usually countered by the remark that you ought to see his own sweet peas! A proper treat last year, and no fancy stuff done beforehand.

To be fair, he was attached to his employers, humored their fancies in horticulture (so far as no actual hard work was involved) but vegetables he knew to be the real stuff of life; a nice Savoy, or a bit of curly kale; flowers were fancy stuff such as ladies liked to go in for, having nothing better to do with their time. He showed his affection by producing presents of the aforementioned asters, salvias, lobelia edging, and summer chrysanthemums.

"Been doing some work at them new houses over at the Development. Want their gardens laid out nice, they do. More plants than they needed so I brought along a few, and I've put 'em in where them old-fashioned roses ain't looking so well."

Thinking of these things, Miss Marple averted her eyes from the garden, and picked up her knitting.

One had to face the fact: St. Mary Mead was not the place it had been. In a sense, of course, nothing was what it had been. You could blame the war (both the wars), or the younger generation, or women going out to work, or the atom bomb, or just the Government—but what one really meant was the simple fact that one was growing old. Miss Marple, who was a very sensible old lady, knew that quite well. It was just that, in a queer way, she felt it more in St. Mary Mead, because it had been her home for so long.

St. Mary Mead, the old-world core of it, was still there. The Blue Boar was there, and the church and the Vicarage and the little nest of Queen Anne and Georgian houses, of which hers was one. Miss Hartnell's house was still there, and also Miss Hartnell, fighting progress to the last gasp. Miss Wetherby had passed on and her house was now inhabited by the bank manager and his family, having been given a face lift by the painting of doors and windows a bright royal blue. There were new people in most of the other old houses, but the houses themselves were little changed in appearance since the people who had bought them had done so because they liked what the house agent called "old-world charm." They just added another bathroom, and spent a good deal of money on plumbing, electric cookers, and dishwashers.

But though the houses looked much as before, the same could hardly be said of the village street. When shops changed hands there, it was with a view to immediate and intemperate modernization. The fishmonger was unrecognizable with new super windows behind which the refrigerated fish gleamed. The butcher had remained conservative—good meat is good meat, if you have the money to pay for it. If not, you take the cheaper cuts and the tough joints and like it! Barnes, the grocer, was still there, unchanged, for which Miss Hartnell and Miss Marple and others daily thanked heaven. So obliging, comfortable chairs to sit in by the counter, and cozy discussions as to cuts of bacon, and varieties of cheese. At the end of the street, however, where Mr. Toms had once had his basket shop stood a glittering new supermarket—anathema to the elderly ladies of St. Mary Mead.

"Packets of things one's never even heard of," exclaimed Miss Hartnell. "All these great packets of breakfast cereal instead of cooking a child a proper breakfast of bacon and eggs. And you're expected to take a basket yourself and go round looking for things—it takes a quarter of an hour sometimes to find all one wants—and usually made up in inconvenient sizes, too much or too little. And then a long queue waiting to pay as you go out. Most tiring. Of course it's all very well for the people from the Development—"

At this point she stopped.

Because, as was now usual, the sentence came to an end there. The Development, Period, as they would say in modern terms. It had an entity of its own, and a capital letter.

II

Miss Marple uttered a sharp exclamation of annoyance. She'd dropped a stitch again. Not only that, she must have dropped it some time ago. Not until now, when she had to decrease for the neck and count the stitches, had she realized the fact. She took up a spare pin, held the knitting sideways to the light and peered anxiously. Even her new spectacles didn't seem to do any good. And that, she reflected, was because obviously there came a time when oculists, in spite of their luxurious waiting rooms, their up-to-date instruments, the bright lights they flashed into your eyes, and the very high fees they charged, couldn't do anything much more for you. Miss Marple reflected with some nostalgia on how good her eyesight had been a few (well, perhaps not a *few)* years ago. From the vantage point of her garden, so admirably placed to see all that was going on in St. Mary Mead, how little had escaped her noticing eye! And with the help of her bird glasses— (an interest in birds was *so* useful)—she had been able to see— She broke off there and let her thoughts run back over the past. Ann Protheroe in her summer frock going along to the Vicarage garden. And Colonel Protheroe— poor man—a very tiresome and unpleasant man, to be sure—but to be murdered like that— She shook her head and went on to thoughts of Griselda, the vicar's pretty young wife. Dear Griselda—such a faithful friend—a Christmas card every year. That attractive baby of hers was a strapping young man now, and with a very good job. Engineering, was it? He always had enjoyed taking his mechanical trains to pieces. Beyond the Vicarage, there had been the stile and the field path with Farmer Giles's cattle beyond in the meadows where now—now . . .

The Development.

And why not? Miss Marple asked herself sternly. These things had to be. The houses were necessary, and they were very well built, or so she had been told. "Planning," or whatever they called it. Though why everything had to be called a Close, she couldn't imagine. Aubrey Close and Longwood Close, and Grandison Close and all the rest of them. Not really Closes at all. Miss Marple knew what a Close was perfectly. Her uncle had been a Canon of Chichester Cathedral. As a child she had gone to stay with him in the Close.

It was like Cherry Baker who always called Miss Marple's old-world overcrowded drawing room the "lounge." Miss Marple corrected her gently, "It's the drawing room, Cherry." And Cherry, because she was young and kind, endeavored to remember, though it was obvious that to her "drawing room" was a very funny word to use—and "lounge" came slipping out. She had of late, however, compromised on "living room." Miss Marple liked Cherry very much. Her name was Mrs. Baker and she came from the Development. She was one of the detachment of young wives who shopped at the supermarket and wheeled prams about the quiet streets of St. Mary Mead. They were all smart and well turned out. Their hair was crisp and curled. They laughed and talked and called to one another. They were like a happy flock of birds. Owing to the insidious snares of installment buying, they were always in need of ready money, though their husbands all earned good wages; and so they came and did housework or cooking. Cherry was a quick and efficient cook, she was an intelligent girl, took telephone calls correctly and was quick to spot inaccuracies in the tradesmen's books. She was not much given to turning mattresses, and as far as washing up went, Miss Marple always now passed the pantry door with her head turned away so as not to observe Cherry's method, which was that of thrusting everything into the sink together and letting loose a snowstorm of detergent on it. Miss Marple had quietly removed her old Worcester tea set from daily circulation and put it in the corner cabinet whence it only emerged on special occasions. Instead she had purchased a modern service with a pattern of pale grey on white and no gilt on it whatsoever to be washed away in the sink.

How different it had been in the past. . . . Faithful Florence, for instance, that grenadier of a parlor-maid—and there had been Amy and Clara and Alice, those "nice little maids"—arriving from St. Faith's Orphanage to be "trained," and then going on to better-paid jobs elsewhere. Rather simple, some of them had been, and frequently adenoidal, and Amy distinctly moronic. They had gossiped and chattered with the other maids in the village and walked out with the fishmonger's assistant, or the under-gardener at the Hall, or one of Mr. Barnes, the grocer's, numerous assistants. Miss Marple's mind went back over them affectionately, thinking of all the little woolly coats she had knitted for their subsequent offspring. They had not been very good with the telephone, and no good at all at arithmetic. On the other hand, they knew how to wash up, and how to make a bed. They had had skills, rather than education. It was odd that nowadays it should be the educated girls who went in for all the domestic chores. Students from abroad, girls *au pair*, university students in the vacation, young married women like Cherry Baker, who lived in spurious Closes on new building developments.

There were still, of course, people like Miss Knight. This last thought came suddenly as Miss Knight's tread overhead made the lusters on the mantelpiece tinkle warningly. Miss Knight had obviously had her afternoon rest and would now go out for her afternoon walk. In a moment she would come to ask Miss Marple if she could get her anything in the town. The thought of Miss Knight brought the usual reaction to Miss Marple's mind. Of course, it was very generous of dear Raymond (her nephew) and nobody could be kinder than Miss Knight, and of course that attack of bronchitis had left her very weak, and Dr. Haydock had said very firmly that she must not go on sleeping alone in the house with only someone coming in daily, but— She stopped there. Because it was no use going on with the thought which was "If only it could have been someone other than Miss Knight." But there wasn't much choice for elderly ladies nowadays. Devoted maidservants had gone out of fashion. In real illness you could have a proper hospital nurse, at vast expense and procured with difficulty, or you could go to hospital. But after that critical phase of illness had passed, you were down to the Miss Knights.

There wasn't, Miss Marple reflected, anything wrong about the Miss Knights other than the fact that they were madly irritating. They were full of kindness, ready to feel affection towards their charges, to humor them, to be bright and cheerful with them and in general to treat them as slightly mentally afflicted children.

"But I," said Miss Marple to herself, "although I may be old, am *not* a mentally afflicted child."

At this moment, breathing rather heavily, as was her custom, Miss Knight bounced brightly into the room. She was a big, rather flabby woman of fifty-six with yellowing grey hair very elaborately arranged, a long thin nose, and below it a good-natured mouth and a weak chin.

"Here we are!" she exclaimed with a kind of beaming boisterousness, meant to cheer and enliven the sad twilight of the aged. "I hope *we've* had our little snooze?"

"*I* have been knitting," Miss Marple replied, putting some emphasis on the pronoun, "and," she went on, confessing her weakness with distaste and shame, "I've dropped a stitch."

"Oh dear, dear," said Miss Knight. "Well, we'll soon put that right, won't we?"

"*You* will," said Miss Marple. "*I*, alas, am unable to do so."

The slight acerbity of her tone passed quite unnoticed. Miss Knight, as always, was eager to help.

"There," she said after a few moments. "There you are, dear. Quite all right now."

Though Miss Marple was perfectly agreeable to be called "dear" (and even "ducks") by the woman at the greengrocer or the girl at the paper shop, it annoyed her intensely to be called "dear" by Miss Knight. Another of those things that elderly ladies have to bear. She thanked Miss Knight politely.

"And now I'm just going out for my wee toddle," said Miss Knight humorously. "Shan't be long."

"Please don't dream of hurrying back," said Miss Marple politely and sincerely.

"Well, I don't like to leave you too long on your own, dear, in case you get moped."

"I assure you I am quite happy," said Miss Marple. "I probably shall have"—she closed her eyes—"a little nap."

"That's right, dear. Anything I can get you?"

Miss Marple opened her eyes and considered.

"You might go into Longdon's and see if the curtains are ready. And perhaps another skein of the blue wool from Mrs. Wisley. And a box of black currant lozenges at the chemist's. And change my book at the library—but don't let them give you anything that isn't on my list. This last one was too terrible. I couldn't read it." She held out *The Spring Awakens*.

"Oh, dear, dear! Didn't you like it? I thought you'd love it. Such a pretty story."

"And if it isn't too far for you, perhaps you wouldn't mind going as far as Halletts and see if they have one of those up-and-down egg whisks—*not* the turn-the-handle kind."

(She knew very well they had nothing of the kind, but Halletts was the farthest shop possible.)

"If all this isn't too much—" she murmured.

But Miss Knight replied with obvious sincerity.

"Not at all. I shall be delighted."

Miss Knight loved shopping. It was the breath of life to her. One met acquaintances, and had the chance of a chat, one gossiped with the assistants, and had the opportunity of examining various articles in the various shops. And one could spend quite a long time engaged in these pleasant occupations without any guilty feeling that it was one's duty to hurry back.

So Miss Knight started off happily, after a last glance at the frail old lady resting so peacefully by the window.

After waiting a few minutes in case Miss Knight should return for a shopping bag, or her purse, or a handkerchief (she was a great forgetter and returner), and also to recover from the slight mental fatigue induced by thinking of so many unwanted things to ask Miss Knight to get, Miss Marple rose briskly to her feet, cast aside her knitting and strode purposefully across the room and into the hall. She took down her summer coat from its peg, a stick from the hall stand, and exchanged her bedroom slippers for a pair of stout walking shoes. Then she left the house by the side door.

"It will take her at least an hour and a half," Miss Marple estimated to herself. "Quite that—with all the people from the Development doing their shopping."

Miss Marple visualized Miss Knight at Longdon's making abortive inquiries *re* curtains. Her surmises were remarkably accurate. At this moment Miss Knight was exclaiming, "Of course, I felt quite sure in my own mind they wouldn't be ready yet. But of course I said I'd come along and see when the old lady spoke about it. Poor old dears, they've got so little to look forward to. One must humor them. And she's a sweet old lady. Failing a little now, it's only to be expected—their faculties get dimmed. Now that's a pretty material you've got there. Do you have it in any other colors?"

A pleasant twenty minutes passed. When Miss Knight had finally departed, the senior assistant remarked with a stiff, "Failing, is she? I'll believe that when I see it for myself. Old Miss Marple has always been as sharp as a needle, and I'd say she still is." She then gave her attention to a young woman in tight trousers and a sailcloth jersey who wanted plastic material with crabs on it for bathroom curtains.

"Emily Waters, that's who she reminds me of," Miss Marple was saying to herself, with the satisfaction it always gave her to match up a human personality with one known in the past. "Just the same bird brain. Let me see, what happened to Emily?"

Nothing much, was her conclusion. She had once nearly got engaged to a curate, but after an understanding of several years the affair had fizzled out. Miss Marple dismissed her nurse attendant from her mind and gave her attention to her surroundings. She had traversed the garden rapidly, only observing as it were from the corner of her eye that Laycock had cut down the old-fashioned roses in a way more suitable to hybrid teas, but she did not allow this to distress her, or distract her from the delicious pleasure of having escaped for an outing entirely on her own. She had a happy feeling of adventure. She turned to the right, entered the Vicarage gate, took the path through the Vicarage garden and came out on the right of way. Where the stile had been there was now an iron swing gate giving on to a tarred asphalt path. This led to a neat little bridge over the stream and on the other side of the stream, where once there had been meadows with cows, there was the Development.

CHAPTER TWO

WITH THE FEELING of Columbus setting out to discover a new world, Miss Marple passed over the bridge, continued on to the path and within four minutes was actually in Aubrey Close.

Of course Miss Marple had seen the Development from the Market Basing Road, that is, had seen from afar its Closes and rows of neat well-built houses, with their television masts and their blue and pink and yellow and green painted doors and windows. But until now it had only had the reality of a map, as it were. She had not been in it and of it. But now she was here, observing the brave new world that was springing up, the world that by all accounts was foreign to all she had known. It was like a neat model built with child's bricks. It hardly seemed real to Miss Marple.

The people, too, looked unreal. The trousered young women, the rather sinister-looking young men and boys, the exuberant bosoms of the fifteen-year-old girls. Miss Marple couldn't help thinking that it all looked terribly depraved. Nobody noticed her much as she trudged along. She turned out of Aubrey Close and was presently in Darlington Close. She went slowly and as she went she listened avidly to the snippets of conversation between mothers wheeling prams, to the girls addressing young men, to the sinister-looking Teds (she supposed they were Teds) exchanging dark remarks with each other. Mothers came out on doorsteps calling to their children who, as usual, were busy doing all the things they had been told not to do. Children, Miss Marple reflected gratefully, never changed. And presently she began to smile, and noted down in her mind her usual series of recognitions.

That woman is just like Carry Edwards—and the dark one is just like that Hooper girl—she'll make a mess of her marriage just as Mary Hooper did. These boys—the dark one is just like Edward Leeke, a lot of wild talk but no harm in him—a nice boy, really—the fair one is Mrs. Bedwell's Josh all over again. Nice boys, both of them. The one like Gregory Binns won't do very well, I'm afraid. I expect he's got the same sort of mother. . . .

She turned a corner into Walsingham Close and her spirits rose every moment.

The new world was the same as the old. The houses were different, the streets were called Closes, the clothes were different, the voices were different, but the human beings were the same as they always had been. And though using slightly different phraseology, the subjects of conversation were the same.

By dint of turning corners in her exploration, Miss Marple had rather lost her sense of direction and had arrived at the edge of the housing estate again. She was now in Carrisbrook Close, half of which was still "under construction." At the first-floor window of a nearly finished house a young couple were standing. Their voices floated down as they discussed the amenities.

"You must admit it's a nice position, Harry."

"Other one was just as good."

"This one's got two more rooms."

"And you've got to pay for 'em."

"Well, I *like* this one."

"You would!"

"Ow, don't be such a spoilsport. You know what Mum said."

"Your Mum never stops saying."

"Don't you say nothing against Mum. Where'd I have been without her? And she might have cut up nastier than she did, I can tell you that. She could have taken you to court."

"Oh, come off it, Lily."

"It's a good view of the hills. You can almost see—" She leaned far out, twisting her body to the left. "You can almost see the reservoir—"

She leaned farther still, not realizing that she was resting her weight on loose boards that had been laid across the sill. They slipped under the pressure of her body, sliding outwards, carrying her with them. She screamed, trying to regain her balance.

"Harry—!"

The young man stood motionless—a foot or two behind her. He took one step backwards—

Desperately, clawing at the wall, the girl righted herself.

"Oo!" She let out a frightened breath. "I near as nothing fell out. Why didn't you get hold of me?"

"It was all so quick. Anyway, you're all right."

"That's all you know about it. I nearly went, I tell you. And look at the front of my jumper, it's all mussed."

Miss Marple went on a little way, then on impulse, she turned back.

Lily was outside in the road waiting for the young man to lock up the house.

Miss Marple went up to her and spoke rapidly in a low voice.

"If I were you, my dear, I shouldn't marry that young man. You want someone whom you can rely upon if you're in danger. You must excuse me for saying this to you—but I feel you ought to be warned."

She turned away and Lily stared after her.

"Well, of all the—"

Her young man approached.

"What was she saying to you, Lil?"

Lily opened her mouth—then shut it again.

"Giving me the gipsy's warning, if you want to know."

She eyed him in a thoughtful manner.

Miss Marple, in her anxiety to get away quickly, turned a corner, stumbled over some loose stones and fell.

A woman came running out of one of the houses.

"Oh, dear, what a nasty spill! I hope you haven't hurt yourself?"

With almost excessive goodwill she put her arms round Miss Marple and tugged her to her feet.

"No bones broken, I hope? There we are. I expect you feel rather shaken."

Her voice was loud and friendly. She was a plump, squarely built woman of about forty, brown hair just turning grey, blue eyes, and a big generous mouth that seemed to Miss Marple's rather shaken gaze to be far too full of white shining teeth.

"You'd better come inside and sit down and rest a bit. I'll make you a cup of tea."

Miss Marple thanked her. She allowed herself to be led through the blue-painted door and into a small room full of bright cretonne-covered chairs and sofas.

"There you are," said her rescuer, establishing her on a cushioned armchair. "You sit quiet and I'll put the kettle on."

She hurried out of the room which seemed rather restfully quiet after her departure. Miss Marple took a deep breath. She was not really hurt, but the fall had shaken her. Falls at her age were not to be encouraged. With luck, however, she thought guiltily, Miss Knight need never know. She moved her arms and legs gingerly. Nothing broken. If she could only get home all right. Perhaps, after a cup of tea—

The cup of tea arrived almost as the thought came to her. Brought on a tray with four sweet biscuits on a little plate.

"There you are." It was placed on a small table in front of her. "Shall I pour it for you? Better have plenty of sugar."

"No sugar, thank you."

"You must have sugar. Shock, you know. I was abroad with ambulances during the war. Sugar's wonderful for shock." She put four lumps in the cup and stirred vigorously. "Now you get that down, and you'll feel as right as rain."

Miss Marple accepted the dictum.

"A kind woman," she thought. "She reminds me of someone—now who is it?"

"You've been very kind to me," she said, smiling.

"Oh, that's nothing. The little ministering angel, that's me. I love helping people." She looked out of the window as the latch of the outer gate clicked. "Here's my husband home, Arthur—we've got a visitor."

She went out into the hall and returned with Arthur who looked rather bewildered. He was a thin pale man, rather slow in speech.

"This lady fell down—right outside our gate, so of course I brought her in."

"Your wife is very kind, Mr.—?"

"Badcock's the name."

"Mr. Badcock. I'm afraid I've given her a lot of trouble."

"Oh, no trouble to Heather. Heather enjoys doing things for people." He looked at her curiously. "Were you on your way anywhere in particular?"

"No, I was just taking a walk. I live in St. Mary Mead, the house beyond the Vicarage. My name is Marple."

"Well, I never!" exclaimed Heather. "So *you're* Miss Marple. I've heard about you. You're the one who does all the murders."

"Heather! What *do* you—"

"Oh, you know what I mean. Not actually do murders—find out about them. That's right, isn't it?"

Miss Marple murmured modestly that she had been mixed up in murders once or twice.

"I heard there have been murders here, in this village. They were talking about it the other night at the Bingo Club. There was one at Gossington Hall. I wouldn't buy a place where there's been a murder. I'd be sure it was haunted."

"The murder wasn't committed in Gossington Hall. A dead body was brought there."

"Found in the library on the hearthrug, that's what they said?"

Miss Marple nodded.

"Did you ever? Perhaps they're going to make a film of it. Perhaps that's why Marina Gregg has bought Gossington Hall."

"Marina Gregg?"

"Yes. She and her husband. I forget his name—he's a producer, I think, or a director—Jason something. But Marina Gregg, she's lovely, isn't she? Of course she hasn't been in so many pictures of late years—she was ill for a long time. But I still think there's never anybody like her. Did you see her in *Carmanella?* And *The Price of Love,* and *Mary of Scotland?* She's not so young any more, but she'll always be a wonderful actress. I've always been a terrific fan of hers. When I was a teen-ager I used to dream about her. The big thrill of my life was when there was a big show in aid of the St. John's Ambulance in Bermuda, and Marina Gregg came to open it. I was mad with excitement, and then on the very day I came down with a temperature and the doctor said I couldn't go. But I wasn't going to be beaten. I didn't actually feel too bad. So I got up and put a lot of make-up on my face and went along. I was introduced to her and she talked to me for quite three minutes and gave me her autograph. It was wonderful. I've never forgotten that day."

Miss Marple stared at her.

"I hope there were no—unfortunate aftereffects?" she said anxiously.

Heather Badcock laughed.

"None at all. Never felt better. What I say is, if you want a thing, you've got to take risks. I always do."

She laughed again, a happy strident laugh.

Arthur Badcock said admiringly, "There's never any holding Heather. She always gets away with things."

"Alison Wilde," murmured Miss Marple, with a nod of satisfaction.

"Pardon?" said Mr. Badcock.

"Nothing. Just someone I used to know."

Heather looked at her inquiringly.

"You reminded me of her, that is all."

"Did I? I hope she was nice."

"She was very nice indeed," said Miss Marple slowly. "Kind, healthy, full of life."

"But she had her faults, I suppose?" laughed Heather. "I have."

"Well, Alison always saw her own point of view so clearly that she didn't always see how things might appear to, or affect, other people."

"Like the time you took in that evacuated family from a condemned cottage and they went off with all our teaspoons," Arthur said.

"But, Arthur!—I couldn't have turned them away. It wouldn't have been kind."

"They were family spoons," said Mr. Badcock sadly. "Georgian. Belonged to my mother's grandmother."

"Oh, do forget those old spoons, Arthur. You do harp so."

"I'm not very good at forgetting, I'm afraid."

Miss Marple looked at him thoughtfully.

"What's your friend doing now?" asked Heather of Miss Marple with kindly interest.

Miss Marple paused a moment before answering.

"Alison Wilde? Oh—she died."

CHAPTER THREE

I

"I'M GLAD TO be back," said Mrs. Bantry. "Although, of course, I've had a wonderful time."

Miss Marple nodded appreciatively, and accepted a cup of tea from her friend's hand.

When her husband, Colonel Bantry, had died some years ago, Mrs. Bantry had sold Gossington Hall and the considerable amount of land attached to it, retaining for herself what had been the East Lodge, a charming porticoed little building replete with inconvenience, where even a gardener had refused to live. Mrs. Bantry had added to it the essentials of modern life, a built-on kitchen of the latest type, a new water supply from the main, electricity, and a bathroom. This had all cost her a great deal, but not nearly so much as an attempt to live at Gossington Hall would have done. She had also retained the essentials of privacy, about three quarters of an acre of garden nicely ringed with trees, so that, as she explained, "Whatever they do with Gossington, I shan't really see it or worry."

For the last few years she had spent a good deal of the year traveling about, visiting children and grandchildren in various parts of the globe, and coming back from time to time to enjoy the privacies of her own home. Gossington Hall itself had changed hands once or twice. It had been run as a guest house, failed, and been bought by four people who had shared it as four roughly divided flats and subsequently quarreled. Finally the Ministry of Health had bought it for some obscure purpose for which they eventually did not want it. The Ministry had now resold it—and it was this sale which the two friends were discussing.

"I have heard rumors, of course," said Miss Marple.

"Naturally," said Mrs. Bantry. "It was even said that Charlie Chaplin and all his children were coming to live here. That would have been wonderful fun; unfortunately there isn't a word of truth in it. No, it's definitely Marina Gregg."

"How very lovely she was," said Miss Marple with a sigh. "I always remember those early films of hers. *Bird of Passage* with that handsome Joel Roberts. And the Mary, Queen of Scots film. And of course it was very sentimental, but I did enjoy *Comin' Thru the Rye*. Oh, dear, that was a long time ago."

"Yes," said Mrs. Bantry. "She must be—what do you think? Forty-five? Fifty?"

Miss Marple thought nearer fifty.

"Has she been in anything lately? Of course I don't go very often to the cinema nowadays."

"Only small parts, I think," said Mrs. Bantry. "She hasn't been a star for quite a long time. She had that bad nervous breakdown. After one of her divorces."

"Such a lot of husbands they all have," said Miss Marple. "It must really be very tiring."

"It wouldn't suit me," said Mrs. Bantry. "After you've fallen in love with a man and married him and got used to his ways and settled down comfortably—to go and throw it all up and start again! It seems to me madness."

"I can't presume to speak," said Miss Marple with a little spinsterish cough, "never having married. But it seems, you know, a pity."

"I suppose they can't help it really," said Mrs. Bantry vaguely. "With the kind of lives they have to live. So public, you know. I met her," she added. "Marina Gregg, I mean, when I was in California."

"What was she like?" Miss Marple asked with interest.

"Charming," said Mrs. Bantry. "So natural and unspoiled." She added thoughtfully, "It's like a kind of livery really."

"What is?"

"Being unspoiled and natural. You learn how to do it, and then you have to go on being it all the time. Just think of the hell of it—never to be able to chuck something and say, 'Oh, for the Lord's sake stop bothering me.' I dare say that in sheer self-defense you have to have drunken parties, or orgies."

"She's had five husbands, hasn't she?" Miss Marple asked.

"At least. An early one that didn't count, and then a foreign prince or count, and then another film star, Robert Truscott, wasn't it? That was built up as a great romance. But it only lasted four years. And then Isidore Wright, the playwright. That was rather serious and quiet, and she had a baby—apparently she'd always longed to have a child—she's even half-adopted a few strays—anyway this was the real thing. Very much built up. Motherhood with a capital M. And then, I believe, it was an imbecile, or queer or something—and it was after that that she had this breakdown and started to take drugs and all that, and threw up her parts."

"You seem to know a lot about her," said Miss Marple.

"Well, naturally," said Mrs. Bantry. "When she bought Gossington I was interested. She married the present man about two years ago, and they say she's quite all right again now. He's a producer—or do I mean a director? I always get mixed. He was in love with her when they were quite young, but he didn't amount to very much in those days. But now, I believe, he's got quite famous. What's his name, now? Jason—Jason something— Jason Hudd, no, Rudd, that's it. They've bought Gossington because it's handy for"—she hesitated—"Elstree?" she hazarded.

Miss Marple shook her head.

"I don't think so," she said. "Elstree's in North London."

"It's the fairly new studios. Hellingforth—that's it. Sounds so Finnish, I always think. About six miles from Market Basing. She's going to do a film on Elizabeth of Austria, I believe."

"What a lot you know," said Miss Marple. "About the private lives of film stars. Did you learn it all in California?"

"Not really," said Mrs. Bantry. "Actually I get it from the extraordinary magazines I read at my hairdresser's. Most of the stars I don't even know by name, but as I said because Marina Gregg and her husband have bought Gossington, I was interested. Really the things those magazines say! I don't suppose half of it is true—probably not a quarter. I don't believe Marina Gregg is a nymphomaniac, I don't think she drinks, probably she doesn't even take drugs, and quite likely she just went away to have a nice rest and didn't have a nervous breakdown at all!—but it's true that she is coming here to live."

"Next week, I heard," said Miss Marple.

"As soon as that? I know she's lending Gossington for a big fête on the twenty-third in aid of St. John's Ambulance Corps. I suppose they've done a lot to the house?"

"Practically everything," said Miss Marple. "Really, it would have been much simpler, and probably cheaper, to have pulled it down and built a new house."

"Bathrooms, I suppose?"

"Six new ones, I hear. And a palm court. And a pool. And what I believe they call picture windows, and they've knocked your husband's study and the library into one to make a music room."

"Arthur will turn in his grave. You know how he hated music. Tone-deaf, poor dear. His face, when some kind friend took us to the opera! He'll probably come back and haunt them!" She stopped and then said abruptly, "Does anyone ever hint that Gossington might be haunted?"

Miss Marple shook her head.

"It isn't," she said with certainty.

"That wouldn't prevent people from saying it was," Mrs. Bantry pointed out.

"Nobody ever has said so." Miss Marple paused and then said, "People aren't really foolish, you know. Not in villages."

Mrs. Bantry shot her a quick look. "You've always stuck to that, Jane. And I won't say that you're not right."

She suddenly smiled.

"Marina Gregg asked me, very sweetly and delicately, if I wouldn't find it very painful to see my old home occupied by strangers. I assured her that it wouldn't hurt me at all. I don't think she quite believed me. But after all, as you know, Jane, Gossington wasn't our home. We weren't brought up there as children—that's what really counts. It was just a house with a nice bit of shooting and fishing attached that we bought when Arthur retired. We thought of it, I remember, as a house that would be nice and easy to run! How we can ever have thought that, I can't imagine! All those staircases and passages. Only four servants! *Only!* Those were the days, ha ha!" She added suddenly: "What's all this about your falling down! That Knight woman ought not to let you go out by yourself."

"It wasn't poor Miss Knight's fault. I gave her a lot of shopping to do and then I—"

"Deliberately gave her the slip? I see. Well, you shouldn't do it, Jane. Not at your age."

"How did you hear about it?"

Mrs. Bantry grinned.

"You can't keep any secrets in St. Mary Mead. You've often told me so. Mrs. Meavy told me."

"Mrs. Meavy?" Miss Marple looked at sea.

"She comes in daily. She's from the Development."

"Oh, the Development." The usual pause happened.

"What were you doing in the Development?" asked Mrs. Bantry curiously.

"I just wanted to see it. To see what the people were like."

"And what did you think they were like?"

"Just the same as everyone else. I don't quite know if that was disappointing or reassuring."

"Disappointing, I should think."

"No. I think it's reassuring. It makes you—well—recognize certain types—so that when anything occurs—one will understand quite well why and for what reason."

"Murder, do you mean?"

Miss Marple looked shocked.

"I don't know why you should assume that I think of murder all the time."

"Nonsense, Jane. Why don't you come out boldly, and call yourself a criminologist and have done with it?"

"Because I am nothing of the sort," said Miss Marple with spirit. "It is simply that I have a certain knowledge of human nature—that is only natural after having lived in a small village all my life."

"You probably have something there," said Mrs. Bantry thoughtfully, "though most people wouldn't agree, of course. Your nephew Raymond always used to say this place was a complete backwater."

"Dear Raymond," said Miss Marple indulgently. She added: "He's always been so kind. He's paying for Miss Knight, you know."

The thought of Miss Knight induced a new train of thought and she rose and said: "I'd better be going back now, I suppose."

"You didn't walk all the way here, did you?"

"Of course not. I came in Inch."

This somewhat enigmatic pronouncement was received with complete understanding. In days very long past, Mr. Inch had been the proprietor of two cabs which met trains at the local station and which were also hired by the local ladies to take them "calling," out to tea parties, and occasionally, with their daughters, to such frivolous entertainments as dances. In the fullness of time, Inch, a cheery red-faced man of seventy-odd, gave place to his son—known as "young Inch" (he was then aged forty-five)—though old Inch still continued to drive such elderly ladies as considered his son too young and irresponsible. To keep up with the times, young Inch abandoned horse vehicles for motorcars. He was not very good with machinery and in due course a certain Mr. Bardwell took over from him. The name Inch persisted. Mr. Bardwell in due course sold out to Mr. Roberts, but in the telephone book *Inch's Taxi Service* was still the official name, and the old ladies of the community continued to refer to their journeys as going somewhere "in Inch," as though they were Jonah and Inch was a whale.

II

"Dr. Haydock called," said Miss Knight reproachfully. "I told him you'd gone to tea with Mrs. Bantry. He said he'd call in again tomorrow."

She helped Miss Marple off with her wraps.

"And now, I expect, we're tired out," she said accusingly.

"*You* may be," said Miss Marple. "*I* am not."

"You come and sit cozy by the fire," said Miss Knight, as usual paying no attention. ("You don't need to take much notice of what the old dears say. I just humor them.") "And how would we fancy a nice cup of Ovaltine? Or Horlicks for a change?"

Miss Marple thanked her and said she would like a small glass of dry sherry. Miss Knight looked disapproving.

"I don't know what the doctor would say to that, I'm sure," she said, when she returned with the glass.

"We will make a point of asking him tomorrow morning," said Miss Marple.

On the following morning Miss Knight met Dr. Haydock in the hall, and did some agitated whispering.

The elderly doctor came into the room rubbing his hands, for it was a chilly morning.

"Here's our doctor to see us," said Miss Knight gaily. "Can I take your gloves, Doctor?"

"They'll be all right here," said Haydock, casting them carelessly on a table. "Quite a nippy morning."

"A little glass of sherry perhaps?" suggested Miss Marple.

"I heard you were taking to drink. Well, you should never drink alone."

The decanter and glasses were already on a small table by Miss Marple. Miss Knight left the room.

Dr. Haydock was a very old friend. He had semi-retired, but came to attend certain of his old patients.

"I hear you've been falling about," he said as he finished his glass. "It won't do, you know, not at your age. I'm warning you. And I hear you didn't want to send for Sandford."

Sandford was Haydock's partner.

"That Miss Knight of yours sent for him anyway—and she was quite right."

"I was only bruised and shaken a little. Dr. Sandford said so. I could have waited quite well until you were back."

"Now look here, my dear. I can't go on for ever. And Sandford, let me tell you, has better qualifications than I have. He's a first-class man."

"The younger doctors are all the same," said Miss Marple. "They take your blood pressure, and whatever's the matter with you, you get some kind of mass-produced variety of new pills. Pink ones, yellow ones, brown ones. Medicine nowadays is just like a supermarket—all packaged up."

"Serve you right if I prescribed leeches, and black draught, and rubbed your chest with camphorated oil."

"I do that myself when I've got a cough," said Miss Marple with spirit, "and very comforting it is."

"We don't like getting old, that's what it is," said Haydock gently. "I hate it."

"You're quite a young man compared to me," said Miss Marple. "And I don't really mind getting old—not that in itself. It's the lesser indignities."

"I think I know what you mean."

"Never being alone! The difficulty of getting out for a few minutes by oneself. And even my knitting—such a comfort that has always been, and I really am a good knitter. Now I drop stitches all the time—and quite often I don't even know I've dropped them."

Haydock loked at her thoughtfully.

The his eyes twinkled.

"There's always the opposite."

"Now what do you mean by that?"

"If you can't knit, what about unraveling for a change? Penelope did."

"I'm hardly in her position."

"But unraveling's rather in your line, isn't it?"

He rose to his feet.

"I must be getting along. What I'd prescribe for you is a nice juicy murder."

"That's an outrageous thing to say!"

"Isn't it? However, you can always make do with the depth the parsley sank into the butter on a summer's day. I always wondered about that. Good old Holmes. A period piece, nowadays, I suppose. But he'll never be forgotten."

Miss Knight bustled in after the doctor had gone.

"There," she said, "we look *much* more cheerful. Did the doctor recommend a tonic?"

"He recommended me to take an interest in murder."

"A nice detective story?"

"No," said Miss Marple. "Real life."

"Goodness," exclaimed Miss Knight. "But there's not likely to be a murder in this quiet spot."

"Murders," said Miss Marple, "can happen anywhere. And do."

"At the Development, perhaps?" mused Miss Knight. "A lot of those Teddy-looking boys carry knives."

But the murder, when it came, was not at the Development.

CHAPTER FOUR

MRS. BANTRY STEPPED back a foot or two, surveyed herself in the glass, made a slight adjustment to her hat (she was not used to wearing hats), drew on a pair of good quality leather gloves and left the lodge, closing the door carefully behind her. She had the most pleasurable anticipations of what lay in front of her. Some three weeks had passed since her talk with Miss Marple. Marina Gregg and her husband had arrived at Gossington Hall and were now more or less installed there.

There was to be a meeting there this afternoon of the main persons involved in the arrangements for the fête in aid of the St. John's Ambulance. Mrs. Bantry was not among those on the committee, but she had received a note from Marina Gregg asking her to come and have tea beforehand. It had recalled their meeting in California and had been signed, "Cordially, Marina Gregg." It had been handwritten, not typewritten. There is no denying that Mrs. Bantry was both pleased and flattered. After all, a celebrated film star is a celebrated film star, and elderly ladies, though they may be of local importance, are aware of their complete unimportance in the world of celebrities. So Mrs. Bantry had the pleased feeling of a child for whom a special treat had been arranged.

As she walked up the drive Mrs. Bantry's keen eyes went from side to side registering her impressions. The place had been smartened up since the days when it had passed from hand to hand. "No expense spared," said Mrs. Bantry to herself, nodding in satisfaction. The drive afforded no view of the flower garden and for that Mrs. Bantry was just as pleased. The flower garden and its special herbaceous border had been her own particular delight in the far-off days when she had lived at Gossington Hall. She permitted regretful and nostalgic memories of her irises. The best iris garden of any in the county, she told herself with a fierce pride.

Faced by a new front door in a blaze of new paint, she pressed the bell. The door was opened with gratifying promptness of what was undeniably an Italian butler. She was ushered by him straight into the room which had been Colonel Bantry's library. This, as she had already heard, had been thrown into one with the study. The result was impressive. The walls were paneled, the floor was parquet. At one end was a grand piano and halfway along the wall was a superb record player. At the other end of the room was

a small island, as it were, which comprised Persian rugs, a tea table and
some chairs. By the tea table sat Marina Gregg, and leaning against the
mantelpiece was what Mrs. Bantry at first thought to be the ugliest man she
had ever seen.

Just a few moments previously when Mrs. Bantry's hand had been
advanced to press the bell, Marina Gregg had been saying in a soft,
enthusiastic voice to her husband:

"This place is right for me, Jinks, just right. It's what I've always wanted.
Quiet. English quiet and the English countryside. I can see myself living
here, living here all my life if need be. And we'll adopt the English way of
life. We'll have afternoon tea every afternoon with China tea and my lovely
Georgian tea service. And we'll look out of the window on those lawns and
that English herbaceous border. I've come home at last, that's what I feel. I
feel that I can settle down here, that I can be quiet and happy. It's going to
be home, this place. That's what I feel. *Home.*"

And Jason Rudd (known to his wife as Jinks) had smiled at her. It was an
acquiescent smile, indulgent, but it held its reserve because, after all, he had
heard it very often before. Perhaps this time it would be true. Perhaps this
was the place that Marina Gregg might feel at home. But he knew her early
enthusiasms so well. She was always so sure that at last she had found
exactly what she wanted. He said in his deep voice:

"That's grand, honey. That's just grand. I'm glad you like it."

"Like it? I adore it. Don't you adore it, too?"

"Sure," said Jason Rudd. "Sure."

It wasn't too bad, he reflected to himself. Good, solidly built, rather ugly
Victorian. It had, he admitted, a feeling of solidity and security. Now that
the worst of its fantastic inconveniences had been ironed out, it would be
quite reasonably comfortable to live in. Not a bad place to come back to
from time to time. With luck, he thought, Marina wouldn't start taking a
dislike to it for perhaps two years to two years and a half. It all depended.

Marina said, sighing softly:

"It's so wonderful to feel well again. Well and strong. Able to cope with
things."

And he said again: "Sure, honey, sure."

And it was at that moment that the door opened and the Italian butler
had ushered in Mrs. Bantry.

Marina Gregg's welcome was all that was charming. She came forward,
hands outstretched, saying how delightful it was to meet Mrs. Bantry again.
And what a coincidence that they should have met that time in San
Francisco and that two years later she and Jinks should actually buy the
house that had once belonged to Mrs. Bantry. And she did hope, she really
did hope that Mrs. Bantry wouldn't mind terribly the way they'd pulled the
house about and done things to it and she hoped she wouldn't feel that they
were terrible intruders living here.

"Your coming to live here is one of the most exciting things that has ever
happened in this place," said Mrs. Bantry cheerfully, and she looked
towards the mantelpiece. Whereupon, almost as an afterthought, Marina
Gregg said:

"You don't know my husband, do you? Jason, this is Mrs. Bantry."

Mrs. Bantry looked at Jason Rudd with some interest. Her first impression that this was one of the ugliest men she had ever seen became qualified. He had interesting eyes. They were, she thought, more deeply sunk in his head than any eyes she had seen. Deep quiet pools, said Mrs. Bantry to herself, and felt like a romantic lady novelist. The rest of his face was distinctly craggy, almost ludicrously out of proportion. His nose jutted upwards and a little red paint would have transformed it into the nose of a clown very easily. He had, too, a clown's big sad mouth. Whether he was at this moment in a furious temper or whether he always looked as though he were in a furious temper she did not quite know. His voice when he spoke was unexpectedly pleasant. Deep and slow.

"A husband," he said, "is always an afterthought. But let me say with my wife that we're very glad to welcome you here. I hope you don't feel that it ought to be the other way about."

"You must get it out of your head," said Mrs. Bantry, "that I've been driven forth from my old home. It never was my old home. I've been congratulating myself ever since I sold it. It was a most inconvenient house to run. I liked the garden, but the house became more and more of a worry. I've had a perfectly splendid time ever since, traveling abroad and going and seing my married daughters and my grandchildren and my friends in all the different parts of the world."

"Daughters," said Marina Gregg, "you have daughters and sons?"

"Two sons and two daughters," said Mrs. Bantry, "and pretty widely spaced. One in Kenya, one in South Africa. One near Texas and the other, thank goodness, in London."

"Four," said Marina Gregg. "Four—and grandchildren?"

"Nine up to date," said Mrs. Bantry. "It's great fun being a grandmother. You don't have any of the worry of parental responsibility. You can spoil them in the most unbridled way—"

Jason Rudd interrupted her. "I'm afraid the sun catches your eyes," he said, and went to a window to adjust the blind. "You must tell us all about this delightful village," he said as he came back.

He handed her a cup of tea.

"Will you have a hot scone or a sandwich, or this cake? We have an Italian cook and she makes quite good pastry and cakes. You see we have quite taken to your English afternoon tea."

"Delicious tea, too," said Mrs. Bantry, sipping the fragrant beverage.

Marina Gregg smiled and looked pleased. The sudden nervous movement of her fingers which Jason Rudd's eye had noticed a minute or two previously, was stilled again. Mrs. Bantry looked at her hostess with great admiration. Marina Gregg's heyday had been before the rise to supreme importance of vital statistics. She could not have been described as Sex Incarnate, or "The Bust" or "The Torso." She had been long and slim and willowy. The bones of her face and head had had some of the beauty associated with those of Garbo. She had brought personality to her pictures rather than mere sex. The sudden turn of her head, the opening of the deep lovely eyes, the faint quiver of her mouth, all these were what brought to one suddenly that feeling of breathtaking loveliness that comes not from regularity of feature but from some sudden magic of the flesh that catches the onlooker unawares. She still had this quality though it was not now so easily apparent. Like many film and stage actresses, she had what seemed to be a habit of turning off personality at will. She could retire into herself, be quiet, gentle, aloof, disappointing to an eager fan. And then suddenly the turn of the head, the movement of the hands, the sudden smile and the magic was there.

One of her greatest pictures had been *Mary, Queen of Scots*, and it was of her performance in that picture that Mrs. Bantry was reminded now as she watched her. Mrs. Bantry's eye switched to the husband. He too was watching Marina. Off guard for a moment, his face expressed clearly his feelings. "Good Lord," said Mrs. Bantry to herself, "the man adores her."

She didn't know why she should feel so surprised. Perhaps because film stars and their love affairs and their devotion were so written up in the press, that one never expected to see the real thing with one's own eyes. On an impulse she said:

"I do hope you'll enjoy it here and that you'll be able to stay here some time. Do you expect to have the house for long?"

Marina opened wide surprised eyes as she turned her head. "I want to stay here always," she said. "Oh, I don't mean that I shan't have to go away a lot. I shall, of course. There's a possibility of my making a film in North Africa next year although nothing's settled yet. No, but this will be my home. I shall come back here. I shall always be able to come back here." She sighed. "That's what's so wonderful. That's what's so very wonderful. To have found a home at last."

"I see," said Mrs. Bantry, but at the same time she thought to herself, "All the same I don't believe for a moment that it will be like that. I don't believe you're the kind that can ever settle down."

Again she shot a quick surreptitious glance at Jason Rudd. He was not scowling now. Instead he was smiling, a sudden very sweet and unexpected smile, but it was a sad smile. "He knows it, too," thought Mrs. Bantry.

The door opened and a woman came in. "Bartletts want you on the telephone, Jason," she said.

"Tell them to call back."

"They said it was urgent."

He sighed and rose. "Let me introduce you to Mrs. Bantry," he said. "Ella Zielinsky, my secretary."

"Have a cup of tea, Ella," said Marina as Ella Zielinsky acknowledged the introduction with a smiling "pleased to meet you."

"I'll have a sandwich," said Ella. "I don't go for China tea."

Ella Zielinsky was, at a guess, thirty-five. She wore a well-cut suit, a ruffled blouse and appeared to breathe self-confidence. She had short-cut black hair and a wide forehead.

"You used to live here, so they tell me," she said to Mrs. Bantry.

"It's a good many years ago now," said Mrs. Bantry. "After my husband's death I sold it, and it's passed through several hands since then."

"Mrs. Bantry really says she doesn't hate the things we've done to it," said Marina.

"I should be frightfully disappointed if you hadn't," said Mrs. Bantry. "I came up here all agog. I can tell you the most splendid rumors have been going around the village."

"Never knew how difficult it was to get hold of plumbers in this country," said Miss Zielinsky, champing a sandwich in a businesslike way. "Not that that's been really my job," she went on.

"Everything is your job," said Marina, "and you know it is, Ella. The domestic staff and the plumbing and arguing with the builders."

"They don't seem ever to have heard of a picture window in this country."

Ella looked towards the window. "It's a nice view, I must admit."

"A lovely old-fashioned rural English scene," said Marina. "This house has got atmosphere."

"It wouldn't look so rural if it wasn't for the trees," said Ella Zielinsky. "That housing estate down there grows while you look at it."

"That's new since my time," said Mrs. Bantry.

"You mean there was nothing but the village when you lived here?"

Mrs. Bantry nodded.

"It must have been hard to do your shopping."

"I don't think so," said Mrs. Bantry. "I think it was frightfully easy."

"I understand having a flower garden," said Ella Zielinsky, "but you folks over here seem to grow all your vegetables as well. Wouldn't it be much easier to buy them—there's a supermarket?"

"It's probably coming to that," said Mrs. Bantry, with a sigh. "They don't taste the same, though."

"Don't spoil the atmosphere, Ella," said Marina.

The door opened and Jason looked in. "Darling," he said to Marina, "I hate to bother you, but would you mind? They just want your private view about this."

Marina sighed and rose. She trailed languidly towards the door. "Always something," she murmured. "I'm so sorry, Mrs. Bantry. I don't really think that this will take longer than a minute or two."

"Atmosphere," said Ella Zielinsky, as Marina went out and closed the door. "Do you think the house has got atmosphere?"

"I can't say I ever thought of it that way," said Mrs. Bantry. "It was just a house. Rather inconvenient in some ways and very nice and cozy in other ways."

"That's what I should have thought," said Ella Zielinsky. She cast a quick look at Mrs. Bantry. "Talking of atmosphere, when did the murder take place here?"

"No murder ever took place here," said Mrs. Bantry.

"Oh, come now. The stories I've heard. There are always stories, Mrs. Bantry. On the hearthrug, right there, wasn't it?" said Miss Zielinsky, nodding towards the fireplace.

"Yes," said Mrs. Bantry. "That was the place."

"So there was a murder?"

Mrs. Bantry shook her head. "The murder didn't take place here. The girl who had been killed was brought here and planted in this room. She'd nothing to do with us."

Miss Zielinsky looked interested.

"Possibly you had a bit of difficulty making people believe that?" she remarked.

"You're quite right there," said Mrs. Bantry.

"When did you find it?"

"The housemaid came in in the morning," said Mrs. Bantry, "with early morning tea. We had housemaids then, you know."

"I know," said Miss Zielinsky, "wearing print dresses that rustled."

"I'm not sure about the print dress," said Mrs. Bantry, "it may have been overalls by then. At any rate, she burst in and said there was a body in the library. I said 'nonsense,' then I woke up my husband and we came down to see."

"And there it was," said Miss Zielinsky. "My, the way things happen." She turned her head sharply towards the door and then back again. "Don't talk about it to Miss Gregg, if you don't mind," she said. "It's not good for her, that sort of thing."

"Of course. I won't say a word," said Mrs. Bantry. "I never do talk about it, as a matter of fact. It all happened so long ago. But won't she— Miss Gregg, I mean—won't she hear it anyway?"

"She doesn't come very much in contact with reality," said Ella Zielinsky. "Film stars can lead a fairly insulated life, you know. In fact very often one has to take care that they do. Things upset them. Things upset her. She's been seriously ill the last year or two, you know. She only started making a comeback a year ago."

"She seems to like the house," said Mrs. Bantry, "and to feel she will be happy here."

"I expect it'll last a year or two," said Ella Zielinsky.

"Not longer than that?"

"Well, I rather doubt it. Marina is one of those people, you know, who are always thinking they've found their heart's desire. But life isn't as easy as that, is it?"

"No," said Mrs. Bantry forcefully, "it isn't."

"It'll mean a lot to him if she's happy here," said Miss Zielinsky. She ate two more sandwiches in an absorbed, rather gobbling fashion in the manner of those who cram food into themselves as though they have an important train to catch. "He's a genius, you know," she went on. "Have you seen any of the pictures he's directed?"

Mrs. Bantry felt slightly embarrassed. She was of the type of woman who when she went to the cinema went entirely for the picture. The long lists of casts, directors, producers, photography and the rest of it passed her by. Very frequently, indeed, she did not even notice the names of the stars. She was not, however, anxious to call attention to this failing on her part.

"I get so mixed up," she said.

"Of course, he's got a lot to contend with," said Ella Zielinsky. "He's got her as well as everything else, and she's not easy. You've got to keep her happy, you see; and it's not really easy, I suppose, to keep people happy. Unless—that is—they—they are—" She hesitated.

"Unless they're the happy kind," suggested Mrs. Bantry. "Some people," she added thoughtfully, "enjoy being miserable."

"Oh, Marina isn't like that," said Ella Zielinsky, shaking her head. "It's more that her ups and downs are so violent. You know—far too happy one moment, far too pleased with everything and delighted with everything and how wonderful she feels. Then, of course, some little thing happens and down she goes to the opposite extreme."

"I suppose that's temperament," said Mrs. Bantry vaguely.

"That's right," said Ella Zielinsky. "Temperament. They've all got it, more or less, but Marina Gregg has got it more than most people. Don't we know it! The stories I could tell you!" She ate the last sandwich. "Thank God I'm only the social secretary."

CHAPTER FIVE

THE THROWING OPEN of the grounds of Gossington Hall for the benefit of the St. John's Ambulance Association was attended by quite an unprecedented number of people. Shilling admission fees mounted up in a highly satisfactory fashion. For one thing, the weather was good, a clear sunny day. But the preponderant attraction was undoubtedly the enormous local curiosity to know exactly what these "film people" had done to Gossington Hall. The most extravagant assumptions were entertained. The swimming pool in particular caused immense satisfaction. Most people's ideas of Hollywood stars were of sun-bathing by a pool in exotic surroundings and in exotic company. That the climate of Hollywood might be more suited to swimming pools than that of St. Mary Mead failed to be considered. After all, England always has one fine hot week in the summer and there is always one day that the Sunday papers publish articles on How to Keep Cool, How to Have Cool Suppers and How to Make Cool Drinks. The pool was almost exactly what everyone had imagined it might be. It was large, its waters were blue, it had a kind of exotic pavilion for changing and was surrounded with a highly artificial plantation of hedges and shrubs. The reactions of the multitude were exactly as might have been expected and hovered over a wide range of remarks.

"O-oh, isn't it lovely!"

"Two penn'orth of splash here, all right!"

"Reminds me of that holiday camp I went to."

"Wicked luxury *I* call it. It oughtn't to be allowed."

"Look at all that fancy marble. It must have cost the earth!"

"Don't see why these people think they can come over here and spend all the money they like."

"Perhaps this'll be on the telly sometime. That'll be fun."

Even Mr. Sampson, the oldest man in St. Mary Mead, boasting proudly of being ninety-six though his relations insisted firmly that he was only eighty-eight, had staggered along supporting his rheumatic legs with a stick, to see the excitement. He gave it his highest praise: "Wicked, this!" He smacked his lips hopefully. "Ah, there'll be a lot of wickedness here, I don't doubt. Naked men and women drinking and smoking what they call in the papers them reefers. There'll be all that, I expect. Ah yes," said Mr. Sampson with enormous pleasure, "there'll be a lot of wickedness."

It was felt that the final seal of approval had been set on the afternoon's entertainment. For an extra shilling people were allowed to go into the house, and study the new music room, the drawing-room, the completely unrecognizable dining-room, now done in dark oak and Spanish leather, and a few other joys.

"Never think this was Gossington Hall, would you, now?" said Mr. Sampson's daughter-in-law.

Mrs. Bantry strolled up fairly late and observed with pleasure that the money was coming in well and that the attendance was phenomenal.

The large marquee in which tea was being served was jammed with people. Mrs. Bantry hoped the buns were going to go round. There seemed some very competent women, however, in charge. She herself made a beeline for the herbaceous border and regarded it with a jealous eye. No expense had been spared on the herbaceous border, she was glad to note, and it was a proper herbaceous border, well planned and arranged and expensively stocked. No personal labors had gone into it, she was sure of that. Some good gardening firm had been given the contract, no doubt. But aided by carte blanche and the weather, they had turned out a very good job.

Looking round her, she felt there was a faint flavor of a Buckingham Palace garden party about the scene. Everybody was craning to see all they could see, and from time to time a chosen few were led into one of the more secret recesses of the house. She herself was presently approached by a willowy young man with long wavy hair.

"Mrs. Bantry? You *are* Mrs. Bantry?"

"I'm Mrs. Bantry, yes."

"Hailey Preston." He shook hands with her. "I work for Mr. Rudd. Will you come up to the second floor? Mr. and Mrs. Rudd are asking a few special friends up there."

Duly honored, Mrs. Bantry followed him. They went in through what had been called in her time the garden door. A red cord cordoned off the bottom of the main stairs. Hailey Preston unhooked it and she passed through. Just in front of her Mrs. Bantry observed Councillor and Mrs. Allcock. The latter who was stout was breathing heavily.

"Wonderful what they've done, isn't it, Mrs. Bantry?" panted Mrs. Allcock. "I'd like to have a look at the bathrooms, I must say, but I suppose I shan't get the chance." Her voice was wistful.

At the top of the stairs Marina Gregg and Jason Rudd were receiving this specially chosen élite. What had once been a spare bedroom had been thrown into the landing so as to make a wide lounge-like effect. Giuseppe the butler was officiating with drinks.

A stout man in livery was announcing guests.

"Councillor and Mrs. Allcock," he boomed.

Marina Gregg was being, as Mrs. Bantry had described her to Miss Marple, completely natural and charming. She could already hear Mrs. Allcock saying later,"—and so unspoiled, you know, in spite of being so famous."

How very nice of Mrs. Allcock to come, *and* the Councillor, and she did hope that they'd enjoy their afternoon. "Jason, please look after Mrs. Allcock."

Councillor and Mrs. Allcock were passed on to Jason and drinks.

"Oh, Mrs. Bantry, it *is* nice of you to come."

"I wouldn't have missed it for the world," said Mrs. Bantry and moved on purposefully towards the martinis.

The young man called Haily Preston ministered to her in a tender manner and then made off, consulting a little list in his hand, to fetch, no doubt, more of the Chosen to the Presence. It was all being managed very well, Mrs. Bantry thought, turning, martini in hand, to watch the next arrivals. The vicar, a lean, ascetic man, was looking vague and slightly bewildered. He said earnestly to Marina Gregg:

"Very nice of you to ask me. I'm afraid, you know, I haven't got a television set myself, but of course I—er—I—well, of course my young people keep me up to the mark."

Nobody knew what he meant. Miss Zielinsky, who was also on duty, administered a lemonade to him with a kindly smile. Mr. and Mrs. Badcock were next up the stairs. Heather Badcock, flushed and triumphant, came a little ahead of her husband.

"Mr. and Mrs. Badcock," boomed the man in livery.

"Mrs. Badcock," said the vicar, turning back, lemonade in hand, "the indefatigable secretary of the association. She's one of our hardest workers. In fact I don't know what St. John's would do without her."

"I'm sure you've been wonderful," said Marina.

"You don't remember me?" said Heather, in an arch manner. "How should you, with all the hundreds of people you meet. And anyway, it was years ago. In Bermuda, of all places in the world. I was there with one of our ambulance units. Oh, it's a long time ago now."

"Of course," said Marina Gregg, once more all charm and smiles.

"I remember it all so well," said Mrs. Badcock. "I was thrilled, you know, absolutely thrilled. I was only a girl at the time. To think there was a chance of seeing Marina Gregg in the flesh—oh! I was a mad fan of yours always."

"It's too kind of you, really too kind of you," said Marina sweetly, her eyes beginning to hover faintly over Heather's shoulder towards the next arrivals.

"I'm not going to detain you," said Heather, "but I must—"

"Poor Marina Gregg," said Mrs. Bantry to herself. "I suppose this kind of thing is always happening to her! The patience they need!"

Heather was continuing in a determined manner with her story.

Mrs. Allcock breathed heavily at Mrs. Bantry's shoulder.

"The changes they've made here! You wouldn't believe till you saw for yourself. What it must have cost . . ."

"—I didn't feel really ill—and I thought I just must—"

"This is vodka." Mrs. Allcock regarded her glass suspiciously. "Mr. Rudd asked if I'd like to try it. Sounds very Russian. I don't think I like it very much . . ."

"—I said to myself; I won't be beaten! I put a lot of make-up on my face—"

"I suppose it would be rude if I just put it down somewhere." Mrs. Allcock sounded desperate.

Mrs. Bantry reassured her kindly.

"Not at all. Vodka ought really to be thrown straight down the throat"—
Mrs. Allcock looked startled—"but that needs practice. Put it down on the
table and get yourself a martini from that tray the butler's carrying."

She turned back to hear Heather Badcock's triumphant peroration.

"I've never forgotten how wonderful you were that day. It was a hundred
times worth it."

Marina's response was this time not so automatic. Her eyes, which had
wavered over Heather Badcock's shoulder, now seemed to be fixed on the
wall midway up the stairs. She was staring and there was something so
ghastly in her expression that Mrs. Bantry half took a step forward. Was the
woman going to faint? What on earth could she be seeing that gave her that
basilisk look? But before she could reach Marina's side, the latter had
recovered herself. Her eyes, vague and unfocused, returned to Heather and
the charm of manner was turned on once more, albeit a shade mechanically.

"What a nice little story. Now, what will you have to drink? Jason! A
cocktail?"

"Well, really I usually have lemonade or orange juice."

"You must have something better than that," said Marina. "This is a
feast day, remember."

"Let me persuade you to an American daiquiri," said Jason, appearing
with a couple in his hand. "They're Marina's favorites, too."

He handed one to his wife.

"I shouldn't drink any more," said Marina. "I've had three already."
But she accepted the glass.

Heather took her drink from Jason. Marina turned away to meet the next
person who was arriving.

Mrs. Bantry said to Mrs. Allcock, "Let's go and see the bathrooms."

"Oh, do you think we can? Wouldn't it look rather rude?"

"I'm sure it wouldn't," said Mrs. Bantry. She spoke to Jason Rudd. "We
want to explore your wonderful new bathrooms, Mr. Rudd. May we satisfy
this purely domestic curiosity?"

"Sure," said Jason, grinning. "Go and enjoy yourselves, girls. Draw
yourselves baths if you like."

Mrs. Allcock followed Mrs. Bantry along the passage.

"That was ever so kind of you, Mrs. Bantry. I must say I wouldn't have
dared myself."

"One has to dare if one wants to get anywhere," said Mrs. Bantry.

They went along the passage, opening various doors. Presently "Ahs"
and "Ohs" began to escape Mrs. Allcock and two other women who had
joined the party.

"I do like the pink one," said Mrs. Allcock. "Oh, I like the pink one a
lot."

"I like the one with the dolphin tiles," said one of the other women.

Mrs. Bantry acted the part of hostess with complete enjoyment. For a
moment she had really forgotten that the house no longer belonged to her.

"All those showers!" said Mrs. Allcock with awe. "Not that I really like
showers. I never know how you keep your head dry."

"It'd be nice to have a peep into the bedrooms," said one of the other
women wistfully, "but I suppose it'd be a bit too nosy. What do you think?"

"Oh, I don't think we could do that," said Mrs. Allcock. They both looked hopefully at Mrs. Bantry.

"Well," said Mrs. Bantry, "no, I suppose we oughtn't to—" Then she took pity on them. "But—I don't think anyone would know if we have one peep." She put her hand on a door handle.

But that had been attended to. The bedrooms were locked. Everyone was very disappointed.

"I suppose they've got to have some privacy," said Mrs. Bantry kindly.

They retraced their steps along the corridor. Mrs. Bantry looked out of one of the landing windows. She noted below her Mrs. Meavy (from the Development) looking incredibly smart in a ruffled organdie dress. With Mrs. Meavy, she noticed, was Miss Marple's Cherry, whose last name for the moment Mrs. Bantry could not remember. They seemed to be enjoying themselves and were laughing and talking.

Suddenly the house felt to Mrs. Bantry old, worn-out and highly artificial. In spite of its new gleaming paint, its alterations, it was in essence a tired old Victorian mansion. "I was wise to go," thought Mrs. Bantry. "Houses are like everything else. There comes a time when they've just had their day. This has had its day. It's been given a face lift, but I don't really think it's done any good."

Suddenly a slight rise in the hum of voices reached her. The two women with her started forward.

"What's happening?" said one. "It sounds as though something's happening."

They stepped back along the corridor towards the stairs. Ella Zielinsky came rapidly along and passed them. She tried a bedroom door and said quickly, "Oh, damn. Of course they've locked them all."

"Is anything the matter?" asked Mrs. Bantry.

"Someone's taken ill," said Miss Zielinsky shortly.

"Oh dear, I'm sorry. Can I do anything?"

"I suppose there's a doctor here somewhere?"

"I haven't seen any of our local doctors," said Mrs. Bantry, "but there's almost sure to be one here."

"Jason's telephoning," said Ella Zielinsky, "but she seems pretty bad."

"Who is it?" asked Mrs. Bantry.

"A Mrs. Badcock, I think."

"Heather Badcock? But she looked so well just now."

Ella Zielinsky said impatiently, "She's had a seizure, or a fit, or something. Do you know if there's anything wrong with her heart or anything like that?"

"I don't really know anything about her," said Mrs. Bantry. "She's new since my day. She comes from the Development."

"The Development? Oh, you mean that housing estate. I don't even know where her husband is or what he looks like."

"Middle-aged, fair, unobtrusive," said Mrs. Bantry. "He came with her so he must be about somewhere."

Ella Zielinsky went into a bathroom. "I don't know really what to give her," she said. "Sal volatile, do you think, something like that?"

"Is she faint?" said Mrs. Bantry.

"It's more than that," said Ella Zielinsky.

"I'll see if there's anything I can do," said Mrs. Bantry. She turned away and walked rapidly back towards the head of the stairs. Turning a corner, she cannoned into Jason Rudd.

"Have you seen Ella?" he said. "Ella Zielinsky?"

"She went along there into one of the bathrooms. She was looking for something. Sal volatile—something like that."

"She needn't bother," said Jason Rudd.

Something in his tone struck Mrs. Bantry. She looked up sharply. "Is it bad?" she said. "Really bad?"

"You could call it that," said Jason Rudd. "The poor woman's dead."

"Dead!" Mrs. Bantry was really shocked. She said, as she had said before. "But she looked so well just now."

"I know. I know," said Jason. He stood there, scowling. "What a thing to happen!"

CHAPTER SIX

I

"HERE WE ARE," said Miss Knight, settling a breakfast tray on the bed table beside Miss Marple. "And how are we this morning? I see we've got our curtains pulled back," she added with a slight note of disapproval in her voice.

"I wake early," said Miss Marple. "You probably will when you're my age," she added.

"Mrs. Bantry rang up," said Miss Knight, "about half an hour ago. She wanted to talk to you but I said she'd better ring up again after you've had your breakfast. I wasn't going to disturb you at that hour, before you'd even had a cup of tea or anything to eat."

"When my friends ring up," said Miss Marple, "I prefer to be told."

"I'm sorry, I'm sure," said Miss Knight, "but it seemed to me very inconsiderate. When you've had your nice tea and your boiled egg and your toast and butter, we'll see."

"Half an hour ago," said Miss Marple thoughtfully, "that would have been—let me see—eight o'clock."

"Much too early," reiterated Miss Knight.

"I don't believe Mrs. Bantry would have rung me up then unless it was for some particular reason," said Miss Marple. "She doesn't usually ring up in the early morning."

"Oh well, dear, don't fuss your head about it," said Miss Knight soothingly. "I expect she'll be ringing up again very shortly. Or would you like me to get her for you?"

"No, thank you," said Miss Marple. "I prefer to eat my breakfast while it's hot."

"Hope I haven't forgotten anything," said Miss Knight cheerfully.

But nothing had been forgotten. The tea had been properly made with boiling water, the egg had been boiled exactly three and three-quarter minutes, the toast was evenly browned, the butter was arranged in a nice little pat and the small jar of honey stood beside it. In many ways undeniably Miss Knight was a treasure. Miss Marple ate her breakfast and enjoyed it. Presently the whirr of a vacuum cleaner began below. Cherry had arrived.

Competing with the whirr of the vacuum cleaner was a fresh tuneful voice singing one of the latest popular tunes of the day. Miss Knight, coming in for the breakfast tray, shook her head.

"I really wish that young woman wouldn't go singing all over the house," she said. "It's not what I call respectful."

Miss Marple smiled a little. "It would never enter Cherry's head that she would have to be respectful," she remarked. "Why should she?"

Miss Knight sniffed and said, "Very different to what things used to be."

"Naturally," said Miss Marple. "Times change. That is a thing which has to be accepted." She added, "Perhaps you'll ring up Mrs. Bantry now and find out what it was she wanted."

Miss Knight bustled away. A minute or two later there was a rap on the door and Cherry entered. She was looking bright and excited and extremely pretty. A plastic overall rakishly patterned with sailors and naval emblems was tied round her dark blue dress.

"Your hair looks nice," said Miss Marple.

"Went for a perm yesterday," said Cherry. "A bit stiff still, but it's going to be all right. I came up to see if you'd heard the news."

"What news?"

"About what happened at Gossington Hall yesterday. You know there was a big do there for the St. John's Ambulance?"

Miss Marple nodded. "What happened?" she asked.

"Somebody died in the middle of it. A Mrs. Badcock. Lives round the corner from us. I don't suppose you'd know her?"

"Mrs. Badcock?" Miss Marple sounded alert. "But I do know her. I think—yes, that was the name—she came out and picked me up when I fell down the other day. She was very kind."

"Oh, Heather Badcock's kind all right," said Cherry. "Overkind, some people say. They call it interfering. Well, anyway, she up and died. Just like that."

"Died! But what of?"

"Search me," said Cherry. "She'd been taken into the house because of her being the secretary of the St. John's Ambulance, I suppose. She and the mayor and a lot of others. As far as I heard, she had a glass of something and about five minutes later she was took bad and died before you could snap your fingers."

"What a shocking occurrence," said Miss Marple. "Did she suffer from heart trouble?"

"Sound as a bell, so they say," Cherry said. "Of course, you never know, do you? I suppose you can have something wrong with your heart and nobody knowing about it. Anyway, I can tell you this. They've not sent her home."

Miss Marple looked puzzled. "What do you mean, not sent her home?"

"The body," said Cherry, her cheerfulness unimpaired. "The doctor said there'd have to be an autopsy. Post-mortem—whatever you call it. He said he hadn't attended her for anything and there was nothing to show the cause of death. Looks funny to me," she added.

"Now what do you mean by funny?" said Miss Marple.

"Well." Cherry considered. "Funny. As though there was something behind it."

"Is her husband terribly upset?"

"Looks as white as a sheet. Never saw a man as badly hit, to look at— that is to say."

Miss Marple's ears, long attuned to delicate nuances, led her to cock her head slightly on one side like an inquisitive bird.

"Was he so very devoted to her?"

"He did what she told him and gave her her own way," said Cherry, "but that doesn't always mean you're devoted, does it? It may mean you haven't got the courage to stick up for yourself."

"You didn't like her?" asked Miss Marple.

"I hardly know her really," said Cherry. "Knew her, I mean. I don't— didn't—dislike her. But she's just not my type. Too interfering."

"You mean inquisitive, nosy?"

"No, I don't," said Cherry. "I don't mean that at all. She was a very kind woman and she was always doing things for people. And she was always quite sure she knew the best thing to do. What they thought about it wouldn't have mattered. I had an aunt like that. Very fond of seedcake herself and she used to bake seedcakes for people and take them to them, and she never troubled to find out whether they liked seedcake or not. There are people can't bear it, just can't stand the flavor of caraway. Well, Heather Badcock was a bit like that."

"Yes," said Miss Marple thoughtfully, "yes, she would have been. I knew someone like that. Such people," she added, "live dangerously—though they don't know it themselves."

Cherry stared at her. "That's a funny thing to say. I don't quite get what you mean."

Miss Knight bustled in. "Mrs. Bantry seems to have gone out," she said. "She didn't say where she was going."

"I can guess where she's going," said Miss Marple. "She's coming here. I shall get up now," she added.

II

Miss Marple had just ensconced herself in her favorite chair by the window when Mrs. Bantry arrived. She was slightly out of breath.

"I've got plenty to tell you, Jane," she said.

"About the fête?" asked Miss Knight. "You went to the fête yesterday, didn't you? I was there myself for a short time early in the afternoon. The tea tent was very crowded. An astonishing lot of people seemed to be there. I didn't catch a glimpse of Marina Gregg, though, which was rather disappointing."

She picked a little dust off a table and said brightly, "Now I'm sure you two want to have a nice little chat together, " and went out of the room.

"She doesn't seem to know anything about it," said Mrs. Bantry. She fixed her friend with a keen glance. "Jane, I believe you *do* know."

"You mean about the death yesterday?"

"You always know everything," said Mrs. Bantry. "I cannot think how."

"Well, really, dear," said Miss Marple, "in the same way one has always known everything. My daily helper, Cherry Baker, brought the news. I expect the butcher will be telling Miss Knight presently."

"And what do you think of it?" said Mrs. Bantry.

"What do I think of what?" said Miss Marple.

"Now don't be aggravating, Jane, you know perfectly what I mean. There's this woman—whatever her name is—"

"Heather Badcock," said Miss Marple.

"She arrives full of life and spirit. I was there when she came. And about a quarter of an hour later she sits down in a chair, says she doesn't feel well, gasps a bit and dies. What do you think of *that?*"

"One mustn't jump to conclusions," said Miss Marple. "The point is, of course, what did a medical man think of it?"

Mrs. Bantry nodded. "There's to be an inquest and a post-mortem," she said. "That shows what they think of it, doesn't it?"

"Not necessarily," said Miss Marple. "Anyone may be taken ill and die suddenly and they have to have a post-mortem to find out the cause."

"It's more than that," said Mrs. Bantry.

"How do you know?" said Miss Marple.

"Dr. Sandford went home and rang up the police."

"Who told you that?" said Miss Marple, with great interest.

"Old Briggs," said Mrs. Bantry. "At least, he didn't tell me. You know he goes down after hours in the evening to see Dr. Sandford's garden, and he was clipping something quite close to the study and he heard the doctor ringing up the police station in Much Benham. Briggs told his daughter and his daughter mentioned it to the postwoman and she told me," said Mrs. Bantry.

Miss Marple smiled. "I see," she said, "that St. Mary Mead has not changed very much from what it used to be."

"The grapevine is much the same," agreed Mrs. Bantry. "Well, now, Jane, tell me what you think?"

"One thinks, of course, of the husband," said Miss Marple reflectively. "Was he there?"

"Yes, he was there. You don't think it would be suicide," said Mrs. Bantry.

"Certainly not suicide," said Miss Marple decisively. "She wasn't the type."

"How did you come across her, Jane?"

"It was the day I went for a walk to the Development, and fell down near her house. She was kindness itself. She was a very kind woman."

"Did you see the husband? Did he look as though he'd like to poison her?

"You know what I mean," Mrs. Bantry went on as Miss Marple showed some slight signs of protesting. "Did he remind you of Major Smith or Bertie Jones or someone you've known years ago who did poison a wife, or tried to?"

"No," said Miss Marple, "he didn't remind me of anyone I know." She added, "But she did."

"Who—Mrs. Badcock?"

"Yes," said Miss Marple, "she reminded me of someone called Alison Wilde."

"And what was Alison Wilde like?"

"She didn't know at all," said Miss Marple slowly, "what the world was like. She didn't know what people were like. She'd never thought about them. and so, you see, she couldn't guard against things happening to her."

"I don't really think I understand a word of what you're saying," said Mrs. Bantry.

"It's very difficult to explain exactly," said Miss Marple apologetically. "It comes really from being self-centered and I don't mean selfish by that," she added. "You can be kind and unselfish and even thoughtful. But if you're like Alison Wilde, you never really know what you may be doing. And so you never know what may happen to you."

"Can't you make that a little clearer?" said Mrs. Bantry.

"Well, I suppose I could give you a sort of figurative example. This isn't anything that actually happened, it's just something I am inventing."

"Go on," said Mrs. Bantry.

"Well, supposing you went into a shop, say, and you knew the proprietress had a son who was the spivvy young juvenile delinquent type. He was there listening while you told his mother about some money you had in the house, or some silver or a piece of jewelry. It was something you were excited and pleased about and you wanted to talk about it. And you also perhaps mention an evening that you were going out. You even say you never lock the house. You're interested in what you're saying, what you're telling her, because it's so very much in your mind. And then, say, on that particular evening you come home because you've forgotten something and there's this bad lot of a boy in the house, caught in the act, and he turns round and coshes you."

"That might happen to almost anybody nowadays," said Mrs. Bantry.

"Not quite," said Miss Marple; "most people have a sense of protection. They realize when it's unwise to say or do something because of the person or persons who are taking in what you say, and because of the kind of character that those people have. But as I say, Alison Wilde never thought of anybody else but herself— She was the sort of person who tells you what they've done and what they've seen and what they've felt and what they've heard. They never mention what any other people said or did. Life is a kind of one-way track—just their own progress through it. Other people seem to them just like—like wallpaper in a room." She paused and then said, "I think Heather Badcock was that kind of person."

Mrs. Bantry said, "You think she was the sort of person who might have butted into something without knowing what she was doing?"

"And without realizing that it was a dangerous thing to do," said Miss

Marple. She added, "It's the only reason I can possibly think of why she would have been killed. If, of course," added Miss Marple, "we are right in assuming that murder *has* been committed."

"You don't think she was blackmailing someone?" Mrs. Bantry suggested.

"Oh, no," Miss Marple assured her. "She was a kind, good woman. She'd never have done anything of *that* kind." She added vexedly, "The whole thing seems to me very unlikely. I suppose it can't have been—"

"Well?" Mrs. Bantry urged her.

"I just wondered if it might have been the wrong murder," said Miss Marple thoughtfully.

The door opened and Dr. Haydock breezed in, Miss Knight twittering behind him.

"Ah, at it already, I see," said Dr. Haydock, looking at the two ladies. "I came in to see how your health was," he said to Miss Marple, "but I needn't ask. I see you've begun to adopt the treatment that I suggested."

"Treatment, Doctor?"

Dr. Haydock pointed a finger at the knitting that lay on the table beside her. "Unraveling," he said. "I'm right, aren't I?"

Miss Marple twinkled very slightly in a discreet, old-ladyish kind of way.

"You will have your joke, Dr. Haydock," she said.

"You can't pull the wool over my eyes, my dear lady. I've known you too many years. Sudden death at Gossington Hall and all the tongues of St. Mary Mead are wagging. Isn't that so? Murder suggested long before anybody even knows the result of the inquest."

"When is the inquest to be held?" asked Miss Marple.

"The day after tomorrow," said Dr. Haydock, "and by that time," he said, "you ladies will have reviewed the whole story, decided on the verdict and decided on a good many other points too, I expect. Well," he added, "I shan't waste my time here. It's no good wasting time on a patient that doesn't need my ministrations. Your cheeks are pink, your eyes are bright, you've begun to enjoy yourself. Nothing like having an interest in life. I'll be on my way." He stomped out again.

"I'd rather have him than Sandford any day," said Mrs. Bantry.

"So would I," said Miss Marple. "He's a good friend, too," she added thoughtfully. "He came, I think, to give me the go-ahead sign."

"Then it *was* murder," said Mrs. Bantry. They looked at each other. "At any rate, the doctors think so."

Miss Knight brought in cups of coffee. For once in their lives, both ladies were too impatient to welcome this interruption. When Miss Knight had gone, Miss Marple started immediately.

"Now then, Dolly, you were there—"

"I practically saw it happen," said Mrs. Bantry, with modest pride.

"Splendid," said Miss Marple. "I mean—well, you know what I mean. So you can tell just exactly what happened from the moment she arrived."

"I'd been taken into the house," said Mrs. Bantry. "Snob status."

"Who took you in?"

"Oh, a willowy-looking young man. I think he's Marina Gregg's secretary or something like that. He took me in, up the staircase. They were having a kind of reunion reception committee at the top of the stairs."

"On the landing?" said Miss Marple, surprised.

"Oh, they've altered all that. They've knocked the dressing-room and bedroom down so that you've got a big sort of alcove, practically a room. It's very attractive-looking."

"I see. And who was there?"

"Marina Gregg, being natural and charming, looking lovely in a sort of willowy grey-green dress. And the husband, of course, and that woman Ella Zielinsky I told you about. She's their social secretary. And there were about—oh, eight or ten people, I should think. Some of them I knew, some of them I didn't. Some I think were from the studios—the ones I didn't know. There was the vicar and Dr. Sandford's wife. He wasn't there himself until later, and Colonel and Mrs. Clittering and the High Sheriff. And I think there was someone from the press there. And a young woman with a big camera taking photographs."

Miss Marple nodded.

"Go on."

"Heather Badcock and her husband arrived just after me. Marina Gregg said nice things to me, then to somebody else, oh, yes—the vicar—and then Heather Badcock and her husband came. She's the secretary, you know, of the St. John's Ambulance. Somebody said something about that and how hard she worked and how valuable she was. And Marina Gregg said some pretty things. Then Mrs. Badcock, who struck me, I must say, Jane, as a rather tiresome sort of woman, began some long rigmarole of how years before she'd met Marina Gregg somewhere. She wasn't awful tactful about it since she urged exactly how long ago and the year it was and everything like that. I'm sure that actresses and film stars and people don't really like being reminded of the exact age they are. Still, she wouldn't think of that, I suppose."

"No," said Miss Marple, "she wasn't the kind of woman who would have thought of that. Well?"

"Well, there was nothing particular in that except for the fact that Marina Gregg didn't do her usual stuff."

"You mean she was annoyed?"

"No, no, I don't mean that. As a matter of fact I'm not at all sure that she heard a word of it. She was staring, you know, over Mrs. Badcock's shoulder, and when Mrs. Badcock had finished her rather silly story of how she got out of a bed of sickness and sneaked out of the house to go and meet Marina and get her autograph, there was a sort of odd silence. Then I saw her face."

"Whose face? Mrs. Badcock's?"

"No. Marina Gregg's. It was as though she hadn't heard a word the Badcock woman was saying. She was staring over her shoulder right at the wall opposite. Staring with—I can't explain it to you—"

"But do try, Dolly," said Miss Marple, "because I think perhaps that this might be important."

"She had a kind of frozen look," said Mrs. Bantry, struggling with words, "as though she'd seen something that—oh, dear me, how hard it is to describe things. Do you remember the Lady of Shallot? *The mirror crack'd from side to side; 'The doom has come upon me,' cried the Lady of Shalott.* Well, that's what she looked like. People laugh at Tennyson nowadays, but the Lady of Shallot always thrilled me when I was young and it still does."

"She had a frozen look," repeated Miss Marple thoughtfully. "And she was looking *over* Mrs. Badcock's shoulder at the wall. What was on that wall?"

"Oh! A picture of some kind, I think," said Mrs. Bantry. "You know, Italian. I think it was a copy of a Bellini Madonna, but I'm not sure. A picture where the Virgin is holding up a laughing child."

Miss Marple frowned. "I can't see that a *picture* could give her that expression."

"Especially as she must see it every day," agreed Mrs. Bantry.

"There were people coming up the stairs still, I suppose?"

"Oh, yes, there were."

"Who were they, do you remember?"

"You mean she might have been looking at one of the people coming up the stairs?"

"Well, it's possible, isn't it?" said Miss Marple.

"Yes—of course— Now let me see. There was the mayor, all dressed up too with his chains and all, and his wife, and there was a man with long hair and one of those funny beards they wear nowadays. Quite a young man. And there was the girl with the camera. She'd taken her position on the stairs so as to get photos of people coming up and having their hands shaken by Marina, and—let me see, two people I didn't know. Studio people, I think, and the Grices from Lower Farm. There may have been others, but that's all I can remember now."

"Doesn't sound very promising," said Miss Marple. "What happened next?"

"I think Jason Rudd nudged her or something because all of a sudden she seemed to pull herself together and she smiled at Mrs. Badcock, and she began to say all the usual things. You know, sweet, unspoilt, natural, charming, the usual bag of tricks."

"And then?"

"And then Jason Rudd gave them drinks."

"What kind of drinks?"

"Daiquiris, I think. He said they were his wife's favorites. He gave one to her and one to the Badcock woman."

"That's very interesting," said Miss Marple. "Very interesting indeed. And what happened after that?"

"I don't know, because I took a gaggle of women to look at the bathrooms. The next thing I knew was when the secretary woman came rushing along and said someone had been taken ill."

CHAPTER SEVEN

THE INQUEST, WHEN it was held, was short and disappointing. Evidence of identification was given by the husband, and the only other evidence was medical. Heather Badcock had died as a result of four grains of hy-ethyldexyl-barbo-quindelorytate, or, let us be frank, some such name! There was no evidence to show how the drug was administered.

The inquest was adjourned for a fortnight.

After it was concluded, Detective-Inspector Frank Cornish joined Arthur Badcock.

"Could I have a word with you, Mr. Badcock?"

"Of course, of course."

Arthur Badcock looked more like a chewed-out bit of string than ever. "I can't understand it," he muttered. "I simply can't understand it."

"I've got a car here," said Cornish. "We'll drive back to your house, shall we? Nicer and more private there."

"Thank you, sir. Yes, yes, I'm sure that would be much better."

They drew up at the neat little blue-painted gate of No. 3 Arlington Close. Arthur Badcock led the way and the inspector followed him. He drew out his latchkey but before he had inserted it into the door, it was opened from inside. The woman who opened it stood back looking slightly embarrassed. Arthur Badcock looked startled.

"Mary," he said.

"I was just getting you ready some tea, Arthur. I thought you'd need it when you came back from the inquest."

"That's very kind of you, I'm sure," said Arthur Badcock gratefully. "Er—" he hesitated. "This is Inspector Cornish, Mrs. Bain. She's a neighbor of mine."

"I see," said Inspector Cornish.

"I'll get another cup," said Mrs. Bain.

She disappeared and rather doubtfully Arthur Badcock showed the inspector into the bright cretonne-covered sitting-room to the right of the hall.

"She's very kind," said Arthur Badcock. "Very kind always."

"You've known her a long time?"

"Oh, no. Only since we came here."

"You've been here two years, I believe, or is it three?"

"Just about three now," said Arthur. "Mrs. Bain only got here about six months ago," he explained. "Her son works near here and so, after her husband's death, she came down to live here and he boards with her."

Mrs. Bain appeared at this point bringing the tray from the kitchen. She was a dark, rather intense-looking woman of about forty years of age. She had gypsy coloring that went with her dark hair and eyes. There was something a little odd about her eyes. They had a watchful look. She put down the tray on the table and Inspector Cornish said something pleasant and noncommittal. Something in him, some professional instinct, was on the alert. The watchful look in the woman's eyes, the slight start she had given when Arthur introduced him had not passed unnoticed. He was familiar with that slight uneasiness in the presence of the police. There were two kinds of uneasiness. One was the kind of natural alarm and distrust as of those who might have offended unwittingly against the majesty of the law, but there was a second kind. And it was the second kind that he felt sure was present here. Mrs. Bain, he thought, had had at some time some connection with the police, something that had left her wary and ill at ease. He made a mental note to find out a little more about Mary Bain. Having set down the tea tray, and refused to partake herself saying she had to get home, she departed.

"Seems a nice woman," said Inspector Cornish.

"Yes, indeed. She's very kind, a very good neighbor, a very sympathetic woman," said Arthur Badcock.

"Was she a great friend of your wife?"

"No. No, I wouldn't say that. They were neighborly and on pleasant terms. Nothing special about it though."

"I see. Now, Mr. Badcock, we want as much information as we can from you. The findings of the inquest have been a shock to you, I expect?"

"Oh, they have, Inspector. Of course I realized that you must think something was wrong, and I almost thought so myself because Heather has always been such a healthy woman. Practically never a day's illness. I said to myself, 'There *must* be something wrong.' But it seems so incredible, if you understand what I mean, Inspector. Really quite incredible. What is this stuff—this hy-ethyl-hex—" he came to a stop.

"There is an easier name for it," said the inspector. "It's sold under a trade name, the trade name of Calmo. Ever come across it?"

Arthur Badcock shook his head, perplexed.

"It's more used in America than here," said the inspector. "They prescribe it very freely over there, I understand."

"What's it for?"

"It induces, or so I understand, a happy and tranquil state of mind," said Cornish. "It's prescribed for those under strain; suffering anxiety, depression, melancholy, sleeplessness and a good many other things. The properly prescribed dose is not dangerous, but overdoses are not to be advised. It would seem that your wife took something like six times the ordinary dose."

Badcock stared. "Heather never took anything like that in her life," he said. "I'm sure of it. She wasn't one for taking medicines anyway. She was never depressed or worried. She was one of the most cheerful women you could possibly imagine."

The inspector nodded. "I see. And no doctor had prescribed anything of this kind for her?"

"No. Certainly not. I'm sure of that."

"Who was her doctor?"

"She's on Dr. Sim's panel, but I don't think she's been to him once since we've been here."

Inspector Cornish said thoughtfully, "So she doesn't seem the kind of woman to have been likely to need such a thing, or to have taken it?"

"She didn't, Inspector, I'm sure she didn't. She must have taken it by a mistake of some kind."

"It's a very difficult mistake to imagine," said Inspector Cornish. "What did she have to eat and drink that afternoon?"

"Well, let me see. For lunch—"

"You needn't go back as far as lunch," said Cornish. "Given in such quantity, the drug would act quickly and suddenly. Tea. Go back to tea."

"Well, we went into the marquee in the grounds. It was a terrible scrum in there, but we managed in the end to get a bun each and a cup of tea. We finished it as quickly as possible because it was very hot in the marquee and we came out again."

"And that's all she had, a bun and a cup of tea there?"

"That's right, sir."

"And after that you went into the house. Is that right?"

"Yes. The young lady came and said that Miss Marina Gregg would be very pleased to see my wife if she would like to come into the house. Of course my wife was delighted. She had been talking about Marina Gregg for days. Everybody was excited. Oh, well, you know that, Inspector, as well as anyone does."

"Yes, indeed," said Cornish. "My wife was excited, too. Why, from all around people were paying their shilling to go in and see Gossington Hall and what had been done there, and hoping to catch a glimpse of Marina Gregg herself."

"The young lady took us into the house," said Arthur Badcock, "and up the stairs. That's where the party was. On the landing up there. But it looked quite different from what it used to look like, so I understand. It was more like a room, a sort of big hollowed-out place with chairs and tables with drinks on them. There were about ten or twelve people there, I suppose."

Inspector Cornish nodded. "And you were received there—by whom?"

"By Miss Marina Gregg herself. Her husband with with her. I've forgotten his name now."

"Jason Rudd," said Inspector Cornish.

"Oh, yes, not that I noticed him at first. Well, anyway, Miss Gregg greeted Heather very nicely and seemed very pleased to see her, and Heather was talking and telling a story of how she'd once met Miss Gregg years ago in the West Indies and everything seemed as right as rain."

"Everything seemed right as rain," echoed the inspector. "And then?"

"And then Miss Gregg said what would we have? And Miss Gregg's husband, Mr. Rudd, got Heather a kind of cocktail. A dickery or something like that."

"A daiquiri."

"That's right, sir. He brought two. One for her and one for Miss Gregg."

"And you, what did you have?"

"I had a sherry."

"I see. And you three stood there drinking your drinks together?"

"Well, not quite like that. You see there were more people coming up the stairs. There was the mayor, for one, and some other people—an American gentleman and lady, I think—so we moved off a bit."

"And your wife drank her daiquiri then?"

"Well, no, not then, she didn't."

"Well, if she didn't drink it then, when did she drink it?"

Arthur Badcock stood frowning in remembrance. "I think—she set it down on one of the tables. She saw some friends there. I think it was someone to do with St. John's Ambulance who'd driven over from Much Benham or somewhere like that. Anyway, they got to talking together."

"And when did she drink her drink?"

Arthur Badcock again frowned. "It was a little after that," he said. "It was getting rather more crowded by then. Somebody jogged Heather's elbow and her glass got spilt."

"What's that?" Inspector Cornish looked up sharply. "Her drink was spilt?"

"Yes, that's how I remember it. . . . She'd picked it up and I think she took a little sip and made rather a face. She didn't really like cocktails, you know, but all the same she wasn't going to be downed by that. Anyway, as she stood there, somebody jogged her elbow and the glass spilled over. It went down her dress and I think it went on Miss Gregg's dress, too. Miss Gregg couldn't have been nicer. She said it didn't matter at all and it would make no stain and she gave Heather a handkerchief to wipe up Heather's dress, and then she passed over the drink she was holding and said, 'Have this, I haven't touched it yet.'"

"She handed over her own drink, did she?" said the inspector. "You're sure of that?"

Arthur Badcock paused a moment while he thought. "Yes, I'm quite sure of that," he said.

"And your wife took the drink?"

"Well, she didn't want to at first, sir. She said, 'Oh, no, I couldn't do that,' and Miss Gregg laughed and said, 'I've had far too much to drink already.'"

"And so your wife took that glass and did what with it?"

"She turned away a little and drank it, rather quick, I think. And then we walked a little way along the corridor, looking at some of the pictures and the curtains. Lovely curtain stuff it was, like nothing we'd seen before. Then I met a pal of mine, Councillor Allcock, and I was just passing the time of day with him when I looked round and saw Heather was sitting in a chair looking rather odd, so I came to her and said, 'What's the matter?' She said she felt a little queer."

"What kind of queerness?"

"I don't know, sir. I didn't have time. Her voice sounded very queer and thick and her head was rolling a little. All of a sudden she made a great half gasp and her head fell forward. She was dead, sir, dead."

CHAPTER EIGHT

I

"ST. MARY MEAD, you say?" Chief Inspector Craddock looked up sharply.

The assistant commissioner was a little surprised.

"Yes," he said, "St. Mary Mead. Why? Does it—"

"Nothing really," said Dermot Craddock.

"It's quite a small place, I understand," went on the other. "Though of course there's a great deal of building development going on there now. Practically all the way from St. Mary Mead to Much Benham, I understand. Hellingforth Studios," he added, "are on the other side of St. Mary Mead, towards Market Basing." He was still looking slightly inquiring. Dermot Craddock felt that he should perhaps explain.

"I know someone living there," he said. "At St. Mary Mead. An old lady.

A very old lady by now. Perhaps she's dead, I don't know. But if not—"

The assistant commissioner took his subordinate's point, or at any rate thought he did.

"Yes," he said, "it would give you an 'in' in a way. One needs a bit of local gossip. The whole thing is a curious business."

"The County have called us in?" Dermot asked.

"Yes. I've got the chief constable's letter here. They don't seem to feel that it's necessarily a local affair. The largest house in the neighborhood, Gossington Hall, was recently sold as a residence for Marina Gregg, the film star, and her husband. They're shooting a film at their new studios, at Hellingforth, in which she is starring. A fête was held in the grounds in aid of St. John's Ambulance. The dead woman—her name is Mrs. Heather Badcock—was the local secretary of this and had done most of the administrative work for the fête. She seems to have been a competent, sensible person, well liked locally."

"One of those bossy women?" suggested Craddock.

"Very possibly," said the assistant commissioner. "Still, in my experience, bossy women seldom get themselves murdered. I can't think why not. When you come to think of it, it's rather a pity. There was a record attendance at the fête, it seems, good weather, everything running to plan. Marina Gregg and her husband held a kind of small private reception in Gossington Hall. About thirty or forty people attended this. The local notables, various people connected with the St. John's Ambulance Association, several friends of Marina Gregg herself, and a few people connected with the studios. All very peaceful, nice and happy. But, fantastically and improbably, Heather Badcock was poisoned there."

Dermot Craddock said thoughtfully, "An odd place to choose."

"That's the chief constable's point of view. If anyone wanted to poison Heather Badcock, why choose that particular afternoon and circumstances? Hundreds of much simpler ways of doing it. A risky business anyway, you know, to slip a dose of deadly poison into a cocktail in the middle of twenty or thirty people milling about. Somebody ought to have seen something."

"It definitely was in the drink?"

"Yes, it was definitely in the drink. We have the particulars here. One of those long inexplicable names that doctors delight in, but actually a fairly common prescription in America."

"In America. I see."

"Oh, this country, too. But these things are handed out much more freely on the other side of the Atlantic. Taken in small doses, beneficial."

"Supplied on prescription or can it be bought freely?"

"No. You have to have a prescription."

"Yes, it's odd," said Dermot. "Heather Badcock have any connection with those film people?"

"None whatever."

"Any member of her own family at this do?"

"Her husband."

"Her husband," said Dermot thoughtfully.

"Yes, one always thinks that way," agreed his superior officer, "but the local man—Cornish, I think his name is—doesn't seem to think there's anything in that, although he does report that Badcock seemed ill at ease and nervous, but he agrees that respectable people often are like that when interviewed by the police. They appear to have been quite a devoted couple."

"In other words, the police there don't think it's their pigeon. Well, it ought to be interesting. I take it I'm going down there, sir?"

"Yes. Better get there as soon as possible, Dermot. Who do you want with you?"

Dermot considered for a moment or two.

"Tiddler, I think," he said thoughtfully. "He's a good man and, what's more, he's a film fan. That might come in useful."

The assistant commissioner nodded. "Good luck to you," he said.

II

"Well!" exclaimed Miss Marple, going pink with pleasure and surprise. "This *is* a surprise. How are you, my dear boy—though you're hardly a boy now. What are you—a Chief Inspector or this new thing they call a Commander?"

Dermot explained his present rank.

"I suppose I need hardly ask what you are doing down here," said Miss Marple. "Our local murder is considered worthy of the attention of Scotland Yard."

"They handed it over to us," said Dermot, "and so, naturally, as soon as I got down here I came to headquarters."

"Do you mean—" Miss Marple fluttered a little.

"Yes, Aunty," said Dermot disrespectfully. "I mean you."

"I'm afraid," said Miss Marple regretfully, "I'm very much out of things nowadays. I don't get out much."

"You get out enough to fall down and be picked up by a woman who's going to be murdered ten days later," said Dermot Craddock.

Miss Marple made the kind of noise that would once have been written down as "tut-tut."

"I don't know where you hear these things," she said.

"You should know," said Dermot Craddock. "You told me yourself that in a village everybody knows everything."

"And just off the record," he added, "did you think she was going to be murdered as soon as you looked at her?"

"Of course not, of course not," exclaimed Miss Marple. "What an idea!"

"You didn't see that look in her husband's eye that reminded you of Harry Simpson or David Jones or somebody you've known years ago, and who subsequently pushed his wife off a precipice?"

"No, I did not!" said Miss Marple. "I'm sure Mr. Badcock would never do a wicked thing of that kind. At least," she added thoughtfully, "I'm nearly sure."

"But human nature being what it is—" murmured Craddock wickedly.

"Exactly," said Miss Marple. She added, "I dare say, after the first natural grief, he won't miss her very much. . . ."

"Why? Did she bully him?"

"Oh, no," said Miss Marple, "but I don't think that she—well, she wasn't a considerate woman. Kind, yes. Considerate—no. She would be fond of him and look after him when he was ill and see to his meals and be a good housekeeper, but I don't think she would ever—well, that she would ever even know what he might be feeling or thinking. That makes rather a lonely life for a man."

"Ah," said Dermot, "and is his life less likely to be lonely in future?"

"I expect he'll marry again," said Miss Marple. "Perhaps quite soon. And probably, which is such a pity, a woman of much the same type. I mean he'll marry someone with a stronger personality than his own."

"Anyone in view?" asked Dermot.

"Not that I know of," said Miss Marple. She added regretfully, "But I know so little."

"Well, what do you *think?*" urged Dermot Craddock. "You've never been backward in thinking things."

"I think," said Miss Marple unexpectedly, "that you ought to go out and see Mrs. Bantry."

"Mrs. Bantry? Who is she? One of the film lot?"

"No," said Miss Marple, "she lives in the East Lodge at Gossington. She was at the party that day. She used to own Gossington at one time. She and her husband, Colonel Bantry."

"She was at the party. And she saw something?"

"I think she must tell you herself what it was she saw. You mayn't think it has any bearing on the matter, but I think it might be—just might be—suggestive. Tell her I sent you to her and—ah, yes, perhaps you'd better just mention the Lady of Shalott."

Dermot Craddock looked at her with his head just slight on one side.

"The Lady of Shallot," he said. "Those are the code words, are they?"

"I don't know that I should put it that way," said Miss Marple, "but it will remind her of what I mean."

Dermot Craddock got up. "I shall be back," he warned her.

"That is very nice of you," said Miss Marple. "Perhaps if you have time, you would come and have tea with me one day. If you still drink tea," she added, rather wistfully. "I know that so many young people nowadays only go out to drinks and things. They think that afternoon tea is a very out-moded affair."

"I'm not as young as all that," said Dermot Craddock. "Yes, I'll come and have tea with you one day. We'll have tea and gossip, and talk about the village. Do you know any of the film stars, by the way, or any of the studio lot?"

"Not a thing," said Miss Marple, "except what I hear," she added.

"Well, you usually hear a good deal," said Dermot Craddock. "Goodbye. It's been very nice to see you."

III

"Oh, how do you do?" said Mrs. Bantry, looking slightly taken aback when Dermot Craddock had introduced himself and explained who he was. "How very exciting to see you. Don't you always have sergeants with you?"

"I've got a sergeant down here, yes," said Craddock. "But he's busy."

"On routine inquiries?" asked Mrs. Bantry hopefully.

"Something of the kind," said Dermot gravely.

"And Jane Marple sent you to me," said Mrs. Bantry, as she ushered him into her small sitting-room. "I was just arranging some flowers," she explained. "It's one of those days when flowers won't do anything you want them to. They fall out, or stick up where they shouldn't stick up or won't lie down where you want them to lie down. So I'm thankful to have a distraction, and especially such an exciting one. So it really was murder, wasn't it?"

"Did you think it was murder?"

"Well, it could have been an accident, I suppose," said Mrs. Bantry. "Nobody's said anything definite, officially, that is. Just that rather silly piece about no evidence to show by whom or in what way the poison was administered. But, of course, we all talk about it as murder."

"And about who did it?"

"That's the odd part of it," said Mrs. Bantry. "We don't. Because I really don't see who *can* have done it."

"You mean as a matter of definite physical fact you don't see who could have done it?"

"Well, no, not that. I suppose it would have been difficult but not impossible. No, I mean I don't see who could have *wanted* to do it."

"Nobody, you think, could have wanted to kill Heather Badcock?"

"Well, frankly," said Mrs. Bantry, "I can't imagine anybody wanting to kill Heather Badcock. I've seen her quite a few times, on local things, you know. Girl Guides and St. John's Ambulance, and various parish things. I found her a rather trying sort of woman. Very enthusiastic about everything and a bit given to overstatement, and just a little bit of a gusher. But you don't want to murder people for that. She was the kind of woman who in the old days if you'd seen her approaching the front door, you'd have hurried out to say to your parlor-maid—which was an institution we had in those days and very useful, too—and told her to say 'Not at home' or 'Not at home to visitors,' if she had conscientious scruples about the truth."

"You mean that one might take pains to avoid Mrs. Badcock, but one would have no urge to remove her permanently."

"Very well put," said Mrs. Bantry, nodding approval.

"She had no money to speak of," mused Dermot, "so nobody stood to gain by her death. Nobody seems to have disliked her to the point of hatred. I don't suppose she was blackmailing anybody."

"She wouldn't have dreamed of doing such a thing, I'm sure," said Mrs. Bantry. "She was the conscientious and high-principled kind."

"And her husband wasn't having an affair with someone else?"

"I shouldn't think so," said Mrs. Bantry. "I only saw him at the party. He looked like a bit of chewed string. Nice but wet."

"Doesn't leave much, does it?" said Dermot Craddock. "One falls back on the assumption that she knew something."

"Knew something?"

"To the detriment of somebody else."

Mrs. Bantry shook her head again. "I doubt it," she said. "I doubt it very much. She struck me as the kind of woman who if she had known anything about anyone, couldn't have helped talking about it."

"Well, that washes that out," said Dermot Craddock, "so we'll come, if we may, to my reasons for coming to see you. Miss Marple, for whom I have the greatest admiration and respect, told me that I was to say to you the Lady of Shalott."

"Oh, *that!*" said Mrs. Bantry.

"Yes," said Craddock. "*That!* Whatever it is."

"People don't read much Tennyson nowadays," said Mrs. Bantry.

"A few echoes come back to me," said Dermot Craddock. "She looked out to Camelot, didn't she?

> "Out flew the web and floated wide;
> The mirror crack'd from side to side;
> 'The curse has come upon me,' cried
> The Lady of Shalott."

"Exactly. She did," said Mrs. Bantry.

"I beg your pardon. Who did? Did what?"

"Looked like that," said Mrs. Bantry.

"Who looked like what?"

"Marina Gregg."

"Ah. Marina Gregg. When was this?"

"Didn't Jane Marple tell you?"

"She didn't tell me anything. She sent me to you."

"That's tiresome of her," said Mrs. Bantry, "because she can always tell things better than I can. My husband always used to say that I was so abrupt that he didn't know what I was talking about. Anyway, it may have been only my fancy. But when you see anyone looking like that you can't help remembering it."

"Please tell me," said Dermot Craddock.

"Well, it was at the party. I call it a party because what can one call things? But it was just a sort of reception up at the top of the stairs where they've made a kind of recess. Marina Gregg was there and her husband. They fetched some of us in. They fetched me, I suppose, because I once owned the house, and they fetched Heather Badcock and her husband because she'd done all the running of the fête, and the arrangements. And we happened to go up the stairs at about the same time, so I was standing there, you see, when I noticed it."

"Quite. When you noticed what?"

"Well, Mrs. Badcock went into a long spiel as people do when they meet celebrities. You know, how wonderful it was, and what a thrill and they'd always hoped to see them. And she went into a long story of how she'd once met her years ago and how exciting it had been. And I thought, in my own mind, you know, what a bore it must be for these poor celebrities to have to say all the right things. And then I noticed that Marina Gregg wasn't saying the right things. She was just staring."

"Staring—at Mrs. Badcock?"

"No—no, it looked as though she'd forgotten Mrs. Badcock altogether. I mean, I don't believe she'd even heard what Mrs. Badcock was saying. She was just staring with what I call this Lady of Shalott look, as though she'd seen something awful. Something frightening, something that she could hardly believe she saw and couldn't bear to see."

"'The curse has come upon me?'" suggested Dermot Craddock helpfully.

"Yes, just that. That's why I called it the Lady of Shalott look."

"But what was she looking *at*, Mrs. Bantry?"

"Well, I wish I knew," said Mrs. Bantry.

"She was at the top of the stairs, you say?"

"She was looking over Mrs. Badcock's head—no, more over one shoulder, I think."

"Straight at the middle of the staircase?"

"It might have been a little to one side."

"And there were people coming up the staircase?"

"Oh, yes, I should think about five or six people."

"Was she looking at one of these people in particular?"

"I can't possibly tell," said Mrs. Bantry. "You see, I wasn't facing that way. I was looking at *her*. My back was to the stairs. I thought perhaps she was looking at one of the pictures."

"But she must know the pictures quite well if she's living in the house."

"Yes, yes, of course. No, I suppose she must have been looking at one of the people. I wonder which."

"We have to try and find out," said Dermot Craddock. "Can you remember at all who the people were?"

"Well, I know the mayor was one of them, and his wife. There was someone who I think was a reporter, with red hair, because I was introduced to him later, but I can't remember his name. I never hear names. Galbraith—something like that. Then there was a big black man. I don't mean a Negro—I just mean very dark, forceful-looking. And an actress with him. A bit overblonde and the minky kind. And old General Barnstaple from Much Benham. He's practically ga-ga by now, poor boy. I don't think *he* could have been anybody's doom. Oh, and the Grices from the farm."

"Those are all the people you can remember?"

"Well, there may have been others. But you see I wasn't—well, I mean I wasn't noticing particularly. I know that the mayor and General Barnstaple and the Americans did arrive about that time. And there were people taking photographs. One I think was a local man, and there was a girl from London, an arty-looking girl with long hair and a rather large camera."

"And you think it was one of those people who brought that look to Marina Gregg's face?"

"I didn't really think anything," said Mrs. Bantry with complete frankness. "I just wondered what on earth made her look like that, and then I didn't think of it any more. But afterwards one remembers about these things. But of course," added Mrs. Bantry with honesty, "I may have imagined it. After all, she may have had a sudden toothache or a safety pin run into her or a sudden violent colic. The sort of thing where you try to go on as usual and not to show anything, but your face can't help looking awful."

Dermot Craddock laughed. "I'm glad to see you're a realist, Mrs. Bantry," he said. "As you say, it may have been something of that kind. But it's certainly just one interesting little fact that might be a pointer."

He shook hands and departed to present his official credentials in Much Benham.

CHAPTER NINE

I

"So LOCALLY YOU'VE drawn a blank?" said Craddock, offering his cigarette case to Frank Cornish.

"Completely," said Cornish. "No enemies, no quarrels, on good terms with her husband."

"No question of another woman or another man?"

The other shook his head. "Nothing of that kind. No hint of scandal anywhere. She wasn't what you'd call the sexy kind. She was on a lot of committees and things like that and there were some local rivalries, but nothing beyond that."

"There wasn't anyone else the husband wanted to marry? No one in the office where he worked?"

"He's in Biddle and Russell, the estate agents and valuers. There's Florrie West with adenoids, and Miss Grundle, who is at least fifty and as plain as a haystack—nothing much there to excite a man. Though for all that I shouldn't be surprised if he did marry again soon."

Craddock looked interested.

"A neighbor," explained Cornish. "A widow. When I went back with him from the inquest, she'd gone in and was making him tea and looking after him generally. He seemed surprised and grateful. If you ask me, she's made up her mind to marry him, but he doesn't know it yet, poor chap."

"What sort of a woman is she?"

"Good-looking," admitted the other. "Not young, but handsome in a gypsyish sort of way. High color. Dark eyes."

"What's her name?"

"Bain. Mrs. Bain. Mary Bain. She's a widow."

"What'd her husband do?"

"No idea. She's got a son working near here who lives with her. She seems a quiet, respectable woman. All the same, I've a feeling I've seen her before." He looked at his watch. "Ten to twelve. I've made an appointment for you at Gossington Hall at twelve o'clock. We'd best be going."

II

Dermot Craddock's eyes, which always looked gently inattentive, were in actuality making a close mental note of the features of Gossington Hall. Inspector Cornish had taken him there, had delivered him over to a young man called Hailey Preston, and had then taken a tactful leave. Since then, Dermot Craddock had been gently nodding at intervals as he listened to the flood of talk emanating from Mr. Preston. Hailey Preston, he gathered, was a kind of public relations or personal assistant, or private secretary, or more likely, a mixture of all three, to Jason Rudd. He talked. He talked freely and at length without much modulation and managing miraculously not to repeat himself too often. He was a pleasant young man, anxious that his own views, reminiscent of those of Dr. Pangloss that all was for the best in the best of all possible worlds, should be shared by anyone in whose company he happened to be. He said several times and in different ways what a terrible shame this had been, how worried everyone had been, how Marina was absolutely prostrated, how Mr. Rudd was more upset than he could possibly say, how it absolutely beat anything that a thing like that should happen, didn't it? Possibly there might have been some kind of allergy to some particular kind of substance? He just put that forward as an idea—allergies were extraordinary things. Chief Inspector Craddock was to count on every possible cooperation that Hellingforth Studios or any of their staff could give. He was to ask any questions he wanted, go anywhere he liked. If they could help in any way, they would do so. They all had the greatest respect for Mrs. Badcock and appreciated her strong social sense and the valuable work she had done for the St. John's Ambulance Association.

He then started again, not in the same words but using the same motifs. No one could have been more eagerly cooperative. At the same time he endeavored to convey how very far this was from the cellophane world of studios; and Mr. Jason Rudd and Miss Marina Gregg, or any of the people in the house who surely were going to do their utmost to help in any way they possibly could. Then he nodded gently some forty-four times. Dermot Craddock took advantage of the pause to say:

"Thank you very much."

It was said quietly but with a kind of finality that brought Mr. Hailey Preston up with a jerk. He said:

"Well—" and paused inquiringly.

"You said I might ask questions?"

"Sure. Sure. Fire ahead."

"Is this where she died?"

"Mrs. Badcock?"

"Mrs. Badcock. Is this the place?"

"Yes, sure. Right here. At least, well, actually I can show you the chair."

They were standing on the landing recess. Hailey Preston walked a short way along the corridor and pointed out a rather phony-looking oak armchair.

"She was sitting right there," he said. "She said she didn't feel well.

Someone went to get her something, and then she just died, right there."

"I see."

"I don't know if she'd seen a physician lately. If she'd been warned that she had anything wrong with her heart—"

"She had nothing wrong with her heart," said Dermot Craddock. "She was a healthy woman. She died of six times the maximum dose of a substance whose official name I will not try to pronounce but which I understood is generally known as Calmo."

"I know, I know," said Hailey Preston. "I take it myself sometimes."

"Indeed? That's very interesting. You find it has a good effect?"

"Marvelous. Marvelous. It bucks you up and it soothes you down, if you understand what I mean. Naturally," he added, "you would have to take it in proper dosage."

"Would there be supplies of this substance in the house?"

He knew the answer to the question, but he put it as though he did not. Hailey Preston's answer was frankness itself.

"Loads of it, I should say. There'll be a bottle of it in most of the bathroom cupboards here."

"Which doesn't make our task easier."

"Of course," said Hailey Preston, "she might have used the stuff herself and taken a dose, and as I say, had an allergy."

Craddock looked unconvinced—Hailey Preston sighed and said:

"You're quite definite about the dosage?"

"Oh, yes. It was a lethal dose and Mrs. Badcock did not take any such things herself. As far as we can make out the only things she ever took were bicarbonate of soda or aspirin."

Hailey Preston shook his head and said, "That sure gives us a problem. Yes, it sure does."

"Where did Mr. Rudd and Miss Gregg receive their guests?"

"Right here." Hailey Preston went to the spot at the top of the stairs.

Chief Inspector Craddock stood beside him. He looked at the wall opposite him. In the center was an Italian Madonna and child. A good copy, he presumed, of some well-known picture. The blue-robed Madonna held aloft the infant Jesus and both the child and the mother were laughing. Little groups of people stood on either side, their eyes upraised to the child. One of the more pleasing Madonnas, Dermot Craddock thought. To the right and left of this picture were two narrow windows. The whole effect was very charming, but it seemed to him that there was emphatically nothing there that could cause a woman to look like the Lady of Shalott whose doom had come upon her.

"People, of course, were coming up the stairs?" he asked.

"Yes. They came in driblets, you know. Not too many at once. I shepherded up some, Ella Zielinsky, that's Mr. Rudd's secretary, brought some of the others. We wanted to make it all pleasant and informal."

"Were you here yourself at the time Mrs. Badcock came up?"

"I'm ashamed to tell you, Chief Inspector Craddock, that I just can't remember. I had a list of names, I went out and I shepherded people in. I introduced them, saw to drinks, then I'd go out and come up with the next batch. At the time I didn't know this Mrs. Badcock by sight, and she wasn't one of the ones on my list to bring up."

"What about a Mrs. Bantry?"

"Ah, yes, she's the former owner of this place, isn't she? I believe she, and Mrs. Badcock and her husband, *did* come up about the same time." He paused. "And the mayor came just about then. He had a big chain on and a wife with yellow hair, wearing royal blue with frills. I remember all of them. I didn't pour drinks for any of them because I had to go down and bring up the next lot."

"Who did pour drinks for them?"

"Why, I can't exactly say. There were three or four of us on duty. I know I went down the stairs just as the mayor was coming up."

"Who else was on the stairs as you went down, if you can remember?"

"Jim Galbraith, one of the newspaper boys who was covering this, and three or four others whom I didn't know. There were a couple of photographers, one of the locals, I don't remember his name, and an arty girl from London, who rather specializes in queer angle shots. Her camera was set right up in that corner so that she could get a view of Miss Gregg receiving. Ah, now let me think, I rather fancy that that was when Ardwyck Fenn arrived."

"And who is Ardwyck Fenn?"

Hailey Preston looked shocked. "He's a big shot, Chief Inspector. A very big shot in the television and moving picture world. We didn't even know he was in this country."

"His turning up was a surprise?"

"I'll say it was," said Preston. "Nice of him to come and quite unexpected."

"Was he an old friend of Miss Gregg's and Mr. Rudd's?"

"He was a close friend of Marina's a good many years ago when she was married to her second husband. I don't know how well Jason knew him."

"Anyway, it was a pleasant surprise when he arrived?"

"Sure it was. We were all delighted."

Craddock nodded and passed from that to other subjects. He made meticulous inquiries about the drinks, their ingredients, how they were served, who served them, what servants and hired servants were on duty. The answer seemed to be, as Inspector Cornish had already hinted was the case, that although any one of thirty people *could* have poisoned Heather Badcock with the utmost ease, yet at the same time any one of the thirty might have been seen doing so! It was, Craddock reflected, a big chance to take.

"Thank you," he said at last, "now I would like, if I may, to speak to Miss Marina Gregg."

Hailey Preston shook his head.

"I'm sorry," he said, "I really am sorry, but that's right out of the question."

Craddock's eyebrows rose.

"Surely!"

"She's prostrated. She's absolutely prostrated. She's got her own physician here looking after her. He wrote out a certificate. I've got it here. I'll show it to you."

Craddock took it and read it.

"I see," he said. He asked, "Does Marina Gregg always have a physician in attendance?"

"They're very high-strung, all these actors and actresses. It's a big strain, this life. It's usually considered desirable in the case of the big shots that they should have a physician who understands their constitution and their nerves. Maurice Gilchrist has a very big reputation. He's looked after Miss Gregg for many years now. She's had a great deal of illness, as you may have read, in the last few years. She was hospitalized for a very long time. It's only about a year ago that she got her strength and health back."

"I see."

Hailey Preston seemed relieved that Craddock was not making any more protest.

"You'll want to see Mr. Rudd?" he suggested. "He'll be—" he looked at his watch—"he'll be back from the studios in about ten minutes if that's all right for you."

"That'll do admirably," said Craddock. "In the meantime, is Dr. Gilchrist actually here in the house?"

"He is."

"Then I'd like to talk to him."

"Why, certainly. I'll fetch him right away."

The young man bustled away. Dermot Craddock stood thoughtfully at the top of the stairs. Of course this frozen look that Mrs. Bantry had described might have been entirely Mrs. Bantry's imagination. She was, he thought, a woman who would jump to conclusions. At the same time he thought it quite likely that the conclusion to which she had jumped was a just one. Without going so far as to look like the Lady of Shalott seeing doom coming upon her, Marina Gregg might have seen something that vexed or annoyed her. Something that had caused her to have been negligent to a guest to whom she was talking. Somebody had come up those stairs, perhaps, who could be described as an unexpected guest—an unwelcome guest?

He turned at the sound of footsteps. Hailey Preston was back, and with him was Dr. Maurice Gilchrist. Dr. Gilchrist was not at all as Dermot Craddock had imagined him. He had no suave bedside manner, neither was he theatrical in appearance. He seemed, on the face of it, a blunt, hearty, matter-of-fact man. He was dressed in tweeds, slightly florid tweeds to the English idea. He had a thatch of brown hair and observant, keen dark eyes.

"Dr. Gilchrist? I am Chief-Inspector Dermot Craddock. May I have a word or two with you in private?"

The doctor nodded. He turned along the corridor and went along it almost to the end, then he pushed the door open and invited Craddock to enter.

"No one will disturb us here," he said.

It was obviously the doctor's own bedroom, a very comfortably appointed one. Dr. Gilchrist indicated a chair and then sat down himself.

"I understand," said Craddock, "that Miss Marina Gregg, according to you, is unable to be interviewed. What's the matter with her, Doctor?"

Gilchrist shrugged his shoulders very slightly.

"Nerves," he said. "If you were to ask her questions now she'd be in a state bordering on hysteria within ten minutes. I can't permit that. If you'd like to send your police doctor to see me, I'd be willing to give him my views. She was unable to be present at the inquest for the same reason."

"How long," asked Craddock, "is such a state of things likely to continue?"

Dr. Gilchrist looked at him and smiled. It was a likeable smile.

"If you want my opinion," he said, "a human opinion, that is, not a medical one, any time within the next forty-eight hours, she'll be not only willing, but asking to see you! She'll be wanting to ask questions. She'll be wanting to answer your questions. They're like that!" He leaned forward. "I'd like to try and make you understand if I can, Chief-Inspector, a little bit what makes these people act the way they do. The motion picture life is a life of continuous strain, and the more successful you are, the greater the strain. You live always, all day, in the public eye. When you're on location, when you're working, it's hard monotonous work with long hours. You're there in the morning, you sit and you wait. You do your small bit, the bit that's being shot over and over again. If you're rehearsing on the stage, you'd be rehearsing as likely as not a whole act, or at any rate, a part of an act. The thing would be in sequence, it would be more or less human and credible. But when you're shooting a picture, everything's taken out of sequence. It's a monotonous, grinding business. It's exhausting. You live in luxury, of course; you have soothing drugs, you have baths and creams and powders and medical attention, you have relaxations and parties and people, but you're always in the public eye. You can't enjoy yourself quietly. You can't really—ever relax."

"I can understand that," said Dermot. "Yes, I can understand."

"And there's another thing," went on Gilchrist. "If you adopt this career, and especially if you're any good at it, you are a certain kind of person. You're a person—or so I've found in my experience—with a skin too few—a person who is plagued the whole time with diffidence. A terrible feeling of inadequacy, of apprehension that you can't do what's required of you. People say that actors and actresses are vain. That isn't true. They're not conceited about themselves; they're obsessed with themselves, yes, but they need reassurance the whole time. They must be continually reassured. Ask Jason Rudd. He'll tell you the same. You have to make them feel they can do it, to assure them they can do it, take them over and over again over the same thing, encouraging them the whole time until you get the effect you want. But they are always doubtful of themselves. And that makes them, in an ordinary, human, unprofessional word: nervy. Damned nervy! A mass of nerves. And the worse their nerves are, the better they are at the job."

"That's interesting," said Craddock. "Very interesting." He paused, adding: "Though I don't see quite why you—"

"I'm trying to make you understand Marina Gregg," said Maurice Gilchrist. "You've seen her pictures, no doubt."

"She's a wonderful actress," said Dermot, "wonderful. She has a personality, a beauty, a sympathy."

"Yes," said Gilchrist, "she has all those, and she's had to work like the devil to produce the effects that she has produced. In the process her nerves get shot to pieces, and she's not actually a strong woman physically. Not as strong as you need to be. She's got one of those temperaments that swing to and fro between despair and rapture. She can't help it. She's made that way. She's suffered a great deal in her life. A large part of the suffering has been her own fault, but some of it hasn't. None of her marriages has been happy, except, I'd say, this last one. She's married to a man now who loves her dearly and who's loved her for years. She's sheltering in that love and she's happy in it. At least, at the moment she's happy in it. One can't say how long all that will last. The trouble with her is that either she thinks that at last she's got to that spot or place or that moment in her life where everything's like a fairy tale come true, that nothing can go wrong, that she'll never be unhappy again; or else she's down in the dumps, a woman whose life is ruined, who's never known love and happiness and who never will again." He added dryly, "If she could only stop halfway between the two, it's be wonderful for her; and the world would lose a fine actress."

He paused, but Dermot Craddock did not speak. He was wondering why Maurice Gilchrist was saying what he did. Why this close detailed analysis of Marina Gregg? Gilchrist was looking at him. It was as though he was urging Dermot to ask one particular question. Dermot wondered very much what the question was that he ought to ask. He said at last slowly, with the air of one feeling his way:

"She's been very much upset by this tragedy happening here?"

"Yes," said Gilchrist, "she has."

"Almost unnaturally so?"

"That depends," said Dr. Gilchrist.

"On what does it depend?"

"On her reason for being so upset."

"I suppose," said Dermot, feeling his way, "that it was a shock, a sudden death happening like that in the midst of a party."

He saw very little response on the face opposite him. "Or might it," he said, "be something more than that?"

"You can't tell, of course," said Dr. Gilchrist, "how people are going to react. You can't tell, however well you know them. They can always surprise you. Marina might have taken this in her stride. She's a soft-hearted creature. She might say, 'Oh, poor, poor woman, how tragic. I wonder how it could have happened.' She could have been sympathetic without really caring. After all, deaths do occasionally occur at studio parties. Or she might, if there wasn't anything very interesting going on, choose—choose unconsciously, mind you—to dramatize herself over it. She might decide to throw a scene. Or there might be some quite different reason."

Dermot decided to take the bull by the horns. "I wish," he said, "you would tell me what you really think?"

"I don't know," said Dr. Gilchrist, "I can't be sure." He paused and then said, "There's professional etiquette, you know. There's the relationship between doctor and patient."

"She has told you something?"

"I don't think I could go as far as that."

"Did Marina Gregg know this woman, Heather Badcock? Had she met her before?"

"I don't think she knew her from Adam," said Dr. Gilchrist. "No. That's not the trouble. If you ask me, it's nothing to do with Heather Badcock."

Dermot said, "This stuff, this Calmo. Does Marina Gregg ever use it herself?"

"Lives on it, pretty well," said Dr. Gilchrist. "So does everyone else around here," he added. "Ella Zielinsky takes it, Hailey Preston takes it, half the boiling takes it—it's the fashion at this moment. They're all much the same, these things. People get tired of one and they try a new one that comes out, and they think it's wonderful, and that it makes all the difference."

"And does it make all the difference?"

"Well," said Gilchrist, "it makes *a* difference. It does its work. It calms you or it peps you up, makes you feel you could do things which otherwise you might fancy that you couldn't. I don't prescribe them more than I can help, but they're not dangerous taken properly. They help people who can't help themselves."

"I wish I knew," said Dermot Craddock, "what it is that you are trying to tell me."

"I'm trying to decide," said Gilchrist, "what is my duty. There are two duties. There's the duty of a doctor to his patient. What his patient says to him is confidential and must be kept so. But there's another point of view. You can fancy that there is danger to a patient. You have to take steps to avoid the danger."

He stopped. Craddock looked at him and waited.

"Yes," said Dr. Gilchrist. "I think I know what I must do. I must ask you, Chief-Inspector Craddock, to keep what I am telling you confidential. Not from your colleagues, of course. But as far as regards the outer world, particularly people in the house here. Do you agree?"

"I can't bind myself," said Craddock. "I don't know what will arise. In general terms, yes, I agree. That is to say, I should imagine that any piece of information you gave me I should prefer to keep to myself and to my colleagues."

"Now listen," said Gilchrist, "this mayn't mean anything at all. Women say anything when they're in the state of nerves Marina Gregg is in now. I'm telling you something which she said to me. There may be nothing in it at all."

"What did she say?" asked Craddock.

"She broke down after this thing happened. She sent for me. I gave her a sedative. I stayed there beside her, holding her hand, telling her to calm down, telling her things were going to be all right. Then, just before she went off into unconsciousness, she said, 'It was meant for *me*, Doctor.'"

Craddock stared. "She said that, did she? And afterwards—the next day?"

"She never alluded to it again. I raised the point once. She evaded it. She said, 'Oh, you must have made a mistake. I'm sure I never said anything like that. I expect I was half doped at the time.'"

"But you think she meant it?"

"She meant it all right," said Gilchrist. "That's not to say that it is so," he added warningly. "Whether someone meant to poison her or meant to poison Heather Badcock, I don't know. You'd probably know better than I would. All I do say is that Marina Gregg definitely thought and believed that that dose was meant for her."

Craddock was silent for some moments. Then he said, "Thank you, Dr. Gilchrist. I appreciate what you have told me and I realize your motive. If what Marina Gregg said to you was founded on fact, it may mean, may it not, that there is still danger to her?"

"That's the point," said Gilchrist. "That's the whole point."

"Have you any reason to believe that that might be so?"

"No, I haven't."

"No idea what her reason for thinking so was?"

"No."

"Thank you."

Craddock got up. "Just one thing more, Doctor. Do you know if she said the same thing to her husband?"

Slowly Gilchrist shook his head. "No," he said, "I'm quite sure of that. She didn't tell her husband."

His eyes met Dermot's for a few moments, then he gave a brief nod of his head and said, "You don't want me any more? All right. I'll go back and have a look at the patient. You shall talk to her as soon as it's possible."

He left the room and Craddock remained, pursing his lips up and whistling very softly beneath his breath.

CHAPTER TEN

"JASON'S BACK NOW," said Hailey Preston. "will you come with me, Chief Inspector? I'll take you to his room."

The room which Jason Rudd used partly for office and partly for a sitting room was on the first floor. It was comfortably but not luxuriously furnished. It was a room which had little personality and no indication of the private tastes or predilection of its user. Jason Rudd rose from the desk at which he was sitting and came forward to meet Dermot. It was wholly unnecessary, Dermot thought, for the room to have a personality; the user of it had so much. Hailey Preston had been an efficient and voluble gasbag. Gilchrist had force and magnetism. But here was a man whom, as Dermot immediately admitted to himself, it would not be easy to read. In the course of his career, Craddock had met and summed up many people. By now he was fully adept in realizing the potentialities and very often reading the thoughts of most people with whom he came in contact. But he felt at once that one would be able to gauge only so much of Jason Rudd's thoughts as Jason Rudd himself permitted. The eyes, deep-set and thoughtful, perceived but would not easily reveal. The ugly, rugged head spoke of an excellent intellect. The clown's face could repel you or attract you. Here, thought Dermot Craddock to himself, is where I sit and listen and take very careful notes.

"Sorry, Chief-Inspector, if you've had to wait for me. I was held up by some small complication over at the studios. Can I offer you a drink?"

"Not just now, thank you, Mr. Rudd."

The clown's face suddenly crinkled into a kind of ironic amusement.

"Not the house to take a drink in, is that what you're thinking?"

"As a matter of fact it wasn't what I was thinking."

"No, no, I suppose not. Well, Chief Inspector, what do you want to know? What can I tell you?"

"Mr. Preston has answered very adequately all the questions I have put to him."

"And that has been helpful to you?"

"Not as helpful as I could wish."

Jason Rudd looked inquiring.

"I've also seen Dr. Gilchrist. He informs me that your wife is not yet strong enough to be asked questions."

"Marina," said Jason Rudd, "is very sensitive. She's subject, frankly, to nerve storms. And murder at such close quarters, is, as you will admit, likely to produce a nerve storm."

"It is not a pleasant experience," Dermot Craddock agreed dryly.

"In any case I doubt if there is anything my wife could tell you that you could not learn equally well from me. I was standing beside her when the thing happened, and frankly I would say that I am a better observer than my wife."

"The first question I would like to ask," said Dermot, "(and it is a question that you have probably answered already but for all that, I would like to ask it again) had you or your wife any previous acquaintance with Heather Badcock?"

Jason Rudd shook his head.

"None whatever. I certainly have never seen the woman before in my life. I had had two letters from her on behalf of the St. John's Ambulance Association, but I had not met her personally until about five minutes before her death."

"But she claimed to have met your wife?"

Jason Rudd nodded.

"Yes, some twelve or thirteen years ago, I gather. In Bermuda. Some big garden party in aid of ambulances, which Marina opened for them, I think, and Mrs. Badcock, as soon as she was introduced, burst into some long rigmarole of how although she was in bed with 'flu, she had got up and had managed to come to this affair and had asked for and got my wife's autograph."

Again the ironical smile crinkled his face.

"That, I may say, is a very common occurrence, Chief Inspector. Large mobs of people are usually lined up to obtain my wife's autograph, and it is a moment that they treasure and remember. Quite understandably, it is an event in their lives. Equally naturally it is not likely that my wife would remember one out of a thousand or so autograph hunters. She had, quite frankly, no recollection of ever having seen Mrs. Badcock before."

"That I can well understand," said Craddock. "Now I have been told, Mr. Rudd, by an onlooker that your wife was slightly distrait during the few moments that Heather Badcock was speaking to her. Would you agree that such was the case?"

"Very possibly," said Jason Rudd. "Marina is not particularly strong. She was, of course, used to what I may describe as her public social work, and could carry out her duties in that line almost automatically. But towards the end of a long day she was inclined occasionally to flag. This may have been such a moment. I did not, I may say, observe anything of the kind myself. No, wait a minute, that is not quite true. I do remember that she was a little slow in making her reply to Mrs. Badcock. In fact I think I nudged her very gently in the ribs."

"Something had perhaps distracted her attention?" said Dermot.

"Possibly, but it may have been just a momentary lapse through fatigue."

Dermot Craddock was silent for a few minutes. He looked out of the window where the view was the somewhat somber one over the woods surrounding Gossington Hall. He looked at the pictures on the walls, and finally he looked at Jason Rudd. Jason Rudd's face was attentive but nothing more. There was no guide to his feelings. He appeared courteous and completely at ease, but he might, Craddock thought, be actually nothing of the kind. This was a man of very high mental caliber. One would not, Dermot thought, get anything out of him that he was not prepared to say unless one put one's cards on the table. Dermot took his decision. He would do just that.

"Has it occurred to you, Mr. Rudd, that the poisoning of Heather Badcock may have been entirely accidental? That the real intended victim was your wife?"

There was a silence. Jason Rudd's face did not change its expression. Dermot waited. Finally Jason Rudd gave a deep sigh and appeared to relax.

"Yes," he said quietly, "you're quite right, Chief Inspector. I have been sure of it all along."

"But you have said nothing to that effect, not to Inspector Cornish, not at the inquest?"

"No."

"Why not, Mr. Rudd?"

"I could answer you very adequately by saying that it was merely a belief on my part unsupported by any kind of evidence. The facts that led me to deduce it were facts equally accessible to the law, which was probably better qualified to decide than I was. I know nothing about Mrs. Badcock personally. She might have enemies, someone might have decided to administer a fatal dose to her on this particular occasion, though it would seem a very curious and farfetched decision. But it might have been chosen conceivably for the reason that at a public occasion of this kind the issues would be more confused, the number of strangers present would be considerable, and just for that reason it would be more difficult to bring home to the person in question the commission of such a crime. All that is true, but I am going to be frank with you, Chief Inspector. That was *not* my reason for keeping silent. I will tell you what that reason was. I didn't want my wife to suspect for one moment that it was she who had narrowly escaped dying by poison."

"Thank you for your frankness," said Dermot. "Not that I quite understand your motive in keeping silent."

"No? Perhaps it is a little difficult to explain. You would have to know Marina to understand. She is a person who badly needs happiness and security. Her life has been highly successful in the material sense. She has won renown artistically, but her personal life has been one of deep unhappiness. Again and again she has thought that she has found happiness and was wildly and unduly elated thereby, and has had her hopes dashed to the ground. She is incapable, Mr. Craddock, of taking a rational, prudent view of life. In her previous marriages she has expected, like a child reading a fairy story, to live happy ever afterwards."

Again the ironic smile changed the ugliness of the clown's face into a strange, sudden sweetness.

"But marriage is not like that, Chief-Inspector. There can be no rapture continued indefinitely. We are fortunate indeed if we can achieve a life of quiet, content, affection, and serene and sober happiness." He added, "Perhaps you are married, Chief-Inspector?"

"I have not so far that good, or bad, fortune," he murmured.

"In our world, the moving picture world, marriage is a fully occupational hazard. Film stars marry often. Sometimes happily, sometimes disastrously, but seldom permanently. In that respect I should not say that Marina has had any undue cause to complain, but to one of her temperament things of that kind matter very deeply. She imbued herself with the idea that she was unlucky, that nothing would ever go right for her. She has always been looking desperately for the same thing: love, happiness, affection, security. She was wildly anxious to have children. According to some medical opinion, the very strength of that anxiety frustrated its object. One very celebrated physician advised the adoption of a child. He said it is often the case that when an intense desire for maternity is assuaged by having adopted a baby, a child is born naturally shortly afterwards. Marina adopted no less than three children. For a time she got a certain amount of happiness and serenity, but it was not the real thing. You can imagine her delight when eleven years ago she found she was going to have a child. Her pleasure and delight were quite indescribable. She was in good health and the doctors assured her that there was every reason to believe that everything would go well. As you may or may not know, the result was tragedy. The child, a boy, was born mentally deficient, imbecile. The result was disastrous. Marina had a complete breakdown and was severely ill for years, confined in a sanatorium. Though her recovery was slow, she did recover. Shortly after that we married and she began once more to take an interest in life and to feel that perhaps she could be happy. It was difficult at first for her to get a worthwhile contract for a picture. Everyone was inclined to doubt whether her health would stand the strain. I had to battle for that." Jason Rudd's lips set firmly together. "Well, the battle was successful. We have started shooting the picture. In the meantime we bought this house and set about altering it. Only about a fortnight ago Marina was saying to me how happy she was, and how she felt at last she was going to be able to settle down to a happy home life, her troubles behind her. I was a little nervous because, as usual, her expectations were too optimistic. But there was no doubt that she was happy. Her nervous symptoms disappeared, there was a calmness and a quietness about her that I had never seen before. Everything was going well until—" he paused. His voice became suddenly bitter. "Until this happened! That woman had to die—*here!* That in itself was shock enough. I couldn't risk—I was determined not to risk—Marina's knowing that an attempt had been made on *her* life. That would have been a second, perhaps fatal, shock. It might have precipitated another mental collapse."

He looked directly at Dermot.

"Do you understand—now?"

"I see your point of view," said Craddock, "but forgive me, isn't there one aspect that you are neglecting? You give me your conviction that an attempt was made to poison your wife. Doesn't that danger still remain? If a poisoner does not succeed, isn't it likely that the attempt may be repeated?"

"Naturally I've considered that," said Jason Rudd, "but I am confident that, being forewarned, so to speak, I can take all reasonable precautions for my wife's safety. I shall watch over her and arrange that others shall watch over her. The great thing, I feel, is that she herself should not know that any danger threatened her."

"And you think," said Dermot cautiously, "that she does not know?"

"Of course not. She has no idea."

"You're sure of that?"

"Certain. Such an idea would never occur to her."

"But it occurred to you," Dermot pointed out.

"That's very different," said Jason Rudd. "Logically, it was the only solution. But my wife isn't logical, and to begin with she could not possibly imagine that anyone would want to do away with her. Such a possibility would simply not occur to her mind."

"You may be right," said Dermot slowly, "but that leaves us now with several other questions. Again, let me put this bluntly. Whom do you suspect?"

"I can't tell you."

"Excuse me, Mr. Rudd, do you mean that you can't or that you won't?"

Jason Rudd spoke quickly. "Can't. Can't every time. It seems to me just as impossible as it would seem to her that anyone would dislike her enough—should have a sufficient grudge against her—to do such a thing. On the other hand, on the sheer, downright evidence of the facts, that is exactly what must have occurred."

"Will you outline the facts to me as you see them?"

"If you like. The circumstances are quite clear. I poured out two daiquiri cocktails from an already prepared jug. I took them to Marina and to Mrs. Badcock. What Mrs. Badcock did I do not know. She moved on, I presume, to speak to someone she knew. My wife had her drink in her hand. At that moment the mayor and his wife were approaching. She put down her glass, as yet untouched, and greeted them. Then there were more greetings. An old friend we'd not seen for years, some other locals and one or two people from the studios. During that time the glass containing the cocktail stood on the table which was situated at that time behind us since we had both moved forward a little to the top of the stairs. One or two photographs were taken of my wife talking to the mayor, which we hoped would please the local population, at the special request of the representatives of the local newspaper. While this was being done I brought some fresh drinks to a few of the last arrivals. During that time my wife's glass must have been poisoned. Don't ask me how it was done, it cannot have been easy to do. On the other hand, it is startling, if anyone has the nerve to do an action openly and unconcernedly, how little people are likely to notice it! You ask me if I have suspicions; all I can say is that at least one of about twenty people might have done it. People, you see, were moving about in little groups, talking, occasionally going off to have a look at the alterations which had been done to the house. There was movement, continual movement. I've thought and I've thought, I've racked my brains but there is nothing, absolutely *nothing* to direct my suspicions to any particular person."

He paused and gave an exasperated sigh.

"I dare say you've heard the next part before."

"I should like to hear it again from you."

"Well, I had come back towards the head of the stairs. My wife had turned towards the table and was just picking up her glass. There was a slight exclamation from Mrs. Badcock. Somebody must have jogged her arm and the glass slipped out of her fingers and was broken on the floor. Marina did the natural hostess's act. Her own skirt had been slightly touched with the liquid. She insisted no harm was done, used her own handkerchief to wipe Mrs. Badcock's skirt and insisted on her having her own drink. If I remember, she said, 'I've had far too much already.' So that was that. But I can assure you of this. The fatal dose could not have been added *after* that, for Mrs. Badcock immediately began to drink from the glass. As you know, four or five minutes later she was dead. I wonder—how I wonder—what the poisoner must have felt when he realized how badly his scheme had failed. . . .'

"All this occurred to you at the time?"

"Of course not. At the time I concluded, naturally enough, that this woman had had some kind of a seizure. Perhaps heart, coronary thrombosis, something of that sort. It never occurred to me that *poisoning* was involved. Would it occur to you—would it occur to anybody?"

"Probably not," said Dermot. "Well, your account is clear enough and you seem sure of your facts. You say you have no suspicion of any particular person. I can't quite accept that, you know."

"I assure you it's the truth."

"Let us approach it from another angle. Who is there who could wish to harm your wife? It all sounds melodramatic if you put it this way, but what enemies has she got?"

Jason Rudd made an expressive gesture.

"Enemies? Enemies? It's so hard to define what one means by an enemy. There's plenty of envy and jealousy in the world my wife and I occupy. There are always people who say malicious things, who'll start a whispering campaign, who will do someone they are jealous of a bad turn if the opportunity occurs. But that doesn't mean that any of those people is a murderer, or indeed even a likely murderer. Don't you agree?"

"Yes, I agree. There must be something beyond petty dislikes or envies. Is there anyone whom your wife has injured, say, in the past?"

Jason Rudd did not rebut this easily. Instead he frowned.

"Honestly, I don't think so," he said at last, "and I may say I've given a lot of thought to that point."

"Anything in the nature of a love affair, an association with some man?"

"There have of course been affairs of that kind. It may be considered, I suppose, that Marina has occasionally treated some man badly. But there is nothing to cause any lasting ill-will. I'm sure of it."

"What about women? Any woman who has had a lasting grudge against Miss Gregg?"

"Well," said Jason Rudd, "you can never tell with women. I can't think of any particular one offhand."

"Who'd benefit financially by your wife's death?"

"Her will benefits various people, but not to any large extent. I suppose the people who'd benefit, as you put it, financially, would be myself as her husband and from another angle, possibly the star who might replace her in this film. Though, of course, the film might be abandoned altogether. These things are very uncertain."

"Well, we need not go into all that now," said Dermot.

"And I have your assurance that Marina will not be told that she is in possible danger?"

"We shall have to go into that matter," said Dermot. "I want to impress upon you that you are taking quite a considerable risk there. However, the matter will not arise for some days since your wife is still under medical care. Now there is one more thing I would like you to do. I would like you to write down for me as accurately as you can every single person who was in that recess at the top of the stairs, or whom you saw coming up the stairs at the time of the murder."

"I'll do my best, but I'm rather doubtful. You'd do far better to consult my secretary, Ella Zielinsky. She has a most accurate memory and also lists of the local people who were there. If you'd like to see her now—"

"I would like to talk to Miss Ella Zielinsky very much," said Dermot.

CHAPTER ELEVEN

I

SURVEYING DERMOT CRADDOCK unemotionally through her large horn-rimmed spectacles, Ella Zielinsky seemed to him almost too good to be true. With quiet businesslike alacrity she whipped out of a drawer a typewritten sheet and passed it across to him.

"I think I can be fairly sure that there are no omissions," she said. "But it is just possible that I may have included one or two names—local names they will be—who were not actually there. That is to say who may have left earlier or who may not have been found and brought up. Actually, I'm pretty sure that it is correct."

"A very efficient piece of work if I may say so," said Dermot.

"Thank you."

"I suppose—I am quite an ignoramus in such things—that you have to attain a high standard of efficiency in your job?"

"One has to have things pretty well taped, yes."

"What exactly does your job comprise? Are you a kind of liaison officer, so to speak, between the studios and Gossington Hall?"

"No. I've nothing to do with the studios, actually, though of course I naturally take messages from there on the telephone or send them. My job is to look after Miss Gregg's social life, her public and private engagements, and to supervise in some degree the running of the house.''

"You like the job?''

"It's extremely well paid and I find it reasonably interesting. I didn't, however, bargain for murder,'' she added dryly.

"Did it seem very incredible to you?''

"So much so that I am going to ask you if you are really sure it *is* murder?''

"Six times the dose of hy-ethyl-mexine, et cetera, could hardly be anything else.''

"It might have been an accident of some kind.''

"And how would you suggest such an accident could have occurred?''

"More easily than you'd imagine, since you don't know the set-up. This house is simply full of drugs of all kinds. I don't mean dope when I say drugs. I mean properly prescribed remedies, but, like most of these things, what they call, I understand, the lethal dose is not very far removed from the therapeutic dose.''

Dermot nodded.

"These theatrical and picture people have the most curious lapses of their intelligence. Sometimes it seems to me that the more of an artistic genius you are, the less common sense you have in everyday life.''

"That may well be.''

"What with all the bottles, cachets, powders, capsules, and little boxes that they carry about with them; what with popping a tranquilizer here and a tonic there and a pep pill somewhere else, don't you think it would be easy enough that the whole thing might get mixed up?''

"I don't see how it could apply in this case.''

"Well, I think it could. Somebody, one of the guests, may have wanted a sedative, or a reviver, and whipped out his or her little container which they carry around and possibly because they hadn't had one for some time, might have put too much in a glass. Then their mind was distracted and they went off somewhere, and let's say this Mrs. What's-her-name comes along, thinks it's her glass, picks it up and drinks it. That's surely a more feasible idea than anything else?''

"You don't think that all those possibilities haven't been gone into, do you?''

"No, I suppose not. But there were a lot of people there and a lot of glasses standing about with drinks in them. It happens often enough, you know, that you pick up the wrong glass and drink out of it.''

"Then you don't think that Heather Badcock was deliberately poisoned? You think that she drank out of somebody else's glass?''

"I can't imagine anything more likely to happen.''

"In that case,'' said Dermot, speaking carefully, "It would have had to be Marina Gregg's glass. You realize that? Marina handed her her own glass.''

"Or what she thought was her own glass,'' Ella Zielinsky corrected him. "You haven't talked to Marina yet, have you? She's extremely vague. She'd pick up any glass that looked as though it were hers, and drink it. I've seen her do it again and again.''

"She takes Calmo?''

"Oh, yes, we all do."

"You too, Miss Zielinsky?"

"I'm driven to it sometimes," said Ella Zielinsky. "These things are rather imitative, you know."

"I shall be glad," said Dermot, "when I am able to talk to Miss Gregg. She—er—seems to be prostrated for a very long time."

"That's just throwing a temperament," said Ella Zielinsky. "She dramatizes herself a good deal, you know. She'd never take murder in her stride."

"As you manage to do, Miss Zielinsky?"

"When everybody about you is in a continual state of agitation," said Ella dryly, "it develops in you a desire to go to the opposite extreme."

"You learn to take a pride in not turning a hair when some shocking tragedy occurs?"

She considered. "It's not a really nice trait, perhaps. But I think if you didn't develop that sense, you'd probably go round the bend yourself."

"Was Miss Gregg—is Miss Gregg a difficult person to work for?"

It was something of a personal question, but Dermot Craddock regarded it as a kind of test. If Ella Zielinsky raised her eyebrows and tacitly demanded what this had to do with the murder of Mrs. Badcock, he would be forced to admit that it had nothing to do with it. But he wondered if Ella Zielinsky might perhaps enjoy telling him what she thought of Marina Gregg.

"She's a great artist. She's got a personal magnetism that comes over on the screen in the most extraordinary way. Because of that, one feels it's rather a privilege to work with her. Taken purely personally, of course, she's hell!"

"Ah," said Dermot.

"She has no kind of moderation, you see. She's up in the air or down in the dumps and everything is always terrifically exaggerated, and she changes her mind and there are an enormous lot of things that one must never mention or allude to because they upset her."

"Such as?"

"Well, naturally mental breakdown, or sanatoriums for mental cases. I think it is quite to be understood that she should be sensitive about that. And anything to do with children."

"Children? In what way?"

"Well, it upsets her to see children, or to hear of people being happy with children. If she hears someone is going to have a baby or has just had a baby, it throws her into a state of misery at once. She can never have another child herself, you see, and the only one she did have is batty. I don't know if you knew that?"

"I had heard it, yes. It's all very sad and unfortunate. But after a good many years you'd think she'd forget about it a little."

"She doesn't. It's an obsession with her. She broods on it."

"What does Mr. Rudd feel about it?"

"Oh, it wasn't his child. It was her last husband's, Isidore Wright's."

"Ah yes, her last husband. Where is he now?"

"He's married again and lives in Florida," said Ella Zielinsky promptly.

"Would you say that Marina Gregg had made many enemies in her life?"

"Not unduly so. Not more than most, that is to say. There are always rows over other women or other men or over contracts or jealousy—all those things."

"She wasn't as far as you know afraid of anyone?"

"Marina? *Afraid* of anyone? I don't think so. Why? Why should she be?"

"I don't know," said Dermot. He picked up the list of names. "Thank you very much, Miss Zielinsky. If there's anything else I want to know, I'll come back. May I?"

"Certainly. I'm only too anxious—we're all only too anxious—to do anything we can to help."

II

"Well, Tom, what have you got for me?"

Detective-Sergeant Tiddler grinned appreciatively. His name was not Tom, it was William, but the combination of Tom Tiddler had always been too much for his colleagues.

"What gold and silver have you picked up for me?" continued Dermot Craddock.

The two were staying at the Blue Boar, and Tiddler had just come back from a day spent at the studios.

"The proportion of gold is very small," said Tiddler. "Not much gossip. No startling rumors. One or two suggestions of suicide."

"Why suicide?"

"They thought she might have had a row with her husband and be trying to make him sorry. That line of country. But that she didn't really mean to go so far as doing herself in."

"I can't see that that's a very hopeful line," said Dermot.

"No, of course it isn't. They know nothing about it, you see. They don't know anything except what they're busy on. It's all highly technical and there's an atmosphere of 'the show must go on,' or as I suppose one ought to say, the picture must go on, or the shooting must go on. I don't know any of the right terms. All they're concerned about is when Marina Gregg will get back to the set. She's mucked up a picture once or twice before by staging a nervous breakdown."

"Do they like her on the whole?"

"I should say they consider her the devil of a nuisance but for all that, they can't help being fascinated by her when she's in the mood to fascinate them. Her husband's besotted about her, by the way."

"What do they think of him?"

"They think he's the finest director or producer or whatever it is that there's ever been."

"No rumors of his being mixed up with some other star or some woman of some kind?"

Tom Tiddler stared. "No," he said, "no. Not a hint of such a thing. Why, do you think there might be?"

"I wondered," said Dermot. "Marina Gregg is convinced that the lethal dose was meant for her."

"Is she now? Is she right?"

"Almost certainly, I should say," Dermot replied. "But that's not the point. The point is that she hasn't told her husband so, only her doctor."

"Do you think she would have told him if—"

"I just wondered," said Craddock, "whether she might have had at the back of her mind an idea that her husband had been responsible. The doctor's manner was a little peculiar. I may have imagined it, but I don't think I did."

"Well, there were no such rumors going about at the studios," said Tom. "You hear that sort of thing soon enough."

"She herself is not embroiled with any other man?"

"No, she seems to be devoted to Rudd."

"No interesting snippets about her past?"

Tiddler grinned. "Nothing to what you can read in a film magazine any day of the week."

"I think I'll have to read a few," said Dermot, "to get the atmosphere."

"The things they say and hint!" said Tiddler.

"I wonder," said Dermot thoughtfully, "if my Miss Marple reads film magazines."

"Is that the old lady who lives in the house by the church?"

"That's right."

"They say she's sharp," said Tiddler. "They say there's nothing goes on here that Miss Marple doesn't hear about. She may not know much about the film people, but she ought to be able to give you the low-down on the Badcocks all right."

"It's not as simple as it used to be," said Dermot. "There's a new social life springing up here. A housing estate, big building development. The Badcocks are fairly new and come from there."

"I didn't hear much about the locals of course," said Tiddler. "I concentrated on the sex life of film stars and such things."

"You haven't brought back very much," grumbled Dermot. "What about Marina Gregg's past, anything about that?"

"Done a bit of marrying in her time, but not more than most. Her first husband didn't like getting the chuck, so they said, but he was a very ordinary sort of bloke. He was a realtor or something like that. What is a realtor, by the way?"

"I think it means in the real estate business."

"Oh well, anyway, he didn't line up as very glamorous so she got rid of him and married a foreign count or prince. That lasted hardly any time at all, but there don't seem to be any bones broken. She just shook him off and teamed up with number three. Film star Robert Truscott. That was said to be a passionate love match. His wife didn't much like letting go of him, but she had to take it in the end. Big alimony. As far as I can make out, everybody's hard up because they've got to pay so much alimony to all their ex-wives."

"But it went wrong?"

"Yes. She was the brokenhearted one, I gather. But another big romance came along a year or two later. Isidore Somebody—a playwright."

"It's an exotic life," said Dermot. "Well, we'll call it a day now. Tomorrow we've got to get down to a bit of hard work."

"Such as?"

"Such as checking a list I've got here. Out of twenty-odd names we ought to be able to do some elimination, and out of what's left we'll have to look for X."

"Any idea who X is?"

"Not in the least. If it isn't Jason Rudd, that is." He added with a wry and ironic smile, "I shall have to go to Miss Marple and get briefed on local matters."

CHAPTER TWELVE

MISS MARPLE WAS pursuing her own method of research.

"It's very kind of you, Mrs. Jameson, very kind of you indeed. I can't tell you how grateful I am."

"Oh, don't mention it, Miss Marple. I'm sure I'm glad to oblige you. I suppose you'll want the latest ones?"

"No, no, not particularly," said Miss Marple. "In fact I think I'd rather have some of the older numbers."

"Well, here you are then," said Mrs. Jameson, "there's a nice armful and I can assure you we shan't miss them. Keep them as long as you like. Now it's too heavy for you to carry. Jenny, how's your perm doing?"

"She's all right, Mrs. Jameson. She's had her rinse and now she's having a good dry-out."

"In that case, dear, you might just run along with Miss Marple here, and carry these magazines for her. No, really, Miss Marple, it's no trouble at all. Always pleased to do anything we can for you."

How kind people were, Miss Marple thought, especially when they'd known you practically all their lives. Mrs. Jameson, after long years of running a hairdressing parlor, had steeled herself to going as far in the cause of progress as to repaint her sign and call herself. "DIANE. Hair Stylist." Otherwise the shop remained much as before and catered in much the same way to the needs of its clients. It turned you out with a nice firm perm: it accepted the task of shaping and cutting for the younger generation and the resultant mess was accepted without too much recrimination. But the bulk of Mrs. Jameson's clientele was a bunch of solid, stick-in-the-mud middle-aged ladies who found it extremely hard to get their hair done the way they wanted it anywhere else.

"Well, I never," said Cherry the next morning, as she prepared to run a virulent Hoover round the lounge as she still called it in her mind. "What's all this?"

"I am trying," said Miss Marple, "to instruct myself a little in the moving picture world."

She laid aside *Movie News* and picked up *Amongst the Stars*.

"It's really very interesting. It reminds one so much of so many things."

"Fantastic lives they must lead," said Cherry.

"Specialized lives," said Miss Marple. "Highly specialized. It reminds me very much of the things a friend of mine used to tell me. She was a hospital nurse. The same simplicity of outlook and all the gossip and the rumors. And good-looking doctors causing any amount of havoc."

"Rather sudden, isn't it, this interest of yours?" said Cherry.

"I'm finding it difficult to knit nowadays," said Miss Marple. "Of course the print of these is rather small, but I can always use a magnifying glass."

Cherry looked at her curiously.

"You're always surprising me," she said. "The things you take an interest in."

"I take an interest in everything," said Miss Marple.

"I mean taking up new subjects at your age."

Miss Marple shook her head.

"They aren't really new subjects. It's human nature I'm interested in, you know, and human nature is much the same whether it's film stars or hospital nurses or people in St. Mary Mead or," she added thoughtfully, "people who live in the Development."

"Can't see much likeness between me and a film star," said Cherry laughing, "more's the pity. I suppose it's Marina Gregg and her husband coming to live at Gossington Hall that set you off on this."

"That and the very sad event that occurred there," said Miss Marple.

"Mrs. Badcock, you mean? It was bad luck, that."

"What do you think of it in the—" Miss Marple paused with the "D" hovering on her lips. "What do you and your friends think about it?" she amended her question.

"It's a queer do," said Cherry. "Looks as though it were murder, doesn't it, though of course the police are too cagey to say so outright. Still, that's what it looks like."

"I don't see what else it could be," said Miss Marple.

"It couldn't be suicide," agreed Cherry, "not with Heather Badcock."

"Did you know her well?"

"No, not really. Hardly at all. She was a bit of a nosy parker you know. Always wanting you to join this, join that, turn up for meetings at so-and-so. Too much energy. Her husband got a bit sick of it sometimes, I think."

"She doesn't seem to have had any real enemies."

"People used to get a bit fed up with her sometimes. The point is, I don't see who could have murdered her unless it was her husband. And he's a very meek type. Still, the worm will turn, or so they say. I've always heard that Crippen was ever so nice a man and that man Haigh, who pickled them all in acid—they said he couldn't have been more charming! So one never knows, does one?"

"Poor Mr. Badcock," said Miss Marple.

"And people say he was upset and nervy at the fête that day—before it happened, I mean—but people always say that kind of thing afterwards. If you ask me, he's looking better now than he's looked in years. Seems to have got a bit more spirit and go in him."

"Indeed?" said Miss Marple.

"Nobody *really* thinks he did it," said Cherry. "Only, if he didn't, who did? I can't help thinking myself it must have been an accident of some kind. Accidents do happen. You think you know all about mushrooms and go out and pick some. One fungus gets in among them and there you are, rolling about in agony and lucky if the doctor gets to you in time."

"Cocktails and glasses of sherry don't seem to lend themselves to accident," said Miss Marple.

"Oh, I don't know," said Cherry. "A bottle of something or other could have got in by mistake. Somebody I knew took a dose of concentrated D.D.T. once. Horribly ill they were."

"Accident," said Miss Marple thoughtfully. "Yes, it certainly seems the best solution. I must say I can't believe that in the case of Heather Badcock it could have been deliberate murder. I won't say it's impossible. Nothing is impossible, but it doesn't seem like it. No, I think the truth lies somewhere here." She rustled her magazines and picked up another one.

"You mean you're looking for some special story about someone?"

"No," said Miss Marple. "I'm just looking for odd mentions of people and a way of life and something—some little something that might help." She returned to her perusal of the magazines and Cherry removed her vacuum cleaner to the upper floor. Miss Marple's face was pink and interested, and being slightly deaf now, she did not hear the footsteps that came along the garden path towards the drawing-room window. It was only when a slight shadow fell on the page that she looked up. Dermot Craddock was standing smiling at her.

"Doing your homework, I see," he remarked.

"Inspector Craddock, how very nice to see you. And how kind to spare time to come and see me. Would you like a cup of coffee, or possibly a glass of sherry?"

"A glass of sherry would be splendid," said Dermot. "Don't you move," he added. "I'll ask for it as I come in."

He went round by the side door and presently joined Miss Marple.

"Well," he said, "is all that bumph giving you ideas?"

"Rather too many ideas," said Miss Marple. "I'm not often shocked, you know, but this does shock me a little."

"What, the private lives of film stars?"

"Oh, no," said Miss Marple, "not *that!* That all seems to be most natural, given the circumstances and the money involved and the opportunities for propinquity. Oh, no, that's natural enough. I mean the way they're written about. I'm rather old-fashioned, you know, and I feel that that really shouldn't be allowed."

"It's news," said Dermot Craddock, "and some pretty nasty things can be said in the way of fair comment."

"I know," said Miss Marple. "It makes me sometimes very angry. I expect you think it's silly of me reading all these. But one does so badly want to be *in* things, and of course sitting here in the house I can't really know as much about things as I would like to."

"That's just what I thought," said Dermot Craddock, "and that's why I've come to tell you about them."

"But, my dear boy, excuse me, would your superiors really approve of that?"

"I don't see why not," said Dermot. "Here," he added, "I have a list. A list of people who were there on that landing during the short time of Heather Badcock's arrival until her death. We've eliminated a lot of people, perhaps precipitately, but I don't think so. We've eliminated the mayor and his wife and Alderman somebody and his wife and a great many of the locals, though we've kept in the husband. If I remember rightly, you were always very suspicious of husbands."

"They are often the obvious suspects," said Miss Marple apologetically, "and the obvious is so often right."

"I couldn't agree with you more," said Craddock.

"But which husband, my dear boy, are you referring to?"

"Which one do you think?" asked Dermot. He eyed her sharply.

Miss Marple looked at him.

"Jason Rudd?" she asked.

"Ah!" said Craddock. "Your mind works just as mine does. I don't think it was Arthur Badcock, because you see, I don't think that Heather Badcock was meant to be killed. I think the intended victim was Marina Gregg."

"That would seem almost certain, wouldn't it?" said Miss Marple.

"And so," said Craddock, "as we both agree on that, the field widens. To tell you who was there on that day, what they saw or said they saw, and where they were or said they were, is only a thing you could have observed for yourself if you'd been there. So my superiors, as you call them, couldn't possibly object to my discussing that with you, could they?"

"That's very nicely put, my dear boy," said Miss Marple.

"I'll give you a little précis of what I was told and then we'll come to the list."

He gave a brief résumé of what he had heard, and then he produced his list.

"It must be one of these," he said. "My godfather Sir Henry Clithering told me that you once had a club here. You called it the Tuesday Night Club. You all dined with each other in turn and then someone would tell a story—a story of some real-life happening which had ended in mystery. A mystery of which only the teller of the tale knew the answer. And every time, so my grandfather told me, you guessed right. So I thought I'd come along and see if you'd do a bit of guessing for me this morning."

"I think that is a rather frivolous way of putting it," said Miss Marple reprovingly, "but there is one question I should like to ask."

"Yes?"

"What about the children?"

"The children? There's only one. An imbecile child in a sanatorium in America. Is that what you mean?"

"No," said Miss Marple, "that's not what I mean. It's very sad of course. One of those tragedies that seem to happen and there's no one to blame for it. No, I meant the children that I've seen mentioned in some article here." She tapped the papers in front of her. "Children that Marina Gregg adopted. Two boys, I think, and a girl. In one case a mother with a lot of children and very little money to bring them up in this country, wrote to her, and asked if she couldn't take a child. There was a lot of very silly false sentiment written about that. About the mother's unselfishness and the wonderful home and education and future the child was going to have. I can't find out much about the other two. One I think was a foreign refugee and the other was some American child. Marina Gregg adopted them at different times. I'd like to know what's happened to them."

Dermot Craddock looked at her curiously. "It's odd that you should think of that," he said. "I did just vaguely wonder about those children myself. But how do you connect them up?"

"Well," said Miss Marple, "as far as I can hear or find out, they're not living with her now, are they?"

"I expect they were provided for," said Craddock. "In fact, I think that the adoption laws would insist on that. There was probably money settled on them in trust."

"So when she got—tired of them," said Miss Marple with a very faint pause before the word "tired," "they were dismissed! After being brought up in luxury with every advantage. Is that it?"

"Probably," said Craddock. "I don't know exactly." He continued to look at her curiously.

"Children feel things, you know," said Miss Marple, nodding her head. "They feel things more than the people around them ever imagine. The sense of hurt, of being rejected, of not belonging. It's a thing that you don't get over just because of advantages. Education is no substitute for it, or comfortable living, or an assured income, or a start in a profession. It's the sort of thing that might rankle."

"Yes. But all the same, isn't it rather farfetched to think that— Well, what exactly do you think?"

"I haven't got as far as that," said Miss Marple. "I just wondered where they were and how old they would be now? Grown up, I should imagine, from what I've read here."

"I could find out, I suppose," said Dermot Craddock slowly.

"Oh, I don't want to bother you in any way, or even to suggest that my little idea's worth while at all."

"There's no harm," said Dermot Craddock, "in having that checked up on." He made a note in his little book. "Now do you want to look at my list?"

"I don't really think I should be able to do anything useful about that. You see, I wouldn't know who the people were."

"Oh, I could give you a running commentary," said Craddock. "Here we are. *Jason Rudd, husband* (husbands always highly suspicious). Everyone says that Jason Rudd adored her. That is suspicious in itself, don't you think?"

"Not necessarily," said Miss Marple with dignity.

"He's been very active in trying to conceal the fact that his wife was the object of an attack. He hadn't hinted any suspicion of such a thing to the police. I don't know why he thinks we're such asses as not to think of it for ourselves. We've considered it from the first. But anyway, that's his story. He was afraid that knowledge of that fact might get to his wife's ears and that she'd go into a panic about it."

"Is she the sort of woman who goes into panics?"

"Yes, she's neurasthenic, throws temperaments, has nervous breakdowns, gets in states."

"That might not mean any lack of courage," Miss Marple objected.

"On the other hand," said Craddock, "if she knows quite well that she was the object of the attack, it's also possible that she may know who did it."

"You mean she knows who did it—but does not want to disclose the fact?"

"I just say it's a possibility, and if so, one rather wonders why not? It looks as though the motive, the root of the matter, was something she didn't want to come to her husband's ear."

"That is certainly an interesting thought," said Miss Marple.

"Here are a few more names. The secretary, Ella Zielinsky. An extremely competent and efficient young woman."

"In love with the husband, do you think?" asked Miss Marple.

"I should think definitely," answered Craddock, "but why should you think so?"

"Well, it so often happens," said Miss Marple. "And therefore not very fond of poor Marina Gregg, I expect?"

"Therefore possible motive for murder," said Craddock.

"A lot of secretaries and employees are in love with their employers' husbands," said Miss Marple, "but very, very few of them try to poison them."

"Well, we must allow for exceptions," said Craddock. "Then there were two local and one London photographer, and two members of the press. None of them seem likely but we will follow them up. There was the woman who was formerly married to Marina Gregg's second or third husband. She didn't like it when Marina Gregg took her husband away. Still, that's about eleven or twelve years ago. It seems unlikely that she'd make a visit here at this juncture on purpose to poison Marina because of that. Then there's a man called Ardwyck Fenn. He was once a very close friend of Marina Gregg's. He hasn't seen her for years. He was not known to be in this part of the world, and it was a great surprise when he turned up on this occasion."

"She would be startled then when she saw him?"

"Presumably yes."

"Startled—and possibly frightened."

"'*The doom has come upon me,*'" said Craddock. "That's the idea. Then there was young Hailey Preston dodging about that day, doing his stuff. Talks a good deal but definitely heard nothing, saw nothing and knew nothing. Almost too anxious to say so. Does anything there ring a bell?"

"Not exactly," said Miss Marple. "Plenty of interesting possibilities. But I'd still like to know a little more about the children."

He looked at her curiously. "You've got quite a bee in your bonnet about that, haven't you?" he said. "All right, I'll find out."

CHAPTER THIRTEEN

I

"I SUPPOSE IT couldn't possibly have been the mayor?" said Inspector Cornish wistfully.

He tapped the paper with the list of names on it with his pencil. Dermot Craddock grinned.

"Wishful thinking?"

"You could certainly call it that," said Cornish. "Pompous, canting old hypocrite!" he went on. "Everybody's got it in for him. Throws his weight about, ultra-sanctimonious, and neck-deep in graft for years past!"

"Can't you ever bring it home to him?"

"No," said Cornish. "He's too slick for that. He's always just on the right side of the law."

"It's tempting, I agree," said Dermot Craddock, "but I think you'll have to banish that rosy picture from your mind, Frank."

"I know, I know," said Cornish. "He's a possible, but a wildly improbable. Who else have we got?"

Both men studied the list again. There were still eight names on it.

"We're pretty well agreed," said Craddock, "that there's nobody missed out from here?" There was a faint question in his voice. Cornish answered it.

"I think you can be pretty sure that's the lot. After Mrs. Bantry came the vicar, and after that the Badcocks. There were then eight people on the stairs. The mayor and his wife, Joshua Grice and his wife from Lower Farm. Donald McNeil of the Much Benham *Herald and Argus,* Ardwyck Fenn, U.S.A., Miss Lola Brewster, U.S.A., moving picture star. There you are. In addition there was an arty photographer from London with a camera set up on the angle of the stairs. If, as you suggest, this Mrs. Bantry's story of Marina Gregg having a 'frozen look' was occasioned by someone she saw on the stairs, you've got to take your pick among that lot. Mayor regretfully out. Grices out—never been away from St. Mary Mead, I should say. That leaves four. Local journalist unlikely, photographer girl had been there for half an hour already, so why should Marina react so late in the day? What does that leave?"

"Sinister strangers from America," said Craddock with a faint smile.

"You've said it."

"They're our best suspects by far, I agree," said Craddock. "They turned up unexpectedly. Ardwyck Fenn was an old flame of Marina's whom she had not seen for years. Lola Brewster was once married to Marina Gregg's third husband, who got a divorce from her in order to marry Marina. It was not, I gather, a very amicable divorce."

"I'd put her down as Suspect Number One," said Cornish.

"Would you, Frank? After a lapse of about fifteen years or so, and having remarried twice herself since then?"

Cornish said that you never knew with women. Dermot accepted that as a general dictum, but remarked that it seemed odd to him to say the least of it.

"But you agree that it lies between them?"

"Possibly. But I don't like it very much. What about the hired help who were serving the drinks?"

"Discounting the 'frozen look' we've heard so much about? Well, we've checked up in a general way. Local catering firm from Market Basing had the job—for the fête, I mean. Actually in the house, there was the butler, Giuseppe, in charge; and two local girls from the studios' canteen. I know both of them. Not overbright, but harmless."

"Pushing it back at me, are you? I'll go and have a word with the reporter chap. He might have seen something helpful. Then to London. Ardwyck Fenn, Lola Brewster—and the photographer girl—what's her name?— Margot Bence. She also might have seen something."

Cornish nodded. "Lola Brewster is my best bet," he said. He looked curiously at Craddock. "You don't seem as sold on her as I am."

"I'm thinking of the difficulties," said Dermot slowly.

"Of putting poison into Marina's glass without anybody seeing her."

"Well, that's the same for everybody, isn't it? It was a mad thing to do."

"Agreed it was a mad thing to do, but it would be a madder thing for someone like Lola Brewster than for anybody else."

"Why?" asked Cornish.

"Because she was a guest of some importance. She's a somebody, a big name. Everyone would be looking at her."

"True enough," Cornish admitted.

"The locals would nudge each other and whisper and stare, and after Marina Gregg and Jason Rudd had greeted her, she'd have been passed on for the secretaries to look after. It wouldn't be easy, Frank. However adroit you were, you couldn't be sure *someone* wouldn't see you. That's the snag there, and it's a big snag."

"As I say, isn't that snag the same for everybody?"

"No," said Craddock. "Oh, no. Far from it. Take the butler now, Giuseppe. He's busy with the drinks and glasses, with pouring things out, with handing them. He could put in a pinch or a tablet or two of Calmo in a glass easily enough."

"Giuseppe?" Frank Cornish reflected. "Do you think he did?"

"No reason to believe so," said Craddock, "but we might find a reason. A nice solid bit of motive, that is to say. Yes, he could have done it. Or one of the catering staff could have done it. Unfortunately they weren't on the spot—a pity."

"Someone might have managed to get himself or herself deliberately planted in the firm for the purpose."

"You mean it might have been as premeditated as all that?"

"We don't know anything about it yet," said Craddock vexedly. "We absolutely don't know the first thing about it. Not until we prise what we want to know out of Marina Gregg, or out of her husband. They *must* know or suspect—but they're not telling. And we don't know yet *why* they're not telling. We've a long way to go."

He paused and then resumed: "Discounting the 'frozen look' which may have been pure coincidence, there are other people who could have done it fairly easily. The secretary woman, Ella Zielinsky. She was also busy with glasses, with handing things to people. Nobody would be watching *her* with any particular interest. The same applies to that willow wand of a young man—I've forgotten his name. Hailey—Hailey Preston? That's right. There would be a good opportunity for either of them. In fact if either of them *had* wanted to do away with Marina Gregg, it would have been far safer to do so on a public occasion."

"Anyone else?"

"Well, there's always the husband," said Craddock.

"Back to husbands again," said Cornish, with a faint smile. "We thought it was that poor devil, Badcock, before we realized that Marina was the intended victim. Now we've transferred our suspicions to Jason Rudd. He seems devoted enough though, I must say."

"He has the reputation of being so," said Craddock, "but one never knows."

"If he wanted to get rid of her, wouldn't divorce be much easier?"

"It would be far more usual," agreed Dermot, "but there may be a lot of ins and outs to this business that we don't know yet."

The telephone rang. Cornish took up the receiver.

"What? Yes? Put them through. Yes, he's here." He listened for a moment, then put his hand over the receiver and looked at Dermot. "Miss Marina Gregg," he said, "is feeling very much better. She is quite ready to be interviewed."

"I'd better hurry along," said Dermot Craddock, "before she changes her mind."

II

At Gossington Hall, Dermot Craddock was received by Ella Zielinsky. She was, as usual, brisk and efficient.

"Miss Gregg is waiting for you, Mr. Craddock," she said.

Dermot looked at her with some interest. From the beginning he had found Ella Zielinsky an intriguing personality. He had said to himself, "A poker face if I ever saw one." She had answered any questions he had asked with the utmost readiness. She had shown no signs of keeping anything back, but what she really thought or felt or even knew about the business, he still had no idea. There seemed to be no chink in the armor of her bright efficiency. She might know no more than she said she did; she might know a good deal. The only thing he was sure of—and he had to admit to himself that he had no reasons to adduce for that surety—was that she was in love with Jason Rudd. It was, as he said, an occupational disease of secretaries. It probably meant nothing. But the fact did at least suggest a motive and he was sure, quite sure, that she was concealing something. It might be love, it might be hate. It might, quite simply, be guilt. She might have taken her opportunity that afternoon, or she might have deliberately planned what she

was going to do. He could see her in the part quite easily, as far as the
execution of it went. Her swift but unhurried movements, moving here and
there looking after guests, handing glasses to one or another, taking glasses
away, her eyes marking the spot where Marina had put her glass down on
the table. And then, perhaps at the very moment when Marina had been
greeting the arrivals from the States, with surprise and joyous cries and
everybody's eyes turned towards their meeting, she could have quietly and
unobtrusively dropped the fatal dose into that glass. It would require
audacity, nerve, swiftness. She would have had all those. Whatever she had
done, she would not have looked guilty while she was doing it. It would
have been a simple, brilliant crime, a crime that could hardly fail to be
successful. But chance had ruled otherwise. In the rather crowded floor
space someone had joggled Heather Badcock's arm. Her drink had been
spilt, and Marina, with her natural impulsive grace, had quickly proffered
her own glass, standing there untouched. And so the wrong woman had
died.

A lot of pure theory, and probably hooey at that, said Dermot Craddock
to himself at the same time as he was making polite remarks to Ella
Zielinsky.

"One thing I wanted to ask you, Miss Zielinsky. The catering was done
by a Market Basing firm, I understand?"

"Yes."

"Why was that particular firm chosen?"

"I really don't know," said Ella. "That doesn't lie among my duties. I
know Mr. Rudd thought it would be more tactful to employ somebody local
rather than to employ a firm from London. The whole thing was really quite
a small affair from our point of view."

"Quite." He watched her as she stood frowning a little and looking down.
A good forehead, a determined chin, a figure which could look quite
voluptuous if it was allowed to do so, a hard mouth, an acquisitive mouth.
The eyes? He looked at them in faint surprise. The lids were reddened. He
wondered. Had she been crying? It looked like it. And yet he could have
sworn she was not the type of young woman to cry. She looked up at him,
and as though she read his thoughts, she took out her handkerchief and blew
her nose heartily.

"You've got a cold," he said.

"Not a cold. Hay fever. It's an allergy of some kind, really. I always get it
at this time of year."

There was a low buzz. There were two phones in the room, one on the
table and one on another table in the corner. It was the latter one that was
beginning to buzz. Ella Zielinsky went over to it and picked up the receiver.

"Yes," she said, "he's here. I'll bring him up at once." She put the
receiver down again. "Marina's ready for you," she said.

III

Marina Gregg received Craddock in a room on the first floor, which was obviously her own private sitting-room opening out of her bedroom. After the accounts of her prostration and her nervous state, Dermot Craddock had expected to find a fluttering invalid. But although Marina was half reclining on a sofa, her voice was vigorous and her eyes were bright. She had very little make-up on, but in spite of this she did not look her age, and he was struck very forcibly by the subdued radiance of her beauty. It was the exquisite line of cheek and jawbone, the way the hair fell loosely and naturally to frame her face. The long sea-green eyes, the penciled eyebrows, owing something to art but more to nature, and the warmth and sweetness of her smile, all had a subtle magic. She said:

"Chief-Inspector Craddock? I've been behaving disgracefully. I do apologize. I just let myself go to pieces after this awful thing. I could have snapped out of it, but I didn't. I'm ashamed of myself." The smile came, rueful, sweet, turning up the corners of the mouth. She extended a hand and he took it.

"It was only natural," he said, "that you should feel upset."

"Well, everyone was upset," said Marina. "I'd no business to make out it was worse for me than anyone else."

"Hadn't you?"

She looked at him for a minute and then nodded. "Yes," she said, "you're very perceptive. Yes, I had." She looked down and with one long forefinger gently stroked the arm of the sofa. It was a gesture he had noticed in one of her films. It was a meaningless gesture, yet it seemed fraught with significance. It had a kind of musing gentleness.

"I'm a coward," she said, her eyes still cast down. "Somebody wanted to kill me, and I didn't want to die."

"Why do you think someone wanted to kill you?"

Her eyes opened wide. "Because it was my glass—*my* drink—that had been tampered with. It was just a mistake that that poor stupid woman got it. That's what's so horrible and tragic. Besides—"

"Yes, Miss Gregg?"

She seemed a little uncertain about saying more.

"You had other reasons perhaps for believing that you were the intended victim?"

She nodded.

"What reasons, Miss Gregg?"

She paused a minute longer before saying, "Jason says I must tell you about it."

"You've confided in him then?"

"Yes . . . I didn't want to at first—but Dr. Gilchrist put it to me that I must. And then I found that he thought so too. He'd thought it all along but—it's rather funny really"—a rueful smile curled her lips again "he didn't want to alarm me by telling me. Really!" Marina sat up with a sudden vigorous movement. "Darling Jinks! Does he think I'm a complete fool?"

"You haven't told me yet, Miss Gregg, why you should think anyone wanted to kill you."

She was silent for a moment and then with a sudden, brusque gesture, she stretched out for her handbag, opened it, took out a piece of paper and thrust it into his hand. He read it. Typed on it was one line of writing: *Don't think you'll escape next time.*

Craddock said sharply, "When did you get this?"

"It was on my dressing-table when I came back from the bath."

"So someone in the house—"

"Not necessarily. Someone could have climbed up the balcony outside my window and pushed it through there. I think they meant it to frighten me still more, but actually it didn't. I just felt furiously angry and sent word to you to come and see me."

Dermot Craddock smiled. "Possibly a rather unexpected result for whoever sent it. Is this the first kind of message like that you've had?"

Again Marina hesitated. Then she said, "No, it isn't."

"Will you tell me about any others?"

"It was three weeks ago, when we first came here. It came from the studio, not here. It was quite ridiculous. It was just a message. Not typewritten that time. In capital letters. It said, 'Prepare to die.'" She laughed. There was perhaps a very faint tinge of hysteria in the laugh. The mirth was genuine enough. "It was so silly," she said. "Of course one often gets crank messages, threats, things like that. I thought it was probably religious, you know. Someone who didn't approve of film actresses. I just tore it up and threw it into the wastepaper basket."

"Did you tell anyone about it, Miss Gregg?"

Marina shook her head. "No, I never said a word to anyone. As a matter of fact, we were having a bit of worry at the moment about the scene we were shooting. I just couldn't have thought of anything but that at the moment. Anyway, as I say, I thought it was either a silly joke or one of those religious cranks who write and disapprove of play-acting and things like that."

"And after that, was there another?"

"Yes. On the day of the fête. One of the gardeners brought it to me, I think. He said someone had left a note for me and was there any answer? I thought perhaps it had to do with the arrangements. I just tore it open. It said, 'Today will be your last day on earth.' I just crumpled it up and said, 'No answer.' Then I called the man back and asked him who gave it to him. He said it was a man with spectacles on a bicycle. Well, I mean, what could you do about that? I thought it was more silliness. I didn't think—I didn't think for a moment it was a real genuine threat."

"Where's that note now, Miss Gregg?"

"I've no idea. I was wearing one of those colored Italian silk coats and I think, as far as I can remember, that I crumpled it up and shoved it into the pocket of it. But it's not there now. It probably fell out."

"And you've no idea who wrote those notes, Miss Gregg? Who inspired them. Not even now?"

Her eyes opened widely. There was a kind of innocent wonder in them that he took note of. He admired it, but he did not believe in it.

"How can I tell? How can I possibly tell?"

"I think you might have quite a good idea, Miss Gregg."

"I haven't. I assure you I haven't."

"You're a very famous person," said Dermot. "You've had great successes. Successes in your profession, and personal successes, too. Men have fallen in love with you, wanted to marry you, have married you. Women have been jealous and envied you. Men have been in love with you and rebuffed by you. It's a pretty wide field, I agree, but I should think you must have some idea who could have written those notes."

"It could have been anybody."

"No, Miss Gregg, it couldn't have been *anybody*. It could possibly have been one of quite a lot of people. It could be someone quite humble, a dresser, an electrician, a servant; or it could be someone among the ranks of your friends, or so-called friends. But you must have some idea. Some name, more than one name, perhaps, to suggest."

The door opened and Jason Rudd came in. Marina turned to him. She swept out an arm appealingly.

"Jinks, darling, Mr. Craddock is insisting that I must know who wrote those horrid notes. And I don't. You know I don't. Neither of us know. We haven't got the least idea."

"Very urgent about that," thought Craddock. "Very urgent. Is Marina Gregg afraid of what her husband might say?"

Jason Rudd, his eyes dark with fatigue and the scowl on his face deeper than usual, came over to join them. He took Marina's hand in his.

"I know it sounds unbelievable to you, Inspector," he said, "but honestly neither Marina nor I has any idea about this business."

"So you're in the happy position of having no enemies, is that it?" The irony was manifest in Dermot's voice.

Jason Rudd flushed a little. "Enemies? That's a very biblical word, Inspector. In that sense, I can assure you I can think of no enemies. People who dislike one, would like to get the better of one, would do a mean turn to one if they could, in malice and uncharitableness, yes. But it's a long step from that to putting an overdose of poison in a drink."

"Just now, in speaking to your wife, I asked her who could have written or inspired those letters. She said she didn't know. But when we come to the actual action, it narrows it down. *Somebody actually put the poison in that glass.* And that's a fairly limited field, you know."

"I saw nothing," said Jason Rudd.

"I certainly didn't," said Marina. "Well, I mean—If I had seen anyone putting anything in my glass, I wouldn't have drunk the stuff, would I?"

"I can't help believing, you know," said Dermot Craddock gently, "that you do know a little more than you're telling me."

"It's not *true*," said Marina. "Tell him that that isn't true, Jason!"

"I assure you," said Jason Rudd, "that I am completely and absolutely at a loss. The whole thing's fantastic. I might believe it was a joke—a joke that had somehow gone wrong—that had proved dangerous, done by a person who never dreamt that it would be dangerous. . . ."

There was a slight question in his voice, then he shook his head. "No. I see that idea doesn't appeal to you."

"There's one more thing I should like to ask you," said Dermot Craddock. "You remember Mr. and Mrs. Badcock's arrival, of course.

They came immediately after the vicar. You greeted them, I understand, Miss Gregg, in the same charming way as you had received all your guests. But I am told by an eyewitness that immediately after greeting them you looked over Mrs. Badcock's shoulder and that you saw something which seemed to alarm you. Is that true, and if so, what was it?"

Marina said quickly, "Of course it isn't true. Alarm me—what should have alarmed me?"

"That's what we want to know," said Dermot Craddock patiently. "My witness is very insistent on the point, you know."

"Who was your witness? What did he or she say they saw?"

"You were looking at the staircase," said Dermot Craddock. "There were people coming up that staircase. There was a journalist, there was Mr. Grice and his wife, elderly residents in this place, there was Mr. Ardwyck Fenn who had just arrived from the States, and there was Miss Lola Brewster. Was it the sight of one of those people that upset you, Miss Gregg?"

"I tell you I wasn't upset." She almost barked the words.

"And yet your attention wavered from greeting Mrs. Badcock. She had said something to you which you left unanswered because you were staring past her at something else."

Marina Gregg took hold on herself. She spoke quickly and convincingly.

"I can explain that, I really can. If you knew anything about acting, you'd be able to understand quite easily. There comes a moment, even when you know a part well—in fact, it usually happens when you *do* know a part well—when you go on with it mechanically. Smiling, making the proper movements and gestures, saying the words with the usual inflections. But your mind isn't on it. And quite suddenly there's a horrible blank moment when you don't know where you are, where you've got to in the play, what you next lines are! Drying up, that's what we call it. Well, that's what happened to me. I'm not terribly strong, as my husband will tell you. I've had a rather strenuous time, and a good deal of nervous apprehension about this film. I wanted to make a success of this fête and to be nice and pleasant and welcoming to everybody. But one does say the same things over and over again, mechanically, to the people who are always saying the same things to you. You know, how they've always wanted to meet you. How they once saw you outside a theater in San Francisco—or traveled in a plane with you. Something silly, really, but one has to be nice about it and say things. Well, as I'm telling you, one does that automatically. One doesn't need to think what to say because one's said it so often before. Suddenly, I think, a wave of tiredness came over me. My brain went blank. Then I realized that Mrs. Badcock had been telling me a long story which I hadn't really heard at all, and was now looking at me in an eager sort of way and that I hadn't answered her or said any of the proper things. It was just tiredness."

"Just tiredness," said Dermot Craddock slowly. "You insist on that, Miss Gregg?"

"Yes, I do. I can't see why you don't believe me."

Dermot Craddock turned towards Jason Rudd. "Mr. Rudd," he said, "I think you're more likely to understand my meaning than your wife is. I am concerned, very much concerned, for your wife's safety. There has been an attempt on her life, there have been threatening letters. That means, doesn't it, that there is someone who was here on the day of the fête and possibly is still here, someone in very close touch with this house and what goes on in it. That person, whoever it is, may be slightly insane. It's not just a question of threats. Threatened men live long, as they say. The same goes for women. But whoever it was didn't stop at threats. A deliberate attempt was made to poison Miss Gregg. Don't you see, in the whole nature of things, that attempt is bound to repeated? There's only one way to achieve safety. That is to give me all the clues you can. I don't say that you *know* who that person is, but I think that you must be able to give a guess or to have a vague idea. Won't you tell me the truth? Or if, which is possible, you yourself do not know the truth, won't you urge your wife to do so? It's in the interests of her own safety that I'm asking you."

Jason Rudd turned his head slowly. "You hear what Inspector Craddock says, Marina," he said. "It's possible, as he says, that you may know something that I do not. If so, for God's sake, don't be foolish about it. If you've the least suspicion of *anyone*, tell it to us now."

"But I haven't." Her voice rose in a wail. "You must believe me."

"Who were you afraid of that day?" asked Dermot.

"I wasn't afraid of anyone."

"Listen, Miss Gregg, of the people on the stairs or coming up it, there were two friends whom you were surprised to see, whom you had not seen for a long time and whom you did not expect to see that day. Mr. Ardwyck Fenn and Miss Brewster. Had you any special emotions when you suddenly saw them coming up the stairs? You didn't know they were coming, did you?"

"No, we'd no idea they were even in England," said Jason Rudd.

"I was delighted," said Marina, "absolutely delighted!"

"Delighted to see Miss Brewster?"

"Well—" she shot him a quick, faintly suspicious glance.

Craddock said, "Lola Brewster was, I believe, originally married to your third husband, Robert Truscott?"

"Yes, that's so."

"He divorced her in order to marry you."

"Oh, everyone knows about that," said Marina Gregg impatiently. "You needn't think it's anything you've found out. There was a bit of a rumpus at the time, but there wasn't any bad feeling about it in the end."

"Did she make threats against you?"

"Well—in a way, yes. But, oh dear, I wish I could explain. No one takes those sort of threats seriously. It was at a party, she'd had a lot of drink. She might have taken a pot shot at me with a pistol if she'd had one. But luckily she didn't. All that was *years* ago! None of these things last, these emotions! They don't, really they don't. That's true, isn't it, Jason?"

"I'd say it was true enough," said Jason Rudd, "and I can assure you, Mr. Craddock, that Lola Brewster had no opportunity on the day of the fête of poisoning my wife's drink. I was close beside her most of the time. The idea that Lola would suddenly, after a long period of friendliness, come to England, and arrive at our house all prepared to poison my wife's drink— why, the whole idea's absurd!"

"I appreciate your point of view," said Craddock.

"It's not only that, it's a matter of *fact* as well. She was nowhere near Marina's glass."

"And your other visitor—Ardwyck Fenn?"

There was, he thought, a very slight pause before Jason Rudd spoke.

"He's a very old friend of ours," he said. "We haven't seen him for a good many years now, though we occasionally correspond. He's quite a big figure in American television."

"Was he an old friend of yours, too?" Dermot Craddock asked Marina.

Her breath came rather quickly as she replied. "Yes, oh yes. He—he was quite a friend of mine always, but I've rather lost sight of him of late years." Then with a sudden quick rush of words, she went on, "If you think that I looked up and saw Ardwyck and was frightened of him, it's nonsense. It's absolute *nonsense*. Why should I be frightened of him, what reason would I have to be frightened of him? We were great friends. I was just very, very pleased when I suddenly saw him. It was a delightful surprise, as I told you. Yes, a delightful surprise." She raised her head, looking at him, her face vivid and defiant.

"Thank you, Miss Gregg," said Craddock quietly. "If you should feel inclined at any moment to take me a little further into your confidence, I should strongly advise you to do so."

CHAPTER FOURTEEN

I

MRS. BANTRY WAS on her knees. A good day for hoeing. Nice dry soil. But hoeing wouldn't do everything. Thistles now, and dandelions. She dealt vigorously with these pests.

She rose to her feet, breathless but triumphant, and looked out over the hedge on to the road. She was faintly surprised to see the dark-haired secretary whose name she couldn't remember coming out of the public call box that was situated near the bus stop on the other side of the road.

What was her name now? It began with a B—or was it an R? No, *Zielinsky,* that was it. Mrs. Bantry remembered just in time, as Ella crossed the road and came into the drive past the Lodge.

"Good morning, Miss Zielinsky," she called in a friendly tone.

Ella Zielinsky jumped. It was not so much a jump, as a shy—the shy of a frightened horse. It surprised Mrs. Bantry.

"Good morning," said Ella, and added quickly: "I came down to telephone. There's something wrong with our line today."

Mrs. Bantry felt more surprise. She wondered why Ella Zielinsky bothered to explain her action. She responded civilly.

"How annoying for you. Do come in and telephone any time you want to."

"Oh—thank you very much . . ." Ella was interrupted by a fit of sneezing.

"You've got hay fever." said Mrs. Bantry with immediate diagnosis. "Try weak bicarbonate of soda and water."

"Oh, that's all right. I have some very good patent stuff in an atomizer. Thank you all the same."

She sneezed again as she moved away, walking briskly up the drive.

Mrs. Bantry looked after her. Then her eyes returned to her garden. She looked at it in a dissatisfied fashion. Not a weed to be seen anywhere.

"Othello's occupation's gone," Mrs. Bantry murmured to herself confusedly. "I dare say I'm a nosy old woman but I would like to know if—"

A moment of irresolution and then Mrs. Bantry yielded to temptation. She was going to be a nosy old woman and the hell with it! She strode indoors to the telephone, lifted the receiver and dialed. A brisk transatlantic voice spoke.

"Gossington Hall."

"This is Mrs. Bantry, at the East Lodge."

"Oh, good morning, Mrs. Bantry. This is Hailey Preston. I met you on the day of the fête. What can I do for you?"

"I thought perhaps I could do something for you. If your telephone's out of order—"

His astonished voice interrupted her.

"Our telephone out of order? There's been nothing wrong with it. Why did you think so?"

"I must have made a mistake," said Mrs. Bantry. "I don't always hear very well," she explained unblushingly.

She put the receiver back, waited a minute, then dialed once more.

"Jane? Dolly here."

"Yes, Dolly. What is it?"

"Well, it seems rather odd. That secretary woman was dialing from the public call box in the road. She took the trouble to explain to me quite unnecessarily that she was doing so because the line at Gossington Hall was out of order. But I've rung up there, and it isn't. . . ."

She paused, and waited for intelligence to pronounce.

"In-deed," said Miss Marple thoughtfully. "Interesting."

"For what reason, do you think?"

"Well, clearly, she didn't want to be overheard—"

"Exactly."

"And there might be quite a number of reasons for that."

"Yes."

"Interesting," said Miss Marple again.

II

Nobody could have been more ready to talk than Donald McNeil. He was an amiable red-headed young man. He greeted Dermot Craddock with pleasure and curiosity.

"How are you getting along," he asked cheerfully, "got any little special tidbit for me?"

"Not as yet. Later perhaps."

"Stalling as usual. You're all the same. Affable oysters! Haven't you come to the stage yet of inviting someone to come and 'assist you in your inquiries'?"

"I've come to you," said Dermot Craddock with a grin.

"Is there a nasty *double-entendre* in that remark? Are you really suspicious that I murdered Heather Badcock and do you think I did it in mistake for Marina Gregg or that I meant to murder Heather Badcock all the time?"

"I haven't suggested anything," said Craddock.

"No, no, you wouldn't do that, would you? You'd be very correct. All right. Let's go into it. I was there. I had opportunity but had I any motive? Ah, that's what you'd like to know. What was my motive?"

"I haven't been able to find one so far," said Craddock.

"That's very gratifying. I feel safer."

"I'm just interested in what you may have seen that day."

"You've had that already. The local police had that straight away. It's humiliating. There I was on the scene of a murder. I practically *saw* the murder committed. I must have and yet I've no idea who did it. I'm ashamed to confess that the first I knew about it was seeing the poor, dear woman sitting on a chair gasping for breath and then pegging out. Of course, it made a very good eyewitness account. It was a good scoop for me—and all that. But I'll confess to you that I feel humiliated that I don't know more. I ought to know more. And you can't kid me that the dose was meant for Heather Badcock. She was a nice woman who talked too much, but nobody ever gets murdered for that—unless of course they give away secrets. But I don't think anybody would ever have told Heather Badcock a secret. She wasn't the kind of woman who'd have been interested in other people's secrets. My view of her is of a woman who invariably talked about *herself.*"

"That seems to be the generally accepted view," agreed Craddock.

"So we come to the famous Marina Gregg. I'm sure there are lots of wonderful motives for murdering Marina. Envy and jealousy and love tangles—all the stuff of drama. But who did it? Someone with a screw loose, I presume. There! You've had my valuable opinion. Is that what you wanted?"

"Not that alone. I understand that you arrived and came up the stairs about the same time as the vicar and the mayor."

"Quite correct. But that wasn't the first time I'd arrived. I'd been there earlier."

"I didn't know that."

"Yes. I was on a kind of roving commission, you know, going here and there. I had a photographer with me. I'd gone down to take a few local shots of the mayor arriving and throwing a hoopla and putting in a peg for buried treasure, and that kind of thing. Then I went back up again, not so much on the job, as to get a drink or two. The drink was good."

"I see. Now can you remember who else was on the staircase when you went up?"

"Margot Bence from London was there with her camera."

"You know her well?"

"Oh, I run against her quite often. She's a clever girl, who makes a success of her stuff. She takes all the fashionable things—first nights, gala performances—specializes in photographs from unusual angles. Arty! She was in a corner of the half landing, very well placed for taking anyone who came up and for taking the greetings going on at the top. Lola Brewster was just ahead of me on the stairs. Didn't know her at first. She's got a new rust-red hair-do. The very latest Fiji Islander type. Last time I saw her it was lank waves falling round her face and chin in a nice shade of auburn. There was a big dark man with her, American. I don't know who he was, but he looked important."

"Did you look at Marina Gregg herself at all as you were coming up?"

"Yes, of course I did."

"She didn't look upset at all or as though she'd had a shock or was frightened?"

"It's odd you should say that. I *did* think for a moment or two she was going to faint."

"I see," said Craddock thoughtfully. "Thanks. There's nothing else you'd like to tell me?"

McNeil gave him a wide innocent stare.

"What could there be?"

"I don't trust you," said Craddock.

"But you seem quite sure I didn't do it. Disappointing. Suppose I turn out to be her first husband. Nobody knows who he was except that he was so insignificant that even his name's been forgotten."

Dermot grinned.

"Married from your prep school?" he asked. "Or possibly in rompers! I must hurry. I've got a train to catch."

III

There was a neatly docketed pile of papers on Craddock's desk at New Scotland Yard. He gave a perfunctory glance through them, then threw a question over his shoulder.

"Where's Lola Brewster staying?"

"At the Savoy, sir. Suite eighteen hundred. She's expecting you."

"And Ardwyck Fenn?"

"He's at the Dorchester. First floor, one ninety."

"Good."

He picked up some cablegrams and read them through again before shoving them into his pocket. He smiled a moment to himself over the last one. "Don't say I don't do my stuff, Aunt Jane," he murmured under his breath.

He went out and made his way to the Savoy.

In Lola Brewster's suite Lola went out of her way to welcome him effusively. With the report he had just read in his mind, he studied her carefully. Quite a beauty still, he thought, in a lush kind of way, what you might call a trifle overblown, perhaps, but they still liked them that way. A completely different type, of course, from Marina Gregg. The amenities over, Lola pushed back her Fiji Islander hair, drew her generous lipsticked mouth into a provocative pout, and flickering blue eyelids over wide brown eyes, said:

"Have you come to ask me a lot more horrible questions? Like that local inspector did."

"I hope they won't be too horrible, Miss Brewster."

"Oh, but I'm sure they will be, and I'm sure the whole thing must have been some terrible mistake."

"Do you really think so?"

"Yes. It's all such nonsense. Do you really mean that someone tried to poison Marina? Who on earth would poison Marina? She's an absolute sweetie, you know. Everybody loves her."

"Including you?"

"I've always been devoted to Marina."

"Oh, come now, Miss Brewster, wasn't there a little trouble about eleven or twelve years ago?"

"Oh, that." Lola waved it away. "I was terribly nervy and distraught, and Rob and I had been having the most frightful quarrels. We were neither of us normal at the moment. Marina just fell wildly in love with him and rushed him off his feet, the poor pet."

"And you minded very much?"

"Well, I thought I did, Inspector. Of course I see now it was one of the best things that ever happened for me. I was really worried about the children, you know. Breaking up our home. I'm afraid I'd already realized that Rob and I were incompatible. I expect you know I got married to Eddie Groves as soon as the divorce went through? I think really I'd been in love with him for a long time, but of course I didn't want to break up my marriage, because of the children. It's so important, isn't it, that children should have a *home?*"

"Yet people say that actually you were terribly upset."

"Oh, people always say things," said Lola vaguely.

"You said quite a lot, didn't you, Miss Brewster? You went around threatening to shoot Marina Gregg, or so I understand."

"I've told you one *says* things. One's *supposed* to say things like that. Of course I wouldn't really shoot *anyone.*"

"In spite of taking a pot shot at Eddie Groves some few years later?"

"Oh, that was because we'd had an argument," said Lola. "I lost my temper."

"I have it on very good authority, Miss Brewster, that you said—and these are your exact words, or so I'm told" (he read from a note-book)—"'That bitch needn't think she'll get away with it. If I don't shoot her now I'll wait and get her in some other way. I don't care how long I wait, years if need be, but I'll get even with her in the end.'"

"Oh, I'm sure I never said anything of the kind." Lola laughed.

"I'm sure, Miss Brewster, that you did."

"People exaggerate so." A charming smile broke over her face. "I was just mad at the moment, you know," she murmured confidentially. "One says all sorts of things when one's mad with people. But you don't really think I'd wait fourteen years and come across to England and look up Marina and drop some deadly poison into her cocktail glass within three minutes of seeing her again?"

Dermot Craddock didn't really think so. It seemed to him wildly improbable. He merely said:

"I'm only pointing out to you, Miss Brewster, that there had been threats in the past and that Marina Gregg was certainly startled and frightened to see someone who came up the stairs that day. Naturally one feels that someone must have been you."

"But darling Marina was delighted to see me! She kissed me and exclaimed how wonderful it was. Oh, really, Inspector, I do think that you're being very, very silly."

"In fact, you were all one big happy family?"

"Well, that's really much more true than all the things you've been thinking."

"And you've no ideas that could help us in any way? No ideas who might have killed her?"

"I tell you nobody would have wanted to kill Marina. She's a very silly woman anyway. Always making terrible fusses about her health, and changing her mind and wanting this, that and the other, and when she's got it being dissatisfied with it! I can't think why people are as fond of her as they are. Jason's always been absolutely mad about her. What that man has to put up with! But there it is. Everybody puts up with Marina, puts themselves out for her. Then she gives them a sad, sweet smile and thanks them! And apparently that makes them feel that the trouble is worth while. I really don't know how she does it. You'd better put the idea that somebody wanted to kill her right out of your head."

"I should like to," said Dermot Craddock. "Unfortunately I can't put it out of my head because, you see, it happened."

"What do you mean, *it happened?* Nobody has killed Marina, have they?"

"No. But the attempt was made."

"I don't believe it for a moment! I expect whoever it was meant to kill the other woman all the time—the one who *was* killed. I expect someone comes into money when she dies."

"She hadn't any money, Miss Brewster."

"Oh, well, there was some other reason. Anyway, I shouldn't worry about Marina if I were you. Marina is *always* all right!"

"Is she? She doesn't look a very happy woman to me."

"Oh, that's because she makes such a song and dance about everything. Unhappy love affairs. Not being able to have any children."

"She adopted some children, didn't she?" said Dermot with a lively remembrance of Miss Marple's urgent voice.

"I believe she did once. It wasn't a great success, I believe. She does these impulsive things and then wishes she hadn't."

"What happened to the children she adopted?"

"I've no idea. They just sort of vanished after a bit. She got tired of them, I suppose, like everything else."

"I see," said Dermot Craddock.

IV

Next—the Dorchester. Suite 190.

"Well, Chief-Inspector—" Ardwyck Fenn looked down at the card in his hand.

"Craddock."

"What can I do for you?"

"I hope you won't mind if I ask you a few questions."

"Not at all. It's this business at Much Benham. No—what's the actual name, St. Mary Mead?"

"Yes. That's right. Gossington Hall."

"Can't think what Jason Rudd wanted to buy a place like that for. Plenty of good Georgian houses in England—or even Queen Anne. Gossington Hall is a purely Victorian mansion. What's the attraction in that, I wonder?"

"Oh, there's some attraction—for some people, that is, in Victorian stability."

"Stability? Well, perhaps you've got something there. Marina, I suppose, had a feeling for stability. It's a thing she never had herself, poor girl, so I suppose that's why she always covets it. Perhaps this place will satisfy her for a bit."

"You know her well, Mr. Fenn?"

Ardwyck Fenn shrugged his shoulders.

"Well? I don't know that I'd say that. I've known her over a long period of years. Known her off and on, that is to say."

Craddock looked at him appraisingly. A dark man, heavily built, shrewd eyes behind thick glasses, heavy jowl and chin. Ardwyck Fenn went on:

"The idea is, I gather, from what I read in the newspapers, that this Mrs. Whatever-her-name-was poisoned by mistake. That the dose was intended for Marina. Is that right?"

"Yes. That's it. The dose was in Marina Gregg's cocktail. Mrs. Badcock spilt hers and Marina handed over her drink to her."

"Well, that seems pretty conclusive. I really can't think, though, who would want to poison Marina. Especially as Lynette Brown wasn't there."

"Lynette Brown?" Craddock looked slightly at sea.

Ardwyck Fenn smiled. "If Marina breaks this contract, throws up this part—Lynette will get it and it would mean a good deal to Lynette to get it. But for all that, I don't imagine she'd send some emissary along with poison. Much too melodramatic an idea."

"It seems a little farfetched," said Dermot dryly.

"Ah, you'd be surprised what women will do when they're ambitious," said Ardwyck Fenn. "Mind you, death mayn't have been intended. It may have been just meant to give her a fright— Enough to knock her out but not to finish her."

Craddock shook his head. "It wasn't a borderline dose," he said.

"People make mistakes in doses, quite big ones."

"Is this really your theory?"

"Oh, no, it isn't. It was only a suggestion. I've no theory. I was only an innocent bystander."

"Was Marina Gregg surprised to see you?"

"Yes, it was a complete surprise to her." He laughed amusedly. "Just couldn't believe her eyes when she saw me coming up the stairs. She gave me a very nice welcome, I must say."

"You hadn't seen her for a long time?"

"Not for four or five years, I should say."

"And some years before that there was a time when you and she were very close friends, I believe?"

"Are you insinuating anything in particular by that remark, Inspector Craddock?"

There was very little change in the voice, but there was something there that had not been there before. A hint of steel, of menace. Dermot felt suddenly that this man would be a very ruthless opponent.

"It would be as well, I think," said Ardwyck Fenn, "that you said exactly what you do mean."

"I'm quite prepared to do so, Mr. Fenn. I have to inquire into the past relations of everyone who was there on that day with Marina Gregg. It seems to have been a matter of common gossip that at the time I have just referred to, you were wildly in love with Marina Gregg."

Ardwyck Fenn shrugged his shoulders.

"One has these infatuations, Inspector. Fortunately, they pass."

"It is said that she encouraged you and that later she turned you down and that you resented the fact."

"It is said—it is said! I suppose you read all that in *Confidential?*"

"It has been told me by quite well-informed and sensible people."

Ardwyck Fenn threw back his head, showing the bull-like line of his neck.

"I had a yen for her at one time, yes," he admitted. "She was a beautiful and attractive woman and still is. To say that I ever threatened her is going a little far. I'm never pleased to be thwarted, Chief-Inspector, and most people who thwart me tend to be sorry that they have done so. But that principle applies mainly in my business life."

"You did, I believe, use your influence to have her dropped from a picture that she was making?"

Fenn shrugged his shoulders.

"She was unsuitable for the role. There was conflict between her and the director. I had money in that picture and I had no intention of jeopardizing it. It was, I assure you, purely a business transaction."

"But perhaps Marina Gregg did not think so?"

"Oh, naturally she did not think so. She would always think that anything like that was personal."

"She actually told certain friends of hers that she was afraid of you, I believe?"

"Did she? How childish. I expect she enjoyed the sensation."

"You think there was no need for her to be afraid of you?"

"Of course not. Whatever personal disappointment I might have had, I soon put it behind me. I've always gone on the principle that where women are concerned there are as good fish in the sea as ever came out of it."

"A very satisfactory way to go through life, Mr. Fenn."

"Yes, I think it is."

"You have a wide knowledge of the moving picture world?"

"I have financial interests in it."

"And therefore you are bound to know a lot about it?"

"Perhaps."

"You are a man whose judgment would be worth listening to. Can you suggest to me any person who is likely to have such a deep grudge against Marina Gregg that they would be willing to do away with her?"

"Probably a dozen," said Ardwyck Fenn, "that is to say, if they didn't have to do anything about it personally. If it was a mere matter of pressing a button in a wall, I dare say there'd be a lot of willing fingers."

"You were there that day. You saw her and talked to her. Do you think that among any of the people who were around you in that brief space of time—from when you arrived to the moment when Heather Badcock died— do you think that among them you can suggest—only suggest, mind you, I'm asking for nothing more than a guess—anyone who might poison Marina Gregg?"

"I wouldn't like to say," said Ardwyck Fenn.

"That means that you have some idea?"

"It means that I have nothing to say on that subject. And that, Chief-Inspector Craddock, is all you'll get out of me."

CHAPTER FIFTEEN

DERMOT CRADDOCK LOOKED down at the last name and address he had written in his notebook. The telephone number had been rung twice for him, but there had been no response. He tried it now once more. He shrugged his shoulders, got up and decided to go and see for himself.

Margot Bence's studio was in a cul-de-sac off the Tottenham Court Road. Beyond the name on a plate on the side of a door, there was little to identify it and certainly no form of advertising. Craddock groped his way to the first floor. There was a large notice here painted in black on a white board. "Margot Bence, Personality Photographer. Please enter."

Craddock entered. There was a small waiting-room but nobody in charge of it. He stood there hesitating, then cleared his throat in a loud and theatrical manner. Since that drew no attention, he raised his voice.

"Anybody here?"

He heard a flap of slippers behind a velvet curtain, the curtain was pushed aside and a young man with exuberant hair and a pink and white face peered round it.

"Terribly sorry, my dear," he said. "I didn't hear you. I had an absolutely new idea and I was just trying it out."

He pushed the velvet curtain farther aside and Craddock followed him into an inner room. This proved to be unexpectedly large. It was clearly the working studio. There were cameras, lights, arc lights, piles of drapery, screens on wheels.

"Such a mess," said the young man, who was almost as willowy as Hailey Preston. "But one finds it very hard to work, I think, unless one *does* get into a mess. Now what were you wanting to see us about?"

"I wanted to see Miss Margot Bence."

"Ah, Margot. Now what a pity. If you'd been half an hour earlier you'd have found her here. She's gone off to produce some photographs of models for *Fashion Dream*. You should have rung up, you know, to make an appointment. Margot's terribly busy these days."

"I did ring up. There was no reply."

"Of course," said the young man. "We took the receiver off. I remember now. It disturbed us." He smoothed down a kind of lilac smock that he was wearing. "Can I do anything for you? Make an appointment? I do a lot of Margot's business arrangements for her. You wanted to arrange for some photography somewhere? Private or business?"

"From that point of view, neither," said Dermot Craddock. He handed his card to the young man.

"How perfectly rapturous," said the young man. "C.I.D.! I believe, you know, I've seen pictures of you. Are you one of the Big Four or the Big Five, or is it perhaps the Big Six nowadays? There's so much crime about, they'd have to increase the numbers, wouldn't they? Oh dear, is that disrespectful? I'm afraid it is. I didn't mean to be disrespectful at all. Now, what do you want Margot for—not to arrest her, I hope."

"I just wanted to ask her one or two questions."

"She doesn't do indecent photographs or anything like that," said the young man anxiously. "I hope nobody's been telling you any stories of that kind, because it isn't true. Margot's very artistic. She does a lot of stage work and studio work. But her studies are terribly, terribly pure—almost prudish, I'd say."

"I can tell you quite simply why I want to speak to Miss Bence," said Dermot. "She was recently an eyewitness of a crime that took place near Much Benham, at a village called St. Mary Mead."

"Oh, my dear, of *course*! I know about *that*. Margot came back and told me about it. Hemlock in the cocktails, wasn't it? Something of that kind. So *bleak* it sounded! But all mixed up with St. John's Ambulance, which doesn't seem so bleak, does it? But haven't you already asked Margot questions about that—or was it somebody else?"

"One always finds there are more questions as the case goes on," said Dermot.

"You mean it develops. Yes, I can quite see that. Murder develops. Yes, like a photograph, isn't it?"

"It's very much like a photograph, really," said Dermot. "Quite a good comparison of yours."

"Well, it's very nice of you to say so, I'm sure. Now about Margot. Would you like to get hold of her right away?"

"If you can help me to do so, yes."

"Well, at the moment," said the young man, consulting his watch, "at the moment she'll be outside Keats' house at Hampstead Heath. My car's outside. Shall I run you up there?"

"That would be very kind of you, Mr.—?"

"Jethroe," said the young man, "Johnny Jethroe."

As they went down the stairs Dermot asked:

"Why Keats' house?"

"Well, you know we don't pose fashion photographs in the studio any more. We like them to seem natural, blown about by the wind. And if possible, some rather unlikely background. You know an Ascot frock against Wandsworth Prison, or a frivolous little suit outside a poet's house."

Mr. Jethroe drove rapidly but skillfully up Tottenham Court Road, through Camden Town and finally to the neighborhood of Hampstead Heath. On the pavement near Keats' house a pretty little scene was being enacted. A slim girl wearing diaphanous organdie was standing clutching an immense black hat. On her knees, a little way behind her, a second girl was holding the first girl's skirt well pulled back so that it clung around her knees and legs. In a deep hoarse voice a girl with a camera was directing operations.

"For goodness' sake, Jane, get your behind down. It's showing behind her right knee. Get down flatter. That's it. No, more to the left. That's right. Now you're masked by the bush. That'll do. Hold it. We'll have one more. Both hands on the back of the hat this time. Head up. Good—now turn round, Elsie. Bend over. More. Bend! *Bend,* you've got to pick up that cigarette case. That's right. That's *heaven!* Got it! Now move over to the left. Same pose, only just turn your head over your shoulder. So."

"I can't see what you want to go taking photographs of my behind for," said the girl called Elsie rather sulkily.

"It's a lovely behind, dear. It looks smashing," said the photographer. "And when you turn your head, your chin comes up like the rising moon over a mountain. I don't think we need bother with any more."

"Hi—Margot," said Mr. Jethroe.

She turned her head. "Oh, it's you. What are you doing here?"

"I brought someone along to see you. Chief Detective-Inspector Craddock, C.I.D."

The girl's eyes turned swiftly on to Dermot. He thought they had a wary, searching look, but that, as he well knew, was nothing extraordinary. It was a fairly common reaction to detective-inspectors. She was a thin girl, all elbows and angles, but was an interesting shape for all that. A heavy curtain of black hair fell down on either side of her face. She looked dirty as well as sallow and not particularly prepossessing to his eyes. But he acknowledged that there was character there. She raised her eyebrows which were slightly raised by art already and remarked:

"And what can I do for you, Detective-Inspector Craddock?"

"How do you do, Miss Bence. I wanted to ask you if you would be so kind as to answer a few questions about that very unfortunate business at Gossington Hall, near Much Benham. You went there, if I remember, to take some photographs."

The girl nodded. "Of course. I remember quite well." She shot him a quick searching look. "I didn't see you there. Surely it was somebody else. Inspector—Inspector—"

"Inspector Cornish?" said Dermot.

"That's right."

"We were called in later."

"You're from Scotland Yard?"

"Yes."

"You butted in and took over from the local people. Is that it?"

"Well, it isn't quite a question of butting in, you know. It's up to the chief constable of the county to decide whether he thinks it'll be better handled by us."

"What makes him decide?"

"It very often turns on whether the case has a local background or whether it's a more—universal one. Sometimes, perhaps, an international one."

"And he decided, did he, that this was an international one?"

"Transatlantic, perhaps, would be a better word."

"They've been hinting that in the papers, haven't they? Hinting that the killer, whoever he was, was out to get Marina Gregg and got some wretched local woman by mistake. Is that true or is it a bit of publicity for their film?"

"I'm afraid there isn't much doubt about it, Miss Bence."

"What do you want to ask me? Have I got to come to Scotland Yard?"

He shook his head. "Not unless you like. We'll go back to your studio if you prefer."

"All right, let's do that. My car's just up the street."

She walked rapidly along the footpath. Dermot went with her. Jethroe called after them.

"So long, darling, I won't butt in. I'm sure you and the inspector are going to talk big secrets." He joined the two models on the pavement and began an animated discussion with them.

Margot got into the car, unlocked the door on the other side, and Dermot Craddock got in beside her. She said nothing at all during the drive back to Tottenham Court Road. She turned down the cul-de-sac and at the bottom of it drove through an open doorway.

"Got my own parking place here," she remarked. "It's a furniture depository place really, but they rent me a bit of space. Parking a car is one of the big headaches in London, as you probably know only too well, though I don't suppose you deal with traffic, do you?"

"No, that's not one of my troubles."

"I should think murder would be infinitely preferable," said Margot Bence.

She led the way back to the studio, motioned him to a chair, offered him a cigarette and sank down on the large ottoman opposite him. From behind the curtain of dark hair she looked at him in a somber questioning way.

"Shoot, stranger," she said.

"You were taking photographs on the occasion of this death, I understand."

"Yes."

"You'd been engaged professionally?"

"Yes. They wanted someone to do a few specialized shots. I do quite a lot of that stuff. I do some work for film studios sometimes, but this time I was just taking photographs of the fête, and afterwards a few shots of special people being greeted by Marina Gregg and Jason Rudd. Local notabilities or other personalities. That sort of thing."

"Yes. I understand that. You had your camera on the stairs, I understand?"

"A part of the time, yes. I got a very good angle from there. You get people coming up the stairs below you and you could swivel round and get Marina shaking hands with them. You could get a lot of different angles without having to move much."

"I know, of course, that you answered some questions at the time as to whether you'd seen anything unusual, anything that might be helpful. They were general questions."

"Have you got more specialized ones?"

"A little more specialized, I think. You had a good view of Marina Gregg from where you were standing?"

She nodded. "Excellent."

"And of Jason Rudd?"

"Occasionally. But he was moving about more. Drinks and things and introducing people to one another. The locals to the celebrities. That kind of thing, I should imagine. I didn't see this Mrs. Baddeley—"

"Badcock."

"Sorry, Badcock. I didn't see her drink the fatal draught or anything like that. In fact, I don't think I really know which she was."

"Do you remember the arrival of the mayor?"

"Oh, yes. I remember the mayor all right. He had on his chain and his robes of office. I got one of him coming up the stairs—a close-up—rather a cruel profile, and then I got him shaking hands with Marina."

"Then you can fix that time at least in your mind. Mrs. Badcock and her husband came up the stairs to Marina Gregg immediately in front of him."

She shook her head. "Sorry. I still don't remember her."

"That doesn't matter so much. I presume that you had a pretty good view of Marina Gregg and that you had your eyes on her and were pointing the camera at her fairly often."

"Quite right. Most of the time. I'd wait till I got just the right moment."

"Do you know a man called Ardwyck Fenn by sight?"

"Oh, yes. I know him well enough. Television network—films, too."

"Did you take a photograph of him?"

"Yes, I got him coming up with Lola Brewster."

"That would be just after the mayor?"

She thought a minute then agreed. "Yes, about then."

"Did you notice that about that time Marina Gregg seemed to feel suddenly ill? Did you notice any unusual expression on her face?"

Margot Bence leant forward, opened a cigarette box and took out a cigarette. She lit it. Although she had not answered Dermot did not press her. He waited, wondering what it was she was turning over in her mind. She said at last, abruptly:

"Why do you ask me that?"

"Because it's a question to which I am very anxious to have an answer—a reliable answer."

"Do you think my answer's likely to be reliable?"

"Yes I do, as a matter of fact. You must have the habit of watching people's faces very closely, waiting for certain expressions, certain propitious moments."

She nodded her head.

"Did you see anything of that kind?"

"Somebody else saw it too, did they?"

"Yes. More than one person, but it's been described rather differently."

"How did the other people describe it?"

"One person has told me that she was taken faint."

Margot Bence shook her head slowly.

"Someone else said that she was startled." He paused a moment then went on, "And somebody else describes her as having a frozen look on her face."

"Frozen," said Margot Bence thoughtfully.

"Do you agree to that last statement?"

"I don't know. Perhaps."

"It was put rather more fancifully still," said Dermot. "In the words of the late poet, Tennyson. *The mirror crack'd from side to side; 'The doom has come upon me,' cried the Lady of Shalott.*"

"There wasn't any mirror," said Margot Bence, "but if there had been it might have cracked." She got up abruptly. "Wait," she said. "I'll do something better than describe it to you. I'll show you."

She pushed aside the curtain at the far end and disappeared for some moments. He could hear her uttering impatient mutterings under her breath.

"What hell it is," she said as she emerged again, "one never can find things when one wants them. I've got it now though."

She came across to him and put a glossy print into his hand. He looked down at it. It was a very good photograph of Marina Gregg. Her hand was clasped in the hand of a woman standing in front of her, and therefore with her back to the camera. But Marina Gregg was not looking at the woman. Her eyes stared not quite into the camera but slightly obliquely to the left. The interesting thing to Dermot Craddock was that the face expressed nothing whatever. There was no fear on it, no pain. The woman portrayed there was staring at something, something she saw, and the emotion it aroused in her was so great that she was physically unable to express it by any kind of facial expression. Dermot Craddock had seen such a look once on a man's face, a man who a second later had been shot dead. . . .

"Satisfied?" asked Margot Bence.

Craddock gave a deep sigh. "Yes, thank you. It's hard, you know, to make up one's mind if witnesses are exaggerating, if they are imagining they see things. But that's not so in this case. There *was* something to see and she saw it." He asked, "Can I keep this picture?"

"Oh, yes, you can have the print. I've got the negative."

"You didn't send it to the press?"

Margot Bence shook her head.

"I rather wonder why you didn't. After all, it's rather a dramatic photograph. Some paper might have paid a good price for it."

"I wouldn't care to do that," said Margot Bence. "If you look into somebody's soul by accident, you feel a bit embarrassed about cashing in."

"Did you know Marina Gregg at all?"

"No."

"You come from the States, don't you?"

"I was born in England. I was trained in America, though. I came over here, oh, about three years ago."

Dermot Craddock nodded. He had known the answers to his questions. They had been waiting for him among the other lists of information on his office table. The girl seemed straightforward enough. He asked:

"Where did you train?"

"Reingarden Studios. I was with Andrew Quilp for a time. He taught me a lot."

"Reingarden Studios and Andrew Quilp." Dermot Craddock was suddenly alert. The names struck a chord of remembrance.

"You lived in Seven Springs, didn't you?"

She looked amused.

"You seem to know a lot about me. Have you been checking up?"

"You're a well-known photographer, Miss Bence. There have been articles written about you, you know. Why did you come to England?"

She shrugged her shoulders.

"Oh, I like a change. Besides, as I told you, I was born in England although I went to the States as a child."

"Quite a young child, I think."

"Five years old, if you're interested."

"I am interested. I think, Miss Bence, you could tell me a little more than you have done."

Her face hardened. She stared at him.

"What do you mean by that?"

Dermot Craddock looked at her and risked it. It wasn't much to go on. Reingarden Studios and Andrew Quilp and the name of one town. But he felt rather as if old Miss Marple were at his shoulder egging him on.

"I think you knew Marina Gregg better than you say."

She laughed. "Prove it. You're imagining things."

"Am I? I don't think I am. And it *could* be proved, you know, with a little time and care. Come now, Miss Bence, hadn't you better admit the truth? Admit that Marina Gregg adopted you as a child and that you lived with her for four years."

She drew her breath in sharply with a hiss.

"You nosy bastard!" she said.

It startled him a little, it was such a contrast to her former manner. She got up, shaking her black head of hair.

"All right, all right, it's true enough! Yes. Marina Gregg took me over to America with her. My mother had eight kids. She lived in a slum somewhere. She was one of hundreds of people, I suppose, who write to any film actress they happen to see or hear about, spilling a hard-luck story, begging her to adopt the child a mother couldn't give advantages to. Oh, it's such a sickening business, all of it."

"There were three of you," said Dermot. "Three children adopted at different times from different places."

"That's right. Me and Rod and Angus. Angus was older than I was, Rod was practically a baby. We had a wonderful life. Oh, a wonderful life! All the advantages!" Her voice rose mockingly. "Clothes and cars and a wonderful house to live in and people to look after us, good schooling and teaching, and delicious food. Everything piled on! And she herself, our 'Mom.' 'Mom' in inverted commas, playing her part, crooning over us, being photographed with us! Ah, such a pretty sentimental picture.''

"But she really wanted children," said Dermot Craddock. "That was real enough, wasn't it? It wasn't just a publicity stunt."

"Oh, perhaps. Yes, I think that was true. She wanted children. But she didn't want *us!* Not really. It was just a glorious bit of play-acting. *'My family' 'So lovely to have a family of my own.'* And Izzy let her do it. He ought to have known better."

"Izzy was Isidore Wright?"

"Yes, her third husband or her fourth, I forget which. He was a wonderful man really. He understood her, I think, and he was worried sometimes about us. He was kind to us. But he didn't pretend to be a father. He didn't feel like a father. He only cared really about his own writing. I've read some of his things since. They're sordid and rather cruel, but they're powerful. I think people will call him a great writer one day."

"And this went on until when?"

Margot Bence's smile curved suddenly. "Until she got sick of that particular bit of play-acting. No, that's not quite true. . . . She found she was going to have a child of her own."

"And then?"

She laughed with sudden bitterness "Then we'd had it! We weren't wanted any more. We'd done very well as little stop-gaps, but she didn't care a damn about us really, not a damn. Oh, she pensioned us off very prettily. With a home and a foster-mother and money for our education and a nice little sum to start us off in the world. Nobody can say that she didn't behave correctly and handsomely. But she'd never wanted *us*—all she wanted was a child of her own."

"You can't blame her for that," said Dermot gently.

"I don't blame her for wanting a child of her own, no! But what about us? She took us away from our own parents, from the places where we belonged. My mother sold me for a mess of pottage, if you like, but she didn't sell me for advantage to herself. She sold me because she was a damn silly woman who thought I'd get 'advantages' and 'education' and have a wonderful life. She thought she was doing the best for me. Best for me? If she only knew."

"You're still very bitter, I see."

"No, I'm not bitter now. I've got over that. I'm bitter because I'm remembering, because I've gone back to those days. We were all pretty bitter."

"All of you?"

"Well, not Rod. Rod never cared about anything. Besides, he was rather small. But Angus felt like I did, only I think he was more revengeful. He said that when he was grown up he would go and kill that baby she was going to have."

"You knew about the baby?"

"Oh, of course I knew. And everyone knows what happened. She went crazy with rapture about having it, and when it was born it was an idiot! Served her right. Idiot or no idiot, she didn't want *us* back again."

"You hate her very much?"

"Why shouldn't I hate her? She did the worst thing to me that anyone can do to anyone else. Let them believe that they're loved and wanted and then show them that it's all a sham."

"What happened to your two—I'll call them brothers, for the sake of convenience."

"Oh, we all drifted apart later. Rod's farming somewhere in the Middle West. He's got a happy nature, and always had. Angus? I don't know. I lost sight of him."

"Did he continue to feel revengeful?"

"I shouldn't think so," said Margot. "It's not the sort of thing you can go on feeling. The last time I saw him, he said he was going on the stage. I don't know whether he did."

"You've remembered, though," said Dermot.

"Yes. I've remembered," said Margot Bence.

"Was Marina Gregg surprised to see you on that day or did she make the arrangements for your photography on purpose to please you?"

"She?" The girl smiled scornfully. "She knew nothing about the arrangements. I was curious to see her, so I did a bit of lobbying to get the job. As I say, I've got some influence with studio people. I wanted to see what she looked like nowadays." She stroked the surface of the table. "She didn't even recognize me. What do you think of that? I was with her for four years. From five years old to nine, and she didn't recognize me."

"Children change," said Dermot Craddock; "they change so much that you'd hardly know them. I have a niece I met the other day and I assure you I'd have passed her in the street."

"Are you saying that to make me feel better? I don't care really. Oh, what the hell, let's be honest. I do care. I did. She had a magic, you know. Marina! A wonderful calamitous magic that took hold of you. You can hate a person and still mind."

"You didn't tell her who you were?"

She shook her head. "No, I didn't tell her. That's the last thing I'd do."

"Did you try and poison her, Miss Bence?"

Her mood changed. She got up and laughed.

"What ridiculous questions you do ask! But I suppose you have to. It's part of your job. No, I can assure you I didn't kill her."

"That isn't what I asked you, Miss Bence."

She looked at him, frowning, puzzled.

"Marina Gregg," he said, "is still alive."

"For how long?"

"What do you mean by that?"

"Don't you think it's likely, Inspector, that someone will try again, and this time—this time, perhaps—they'll succeed?"

"Precautions will be taken."

"Oh, I'm sure they will. The adoring husband will look after her, won't he, and make sure that no harm comes to her?"

He was listening carefully to the mockery in her voice.

"What did you mean when you said you didn't ask me that?" she said, harking back suddenly.

"I asked you if you tried to kill her. You replied that you didn't kill her. That's true enough, but someone died, someone was killed."

"You mean I tried to kill Marina and instead I killed Mrs. What's-her-name. If you'd like me to make it quite clear, I didn't try to poison Marina and I didn't poison Mrs. Badcock."

"But you know perhaps who did?"

"I don't know anything, Inspector, I assure you."

"But you have some idea?"

"Oh, one always has ideas." She smiled at him, a mocking smile. "Among so many people it might be, mightn't it, the black-haired robot of a secretary, the elegant Hailey Preston, servants, maids, a masseur, the hairdresser, someone at the studios, so many people—*and one of them mightn't be what he or she pretended to be?*"

Then as he took an unconscious step towards her, she shook her head vehemently.

"Relax, Inspector," she said. "I'm only teasing you. Somebody's out for Marina's blood, but who it is I've no idea. Really. I've no idea at all."

CHAPTER SIXTEEN

I

AT NO. 16 Aubrey Close, young Mrs. Baker was talking to her husband. Jim Baker, a big good-looking blond giant of a man, was intent on assembling a model construction unit.

"Neighbors!" said Cherry. She gave a toss of her black curly head. "Neighbors!" she said again with venom.

She carefully lifted the frying pan from the stove, then neatly shot its contents on to two plates, one rather fuller than the other. She placed the fuller one before her husband.

"Mixed grill," she announced.

Jim looked up and sniffed appreciatively.

"That's something like," he said. "What is today? My birthday?"

"You have to be well nourished," said Cherry.

She was looking very pretty in a cerise and white striped apron with little frills on it. Jim Baker shifted the component parts of a stratocruiser to make room for his meal. He grinned at his wife and asked:

"Who says so?"

"My Miss Marple for one!" said Cherry. "And if it comes to that," she added, sitting down opposite Jim and pulling her plate towards her, "I should say she could do with a bit more solid nourishment herself. That old cat of a White Knight of hers, gives her nothing but carbohydrates. It's all she can think of! A 'nice custard,' a 'nice bread and butter pudding,' a 'nice macaroni cheese.' Squashy puddings with pink sauce. And gas, gas, gas, all day. Talks her head off, she does."

"Oh, well," said Jim vaguely, "it's invalid diet, I suppose."

"Invalid diet!" said Cherry and snorted. "Miss Marple isn't an invalid—she's just old. Always interfering, too."

"Who, Miss Marple?"

"No. That Miss Knight. Telling me how to do things! She even tries to tell me how to cook! I know a lot more about cooking than she does."

"You're tops for cooking, Cherry," said Jim appreciatively.

"There's something *to* cooking," said Cherry, "something you can get your teeth into."

Jim laughed. "I'm getting my teeth into this all right. Why did your Miss Marple say that I needed nourishing? Did she think I looked run-down, the other day when I came in to fix that bathroom shelf?"

Cherry laughed. "I'll tell you what she said to me. She said 'You've got a handsome husband, my dear. A *very* handsome husband.' Sounds like one of those period books they read aloud on the telly."

"I hope you agreed with her?" said Jim with a grin.

"I said you were all right."

"All right, indeed! That's a nice lukewarm way of talking."

"And then she said, 'You must take care of your husband, my dear. Be sure you feed him properly. Men need plenty of good meat meals, well cooked.'"

"Hear, hear!"

"And she told me to be sure and prepare fresh food for you and not buy ready-made pies and things and slip them in the oven to warm up. Not that I do that often," added Cherry virtuously.

"You can't do it too seldom for me," said Jim. "They don't taste a bit the same."

"So long as you notice what you eat," said Cherry, "and aren't so taken up with those stratocruisers and things you're always building. And don't tell me you bought that set as a Christmas present for your nephew Michael. You bought it so that you could play with it yourself."

"He's not quite old enough for it yet," said Jim apologetically.

"And I suppose you're going on dithering about with it all the evening. What about some music? Did you get that new record you were talking about?"

"Yes, I did. Tchaikovski 1812."

"That's the loud one with the battle, isn't it?" said Cherry. She made a face. "Our Mrs. Hartwell won't half like that! Neighbors! I'm fed up with neighbors. Always grousing and complaining. I don't know which is the worst. The Hartwells or the Barnabys. The Hartwells start rapping on the wall as early as twenty to eleven sometimes. It's a bit thick! After all, even the telly and the B.B.C. go on later than that. Why shouldn't we have a bit of music if we like? And always asking us to turn it down low."

"You can't turn these things down low," said Jim with authority. "You don't get the tone unless you've got the volume. Everyone knows that. It's absolutely recognized in musical circles. And what about their cat—always coming over into our garden, digging up the beds, just when I've got it nice."

"I tell you what, Jim. I'm fed up with this place."

"You didn't mind your neighbors up in Huddersfield," remarked Jim.

"It wasn't the same there," said Cherry. "I mean, you're all independent there. If you're in trouble, somebody'd give you a hand and you'd give a hand to them. But you don't interfere. There's something about a new estate like this that makes people look sideways at their neighbors. Because we're all new, I suppose. The amount of backbiting and tale-telling and writing to the council and one thing and another round here beats me! People in real towns are too busy for it."

"You may have something there, my girl."

"D'you like it here, Jim?"

"The job's all right. And after all, this is a brand-new house. I wish there was a bit more room in it so that I could spread myself a bit more. It would be fine if I could have a workshop."

"I thought it was lovely at first," said Cherry, "but now I'm not so sure. The house is all right and I love the blue paint and the bathroom's nice, but I don't like the people and the *feeling* round here. Some of the people are nice enough. Did I tell you that Lily Price and that Harry of hers have broken off? It was a funny business that day in that house they went to look over. You know when she more or less fell out of the window. She said Harry just stood there like a stuck pig."

"I'm glad she's broken off with him. He's a no-good if I ever saw one," said Jim.

"No good marrying a chap just because a baby's on the way," said Cherry. "He didn't want to marry her, you know. He's not a very nice fellow. Miss Marple said he wasn't," she added thoughtfully. "She spoke to Lily about him. Lily thought she was crackers."

"Miss Marple? I didn't know she'd ever seen him?"

"Oh, yes, she was round here walking the day she fell down and Mrs. Badcock picked her up and took her into her house. Do you think Arthur and Mrs. Bain will make a match of it?"

Jim frowned as he picked up a bit of stratocruiser and consulted the instructional diagram.

"I do wish you'd listen when I'm talking," said Cherry.

"What did you say?"

"Arthur Badcock and Mary Bain."

"For the Lord's sake, Cherry, his wife's only just dead! You women! I've heard he's in a terrible state of nerves still—jumps if you speak to him."

"I wonder why. . . . I shouldn't have thought he'd take it that way, would you?"

"Can you clear off this end of the table a bit?" said Jim, relinquishing even a passing interest in the affairs of his neighbors. "Just so that I can spread some of these pieces out a bit."

Cherry heaved an exasperated sigh.

"To get any attention round here, you have to be a super jet, or a turbo prop," she added bitterly. "You and your constructional models!"

She piled the tray with the remains of supper and carried it over to the sink. She decided not to wash up, a necessity of daily life she always put off as long as possible. Instead, she piled everything into the sink, haphazard, slipped on a corduroy jacket and went out of the house, pausing to call over her shoulder:

"I'm just going to slip along to see Gladys Dixon. I want to borrow one of her *Vogue* patterns."

"All right, old girl." Jim bent over his model.

Casting a venomous look at her next-door neighbor's front door as she passed, Cherry went round the corner into Blenheim Close and stopped at No. 16. The door was open and Cherry tapped on it and went into the hall calling out:

"Is Gladdy about?"

"Is that you, Cherry?" Mrs. Dixon looked out of the kitchen. "She's upstairs in her room, dressmaking."

"Right, I'll go up."

Cherry went upstairs to a small bedroom in which Gladys, a plump girl with a plain face, was kneeling on the floor, her cheeks flushed, and several pins in her mouth, tacking up a paper pattern.

"Hello, Cherry. Look, I got a lovely bit of stuff at Harper's sale in Much Benham. I'm going to do that crossover pattern with frills again, the one I did in Terylene before."

"That'll be nice," said Cherry.

Gladys rose to her feet, panting a little.

"Got indigestion now," she said.

"You oughtn't to do dressmaking right after supper," said Cherry, "bending over like that."

"I suppose I ought to slim a bit," said Gladys. She sat down on the bed.

"Any news from the studios?" asked Cherry, always avid for film news.

"Nothing much. There's a lot of talk still. Marina Gregg came back on the set yesterday—and she created something frightful."

"About what?"

"She didn't like the taste of her coffee. You know, they have coffee in the middle of the morning. She took one sip and said there was something wrong with it. Which was nonsense, of course. There couldn't have been. It comes in a jug straight from the canteen. Of course I always put hers in a special china cup, rather posh—different from the others—but it's the same coffee. So there couldn't have been anything wrong with it, could there?"

"Nerves, I suppose," said Cherry. "What happened?"

"Oh, nothing. Mr. Rudd just calmed everyone down. He's wonderful that way. He took the coffee from her and poured it down the sink."

"That seems rather stupid," said Cherry slowly.

"Why—what do you mean?"

"Well, if there was anything wrong with it—now nobody will ever know."

"Do you think there really might have been?" asked Gladys, looking alarmed.

"Well"—Cherry shrugged her shoulders"there was something wrong with her cocktail the day of the fête wasn't there, so why not the coffee? If at first you don't succeed, try, try, again."

Gladys shivered.

"I don't half like it, Cherry," she said. "Somebody's got it in for her all right. She's had more letters, you know, threatening her—and there was that bust business the other day."

"What bust business?"

"A marble bust. On the set. It's a corner of a room in some Austrian palace or other. Funny name like Shotbrown. Pictures and china and marble busts. This one was up on a bracket—suppose it hadn't been pushed

back enough. Anyway, a heavy lorry went past out in the road and jarred it
off—right on to the chair where Marina sits for her big scene with Count
Somebody-or-other. Smashed it to smithereens! Lucky they weren't shooting at the time. Mr. Rudd, he said not to say a word about it to her, and he
put another chair there, and when she came yesterday and asked why the
chair had been changed, he said the other chair was the wrong period, and
this gave a better angle for the camera. But he didn't half like it—I can tell
you that."

The two girls looked at each other.

"It's exciting in a way," said Cherry slowly. "And yet—it isn't. . . ."

"I think I'm going to give up working in the canteen at the studios," said
Gladys.

"Why? Nobody wants to poison you or drop marble busts on your head!"

"No. But it's not always the person who's meant to get done in who gets
done in. It may be someone else. Like Heather Badcock that day."

"True enough," said Cherry.

"You know," said Gladys, "I've been thinking. I was up at the Hall that
day, helping. I was quite close to them at the time."

"When Heather died?"

"No, when she spilt the cocktail. All down her dress. A lovely dress it was,
too, royal blue nylon taffeta. She'd got it quite new for the occasion. And it
was funny."

"What was funny?"

"I didn't think anything of it at the time. But it does seem funny when I
think it over."

Cherry looked at her expectantly. She accepted the adjective "funny" in
the sense that it was meant. It was not intended humorously.

"For goodness' sake, what was funny?" she demanded.

"I'm almost sure she did it on purpose."

"Spilt the cocktail on purpose?"

"Yes. And I do think that was funny, don't you?"

"On a brand-new dress? I don't believe it."

"I wonder now," said Gladys, "what Arthur Badcock will do with all
Heather's clothes. That dress would clean all right. Or I could take out half
a breadth, it's a lovely full skirt. Do you think Arthur Badcock would think
it very awful of me if I wanted to buy it off him? It would need hardly any
alteration—and it's lovely stuff."

"You wouldn't"—Cherry hesitated "mind?"

"Mind what?"

"Well—having a dress that a woman had died in—I mean died that
way. . . ."

Gladys stared at her.

"I hadn't thought of that," she admitted. She considered for a moment or
two. Then she cheered up.

"I can't see that it really matters," she said. "After all, every time you
buy something secondhand, somebody's usually worn it who has died,
haven't they?"

"Yes. But it's not quite the same."

"I think you're being fanciful," said Gladys. "It's a lovely bright shade of
blue, and really expensive stuff. About that funny business," she continued

thoughtfully, "I think I'll go up to the hall tomorrow morning on my way to work and have a word with Mr. Giuseppe about it."

"Is he the Italian butler?"

"Yes. He's awfully handsome. Flashing eyes. He's got a terrible temper. When we go and help there, he chivvies us girls something terrible." She giggled. "But none of us really mind. He can be awfully nice sometimes. . . . Anyway, I might just tell him about it, and ask him what I ought to do."

"I don't see that you've got anything to tell," said Cherry.

"Well—it was funny," said Gladys, defiantly clinging to her favorite adjective.

"*I* think," said Cherry, "that you just want an excuse to go and talk to Mr. Giuseppe—and you'd better be careful, my girl. You know what these Italians are like! Affiliation orders all over the place. Hot-blooded and passionate, that's what they are."

Gladys sighed ecstatically.

Cherry looked at her friend's fat slightly spotty face and decided that her warnings were unnecessary. Mr. Giuseppe, she thought, would have better fish to fry elsewhere.

II

"Aha!" said Dr. Haydock, "unraveling, I see."

He looked from Miss Marple to a pile of fluffy white fleecy wool.

"You advised me to try unraveling if I couldn't knit," said Miss Marple. "You seem to have been very thorough about it."

"I made a mistake in the pattern right at the beginning. That made the whole thing go out of proportion, so I've had to unravel it all. It's a very elaborate pattern, you see."

"What are elaborate patterns to you? Nothing at all."

"I ought really, I suppose, with my bad eyesight, to stick to plain knitting."

"You'd find that very boring. Well, I'm flattered that you took my advice."

"Don't I always take your advice, Dr. Haydock?"

"You do when it suits you," said Dr. Haydock.

"Tell me, Doctor, was it really knitting you had in mind when you gave me that advice?"

"How are you getting on with unraveling the murder?" he asked.

He met the twinkle in her eyes and twinkled back at her.

"I'm afraid my faculties aren't quite what they were," said Miss Marple, shaking her head with a sigh.

"Nonsense," said Dr. Haydock. "Don't tell me you haven't formed some conclusions."

"Of course I have formed conclusions. Very definite ones."

"Such as?" asked Haydock inquiringly.

"If the cocktail glass was tampered with that day—and I don't see quite how that could have been done—"

"Might have had the stuff ready in an eyedropper," suggested Haydock.

"You are so professional," said Miss Marple admiringly. "But even then it seems to me so very peculiar that nobody saw it happen."

"Murder should not only be done, but be seen to be done! Is that it?"

"You know exactly what I mean," said Miss Marple.

"That was a chance the murderer had to take," said Haydock.

"Oh, quite so. I'm not disputing that for a moment. But there were, I have found by inquiry and adding up the persons, at least eighteen to twenty people on the spot. It seems to me that among twenty people somebody must have seen that action occur."

Haydock nodded. "One would think so, certainly. But obviously no one did."

"I wonder," said Miss Marple thoughtfully.

"What have you got in mind exactly?"

"Well, there are three possibilities. I'm assuming that at least one person would have seen something. One out of twenty. I think it's only reasonable to assume that."

"I think you're begging the question," said Haydock, "and I can see looming ahead one of those terrible exercises in probability where six men have white hats and six men have black and you have to work it out by mathematics how likely it is that the hats will get mixed up and in what proporrtion. If you start thinking about things like that, you would go round the bend. Let me assure you of that!"

"I wasn't thinking of anything like that," said Miss Marple. "I was just thinking of what is likely—"

"Yes," said Haydock thoughtfully, "you're very good at that. You always have been."

"It *is* likely, you know," said Miss Marple, "that out of twenty people one at least should be an observant one."

"I give in," said Haydock. "Let's have the three possibilities."

"I'm afraid I'll have to put them rather sketchily," said Miss Marple. "I haven't quite thought it out. Inspector Craddock, and probably Frank Cornish before him, will have questioned everybody who was there, so the natural thing would be that whoever saw anything of the kind would have said so at once."

"Is that one of the possibilities?"

"No, of course it isn't," said Miss Marple, "because it hasn't happened. What you have to account for is if one person did see something, why didn't that person say so?"

"I'm listening."

"Possibility One," said Miss Marple, her cheeks going pink with animation. "The person who saw it didn't realize what they had seen. That would mean, of course, that it would have to be a rather stupid person. Someone, let us say, who can use their eyes but not their brains. The sort of person who, if you asked them "Did you see anyone put anything in Marina Gregg's glass?' would answer, 'Oh, no,' but if you said 'Did you see anyone put their hand over the top of Marina Gregg's glass?" would say 'Oh, yes, of course I did!'"

Haydock laughed. "I admit," he said, "that one never quite allows for the moron in our midst. All right, I grant you Possibility One. The moron saw it, the moron didn't grasp what the action meant. And the second possibility?"

"This one's very farfetched, but I do think it is just a possibility. It might have been a person whose action in putting something in a glass was natural."

"Wait, wait, explain that a little more clearly."

"It seems to me nowadays," said Miss Marple, "that people are always adding things to what they eat and drink. In my young day it was considered to be very bad manners to take medicines with one's meals. It was on a par with blowing your nose at the dinner table. It just wasn't done. If you had to take pills or capsules, or a spoonful of something, you went out of the room to do so. That's not the case now. When staying with my nephew Raymond, I observed some of his guests seemed to arrive with quite a quantity of little bottles of pills and tablets. They take them with food, or before food, or after food. They keep aspirins and such things in their handbags and take them the whole time—with cups of tea or with their after-dinner coffee. You understand what I mean?"

"Oh, yes," said Dr. Haydock, "I've got your meaning now and it's interesting. You mean that someone—" he stopped. "Let me have it in your own words."

"I meant," said Miss Marple, "that it would be quite possible, audacious but possible, for someone to pick up that glass which as soon as it was in his hand or her hand, of course, would be assumed to be his or her own drink and to add whatever was added quite openly. In that case, you see, people wouldn't think twice of it."

"He—or she—couldn't be sure of that, though," Haydock pointed out.

"No," agreed Miss Marple, "it would be a gamble, a risk—but it could happen. And then," she went on, "there's the third possibility."

"Possibility One, a moron," said the doctor. "Possibility Two, a gambler—what's Possibility Three?"

"Somebody saw what happened and has held their tongue deliberately."

Haydock frowned. "For what reason?" he asked. "Are you suggesting blackmail? If so—"

"If so," said Miss Marple, "it's a very dangerous thing to do."

"Yes, indeed." He looked sharply at the placid old lady with the white fleecy wool on her lap. "Is the third possibility the one you consider the most probable one?"

"No," said Miss Marple, "I wouldn't go so far as that. I have, at the moment, insufficient grounds. Unless," she added carefully, "someone else gets killed."

"Do you think someone else is going to get killed?"

"I hope not," said Miss Marple, "I trust and pray not. But it so often happens, Dr. Haydock. That's the sad and frightening thing. It so often happens."

CHAPTER SEVENTEEN

ELLA PUT DOWN the receiver, smiled to herself and came out of the public telephone box. She was pleased with herself.

"Chief-Inspector God Almighty Craddock!" she said to herself. "I'm twice as good as he is at the job. Variations on the theme of: 'Fly, all is discovered!'"

She pictured to herself with a good deal of pleasure the reactions recently suffered by the person at the other end of the line. That faint menacing whisper coming through the receiver. *"I saw you . . ."*

She laughed silently, the corners of her mouth curving up in a feline cruel line. A student of psychology might have watched her with some interest. Never until the last few days had she had this feeling of power. She was hardly aware herself of how much the heady intoxication of it affected her. . . .

She passed the East Lodge and Mrs. Bantry, busy as usual in the garden, waved a hand to her.

"Damn that old woman," thought Ella. She could feel Mrs. Bantry's eyes following her as she walked up the drive.

A phrase came into her head for no particular reason.

The pitcher goes to the well once too often . . .

Nonsense. Nobody could suspect that it was she who had whispered those menacing words. . . .

She sneezed.

"Damn this hay fever," said Ella Zielinsky.

When she came into her office, Jason Rudd was standing by the window. He wheeled round.

"I couldn't think where you were."

"I had to go and speak to the gardener. There were—" she broke off as she caught sight of his face.

She asked sharply: "What is it?"

His eyes seemed set deeper in his face than ever. All the gaiety of the clown was gone. This was a man under strain. She had seen him under strain before, but never looking like this.

She said again, "What is it?"

He held a sheet of paper out to her. "It's the analysis of that coffee. The coffee that Marina complained about and wouldn't drink."

"You sent it to be analyzed?" She was startled. "But you poured it away down the sink. I saw you."

His wide mouth curled up in a smile. "I'm pretty good at sleight of hand, Ella," he said. "You didn't know that, did you? Yes, I poured most of it away, but I kept a little and I took it along to be analyzed."

She looked down at the paper in her hand.

"Arsenic." She sounded incredulous.

"Yes, arsenic."

"So Marina was right about it tasting bitter?"

"She wasn't right about that. Arsenic has no taste. But her instinct was quite right."

"And we thought she was just being hysterical!"

"She is hysterical! Who wouldn't be? She has a woman drop dead at her feet practically. She gets threatening notes—one after another—there's not been anything today, has there?"

Ella shook her head.

"Who plants the damned things? Oh, well, I suppose it's easy enough— all these open windows. Anyone could slip in."

"You must mean we ought to keep the house barred and locked? But it's such hot weather. There's a man posted in the grounds, after all."

"Yes, and I don't want to frighten her more than she's frightened already. Threatening notes don't matter two hoots. But arsenic, Ella, arsenic's different. . . ."

"Nobody could tamper with food here in the house."

"Couldn't they, Ella? Couldn't they?"

"Not without being seen. No unauthorized person—"

He interrupted.

"People will do things for money, Ella."

"Hardly murder!"

"Even that. And they mightn't realize it *was* murder . . . The servants . . ."

"I'm sure the servants are all right."

"Giuseppe now. I doubt if I'd trust Giuseppe very far if it came to the question of money . . . He's been with us some time, of course, but—"

"Must you torture yourself like this, Jason?"

He flung himself down in the chair. He leaned forward, his long arms hanging down between his knees.

"What to do?" he said slowly and softly. "My God, what to do?"

Ella did not speak. She sat there watching him.

"She was happy here," said Jason. He was speaking more to himself than to Ella. He stared down between his knees at the carpet. If he had looked up, the expression on her face might perhaps have surprised him.

"She was happy," he said again. "She hoped to be happy and she *was* happy. She was saying so that day, the day Mrs. What's-her-name—"

"Bantry?"

"Yes. The day Mrs. Bantry came to tea. She said it was 'so peaceful.' She said that at last she'd found a place where she could settle down and be happy and feel secure. My goodness, secure!"

"Happy ever after?" Ella's voice held a slight tone of irony. "Yes, put like that, it sounds just like a fairy story."

"At any rate she believed it."

"But you didn't," said Ella. "You never thought it would be like that?"

Jason Rudd smiled. "No. I didn't go the whole hog. But I did think that for a while, a year—two years—there might be a period of calm and content. It might have made a new woman of her. It might have given her confidence in herself. She can be happy, you know. When she is happy she's like a child. Just like a child. And now—*this* had to happen to her."

Ella moved restlessly. "Things have to happen to all of us," she said brusquely. "That's the way life is. You just have to take it. Some of us can, some of us can't. She's the kind that can't."

She sneezed.

"Your hay fever bad again?"

"Yes. By the way, Giuseppe's gone to London."

Jason looked faintly surprised.

"To London? Why?"

"Some kind of family trouble. He's got relations in Soho, and one of them's desperately ill. He went to Marina about it and she said it was all right, so I gave him the day off. He'll be back sometime tonight. You don't mind, do you?"

"No," said Jason. "I don't mind. . . ."

He got up and walked up and down.

"If I could take her away . . . now . . . at once."

"Scrap the picture? But just think—"

His voice rose.

"I can't think of anything but Marina. Don't you understand? She's in danger. That's all I can think about."

She opened her mouth impulsively, then closed it.

She gave another muffled sneeze and rose.

"I'd better get my atomizer."

She left the room and went to her bedroom, a word echoing in her mind. *Marina . . . Marina . . . Marina . . .* Always Marina . . .

Fury rose up in her. She stilled it. She went into the bathroom and picked up the spray she used.

She inserted the nozzle into one nostril and squeezed.

The warning came a second too late. . . . Her brain recognized the unfamiliar odor of bitter almonds . . . but not in time to paralyze the squeezing fingers. . . .

CHAPTER EIGHTEEN

I

Frank Cornish replaced the receiver.

"Miss Brewster is out of London for the day," he announced.

"Is she now?" said Craddock.

"Do you think she—"

"I don't know. I shouldn't think so, but I don't know. Ardwyck Fenn?"

"Out. I left word for him to ring you. And Margot Bence, Personality Photographer, has got an assignment somewhere in the country. Her pansy partner didn't know where—or said he didn't. And the butler's hooked it to London."

"I wonder," said Craddock thoughtfully, "if the butler has hooked it for good. I always suspect dying relatives. Why was he suddenly anxious to go to London today?"

"He could have put the cyanide in the atomizer easily enough before he left."

"Anybody could."

"But I think he's indicated. It could hardly be someone from outside."

"Oh, yes, it could. You'd have to judge your moment. You could leave a car in one of the side drives, wait until everyone is in the dining-room, say, and slip in through a window and upstairs. The shrubberies come close up to the house."

"Damn risky."

"This murderer doesn't mind taking risks, you know. That's been apparent all along."

"We've had a man on duty in the grounds."

"I know. One man wasn't enough. So long as it was a question of these anonymous letters, I didn't feel so much urgency. Marina Gregg herself is being well guarded. It never occurred to me that anyone else was in danger. I—"

The telephone rang. Cornish took the call.

"It's the Dorchester. Mr. Ardwyck Fenn is on the line."

He proffered the receiver to Craddock who took it.

"Mr. Fenn? This is Craddock here."

"Ah, yes. I heard you had rung me. I have been out all day."

"I am sorry to tell you, Mr. Fenn, that Miss Zielinsky died this morning—of cyanide poisoning."

"Indeed? I am shocked to hear it. An accident? Or not an accident?"

"Not an accident. Prussic acid had been put in an atomizer she was in the habit of using."

"I see. Yes, I see . . ." There was a short pause. "And why, may I ask, should you ring me about this distressing occurence?"

"You knew Miss Zielinsky, Mr. Fenn."

"Certainly I knew her. I have known her for some years. But she was not an intimate friend."

"We hoped that you could, perhaps, assist us?"

"In what way?"

"We wondered if you could suggest any motive for her death. She is a stranger in this country. We know very little about her friends and associates and the circumstances of her life."

"I would suggest that Jason Rudd is the person to question about that."

"Naturally. We have done so. But there might be an off-chance that you might know something about her that he does not."

"I'm afraid that is not so. I know next to nothing about Ella Zielinsky except that she was a most capable young woman, and first-class at her job. About her private life I know nothing at all."

"So you have no suggestions to make?"

Craddock was ready for the decisive negative, but to his surprise it did not come. Instead there was a pause. He could hear Ardwyck Fenn breathing rather heavily at the other end.

"Are you still there, Chief-Inspector?"

"Yes, Mr. Fenn. I'm here."

"I have decided to tell you something that may be of assistance to you. When you hear what it is, you will realize that I have every reason to keep it to myself. But I judge that in the end that might be unwise. The facts are these. A couple of days ago I received a telephone call. A voice spoke to me in a whisper. It said—I am quoting now—*I saw you . . . I saw you put the tablets in the glass . . . You didn't know there had been an eyewitness, did you? That's all for now—very soon you will be told what you have to do.*"

Craddock uttered an ejaculation of astonishment.

"Surprising, was it not, Mr. Craddock? I will assure you categorically that the accusation was entirely unfounded. I did *not* put tablets in anybody's glass. I defy anyone to prove that I did. The suggestion is utterly absurd. But it would seem, would it not, that Miss Zielinsky was embarking on blackmail."

"You recognized her voice?"

"You cannot recognize a whisper. But it was Ella Zielinsky all right."

"How do you know?"

"The whisperer sneezed heavily before ringing off. I knew that Miss Zielinsky suffered from hay fever."

"And you think—what?"

"I think that Miss Zielinsky got hold of the wrong person at her first attempt. It seems to me possible that she was more successful later. Blackmail can be a dangerous game."

Craddock pulled himself together.

"I must thank you very much for your statement, Mr. Fenn. As a matter of form, I shall have to check upon your movements today."

"Naturally. My chauffeur will be able to give you precise information."

Craddock rang off and repeated what Fenn had said. Cornish whistled.

"Either that lets him out completely. Or else—"

"Or else it's a magnificent piece of bluff. It could be. He's the kind of man who has the nerve for it. If there's the least chance that Ella Zielinsky left a record of her suspicions, then his taking the bull by the horns is a magnificent bluff."

"And his alibi?"

"We've come across some very good faked alibis in our time," said Craddock. "He could afford to pay a good sum for one."

II

It was past midnight when Giuseppe returned to Gossington. He took a taxi from Much Benham, as the last train on the branch line to St. Mary Mead had gone.

He was in very good spirits. He paid off the taxi at the gate, and took a short cut through the shrubbery. He opened the back door with his key. The house was dark and silent. Giuseppe shut and bolted the door. As he turned to the stair which led up to his own comfortable suite of bed and bath, he noticed that there was a draft. A window open somewhere, perhaps. He decided not to bother. He went upstairs smiling and fitted a key into his door. He always kept his suite locked. As he turned the key and pushed the door open he felt the pressure of a hard round ring in his back. A voice said, "Put your hands up and don't scream."

Giuseppe threw his hands up quickly. He was taking no chances. Actually there was no chance to take.

The trigger was pressed—once—twice.

Giuseppe fell forward. . . .

Bianca lifted her head from her pillow.

Was that a shot? . . . She was almost sure she had heard a shot. . . . She waited some minutes. Then she decided she had been mistaken and lay down again.

CHAPTER NINETEEN

I

"It's too dreadful," said Miss Knight. She put down her parcels and gasped for breath.

"Something has happened?" asked Miss Marple.

"I really don't like to tell you about it, dear, I really don't. It might be a shock to you."

"If you don't tell me," said Miss Marple, "somebody else will."

"Dear, dear, that's true enough," said Miss Knight. "Yes, that's terribly true. Everybody talks too much, they say. And I'm sure there's a lot in that. I never repeat anything myself. Very careful I am."

"You were saying," said Miss Marple, "that something rather terrible had happened?"

"It really quite bowled me over," said Miss Knight. "Are you sure you don't feel the draft from that window, dear?"

"I like a little fresh air," said Miss Marple.

"Ah, but we mustn't catch cold, must we?" said Miss Knight archly. "I'll tell you what. I'll just pop out and make you a nice eggnog. We'd like that, wouldn't we?"

"I don't know whether *you* would like it," said Miss Marple. "*I* should be delighted for you to have it if you would like it."

"Now, now," said Miss Knight, shaking her finger, "so fond of our joke, aren't we?"

"But you were going to tell me something," said Miss Marple.

"Well, you mustn't worry about it," said Miss Knight, "and you mustn't let it make you nervous in any way, because I'm sure it's nothing to do with *us.* But with all these American gangsters and things like that, well, I suppose it's nothing to be surprised about."

"Somebody else has been killed," said Miss Marple, "is that it?"

"Oh, that's very sharp of you, dear. I don't know what should put such a thing into your head."

"As a matter of fact," said Miss Marple thoughtfully, "I've been expecting it."

"Oh, really!" exclaimed Miss Knight.

"Somebody always sees something," said Miss Marple, "only sometimes it takes a little while for them to realize what it is they have seen. Who is it who's dead?"

"The Italian butler. He was shot last night."

"I see," said Miss Marple thoughtfully. "Yes, very likely, of course, but I should have thought that he'd have realized before now the importance of what he saw—"

"Really!" exclaimed Miss Knight. "You talk as though you knew all about it. Why should he have been killed?"

"I expect," said Miss Marple thoughtfully, "that he tried to blackmail somebody."

"He went to London yesterday, they say."

"Did he now," said Miss Marple, "that's very interesting, and suggestive too, I think."

Miss Knight departed to the kitchen intent on the concoction of nourishing beverages. Miss Marple remained sitting thoughtfully till disturbed by the loud aggressive humming of the vacuum cleaner, assisted by Cherry's voice singing the latest favorite ditty of the moment, "I Said to You and You Said to Me."

Miss Knight popped her head round the kitchen door.

"Not quite so much noice, please, Cherry," she said. "You don't want to disturb dear Miss Marple, do you? You mustn't be thoughtless, you know."

She shut the kitchen door again as Cherry remarked, either to herself or the world at large, "And who said you could call me Cherry, you old jelly-bag?" The vacuum continued to whine while Cherry sang in a more subdued voice. Miss Marple called in a high clear voice:

"Cherry, come here a minute."

Cherry switched off the vacuum and opened the drawing-room door.

"I didn't mean to disturb you by singing, Miss Marple."

"Your singing is much pleasanter than the horrid noise that vacuum makes," said Miss Marple, "But I know one has to go with the times. It would be no use on earth asking any of you young people to use the dustpan and brush in the old-fashioned way."

"What, get down on my knees with a dustpan and brush?" Cherry registered alarm and surprise.

"Quite unheard of, I know," said Miss Marple. "Come in and shut the door. I called you because I wanted to talk to you."

Cherry obeyed and came towards Miss Marple looking inquiringly at her.

"We've not much time," said Miss Marple. "That old—Miss Knight, I mean—will come in any moment with an egg drink of some kind."

"Good for you, I expect. It'll pep you up," said Cherry encouragingly.

"Had you heard," asked Miss Marple, "that the butler at Gossington Hall was shot last night?"

"What, the Italian?" demanded Cherry.

"Yes. His name is Giuseppe, I understand."

"No," said Cherry, "I hadn't heard *that*. I heard that Mr. Rudd's secretary had a heart attack yesterday, and somebody said she was actually dead—but I suspect that was just a rumor. Who told you about the butler?"

"Miss Knight came back and told me."

"Of course I haven't seen anyone to speak to this morning," said Cherry, "not before coming along here. I expect the news has only just got round. Was he bumped off?" she demanded.

"That seems to be assumed," said Miss Marple, "whether rightly or wrongly, I don't quite know."

"This is a wonderful place for talk," said Cherry. "I wonder if Gladys got to see him or not," she added thoughtfully.

"Gladys?"

"Oh, a sort of friend of mine. She lives a few doors away. Works in the canteen at the studios."

"And she talked to you about Giuseppe?"

"Well, there was something that struck her as a bit funny, and she was going to ask him what he thought about it. But if you ask me, it was an excuse—she's a bit sweet on him. Of course he's quite handsome and Italians do have a way with them—I told her to be careful about him, though. You know what Italians are."

"He went to London yesterday," said Miss Marple, "and only returned in the evening, I understand."

"I wonder if she managed to get to see him before he went?"

"Why did she want to see him, Cherry?"

"It was just something which she felt was a bit funny," said Cherry. Miss Marple looked at her inquiringly. She was able to take the word "funny" at the valuation it usually had for the Gladyses of the neighborhood.

"She was one of the girls who helped at the party there," explained Cherry. "The day of the fête. You know, when Mrs. Badcock got hers."

"Yes?" Miss Marple was looking more alert than ever, much as a fox terrier might look at a waiting rathole.

"And there was something that she saw that struck her as a bit funny."

"Why didn't she go to the police about it?"

"Well, she didn't really think it meant anything, you see," explained Cherry. "Anyway, she thought she'd better ask Mr. Giuseppe first."

"What was it that she saw that day?"

"Frankly," said Cherry, "what she told me seemed nonsense! I've wondered, perhaps, if she was just putting me off—and what she was going to see Mr. Giuseppe about was something quite different."

"What *did* she say?" Miss Marple was patient and pursuing.

Cherry frowned. "She was talking about Mrs. Badcock and the cocktail and she said she was quite near her at the time. And she said she did it herself."

"Did what herself."

"Spilt her cocktail all down her dress, and ruined it."

"You mean it was clumsiness?"

"No, not clumsiness. Gladys said she did it on *purpose*—that she *meant* to do it. Well, I mean, that doesn't make sense, does it, however you look at it?"

Miss Marple shook her head, perplexed. "No," she said. "Certainly not—no, I can't see any sense in that."

"She'd got on a new dress, too," said Cherry. "That's how the subject came up. Gladys wondered whether she'd be able to buy it. Said it ought to clean all right but she didn't like to go and ask Mr. Badcock herself. She's very good at dressmaking, Gladys is, and she said it was lovely stuff. Royal blue artificial taffeta; and she said even if the stuff *was* ruined where the cocktail stained it, she could take out a seam—half a breadth say—because it was one of those full skirts."

Miss Marple considered this dressmaking problem for a moment and then set it aside.

"But you think your friend Gladys might have been keeping something back?"

"Well, I just wondered because I don't see if that's all she saw—Heather Badcock deliberately spilling her cocktail over herself—I don't see that there'd be anything to ask Mr. Giuseppe about, do you?"

"No, I don't" said Miss Marple. "But it's always interesting when one doesn't see," she added. "If you don't see what a thing means, you must be looking at it wrong way round, unless of course you haven't got full information. Which is probably the case here." She sighed. "It's a pity she didn't go straight to the police."

The door opened and Miss Knight bustled in holding a tall tumbler with a delicious pale yellow froth on top.

"Now here you are, dear," she said, "a nice little treat. We're going to enjoy this."

She pulled forward a little table and placed it beside her employer. Then she turned a glance on Cherry. "The vacuum cleaner," she said coldly, "is left in a most difficult position in the hall. I nearly fell over it. *Anyone* might have an accident."

"Righty-ho," said Cherry. "I'd better get on with things."

She left the room.

"Really," said Miss Knight, "that Mrs. Baker! I'm continually having to speak to her about something or other. Leaving vacuum cleaners all over the place and coming in here chattering to you when you want to be quiet."

"I called her in," said Miss Marple. "I wanted to speak to her."

"Well, I hope you mentioned the way the beds are made," said Miss Knight. "I was quite shocked when I came to turn down your bed last night. I had to make it all over again."

"That was very kind of you," said Miss Marple.

"Oh, I never grudge being helpful," said Miss Knight. "That's why I'm here, isn't it? To make a certain person we know as comfortable and happy as possible. Oh, dear, dear," she added, "you've pulled out a lot of your knitting again."

Miss Marple leaned back and closed her eyes. "I'm going to have a little rest," she said. "Put the glass here—thank you. And please don't come in and disturb me for at least three-quarters of an hour."

"Indeed I won't, dear," said Miss Knight. "And I'll tell that Mrs. Baker to be very quiet."

She bustled out purposefully.

II

The good-looking young American glanced round him in a puzzled way. The ramifications of the housing estate perplexed him.

He addressed himself politely to an old lady with white hair and pink cheeks who seemed to be the only human being in sight.

"Excuse me, ma'am, but could you tell me where to find Blenheim Close?"

The old lady considered him for a moment. He had just begun to wonder if she was deaf, and had prepared himself to repeat his demand in a louder voice, when she spoke.

"Along here to the right, then turn left, second to the right again, and straight on. What number do you want?"

"Number sixteen." He consulted a small piece of paper. "Gladys Dixon."

"That's right," said the old lady. "But I believe she works at the Hellingforth Studios. In the canteen. You'll find her there if you want her."

"She didn't turn up this morning," explained the young man. "I want to get hold of her to come up to Gossington Hall. We're very shorthanded there today."

"Of course," said the old lady. "The butler was shot last night, wasn't he?"

The young man was slightly staggered by this reply.

"I guess news gets round pretty quickly in these parts," he said.

"It does indeed," said the old lady. "Mr. Rudd's secretary died of some kind of seizure yesterday, too, I understand."

She shook her head. "Terrible. Quite terrible. What are we coming to?"

CHAPTER TWENTY

I

A LITTLE LATER in the day yet another visitor found his way to 16 Blenheim Close. Detective-Sergeant William (Tom) Tiddler.

In reply to his sharp knock on the smart yellow-painted door, it was opened to him by a girl of about fifteen. She had long straggly fair hair and was wearing tight black pants and an orange sweater.

"Miss Gladys Dixon live here?"

"You want Gladys? You're unlucky. She isn't here."

"Where is she? Out for the evening?"

"No. She's gone away. Bit of a holiday like."

"Where's she gone to?"

"That's telling," said the girl.

Tom Tiddler smiled at her in his most ingratiating manner. "May I come in? Is your mother at home?"

"Mum's out at work. She won't be in until half-past seven. But she can't tell you any more than I can. Gladys has gone off for a holiday."

"Oh, I see. When did she go?"

"This morning. All of a sudden like. Said she'd got the chance of a free trip."

"Perhaps you wouldn't mind giving me her address."

The fair-haired girl shook her head. "Haven't got an address," she said. "Gladys said she'd send us her address as soon as she knew where she was going to stay. As like as not she won't, though," she added. "Last summer she went to Newquay and never sent us as much as a postcard. She's slack that way and besides, she says, why do mothers have to bother all the time?"

"Did somebody stand her this holiday?"

"Must have," said the girl. "She's pretty hard up at the moment. Went to the sales last week."

"And you've no idea at all who gave her this trip or—er—paid for her going there?"

The fair girl bristled suddenly.

"Now don't you get any wrong ideas. Our Gladys isn't that sort. She and her boy friend may like to go to the same place for holidays in August, but there's nothing wrong about it. She pays for herself. So don't you get ideas, mister."

Tiddler said meekly that he wouldn't get ideas but he would like the address if Gladys Dixon should send a postcard.

He returned to the station with the result of his various inquiries. From the studios, he had learnt that Gladys Dixon had rung up that day and said she wouldn't be able to come to work for about a week. He had also learned some other things.

"No end of a shemozzle there's been there lately," he said. "Marina Gregg's been having hysterics most days. Said some coffee she was given was poisoned. Said it tasted bitter. Awful state of nerves she was in. Her husband took it and threw it down the sink and told her not to make so much fuss."

"Yes?" said Craddock. It seemed plain there was more to come.

"But word went round as Mr. Rudd didn't throw it all away. He kept some and had it analyzed and it was poison."

"It sounds to me," said Craddock, "very unlikely. I'll have to ask him about that."

II

Jason Rudd was nervous, irritable.

"Surely, Inspector Craddock," he said, "I was only doing what I had a perfect right to do."

"If you suspected anything was wrong with that coffee, Mr. Rudd, it would have been much better if you'd turned it over to us."

"The truth of it is that I didn't suspect for a moment that anything was wrong with it."

"In spite of your wife saying that it tasted odd?"

"Oh, that!" A faintly rueful smile came to Rudd's face. "Ever since the date of the fête everything that my wife has eaten or drunk has tasted odd. What with that and the threatening notes that have been coming—"

"There have been more of them?"

"Two more. One through the window down there. The other one was slipped in the letter box. Here they are if you would like to see them."

Craddock looked. They were printed, as the first one had been. One ran: *It won't be long now. Prepare yourself.*

The other had a rough drawing of a skull and crossbones and below it was written: *This means you, Marina.*

Craddock's eyebrows rose.

"Very childish," he said.

"Meaning you discount them as dangerous?"

"Not at all," said Craddock. "A murderer's mind usually is childish. You've really no idea at all, Mr. Rudd, who sent these?"

"Not the least," said Jason. "I can't help feeling it's more like a macabre joke than anything else. It seemed to me perhaps—" he hesitated.

"Yes, Mr. Rudd?"

"It could be somebody local, perhaps, who—who had been excited by the poisoning on the date of the fête. Someone, perhaps, who has a grudge against the acting profession. There are rural pockets where acting is considered to be one of the devil's weapons."

"Meaning that you think Miss Gregg is not actually threatened? But what about this business of the coffee?"

"I don't even know how you got to hear about that," said Rudd with some annoyance.

Craddock shook his head.

"Everything's talked about. It always comes to one's ears sooner or later. But you should have come to us. Even when you got the result of the analysis you didn't let us know, did you?"

"No," said Jason. "No, I didn't. But I had other things to think about. Poor Ella's death, for one thing. And now this business of Giuseppe. Inspector Craddock, when can I get my wife away from here? She's half frantic."

"I can understand that. But there will be the inquests to attend."

"You do realize that her life is still in danger?"

"I hope not. Every precaution will be taken—"

"Every precaution! I've heard that before, I think . . . I must get her away from here, Craddock. I *must.*"

III

Marina was lying on the chaise longue in her bedroom, her eyes closed. She looked grey with strain and fatigue.

Her husband stood there for a moment looking at her. Her eyes opened.

"Was that that Craddock man?"

"Yes."

"What did he come about? Ella?"

"Ella—and Giuseppe."

Marina frowned.

"Giuseppe? Have they found out who shot him?"

"Not yet."

"It's all like a nightmare. . . . Did he say we could go away?"

"He said—not yet."

"Why not? We must. Didn't you make him see that I can't go on waiting day after day for someone to kill me? It's fantastic."

"Every precaution will be taken."

"They said that before. Did it stop Ella being killed? Or Giuseppe? Don't you see, they'll get me in the end. . . . There was something in my coffee that day at the studio. I'm sure there was. . . . If only you hadn't poured it away! If we'd kept it, we could have had it analyzed or whatever you call it. We'd have known for sure. . . ."

"Would it have made you happier to know for sure?"

She stared at him, the pupils of her eyes widely dilated.

"I don't see what you mean. If they'd known for sure that someone was trying to poison me, they'd have let us leave here, they'd have let us get away."

"Not necessarily."

"But I can't go on like this! I can't . . . I can't . . . You must help me, Jason. You must do *something*. I'm frightened. I'm so terribly frightened . . . There's an enemy here. And I don't know who it is . . . It might be anyone—anyone. At the studios—or here in the house. Someone who hates me—but why? . . . why? . . . Someone who wants me dead . . . But who is it? Who is it? I thought—I was almost sure—it was Ella. But now—"

"You thought it was Ella?" Jason sounded astonished. "But why?"

"Because she hated me—oh, yes, she did. Don't men ever see these things? She was madly in love with you. I don't believe you had the least idea of it. But it can't be Ella, because Ella's dead. Oh Jinks, Jinks—do help me—get me away from here—let me go somewhere safe . . . safe . . ."

She sprang up and walked rapidly up and down, turning and twisting her hands.

The director in Jason was full of admiration for those passionate, tortured movements. I must remember them, he thought. For Hedda Gabler, perhaps? Then, with a shock, he remembered that it was his wife he was watching.

He went to her and put his arms round her.

"It's all right, Marina—all right. I'll look after you."

"We must go away from this hateful house—at once. I hate this house—hate it."

"Listen, we can't go away immediately."

"Why not? Why *not?*"

"Because," said Rudd, "death causes complications . . . and there's something else to consider. Will running away do any good?"

"Of course it will. We'll get away from this person who hates me."

"If there's anyone who hates you that much, they could follow you easily enough."

"You mean—you mean—I shall never get away? I shall never be safe again?"

"Darling—it will be all right. I'll look after you. I'll keep you safe."

She clung to him.

"Will you, Jinks? Will you see that nothing happens to me?"

She sagged against him, and he laid her down gently on the chaise longue.

"Oh, I'm a coward," she murmured, "a coward . . . If I knew who it was—and why? . . . Get me my pills—the yellow ones—not the brown. I must have something to calm me."

"Don't take too many, for God's sake, Marina."

"All right—all right . . . Sometimes they don't have any effect any more. . . ." She looked up in his face.

She smiled, a tender exquisite smile.

"You'll take care of me, Jinks? Swear you'll take care of me . . ."

"Always," said Jason Rudd. "To the bitter end."

"You looked so—so odd when you said that."

Her eyes opened wide.

"Did I? How did I look?"

"I can't explain. Like—like a clown laughing at something terribly sad, that no one else has seen. . . ."

CHAPTER TWENTY-ONE

IT WAS A TIRED and depressed Inspector Craddock who came to see Miss Marple the following day.

"Sit down and be comfortable," she said. "I can see you've had a very hard time."

"I don't like to be defeated," said Inspector Craddock. "Two murders within twenty-four hours. Ah, well, I'm poorer at my job than I thought I was. Give me a nice cup of tea, Aunt Jane, with some thin bread and butter and soothe me with your earliest remembrances of St. Mary Mead."

Miss Marple clicked her tongue in a sympathetic manner.

"Now it's no good talking like that, my dear boy, and I don't think tea and bread and butter is at all what you want. Gentlemen, when they've had a disappointment, want something stronger than tea."

As usual, Miss Marple said the word "gentlemen" in the way of someone describing a foreign species.

"I should advise a good stiff whisky and soda," she said.

"Would you really, Aunt Jane? Well, 1 won't say no."

"And I shall get it for you myself," said Miss Marple, rising to her feet.

"Oh, no, don't do that. Let me. Or what about Miss What's-her-name?"

"We don't want Miss Knight fussing about here," said Miss Marple. "She won't be bringing my tea for another twenty minutes, so that gives us a little peace and quiet. Clever of you to come to the window and not through the front door. Now we can have a nice quiet little time by ourselves."

She went to a corner cupboard, opened it and produced a bottle, a syphon of soda water and a glass.

"You are full of surprises," said Dermot Craddock. "I'd no idea that's what you kept in your corner cupboard. Are you quite sure you're not a secret drinker, Aunt Jane?"

"Now, now," Miss Marple admonished him. "I have never been an advocate of teetotalism. A little strong drink is always advisable on the premises in case there is a shock or an accident. Invaluable at such times. Or, of course, if a gentleman should arrive suddenly. There!" said Miss Marple, handing him her remedy with an air of quiet triumph. "And you don't need to joke any more. Just sit quietly there and relax."

"Wonderful wives there must have been in your young days," said Dermot Craddock.

"I'm sure, my dear boy, you would find the young lady of the type you refer to as a very inadequate helpmeet nowadays. Young ladies were not encouraged to be intellectual, and very few of them had university degrees or any kind of academic distinction."

"There are things that are preferable to academic distinctions," said Dermot. "One of them is knowing when a man wants a whisky and soda and giving it to him."

Miss Marple smiled at him affectionately.

"Come," she said. "Tell me about it. Or as much as you are allowed to tell me."

"I think you probably know as much as I do. And very likely you have something up your sleeve. How about your dog's-body, your dear Miss Knight? What about her having committed the crime?"

"Now why should Miss Knight have done such a thing?" demanded Miss Marple, surprised.

"Because she's the most unlikely person," said Dermot. "It so often seems to hold good when you produce your answer."

"Not at all," said Miss Marple with spirit. "I have said over and over again, not only to you, my dear Dermot—if I may call you so—that it is always the *obvious* person who has done the crime. One thinks so often of the wife or the husband and so very often it *is* the wife or the husband."

"Meaning Jason Rudd?" He shook his head. "That man adores Marina Gregg."

"I was speaking generally," said Miss Marple, with dignity. "First we had Mrs. Badcock apparently murdered. One asked oneself who could have done such a thing and the first answer would naturally be the husband. So one had to examine that possibility. Then we decide that the real object of the crime was Marina Gregg and there again we have to look for the person most intimately connected with Marina Gregg, starting, as I say, with the

husband. Because there is no doubt about it that husbands do, very
frequently, want to make away with their wives, though sometimes, of
course, they only *wish* to make away with their wives and do not actually do
so. But I agree with you, my dear boy, that Jason Rudd really cares with all
his heart for Marina Gregg. It *might* be very clever acting, though I can
hardly believe that. And one certainly cannot see a motive of any kind for
his doing away with her. If he wanted to marry somebody else there could, I
should say, be nothing more simple. Divorce, if I may say so, seems second
nature to film stars. A practical advantage does not seem to arise either. He
is not a poor man by any means. He has his own career, and is, I
understand, most successful in it. So we must go farther afield. But it
certainly is difficult. Yes, very difficult."

"Yes," said Craddock, "it must hold particular difficulties for you
because of course this film world is entirely new to you. You don't know the
local scandals and animosities and all the rest of it."

"I know a little more than you may think," said Miss Marple. "I have
studied very closely various numbers of *Confidential, Film Life, Film Talk* and
Film Topics."

Dermot Craddock laughed. He couldn't help it.

"I must say," he said, "it tickles me to see you sitting there and telling me
what your course of literature has been."

"I found it very interesting," said Miss Marple. "They're not particularly
well written, if I may say so. But it really is disappointing in a way that it is
all so much the same as it used to be in my young days. *Modern Society* and
Tit Bits and all the rest of them. A lot of gossip. A lot of scandal. A great
preoccupation with who is in love with who, and all the rest of it. Really,
you know, practically exactly the same sort of thing that goes on in St. Mary
Mead. And in the Development, too. Human nature, I mean, is just the
same everywhere. One comes back, I think, to the question of who could
have been likely to want to kill Marina Gregg, to want to so much that
having failed once they sent threatening letters and made repeated attempts
to do so. Someone perhaps a little—" very gently she tapped her forehead.

"Yes," said Craddock, "that certainly seems indicated. And of course it
doesn't always show."

"Oh, I know," agreed Miss Marple fervently. "Old Mrs. Pike's second
boy, Alfred, *seemed* perfectly rational and normal. Almost painfully prosaic,
if you know what I mean, but actually, it seems, he had the most abnormal
psychology, or so I understand. Really positively dangerous. He seems quite
happy and contented, so Mrs. Pike told me, now that he is in Fairways
Mental Home. They understand him there, and the doctors think him a
most interesting case. That of course pleases him very much. Yes, it all
ended quite happily, but she had one or two very near escapes."

Craddock revolved in his mind the possibility of a parallel between
someone in Marina Gregg's entourage and Mrs. Pike's second son.

"The Italian butler," continued Miss Marple, "the one who was killed.
He went to London, I understand, on the day of his death. Does anyone
know what he did there—if you are allowed to tell me, that is," she added
conscientiously.

"He arrived in London at eleven-thirty in the morning," said Craddock,
"and what he did in London nobody knows until at a quarter to two he

visited his bank and made a deposit of five hundred pounds in cash. I may say that there was no confirmation of his story that he went to London to visit an ill relative or a relative who had got into trouble. None of his relatives there had seen him."

Miss Marple nodded her head appreciatively.

"Five hundred pounds," she said. "Yes, that's quite an interesting sum, isn't it? I should imagine it would be the first installment of a good many other sums, wouldn't you?"

"It looks that way," said Craddock.

"It was probably all the ready money the person he was threatening could raise. He may have pretended to be satisfied with that, or he may have accepted it as a down payment and the victim may have promised to raise further sums in the immediate future. It seems to knock out the idea that Marina Gregg's killer could have been someone in humble circumstances who had a private vendetta against her. It would also knock out, I should say, the idea of someone who'd obtained work as a studio helper or attendant or a servant or a gardener. Unless"—Miss Marple pointed out—"such a person may have been the active agent whereas the employing agent may not have been in the neighborhood. Hence the visit to London."

"Exactly. We have in London Ardwyck Fenn, Lola Brewster and Margot Bence. All three were present at the party. All three of them could have met Giuseppe at an arranged meeting-place somewhere in London between the hours of eleven and a quarter to two. Ardwyck Fenn was out of his office during those hours. Lola Brewster had left her suite to go shopping, Margot Bence was not in her studio. By the way—"

"Yes?" said Miss Marple. "Have you something to tell me?"

"You asked me," said Dermot, "about the children. The children that Marina Gregg adopted before she knew she could have a child of her own."

"Yes, I did."

Craddock told her what he had learned.

"Margot Bence," said Miss Marple softly. "I had a feeling, you know, that it had something to do with children. . . ."

"I can't believe that after all these years—"

"I know, I know. One never can. But do you really, my dear Dermot, know very much about children? Think back to your own childhood. Can't you remember some incident, some happening that caused you grief, or a passion quite incommensurate with its real importance? Some sorrow or passionate resentment that has really never been equalled since? There was such a clever book, you know, written by that brilliant writer, Mr. Richard Hughes. I forget the name of it but it was about some children who had been through a hurricane. Oh, yes—the hurricane in Jamaica. What made a vivid impression on them was their cat rushing madly through the house. It was the only thing they remembered. But the whole of the horror and excitement and fear that they had experienced was bound up in that one incident."

"It's odd you should say that," said Craddock thoughtfully.

"Why, has it made you remember something?"

"I was thinking of when my mother died. I was five I think. Five or six. I was having dinner in the nursery, jam roll pudding. I was very fond of jam roll pudding. One of the servants came in and said to my nursery governess,

'Isn't it awful? There's been an accident and Mrs. Craddock has been killed.' . . . Whenever I think of my mother's death, d'you know what I see?"

"What?"

"A plate with jam roll pudding on it, and I'm staring at it. Staring at it and I can see as well now as then, how the jam oozed out of it at one side. I didn't cry or say anything. I remember just sitting there as though I'd been frozen stiff, staring at the pudding. And d'you know, even now if I see in a shop or a restaurant or in anyone's house a portion of jam roll pudding, a whole wave of horror and misery and despair comes over me. Sometimes for a moment I don't remember *why*. Does that seem very crazy to you?"

"No," said Miss Marple, "it seems entirely natural. It's very interesting, that. It's given me a sort of idea. . . ."

The door opened and Miss Knight appeared bearing the tea tray.

"Dear, dear," she exclaimed, "and so we've got a visitor, have we? How very nice. How do you do, Inspector Craddock. I'll just fetch another cup."

"Don't bother," Dermot called after her, "I've had a drink instead."

Miss Knight popped her head back round the door.

"I wonder—could you just come here a minute, Mr. Craddock?"

Dermot joined her in the hall. She went to the dining-room and shut the door.

"You will be careful, won't you?" she said.

"Careful? In what way, Miss Knight?"

"Our old dear in there. You know, she's so interested in everything, but it's not very good for her to get excited over murders and nasty things like that. We don't want her to brood and have bad dreams. She's very old and frail, and she really must lead a very sheltered life. She always has, you know. I'm sure all this talk of murders and gangsters and things like that is very, very bad for her."

Dermot looked at her with faint amusement.

"I don't think," he said gently, "that anything that you or I could say about murders is likely unduly to excite or shock Miss Marple. I can assure you, my dear Miss Knight, that Miss Marple can contemplate murder and sudden death and indeed crime of all kinds with the utmost equanimity."

He went back to the drawing-room, and Miss Knight, clucking a little in an indignant manner, followed him. She talked briskly during tea with an emphasis on political news in the paper and the most cheerful subjects she could think of. When she finally removed the tea tray and shut the door behind her, Miss Marple drew a deep breath.

"At last we've got some peace," she said. "I hope I shan't murder that woman someday. Now listen, Dermot, there are some things I want to know."

"Yes? What are they?"

"I want to go over very carefully exactly what happened on the day of the fête. Mrs. Bantry has arrived, and the vicar shortly after her. Then come Mr. and Mrs. Badcock, and on the stairs at that time were the mayor and his wife, this man Ardwyck Fenn, Lola Brewster, a reporter from the *Herald and Argus* of Much Benham, and this photographer girl, Margot Bence. Margot Bence, you said, had her camera at an angle on the stairs and was taking photographs of the proceedings. Have you seen any of those photographs?"

"Actually I brought one to show you."

He took from his pocket an unmounted print. Miss Marple looked at it steadfastly. It showed Marina Gregg with Jason Rudd a little behind her to one side. Arthur Badcock, his hand to his face, looking slightly embarrassed, was standing back, while his wife had Marina Gregg's hand in hers and was looking up at her and talking. Marina was not looking at Mrs. Badcock. She was staring over her head looking, it seemed, full into the camera, or possibly just slightly to the left of it.

"*Very* interesting," said Miss Marple. "I've had descriptions, you know, of what this look was on her face. A frozen look. Yes, that describes it quite well. A look of doom. I'm not really so sure about that. It's more a kind of paralysis of feeling rather than apprehension of doom. Don't you think so? I wouldn't say it was actually fear, would you, although fear of course might take you that way. It might paralyze you. But I don't think it was fear. I think rather that it was *shock*. Dermot, my dear boy, I want you to tell me if you've got notes of it, what exactly Heather Badcock said to Marina Gregg on that occasion. I know roughly the gist of it, of course, but how near can you get to the actual words? I suppose you had accounts of it from different people."

Dermot nodded.

"Yes. Let me see. Your friend Mrs. Bantry, then Jason Rudd and I think Arthur Badcock. As you say, they varied a little in wording, but the gist of them was the same."

"I know. It's the variations that I want. I think it might help us."

"I don't see how," said Dermot, "though perhaps you do. Your friend Mrs. Bantry was probably the most definite on the point. As far as I remember—wait—I carry a good many of my jottings around with me."

He took out a small notebook from his pocket, looked through it to refresh his memory.

"I haven't got the exact words here," he said, "but I made a rough note. Apparently Mrs. Badcock was very cheerful, rather arch, and delighted with herself. She said something like 'I can't tell you how wonderful this is for me. You won't remember, but years ago in Bermuda—I got up from bed when I had chicken pox and came along to see you and you gave me an autograph and it's one of the proudest days of my life which I have never forgotten.'"

"I see," said Miss Marple, "she mentioned the place but not the date, did she?"

"Yes."

"And what did Rudd say?"

"Jason Rudd? He said that Mr. Badcock told his wife that she'd got up from bed when she had the 'flu and had come to meet Marina and that she still had her autograph. It was a shorter account than your friend's, but the gist of it was the same."

"Did he mention the time and place?"

"No. I don't think he did. I think he said roughly that it was some ten or twelve years ago."

"I see. And what about Mr. Badcock?"

"Mr. Badcock said that Heather was extremely excited and anxious to meet Miss Gregg, that she was a great fan of Marina Gregg's and that she'd told him that once when she was ill as a girl she managed to get up and meet Miss Gregg and get her autograph. He didn't go into any close particulars, as it was evidently in the days before he was married to his wife. He impressed me as not thinking the incident of much importance."

"I see," said Miss Marple. "Yes, I see . . ."

"And what do you see?" asked Craddock.

"Not quite as much as I'd like to yet," said Miss Marple honestly, "but I have a sort of feeling if I only knew why she'd ruined her new dress—"

"Who—Mrs. Badcock?"

"Yes. It seems to me such a very odd thing—such an inexplicable one unless—of course— Dear me, I think I must be *very* stupid!"

Miss Knight opened the door and entered, switching the light on as she did so.

"I think we want a little light in here," she said brightly.

"Yes," said Miss Marple, "you are so right, Miss Knight. That is exactly what we did want. A little light. I think, you know, that at last we've got it."

The tête-à-tête ended and Craddock rose to his feet.

"There only remains one thing," he said, "and that is for you to tell me just what particular memory from your own past is agitating your mind now."

"Everyone always teases me about that," said Miss Marple, "but I must say that I was reminded just for a moment of the Lauristons' parlormaid."

"The Lauristons' parlormaid?" Craddock looked completely mystified.

"She had, of course, to take messages on the telephone," said Miss Marple, "and she wasn't very good at it. She used to get the general *sense* right, if you know what I mean, but the way she wrote it down used to make quite nonsense of it sometimes. I suppose, really, because her grammar was so bad. The result was that some very unfortunate incidents occurred. I remember one in particular. A Mr. Burroughs, I think it was, rang up and said he had been to see Mr. Elvaston about the fence being broken down but he said that the fence wasn't his business at all to repair. It was on the other side of the property and he said he would like to know if that was really the case before proceeding further as it would depend on whether he was liable or not and it was important for him to know the proper lie of the land before instructing solicitors. A very obscure message, as you see. It confused rather than enlightened."

"If you're talking about parlormaids," said Miss Knight with a little laugh, "that must have been a *very* long time ago. I haven't even heard of a parlormaid for many years now."

"It was a good many years ago," said Miss Marple, "but nevertheless human nature was very much the same then as it is now. Mistakes were made for very much the same reasons. Oh dear," she added, "I *am* thankful that that girl is safely in Bournemouth."

"The girl? What girl?" asked Dermot.

"That girl who did dressmaking and went up to see Giuseppe that day. What was her name—Gladys something."

"Gladys Dixon?"

"Yes, that's the name."

"She's in *Bournemouth*, do you say? How on earth do you know that?"

"I know," said Miss Marple, "because I sent her there."

"What?" Dermot stared at her. "You? Why?"

"I went out to see her," said Miss Marple, "and I gave her some money and told her to take a holiday and not to write home."

"Why on earth did you do that?"

"Because I didn't want her to be killed, of course," said Miss Marple, and blinked at him placidly.

CHAPTER TWENTY-TWO

"SUCH A SWEET letter from Lady Conway," Miss Knight said two days later as she deposited Miss Marple's breakfast tray. "You remember my telling you about her? Just a little, you know—" she tapped her forehead "wanders sometimes. And her memory's bad. Can't recognize her relations always and tells them to go away."

"That might be shrewdness really," said Miss Marple, "rather than a loss of memory."

"Now, now," said Miss Knight, "aren't we being naughty to make suggestions like that? She's spending the winter at the Belgrave Hotel in Llandudno. *Such* a nice residential hotel. Splendid grounds and a very nice glassed-in terrace. She's most anxious for me to come and join her there." She sighed.

Miss Marple sat herself upright in bed.

"But please," she said, "if you are wanted—if you are needed there and would like to go—"

"No, no, I couldn't hear of it," cried Miss Knight. "Oh, no, I never meant anything like that. Why, what would Mr. Raymond West say? He explained to me that being here might turn out to be a permanency. I should never dream of not fulfilling my obligations. I was only just mentioning the fact in passing, so don't worry, dear," she added, patting Miss Marple on the shoulder. "We're going to be looked after and cosseted and made very happy and comfortable always."

She went out of the room. Miss Marple sat with an air of determination, staring at her tray and failing to eat anything. Finally she picked up the receiver of the telephone and dialed with vigor.

"Dr. Haydock?"

"Yes."

"Jane Marple here."

"And what's the matter with you? In need of my professional services?"

"No," said Miss Marple. "But I want to see you as soon as possible."

When Dr. Haydock came, he found Miss Marple still in bed waiting for him.

"You look the picture of health," he complained.

"That is why I wanted to see you," said Miss Marple. "To tell you that I am perfectly well."

"An unusual reason for sending for the doctor."

"I'm quite strong, I'm quite fit, and it's absurd to have anybody living in the house. So long as someone comes every day and does the cleaning and all that I don't see any need at all for having someone living here permanently."

"I dare say you don't, but I do," said Dr. Haydock.

"It seems to me you're turning into a regular old fussbudget," said Miss Marple unkindly.

"And don't call me names!" said Dr. Haydock. "You're a very healthy woman for your age; you were pulled down a bit by bronchitis, which isn't good for the elderly. But to stay alone in a house at your age is a risk. Supposing you fall down the stairs one evening or fall out of bed or slip in the bath. There you'd lie and nobody know about it."

"One can imagine anything," said Miss Marple. "Miss Knight might fall down the stairs and I'd fall over her rushing out to see what had happened."

"It's no good your bullying me," said Dr. Haydock. "You're an old lady and you've got to be looked after in a proper manner. If you don't like this woman you've got, change her and get somebody else."

"That's not always so easy," said Miss Marple.

"Find some old servant of yours, someone that you like, and who's lived with you before. I can see this old hen irritates you. She'd irritate me. There must be some old servant somewhere. That nephew of yours is one of the best-selling authors of the day. He'd make it worth her while if you found the right person."

"Of course dear Raymond would do anything of that kind. He is most generous," said Miss Marple. "But it's not so easy to find the right person. Young people have their own lives to live, and so many of my faithful old servants, I am sorry to say, are dead."

"Well, you're not dead," said Dr. Haydock, "and you'll live a good deal longer if you take proper care of yourself."

He rose to his feet.

"Well," he said. "No good my stopping here. You look as fit as a fiddle. I shan't waste time taking your blood pressure or feeling your pulse or asking you questions. You're thriving on all this local excitement, even if you can't get about to poke your nose in as much as you'd like to do. Good-bye, I've got to go now and do some real doctoring. Eight to ten cases of German measles, half a dozen whooping coughs, and a suspected scarlet fever as well as my regulars!"

Dr. Haydock went out breezily— But Miss Marple was frowning . . . Something that he had said . . . what was it? Patients to see . . . the usual village ailments . . . village ailments? Miss Marple pushed her breakfast tray farther away with a purposeful gesture. Then she rang up Mrs. Bantry.

"Dolly? Jane here. I want to ask you something. Now pay attention. Is it true that you told Inspector Craddock that Heather Badcock told Marina Gregg a long pointless story about how she had chicken pox and got up in spite of it to go and meet Marina and get her autograph?"

"That was it more or less."

"Chicken pox?"

"Well, something like that. Mrs. Allcock was talking to me about vodka at the time, so I wasn't really listening closely."

"You're sure"—Miss Marple took a breath—"that she didn't say whooping cough?"

"Whooping cough?" Mrs. Bantry sounded astounded. "Of course not. She wouldn't have had to powder her face and do it up for whooping cough."

"I see—what's what you went by—her special mention of make-up?"

"Well, she laid stress on it—she wasn't the making-up kind. But I think you're right, it wasn't chicken pox . . . nettlerash, perhaps."

"You only say that," said Miss Marple coldly, "because you once had nettlerash yourself and couldn't go to a wedding. You're hopeless, Dolly, quite hopeless."

She put the receiver down with a bang, cutting off Mrs. Bantry's astonished protest of "Really, Jane."

Miss Marple made a ladylike noise of vexation like a cat sneezing to indicate profound disgust. Her mind reverted to the problem of her own domestic comfort. Faithful Florence? Could faithful Florence, that grenadier of a former parlormaid, be persuaded to leave her comfortable small house and come back to St. Mary Mead to look after her erstwhile mistress? Faithful Florence had always been very devoted to her. But Faithful Florence was very attached to her own little house. Miss Marple shook her head vexedly. A gay rat-a-tat sounded at the door. On Miss Marple's calling, "Come in," Cherry entered.

"Come for your tray," she said. "Has anything happened? You're looking rather upset, aren't you?"

"I feel so helpless," said Miss Marple. "Old and helpless."

"Don't worry," said Cherry, picking up the tray. "You're very far from helpless. You don't know the things I hear about you in this place! Why, practically everybody in the Development knows about you now. All sorts of extraordinary things you've done. *They* don't think of you as the old and helpless kind. It's she puts it into your head."

"She?"

Cherry gave a vigorous nod of her head backwards towards the door behind her.

"Pussy, pussy," she said. "Your Miss Knight. Don't you let her get you down."

"She's very kind," said Miss Marple. "Really very kind," she added, in the tone of one who convinces herself.

"Care killed the cat, they say," said Cherry. "You don't want kindness rubbed into your skin, so to speak, do you?"

"Oh, well," said Miss Marple, sighing, "I suppose we all have our troubles."

"I should say we do," said Cherry. "I oughtn't to complain but I feel sometimes that if I live next door to Mrs. Hartwell any longer there's going to be a regrettable incident. Sour-faced old cat, always gossiping and complaining. Jim's pretty fed up, too. He had a first-class row with her last night. Just because we had the *Messiah* on a bit loud. You can't object to the *Messiah*, can you? I mean, it's religious."

"Did she object?"

"She created something terrible," said Cherry. "Banged on the wall and shouted and one thing and another."

"Do you have to have your music tuned in so loud?" asked Miss Marple.

"Jim likes it that way," said Cherry. "He says you don't get the tone unless you have full volume."

"It might," suggested Miss Marple, "be a little trying for anyone if they weren't musical."

"It's these houses being semi-detached," said Cherry. "Thin as anything, the walls. I'm not so keen really on all this new building, when you come to think of it. It looks all very prissy and nice but you can't express your personality without somebody being down on you like a ton of bricks."

Miss Marple smiled at her.

"You've got a lot of personality to express, Cherry," she said.

"D'you think so?" Cherry was pleased and she laughed. "I wonder," she began. Suddenly she looked embarrassed. She put down the tray and came back to the bed.

"I wonder if you'd think it cheek if I asked you something? I mean— you've only got to say 'out of the question' and that's that."

"Something you want me to do?"

"Not quite. It's those rooms over the kitchen. They're never used nowadays, are they?"

"No."

"Used to be a gardener and wife there once, so I heard. But that's old stuff. What I wondered—what Jim and I wondered—is if we could have them. Come and live here, I mean."

Miss Marple stared at her in astonishment.

"But your beautiful new house in the Development?"

"We're both fed up with it. We like gadgets, but you can have gadgets anywhere—and there would be a nice lot of room here, especially if Jim could have the room over the stables. He'd fix it up like new, and he could have all his construction models there, and wouldn't have to clear them away all the time. And if we had our stereogram there too, you'd hardly hear it."

"Are you really serious about this, Cherry?"

"Yes, I am. Jim and I, we've talked about it a lot. Jim could fix things for you any time—you know, plumbing or a bit of carpentry. And I'd look after you every bit as well as your Miss Knight does. I know you think I'm a bit slap-dash—but I'd try and take trouble with the beds and the washing-up— and I'm getting quite a dab at cooking. Did Beef Stroganoff last night, it's quite easy, really."

Miss Marple contemplated her.

Cherry was looking like an eager kitten—vitality and joy of life radiated from her. Miss Marple thought once more of Faithful Florence. Faithful Florence would, of course, keep the house far better. (Miss Marple put no faith in Cherry's promise.) But she was at least sixty-five—perhaps more. And would she really want to be uprooted? She might accept that out of her very real devotion for Miss Marple. But did Miss Marple really want sacrifices made for her? Wasn't she already suffering from Miss Knight's conscientious devotion to duty?

Cherry, however inadequate in her housework, wanted to come. And she had the qualities that to Miss Marple at this moment seemed of supreme importance.

Warm-heartedness, vitality, and a deep interest in everything that was going on.

"I don't want, of course," said Cherry, "to go behind Miss Knight's back in any way."

"Never mind about Miss Knight," said Miss Marple, coming to a decision. "She'll go off to someone called Lady Conway at a hotel in Llandudno—and enjoy herself thoroughly. We'll have to settle a lot of details, Cherry, and I shall want to talk to your husband—but if you really think you'd be happy. . . ."

"It'll suit us down to the ground," said Cherry. "And you really can rely on me doing things properly. I'll even use the dustpan and brush if you like."

Miss Marple laughed at this supreme offer.

Cherry picked up the breakfast tray again.

"I must get cracking. I got here late this morning—hearing about poor Arthur Badcock."

"Arthur Badcock? What happened to him?"

"Haven't you heard? He's up at the police station now," said Cherry. "They asked him if he'd come and 'assist them with their inquiries,' and you know what that always means."

"When did this happen?" demanded Miss Marple.

"This morning," said Cherry. "I suppose," she added, "that it got out about his once having been married to Marina Gregg."

"What!" Miss Marple sat up again. "Arthur Badcock was once married to Marina Gregg?"

"That's the story," said Cherry. "Nobody had any idea of it. It was Mr. Upshaw put it about. He's been to the States once or twice on business for his firm and so he knows a lot of gossip from over there. It was a long time ago, you know. Really before she'd begun her career. They were only married a year or two and then she won a film award and of course he wasn't good enough for her then, so they had one of these easy American divorces and he just faded out, as you might say. He's the fading-out kind, Arthur Badcock. He wouldn't make a fuss. He changed his name and came back to England. It's all ever so long ago. You wouldn't think anything like that mattered nowadays, would you? Still, there it is. It's enough for the police to go on, I suppose."

"Oh no," said Miss Marple. "Oh *no*. This mustn't happen. If I could only think what to do— Now, let me see." She made a gesture to Cherry. "Take the tray away, Cherry, and send Miss Knight up to me. I'm going to get up."

Cherry obeyed. Miss Marple dressed herself with fingers that fumbled slightly. It irritated her when she found excitement of any kind affected her. She was just hooking up her dress when Miss Knight entered.

"Did you want me? Cherry said—"

Miss Marple broke in incisively.

"Get Inch," she said.

"I beg your pardon," said Miss Knight, startled.

"Inch," said Miss Marple, "get Inch. Telephone for him to come at once."

"Oh, oh, I see. You mean the taxi people. But his name's Roberts, isn't it?"

"To me," said Miss Marple, "he is Inch and always will be. But anyway get him. He's to come here at once."

"You want to go for a little drive?"

"Just get him, can you?" said Miss Marple, "and hurry please."

Miss Knight looked at her doubtfully and proceeded to do as she was told.

"We are feeling all right, dear, aren't we?" she said anxiously.

"We are both feeling very well," said Miss Marple, "and I am feeling particularly well. Inertia does not suit me, and never has. A practical course of action, that is what I have been wanting for a long time."

"Has that Mrs. Baker been saying something that has upset you?"

"Nothing has upset me," said Miss Marple. "I feel particularly well. I am annoyed with myself for being stupid. But really, until I got a hint from Dr. Haydock this morning—Now I wonder if I remember rightly. Where is that medical book of mine?" She gestured Miss Knight askde and walked firmly down the stairs. She found the book she wanted on a shelf in the drawing-room. Taking it out she looked up the index, murmured "Page two hundred ten," turned to the page in question, read for a few moments then nodded her head, satisfied.

"Most remarkable," she said, "most curious. I don't suppose anybody would ever have thought of it. I didn't myself, until the two things came together, so to speak."

Then she shook her head, and a little line appeared between her eyes. "If only there was *someone* . . ."

She went over in her mind the various accounts she had been given on that particular scene . . .

Her eyes widened in thought. There was someone—but would he, she wondered, be any good? One never knew with the vicar. He was quite unpredictable.

Nevertheless she went to the telephone and dialed.

"Good morning, Vicar, this is Miss Marple."

"Oh, yes, Miss Marple—anything I can do for you?"

"I wonder if you could help me on a small point. It concerns the day of the fête when poor Mrs. Badcock died. I believe you were standing quite near Miss Gregg when Mr. and Mrs. Badcock arrived."

"Yes—yes—I was just before them, I think. Such a tragic day."

"Yes, indeed. And I believe that Mrs. Badcock was recalling to Miss Gregg that they had met before in Bermuda. She had been ill in bed and had got up specially."

"Yes, yes, I do remember.."

"And do you remember if Mrs. Badcock mentioned the illness she was suffering from?"

"I think now—let me see—yes, it was measles—at least not real measles—German measles—a much less serious disease. Some people hardly feel ill at all with it. I remember my cousin Caroline . . ."

Miss Marple cut off reminiscences of Cousin Caroline by saying firmly: "Thank you so much, Vicar," and replacing the receiver.

There was an awed expression on her face. One of the great mysteries of St. Mary Mead was what made the vicar remember certain things—only outstripped by the greater mystery of what the vicar could manage to forget!

"The taxi's here, dear," said Miss Knight, bustling in. "It's a very old one, and not too clean. I should say. I don't really like you driving in a thing like that. You might pick up some germ or other."

"Nonsense," said Miss Marple. Setting her hat firmly on her head and buttoning up her summer coat, she went out to the waiting taxi.

"Good morning, Roberts," she said.

"Good morning, Miss Marple. You're early this morning. Where do you want to go?"

"Gossington Hall, please," said Miss Marple.

"I'd better come with you, hadn't I, dear," said Miss Knight. "It won't take me a minute just to slip on outdoor shoes."

"No, thank you," said Miss Marple firmly. "I'm going by myself. Drive on, Inch. I mean Roberts."

Mr. Roberts drove on, merely remarking:

"Ah, Gossington Hall. Great changes there and everywhere nowadays. All that development. Never thought anything like that'd come to St. Mary Mead."

Upon arrival at Gossington Hall, Miss Marple rang the bell and asked to see Mr. Jason Rudd.

Giuseppe's successor, a rather shaky-looking elderly man, conveyed doubt.

"Mr. Rudd," he said, "does not see anybody without an appointment, madam. And today especially—"

"I have no appointment," said Miss Marple, "but I will wait," she added.

She stepped briskly past him into the hall and sat down on a hall chair.

"I'm afraid it will be quite impossible this morning, madam."

"In that case," said Miss Marple, "I shall wait until this afternoon."

Baffled, the new butler retired. Presently a young man came to Miss Marple. He had a pleasant manner and a cheerful, slightly American voice.

"I've seen you before," said Miss Marple. "In the Development. You asked me the way to Blenheim Close."

Hailey Preston smiled good-naturedly. "I guess you did your best, but you misdirected me badly."

"Dear me, did I?" said Miss Marple. "So many Closes, aren't there? Can I see Mr. Rudd?"

"Why, now, that's too bad," said Hailey Preston. "Mr. Rudd's a very busy man and he's—er—fully occupied this morning and really can't be disturbed."

"I'm sure he's very busy," said Miss Marple. "I came here quite prepared to wait."

"Why, I'd suggest now," said Hailey Preston, "that you should tell me what it is you want. I deal with these things for Mr. Rudd, you see. Everyone has to see me first."

"I'm afraid," said Miss Marple, "that I want to see Mr. Rudd himself. And," she added, "I shall wait here until I do."

She settled herself more firmly in the large oak chair.

Hailey Preston hesitated, started to speak, finally turned away and went upstairs.

He returned with a large man in tweeds.

"This is Dr. Gilchrist, Miss—er—"

"Miss Marple."

"So you're Miss Marple," said Dr. Gilchrist. He looked at her with a good deal of interest.

Hailey Preston slipped away with celerity.

"I've heard about you," said Dr. Gilchrist. "From Dr. Haydock."

"Dr. Haydock is a very old friend of mine."

"He certainly is. Now you want to see Mr. Jason Rudd? Why?"

"It is necessary that I should," said Miss Marple.

Dr. Gilchrist's eyes appraised her.

"And you're camping here until you do?" he asked.

"Exactly."

"You would, too," said Dr. Gilchrist. "In that case I will give you a perfectly good reason why you cannot see Mr. Rudd. His wife died last night in her sleep."

"Dead!" exclaimed Miss Marple. "How?"

"An overdose of sleeping stuff. We don't want the news to leak out to the press for a few hours. So I'll ask you to keep this knowledge to yourself for the moment."

"Of course. Was it an accident?"

"That is definitely my view," said Dr. Gilchrist.

"But it could be suicide."

"It could—but most unlikely."

"Or someone could have given it to her?"

Gilchrist shrugged his shoulders.

"A most remote contingency. And a thing," he added firmly, "that would be quite impossible to prove."

"I see," said Miss Marple. She took a deep breath. "I'm sorry, but it's more necessary than ever that I should see Mr. Rudd."

Gilchrist looked at her.

"Wait here," he said.

CHAPTER TWENTY-THREE

JASON RUDD LOOKED up as Gilchrist entered.

"There's an old dame downstairs," said the doctor; "looks about a hundred. Wants to see you. Won't take no and says she'll wait. She'll wait till this afternoon, I gather, or she'll wait till this evening and she's quite capable, I should say, of spending the night here. She's got something she badly wants to say to you. I'd see her if I were you."

Jason Rudd looked up from his desk. His face was white and strained.

"Is she mad?"

"No. Not in the least."

"I don't see why I— Oh, all right—send her up. What does it matter."

Gilchrist nodded, went out of the room and called to Hailey Preston.

"Mr. Rudd can spare you a few minutes now, Miss Marple," said Hailey Preston, appearing again by her side.

"Thank you. That's very kind of him," said Miss Marple as she rose to her feet. "Have you been with Mr. Rudd long?" she asked.

"Why, I've worked with Mr. Rudd for the last two and a half years. My job is public relations generally."

"I see." Miss Marple looked at him thoughtfully. "You remind me very much," she said, "of someone I knew called Gerald French."

"Indeed? What did Gerald French do?"

"Not very much," said Miss Marple, "but he was a very good talker." She sighed. "He had had an unfortunate past."

"You don't say," said Hailey Preston, slightly ill at ease. "What kind of a past?"

"I won't repeat it," said Miss Marple. "He didn't like it talked about."

Jason Rudd rose from his desk and looked with some surprise at the slender elderly lady who was advancing towards him.

"You wanted to see me?" he said. "What can I do for you?"

"I am very sorry about your wife's death," said Miss Marple. "I can see it has been a great grief to you, and I want you to believe that I should not intrude upon you now or offer you sympathy unless it was absolutely necessary. But there are things that need badly to be cleared up unless an innocent man is going to suffer."

"An innocent man? I don't understand you."

"Arthur Badcock," said Miss Marple. "He is with the police now, being questioned."

"Questioned in connection with my wife's death? But that's absurd, completely absurd. He's never been near the place. He didn't even know her."

"I think he knew her," said Miss Marple. "He was married to her once."

"Arthur Badcock? But—he was—he was Heather Badcock's husband. Aren't you perhaps"—he spoke kindly and apologetically—"making a little mistake?"

"He was married to both of them," said Miss Marple. "He was married to your wife when she was very young, before she went into pictures."

Jason Rudd shook his head.

"My wife was first married to a man called Alfred Beadle. He was in real estate. They were not suited and they parted almost immediately."

"Then Alfred Beadle changed his name to Badcock," said Miss Marple. "He's in a real estate firm here. It's odd how some people never seem to like to change their job and want to go on doing the same thing. I expect really that's why Marina Gregg felt that he was no use to her. He couldn't have kept up with her."

"What you've told me is most surprising."

"I can assure you that I am not romancing or imagining things. What I'm telling you is sober fact. These things get round very quickly in a village, you know, though they take a little longer," she added, "in reaching the Hall."

"Well," Jason Rudd stalled, uncertain what to say, then he accepted the position, "and what do you want me to do for you, Miss Marple?" he asked.

"I want, if I may, to stand on the stairs at the spot where you and your wife received guests on the day of the fête."

He shot a quick doubtful glance at her. Was this, after all, just another sensation-seeker? But Miss Marple's face was grave and composed.

"Why certainly," he said, "if you want to do so. Come with me."

He led her to the staircase head and paused in the hollowed-out bay at the top of it.

"You've made a good many changes in the house since the Bantrys were here," said Miss Marple. "I like this. Now, let me see. The tables would be about here, I suppose, and you and your wife would be standing—"

"My wife stood here." Jason Rudd showed her the place. "People came up the stairs, she shook hands with them and passed them on to me."

"She stood here," said Miss Marple.

She moved over and took her place where Marina Gregg had stood. She remained there quite quietly without moving. Jason Rudd watched her. He was perplexed but interested. She raised her right hand slightly as though shaking hands, looked down the stairs as though to see people coming up it. Then she looked straight ahead of her. On the wall halfway up the stairs was a large picture, a copy of an Italian Old Master. On either side of it were narrow windows, one giving out on the garden and the other giving on to the end of the stables and the weathercock. But Miss Marple looked at neither of these. Her eyes were fixed on the picture itself.

"Of course you always hear a thing right the first time," she said. "Mrs. Bantry told me that your wife stared at the picture and her face 'froze,' as she put it." She looked at the rich red and blue robes of the Madonna, a Madonna with her head slightly back, laughing up at the Holy Child that she was holding up in her arms. "Bellini's 'Laughing Madonna,'" she said. "A religious picture, but also a painting of a happy mother with her child. Isn't that so, Mr. Rudd?"

"I would say so, yes."

"I understand now," said Miss Marple. "I understand quite well. The whole thing is really very simple, isn't it?" She looked at Jason Rudd.

"Simple?"

"I think you know how simple it is," said Miss Marple.

There was a peal on the bell below.

"I don't think," said Jason Rudd, "I quite understand." He looked down the stairway. There was a sound of voices.

"I know that voice," said Miss Marple. "It's Inspector Craddock's voice, isn't it?"

"Yes, it seems to be Inspector Craddock."

"He wants to see you, too. Would you mind very much if he joined us?"

"Not at all as far as I am concerned. Whether he will agree—"

"I think he will agree," said Miss Marple. "There's really not much time now to be lost, is there? We've got to the moment when we've got to understand just how everything happened."

"I thought you said it was simple," said Jason Rudd.

"It was so simple," said Miss Marple, "that one just couldn't see it."

The decayed butler arrived at this moment up the stairs.

"Inspector Craddock is here, sir," he said.

"Ask him to join us here, please," said Jason Rudd.

The butler disappeared again and a moment or two later Dermot Craddock came up the stairs.

"You!" he said to Miss Marple. "How did you get here?"

"I came in Inch," said Miss Marple, producing the usual confused effect that that remark always caused.

From slightly behind her, Jason Rudd rapped his forehead interrogatively. Dermot Craddock shook his head.

"I was saying to Mr. Rudd," said Miss Marple, "—has that butler gone away—"

Dermot Craddock cast a look down the stairs.

"Oh, yes," he said, "he's not listening. Sergeant Tiddler will see to that."

"Then that is all right," said Miss Marple. "We could, of course, have gone into a room to talk, but I prefer it like this. Here we are on the spot where the thing happened, which makes it so much easier to understand."

"You are talking," said Jason Rudd, "of the day of the fête here, the day when Heather Badcock was poisoned."

"Yes," said Miss Marple, "and I'm saying that it is all very simple if one only looks at it in the proper way. It all began, you see, with Heather Badcock being the kind of person she was. It was inevitable, really, that something of that kind should someday happen to Heather."

"I don't understand what you mean," said Jason Rudd, "I don't understand at all."

"No, it has to be explained a little. You see, when my friend Mrs. Bantry, who was here, described the scene to me, she quoted a poem that was a great favorite in my youth, a poem of dear Lord Tennyson's, 'The Lady of Shalott.'" She raised her voice a little.

> "The mirror crack'd from side to side;
>   'The curse is come upon me,' cried
> The Lady of Shalott.

"That's what Mrs. Bantry saw, or thought she saw, though actually she misquoted and said doom instead of curse—perhaps a better word in the circumstances. She saw your wife speaking to Heather Badcock and heard Heather Badcock speaking to your wife and she saw this look of doom on your wife's face."

"Haven't we been over that a great many times?" said Jason Rudd.

"Yes, but we shall have to go over it once more," said Miss Marple. "There was that expression on your wife's face and she was looking not at Heather Badcock but at that picture. At a picture of a laughing, happy mother holding up a happy child. The mistake was that though there was doom foreshadowed in Marina Gregg's face, it was not upon her the doom would come. The doom was to come upon Heather. Heather was doomed from the first moment that she began talking and boasting of an incident in the past."

"Could you make yourself a little clearer?" said Dermot Craddock.

Miss Marple turned to him.

"Of course I will. This is something that you know nothing about. You couldn't know about it, because nobody has told you what it was that Heather Badcock actually said."

"But they have," protested Dermot. "They've told me over and over again. Several people have told me."

"Yes," said Miss Marple, "but you don't know because, you see, Heather Badcock didn't tell it to you."

"She hardly could tell it to me seeing she was dead when I arrived here," said Dermot.

"Quite so," said Miss Marple. "All you know is that she was ill but she got up from bed and came along to a celebration of some kind where she met Marina Gregg and spoke to her and asked for an autograph and was given one."

"I know," said Craddock with slight impatience. "I've heard all that."

"But you didn't hear the one operative phrase, because no one thought it was important," said Miss Marple. "Heather Badcock was ill in bed—with *German measles.*"

"German measles? What on earth has that got to do with it?"

"It's a very slight illness, really," said Miss Marple. "It hardly makes you feel ill at all. You have a rash which is easy to cover up with powder, and you have a little fever, but not very much. You feel quite well enough to go out and see people if you want to. And of course in repeating all this the fact that it was German measles didn't strike people particularly. Mrs. Bantry, for instance, just said that Heather had been ill in bed and mentioned chicken pox and nettlerash. Mr. Rudd here said that it was 'flu, but of course he did that on purpose. But I think myself that what Heather Badcock said to Marina Gregg was that she had had German measles and got up from bed and went off to meet Marina. And that's really the answer to the whole thing, because, you see, German measles is extremely infectious. People catch it very easily. And there's one thing about it which you've got to remember. If a woman contracts it in the first four months of—" Miss Marple spoke the next word with a slight Victorian modesty"of—er—pregnancy, it may have a terribly serious effect. It may cause an unborn child to be born blind or to be born mentally affected."

She turned to Jason Rudd.

"I think I am correct in saying, Mr. Rudd, that your wife had a child who was born mentally afflicted and that she had never really recovered from the shock. She had always wanted a child, and when at last the child came, this was the tragedy that happened. A tragedy she had never forgotten, that she had not allowed herself to forget, and which ate into her as a kind of deep sore, an obsession."

"It's quite true," said Jason Rudd. "Marina developed German measles early on in her pregnancy and was told by the doctor that the mental affliction of her child was due to that cause. It was not a case of inherited insanity or anything of that kind. He was trying to be helpful, but I don't think it helped her much. She never knew how or when or from whom she had contracted the disease."

"Quite so," said Miss Marple, "she never knew until one afternoon here when a perfectly strange woman came up those stairs and told her the fact—told her, what was more—with a great deal of pleasure! With an air of being proud of what she'd done. *She* thought she'd been resourceful and brave and shown a lot of spirit in getting up from her bed, covering her face with make-up, and going along to meet the actress on whom she had such a crush and obtaining her autograph. It was a thing she had boasted of all through her life. Heather Badcock meant no harm. She never did mean harm, but there is no doubt that people like Heather Badcock (and like my old friend Alison Wilde), are capable of doing a lot of harm because they lack—not kindness, they have kindness—but any real consideration for the way their actions may affect other people. She thought always of what an action meant to *her,* never sparing a thought to what it might mean to somebody else."

Miss Marple nodded her head gently.

"So she died, you see, for a simple reason out of her own past. You must imagine what that moment meant to Marina Gregg. I think Mr. Rudd understands it very well. I think she had nursed all those years a kind of hatred for the unknown person who had been the cause of her tragedy. And here suddenly she meets that person face to face. And a person who is gay, jolly and pleased with herself. It was too much for her. If she had had time to think, to calm down, to be persuaded to relax—but she gave herself no time. Here was this woman who had destroyed her happiness and destroyed the sanity and health of her child. She wanted to punish her. She wanted to kill her. And unfortunately the means were to hand. She carried with her that well-known specific, Calmo. A somewhat dangerous drug because you had to be careful of the exact dosage. It was very easy to do. She put the stuff into her own glass. If by any chance anyone noticed what she was doing, they were probably so used to her pepping herself up or soothing herself down in any handy liquid that they'd hardly noticed it. It's possible that one person did see her, but I rather doubt it. I think that Miss Zielinsky did no more than guess. Marina Gregg put her glass down on the table and presently she managed to jog Heather Badcock's arm so that Heather Badcock spilt her own drink all down her new dress. And that's where the element of puzzle has come into the matter, owing to the fact that people cannot remember to use their pronouns properly.

"It reminds me so much of that parlormaid I was telling you about," she added to Dermot. "I only had the account, you see, of what Gladys Dixon said to Cherry which simply was that she was worried about the ruin of Heather Badcock's dress with the cocktail spilt down it. What seemed so funny, she said, was that she did it on purpose. But the 'she' that Gladys referred to was not Heather Badcock, it was Marina Gregg. As Gladys said: 'She did it on purpose!' She jogged Heather's arm. Not by accident but because she *meant* to do so. We do know that she must have been standing very close to Heather because we have heard that she mopped up both Heather's dress and her own before pressing her cocktail on Heather. It was really," said Miss Marple meditatively, "a very perfect murder; because, you see, it was committed on the spur of the moment without pausing to think or reflect. She wanted Heather Badcock dead and a few minutes later Heather Badcock *was* dead. She didn't realize, perhaps, the seriousness of what she'd done and certainly not the danger of it until afterwards. But she realized it then. She was afraid, horribly afraid. Afraid that someone had seen her dope her own glass, that someone had seen her deliberately jog Heather's elbow, afraid that someone would accuse her of having poisoned Heather. She could see only one way out. To insist that the murder had been aimed at *her,* that *she* was the prospective victim. She tried that idea first on her doctor. She refused to let him tell her husband because I think she knew that her husband would not be deceived. She did fantastic things. She wrote notes to herself and arranged to find them in extraordinary places and at extraordinary moments. She doctored her own coffee at the studios one day. She did things that could really have been seen through fairly easily if one had happened to be thinking that way. They were seen through by one person."

"This is only a theory of yours," said Jason Rudd.

She looked at Jason Rudd.

"You can put it that way, if you like," said Miss Marple, "but you know quite well, don't you, Mr. Rudd, that I'm speaking the truth. You know, because you knew from the first. You knew because you heard that mention of German measles. You knew and you were frantic to protect her. But you didn't realize how much you would have to protect her from. You didn't realize that it was not only a question of hushing up one death, the death of a woman whom you might say quite fairly had brought her death on herself. But there were other deaths—the death of Giuseppe, a blackmailer, it is true, but a human being. And the death of Ella Zielinsky of whom I expect you were fond. You were frantic to protect Marina and also to prevent her from doing harm. All you wanted was to get her safely away somewhere. You tried to watch her all the time, to make sure that nothing more should happen."

She paused, and then coming nearer to Jason Rudd, she laid a gentle hand on his arm.

"I am very sorry for you," she said, "very sorry. I do realize the agony you've been through. You cared for her so much, didn't you?"

Jason Rudd turned slightly away.

"That," he said, "is, I believe, common knowledge."

"She was such a beautiful creature," said Miss Marple gently. "She had such a wonderful gift. She had a great power of love and hate, but no stability. That's what's so sad for anyone, to be born with no stability. She couldn't let the past go and she could never see the future as it really was, only as she imagined it to be. She was a great actress and a beautiful and very unhappy woman. What a wonderful Mary, Queen of Scots she was! I shall never forget her."

Sergeant Tiddler appeared suddenly on the stairs.

"Sir," he said, "can I speak to you a moment?"

Craddock turned.

"I'll be back," he said to Jason Rudd, then he went towards the stairs.

"Remember," Miss Marple called after him, "poor Arthur Badcock had nothing to do with this. He came to the fête because he wanted to have a glimpse of the girl he had married long ago. I should say she didn't even recognize him. Did she?" she asked Jason Rudd.

"I don't think so. She certainly never said anything to me. I don't think," he added thoughtfully, "she would recognize him."

"Probably not," said Miss Marple. "Anyway," she added, "he's quite innocent of wanting to kill her or anything of that kind. Remember that," she added to Dermot Craddock as he went down the stairs.

"He's not been in any real danger, I can assure you," said Craddock, "but of course when we found out that he had actually been Miss Marina Gregg's first husband we naturally had to question him on the point. Don't worry about him, Aunt Jane," he added in a low murmur, then he hurried down the stairs.

Miss Marple turned to Jason Rudd. He was standing there like a man in a daze, his eyes far away.

"Would you allow me to see her?" said Miss Marple.

He considered her for a moment or two, then he nodded.

"Yes, you can see her. You seem to—understand her very well."

He turned and Miss Marple followed him. He preceded her into the big bedroom and drew the curtains slightly aside.

Marina Gregg lay in the great white shell of the bed—her eyes closed, her hands folded.

So, Miss Marple thought, might the Lady of Shalott have lain in the boat that carried her down to Camelot. And there, standing musing, was a man with a rugged, ugly face, who might pass as a Lancelot of a later day.

Miss Marple said gently, "It's very fortunate for her that she—took an overdose. Death was really the only way of escape left to her. Yes—very fortunate she took that overdose—or—*was given it?*"

His eyes met hers, but he did not speak.

He said brokenly, "She was—so lovely—and she had suffered so much."

Miss Marple looked back again at the still figure.

She quoted softly the last lines of the poem:

> "He said: 'She has a lovely face;
> God in His mercy lend her grace,
> The Lady of Shalott.'"

A Caribbean Mystery

To my old friend
John Cruikshank Rose
with happy memories of my visit
to the West Indies

CHAPTER ONE
Major Palgrave Tells a Story

"TAKE ALL THIS business about Kenya," said Major Palgrave. "Lots of chaps gabbing away who know nothing about the place! Now *I* spent fourteen years of my life there. Some of the best years of my life, too—"

Old Miss Marple inclined her head.

It was a gentle gesture of courtesy. Whilst Major Palgrave proceeded with the somewhat uninteresting recollections of a lifetime, Miss Marple peacefully pursued her own thoughts. It was a routine with which she was well acquainted. The locale varied. In the past, it had been predominantly India. Majors, Colonels, Lieutenant-Generals—and a familiar series of words: *Simla. Bearers. Tigers. Chota Hazri—Tiffin. Khitmagars,* and so on. With Major Palgrave the terms were slightly different. *Safari. Kikuyu. Elephants. Swahili.* But the pattern was essentially the same. An elderly man who needed a listener so that he could, in memory, relive days in which he had been happy. Days when his back had been straight, his eyesight keen, his hearing acute. Some of these talkers had been handsome soldierly old boys, some again had been regrettably unattractive; and Major Palgrave, purple of face, with a glass eye, and the general appearance of a stuffed frog, belonged in the latter category.

Miss Marple had bestowed on all of them the same gentle charity. She had sat attentively, inclining her head from time to time in gentle agreement, thinking her own thoughts and enjoying what there was to enjoy: in this case the deep blue of a Caribbean Sea.

So kind of dear Raymond,—she was thinking gratefully, so really and truly kind . . . Why he should take so much trouble about his old aunt, she really did not know. Conscience, perhaps; family feeling? Or possibly he was truly fond of her . . .

She thought, on the whole, that he *was* fond of her—had always had been—in a slightly exasperated and contemptuous way! Always trying to bring her up to date. Sending her books to read. Modern novels. So difficult—all about such unpleasant people, doing such very odd things and not, apparently, even enjoying them. "Sex" as a word had not been much mentioned in Miss Marple's young days; but there had been plenty of it—not talked about so much—but enjoyed far more than nowadays, or so it seemed to her. Though usually labelled Sin, she couldn't help feeling that

that was preferable to what it seemed to be nowadays—a kind of Duty.

Her glance strayed for a moment to the book on her lap lying open at page twenty-three which was as far as she had got (and indeed as far as she felt like getting!).

"Do you mean that you've had no sexual experience at ALL?" demanded the young man incredulously. "At *nineteen?* But you *must.* It's vital."

The girl hung her head unhappily, her straight greasy hair fell forward over her face.

"I know," she muttered, "I know."

He looked at her, stained old jersey, the bare feet, the dirty toe nails, the smell of rancid fat . . . He wondered why he found her so maddeningly attractive.'

Miss Marple wondered too! And really! To have sex experience urged on you exactly as though it was an iron tonic! Poor young things . . .

"My dear Aunt Jane, why must you bury your head in the sand like a very delightful ostrich? All bound up in this idyllic rural life of yours. REAL LIFE—that's what matters."

Thus Raymond—and his Aunt Jane had looked properly abashed—and said "Yes," she was afraid she *was* rather old-fashioned.

Though really rural life was far from idyllic. People like Raymond were so ignorant. In the course of her duties in a country parish, Jane Marple had acquired quite a comprehensive knowledge of the facts of rural life. She had no urge to *talk* about them, far less to *write* about them—but she knew them. Plenty of sex, natural and unnatural. Rape, incest, perversions of all kinds. (Some kinds, indeed, that even the clever young men from Oxford who wrote books didn't seem to have heard about.)

Miss Marple came back to the Caribbean and took up the thread of what Major Palgrave was saying . . .

"A very unusual experience," she said encouragingly. "*Most* interesting."

"I could tell you a lot more. Some of the things, of course, not fit for a lady's ears—"

With the ease of long practice, Miss Marple dropped her eyelids in a fluttery fashion, and Major Palgrave continued his bowdlerized version of tribal customs while Miss Marple resumed her thoughts of her affectionate nephew.

Raymond West was a very successful novelist and made a large income, and he conscientiously and kindly did all he could to alleviate the life of his elderly aunt. The preceding winter she had had a bad go of pneumonia, and medical opinion had advised sunshine. In lordly fashion Raymond had suggested a trip to the West Indies. Miss Marple had demurred—at the expense, the distance, the difficulties of travel, and at abandoning her house in St. Mary Mead. Rayomd had dealt with everything. A friend who was writing a book wanted a quiet place in the country. "He'll look after the house all right. He's very house proud. He's a queer. I mean—"

He had paused, slightly embarrassed—but surely even dear old Aunt Jane must have heard of queers.

He went on to deal with the next points. Travel was nothing nowadays. She would go by air—another friend, Diana Horrocks, was going out to Trinidad and would see Aunt Jane was all right as far as there, and at St.

Honoré she would stay at the Golden Palm Hotel which was run by the Sandersons. Nicest couple in the world. They'd see she was all right. He'd write to them straightaway.

As it happened the Sandersons had returned to England. But their successors, the Kendals, had been very nice and friendly and had assured Raymond that he need have no qualms about his aunt. There was a very good doctor on the island in case of emergency and they themselves would keep an eye on her and see to her comfort.

They had been as good as their word, too. Molly Kendal was an ingenuous blonde of twenty odd, always apparently in good spirits. She had greeted the old lady warmly and did everything to make her comfortable. Tim Kendal, her husband, lean, dark and in his thirties, had also been kindness itself.

So there she was, thought Miss Marple, far from the rigors of the English climate, with a nice little bungalow of her own, with friendly smiling West Indian girls to wait on her, Tim Kendal to meet her in the diningroom and crack a joke as he advised her about the day's menu, and an easy path from her bungalow to the sea front and the bathing beach where she could sit in a comfortable basket chair and watch the bathing. There were even a few elderly guests for company. Old Mr. Rafiel, Dr. Graham, Canon Prescott and his sister, and her present cavalier Major Palgrave.

What more could an elderly lady want?

It is deeply to be regretted, and Miss Marple felt guilty even admitting it to herself, but she was not as satisfied as she ought to be.

Lovely and warm, yes—and *so* good for her rheumatism—and beautiful scenery, though perhaps—a trifle monotonous? So *many* palm trees. Everything the same every day—never anything *happening*. Not like St. Mary Mead where something was always happening. Her nephew had once compared life in St. Mary Mead to scum on a pond, and she had indignantly pointed out that smeared on a slide under the microscope there would be plenty of life to be observed. Yes, indeed, in St. Mary Mead, there was always something going on. Incident after incident flashed through Miss Marple's mind, the mistake in old Mrs. Linnett's cough mixture—that very odd behavior of young Polegate—the time when Georgy Wood's mother had come down to see him—(but *was* she his mother—?) the real cause of the quarrel between Joe Arden and his wife. So many interesting human problems—giving rise to endless pleasurable hours of speculation. If only there were something here that she could—well—get her teeth into.

With a start she realized that Major Palgrave had abandoned Kenya for the North West Frontier and was relating his experiences as a subaltern. Unfortunately he was asking her with great earnestness: "Now don't you agree?"

Long practice had made Miss Marple quite an adept at dealing with that one.

"I don't really feel that I've got sufficient experience to judge. I'm afraid I've led rather a sheltered life."

"And so you should, dear lady, so you should," cried Major Palgrave gallantly.

"You've had such a very varied life," went on Miss Marple, determined to make amends for her former pleasurable inattention.

"Not bad," said Major Palgrave, complacently. "Not bad at all." He looked round him appreciatively. "Lovely place, this."

"Yes, indeed," said Miss Marple and was then unable to stop herself going on: "Does anything ever happen here, I wonder?"

Major Palgrave stared.

"Oh rather. Plenty of scandals—eh what? Why, I could tell you——"

But it wasn't really scandals Miss Marple wanted. Nothing to get your teeth into in scandals nowadays. Just men and women changing partners, and calling attention to it, instead of trying decently to hush it up and be properly ashamed of themselves.

"There was even a murder here a couple of years ago. Man called Harry Western. Made a big splash in the papers. Daresay you remember it."

Miss Marple nodded without enthusiasm. It had not been her kind of murder. It had made a big splash mainly because everyone concerned had been very rich. It had seemed likely enough that Harry Western had shot the Count de Ferrari, his wife's lover, and equally likely that his well-arranged alibi had been bought and paid for. Everyone seemed to have been drunk, and there was a fine scattering of dope addicts. Not really interesting people, thought Miss Marple—although no doubt very spectacular and attractive to *look* at. But definitely not *her* cup of tea.

"And if you ask me, that wasn't the only murder about that time." He nodded and winked. "I had my suspicions—oh!—well——"

Miss Marple dropped her ball of wool, and the Major stooped and picked it up for her.

"Talking of murder," he went on. "I once came across a very curious case—not exactly personally."

Miss Marple smiled encouragingly.

"Lot of chaps talking at the club one day, you know, and a chap began telling a story. Medical man he was. One of his cases. Young fellow came and knocked him up in the middle of the night. His wife had hanged herself. They hadn't got a telephone, so after the chap had cut her down and done what he could, he'd got out his car and hared off looking for a doctor. Well, she wasn't dead but pretty far gone. Anyway, she pulled through. Young fellow seemed devoted to her. Cried like a child. He'd noticed that she'd been odd for some time, fits of depression and all that. Well, that was that. Everything seemed all right. But actually, about a month later, the wife took an overdose of sleeping stuff and passed out. Sad case."

Major Palgrave paused, and nodded his head several times. Since there was obviously more to come Miss Marple waited.

"And that's that, you might say. Nothing there. Neurotic woman, nothing out of the usual. But about a year later, this medical chap was swapping yarns with a fellow medico, and the other chap told him about a woman who'd tried to drown herself, husband got her out, got a doctor, they pulled her round—and then a few weeks later she gassed herself.

"Well, a bit of a coincidence—eh? Same sort of story. My chap said— 'I had a case rather like that. Name of Jones (or whatever the name was)— What was your man's name?' 'Can't remember. Robinson I think. Certainly not Jones.'

"Well, the chaps looked at each other and said it was pretty odd. And then my chap pulled out a snapshot. He showed it to the second chap.

'That's the fellow,' he said— 'I'd gone along the next day to check up on the particulars, and I noticed a magnificent species of hibiscus just by the front door, a variety I'd never seen before in this country. My camera was in the car and I took a photo. Just as I snapped the shutter the husband came out of the front door so I got him as well. Don't think he realized it. I asked him about the hibiscus but he couldn't tell me its name.' Second medico looked at the snap. He said: 'It's a bit out of focus—But I could swear—at any rate I'm almost sure—*it's the same man.*'

"Don't know if they followed it up. But if so they didn't get anywhere. Expect Mr. Jones or Robinson covered his tracks too well. But queer story, isn't it? Wouldn't think things like that could happen."

"Oh yes, I would," said Miss Marple placidly. "Practically every day."

"Oh, come, come. That's a bit fantastic."

"If a man gets a formula that works—he won't stop. He'll go on."

"Brides in the bath—eh?"

"That kind of thing, yes."

"Doctor let me have that snap just as a curiosity——"

Major Palgrave began fumbling through an over-stuffed wallet murmuring to himself: "Lots of things in here—don't know why I keep all these things . . ."

Miss Marple thought she did know. They were part of the Major's stock-in-trade. They illustrated his repertoire of stories. The story he had just told, or so she suspected, had not been originally like that—it had been worked up a good deal in repeated telling.

The Major was still shuffling and muttering—"Forgotten all about *that* business. Good-looking woman *she* was, you'd never suspect—Now *where*— Ah—that takes my mind back—what tusks! I must show you——"

He stopped—sorted out a small photographic print and peered down at it.

"Like to see the picture of a murderer?"

He was about to pass it to her when his movement was suddenly arrested. Looking more like a stuffed frog than ever, Major Palgrave appeared to be staring fixedly over her right shoulder—from whence came the sound of approaching footsteps and voices.

"Well, I'm damned—I mean——" He stuffed everything back into his wallet and crammed it into his pocket.

His face went an ever deeper shade of purplish red— He exclaimed in a loud, artificial voice.

"As I was saying—I'd like to have shown you those elephant tusks— Biggest elephant I've ever shot— Ah, hallo!" His voice took on a somewhat spurious hearty note.

"Look who's here! The great quartette—Flora and Fauna— What luck have you had today—Eh?"

The approaching footsteps resolved themselves into four of the hotel guests whom Miss Marple already knew by sight. They consisted of two married couples and though Miss Marple was not as yet acquainted with their surnames, she knew that the big man with the upstanding bush of thick grey hair was addressed as "Greg," that the golden blonde woman, his wife, was known as Lucky—and that the other married couple, the dark lean man and the handsome but rather weather-beaten woman, were

Edward and Evelyn. They were botanists, she understood, and also interested in birds.

"No luck at all," said Greg—"At least no luck in getting what we were after."

"Don't know if you know Miss Marple? Colonel and Mrs. Hillingdon and Greg and Lucky Dyson."

They greeted her pleasantly and Lucky said loudly that she'd die if she didn't have a drink at once or sooner.

Greg hailed Tim Kendal who was sitting a little way away with his wife poring over some account books.

"Hi, Tim. Get us some drinks." He addressed the others. "Planters Punch?"

They agreed.

"Same for you, Miss Marple?"

Miss Marple said Thank you, but she would prefer fresh lime.

"Fresh lime it is," said Tim Kendal, "and five Planters Punches."

"Join us, Tim?"

"Wish I could. But I've got to fix up these accounts. Can't leave Molly to cope with everything. Steel band to-night, by the way."

"Good," cried Lucky. "Damn it," she winced, "I'm all over thorns. Ouch! Edward deliberately rammed me into a thorn bush!"

"Lovely pink flowers," said Hillingdon.

"And lovely long thorns. Sadistic brute, aren't you, Edward?"

"Not like me," said Greg, grinning. "Full of the milk of human kindness."

Evelyn Hillingdon sat down by Miss Marple and started talking to her in an easy pleasant way.

Miss Marple put her knitting down on her lap. Slowly and with some difficulty, owing to rheumatism in the neck, she turned her head over her right shoulder to look behind her. At some little distance there was the large bungalow occupied by the rich Mr. Rafiel. But it showed no sign of life.

She replied suitably to Evelyn's remarks (really, how kind people were to her!) but her eyes scanned thoughtfully the faces of the two men.

Edward Hillingdon looked a nice man. Quiet but with a lot of charm . . . And Greg—Big, boisterous, happy-looking. He and Lucky were Canadian or American, she thought.

She looked at Major Palgrave, still acting a *bonhomie* a little larger than life.

Interesting . . .

CHAPTER TWO
Miss Marple Makes Comparisons

I

IT WAS VERY gay that evening at the Golden Palm Hotel.

Seated at her little corner table, Miss Marple looked round her in an interested fashion. The dining-room was a large room open on three sides to the soft warm scented air of the West Indies. There were small table lamps, all softly colored. Most of the women were in evening dress; light cotton prints out of which bronzed shoulders and arms emerged. Miss Marple herself had been urged by her nephew's wife, Joan, in the sweetest way possible, to acccept "a small check."

"Because, Aunt Jane, it will be rather hot out there, and I don't expect you have any very thin clothes."

Jane Marple had thanked her and had accepted the check. She came of the age when it was natural for the old to support and finance the young, but also for the middle-aged to look after the old. She could not, however, force herself to buy anything very *thin!* At her age she seldom felt more than pleasantly warm even in the hottest weather, and the temperature of St. Honoré was not really what is referred to as "tropical heat." This evening she was attired in the best traditions of the provincial gentlewomen of England—grey lace.

Not that she was the only elderly person present. There were representatives of all ages in the room. There were elderly tycoons with young third or fourth wives. There were middle-aged couples from the North of England. There was a gay family from Caracas complete with children. The various countries of South America were well represented, all chattering loudly in Spanish or Portuguese. There was a solid English background of two clergymen, one doctor and one retired judge. There was even a family of Chinese. The dining-room service was mainly done by women, tall black girls of proud carriage, dressed in crisp white; but there was an experienced Italian head waiter in charge, and a French wine waiter, and there was the attentive eye of Tim Kendal watching over everything, pausing here and there to have a social word with people at their tables. His wife seconded him ably. She was a good-looking girl. Her hair was a natural golden blonde and she had a wide generous mouth that laughed easily. It was very seldom that Molly Kendal was out of temper. Her staff worked for her enthusiastically, and she adapted her manner carefully to suit her different guests. With the elderly men she laughed and flirted; she congratulated the younger women on their clothes.

"Oh what a smashing dress you've got on tonight, Mrs. Dyson. I'm so jealous I could tear it off your back." But she looked very well in her own dress, or so Miss Marple thought; a white sheath, with a pale green embroidered silk shawl thrown over her shoulders. Lucky was fingering the shawl. "Lovely color! I'd like one like it." "You can get them at the shop here," Molly told her and passed on. She did not pause by Miss Marple's table. Elderly ladies she usually left to her husband. "The old dears like a man much better," she used to say.

Tim Kendal came and bent over Miss Marple.

"Nothing special you want, is there?" he asked. "Because you've only got to tell me—and I could get it specially cooked for you. Hotel food, and semi-tropical at that, isn't quite what you're used to at home, I expect?"

Miss Marple smiled and said that that was one of the pleasures of coming abroad.

"That's all right, then. But if there *is* anything——"

"Such as?"

"Well—" Tim Kendal looked a little doubtful—"Bread and butter pudding?" he hazarded.

Miss Marple smiled and said that she thought she could do without bread and butter pudding very nicely for the present.

She picked up her spoon and began to eat her passion fruit sundae with cheerful appreciation.

Then the steel band began to play. The steel bands were one of the main attractions of the islands. Truth to tell, Miss Marple could have done very well without them. She considered that they made a hideous noise, unnecessarily loud. The pleasure that everyone else took in them was undeniable, however, and Miss Marple, in the true spirit of her youth, decided that as they had to be, she must manage somehow to learn to like them. She could hardly request Tim Kendal to conjure up from somewhere the muted strains of the "Blue Danube." (So graceful—waltzing.) Most peculiar, the way people danced nowadays. Flinging themselves about, seeming quite *contorted*. Oh well, young people must enjoy—— Her thoughts were arrested. Because, now she came to think of it, very few of these people *were* young. Dancing, lights, the music of a band (even a steel band) all that surely was for *youth*. But where was youth? Studying, she supposed, at universities, or doing a job—with a fortnight's holiday a year. A place like this was too far away and too expensive. This gay and carefree life was all for the thirties and the forties—and the old men who were trying to live up (or down) to their young wives. It seemed, somehow, a *pity*.

Miss Marple sighed for youth. There was Mrs. Kendal, of course. She wasn't more than twenty-two or three, probably, and she seemed to be enjoying herself—but even so, it was a *job* she was doing.

At a table nearby Canon Prescott and his sister were sitting. They motioned to Miss Marple to join them for coffee and she did so. Miss Prescott was a thin severe-looking woman, the Canon was a round, rubicund man, breathing geniality.

Coffee was brought, and chairs were pushed a little way away from the tables. Miss Prescott opened a work bag and took out some frankly hideous table mats that she was hemming. She told Miss Marple all about the day's events. They had visited a new Girls' School in the morning. After an afternoon's rest, they had walked through a cane plantation to have tea at a *pension* where some friends of theirs were staying.

Since the Prescotts had been at the Golden Palm longer than Miss Marple, they were able to enlighten her as to some of her fellow guests.

That very old man, Mr. Rafiel. He came every year. Fantastically rich!

Owned an enormous chain of supermarkets in the North of England. The young woman with him was his secretary, Esther Walters—a widow. (Quite all *right*, of course. Nothing improper. After all, he was nearly eighty!)

Miss Marple accepted the propriety of the relationship with an understanding nod and the Canon remarked:

"A very nice young woman; her mother, I understand, is a widow and lives in Chichester."

"Mr. Rafiel has a valet with him, too. Or rather a kind of Nurse Attendant—he's a qualified masseur, I believe. Jackson, his name is. Poor Mr. Rafiel is practically paralyzed. So sad—with all that money, too."

"A generous and cheerful giver," said Canon Prescott approvingly.

People were regrouping themselves round about, some going farther from the steel band, others crowding up to it. Major Palgrave had joined the Hillingdon-Dyson quartette.

"Now those people——" said Miss Prescott, lowering her voice quite unnecessarily since the steel band easily drowned it.

"Yes, I was going to ask you about them."

"They were here last year. They spend three months every year in the West Indies, going round the different islands. The tall thin man is Colonel Hillingdon and the dark woman is his wife—they are botanists. The other two, Mr. and Mrs. Gregory Dyson—they're American. He writes on butterflies, I believe. And all of them are interested in birds."

"So nice for people to have open-air hobbies," said Canon Prescott genially.

"I don't think they'd like to hear you call it hobbies, Jeremy," said his sister. "They have articles printed in the *National Geographic* and in the *Royal Horticultural Journal*. They take themselves very seriously."

A loud outburst of laughter came from the table they had been observing. It was loud enough to overcome the steel band. Gregory Dyson was leaning back in his chair and thumping the table, his wife was protesting, and Major Palgrave emptied his glass and seemed to be applauding.

They hardly qualified for the moment as people who took themselves seriously.

"Major Palgrave should not drink so much," said Miss Prescott acidly. "He has blood pressure."

A fresh supply of Planters Punches were brought to the table.

"It's so nice to get people sorted out," said Miss Marple. "When I met them this afternoon I wasn't sure which was married to which."

There was a slight pause. Miss Prescott coughed a small dry cough, and said—"Well, as to that——"

"Joan," said the Canon in an admonitory voice. "Perhaps it would be wise to say no more."

"Really, Jeremy, I wasn't going to say *anything*. Only that last year, for some reason or other—I really don't know *why*—we got the idea that Mrs. Dyson was Mrs. Hillingdon until someone told us she wasn't."

"It's odd how one gets impressions, isn't it?" said Miss Marple innocently. Her eyes met Miss Prescott's for a moment. A flash of womanly understanding passed between them.

A more sensitive man than Canon Prescott might have felt that he was *de trop*.

Another signal passed between the women. It said as clearly as if the words had been spoken: *"Some other time . . ."*

"Mr. Dyson calls his wife 'Lucky.' Is that her real name or a nickname?" asked Miss Marple.

"It can hardly be her real name, I should think."

"I happened to ask him," said the Canon. "He said he called her Lucky because she was his good luck piece. If he lost her, he said, he'd lose his luck. Very nicely put, I thought."

"He's very fond of joking," said Miss Prescott.

The Canon looked at his sister doubtfully.

The steel band outdid itself with a wild burst of cacophony and a troupe of dancers came racing on to the floor.

Miss Marple and the others turned their chairs to watch. Miss Marple enjoyed the dancing better than the music; she liked the shuffling feet and the rhythmic sway of the bodies. It seemed, she thought, very *real*. It had a kind of power of understatement.

Tonight, for the first time, she began to feel slightly at home in her new environment. . . . Up to now, she had missed what she usually found so easily, points of resemblance in the people she met, to various people known to her personally. She had, possibly, been dazzled by the gay clothes and the exotic coloring; but soon, she felt, she would be able to make some interesting comparisons.

Molly Kendal, for instance, was like that nice girl whose name she couldn't remember, but who was a conductress on the Market Basing bus. Helped you in, and never rang the bus on until she was sure you'd sat down safely. Tim Kendal was just a little like the head waiter at the Royal George in Medchester. Self-confident, and yet, at the same time, worried. (He had had an ulcer, she remembered.) As for Major Palgrave, he was indistinguishable from General Leroy, Captain Flemming, Admiral Wicklow and Commander Richardson. She went on to someone more interesting. Greg for instance? Greg was difficult because he was American. A dash of Sir George Trollope, perhaps, always so full of jokes at the Civil Defense meetings—or perhaps Mr. Murdoch the butcher. Mr. Murdoch had had rather a bad reputation, but some people said it was just gossip, and that Mr. Murdoch himself liked to encourage the rumors! 'Lucky' now? Well, that was easy—Marleen at the Three Crowns. Evelyn Hillingdon? She couldn't fit Evelyn in precisely. In appearance she fitted many roles—tall thin weatherbeaten Englishwomen were plentiful. Lady Caroline Wolfe, Peter Wolfe's first wife, who had committed suicide? Or there was Leslie James—that quiet woman who seldom showed what she felt and who had sold up her house and left without ever telling anyone she was going. Colonel Hillingdon? No immediate clue there. She'd have to get to know him a little first. One of those quiet men with good manners. You never knew what they were thinking about. Sometimes they surprised you. Major Harper, she remembered, had quietly cut his throat one day. Nobody had ever known why. Miss Marple thought that she did know—but she'd never been quite sure. . . .

Her eyes strayed to Mr. Rafiel's table. The principal thing known about Mr. Rafiel was that he was incredibly rich, he came every year to the West

Indies, he was semi-paralyzed and looked like a wrinkled old bird of prey. His clothes hung loosely on his shrunken form. He might have been seventy or eighty, or even ninety. His eyes were shrewd and he was frequently rude, but people seldom took offense, partly because he was so rich, and partly because of his overwhelming personality which hypnotized you into feeling that somehow, Mr. Rafiel had the right to be rude if he wanted to.

With him sat his secretary, Mrs. Walters. She had corn-colored hair, and a pleasant face. Mr. Rafiel was frequently very rude to her, but she never seemed to notice it—She was not so much subservient, as oblivious. She behaved like a well-trained hospital nurse. Possibly, thought Miss Marple, she had been a hospital nurse.

A young man, tall and good-looking, in a white jacket, came to stand by Mr. Rafiel's chair. The old man looked up at him, nodded, then motioned him to a chair. The young man sat down as bidden. "Mr. Jackson, I presume," said Miss Marple to herself—"His valet-attendant."

She studied Mr. Jackson with some attention.

II

In the bar, Molly Kendal stretched her back, and slipped off her high-heeled shoes. Tim came in from the terrace to join her. They had the bar to themselves for the moment.

"Tired, darling?" he asked.

"Just a bit. I seem to be feeling my feet tonight."

"Not too much for you, is it? All this? I know it's hard work." He looked at her anxiously.

She laughed. "Oh Tim, don't be ridiculous. I love it here. It's gorgeous. The kind of dream I've always had, come true."

"Yes, it would be all right—if one was just a guest. But running the show—that's work."

"Well, you can't have anything for nothing, can you?" said Molly Kendal reasonably.

Tim Kendal frowned.

"You think it's going all right? A success? We're making a go of it?"

"Of course we are."

"You don't think people are saying, 'It's not the same as when the Sandersons were here.'"

"Of course *someone* will be saying that—they always do! But only some old stick-in-the-mud. I'm sure that we're far better at the job than they were. We're more glamorous. You charm the old pussies and manage to look as though you'd like to make love to the desperate forties and fifties, and I ogle the old gentlemen and make them feel sexy dogs—or play the sweet little daughter the sentimental ones would love to have had. Oh, we've got it all taped splendidly."

Tim's frown vanished.

"As long as *you* think so. I get scared. We've risked everything on making a job of this. I chucked my job——"

"And quite right to do so," Molly put in quickly. "It was soul-destroying."

He laughed and kissed the tip of her nose.

"I tell you we've got it taped," she repeated. "Why do you always worry?"

"Made that way, I suppose. I'm always thinking—suppose something should go wrong."

"What sort of thing——"

"Oh I don't know. Somebody might get drowned."

"Not they. It's one of the safest of all the beaches. And we've got that hulking Swede always on guard."

"I'm a fool," said Tim Kendal. He hesitated—and then said, "You—haven't had any more of those dreams, have you?"

"That was shellfish," said Molly, and laughed.

CHAPTER THREE
A Death in the Hotel

MISS MARPLE HAD her breakfast brought to her in bed as usual. Tea, a boiled egg, and a slice of paw-paw.

The fruit on the island, thought Miss Marple, was rather disappointing. It seemed always to be paw-paw. If she could have a nice apple now—but apples seemed to be unknown.

Now that she had been here a week, Miss Marple had cured herself of the impulse to ask what the weather was like. The weather was always the same—fine. No interesting variations.

"The many splendored weather of an English day," she murmured to herself and wondered if it was a quotation, or whether she had made it up.

There were, of course, hurricanes, or so she understood. But hurricanes were not weather in Miss Marple's sense of the word. They were more in the nature of an Act of God. There was rain, short violent rainfall that lasted five minutes and stopped abruptly. Everything and everyone was wringing wet, but in another five minutes they were dry again.

The black West Indian girl smiled and said Good Morning as she placed the tray on Miss Marple's knees. Such lovely white teeth and so happy and smiling. Nice natures, all these girls, and a pity they were so averse to getting married. It worried Canon Prescott a good deal. Plenty of christenings, he said, trying to console himself, but no weddings.

Miss Marple ate her breakfast and decided how she would spend her day. It didn't really take much deciding. She would get up at her leisure, moving slowly because it was rather hot and her fingers weren't as nimble as they used to be. Then she would rest for ten minutes or so, and she would take her knitting and walk slowly along towards the hotel and decide where she would settle herself. On the terrace overlooking the sea? Or should she go on to the bathing beach to watch the bathers and the children? Usually it was the latter. In the afternoon, after her rest, she might take a drive. It really didn't matter very much.

Today would be a day like any other day, she said to herself.

Only, of course, it wasn't.

Miss Marple carried out her program as planned and was slowly making her way along the path towards the hotel when she met Molly Kendal. For once that sunny young woman was not smiling. Her air of distress was so unlike her that Miss Marple said immediately:

"My dear, is anything wrong?"

Molly nodded. She hesitated and then said: "Well, you'll have to know—everyone will have to know. It's Major Palgrave. He's dead."

"Dead?"

"Yes. He died in the night."

"Oh dear, I *am* sorry."

"Yes, it's horrid having a death here. It makes everyone depressed. Of course—he *was* quite old."

"He seemed quite well and cheerful yesterday," said Miss Marple, slightly resenting this calm assumption that everyone of advanced years was liable to die at any minute.

"He seemed quite healthy," she added.

"He had high blood pressure," said Molly.

"But surely there are things one takes nowadays—some kind of pill. Science is so wonderful."

"Oh yes, but perhaps he forgot to take his pills, or took too many of them. Like insulin, you know."

Miss Marple did not think that diabetes and high blood pressure were at all the same kind of thing. She asked:

"What does the doctor say?"

"Oh, Dr. Graham, who's practically retired now, and lives in the hotel, took a look at him, and the local people came officially, of course, to give a death certificate, but it all seems quite straightforward. This kind of thing is quite liable to happen when you have high blood pressure, especially if you overdo the alcohol, and Major Palgrave was really very naughty that way. Last night, for instance."

"Yes, I noticed," said Miss Marple.

"He probably forgot to take his pills. It is bad luck for the old boy—but people can't live forever, can they? But it's terribly worrying—for me and Tim, I mean. People might suggest it was something in the food."

"But surely the symptoms of food poisoning and of blood pressure are *quite* different?"

"Yes. But people do *say* things so easily. And if people decided the food was bad—and left—or told their friends——"

"I really don't think you need worry," said Miss Marple kindly. "As you say, an elderly man like Major Palgrave—he must have been over seventy—is quite liable to die. To most people it will seem quite an ordinary occurrence—sad, but not out of the way at all."

"If only," said Molly unhappily, "it hadn't been so *sudden*."

Yes, it had been very sudden, Miss Marple thought as she walked slowly on. There he had been last night, laughing and talking in the best of spirits with the Hillingdons and the Dysons.

The Hillingdons and the Dysons. . . . Miss Marple walked more slowly still . . . Finally she stopped abruptly. Instead of going to the bathing beach she settled herself in a shady corner of the terrace. She took out her knitting and the needles clicked rapidly as though they were trying to match the speed of her thoughts. *She didn't like it—no she didn't like it. It came so pat.*

She went over the occurrences of yesterday in her mind.

Major Palgrave and his stories . . .

That was all as usual and one didn't need to listen very closely . . . Perhaps, though, it would have been better if she had.

Kenya—he had talked about Kenya and then India—the North West Frontier—and then—for some reason they had got on to murder— And even *then* she hadn't really been listening . . .

Some famous case that had taken place out here—that had been in the newspapers—

It was after that—when he picked up her ball of wool—that he had begun telling her about a snapshot—*A snapshot of a murderer*—that is what he had said.

Miss Marple closed her eyes and tried to remember just exactly how that story had gone.

It had been rather a confused story—told to the Major in his Club—or in somebody else's club—told him by a doctor—who had heard it from another doctor—and one doctor had taken a snapshot of someone coming through a front door—someone who was a murderer—

Yes, that was it—the various details were coming back to her now—

And he had offered to show her that snapshot— He had got out his wallet and begun hunting through its contents—talking all the time—

And then still talking, he had looked up—had looked—not at her—but at something behind her—behind her right shoulder to be accurate. And he had stopped talking, his face had gone purple—and he had started stuffing back everything into his wallet with slightly shaky hands and had begun talking in a loud unnatural voice about elephant tusks!

A moment or two later the Hillingdons and the Dysons had joined them. . . .

It was then that she had turned her head over her right shoulder to look . . . But there had been nothing and nobody to see. To her left, some distance away, in the direction of the hotel, there had been Tim Kendal and his wife; and beyond them a family group of Venezuelans. But Major Palgrave had not been looking in that direction . . .

Miss Marple meditated until lunch time.

After lunch she did not go for a drive.

Instead she sent a message to say that she was not feeling very well, and to ask if Dr. Graham would be kind enough to come and see her.

CHAPTER FOUR
Miss Marple Seeks Medical Attention

DR. GRAHAM WAS a kindly elderly man of about sixty-five. He had practiced in the West Indies for many years, but was now semi-retired, and left most of his work to his West Indian partners. He greeted Miss Marple pleasantly and asked her what the trouble was. Fortunately at Miss Marple's age, there was always some ailment that could be discussed with slight exaggerations on the patient's part. Miss Marple hesitated between "her shoulder" and "her knee," but finally decided upon the knee. Miss Marple's knee, as she would have put it to herself, was always with her.

Dr. Graham was exceedingly kindly but he refrained from putting into words the fact that at her time of life such troubles were only to be expected. He prescribed for her one of the brands of useful little pills that form the basis of a doctor's prescriptions. Since he knew by experience that many elderly people could be lonely when they first came to St. Honoré, he remained for a while gently chatting.

"A very nice man," thought Miss Marple to herself, "and I really feel rather ashamed of having to tell him lies. But I don't quite see what else I can do."

Miss Marple had been brought up to have a proper regard for truth and was indeed by nature a very truthful person. But on certain occasions, when she considered it her duty so to do, she could tell lies with a really astonishing verisimilitude.

She cleared her throat, uttered an apologetic little cough, and said, in an old ladyish and slightly twittering manner:

"There is something, Dr. Graham, I would like to ask you. I don't really like mentioning it—but I don't quite see what else I am to do—although of course it's *quite* unimportant really. But you see, it's important to *me*. And I hope you will understand and not think what I am asking is tiresome or—or unpardonable in any way."

To this opening Dr. Graham replied kindly: "Something is worrying you? Do let me help."

"It's connected with Major Palgrave. *So* sad about his dying. It was quite a shock when I heard it this morning."

"Yes," said Dr. Graham, "it was very sudden, I'm afraid. He seemed in such good spirits yesterday." He spoke kindly, but conventionally. To him, clearly, Major Palgrave's death was nothing out of the way. Miss Marple wondered whether she was really making something out of nothing. Was this suspicious habit of mind growing on her? Perhaps she could no longer trust her own judgment. Not that it was judgment really, only suspicion. Anyway she was in for it now! She must go ahead.

"We were sitting talking together yesterday afternoon," she said. "He was telling me about his very varied and interesting life. So many strange parts of the globe."

"Yes indeed," said Dr. Graham, who had been bored many times by the Major's reminiscences.

"And then he spoke of his family, boyhood rather, and I told him a little about my own nephews and nieces and he listened very sympathetically. And I showed him a snapshot I had with me of one of my nephews. Such a dear boy—at least not exactly a boy now, but always a boy to *me* if you understand."

"Quite so," said Dr. Graham, wondering how long it would be before the old lady was going to come to the point.

"I had handed it to him and he was examining it when quite suddenly those people—those very nice people—who collect wild flowers and butterflies, Colonel and Mrs. Hillingdon I think the name is——"

"Oh yes? The Hillingdons and the Dysons."

"Yes, that's right. They came suddenly along laughing and talking. They sat down and ordered drinks and we all talked together. Very pleasant it was. But without thinking, Major Palgrave must have put back my snapshot into his wallet and returned it to his pocket. I wasn't paying very much attention at the time but I remembered afterward and I said to myself— 'I mustn't forget to ask the Major to give me back my picture of Denzil.' I *did* think of it last night while the dancing and the band was going on, but I didn't like to interrupt him just then, because they were having such a merry party together and I thought 'I will remember to ask him for it in the morning.' Only this morning——" Miss Marple paused—out of breath.

"Yes, yes," said Dr. Graham, "I quite understand. And you—well, naturally you want the snapshot back. Is that it?"

Miss Marple nodded her head in eager agreement.

"Yes. That's it. You see, it is the only one I have got and I haven't got the negative. And I would hate to lose that snapshot, because poor Denzil died some five or six years ago, and he was my favorite nephew. This is the only picture I have to remind me of him. I wondered—I hoped—it is rather tiresome of me to ask—whether you could possibly manage to get hold of it for me? I don't really know who else to ask, you see. I don't know who'll attend to all his belongings and things like that. It is all so difficult. They would think it such a nuisance of me. You see, they don't understand. Nobody could quite understand what this snapshot means to me."

"Of course, of course," said Dr. Graham. "I quite understand. A most natural feeling on your part. Actually, I am meeting the local authorities shortly—the funeral is tomorrow, and someone will be coming from the Administrator's office to look over his papers and effects before communicating with the next of kin—all that sort of thing— If you could describe this snapshot."

"It was just the front of a house," said Miss Marple. "And someone—Denzil, I mean—was just coming out of the front door. As I say it was taken by one of my other nephews who is very keen on flower shows—and he was photographing a hibiscus, I think, or one of those beautiful—something like antipasto—lilies. Denzil just happened to come out of the front door at that time. It wasn't a very good photograph of him—just a trifle blurred— But I liked it, and have always kept it."

"Well," said Dr. Graham, "that seems clear enough. I think we'll have no difficulty in getting back your picture for you, Miss Marple."

He rose from his chair. Miss Marple smiled up at him.

"You are very kind, Dr. Graham, very kind *indeed*. You do understand, don't you?"

"Of course I do, of course I do," said Dr. Graham, shaking her warmly by the hand. "Now don't you worry. Exercise that knee every day gently but not too much, and I'll send you round these tablets. Take one three times a day."

CHAPTER FIVE
Miss Marple Makes a Decision

THE FUNERAL SERVICE was said over the body of the late Major Palgrave on the following day. Miss Marple attended in company with Miss Prescott. The Canon read the service—after that life went on as usual.

Major Palgrave's death was already only an incident, a slightly unpleasant incident, but one that was soon forgotten. Life here was sunshine, sea, and social pleasures. A grim visitor had interrupted these activities, casting a momentary shadow, but the shadow was now gone. After all, nobody had known the deceased very well. He had been rather a garrulous elderly man of the club-bore type, always telling you personal reminiscences that you had no particular desire to hear. He had had little to anchor himself to any particular part of the world. His wife had died many years ago. He had had a lonely life and a lonely death. But it had been the kind of loneliness that spends itself in living amongst people, and in passing the time that way not unpleasantly. Major Palgrave might have been a lonely man, he had also been quite a cheerful one. He had enjoyed himself in his own particular way. And now he was dead, buried, and nobody cared very much, and in another week's time nobody would even remember him or spare him a passing thought.

The only person who could possibly be said to miss him was Miss Marple. Not indeed out of any personal affection, but he represented a kind of life that she knew. As one grew older, so she reflected to herself, one got more and more into the habit of listening; listening possibly without any great interest, but there had been between her and the Major the gentle give and take of two old people. It had had a cheerful, human quality. She did not actually mourn Major Palgrave but she missed him.

On the afternoon of the funeral, as she was sitting knitting in her favorite spot, Dr. Graham came and joined her. She put her needles down and greeted him. He said at once, rather apologetically:

"I am afraid I have rather disappointing news, Miss Marple."

"Indeed? About my——"

"Yes. We haven't found that precious snapshot of yours. I'm afraid that will be a disappointment to you."

"Yes. Yes it is. But of course it does not *really* matter. It was a sentimentality. I do realize that now. It wasn't in Major Palgrave's wallet?"

"No. Nor anywhere else among his things. There were a few letters and newspaper clippings and odds and ends, and a few old photographs, but no sign of a snapshot such as you mentioned."

"Oh dear," said Miss Marple. "Well, it can't be helped . . . Thank you very much, Dr. Graham, for the trouble you've taken."

"Oh it was no trouble, indeed. But I know quite well from my own experience how much family trifles mean to one, especially as one is getting older."

The old lady was really taking it very well, he thought. Major Palgrave, he presumed, had probably come across the snapshot when taking something out of his wallet, and not even realizing how it had come there, had torn it up as something of no importance. But of course it was of great importance to this old lady. Still, she seemed quite cheerful and philosophical about it.

Internally, however, Miss Marple was far from being either cheerful or philosophical. She wanted a little time in which to think things out, but she was also determined to use her present opportunities to the fullest effect.

She engaged Dr. Graham in conversation with an eagerness which she did not attempt to conceal. That kindly man, putting down her flow of talk to the natural loneliness of an old lady, exerted himself to divert her mind from the loss of the snapshot, by conversing easily and pleasantly about life in St. Honoré, and the various interesting places perhaps Miss Marple might like to visit. He hardly knew himself how the conversation drifted back to Major Palgrave's decease.

"It seems so sad," said Miss Marple, "to think of anyone dying like this away from home. Though I gather, from what he himself told me, that he had no immediate family. It seems he lived by himself in London."

"He traveled a fair amount, I believe," said Dr. Graham. "At any rate in the winters. He didn't care for our English winters. Can't say I blame him."

"No, indeed," said Miss Marple. "And perhaps he had some special reason like a weakness of the lungs or something which made it necessary for him to winter abroad?"

"Oh no, I don't think so."

"He had high blood pressure, I believe. So sad nowadays. One hears so much of it."

"He spoke about it to you, did he?"

"Oh no. No, *he* never mentioned it. It was somebody else who told me."

"Ah, really."

"I suppose," went on Miss Marple, "that death was to be expected under those circumstances."

"Not necessarily," said Dr. Graham. "There are methods of controlling blood pressure nowadays."

"His death *seemed* very sudden—but I suppose *you* weren't surprised."

"Well I wasn't particularly surprised in a man of that age. But I certainly didn't expect it. Frankly, he always seemed to me in very good form, but I hadn't ever attended him professionally. I'd never taken his blood pressure or anything like that."

"Does one know—I mean, does a doctor know—when a man has high blood pressure just by looking at him?" Miss Marple inquired with a kind of dewy innocence.

"Not just by looking," said the doctor, smiling. "One has to do a bit of testing."

"Oh I see. That dreadful thing when you put a rubber band round somebody's arm and blow it up—I dislike it *so* much. But my doctor said that my blood pressure was really very good for my age."

"Well that's good hearing," said Dr. Graham.

"Of course, the Major *was* rather fond of Planters Punch," said Miss Marple thoughtfully.

"Yes. Not the best thing with blood pressure—alcohol."

"One takes tablets, doesn't one, or so I have heard?"

"Yes. There are several on the market. There was a bottle of one of them in his room—Serenite."

"How wonderful science is nowadays," said Miss Marple. "Doctors can do so much, can't they?"

"We all have one great competitor," said Dr. Graham. "Nature, you know. And some of the good old-fashioned home remedies come back from time to time."

"Like putting cobwebs on a cut?" said Miss Marple. "We always used to do that when I was a child."

"Very sensible," said Dr. Graham.

"And a linseed poultice on the chest and rubbing in camphorated oil for a bad cough."

"I see you know it all!" said Dr. Graham laughing. He got up. "How's the knee? Not been too troublesome?"

"No, it seems much, much better."

"Well, we won't say whether that's Nature or my pills," said Dr. Graham. "Sorry I couldn't have been of more help to you."

"But you have been most kind—I am really ashamed of taking up your time— Did you say that there were no photographs in the Major's wallet?"

"Oh yes—a very old one of the Major himself as quite a young man on a polo pony—and one of a dead tiger— He was standing with his foot on it. Snaps of that sort—memories of his younger days— But I looked very carefully, I assure you, and the one you describe of your nephew was definitely not there——"

"Oh I'm sure you looked carefully—I didn't mean that—I was just interested— We all tend to keep such very odd things——"

"Treasures from the past," said the doctor smiling.

He said good-bye and departed.

Miss Marple remained looking thoughtfully at the palm trees and the sea. She did not pick up her knitting again for some minutes. She had a fact now. She had to think about that fact and what it meant. The snapshot that the Major had brought out of his wallet and replaced so hurriedly was *not there after he died*. It was not the sort of thing the Major would throw away. He had replaced it in his wallet and it ought to have been in his wallet after his death. Money might have been stolen, but no one would want to steal a snapshot. Unless, that is, they had a special reason for so doing. . . .

Miss Marple's face was grave. She had to take a decision. Was she, or was she not, going to allow Major Palgrave to remain quietly in his grave? Might it not be better to do just that? She quoted under her breath. "Duncan is dead. After Life's fitful fever he sleeps well!" Nothing could hurt

Major Palgrave now. He had gone where danger could not touch him. Was it just a coincidence that he should have died on that particular night? Or was it just possibly *not* a coincidence? Doctors accepted the deaths of elderly men so easily. Especially since in his room there had been a bottle of the tablets that people with high blood pressure had to take every day of their lives. But if someone had taken the snapshot from the Major's wallet, that same person could have put that bottle of tablets in the Major's room. She herself never remembered *seeing* the Major take tablets; he had never spoken about his blood pressure to her. The only thing he had ever said about his health was the admission—"Not as young as I was." He had been occasionally a little short of breath, a trifle asthmatic, nothing else. But someone had mentioned that Major Palgrave had high blood pressure—Molly? Miss Prescott? She couldn't remember.

Miss Marple sighed, then admonished herself in words, though she did not speak those words aloud.

"Now, Jane, what are you suggesting or thinking? Are you, perhaps, just making the whole thing up? Have you *really* got anything to build on?"

She went over, step by step, as nearly as she could, the conversation between herself and the Major on the subject of murder and murderers.

"Oh dear," said Miss Marple. "Even if—really, I *don't* see how I *can* do anything about it——"

But she knew that she meant to try.

CHAPTER SIX
In the Small Hours

I

MISS MARPLE WOKE early. Like many old people she slept lightly and had periods of wakefulness which she used for the planning of some action or actions to be carried out on the next or following days. Usually, of course, these were of a wholly private or domestic nature, of little interest to anybody but herself. But this morning Miss Marple lay thinking soberly and constructively of murder, and what, if her suspicions were correct, she could do about it. It wasn't going to be easy. She had one weapon and one weapon only, and that was conversation.

Old ladies were given to a good deal of rambling conversation. People were bored by this, but certainly did not suspect them of ulterior motives. It would not be a case of asking direct questions. (Indeed, she would have found it difficult to know what questions to ask!) It would be a question of finding out a little more about certain people. She reviewed these certain people in her mind.

She could find out, possibly, a little more about Major Palgrave, but would that really help her? She doubted if it would. If Major Palgrave had been killed it was not because of secrets in his life or to inherit his money or for revenge upon him. In fact, although he was the victim, it was one of those rare cases where a greater knowledge of the victim does not help you or lead you in any way to his murderer. The point, it seemed to her, and the sole point, was that Major Palgrave talked too much!

She had learnt one rather interesting fact from Dr. Graham. He had had in his wallet various photographs; one of himself in company with a polo pony, one of a dead tiger, also one or two other shots of the same nature. Now why did Major Palgrave carry these about with him? Obviously, thought Miss Marple, with long experience of old Admirals, Brigadier-Generals and mere Majors behind her, because he had certain stories which he enjoyed telling to people. Starting off with "Curious thing happened once when I was out tiger shooting in India . . ." Or a reminiscence of himself and a polo pony. Therefore this story about a suspected murderer would in due course be illustrated by the production of the snapshot from his wallet.

He had been following that pattern in his conversation with her. The subject of murder having come up, and to focus interest on his story, he had done what he no doubt usually did, produced his snapshot and said something in the nature of "Wouldn't think this chap was a murderer, would you?"

The point was that it had been a *habit* of his. This murderer story was one of his regular repertoire. If any reference to murder came up, then away went the Major, full steam ahead.

In that case reflected Miss Marple, he might *already* have told his story to someone else here. Or to more than one person— If that were so, then she herself might learn from that person what the further details of the story had been, possibly what the person in the snapshot had looked like.

She nodded her head in satisfaction— That would be a beginning.

And, of course, there were the people she called in her mind the "Four Suspects." Though really, since Major Palgrave had been talking about a *man*—there were only two. Colonel Hillingdon or Mr. Dyson, very unlikely looking murderers, but then murderers so often *were* unlikely. Could there have been anyone else? She had seen no one when she turned her head to look. There was the bungalow of course. Mr. Rafiel's bungalow. Could somebody have come out of the bungalow and gone in again before she had had time to turn her head? If so, it could only have been the valet-attendant. What was his name? Oh yes, Jackson. Could it have been *Jackson* who had come out of the door? That would have been the same pose as the photograph. *A man coming out of a door.* Recognition might have struck suddenly. Up till then, Major Palgrave would not have looked at Arthur Jackson, valet-attendant, with any interest. His roving and curious eye was essentially a snobbish eye—Arthur Jackson was not a *pukka sahib*—Major Palgrave would not have glanced at him twice.

Until, perhaps, he had had the snapshot in his hand, and had looked over Miss Marple's right shoulder and had seen a man coming out of a door . . .?

Miss Marple turned over on her pillow—Program for tomorrow—or rather for today—Further investigation of the Hillingdons, the Dysons and Arthur Jackson, valet-attendant.

II

Dr. Graham also woke early. Usually he turned over and went to sleep again. But today he was uneasy and sleep failed to come. This anxiety that made it so difficult to go to sleep again was a thing he had not suffered from for a long time. What was causing this anxiety? Really, he couldn't make it out. He lay there thinking it over. Something to do with—something to do with—yes, Major Palgrave. Major Palgrave's death? He didn't see, though, what there could be to make him uneasy there. Was it something that that twittery old lady had said? Bad luck for her about her snapshot. She'd taken it very well. But now what was it she had said, what chance word of hers had it been, that had given him this funny feeling of uneasiness? After all, there was nothing *odd* about the Major's death. Nothing at all. At least he supposed there was nothing at all.

It was quite clear that in the Major's state of health—a faint check came in his thought process. Did he really know much *about* Major Palgrave's state of health? Everybody *said* that he'd suffered from high blood pressure. But he himself had never had any conversation with the Major about it. But then he'd never had much conversation with Major Palgrave anyway. Palgrave was an old bore and he avoided old bores. Why on earth should he have this idea that perhaps everything *mightn't* be all right? Was it that old woman? But after all she hadn't *said* anything. Anyway, it was none of his business. The local authorities were quite satisfied. There had been that bottle of Serenite tablets, and the old boy had apparently talked to people about his blood pressure quite freely.

Dr. Graham turned over in bed and soon went to sleep again.

III

Outside the hotel grounds, in one of a row of shanty cabins beside a creek, the girl Victoria Johnson rolled over and sat up in bed. The St. Honoré girl was a magnificent creature with a torso of black marble such as a sculptor would have enjoyed. She ran her fingers through her dark, tightly curling hair. With her foot she nudged her sleeping companion in the ribs.

"Wake up, man."

The man grunted and turned.

"What you want? It's not morning."

"Wake up, man. I want to talk to you."

The man sat up, stretched, showed a wide mouth and beautiful teeth.

"What's worrying you, woman?"

"That Major man who died. Something I don't like. Something wrong about it."

"Ah, what d'you want to worry about that? He was old. He died."

"Listen, man. It's them pills. Them pills the doctor asked me about."

"Well, what about them? He took too many maybe."

"No. It's not that. Listen." She leant towards him, talking vehemently. He yawned and lay down again.

"There's nothing in that. What're you talking about?"

"All the same, I'll speak to Mrs. Kendal about it in the morning. I think there's something wrong there somewhere."

"Shouldn't bother," said the man who, without benefit of ceremony, she considered as her present husband. "Don't let's look for trouble," he said and rolled over on his side yawning.

CHAPTER SEVEN
Morning on the Beach

I

IT WAS MID morning on the beach below the hotel.

Evelyn Hillingdon came out of the water and dropped on the warm golden sand. She took off her bathing cap and shook her dark head vigorously. The beach was not a very big one. People tended to congregate there in the mornings and about 11:30 there was always something of a social reunion. To Evelyn's left in one of the exotic-looking modern basket chairs lay Señora de Caspearo, a handsome woman from Venezuela. Next to her was old Mr. Rafiel who was by now the doyen of the Golden Palm Hotel and held the sway that only an elderly invalid of great wealth could attain. Esther Walters was in attendance on him. She usually had her shorthand notebook and pencil with her in case Mr. Rafiel should suddenly think of urgent business cables which must be got off at once. Mr. Rafiel in beach attire was incredibly desiccated, his bones draped with festoons of dry skin. Though looking like a man on the point of death, he had looked exactly the same for at least the last eight years—or so it was said in the islands. Sharp blue eyes peered out of his wrinkled cheeks, and his principal pleasure in life was denying robustly anything that anyone else said.

Miss Marple was also present. As usual she sat and knitted and listened to what went on, and very occasionally joined in the conversation. When she did so, everyone was surprised because they had usually forgotten that she was there! Evelyn Hillingdon looked at her indulgently, and thought that she was a nice old pussy.

Señora de Caspearo rubbed some more oil on her long beautiful legs and hummed to herself. She was not a woman who spoke much. She looked discontentedly at the flask of sun oil.

"This is not so good as Frangipanio," she said, sadly. "One cannot get it here. A pity." Her eyelids drooped again.

"Are you going in for your dip now, Mr. Rafiel?" asked Esther Walters.

"I'll go in when I'm ready," said Mr. Rafiel, snappishly.

"It's half past eleven," said Mrs. Walters.

"What of it?" said Mr. Rafiel. "Think I'm the kind of man to be tied by the clock? Do this at the hour, do this at twenty minutes past, do that at twenty to—bah!"

Mrs. Walters had been in attendance on Mr. Rafiel long enough to have adopted her own formula for dealing with him. She knew that he liked a good space of time in which to recover from the exertion of bathing and she had therefore reminded him of the time, allowing a good ten minutes for him to rebut her suggestion and then be able to adopt it without seeming to do so.

"I don't like these espadrilles," said Mr. Rafiel raising a foot and looking at it. "I told that fool Jackson so. The man never pays attention to a word I say."

"I'll fetch you some others, shall I, Mr. Rafiel?"

"No, you won't, you'll sit here and keep quiet. I hate people rushing about like clucking hens."

Evelyn shifted slightly in the warm sand, stretching her arms.

Miss Marple, intent on her knitting—or so it seemed—stretched out a foot, then hastily she apologized.

"I'm so sorry, so very sorry, Mrs. Hillingdon. I'm afraid I kicked you."

"Oh, it's quite all right," said Evelyn. "This beach gets rather crowded."

"Oh, please don't move. Please. I'll move my chair a little back so that I won't do it again."

As Miss Marple resettled herself, she went on talking in a childish and garrulous manner.

"It still seems so wonderful to be *here!* I've never been to the West Indies before, you know. I thought it was the kind of place I never should come to and here I am. All by the kindness of my dear nephew. I suppose you know this part of the world very well, don't you, Mrs. Hillingdon?"

"I have been in this island once or twice before and of course in most of the others."

"Oh yes. Butterflies isn't it, and wild flowers? You and your—your friends—or are they relations?"

"Friends. Nothing more."

"And I suppose you go about together a great deal because of your interests being the same?"

"Yes. We've traveled together for some years now."

"I suppose you must have had some rather exciting adventures sometimes?"

"I don't think so," said Evelyn. Her voice was unaccentuated, slightly bored. "Adventures always seem to happen to other people." She yawned.

"No dangerous encounters with snakes or with wild animals or with natives gone berserk?"

('What a fool I sound,') thought Miss Marple.

"Nothing worse than insect bites," Evelyn assured her.

"Poor Major Palgrave, you know, was bitten by a snake once," said Miss Marple, making a purely fictitious statement.

"Was he?"

"Did he never tell you about it?"

"Perhaps. I don't remember."

"I suppose you knew him quite well, didn't you?"

"Major Palgrave? No, hardly at all."

"He always had so many interesting stories to tell."

"Ghastly old bore," said Mr. Rafiel. "Silly fool, too. He needn't have died if he'd looked after himself properly."

"Oh come now, Mr. Rafiel," said Mrs. Walters.

"I know what I'm talking about. If you look after your health properly you're all right anywhere. Look at me. The doctors gave *me* up years ago. All right, I said, I've got my own rules of health and I shall keep to them. And here I am."

He looked round proudly.

It did indeed seem rather a miracle that he should be there.

"Poor Major Palgrave had high blood pressure," said Mrs. Walters.

"Nonsense," said Mr. Rafiel.

"Oh, but he did," said Evelyn Hillingdon. She spoke with sudden, unexpected authority.

"Who says so?" said Mr. Rafiel. "Did he tell you so?"

"Somebody said so."

"He looked very red in the face," Miss Marple contributed.

"Can't go by that," said Mr. Rafiel. "And anyway he *didn't* have high blood pressure because he told me so."

"What do you mean, he told you so?" said Mrs. Walters. "I mean, you can't exactly tell people you *haven't* got a thing."

"Yes you can. I said to him once when he was downing all those Planters Punches, and eating too much, I said, 'You ought to watch your diet and your drink. You've got to think of your blood pressure at your age.' And he said he'd nothing to look out for in that line, that his blood pressure was very good for his age."

"But he took some stuff for it, I believe," said Miss Marple, entering the conversation once more. "Some stuff called—oh, something like—was it Serenite?"

"If you ask me," said Evelyn Hillingdon, "I don't think he ever liked to admit that there could be anything the matter with him or that he could be ill. I think he was one of those people who are afraid of illness and therefore deny there's ever anything wrong with them."

It was a long speech for her. Miss Marple looked thoughtfully down at the top of her dark head.

"The trouble is," said Mr. Rafiel dictatorially, "everybody's too fond of knowing other people's ailments. They think everybody over fifty is going to die of hypertension or coronary thrombosis or one of those things— poppycock! If a man says there's nothing much wrong with him I don't suppose there is. A man ought to know about his own health. What's the time? Quarter to twelve? I ought to have had my dip long ago. Why can't you remind me about these things, Esther?"

Mrs. Walters made no protest. She rose to her feet and with some deftness assisted Mr. Rafiel to his. Together they went down the beach, she supporting him carefully. Together they stepped into the sea.

Señora de Caspearo opened her eyes and murmured: "How ugly are old men! Oh how they are ugly! They should all be put to death at forty, or perhaps thirty-five would be better. Yes?"

Edward Hillingdon and Gregory Dyson came crunching down the beach.

"What's the water like, Evelyn?"

"Just the same as always."

"Never much variation, is there? Where's Lucky?"

"I don't know," said Evelyn.

Again Miss Marple looked down thoughtfully at the dark head.

"Well, now I give my imitation of a whale," said Gregory. He threw off his gaily patterned Bermuda shirt and tore down the beach, flinging himself, puffing and panting, into the sea, doing a fast crawl. Edward Hillingdon sat down on the beach by his wife. Presently he asked, "Coming in again?"

She smiled—put on her cap—and they went down the beach together in a much less spectacular manner.

Señora de Caspearo opened her eyes again.

"I think at first those two they are on their honeymoon, he is so charming to her, but I hear they have been married eight—nine years. It is incredible, is it not?"

"I wonder where Mrs. Dyson is?" said Miss Marple.

"That Lucky? She is with some man."

"You—you think so?"

"It is certain," said Señora de Caspearo. "She is that type. But she is not so young any longer—Her husband—already his eyes go elsewhere—He makes passes—here, there, all the time. I know."

"Yes," said Miss Marple, "I expect you would know."

Señora de Caspearo shot a surprised glance at her. It was clearly not what she had expected from that quarter.

Miss Marple, however, was looking at the waves with an air of gentle innocence.

II

"May I speak to you, ma'am, Mrs. Kendal?"

"Yes, of course," said Molly. She was sitting at her desk in the office.

Victoria Johnson tall, and buoyant in her crisp white uniform came in farther and shut the door behind her with a somewhat mysterious air.

"I like to tell you something, please, Mrs. Kendal."

"Yes, what is it. Is anything wrong?"

"I don't know that. Not for sure. It's the old gentleman who died. The Major gentleman. He die in his sleep."

"Yes, yes. What about it?"

"There was a bottle of pills in his room. Doctor, he asked me about them."

"Yes?"

"The doctor said— 'Let me see what he has here on the bathroom shelf,' and he looked, you see. He see there was tooth powder and indigestion pills and aspirin and cascara pills, and then these pills in a bottle called Serenite."

"Yes," repeated Molly yet again.

"And the doctor looked at them. He seemed quite satisfied, and nodded his head. But I get to thinking afterwards. Those pills weren't there before. I've not seen them in his bathroom before. The others, yes. The tooth powder and the aspirin and the after shave lotion and all the rest. But those pills, those Serenite pills, I never noticed them before."

"So you think——" Molly looked puzzled.

"I don't know what to think," said Victoria. "I just think it's not right, so I think I better tell you about it. Perhaps you tell doctor? Perhaps it means something. Perhaps *someone* put those pills there so he take them and he died."

"Oh, I don't think that's likely at all," said Molly.

Victoria shook her dark head. "You never know. People do bad things."

Molly glanced out of the window. The place looked like an earthly paradise. With its sunshine, its sea, its coral reef, its music, its dancing, it seemed a Garden of Eden. But even in the Garden of Eden, there had been a shadow—the shadow of the Serpent—*Bad things*—how hateful to hear those words.

"I'll make inquiries, Victoria," she said sharply. "Don't worry. And above all don't go starting a lot of silly rumors."

Tim Kendal came in, just as Victoria was, somewhat unwillingly, leaving.

"Anything wrong, Molly?"

She hesitated—but Victoria might go to him— She told him what the girl had said.

"I don't see what all this rigmarole—what *were* these pills anyway?"

"Well, I don't really know, Tim. Dr. Robertson when he came said they—were something to do with blood pressure, I think."

"Well, that would be all right, wouldn't it? I mean, he *had* high blood pressure, and he *would* be taking things for it, wouldn't he? People do. I've seen them, lots of times."

"Yes," Molly hesitated, "but Victoria seemed to think that he might have taken one of these pills and it would have killed him."

"Oh darling, that is a bit *too* melodramatic! You mean that somebody might have changed his blood pressure pills for something else, and that they poisoned him?"

"It does sound absurd," said Molly apologetically, "when you say it like that. But that seemed to be what Victoria thought!"

"Silly girl! We *could* go and ask Dr. Graham about it, I suppose he'd know. But really it's such nonsense that it's not worth bothering him."

"That's what I think."

"What on earth made the girl think anybody would have changed the pills. You mean, put different pills into the same bottle?"

"I didn't quite gather," said Molly, looking rather helpless. "Victoria seemed to think that was the first time that Serenite bottle had been there."

"Oh but that's nonsense," said Tim Kendal. "He had to take those pills all the time to keep his blood pressure down." And he went off cheerfully to consult with Fernando the *maître d'hôtel*.

But Molly could not dismiss the matter so lightly. After the stress of lunch was over she said to her husband:

"Tim—I've been thinking— If Victoria is going around talking about this perhaps we ought just to ask someone about it?"

"My dear girl! Robertson and all the rest of them came and looked at everything and asked all the questions they wanted at the time."

"Yes, but you know how they work themselves up, these girls—"

"Oh, all right! I'll tell you what—we'll go and ask Graham—he'll know."

Dr. Graham was sitting on his loggia with a book. The young couple came in and Molly plunged into her recital. It was a little incoherent and Tim took over.

"Sounds rather idiotic," he said apologetically, "but as far as I can make out, this girl has got it into her head that someone put some poison tablets in the—what's the name of the stuff—Sera—somthing bottle."

"But why should she get this idea into her head?" asked Dr. Graham. "Did she see anything or hear anything or—I mean, why should she think so?"

"I don't know," said Tim rather helplessly. "Was it a different bottle? Was that it, Molly?"

"No," said Molly. "I think what she said was that there was a bottle there labeled—Seven—Seren——"

"Serenite," said the doctor. "That's quite right. A well-known preparation. He'd been taking it regularly."

"Victoria said she'd never seen it in his room before."

"Never seen it in his room before?" said Graham sharply. "What does she mean by that?"

"Well, that's what she *said*. She said there were all sorts of things on the bathroom shelf. You know, tooth powder, aspirin and after shave and— oh—she rattled them off gaily. I suppose she's always cleaning them and so she knows them all off by heart. But this one—the Serenite—she hadn't seen it there until the day after he died."

"That's very odd," said Dr. Graham, rather sharply. "Is she sure?"

The unusual sharpness of his tone made both of the Kendals look at him. They had not expected Dr. Graham to take up quite this attitude.

"She sounded sure," said Molly slowly.

"Perhaps she just wanted to be sensational," suggested Tim.

"I think perhaps," said Dr. Graham, "I'd better have a few words with the girl myself."

Victoria displayed a distinct pleasure at being allowed to tell her story.

"I don't want to get in no trouble," she said. "*I* didn't put that bottle there and I don't know who did."

"But you think it *was* put there?" asked Graham.

"Well, you see, Doctor, it *must* have been put there if it wasn't there before."

"Major Palgrave could have kept it in a drawer—or a dispatch-case, something like that."

Victoria shook her head shrewdly.

"Wouldn't do that if he was taking it all the time, would he?"

"No," said Graham reluctantly. "No, it was stuff he would have to take several times a day. You never saw him taking it or anything of that kind?"

"He didn't have it there before. I just thought—word got round as that stuff had something to do with his death, poisoned his blood or something, and I thought maybe he had an enemy put it there so as to kill him."

"Nonsense, my girl," said the doctor robustly. "Sheer nonsense."

Victoria looked shaken.

"You say as this stuff was medicine, good medicine?" she asked doubtfully.

"Good medicine, and what is more, *necessary* medicine," said Dr. Graham. "So you needn't worry, Victoria. I can assure you there was nothing wrong with that medicine. It was the proper thing for a man to take who had his complaint."

"Surely you've taken a load off my mind," said Victoria. She showed white teeth at him in a cheerful smile.

But the load was not taken off Dr. Graham's mind. That uneasiness of his that had been so nebulous was now becoming tangible.

CHAPTER EIGHT
A Talk with Esther Walters

"This place isn't what it used to be," said Mr. Rafiel, irritably, as he observed Miss Marple approaching the spot where he and his secretary were sitting. "Can't move a step without some old hen getting under your feet. What do old ladies want to come to the West Indies for?"

"Where do you suggest they should go?" asked Esther Walters.

"To Cheltenham," said Mr. Rafiel promptly. "Or Bournemouth," he offered, "or Torquay or Llandrindod Wells. Plenty of choice. They like it there—they're quite happy."

"They can't often afford to come to the West Indies, I suppose," said Esther. "It isn't everyone who is as lucky as you are."

"That's right," said Mr. Rafiel. "Rub it in. Here am I, a mass of aches and pains and disjoints. You grudge me any alleviation! And you don't do any work— Why haven't you typed out those letters yet?"

"I haven't had time."

"Well, get on with it, can't you? I bring you out here to do a bit of work, not to sit about sunning yourself and showing off your figure."

Some people would have considered Mr. Rafiel's remarks quite insupportable but Esther Walters had worked for him for some years and she knew well enough that Mr. Rafiel's bark was a great deal worse than his bite. He was a man who suffered almost continual pain, and making disagreeable remarks was one of his ways of letting off steam. No matter what he said she remained quite imperturbable.

"Such a lovely evening, isn't it?" said Miss Marple, pausing beside them.

"Why not?" said Mr. Rafiel. "That's what we're here for, isn't it?"

Miss Marple gave a tinkly little laugh.

"You're so severe—of course the weather *is* a very English subject of conversation—one forgets— Oh dear—this is the wrong colored wool." She deposited her knitting bag on the garden table and trotted towards her own bungalow.

"Jackson!" yelled Mr. Rafiel.

Jackson appeared.

"Take me back inside," said Mr. Rafiel. "I'll have my massage now before that chattering hen comes back. Not that massage does me a bit of good," he added. Having said which, he allowed himself to be deftly helped to his feet and went off with the masseur beside him into his bungalow.

Esther Walters looked after them and then turned her head as Miss Marple came back with a ball of wool to sit down near her.

"I hope I'm not disturbing you?" said Miss Marple.

"Of course not," said Esther Walters, "I've got to go off and do some typing in a minute, but I'm going to enjoy another ten minutes of the sunset first."

Miss Marple sat down and in a gentle voice began to talk. As she talked, she summed up Esther Walters. Not at all glamorous, but could be attractive looking if she tried. Miss Marple wondered why she didn't try. It could be, of course, because Mr. Rafiel would not have liked it, but Miss Marple didn't think Mr. Rafiel would really mind in the least. He was so completely taken up with himself that so long as he was not personally neglected, his secretary might have got herself up like a houri in Paradise without his objecting. Besides, he usually went to bed early and in the evening hours of steel bands and dancing, Esther Walters might easily have—Miss Marple paused to select a word in her mind, at the same time conversing cheerfully about her visit to Jamestown.— Ah yes, *blossomed*. Esther Walters might have blossomed in the evening hours.

She led the conversation gently in the direction of Jackson.

On the subject of Jackson Esther Walters was rather vague.

"He's very competent," she said. "A fully trained masseur."

"I suppose he's been with Mr. Rafiel a long time?"

"Oh no—about nine months, I think——"

"Is he married?" Miss Marple hazarded.

"Married? I don't think so," said Esther slightly surprised. "He's never mentioned it if so——

"No," she added. "Definitely *not* married, I should say." And she showed amusement.

Miss Marple interpreted that by adding to it in her own mind the following sentence—"At any rate he doesn't behave as though he were married."

But then, how many married men there were who behaved as though they weren't married!! Miss Marple could think of a dozen examples!

"He's quite good looking," she said thoughtfully.

"Yes—I suppose he is," said Esther without interest.

Miss Marple considered her thoughtfully. Uninterested in men? The kind of woman, perhaps, who was only interested in one man— A widow, they had said.

She asked—"Have you worked for Mr. Rafiel long?"

"Four or five years. After my husband died, I had to take a job again. I've got a daughter at school and my husband left me very badly off."

"Mr. Rafiel must be a difficult man to work for?" Miss Marple hazarded.

"Not really, when you get to know him. He flies into rages and is very contradictory. I think the real trouble is he gets tired of people. He's had five different valet-attendants in two years. He likes having someone new to bully. But he and I have always got on very well."

"Mr. Jackson seems a very obliging young man?"

"He's very tactful and resourceful," said Esther. "Of course, he's sometimes a little——" She broke off.

Miss Marple considered. "Rather a difficult position sometimes?" she suggested.

"Well, yes. Neither one thing nor the other. However—" she smiled—"I think he manages to have quite a good time."

Miss Marple considered this also. It didn't help her much. She continued her twittering conversation and soon she was hearing a good deal about that nature-loving quartet, the Dysons and the Hillingdons.

"The Hillingdons have been here for the last three or four years at least," said Esther, "but Gregory Dyson has been here much longer than that. He knows the West Indies very well. He came here, originally, I believe, with his first wife. She was delicate and had to go abroad in the winters, or go somewhere warm, at any rate."

"And she died? Or was it divorce?"

"No. She died. Out here, I believe. I don't mean this particular island but one of the West Indies islands. There was some sort of trouble, I believe, some kind of scandal or other. He never talks about her. Somebody else told me about it. They didn't, I gather, get on very well together."

"And then he married this wife. 'Lucky.'" Miss Marple said the word with faint dissatisfaction as if to say 'Really, a most incredible name!'

"I believe she was a relation of his first wife."

"Have they known the Hillingdons a great many years?"

"Oh, I think only since the Hillingdons came out here. Three or four years, not more."

"The Hillingdons seem very pleasant," said Miss Marple. "Quiet, of course."

"Yes. They're both quiet."

"Everyone says they're very devoted to each other," said Miss Marple. The tone of her voice was quite noncommittal but Esther Walters looked at her sharply.

"But you don't think they are?" she said.

"You don't really think so yourself, do you, my dear?"

"Well, I've wondered sometimes . . ."

"Quiet men, like Colonel Hillingdon," said Miss Marple, "are often attracted to flamboyant types." And she added, after a significant pause "Lucky—such a curious name. Do you think Mr. Dyson has any idea of—of what might be going on?"

'Old scandal-monger,' thought Esther Walters. 'really, these old women!' She said rather coldly, "I've no idea."

Miss Marple shifted to another subject. "It's very sad about poor Major Palgrave isn't it?" she said.

Esther Walters agreed, though in a somewhat perfunctory fashion.

"The people I'm really sorry for are the Kendals," she said.

"Yes, I suppose it is really rather unfortunate when something of that kind happens in a hotel."

"People come here, you see, to enjoy themselves, don't they?" said Esther. "To forget about illnesses and deaths and income tax and frozen pipes and all the rest of it. They don't like—" she went on, with a sudden flash of an entirely different manner—"any reminders of mortality."

Miss Marple laid down her knitting. "Now that is very well put, my dear," she said, "very well put indeed. Yes, it is as you say."

"And you see they're quite a young couple," went on Esther Walters. "They only just took over from the Sandersons six months ago and they're terribly worried about whether they're going to succeed or not, because they haven't had much experience."

"And you think this might be really disadvantageous to them?"

"Well, no, I don't, frankly," said Esther Walters. "I don't think people remember anything for more than a day or two, not in this atmosphere of 'we've-all-come-out-here-to-enjoy-ourselves-let's-get-on-with-it.' I think a death just gives them a jolt for about twenty-four hours or so and then they don't think of it again once the funeral is over. Not unless they're reminded of it, that is. I've told Molly so, but of course she is a worrier."

"Mrs. Kendal is a worrier? She always seems so carefree."

"I think a lot of that is put on," said Esther slowly. "Actually, I think she's one of those anxious sort of people who can't help worrying all the time that things *may* go wrong."

"I should have thought *he* worried more than she did."

"No, I don't think so. I think she's the worrier and he worries because she worries if you know what I mean."

"That is interesting," said Miss Marple.

"I think Molly wants desperately to try and appear very gay and to be enjoying herself. She works at it very hard but the effort exhausts her. Then she has these odd fits of depression. She's not—well not really well-balanced."

"Poor child," said Miss Marple. "There certainly are people like that, and very often outsiders don't suspect it."

"No, they put on such a good show, don't they? However," Esther added, "I don't think Molly has really anything to worry about in this case. I mean, people are dying of coronary thrombosis or cerebral hemorrhage or things of that kind all the time nowadays. Far more than they used to, as far as I can see. It's only food poisoning or typhoid or something like that, that makes people get het up."

"Major Palgrave never mentioned to *me* that he had high blood pressure," said Miss Marple. "Did he to you?"

"He said so to somebody—I don't know who—It may have been to Mr. Rafiel. I know Mr. Rafiel says just the opposite—but then he's like that! Certainly Jackson mentioned it to me once. He said the Major ought to be more careful over the alcohol he took."

"I see," said Miss Marple, thoughtfully. She went on: "I expect you found him rather a boring old man? He told a lot of stories and I expect repeated himself a good deal."

"That's the worst of it," said Esther. "You do hear the same story again and again unless you can manage to be quick enough to fend it off."

"Of course *I* didn't mind so much," said Miss Marple, "because I'm used to that sort of thing. If I get stories told to me rather often, I don't really mind hearing them again because I've usually forgotten them."

"There is that," said Esther and laughed cheerfully.

"There was one story he was very fond of telling," said Miss Marple, "about a murder. I expect he told you that, didn't he?"

Esther Walters opened her handbag and started searching through it. She drew out her lipstick saying, "I thought I'd lost it." Then she asked, "I beg your pardon, what did you say?"

"I asked if Major Palgrave told you his favorite murder story?"

"I believe he did, now I come to think of it. Something about someone who gassed themselves, wasn't it? Only really it was the *wife* who gassed him. I mean she'd given him a sedative of some kind and then stuck his head in the gas oven. Was that it?"

"I don't think that was exactly it," said Miss Marple. She looked at Esther Walters thoughtfully.

"He told such a lot of stories," said Esther Walters, apologetically, "and as I said, one didn't always listen."

"He had a snapshot," said Miss Marple, "that he used to show people."

"I believe he did . . . I can't remember what it was now. Did he show it to you?"

"No," said Miss Marple. "He didn't show it to me. We were interrupted——"

CHAPTER NINE
Miss Prescott and Others

"THE STORY *I* heard," began Miss Prescott, lowering her voice, and looking carefully around.

Miss Marple drew her chair a little closer. It had been some time before she had been able to get together with Miss Prescott for a heart-to-heart chat. This was owing to the fact that clergymen are very strong family men so that Miss Prescott was nearly always accompanied by her brother, and there was no doubt that Miss Marple and Miss Prescott found it less easy to take their back hair down in a good gossip when the jovial Canon was of their company.

"It seems," said Miss Prescott, "though of course I don't want to talk any scandal and I really know *nothing* about it——"

"Oh, I *quite* understand," said Miss Marple.

"It seems there was some scandal when his first wife was still alive! Apparently this woman, Lucky—such a name!—who I think was a cousin of his first wife, came out here and joined them and I think did some work with him on flowers or butterflies or whatever it was. And people talked a lot because they got on so well together—if you know what I mean."

"People do *notice* things so much, don't they," said Miss Marple.

"And then of course, when his wife died rather suddenly——"

"She died here, on this island?"

"No. No, I think they were in Martinique or Tobago at the time."

"I see."

"But I gathered from some other people who were there at the time, and who came on here and talked about things, that the doctor wasn't very satisfied."

"Indeed," said Miss Marple, with interest.

"It was only *gossip*," of course, "but—well, Mr. Dyson certainly married again *very quickly*." She lowered her voice again. "Only a *month* I believe."

"Only a month," said Miss Marple.

The two women looked at each other. "It seemed—unfeeling," said Miss Prescott.

"Yes," said Miss Marple. "It certainly did." She added delicately, "Was there—any money?"

"I don't really know. He makes his little joke—perhaps you've heard him—about this wife being his 'lucky piece'——"

"Yes, I've heard him," said Miss Marple.

"And some people think that means that he was lucky to marry a rich wife. Though, of course," said Miss Prescott with the air of one being entirely fair, "she's very good-looking too, if you care for that type. And I think myself that it was the *first* wife who had the money."

"Are the Hillingdons well off?"

"Well, I think they're *well off*. I don't mean fabulously rich, I just mean well off. They have two boys at Public School and a very nice place in England, I believe, and they travel most of the winter."

The Canon appearing at this moment to suggest a brisk walk, Miss Prescott rose to join her brother. Miss Marple remained sitting there.

A few minutes later Gregory Dyson passed her striding along towards the hotel. He waved a cheerful hand as he passed.

"Penny for your thoughts," he called out.

Miss Marple smiled gently, wondering how he would have reacted if she had replied:

"I was wondering if you were a murderer."

It really seemed most probable that he was. It all fitted in so nicely— This story about the death of the first Mrs. Dyson— Major Palgrave had certainly been talking about a wife killer—with special reference to the "Brides in the bath Case."

Yes—it fitted—the only objection was that it fitted almost too well. But Miss Marple reproved herself for this thought— Who was she to demand Murders Made to Measure?

A voice made her jump—a somewhat raucous one.

"Seen Greg any place, Miss—er——"

Lucky, Miss Marple thought, was not in a good temper.

"He passed by just now—going towards the hotel."

"I'll bet!" Lucky uttered an irritated ejaculation and hurried on.

"Forty, if she's a day, and looks it this morning," thought Miss Marple.

Pity invaded her—Pity for the Luckys of the world—who were so vulnerable to Time—

At the sound of a noise behind her, she turned her chair round—

Mr. Rafiel, supported by Jackson, was making his morning appearance and coming out of his bungalow—

Jackson settled his employer in his wheel chair and fussed round him. Mr. Rafiel waved his attendant away impatiently and Jackson went off in the direction of the hotel.

Miss Marple lost no time—Mr. Rafiel was never left alone for long—Probably Esther Walters would come and join him. Miss Marple wanted a word alone with Mr. Rafiel and now, she thought, was her chance. She would have to be quick about what she wanted to say. There could be no leading up to things. Mr. Rafiel was not a man who cared for the idle twittering conversation of old ladies. He would probably retreat again into his bungalow, definitely regarding himself the victim of persecution. Miss Marple decided to plump for downrightness.

She made her way to where he was sitting, drew up a chair, sat down, and said:

"I want to ask you something, Mr. Rafiel."

"All right, all right," said Mr. Rafiel, "let's have it. What do you want—a subscription, I suppose? Missions in Africa or repairing a church, something of that kind?"

"Yes," said Miss Marple. "I am interested in several objects of that nature, and I shall be delighted if you will give me a subscription for them. But that wasn't actually what I was going to ask you. What I was going to ask you was if Major Palgrave ever told you a story about a murder."

"Oho," said Mr. Rafiel. "So he told it to you too, did he? And I suppose you fell for it, hook line and sinker."

"I didn't really know what to think," said Miss Marple. "What exactly did he tell you?"

"He prattled on," said Mr. Rafiel, "about a lovely creature, Lucrezia Borgia reincarnated. Beautiful, young, golden-haired, everything."

"Oh," said Miss Marple slightly taken aback, "and who did she murder?"

"Her husband, of course," said Mr. Rafiel, "who do you think?"

"Poison?"

"No, I think she gave him a sleeping draught and then stuck him in a gas oven. Resourceful female. Then she said it was suicide. She got off quite lightly. Diminished responsibility or something. That's what it's called nowadays if you're a good-looking woman, or some miserable young hooligan whose mother's been too fond of him. Bah!"

"Did the Major show you a snapshot?"

"What—a snapshot of the woman? No. Why should he?"

"Oh——" said Miss Marple.

She sat there, rather taken aback. Apparently Major Palgrave spent his life telling people not only about tigers he had shot and elephants he had hunted but also about murderers he had met. Perhaps he had a whole repertoire of murder stories. One had to face it— She was startled by Mr. Rafiel suddenly giving a roar of "Jackson!" There was no response.

"Shall I find him for you?" said Miss Marple rising.

"You won't find him. Tom-catting somewhere, that's what he does. No good, that fellow. Bad character. But he suits me all right."

"I'll go and look for him," said Miss Marple.

Miss Marple found Jackson on the far side of the hotel terrace having a drink with Tim Kendal.

"Mr. Rafiel is asking for you," she said.

Jackson made an expressive grimace, drained his glass, and rose to his feet.

"Here we go again," he said. "No peace for the wicked— Two telephone calls and a special diet order—I thought that might give me a quarter of an hour's alibi— Apparently not! Thank you, Miss Marple. Thanks for the drink, Mr. Kendal."

He strode away.

"I feel sorry for that chap," said Tim. "I have to stand him a drink now and then, just to cheer him up— Can I offer you something, Miss Marple— How about fresh lime? I know you're fond of that."

"Not just now, thank you— I suppose looking after someone like Mr. Rafiel must always be rather exacting. Invalids are frequently difficult——"

"I didn't mean only that— It's very well paid and you expect to put up with a good deal of crotchetiness—old Rafiel's not really a bad sort. I meant more that——" he hesitated.

Miss Marple looked inquiring.

"Well—how shall I put it—it's difficult for him socially. People are so damned snobbish—there's no one here of his class. He's better than a servant—and below the average visitor—or they think he is. Rather like the Victorian governess. Even the secretary woman, Mrs. Walters—feels she's a cut above him. Makes things difficult." Tim paused, then said with feeling: "It's really awful the amount of social problems there are in a place like this."

Dr. Graham passed them— He had a book in his hand. He went and sat at a table overlooking the sea.

"Dr. Graham looks rather worried," remarked Miss Marple.

"Oh! We're all worried."

"You too? Because of Major Palgrave's death?"

"I've left off worrying about that. People seem to have forgotten it—taken it in their stride. No—it's my wife—Molly— Do you know anything about dreams?"

"Dreams?" Miss Marple was surprised.

"Yes—bad dreams—nightmares, I suppose. Oh, we all get that sort of thing sometimes. But Molly—she seems to have them nearly all the time. They frighten her. Is there anything one can do about them? Take for them? She's got some sleeping pills, but she says they make it worse—she struggles to wake up and can't."

"What are the dreams about?"

"Oh, something or someone chasing her— Or watching her and spying on her—she can't shake off the feeling even when she's awake."

"Surely a doctor——"

"She's got a thing against doctors. Won't hear of it— Oh well—I daresay it will all pass off— But we were so happy. It was all such fun— And now, just lately— Perhaps old Palgrave's death upset her. She seems like a different person since . . ."

He got up.

"Must get on with the daily chores—are you sure you won't have that fresh lime?"

Miss Marple shook her head.

She sat there, thinking. Her face was grave and anxious.

She glanced over at Dr. Graham.

Presently she came to a decision.

She rose and went across to his table.

"I have got to apologize to you, Dr. Graham," she said.

"Indeed?" The doctor looked at her in kindly surprise. He pulled forward a chair and she sat down.

"I am afraid I have done the most disgraceful thing," said Miss Marple. "I told you, Dr. Graham, a deliberate lie."

She looked at him apprehensively.

Dr. Graham did not look at all shattered, but he did look a little surprised.

"Really?" he said. "Ah well, you mustn't let that worry you too much."

What had the dear old thing been telling lies about, he wondered; her age? Though as far as he could remember she hadn't mentioned her age.

"Well, let's hear about it," he said, since she clearly wished to confess.

"You remember my speaking to you about a snapshot of my nephew, one that I showed to Major Palgrave, and that he didn't give back to me?"

"Yes, yes, of course I remember. Sorry we couldn't find it for you."

"There wasn't any such thing," said Miss Marple, in a small, frightened voice.

"I beg your pardon?"

"There wasn't any such thing. I made up that story, I'm afraid."

"You made it up?" Dr. Graham looked slightly annoyed. "Why?"

Miss Marple told him. She told him quite clearly, without twittering. She told him about Major Palgrave's murder story and how he'd been about to show her this particular snapshot and his sudden confusion and then she went on to her own anxiety and to her final decision to try somehow to obtain a view of it.

"And really, I couldn't see *any* way of doing so without telling you something that was quite untrue," she said, "I do hope you will forgive me."

"You thought that what he had been about to show you was a picture of a murderer?"

"That's what he said it was," said Miss Marple. "At least he said it was given him by this acquaintance who had told him the story about a man who was a murderer."

"Yes, yes. And—excuse me—you believed him?"

"I don't know if I really believed him or not at the time," said Miss Marple. "But then, you see, the next day he died."

"Yes," said Dr. Graham, struck suddenly by the clarity of that one sentence. *The next day he died. . . .*

"And the snapshot had disappeared."

Dr. Graham looked at her. He didn't know quite what to say.

"Excuse me, Miss Marple," he said at last, "but is what you're telling me now—is it really true this time?"

"I don't wonder your doubting me," said Miss Marple. "I should, in your place. Yes, it is true what I am telling you now, but I quite realize that you have only my word for it. Still, even if you don't believe me, I thought I ought to tell you."

"Why?"

"I realized that you ought to have the fullest information possible— In case——"

"In case what?"

"In case you decided to take any steps about it."

CHAPTER TEN
A Decision in Jamestown

DR. GRAHAM WAS in Jamestown, in the Administrator's office; sitting at a table opposite his friend Daventry, a grave young man of thirty-five.

"You sounded rather mysterious on the phone, Graham," said Daventry. "Anything special the matter?"

"I don't know," said Dr. Graham, "but I'm worried."

Daventry looked at the other's face, then he nodded as drinks were brought in. He spoke lightly of a fishing expedition he had made lately. Then when the servant had gone away, he sat back in his chair and looked at the other man.

"Now then," he said, "let's have it."

Dr. Graham recounted the facts that had worried him. Daventry gave a slow long whistle.

"I see. You think maybe there's something funny about old Palgrave's death? You're no longer sure that it was just natural causes? Who certified the death? Robertson, I suppose. He didn't have any doubts, did he?"

"No, but I think he may have been influenced in giving the certificate by the fact of the Serenite tablets in the bathroom. He asked me if Palgrave had mentioned that he suffered from hypertension, and I said No, I'd never had any medical conversation with him myself, but apparently he had talked about it to other people in the hotel. The whole thing—the bottle of tablets, and what Palgrave had said to people—it all fitted in—no earthly reason to suspect anything else. It was a perfectly natural inference to make—but I think now it may not have been correct. If it had been my business to give the certificate, I'd have given it without a second thought. The appearances are quite consistent with his having died from that cause. I'd never have thought about it since if it hadn't been for the odd disappearance of that snapshot . . ."

"But look here, Graham," said Daventry, "if you will allow me to say so, aren't you relying a little too much on a rather fanciful story told you by an elderly lady. You know what these elderly ladies are like. They magnify some small detail and work the whole thing up."

"Yes, I know," said Dr. Graham, unhappily. "I know that. I've said to myself that it may be so, that it probably *is* so. But I can't quite convince myself. She was so very clear and detailed in her statement."

"The whole thing seems wildly improbable to me," said Daventry. "Some old lady tells a story about a snapshot that ought not to be there—no I'm getting mixed myself—I mean the other way about don't I?—but the only thing you've really got to go on is that a chambermaid says that a bottle of pills which the authorities had relied on for evidence, wasn't in the Major's room the day before his death. But there are a hundred explanations for that. He might always have carried those pills about in his pocket."

"It's possible, I suppose, yes."

"Or the chambermaid may have made a mistake and she simply hadn't noticed them before——"

"That's possible, too."

"Well, then."

Graham said slowly:

"The girl was very positive."

"Well, the St. Honoré people are very excitable, you know. Emotional. Work themselves up easily. Are you thinking that she knows—a little more than she has said?"

"I think it might be so," said Dr. Graham slowly.

"You'd better try and get it out of her, if so. We don't want to make an unnecessary fuss—unless we've something definite to go on. If he didn't die of blood pressure, what do you think it was?"

"There are too many things it might be nowadays," said Dr. Graham.

"You mean things that don't leave recognizable traces?"

"Not everyone," said Dr. Graham dryly, "is so considerate as to use arsenic."

"Now let's get things quite clear—what's the suggestion? That a bottle of pills was substituted for the real ones? And that Major Palgrave was poisoned in that way?"

"No—it's not like that. That's what the girl—Victoria Something thinks— But she's got it all wrong— If it was decided to get rid of the Major—quickly—he would have been given something—most likely in a drink of some kind. Then to make it appear a natural death, a bottle of the tablets prescribed to relieve blood pressure was put in his room. And the rumor was put about that he suffered from high blood pressure."

"Who put the rumor about?"

"I've tried to find out—with no success— It's been too cleverly done. A says 'I *think* B told me'—B, asked, says 'No, I didn't say so but I do remember C mentioning it one day.' C says 'Several people talked about it—one of them, I think, was A.' And there we are, back again."

"Someone was clever?"

"Yes. As soon as the death was discovered, everybody seemed to be talking about the Major's high blood pressure and repeating round what other people had said."

"Wouldn't it have been simpler just to poison him and let it go at that?"

"No. That might have meant inquiry—possibly an autopsy— This way, a doctor would accept the death and give a certificate—as he did."

"What do you want me to do? Go to the C.I.D.? Suggest they dig the chap up? It'd make a lot of stink——"

"It could be kept quite quiet."

"Could it? In St. Honoré? Think again! The grapevine would be on to it before it had happened. All the same," Daventry sighed— "I suppose we'll have to do something. But if you ask me, it's all a mare's nest!"

"I devoutly hope it is," said Dr. Graham.

CHAPTER ELEVEN
Evening at the Golden Palm

I

MOLLY REARRANGED A few of the table decorations in the dining-room, removed an extra knife, straightened a fork, reset a glass or two, stood back to look at the effect and then walked out on to the terrace outside. There was no one about just at present and she strolled to the far corner and stood by the balustrade. Soon another evening would begin. Chattering, talking, drinking, all so gay and carefree, the sort of life she had longed for and, up to a few days ago, had enjoyed so much. Now even Tim seemed anxious and worried. Natural, perhaps, that he should worry a little. It was important that this venture of theirs should turn out all right. After all, he had sunk all he had in it.

But that, thought Molly, is not *really* what's worrying him. It's *me*. But I don't see, said Molly to herself, why he should worry about *me*. Because he did worry about her. That she was quite sure of. The questions he put, the quick nervous glance he shot at her from time to time. But why? thought Molly. "I've been very careful," she summed up things in her mind. She didn't understand it really herself. She couldn't remember when it had begun. She wasn't even very sure what it was. She'd begun to be frightened of people. She didn't know why. What could they do to her? What should they want to do to her?

She nodded her head, then started violently as a hand touched her arm. She spun round to find Gregory Dyson, slightly taken aback, looking apologetic.

"Ever so sorry. Did I startle you, little girl?"

Molly hated being called 'little girl.' She said quickly and brightly: "I didn't hear you coming, Mr. Dyson, so it made me jump."

"Mr. Dyson? We're very formal tonight. Aren't we all one great happy family here? Ed and me and Lucky and Evelyn and you and Tim and Esther Walters and old Rafiel. All the lot of us one happy family."

'He's had plenty to drink already,' thought Molly. She smiled at him pleasantly.

"Oh! I come over the heavy hostess sometimes," she said, lightly. "Tim and I think it's more polite not to be too handy with Christian names."

"Aw! we don't want any of that stuffed-shirt business. Now then, Molly my lovely, have a drink with me."

"Ask me later," said Molly. "I have a few things to get on with."

"Now don't run away." His arm fastened round her arm. "You're a lovely girl, Molly. I hope Tim appreciates his good luck."

"Oh, I see to it that he does," said Molly cheerfully.

"I could go for you, you know, in a big way." He leered at her—"though I wouldn't let my wife hear me say so."

"Did you have a good trip this afternoon?"

"I suppose so. Between you and me I get a bit fed up sometimes. You can get tired of the birds and butterflies. What say you and I go for a little picnic on our own one day?"

"We'll have to see about that," said Molly gaily. "I'll be looking forward to it."

With a light laugh she escaped, and went back into the bar.

"Hallo, Molly," said Tim, "you seem in a hurry. Who's that you've been with out there?"

He peered out.

"Gregory Dyson."

"What does he want?"

"Wanted to make a pass at me," said Molly.

"Blast him," said Tim.

"Don't worry," said Molly. "I can do all the blasting necessary."

Tim started to answer her, caught sight of Fernando and went over to him shouting out some directions. Molly slipped away through the kitchen, out through the kitchen door and down the steps to the beach.

Gregory Dyson swore under his breath. Then he walked slowly back in the direction of his bungalow. He had nearly got there when a voice spoke to him from the shadow of one of the bushes. He turned his head, startled. In the gathering dusk he thought for a moment that it was a ghostly figure that stood there. Then he laughed. It had looked like a faceless apparition but that was because, though the dress was white, the face was black.

Victoria stepped out of the bushes on to the path.

"Mr. Dyson, please?"

"Yes. What is it?"

Ashamed of being startled, he spoke with a touch of impatience.

"I brought you this, sir." She held out her hand. In it was a bottle of tablets. "This belongs to you, doesn't it. Yes?"

"Oh, my bottle of Serenite tablets. Yes, of course. Where did you find it?"

"I found it where it had been put. In the gentleman's room."

"What do you mean—in the gentleman's room?"

"The gentleman who is dead," she added gravely. "I do not think he sleeps very well in his grave."

"Why the devil not?" asked Dyson.

Victoria stood looking at him.

"I still don't know what you're talking about. You mean you found this bottle of tablets in Major Palgrave's bungalow?"

"That is right, yes. After the doctor and the Jamestown people go away, they give me all the things in his bathroom to throw away. The toothpaste and the lotions, and all the other things—including this."

"Well, why didn't you throw it away?"

"Because these are yours. You missed them. You remember, you asked about them?"

"Yes—well—yes, I did. I—I thought I'd just mislaid them."

"No, you did not mislay them. They were taken from your bungalow and put in Major Palgrave's bungalow."

"How do you know?" He spoke roughly.

"I know. I saw." She smiled at him in a sudden flash of white teeth. "Someone put them in the dead gentleman's room. Now I give them back to you."

"Here—wait. What do you mean? What—who did you see?"

She hurried away, back into the darkness of the bushes. Greg made as to move after her and then stopped. He stood stroking his chin.

"What's the matter, Greg? Seen a ghost?" asked Mrs. Dyson, as she came along the path from their bungalow.

"Thought I had for a minute or two."

"Who was that you were talking to?"

"The colored girl who does our place. Victoria, her name is, isn't it?"

"What did she want? Making a pass at you?"

"Don't be stupid, Lucky. That girl's got some idiotic idea into her head."

"Idea about what?"

"You remember I couldn't find my Serenite the other day?"

"You said you couldn't."

"What do you mean 'I said I couldn't'?"

"Oh, for heck's sake, have you got to take me up on everything?"

"I'm sorry," said Greg. "Everybody goes about being so damn' mysterious." He held out his hand with the bottle in it. "That girl brought them back to me."

"Had she pinched them?"

"No. She—found them somewhere I think."

"Well, what of it? What's the mystery about?"

"Oh nothing," said Greg. "She just riled me, that's all."

"Look here, Greg, what is this stuff all about? Come along and have a drink before dinner."

II

Molly had gone down to the beach. She pulled out one of the old basket chairs, one of the more rickety ones that were seldom used. She sat in it for a while looking at the sea, then suddenly she dropped her head in her hands and burst into tears. She sat there sobbing unrestrainedly for some time. Then she heard a rustle close by her and glanced up sharply to see Mrs. Hillingdon looking down at her.

"Hallo, Evelyn, I didn't hear you. I—I'm sorry."

"What's the matter, child?" said Evelyn. "Something gone wrong?" She pulled another chair forward and sat down. "Tell me."

"There's nothing wrong," said Molly. "Nothing at all."

"Of course there is. You wouldn't sit and cry here for nothing. Can't you tell me? Is it—some trouble between you and Tim?"

"Oh *no*."

"I'm glad of that. You always look so happy together."

"Not more than you do," said Molly. "Tim and I always think how wonderful it is that you and Edward should seem so happy together after being married so many years."

"Oh, that," said Evelyn. Her voice was sharp as she spoke but Molly hardly noticed.

"People bicker so," she said, "and have such rows. Even if they're quite fond of each other they still seem to have rows and not to mind a bit whether they have them in public or not."

"Some people like living that way," said Evelyn. "It doesn't really mean anything."

"Well, I think it's horrid," said Molly.

"So do I, really," said Evelyn.

"But to see you and Edward——"

"Oh it's no good, Molly. I can't let you go on thinking things of that kind. Edward and I—" she paused. "If you want to know the truth, we've hardly said a word to each other in private for the last three years."

"What!" Molly stared at her, appalled. "I—I can't believe it."

"Oh, we both put up quite a good show," said Evelyn. "We're neither of us the kind that like having rows in public. And anyway there's nothing really to have a row about."

"But what went wrong?" asked Molly.

"Just the usual."

"What do you mean by the usual? Another——"

"Yes, another woman in the case, and I don't suppose it will be difficult for you to guess who the woman is."

"Do you mean Mrs. Dyson—Lucky?"

Evelyn nodded.

"I know they always flirt together a lot," said Molly, "but I thought that was just . . ."

"Just high spirits?" said Evelyn. "Nothing behind it?"

"But why—" Molly paused and tried again. "But didn't you—oh I mean, well I suppose I oughtn't to ask."

"Ask anything you like," said Evelyn. "I'm tired of never saying a word, tired of being a well-bred happy wife. Edward just lost his head completely about Lucky. He was stupid enough to come and tell me about it. It made him feel better I suppose. Truthful. Honorable. All that sort of stuff. It didn't occur to him to think that it wouldn't make *me* feel better."

"Did he want to leave you?"

Evelyn shook her head. "We've got two children, you know," she said. "Children whom we're both very fond of. They're at school in England. We didn't want to break up the home. And then of course, Lucky didn't want a divorce either. Greg's a very rich man. His first wife left a lot of money. So we agreed to live and let live—Edward and Lucky in happy immorality,

Greg in blissful ignorance, and Edward and I just good friends." She spoke with scalding bitterness.

"How—how can you bear it?"

"One gets used to anything. But sometimes——"

"Yes?" said Molly.

"Sometimes I'd like to kill that woman."

The passion behind her voice startled Molly.

"Don't let's talk any more about me," said Evelyn. "Let's talk about you. I want to know what's the matter."

Molly was silent for some moments and then she said, "It's only—it's only that I think there's something wrong about me."

"Wrong? What do you mean?"

Molly shook her head unhappily. "I'm frightened," she said. "I'm terribly frightened."

"Frightened of what?"

"Everything," said Molly. "It's—growing on me. Voices in the bushes, footsteps—or things that people say. As though someone were watching me all the time, spying on me. Somebody hates me. That's what I keep feeling. Somebody hates me."

"My dear child." Evelyn was shocked and startled. "How long has this been going on?"

"I don't know. It came—it started by degrees. And there have been other things too."

"What sort of things?"

"There are times," said Molly slowly, "that I can't account for, that I can't remember."

"Do you mean you have blackouts—that sort of thing."

"I suppose so. I mean sometimes it's—oh, say it's five o'clock—and I can't remember anything since about half past one or two."

"Oh my dear, but that's just that you've been asleep. Had a doze."

"No," said Molly, "it's not like that at all. Because you see, at the end of the time it's not as though I'd just dozed off. I'm in a different *place*. Sometimes I'm wearing different clothes and sometimes I seem to have been doing things—even saying things to people, talking to someone, and not remembering that I've done so."

Evelyn looked shocked. "But, Molly, my dear, if this is so, then you ought to see a doctor."

"I won't see a doctor! I don't want to. I wouldn't go *near* a doctor."

Evelyn looked sharply down into her face, then she took the girl's hand in hers.

"You may be frightening yourself for nothing, Molly. You know there are all kinds of nervous disorders that aren't really serious at all. A doctor would soon reassure you."

"He mightn't. He might say that there was something really wrong with me."

"Why should there be anything wrong with you?"

"Because—" Molly spoke and then was silent, "—no reason, I suppose," she said.

"Couldn't your family—haven't you any family, any mother or sisters or someone who could come out here?"

"I don't get on with my mother. I never have. I've got sisters. They're married but I suppose—I suppose they could come if I wanted them. But I don't want them. I don't want anyone—anyone except Tim."

"Does Tim know about this? Have you told him?"

"Not really," said Molly. "But he's anxious about me and he watches me. It's as though he were trying to—to help me or to shield me. But if he does that it means I want shielding, doesn't it?"

"I think a lot of it may be imagination but I still think you ought to see a doctor."

"Old Dr. Graham? He wouldn't be any good."

"There are other doctors on the island."

"It's all right, really," said Molly. "I just—mustn't think of it. I expect, as you say, it's all imagination. Good gracious, it's getting frightfully late. I ought to be on duty now in the dining-room. I—I must go back."

She looked sharply and almost offensively at Evelyn Hillingdon, and then hurried off. Evelyn stared after her.

CHAPTER TWELVE
Old Sins Cast Long Shadows

I

"I THINK AS I am on to something, man."

"What's that you say, Victoria?"

"I think I'm on to something. It may mean money. Big money."

"Now look, girl, you be careful, you'll not tangle yourself up in something. Maybe I'd better tackle what it is."

Victoria laughed, a deep rich chuckle.

"You wait and see," she said. "I know how to play this hand. It's money, man, it's big money. Something I see, and something I guess. I think I guess right."

And again the soft rich chuckle rolled out on the night.

II

"Evelyn . . ."

"Yes?"

Evelyn Hillingdon spoke mechanically, without interest. She did not look at her husband.

"Evelyn, would you mind if we chucked all this and went home to England?"

She had been combing her short dark hair. Now her hands came down from her head sharply. She turned towards him.

"You mean—but we've only just come. We've not been out here in the islands for more than three weeks."

"I know. But—would you mind?"

Her eyes searched him incredulously.

"You really want to go back to England. Back home?"

"Yes."

"Leaving—Lucky."

He winced.

"You've known all the time, I suppose, that—that it was still going on?"

"Pretty well. Yes."

"You've never said anything."

"Why should I? We had the whole thing out years ago. Neither of us wanted to make a break. So we agreed to go our separate ways—but keep up the show in public." Then she added before he could speak, "But why are you so set on going back to England *now?*"

"Because I'm at breaking point. I can't stick it any longer, Evelyn. I can't." The quiet Edward Hillingdon was transformed. His hands shook, he swallowed, his calm unemotional face seemed distorted by pain.

"For God's sake, Edward, what's the *matter?*"

"Nothing's the matter except that I want to get out of here——"

"You fell wildly in love with Lucky. And now you've got over it. Is that what you're telling me?"

"Yes. I don't suppose you'll ever feel the same."

"Oh let's not go into that now! I want to understand what's upsetting you so much, Edward."

"I'm not particularly upset."

"But you are. Why?"

"Isn't it obvious?"

"No, it isn't," said Evelyn. "Let's put it in plain concrete terms. You've had an affair with a woman. That happens often enough. And now it's over. Or isn't it over? Perhaps it isn't over on *her* side. Is that it? Does Greg know about it? I've often wondered."

"I don't know," said Edward. "He's never said anything. He always seems friendly enough."

"Men can be extraordinarily obtuse," said Evelyn thoughtfully. "Or else— Perhaps Greg has got an outside interest of his own!"

"He's made passes at you, hasn't he?" said Edward. "Answer me—I know he has——"

"Oh yes," said Evelyn, carelessly, "but he makes passes at everybody. That's just Greg. It doesn't ever really mean much, I imagine. It's just part of the Greg he-man act."

"Do you care for him, Evelyn? I'd rather know the truth."

"Greg? I'm quite fond of him—he amuses me. He's a good friend."

"And that's all? I wish I could believe you."

"I can't really see how it can possibly matter to you," said Evelyn dryly.

"I suppose I deserve that."

Evelyn walked to the window, looked out across the veranda and came back again.

"I wish you would tell me what's *really* upsetting you, Edward."

"I've told you."

"I wonder."

"You can't understand, I suppose, how extraordinary a temporary madness of this kind can seem to you after you've got over it."

"I can try, I suppose. But what's worrying me now is that Lucky seems to have got some kind of stranglehold upon you. She's not just a discarded mistress. She's a tigress with claws. You *must* tell me the truth, Edward. It's the only way if you want me to stand by you."

Edward said in a low voice: "If I don't get away from her soon—I shall kill her."

"Kill Lucky? Why?"

"Because of what she made me do . . ."

"What did she make you do?"

"I helped her to commit a murder——"

The words were out— There was silence— Evelyn stared at him.

"Do you know what you are saying?"

"Yes. I didn't know I was doing it. There were things she asked me to get for her—at the chemist's. I didn't know—I hadn't the least idea what she wanted them for— She got me to copy out a prescription she had . . ."

"When was this?"

"Four years ago. When we were in Martinique. When—when Greg's wife——"

"You mean Greg's first wife—Gail? You mean Lucky poisoned her?"

"Yes—and I helped her. When I realized——"

Evelyn interrupted him.

"When you realized what had happened, Lucky pointed out to you that *you* had written out the prescription, that *you* had got the drugs, that you and she were in it together? Is that right?"

"Yes. She said she had done it out of pity—that Gail was suffering—that she had begged Lucky to get something that would end it all."

"A mercy killing! I see. And you believed *that?*"

Edward Hillingdon was silent a moment—then he said:

"No—I didn't really—not deep down—I accepted it because I *wanted* to believe it—because I was infatuated with Lucky."

"And afterwards—when she married Greg—did you still believe it?"

"I'd made myself believe it by then."

"And Greg—how much did he know about it all?"

"Nothing at all."

"That I find hard to believe!"

Edward Hillingdon broke out—

"Evelyn, I've *got* to get free of it all! That woman taunts me still with what I did. She knows I don't care for her any longer. Care for her?— I've come to hate her— But she makes me feel I'm tied to her—by the thing we did together——"

Evelyn walked up and down the room—then she stopped and faced him.

"The entire trouble with you, Edward, is that you are ridiculously sensitive—and also incredibly suggestible. That devil of a woman has got you just where she wants you by playing on your sense of guilt— And I'll tell you this in plain Bible terms, the guilt that weighs on you is the guilt of adultery—not murder— You were guilt-stricken about your affair with Lucky—and then she made a cat's-paw of you for her murder scheme, and managed to make you feel you shared her guilt. You *don't*."

"Evelyn" . . . He stepped towards her—

She stepped back a minute—and looked at him searchingly.

"Is this all true, Edward— *Is* it? Or are you making it up?"

"Evelyn! Why on earth should I do such a thing?"

"I don't know," said Evelyn Hillingdon slowly—"It's just perhaps— because I find it hard to trust—anybody. And because— Oh! I don't know— I've got, I suppose, so that I don't know the truth when I hear it."

"Let's chuck all this— Go back home to England."

"Yes— We will— But not now."

"Why not?"

"We must carry on as usual—just for the present. It's important. Do you understand, Edward? Don't let Lucky have an inkling of what we're up to——"

CHAPTER THIRTEEN
Exit Victoria Johnson

THE EVENING WAS drawing to a close. The steel band was at last relaxing its efforts. Tim stood by the dining-room looking over the terrace. He extinguished a few lights on tables that had been vacated.

A voice spoke behind him. "Tim, can I speak to you a moment?"

Tim Kendal started.

"Hallo, Evelyn, is there anything I can do for you?"

Evelyn looked round.

"Come to this table here, and let's sit down a minute."

She led the way to a table at the extreme end of the terrace. There were no other people near them.

"Tim, you must forgive me talking to you, but I'm worried about Molly."

His face changed at once.

"What about Molly?" he said stiffly.

"I don't think she's awfully well. She seems upset."

"Things do seem to upset her rather easily just lately."

"She ought to see a doctor, I think."

"Yes, I know, but she doesn't want to. She'd hate it."

"Why?"

"Eh? What d'you mean?"

"I said why? Why should she hate seeing a doctor?"

"Well," said Tim rather vaguely, "People do sometimes, you know. It's—well, it sort of makes them feel frightened about themselves."

"You're worried about her yourself, aren't you, Tim?"

"Yes. Yes, I am rather."

"Isn't there anyone of her family who could come out here to be with her?"

"No. That'd make things worse, far worse."

"What *is* the trouble—with her family, I mean?"

"Oh, just one of those things. I suppose she's just highly strung and—she didn't get on with them—particularly her mother. She never has. They're—they're rather an odd family in some ways and she cut loose from them. Good thing she did, I think."

Evelyn said hesitantly—"She seems to have had blackouts, from what she told me, and to be frightened of people. Almost like persecution mania."

"Don't say that," said Tim angrily. "Persecution mania! People always say that about people. Just because she—well—maybe she's a bit nervy. Coming out here to the West Indies. All the dark faces. You know, people are rather queer, sometimes, about the West Indies and colored people."

"Surely not girls like Molly?"

"Oh, how does one know the things people are frightened of? There are people who can't be in the room with cats. And other people who faint if a caterpillar drops on them."

"I hate suggesting it—but don't you think perhaps she ought to see a—well, a psychiatrist?"

"*No!*" said Tim explosively. "I won't have people like that monkeying about with her. I don't believe in them. They make people worse. If her mother had left psychiatrists alone . . ."

"So there *was* trouble of that kind in her family—was there? I mean a history of—" she chose the word carefully—"instability."

"I don't want to talk about it— I took her away from it all and she was all right, quite all right. She has just got into a nervous state. . . . But these things aren't hereditary. Everybody knows that nowadays. It's an exploded idea. Molly's perfectly sane. It's just that—oh! I believe it was that wretched old Palgrave dying that started it all off."

"I see," said Evelyn thoughtfully. "But there was nothing really to worry anyone in Major Palgrave's death, was there?"

"No of course there wasn't. But it's a kind of shock when somebody dies suddenly."

He looked so desperate and defeated that Evelyn's heart smote her. She put her hand on his arm.

"Well, I hope you know what you're doing, Tim, but if I could help in any way—I mean if I could go with Molly to New York—I could fly with her there or Miami or somewhere where she could get really first-class medical advice."

"It's very good of you, Evelyn, but Molly's all right. She's getting over it, anyway."

Evelyn shook her head in doubt. She turned away slowly and looked along the line of the terrace. Most people had gone by now to their bungalows. Evelyn was walking toward her table to see if she'd left anything behind there, when she heard Tim give an exclamation. She looked up sharply. He was staring towards the steps at the end of the terrace and she followed his gaze. Then she too caught her breath.

Molly was coming up the steps from the beach. She was breathing with deep, sobbing breaths, her body swayed to and fro as she came, in a curious directionless run. Tim cried,

"Molly! What's the matter?"

He ran towards her and Evelyn followed him. Molly was at the top of the steps now and she stood there, both hands behind her back. She said in sobbing breaths:

"I found her. . . . She's there in the bushes . . . There in the bushes . . . And look at my hands—look at my *hands."* She held them out and Evelyn caught her breath as she saw the queer dark stains. They looked dark in the subdued lighting but she knew well enough that their real color was red.

"What's happened, Molly?" cried Tim.

"Down there," said Molly. She swayed on her feet. "In the bushes . . ."

Tim hesitated, looked at Evelyn, then shoved Molly a little towards Evelyn and ran down the steps. Evelyn put her arm round the girl.

"Come. Sit down, Molly. Here. You'd better have something to drink."

Molly collapsed in a chair and leaned forward on the table, her forehead on her crossed arms. Evelyn did not question her any more. She thought it better to leave her time to recover.

"It'll be all right, you know," said Evelyn gently. "It'll be all right."

"I don't know," said Molly. "I don't know what happened. I don't know anything. I can't remember. I—" she raised her head suddenly. "What's the matter with me? What's the *matter* with me?"

"It's all right, child. It's all right."

Tim was coming slowly up the steps. His face was ghastly. Evelyn looked up at him, raising her eyebrows in a query.

"It's one of our girls," he said. "What's-her-name—Victoria. Somebody's put a knife in her."

CHAPTER FOURTEEN
Inquiry

I

MOLLY LAY ON her bed. Dr. Graham and Dr. Robertson, the West Indian police doctor stood on one side—Tim on the other. Robertson had his hand on Molly's pulse— He nodded to the man at the foot of the bed, a slender dark man in police uniform, Inspector Weston of the St. Honoré Police Force.

"A bare statement—no more," the doctor said.

The other nodded.

"Now, Mrs. Kendal—just tell us how you came to find this girl."

For a moment or two it was as though the figure on the bed had not heard. Then she spoke in a faint, faraway voice.

"In the bushes—white. . . ."

"You saw something white—and you looked to see what it was? Is that it?"

"Yes—white—lying there—I tried—tried to lift—she—it—blood—blood all over my hands."

She began to tremble.

Dr. Graham shook his head at them. Robertson whispered—"She can't stand much more."

"What were you doing on the beach path, Mrs. Kendal?"

"Warm—nice—by the sea——"

"You knew who the girl was?"

"Victoria—nice—nice girl—laughs—she used to laugh—oh! and now she won't— She won't ever laugh again. I'll never forget it—I'll never forget it——" Her voice rose hysterically.

"Molly—don't." It was Tim.

"Quiet—Quiet—." Dr. Robertson spoke with a soothing authority— "Just relax—relax— Now just a small prick—"

He withdrew the hypodermic.

"She'll be in no fit condition to be questioned for at least twenty-four hours," he said—"I'll let you know when."

II

The big handsome Negro looked from one to the other of the men sitting at the table.

"Ah declare to God," he said. "That's all I know. I don't know nothing but what Ah've told you."

The perspiration stood out on his forehead. Daventry sighed. The man presiding at the table, Inspector Weston of the St. Honoré C.I.D., made a gesture of dismissal. Big Jim Ellis shuffled out of the room.

"It's not all he knows, of course," Weston said. He had the soft Island voice. "But it's all we shall learn from him."

"You think he's in the clear himself?" asked Daventry.

"Yes. They seem to have been on good terms together."

"They weren't married?"

A faint smile appeared on Lieutenant Weston's lips. "No," he said, "they weren't married. We don't have so many marriages on the Island. They christen the children, though. He's had two children by Victoria."

"Do you think he was in it, whatever it was, with her?"

"Probably not. I think he'd have been nervous of anything of that kind. And I'd say, too, that what she did know wasn't very much."

"But enough for blackmail?"

"I don't know that I'd even call it that. I doubt if the girl would even understand that word. Payment for being discreet isn't thought of as blackmail. You see, some of the people who stay here are the rich playboy lot and their morals won't bear much investigation." His voice was slightly scathing.

"We get all kinds, I agree," said Daventry. "A woman, maybe, doesn't want it known that she's sleeping around, so she gives a present to the girl who waits on her. It's tacitly understood that the payment's for discretion."

"Exactly."

"But this," objected Daventry, "wasn't anything of *that* kind. It was murder."

"I should doubt, though, if the girl knew it was serious. She saw something, some puzzling incident, something to do presumably with this bottle of pills. It belonged to Mr. Dyson, I understand. We'd better see him next."

Gregory came in with his usual hearty air.

"Here I am," he said, "what can I do to help? Too bad about this girl. She was a nice girl. We both liked her. I suppose it was some sort of quarrel or other with a man, but she seemed quite happy and no signs of being in trouble about anything. I was kidding her only last night."

"I believe you take a preparation, Mr. Dyson, called Serenite?"

"Quite right. Little pink tablets."

"You have them on prescription from a physician?"

"Yes. I can show it to you if you like. Suffer a bit from high blood pressure, like so many people do nowadays."

"Very few people seem to be aware of that fact."

"Well, I don't go talking about it. I—well, I've always been well and hearty and I never like people who talk about their ailments all the time."

"How many of the pills do you take?"

"Two, three times a day."

"Do you have a fairly large stock with you?"

"Yes. I've got about half a dozen bottles. But they're locked up, you know, in a suitcase. I only keep one out, the one that's in current use."

"And you missed this bottle a short time ago, so I hear?"

"Quite right."

"And you asked this girl, Victoria Johnson, whether she'd seen it?"

"Yes, I did."

"And what did she say?"

"She said the last time she'd seen it was on the shelf in our bathroom. She said she'd look around."

"And after that?"

"She came and returned the bottle to me some time later. She said was this the bottle that was missing?"

"And you said?"

"I said 'that's it, all right, where did you find it?' And she said it was in old Major Palgrave's room. I said 'how on earth did it get there?'"

"And what did she answer to that?"

"She said she didn't know, but——" he hesitated.

"Yes, Mr. Dyson?"

"Well, she gave me the feeling that she did know a little more than she was saying, but I didn't pay much attention. After all, it wasn't very important. As I say, I've got other bottles of the pills with me. I thought perhaps I'd left it around in the restaurant or somewhere and old Palgrave picked it up for some reason. Perhaps he put it in his pocket meaning to return it to me, then forgot."

"And that's all you know about it, Mr. Dyson?"

"That's all I know. Sorry to be so unhelpful. Is it important? Why?"

Weston shrugged his shoulders. "As things are, anything may be important."

"I don't see where pills come in. I thought you'd want to know about what my movements were when this wretched girl was stabbed. I've written them all down as carefully as I can."

Weston looked at him thoughtfully.

"Indeed? That was very helpful of you, Mr. Dyson."

"Save everybody trouble, I thought," said Greg. He shoved a piece of paper across the table.

Weston studied it and Daventry drew his chair a little closer and looked over his shoulder.

"That seems very clear," said Weston, after a moment or two. "You and your wife were together changing for dinner in your bungalow until ten minutes to nine. You then went along to the terrace where you had drinks with Señora de Caspearo. At quarter past nine Colonel and Mrs. Hillingdon joined you and you went in to dine. As far as you can remember, you went off to bed at about half past eleven."

"Of course," said Greg. "I don't know what time the girl was actually killed——?"

There was a faint semblance of a question in the words. Lieutenant Weston, however, did not appear to notice it.

"Mrs. Kendal found her, I understand? Must have been a very nasty shock for her."

"Yes. Dr. Robertson had to give her a sedative."

"This was quite late, wasn't it, when most people had trundled off to bed?"

"Yes."

"Had she been dead long? When Mrs. Kendal found her, I mean?"

"We're not quite certain of the exact time yet," said Weston smoothly.

"Poor little Molly. It must have been a nasty shock for her. Matter of fact, I didn't notice *her* about last night. Thought she might have had a headache or something and was lying down."

"When was the last time you *did* see Mrs. Kendal?"

"Oh, quite early, before I went to change. She was playing about with some of the table decorations and things. Rearranging the knives."

"I see."

"She was quite cheerful then," said Greg. "Kidding and all that. She's a great girl. We're all very fond of her. Tim's a lucky fellow."

"Well, thank you, Mr. Dyson. You can't remember anything more than you've told us about what the girl Victoria said when she returned the tablets?"

"No . . . It was just as I say. Asked me were these the tablets I'd been asking for. Said she'd found them in old Palgrave's room."

"She'd no idea who put them there?"

"Don't think so—can't remember, really."

"Thank you, Mr. Dyson."

Gregory went out.

"Very thoughtful of him," said Weston, gently tapping the paper with his fingernail, "to be so anxious to want us to know for sure exactly where he was last night."

"A little over-anxious do you think?" asked Daventry.

"That's very difficult to tell. There are people, you know, who are naturally nervous about their own safety, about being mixed up with anything. It isn't necessarily because they have any guilty knowledge. On the other hand it might be just that."

"What about opportunity? Nobody's really got much of an alibi, what with the band and the dancing and the coming and going. People are getting up, leaving their tables, coming back. Women go to powder their noses. Men take a stroll. Dyson could have slipped away. Anybody could have slipped away. But he does seem rather anxious to prove that *he* didn't." He looked thoughtfully down at the paper. "So Mrs. Kendal was rearranging knives on the table," he said. "I rather wonder if he dragged that in on purpose."

"Did it sound like it to you?"

The other considered. "I think it's possible."

Outside the room where the two men were sitting, a noise had arisen. A high voice was demanding admittance shrilly.

"I've got something to tell. I've got something to tell. You take me in to where the gentlemen are. You take me in to where the policeman is."

A uniformed policeman pushed open the door.

"It's one of the cooks here," he said, "very anxious to see you. Says he's got something you ought to know."

A frightened dark man in a cook's cap pushed past him and came into the room. It was one of the minor cooks. A Cuban, not a native of St. Honoré.

"I tell you something. I tell you," he said. "She come through my kitchen, she did, and she had a knife with her. A knife, I tell you. She had a knife in her hand. She come through my kitchen and out the door. Out into the garden. I saw her."

"Now calm down," said Daventry, "calm down. Who are you talking about?"

"I tell you who I'm talking about. I'm talking about the boss's wife. Mrs. Kendal. I'm talking about her. She have a knife in her hand and she go out into the dark. Before dinner that was—and *she didn't come back.*"

CHAPTER FIFTEEN
Inquiry Continued

I

"CAN WE HAVE a word with you, Mr. Kendal?"

"Of course." Tim looked up from his desk. He pushed some papers aside and indicated chairs. His face was drawn and miserable. "How are you getting on? Got any forwarder? There seems to be a doom in this place.

People are wanting to leave, you know, asking about air passages. Just when it seemed everything was being a success. Oh lord, you don't know what it means, this place, to me and to Molly. We staked everything on it."

"It's very hard on you, I know," said Inspector Weston. "Don't think that we don't sympathize."

"If it all could be cleared up quickly," said Tim. "This wretched girl Victoria—Oh! I oughtn't to talk about her like that. She was quite a good sort, Victoria was. But—but there must be some quite simple reason, some—kind of intrigue, or love affair she had. Perhaps her husband——"

"Jim Ellis wasn't her husband, and they seemed a settled sort of couple."

"If it could only be cleared up *quickly,*" said Tim again. "I'm sorry. You wanted to talk to me about something, ask me something."

"Yes. It was about last night. According to medical evidence Victoria was killed some time between 10:30 p.m. and midnight. Alibis under the circumstances that prevail here, are not very easy to prove. People are moving about, dancing, walking away from the terrace, coming back. It's all very difficult."

"I suppose so. But does that mean that you definitely consider Victoria was killed by one of the guests here?"

"Well, we have to examine that possibility, Mr. Kendal. What I want to ask you particularly about, is a statement made by one of your cooks."

"Oh? Which one? What does he say?"

"He's a Cuban, I understand."

"We've got two Cubans and a Puerto Rican."

"This man Enrico states that your wife passed through the kitchen on her way from the dining-room, and went out into the garden and that she was carrying a knife."

Tim stared at him.

"Molly, carrying a knife? Well, why shouldn't she? I mean—why—you don't think—what are you trying to suggest?"

"I am talking of the time before people had come into the dining-room. It would be, I suppose, some time about 8:30. You yourself were in the dining-room talking to the head waiter, Fernando, I believe."

"Yes." Tim cast his mind back. "Yes, I remember."

"And your wife came in from the terrace?"

"Yes, she did," Tim agreed. "She always went out to look over the tables. Sometimes the boys set things wrong, forgot some of the cutlery, things like that. Very likely that's what it was. She may have been rearranging cutlery or something. She might have had a spare knife or a spoon, something like that in her hand."

"And she came from the terrace into the dining-room. Did she speak to you?"

"Yes, we had a word or two together."

"What did she say? Can you remember?"

"I think I asked her who she'd been talking to. I heard her voice out there."

"And who did she say she'd been talking to?"

"Gregory Dyson."

"Ah. Yes. That is what *he* said."

Tim went on, "He'd been making a pass at her, I understand. He was a bit given to that kind of thing. It annoyed me and I said 'Blast him' and

Molly laughed and said she could do all the blasting that needed to be done. Molly's a very clever girl that way. It's not always an easy position, you know. You can't offend guests, and so an attractive girl like Molly has to pass things off with a laugh and a shrug. Gregory Dyson finds it difficult to keep his hands off any good-looking woman."

"Had there been any altercation between them?"

"No, I don't think so. I think, as I say, she just laughed it off as usual."

"You can't say definitely whether she had a knife in her hand or not?"

"I can't remember—I'm almost sure she didn't— In fact quite sure she didn't."

"But you said just now . . ."

"Look here, what I meant was that if she was in the dining-room or in the kitchen it's quite likely she might have picked up a knife or had one in her hand. Matter of fact I can remember quite well, she came in from the dining-room and she had *nothing* in her hand. *Nothing at all.* That's definite."

"I see," said Weston.

Tim looked at him uneasily.

"What on earth is this you're getting at? What did that damn' fool Enrico—Manuel—whichever it was—say?"

"He said your wife came out into the kitchen, that she looked upset, that she had a knife in her hand."

"He's just dramatizing."

"Did you have any further conversation with your wife during dinner or after?"

"No, I don't think I did really. Matter of fact I was rather busy."

"Was your wife there in the dining-room during the meal?"

"I—oh—yes, we always move about among the guests and things like that. See how things are going on."

"Did you speak to her at all?"

"No, I don't think I did . . . We're usually fairly busy. We don't always notice what the other one's doing and we certainly haven't got time to talk to each other."

"Actually you don't remember speaking to her until she came up the steps three hours later, after finding the body?"

"It was an awful shock for her. It upset her terribly."

"I know. A very unpleasant experience. How did she come to be walking along the beach path?"

"After the stress of dinner being served, she often does go for a turn. You know, get away from the guests for a minute or two, get a breather."

"When she came back, I understand you were talking to Mrs. Hillingdon."

"Yes. Practically everyone else had gone to bed."

"What was the subject of your conversation with Mrs. Hillingdon?"

"Nothing particular. Why? What's she been saying?"

"So far she hasn't said anything. We haven't asked her."

"We were just talking of this and that. Molly, and hotel running, and one thing and another."

"And then—your wife came up the steps of the terrace and told you what had happened?"

"Yes."

"There was blood on her hands?"

"Of course there was! She'd bent over the girl, tried to lift her, couldn't understand what had happened, what was the matter with her. Of course there was blood on her hands! Look here, what the hell are you suggesting? You *are* suggesting something?"

"Please calm down," said Daventry. "It's all a great strain on you I know, Tim, but we have to get the facts clear. I understand your wife hasn't been feeling very well lately?"

"Nonsense—she's all right. Major Palgrave's death upset her a bit. Naturally. She's a sensitive girl."

"We shall have to ask her a few questions as soon as she's fit enough," said Weston.

"Well, you can't now. The doctor gave her a sedative and said she wasn't to be disturbed. I won't have her upset and brow-beaten, d'you hear?"

"We're not going to do any brow-beating," said Weston. "We've just got to get the facts clear. We won't disturb her at present, but as soon as the doctor allows us, we'll have to see her." His voice was gentle—inflexible.

Tim looked at him, opened his mouth, but said nothing.

II

Evelyn Hillingdon, calm and composed as usual, sat down in the chair indicated. She considered the few questions asked her, taking her time over it. Her dark, intelligent eyes looked at Weston carefully.

"Yes," she said, "I was talking to Mr. Kendal on the terrace when his wife came up the steps and told us about the murder."

"Your husband wasn't there?"

"No, he had gone to bed."

"Had you any special reason for your conversation with Mr. Kendal?"

Evelyn raised her finely pencilled eyebrows— It was a definite rebuke. She said coldly:

"What a very odd question. No—there was nothing special about our conversation."

"Did you discuss the matter of his wife's health?"

Again Evelyn took her time.

"I really can't remember," she said at last.

"Are you sure of that?"

"Sure that I can't remember? What a curious way of putting it—one talks about so many things at different times."

"Mrs. Kendal has not been in good health lately, I understand."

"She looked quite all right—a little tired, perhaps. Of course running a place like this means a lot of worries, and she is quite inexperienced. Naturally, she gets flustered now and then."

"Flustered." Weston repeated the word. "That was the way you would describe it?"

"It's an old-fashioned word, perhaps, but just as good as the modern jargon we use for everything— A 'virus infection' for a bilious attack—an 'anxiety neurosis' for the minor bothers of daily life——"

Her smile made Weston feel slightly ridiculous. He thought to himself that Evelyn Hillingdon was a clever woman. He looked at Daventry whose face remained unmoved and wondered what he thought.

"Thank you, Mrs. Hillingdon," said Weston.

III

"We don't want to worry you, Mrs. Kendal, but we have to have your account of just how you came to find this girl. Dr. Graham says you are sufficiently recovered to talk about it now."

"Oh yes," said Molly, "I'm really quite all right again." She gave them a small nervous smile. "It was just the shock— It *was* rather awful, you know."

"Yes, indeed it must have been—I understand you went for a walk after dinner."

"Yes—I—often do."

Her eyes shifted, Daventry noticed, and the fingers of her hands twined and untwined about each other.

"What time would that have been, Mrs. Kendal?" asked Weston.

"Well, I don't really know—we don't go much by the time."

"The steel band was still playing?"

"Yes—at least—I think so—I can't remember."

"And you walked—which way?"

"Oh, along the beach path."

"To the left or the right?"

"Oh! First one way—and then the other—I—I—really didn't notice."

"Why didn't you notice, Mrs. Kendal?"

She frowned.

"I suppose I was—well—thinking of things."

"Thinking of anything particular?"

"No—No—Nothing particular— Just things that had to be done—seen to—in the hotel." Again that nervous twining and untwining of fingers. "And then—I noticed something white—in a clump of hibiscus bushes— and I wondered what it was. I stopped and—and pulled——" She swallowed convulsively— "And it was her—Victoria—all huddled up—and I tried to raise her head up and I got—blood—on my hands."

She looked at them and repeated wonderingly as though recalling something impossible:

"Blood—on my hands."

"Yes—Yes— A very dreadful experience. There is no need for you to tell us more about that part of it— How long had you been walking, do you think, when you found her——"

"I don't know—I have no idea."

"An hour? Half an hour? Or more than an hour——"

"I don't know," Molly repeated.

Daventry asked in a quiet everyday voice:

"Did you take a knife with you on your—walk?"

"A knife?" Molly sounded surprised. "Why should I take a knife?"

"I only ask because one of the kitchen staff mentioned that you had a knife in your hand when you went out of the kitchen into the garden."

Molly frowned.

"But I didn't go out of the kitchen—oh you mean earlier—before dinner—I—I don't *think* so——"

"You had been rearranging the cutlery on the tables, perhaps."

"I have to, sometimes. They lay things wrong—not enough knives—or too many. The wrong number of forks and spoons—that sort of thing."

"And did that happen on this particular evening?"

"It may have done—something like that— It's really automatic. One doesn't think, or remember——"

"So you may have gone out of the kitchen that evening carrying a knife in your hand?"

"I don't think I did—I'm sure I didn't—" She added— "Tim was there—he would know. Ask him."

"Did you like this girl—Victoria—was she good at her work?" asked Weston.

"Yes—she was a very nice girl."

"You had had no dispute with her?"

"Dispute? No."

"She had never threatened you—in any way?"

"Threatened me? What do you mean?"

"It doesn't matter— You have no idea of who could have killed her? No idea at all?"

"None." She spoke positively.

"Well, thank you, Mrs. Kendal." He smiled. "It wasn't so terrible, was it?"

"That's all?"

"That's all for now."

Daventry got up, opened the door for her, and watched her go out.

"Tim would know," he quoted as he returned to his chair. "And Tim says definitely that she *didn't* have a knife."

Weston said gravely:

"I think that that is what any husband would feel called upon to say."

"A table knife seems a very poor type of knife to use for murder."

"But it was a *steak* knife, Mr. Daventry. Steaks were on the menu that evening. Steak knives are kept sharp."

"I really can't bring myself to believe that that girl we've just been talking to is a red-handed murderess, Weston."

"It is not necessary to believe it yet. It could be that Mrs. Kendal went out into the garden before dinner, clasping a knife she had taken off one of the tables because it was superfluous—she might not even have noticed she was holding it, and she could have put it down somewhere—or dropped it— It could have been found and used by someone else— I, too, think her an unlikely murderess."

"All the same," said Daventry thoughtfully, "I'm pretty sure she is not telling all she knows. Her vagueness over time is odd—where was she—what was she doing out there? Nobody, so far, seems to have noticed her in the dining-room that evening."

"The husband was about as usual—but not the wife——"

"You think she went to meet someone—Victoria Johnson?"

"Perhaps—or perhaps she saw whoever it was who did go to meet Victoria."

"You're thinking of Gregory Dyson?"

"We know he was talking to Victoria earlier— He may have arranged to meet her again later—everyone moved around freely on the terrace, remember—dancing, drinking—in and out of the bar."

"No alibi like a steel band," said Daventry wryly.

CHAPTER SIXTEEN
Miss Marple Seeks Assistance

IF ANYBODY HAD been there to observe the gentle-looking elderly lady who stood meditatively on the loggia outside her bungalow, they would have thought she had nothing more on her mind than deliberation on how to arrange her time that day— An expedition, perhaps, to Castle Cliff—a visit to Jamestown—a nice drive and lunch at Pelican Point—or just a quiet morning on the beach—

But the gentle old lady was deliberating quite other matters—she was in militant mood.

"Something has got to be done," said Miss Marple to herself.

Moreover, she was convinced that there was no time to be lost— There was urgency.

But who was there that she could convince of that fact? Given time, she thought she could find out the truth by herself.

She had found out a good deal. But not enough—not nearly enough. And time was short.

She realized, bitterly, that here on this Paradise of an island, she had none of her usual allies.

She thought regretfully of her friends in England—Sir Henry Clithering—always willing to listen indulgently—his godson Dermot, who in spite of his increased status at Scotland Yard, was still ready to believe that when Miss Marple voiced an opinion there was usually something behind it.

But would that soft-voiced native police officer pay any attention to an old lady's urgency? Dr. Graham? But Dr. Graham was not what she needed—too gentle and hesitant, certainly not a man of quick decisions and rapid actions.

Miss Marple, feeling rather like a humble deputy of the Almighty, almost cried aloud her need in Biblical phrasing.

Who will go for me?

Whom shall I send?

The sound that reached her ears a moment later was not instantly recognized by her as an answer to prayer—far from it— At the back of her mind it registered only as a man possibly calling his dog.

"Hi!"

Miss Marple, lost in perplexity, paid no attention.

"Hi!" The volume thus increased, Miss Marple looked vaguely round.

"HI!" called Mr. Rafiel impatiently. He added—"You—there——"

Miss Marple had not at first realized that Mr. Rafiel's "Hi You" was addressed to her. It was not a method that anyone had ever used before to summon her. It was certainly not a gentlemanly mode of address. Miss Marple did not resent it, because people seldom did resent Mr. Rafiel's somewhat arbitrary method of doing things. He was a law unto himself and people accepted him as such. Miss Marple looked across the intervening space between her bungalow and his. Mr. Rafiel was sitting outside on his loggia and he beckoned her.

"You were calling me?" she asked.

"Of course I was calling you," said Mr. Rafiel. "Who did you think I was calling—a cat? Come over here."

Miss Marple looked round for her handbag, picked it up, and crossed the intervening space.

"I can't come to you unless someone helps me," explained Mr. Rafiel, "so you've got to come to me."

"Oh yes," said Miss Marple, "I quite understand *that.*"

Mr. Rafiel pointed to an adjacent chair. "Sit down," he said, "I want to talk to you. Something damned odd is going on in this island."

"Yes, indeed," agreed Miss Marple, taking the chair as indicated. By sheer habit she drew her knitting out of her bag.

"Don't start knitting again," said Mr. Rafiel, "I can't stand it. I hate women knitting. It irritates me."

Miss Marple returned her knitting to her bag. She did this with no undue air of meekness, rather with the air of one who makes allowances for a fractious patient.

"There's a lot of chit-chat going on," said Mr. Rafiel, "and I bet you're in the forefront of it. You and the parson and his sister."

"It is, perhaps, only natural that there should be chit-chat," said Miss Marple with spirit, "given the circumstances."

"This Island girl gets herself knifed. Found in the bushes. *Might* be ordinary enough. That chap she was living with might have got jealous of another man—or he's got himself another girl and she got jealous and they had a row. Sex in the tropics. That sort of stuff. What do you say?"

"No," said Miss Marple, shaking her head.

"The authorities don't think so, either."

"They would say more to you," pointed out Miss Marple, "than they would say to me."

"All the same, I bet you know more about it than I do. You've listened to the tittle-tattle."

"Certainly I have," said Miss Marple.

"Nothing much else to do, have you, except listen to tittle-tattle?"

"It is often informative and useful."

"D'you know," said Mr. Rafiel, studying her attentively, "I made a mistake about you. I don't often make mistakes about people. There's a lot more to you than I thought there was. All these rumors about Major Palgrave and the stories he told. You think he was bumped off, don't you?"

"I very much fear so," said Miss Marple.

"Well, he was," said Mr. Rafiel.

Miss Marple drew a deep breath. "That is definite, is it?" she asked.

"Yes, it's definite enough. I had it from Daventry. I'm not breaking a confidence because the facts of the autopsy will have to come out. You told Graham something, he went to Daventry, Daventry went to the Administrator, the C.I.D. were informed, and between them they agreed that things looked fishy, so they dug up old Palgrave and had a look."

"And they found?" Miss Marple paused interrogatively.

"They found he'd had a lethal dose of something that only a doctor could pronounce properly. As far as I remember it sounds vaguely like di-flor, hexagonal-ethylcarbenzol. That's not the right name. But that's roughly what it *sounds* like. The police doctor put it that way so that nobody should know, I suppose, what it really *was*. The stuff's probably got some quite simple nice easy name like Evipan or Veronal or Easton's Syrup or something of that kind. This is its official name to baffle laymen with. Anyway, a sizeable dose of it, I gather, would produce death, and the signs would be much the same as those of high blood pressure aggravated by over indulgence in alcohol on a gay evening. In fact, it all looked perfectly natural and nobody questioned it for a moment. Just said 'poor old chap' and buried him quick. Now they wonder if he ever had high blood pressure at all. Did he ever say he had to you?"

"No."

"Exactly! And yet everyone seems to have taken it as a fact."

"Apparently he told people he had."

"It's like seeing ghosts," said Mr. Rafiel. "You never meet the chap who's seen the ghost himself. It's always the second cousin of his aunt, or a friend, or a friend of a friend. But leave that for a moment. They thought he had blood pressure, because there was a bottle of tablets controlling blood pressure found in his room but—and now we're coming to the point—I gather that this girl who was killed went about saying that that bottle was put there by somebody else, and that *actually* it belonged to that fellow Greg."

"Mr. Dyson *has* got blood pressure. His wife mentioned it," said Miss Marple.

"So it was put in Palgrave's room to suggest that he suffered from blood pressure and to make his death seem natural."

"Exactly," said Miss Marple. "And the story was put about, very cleverly, that he had frequently mentioned to people that he had high blood pressure. But you know, it's very easy to put about a story. Very easy. I've seen a lot of it in my time."

"I bet you have," said Mr. Rafiel.

"It only needs a murmur here and there," said Miss Marple. "You don't say it of your own knowledge, you just say that Mrs. B. told you that Colonel C. told her. It's always at second hand or third hand or fourth hand and it's very difficult to find out who was the original whisperer. Oh yes, it can be done. And the people you say it to go on and repeat it to others as if they know it of their own knowledge."

"Somebody's been clever," said Mr. Rafiel thoughtfully.

"Yes," said Miss Marple, "I think somebody's been quite clever."

"This girl saw something, or knew something, and tried blackmail, I suppose," said Mr. Rafiel.

"She mayn't have thought of it as blackmail," said Miss Marple. "In these large hotels, there are often things the maids know that some people would rather not have repeated. And so they hand out a larger tip or a little present of money. The girl possibly didn't realize at first the importance of what she knew."

"Still, she got a knife in her back all right," said Mr. Rafiel brutally.

"Yes. Evidently someone couldn't afford to let her talk."

"Well? Let's hear what you think about it all."

Miss Marple looked at him thoughtfully.

"Why should you think I know any more than you do, Mr. Rafiel?"

"Probably you don't," said Mr. Rafiel, "but I'm interested to hear your ideas about what you do know."

"But why?"

"There's not very much to do out here," said Mr. Rafiel, "except make money."

Miss Marple looked slightly surprised.

"Make money? Out here?"

"You can send out half a dozen cables in code every day if you like," said Mr. Rafiel. "That's how I amuse myself."

"Take-over bids?" Miss Marple asked doubtfully, in the tone of one who speaks a foreign language.

"That kind of thing," agreed Mr. Rafiel. "Pitting your wits against other people's wits. The trouble is it doesn't occupy enough time, so I've got interested in this business. It's aroused my curiosity. Palgrave spent a good deal of his time talking to you. Nobody else would be bothered with him, I expect. What did he say?"

"He told me a good many stories," said Miss Marple.

"I know he did. Damn' boring, most of them. And you hadn't only got to hear them once. If you got anywhere within range you heard them three or four times over."

"I know," said Miss Marple. "I'm afraid that does happen when gentlemen get older."

Mr. Rafiel looked at her very sharply.

"I don't tell stories," he said. "Go on. It started with one of Palgrave's stories, did it?"

"He said he knew a murderer," said Miss Marple. "There's nothing really special about that," she added in her gentle voice, "because I suppose it happens to nearly everybody."

"I don't follow you," said Mr. Rafiel.

"I don't mean specifically," said Miss Marple, "but surely, Mr. Rafiel, if you cast over in your mind your recollections of various events in your life, hasn't there nearly always been an occasion when somebody has made some careless reference such as 'Oh yes I knew the So-and-So's quite well—he died very suddenly and they always say his wife did him in, but I daresay that's just gossip.' You've heard people say something like that, haven't you?"

"Well, I suppose so—yes, something of the kind. But not—well, not seriously."

"Exactly," said Miss Marple, "but Major Palgrave was a very serious man. I think he enjoyed telling this story. He said he had a snapshot of the murderer. He was going to show it to me but—actually—he didn't."

"Why?"

"Because he saw something," said Miss Marple. "Saw someone, I suspect. His face got very red and he shoved back the snapshot into his wallet and began talking on another subject."

"Who did he see?"

"I've thought about that a good deal," said Miss Marple. "I was sitting outside my bungalow, and he was sitting nearly opposite me and—whatever he saw, he saw over my right shoulder."

"Someone coming along the path then from behind you on the right, the path from the creek and the car park——"

"Yes."

"*Was* anyone coming along the path?"

"Mr. and Mrs. Dyson and Colonel and Mrs. Hillingdon."

"Anybody else?"

"Not that I can find out. Of course, your bungalow would also be in his line of vision. . . ."

"Ah. Then we include—shall we say—Esther Walters and my chap, Jackson. Is that right? Either of them, I suppose, *might* have come out of the bungalow and gone back inside again without your seeing them."

"They might have," said Miss Marple, "I didn't turn my head at once."

"The Dysons, the Hillingdons, Esther, Jackson. One of them's a murderer. Or of course, myself," he added; obviously as an afterthought.

Miss Marple smiled faintly.

"And he spoke of the murderer as a *man?*"

"Yes."

"Right. That cuts out Evelyn Hillingdon, Lucky and Esther Walters. So your murderer, allowing that all this far-fetched nonsense is true, your murderer is Dyson, Hillingdon or my smooth-tongued Jackson."

"Or yourself," said Miss Marple.

Mr. Rafiel ignored this last point.

"Don't say things to irritate me," he said. "I'll tell you the first thing that strikes me, and which you don't seem to have thought of. *If* it's one of those three, why the devil didn't old Palgrave recognize him before? Dash it all, they've all been sitting round looking at each other for the last two weeks. That doesn't seem to make sense."

"I think it could," said Miss Marple.

"Well, tell me how."

"You see, in Major Palgrave's story he hadn't seen this man *himself* at any time. It was a story told to him by a doctor. The doctor gave him the snapshot as a curiosity. Major Palgrave may have looked at the snapshot fairly closely at the time but after that he'd just stack it away in his wallet and keep it as a souvenir. Occasionally, perhaps, he'd take it out and show it to someone he was telling the story to. And another thing, Mr. Rafiel, we don't know how long ago this happened. He didn't give me any indication of that when he was telling the story. I mean this may have been a story he's been telling to people for *years*. Five years—ten years—longer still perhaps. Some of his tiger stories go back about twenty years."

"They would!" said Mr. Rafiel.

"So I don't suppose for a moment that Major Palgrave would recognize the face in the snapshot if he came across the man casually. What I think happened, what I'm almost sure *must* have happened, is that as he told his story he fumbled for the snapshot, took it out, looked down at it studying the face and then looked up to see *the same face,* or one with a strong resemblance coming towards him from a distance of about ten or twelve feet away."

"Yes," said Mr. Rafiel consideringly, "Yes, that's possible."

"He was taken aback," said Miss Marple, "and he shoved it back in his wallet and began to talk loudly about something else."

"He couldn't have been sure," said Mr. Rafiel, shrewdly.

"No," said Miss Marple, "he couldn't have been sure. But of course afterwards he would have studied the snapshot very carefully and would have looked at the man and tried to make up his mind whether it was just a likeness or whether it could actually be the same person."

Mr. Rafiel reflected a moment or two, then he shook his head.

"There's something wrong here. The motive's inadequate. Absolutely inadequate. He was speaking to you loudly, was he?"

"Yes," said Miss Marple, "quite loudly. He always did."

"True enough. Yes, he did shout. So whoever was approaching would hear what he said?"

"I should imagine you could hear it for quite a good radius round."

Mr. Rafiel shook his head again. He said, "It's fantastic, too fantastic. Anybody would laugh at such a story. Here's an old booby telling a story about another story somebody told him, and showing a snapshot, and all of it centering round a murder which had taken place years ago! Or at any rate, a year or two. How on earth can *that* worry the man in question. No evidence, just a bit of hearsay, a story at third hand. He could even admit a likeness, he could say: 'Yes, I *do* look rather like that fellow, don't I! Ha, ha!' Nobody's going to take old Palgrave's identification seriously. Don't tell me so, because I won't believe it. No, the chap, if it *was* the chap, had nothing to fear—nothing whatever. It's the kind of accusation he can just laugh off. Why on earth should he proceed to murder old Palgrave? It's absolutely unnecessary. You must see that."

"Oh I do see that," said Miss Marple. "I couldn't agree with you more. That's what makes me uneasy. So very uneasy that I really couldn't sleep last night."

Mr. Rafiel stared at her. "Let's hear what's on your mind," he said quietly.

"I may be entirely wrong," said Miss Marple hesitantly.

"Probably you are," said Mr. Rafiel with his usual lack of courtesy, "but at any rate let's hear what you've thought up in the small hours."

"There could be a very powerful motive if——"

"If what?"

"If there was going to be—quite soon—*another murder.*"

Mr. Rafiel stared at her. He tried to pull himself up a little in his chair.

"Let's get this clear," he said.

"I am so bad at explaining." Miss Marple spoke rapidly and rather incoherently. A pink flush rose to her cheeks. "Supposing there was a murder planned. If you remember, the story Major Palgrave told me concerned a man whose wife died under suspicious circumstances. Then, after a certain lapse of time, there was another murder under exactly the same circumstances. A man of a different name had a wife who died in much the same way and the doctor who was telling it recognized him as the same man, although he'd changed his name. Well, it does look, doesn't it, as though this murderer might be the kind of murderer who made a habit of the thing?"

"You mean like Smith, *Brides in the Bath,* that kind of thing. Yes."

"As far as I can make out," said Miss Marple, "and from what I have heard and read, a man who does a wicked thing like this and gets away with it the first time, is, alas, *encouraged.* He thinks it's easy, he thinks he's clever. And so he repeats it. And in the end, as you say, like Smith and the Brides in the Bath, it becomes a *habit.* Each time in a different place and each time the man changes his name. But the crimes themselves are all very much alike. So it seems to me, although I may be quite wrong——"

"But you don't think you are wrong, do you?" Mr. Rafiel put in shrewdly.

Miss Marple went on without answering. "——that if that *were* so and if this—this person had got things all lined up for a murder out here, for getting rid of *another* wife, say, and if this is crime three or four, well then, the Major's story *would* matter because the murderer couldn't afford to have any similarity pointed out. If you remember, that was exactly the way Smith got caught. The circumstances of a crime attracted the attention of somebody who compared it with a newspaper clipping of some other case. So you do see, don't you, that if this wicked person has got a crime planned, arranged, and shortly about to take place, he couldn't afford to let Major Palgrave go about telling this story and showing that snapshot."

She stopped and looked appealingly at Mr. Rafiel.

"So you see he had to do something very quickly, as quickly as possible."

Mr. Rafiel spoke, "In fact, that very same night, eh?"

"Yes," said Miss Marple.

"Quick work," said Mr. Rafiel, "but it could be done. Put the tablets in old Palgrave's room, spread the blood pressure rumor about and add a little of our fourteen syllable drug to a Planters Punch. Is that it?"

"Yes— But that's all over—we needn't worry about it. It's the *future.* It's now. With Major Palgrave out of the way and the snapshot destroyed, *this man will go on with his murder as planned.*"

Mr. Rafiel whistled.

"You've got it all worked out, haven't you?"

Miss Marple nodded. She said in a most unaccustomed voice, firm and almost dictatorial, "And we've got to stop it. *You've* got to stop it, Mr. Rafiel."

"Me?" said Mr. Rafiel, astonished, "why me?"

"Because you're rich and important," said Miss Marple, simply. "People will take notice of what you say or suggest. They wouldn't listen to me for a moment. They would say that I was an old lady imagining things."

"They might at that," said Mr. Rafiel. "More fools if they did. I must say, though, that nobody would think you had any brains in your head to hear your usual line of talk. Actually, you've got a logical mind. Very few women have." He shifted himself uncomfortably in his chair. "Where the hell's Esther or Jackson?" he said. "I need resettling. No, it's no good your doing it. You're not strong enough. I don't know what they mean, leaving me alone like this."

"I'll go and find them."

"No, you won't. You'll stay here—and thrash this out. Which of them is it? The egregious Greg? The quiet Edward Hillingdon or my fellow Jackson? It's got to be one of the three, hasn't it?"

CHAPTER SEVENTEEN
Mr. Rafiel Takes Charge

"I DON'T KNOW," said Miss Marple.

"What do you mean? What have we been talking about for the last twenty minutes?"

"It has occurred to me that I may have been wrong."

Mr. Rafiel stared at her.

"Scatty after all!" he said disgustedly. "And you sounded so sure of yourself."

"Oh, I am sure—about the *murder*. It's the *murderer* I'm not sure about. You see I've found out that Major Palgrave had more than one murder story—you told me yourself he'd told you one about a kind of Lucrezia Borgia——"

"So he did—at that. But that was quite a different kind of story."

"I know. And Mrs. Walters said he had one about someone being gassed in a gas oven——"

"But the story he told you——"

Miss Marple allowed herself to interrupt—a thing that did not often happen to Mr. Rafiel.

She spoke with desperate earnestness and only moderate incoherence.

"Don't you see—it's so difficult to be *sure*. The whole point is that—so often—one doesn't *listen*. Ask Mrs. Walters—she said the same thing—you listen to begin with—and then your attention flags—your mind wanders—and suddenly you find you've missed a bit. I just wonder if possibly there may have been a gap—a very small one—between the story he was telling me—about a *man*—and the moment when he was getting out his wallet and saying— 'Like to see a picture of a murderer.'"

"But you thought it was a picture of the man he had been talking about?"

"I thought so—yes. It never occurred to me that it mightn't have been. But now—how can I be *sure?*"

Mr. Rafiel looked at her very thoughtfully. . . .

"The trouble with you is," he said, "that you're too conscientious. Great mistake— Make up your mind and don't shilly shally. You didn't shilly shally to begin with. If you ask me, in all this chit-chat you've been having with the parson's sister and the rest of them, you've got hold of something that's unsettled you."

"Perhaps you're right."

"Well, cut it out for the moment. Let's go ahead with what you had to begin with. Because, nine times out of ten, one's original judgments are right—or so I've found. We've got three suspects. Let's take 'em out and have a good look at them. Any preference?"

"I really haven't," said Miss Marple, "all three of them seem so very unlikely."

"We'll take Greg first," said Mr. Rafiel. "Can't stand the fellow. Doesn't make him a murderer, though. Still, there *are* one or two points against him. Those blood pressure tablets belonged to him. Nice and handy to make use of."

"That would be a little obvious, wouldn't it?" Miss Marple objected.

"I don't know that it would," said Mr. Rafiel. "After all, the main thing was to do something *quickly,* and he'd got the tablets. Hadn't much time to go looking round for tablets that somebody else might have. Let's say it's Greg. All right. *If* he wanted to put his dear wife Lucky out of the way— (Good job, too, I'd say. In fact I'm in sympathy with him) I can't actually see his motive. From all accounts he's rich. Inherited money from his first wife who had pots of it. He qualifies on that as a possible wife murderer all right. But that's over and done with. He got away with it. But Lucky was his first wife's poor relation. No money there, so if he wants to put *her* out of the way it must be in order to marry somebody else. Any gossip going around about that?"

Miss Marple shook her head.

"Not that I have heard. He—er—has a very gallant manner with *all* the ladies."

"Well, that's a nice, old-fashioned way of putting it," said Mr. Rafiel. "All right, he's a stoat. He makes passes. Not enough! We want more than that. Let's go on to Edward Hillingdon. Now there's a dark horse, if ever there was one."

"He is not, I think, a happy man," offered Miss Marple.

Mr. Rafiel looked at her thoughtfully.

"Do you think a murderer ought to be a happy man?"

Miss Marple coughed.

"Well, they usually have been in my experience."

"I don't suppose your experience has gone very far," said Mr. Rafiel.

In this assumption, as Miss Marple could have told him, he was wrong. But she forbore to contest his statement. Gentlemen, she knew, did not like to be put right in their facts.

"I rather fancy Hillingdon myself," said Mr. Rafiel. "I've an idea that there is something a bit odd going on between him and his wife. You noticed it at all?"

"Oh yes," said Miss Marple, "I have noticed it. Their behavior is perfect in public, of course, but that one would expect."

"You probably know more about those sort of people than I would," said Mr. Rafiel. "Very well, then, everything is in perfectly good taste but it's a probability that, in a gentlemanly way, Edward Hillingdon is contemplating doing away with Evelyn Hillingdon. Do you agree?"

"If so," said Miss Marple, "there must be another woman."

"But what woman?"

Miss Marple shook her head in a dissatisfied manner.

"I can't help feeling—I really can't—that it's not all quite as simple as that."

"Well, who shall we consider next—Jackson? We leave me out of it."

Miss Marple smiled for the first time.

"And why do we leave you out of it, Mr. Rafiel?"

"Because if you want to discuss the possibilities of my being a murderer you'd have to do it with somebody else. Waste of time talking about it to me. And anyway, I ask you, am I cut out for the part? Helpless, hauled out of bed like a dummy, dressed, wheeled about in a chair, shuffled along for a walk. What earthly chance have *I* of going and murdering anyone?"

"Probably as good a chance as anyone else," said Miss Marple vigorously.

"And how do you make that out?"

"Well, you would agree yourself, I think, that you have brains?"

"Of course I've got brains," declared Mr. Rafiel. "A good deal more than anybody else in this community, I'd say."

"And having brains," went on Miss Marple, "would enable you to overcome the physical difficulties of being a murderer."

"It would take some doing!"

"Yes," said Miss Marple, "it would take some doing. But then, I think, Mr. Rafiel, you would enjoy that."

Mr. Rafiel stared at her for quite a long time and then he suddenly laughed.

"You've got a nerve!" he said. "Not quite the gentle fluffy old lady you look, are you? So you really think I'm a murderer?"

"No," said Miss Marple, "I do not."

"And why?"

"Well, really, I think just *because* you have got brains. Having brains, you can get most things you want without having recourse to murder. Murder is stupid."

"And anyway who the devil should I want to murder?"

"That would be a very interesting question," said Miss Marple. "I have not yet had the pleasure of sufficient conversation with you to evolve a theory as to that."

Mr. Rafiel's smile broadened.

"Conversations with you might be dangerous," he said.

"Conversations are always dangerous, if you have something to hide," said Miss Marple.

"You may be right. Let's get on to Jackson. What do you think of Jackson?"

"It is difficult for me to say. I have not had the opportunity really of *any* conversation with him."

"So you've no views on the subject?"

"He reminds me a little," said Miss Marple reflectively, "of a young man in the Town Clerk's office near where I live, Jonas Parry."

"And?" Mr. Rafiel asked and paused.

"He was not," said Miss Marple, "very satisfactory."

"Jackson's not wholly satisfactory either. He suits me all right. He's first class at his job, and he doesn't mind being sworn at. He knows he's damn' well paid and so he puts up with things. I wouldn't employ him in a position of trust, but I don't have to trust him. Maybe his past is blameless, maybe it isn't. His references were all right but I discern—shall I say, a note of reserve. Fortunately, I'm not a man who has any guilty secrets, so I'm not a subject for blackmail."

"No secrets?" said Miss Marple, thoughtfully. "Surely, Mr. Rafiel, you have business secrets?"

"Not where Jackson can get at them. No. Jackson is a smooth article, one might say, but I really don't see him as a murderer. I'd say that wasn't his line at all."

He paused a minute and then said suddenly, "Do you know, if one stands back and takes a good look at all this fantastic business, Major Palgrave and his ridiculous stories and all the rest of it, the *emphasis* is entirely wrong. *I'm* the person who ought to be murdered."

Miss Marple looked at him in some surprise.

"Proper type casting," explained Mr. Rafiel. "Who's the victim in murder stories? Elderly men with lots of money."

"And lots of people with a good reason for wishing him out of the way, so as to get that money," said Miss Marple. "Is that true also?"

"Well——" Mr. Rafiel considered. "I can count up to five or six men in London who wouldn't burst into tears if they read my obituary in *The Times*. But they wouldn't go so far as to do anything to bring about my demise. After all, why should they? I'm expected to die any day. In fact the bug— blighters are astonished that I've lasted so long. The doctors are surprised too."

"You have of course, a great will to live," said Miss Marple.

"You think that's odd, I suppose," said Mr. Rafiel.

Miss Marple shook her head.

"Oh no," she said, "I think it's quite natural. Life is more worth living, more full of interest when you are likely to lose it. It shouldn't be, perhaps, but it is. When you're young and strong and healthy, and life stretches ahead of you, living isn't really important at all. It's young people who commit suicide easily, out of despair from love, sometimes from sheer anxiety and worry. But old people know how valuable life is and how interesting."

"Hah!" said Mr. Rafiel, snorting. "Listen to a couple of old crocks."

"Well, what I said is true, isn't it?" demanded Miss Marple.

"Oh, yes," said Mr. Rafiel, "it's true enough. But don't you think I'm right when I say that I ought to be cast as the victim?"

"It depends on who has reason to gain by your death," said Miss Marple.

"Nobody, really," said Mr. Rafiel. "Apart, as I've said, from my competition in the business world who, as I have also said, can count comfortably on my being out of it before very long. I'm not such a fool as to leave a lot of money divided up among my relations. Precious little they'd get of it after the Government had taken practically the lot. Oh no, I've attended to all that years ago. Settlements, trusts and all the rest of it."

"Jackson, for instance, wouldn't profit by your death?"

"He wouldn't get a penny," said Mr. Rafiel cheerfully. "I pay him double the salary that he'd get from anyone else. That's because he has to put up with my bad temper; and he knows quite well that he will be the loser when I die."

"And Mrs. Walters?"

"The same goes for Esther. She's a good girl. First-class secretary, intelligent, good-tempered, understands my ways, doesn't turn a hair if I fly off the handle, couldn't care less if I insult her. Behaves like a nice nursery governess in charge of an outrageous and obstreperous child. She irritates me a bit sometimes, but who doesn't? There's nothing outstanding about her. She's rather a commonplace young woman in many ways, but I couldn't have anyone who suited me better. She's had a lot of trouble in her life. Married a man who wasn't much good. I'd say she never had much judgment when it came to men. Some women haven't. They fall for anyone who tells them a hard luck story. Always convinced that all the man needs is proper female understanding. That, once married to her, he'll pull up his socks and make a go of life! But of course that type of man never does. Anyway, fortunately her unsatisfactory husband died; drank too much at a party one night and stepped in front of a bus. Esther had a daughter to support and she went back to her secretarial job. She's been with me five years. I made it quite clear to her from the start that she need have no expectations from me in the event of my death. I paid her from the start a very large salary, and that salary I've augmented by as much as a quarter as much again each year. However decent and honest people are, one should never trust *anybody*—that's why I told Esther quite clearly that she'd nothing to hope for from my death. Every year I live she'll get a bigger salary. If she puts most of that aside every year—and that's what I think she has done—she'll be quite a well-to-do woman by the time I kick the bucket. I've made myself responsible for her daughter's schooling and I've put a sum in trust for the daughter which she'll get when she comes of age. So Mrs. Esther Walters is very comfortably placed. My death, let me tell you, would mean a serious financial loss to her." He looked very hard at Miss Marple. "She fully realizes all that. She's very sensible, Esther is."

"Do she and Jackson get on?" asked Miss Marple.

Mr. Rafiel shot a quick glance at her.

"Noticed something, have you?" he said. "Yes, I think Jackson's done a bit of tom-catting around, with an eye in her direction, especially lately. He's a good-looking chap, of course, but he hasn't cut any ice in that direction. For one thing, there's class distinction. She's just a cut above him. Not very much. If she was *really* a cut above him it wouldn't matter, but the lower middle class—they're very particular. Her mother was a school teacher and her father a bank clerk. No, she won't make a fool of herself about Jackson. Dare say he's after her little nest egg, but he won't get it."

"Hush—she's coming now!" said Miss Marple.

They both looked at Esther Walters as she came along the hotel path towards them.

"She's quite a good-looking girl, you know," said Mr. Rafiel, "but not an atom of glamor. I don't know why, she's quite nicely turned out."

Miss Marple sighed, a sigh that any woman will give however old at what might be considered wasted opportunities. What was lacking in Esther had been called by so many names during Miss Marple's span of existence. 'Not really attractive to men.' 'No S.A.' 'Lacks Come-hither in her eye.' Fair hair, good complexion, hazel eyes, quite a good figure, pleasant smile, but lacking something that makes a man's head turn when he passes a woman in the street.

"She ought to get married again," said Miss Marple, lowering her voice.

"Of course she ought. She'd make a man a good wife."

Esther Walters joined them and Mr. Rafiel said, in a slightly artificial voice,

"So there you are at last! What's been keeping you?"

"Everyone seemed to be sending cables this morning," said Esther. "What with that, and people trying to check out——"

"Trying to check out, are they? A result of this murder business?"

"I suppose so. Poor Tim Kendal is worried to death."

"And well he might be. Bad luck for that young couple, I must say."

"I know. I gather it was rather a big undertaking for them to take on this place. They've been worried about making a success of it. They were doing very well, too."

"They were doing a good job," agreed Mr. Rafiel.

"He's very capable and a damned hard worker. She's a very nice girl—attractive too. They've both worked like blacks, though that's an odd term to use out here, for blacks don't work themselves to death at all, so far as I can see. Was looking at a fellow shinning up a coconut tree to get his breakfast, then he goes to sleep for the rest of the day. Nice life."

He added, "We've been discussing the murder here."

Esther Walters looked slightly startled. She turned her head towards Miss Marple.

"I've been wrong about her," said Mr. Rafiel, with characteristic frankness. "Never been much of a one for the old pussies. All knitting wool and tittle-tattle. But this one's got something. Eyes and ears, and she uses them."

Esther Walters looked apologetically at Miss Marple, but Miss Marple did not appear to take offense.

"That's really meant to be a compliment, you know," Esther explained.

"I quite realize that," said Miss Marple. "I realize, too, that Mr. Rafiel is privileged, or thinks he is."

"What do you mean—privileged?" asked Mr. Rafiel.

"To be rude if you want to be rude," said Miss Marple.

"Have I been rude?" said Mr. Rafiel, surprised. "I'm sorry if I've offended you."

"You haven't offended me," said Miss Marple, "I make allowances."

"Now, don't be nasty. Esther, get a chair and bring it here. Maybe you can help."

Esther walked a few steps to the balcony of the bungalow and brought over a light basket chair.

"We'll go on with our consultation," said Mr. Rafiel. "We started with old Palgrave, deceased, and his eternal stories."

"Oh dear," sighed Esther. "I'm afraid I used to escape from him whenever I could."

"Miss Marple was more patient," said Mr. Rafiel. "Tell me, Esther, did he ever tell you a story about a murderer?"

"Oh yes," said Esther. "Several times."

"What was it exactly? Let's have *your* recollection."

"Well——" Esther paused to think. "The trouble is," she said apologetically, "I didn't really listen very closely. You see, it was rather like that terrible story about the lion in Rhodesia which used to go on and on. One did get rather in the habit of not listening."

"Well, tell us what you *do* remember."

"I think it arose out of some murder case that had been in the papers. Major Palgrave said that he'd had an experience not every person had had. He'd actually met a murderer face to face."

"Met?" Mr. Rafiel exclaimed. "Did he actually use the word 'Met'?"

Esther looked confused.

"I think so." She was doubtful. "Or he may have said, 'I can point you out a murderer.'"

"Well, which was it? There's a difference."

"I can't really be sure . . . I *think* he said he'd show me a picture of someone."

"That's better."

"And then he talked a lot about Lucrezia Borgia."

"Never mind Lucrezia Borgia. We know all about her."

"He talked about poisoners and that Lucrezia was very beautiful and had red hair. He said there were probably far more women poisoners going about the world than anyone knew."

"That I fear is *quite* likely," said Miss Marple.

"And he talked about poison being a woman's weapon."

"Seems to have been wandering from the point a bit," said Mr. Rafiel.

"Well, of course, he always did wander from the point in his stories. And then one used to stop listening and just say 'Yes' and 'Really?' and 'You don't say so.'"

"What about this picture he was going to show you?"

"I don't remember. It may have been something he'd seen in the paper——"

"He didn't actually show you a snapshot?"

"A snapshot? No." She shook her head. "I'm quite sure of that. He did say that she was a good-looking woman, and you'd never think she was a murderer to look at her."

"She?"

"There you are," exclaimed Miss Marple. "It makes it all so confusing."

"He was talking about a woman?" Mr. Rafiel asked.

"Oh yes."

"The snapshot was a snapshot of a woman?"

"Yes."

"It can't have been!"

"But it was," Esther persisted. "He said 'She's here in this island. I'll point her out to you, and then I'll tell you the whole story.'"

Mr. Rafiel swore. In saying what he thought of the late Major Palgrave he did not mince his words.

"The probabilities are," he finished, "that not a word of anything he said was true!"

"One does begin to wonder," Miss Marple murmured.

"So there we are," said Mr. Rafiel. "The old booby started telling you hunting tales. Pig sticking, tiger shooting, elephant hunting, narrow escapes from lions. One or two of them might have been fact. Several of them were fiction, and others had happened to somebody else! Then he gets on to the subject of murder and he tells one murder story to cap another murder story. And what's more he tells them all as if they'd happened to *him*. Ten to one most of them were a hash up of what he'd read in the paper, or seen on T.V."

He turned accusingly on Esther. "You admit that you weren't listening closely. Perhaps you misunderstood what he was saying."

"I'm certain he was talking about a woman," said Esther obstinately, "because of course I wondered who it was."

"Who do you think it was?" asked Miss Marple.

Esther flushed and looked slightly embarrassed.

"Oh, I didn't really—I mean, I wouldn't like to——"

Miss Marple did not insist. The presence of Mr. Rafiel, she thought, was inimical to her finding out exactly what suppositions Esther Walters had made. That could only be cosily brought out in a tête-à-tête between two women. And there was, of course, the possibility that Esther Walters was lying. Naturally, Miss Marple did not suggest this aloud. She registered it as a possibility but she was not inclined to believe in it. For one thing she did not think that Esther Walters was a liar (though one never knew) and for another, she could see no point in such a lie.

"But *you* say," Mr. Rafiel was now turning upon Miss Marple, "*you* say that he told you this yarn about a murderer and that he then said he had a picture of him which he was going to show you."

"I thought so, yes."

"You thought so? You were sure enough to begin with!"

Miss Marple retorted with spirit.

"It is never easy to repeat a conversation and be entirely accurate in what the other party to it has said. One is always inclined to jump at what you think they *meant*. Then, afterwards, you put actual words into their mouths. Major Palgrave told me this story, yes. He told me that the man who told it to him, this doctor, had shown him a snapshot of the murderer; but if I am to be quite honest I must admit that what he actually said to me was 'Would you like to see a snapshot of a murderer?' and naturally I assumed that it was the same snapshot he had been talking about. That it was the snapshot of that particular murderer. But I have to admit that it is possible—only remotely possible, but still possible—that by an association of ideas in his mind he leaped from the snapshot he had been shown in the past, to a snapshot he had taken recently of someone here whom he was convinced was a murderer."

"Women!" snorted Mr. Rafiel, in exasperation. "You're all the same, the whole blinking lot of you! Can't be accurate. You're never exactly *sure* of what a thing was. And now," he added irritably, "where does *that* leave us?" He snorted. "Evelyn Hillingdon, or Greg's wife, Lucky? The whole thing is a mess."

There was a slight apologetic cough. Arthur Jackson was standing at Mr. Rafiel's elbow. He had come so noiselessly that nobody had noticed him.

"Time for your massage, sir," he said.

Mr. Rafiel displayed immediate temper.

"What do you mean by sneaking up on me in that way and making me jump? I never heard you."

"Very sorry, sir."

"I don't think I'll have any massage today. It never does me a damn' bit of good."

"Oh come sir, you mustn't say that." Jackson was full of professional cheerfulness. "You'd soon notice it if you left it off."

He wheeled the chair deftly round.

Miss Marple rose to her feet, smiled at Esther and went down to the beach.

CHAPTER EIGHTEEN
Without Benefit of Clergy

THE BEACH WAS rather empty this morning. Greg was splashing in the water in his usual noisy style, Lucky was lying on her face on the beach with a sun-tanned back well oiled and her blonde hair splayed over her shoulders. The Hillingdons were not there. Señora de Caspearo, with an assorted bag of gentlemen in attendance was lying face upwards and talking deep-throated, happy Spanish. Some French and Italian children were playing at the water's edge and laughing. Canon and Miss Prescott were sitting in beach chairs observing the scene. The Canon had his hat tilted forward over his eyes and seemed half asleep. There was a convenient chair next to Miss Prescott and Miss Marple made for it and sat down.

"Oh dear," she said, with a deep sigh.

"I know," said Miss Prescott.

It was their joint tribute to violent death.

"That poor girl," said Miss Marple.

"Very sad," said the Canon. "Most deplorable."

"For a moment or two," said Miss Prescott, "we really thought of leaving, Jeremy and I. But then we decided against it. It would not really be fair, I felt, on the Kendals. After all, it's not *their* fault— It might have happened anywhere."

"In the midst of life we are in death," said the Canon solemnly.

"It's very important, you know," said Miss Prescott, "that they should make a go of this place. They have sunk all their capital in it."

"A very sweet girl," said Miss Marple, "but not looking at all well lately."

"Very nervy," agreed Miss Prescott. "Of course her family——" she shook her head.

"I really think, Joan," said the Canon in mild reproof, "that there are some things——"

"Everybody knows about it," said Miss Prescott. "Her family live in our part of the world. A great-aunt—most peculiar—and one of her uncles took off all his clothes in one of the tube stations. Green Park, I believe it was."

"Joan, that is a thing that should *not* be repeated."

"Very sad," said Miss Marple, shaking her head, "though I believe not an uncommon form of madness. I know when we were working for the Armenian relief, a most respectable elderly clergyman was afflicted the same way. They telephoned his wife and she came along at once and took him home in a cab, wrapped in a blanket."

"Of course, Molly's immediate family's all right," said Miss Prescott. "She never got on very well with her mother, but then so few girls seem to get on with their mothers nowadays."

"Such a pity," said Miss Marple, shaking her head, "because really a young girl needs her mother's knowledge of the world and experience."

"Exactly," said Miss Prescott with emphasis. "Molly, you know, took up with some man—*quite* unsuitable, I understand."

"It so often happens," said Miss Marple.

"Her family disapproved, naturally. *She* didn't tell them about it. They heard about it from a complete outsider. Of course her mother said she must bring him along so that they met him properly. This, I understand, the girl refused to do. She said it was humiliating to him. Most insulting to be made to come and meet her family and be looked over. Just as though you were a horse, she said."

Miss Marple sighed. "One does need so much *tact* when dealing with the young," she murmured.

"Anyway there it was! They forbade her to see him."

"But you can't *do* that nowadays," said Miss Marple. "Girls have jobs and they meet people whether anyone forbids them or not."

"But then, very fortunately," went on Miss Prescott, "she met Tim Kendal, and the other man sort of faded out of the picture. I can't *tell* you how relieved the family was."

"I hope they didn't show it too plainly," said Miss Marple. "That so often puts girls off from forming suitable attachments."

"Yes, indeed."

"One remembers oneself——" murmured Miss Marple, her mind going back to the past. A young man she had met at a croquet party. He had seemed so nice—rather gay, almost *Bohemian* in his views. And then he had been unexpectedly warmly welcomed by her father. He had been suitable, eligible; he had been asked freely to the house more than once, and Miss Marple had found that, after all, he was *dull*. Very dull.

The Canon seemed safely comatose and Miss Marple advanced tentatively to the subject she was anxious to pursue.

"Of course you know so much about this place," she murmured. "You have been here several years running, have you not?"

"Well, last year and two years before that. We like St. Honoré very much. Always such nice people here. Not the flashy, ultra-rich set."

"So I suppose you know the Hillingdons and the Dysons well!"

"Yes, fairly well."

Miss Marple coughed and lowered her voice slightly.

"Major Palgrave told me such an interesting story," she said.

"He had a great repertoire of stories, hadn't he? Of course he had traveled very widely. Africa, India, even China I believe."

"Yes indeed," said Miss Marple. "But I didn't mean one of *those* stories. This was a story concerned with—well, with one of the people I have just mentioned."

"Oh!" said Miss Prescott. Her voice held meaning.

"Yes. Now I wonder——" Miss Marple allowed her eyes to travel gently round the beach to where Lucky lay sunning her back. "Very beautifully tanned, isn't she," remarked Miss Marple. "And her hair. Most attractive. Practically the same color as Molly Kendal's, isn't it?"

"The only difference," said Miss Prescott, "is that Molly's is natural and Lucky's comes out of a bottle!"

"Really, Joan," the Canon protested, unexpectedly awake again. "Don't you think that is *rather* an uncharitable thing to say?"

"It's not uncharitable," said Miss Prescott, acidly. "Merely a *fact*."

"It looks very nice to *me*," said the Canon.

"Of course. That's why she does it. But I assure you, my dear Jeremy, it wouldn't deceive any *woman* for a moment. Would it?" She appealed to Miss Marple.

"Well, I'm afraid——" said Miss Marple, "of course I haven't the experience that you have—but I'm afraid—yes I should say definitely *not natural*. The appearance at the roots every fifth or sixth day——" She looked at Miss Prescott and they both nodded with quiet female assurance.

The Canon appeared to be dropping off again.

"Major Palgrave told me a really extraordinary story," murmured Miss Marple, "about—well I couldn't quite make out. I am a little deaf sometimes. He appeared to be saying or hinting——" she paused.

"I know what you mean. There was a great deal of talk at the time——"

"You mean at the time that——"

"When the first Mrs. Dyson died. Her death was quite unexpected. In fact, everybody thought she was a *malade imaginaire*—a hypochondriac. So when she had this attack and died so unexpectedly, well, of course, people did talk."

"There wasn't—any—trouble at the time?"

"The doctor was puzzled. He was quite a young man and he hadn't had much experience. He was what I call one of those antibiotics-for-all men. You know, the kind that doesn't bother to look at the patient much, or worry what's the matter with him. They just give them some kind of pill out of a bottle and if they don't get better, then they try a different pill. Yes, I believe he *was* puzzled, but it seemed she had had gastric trouble before. At least her husband said so, and there seemed no reason for believing anything was *wrong*."

"But you yourself think——"

"Well, I always try to keep an open mind, but one does *wonder*, you know. And what with various things people said——"

"Joan!" The Canon sat up. He looked belligerent. "I don't like—I really don't like to hear this kind of ill-natured gossip being repeated. We've always set our faces against that kind of thing. See no evil, hear no evil, speak no evil—and what is more, *think* no evil! That should be the motto of every Christian man and woman."

The two women sat in silence. They were rebuked, and in deference to their training they deferred to the criticism of a man. But inwardly they were frustrated, irritated and quite unrepentant. Miss Prescott threw a frank glance of irritation towards her brother. Miss Marple took out her knitting and looked at it. Fortunately for them Chance was on their side.

"*Mon père,*" said a small shrill voice. It was one of the French children who had been playing at the water's edge. She had come up unnoticed, and was standing by Canon Prescott's chair.

"*Mon père,*" she fluted.

"Eh? Yes, my dear? *Oui, qu'est-ce qu'il y a, ma petite?*"

The child explained. There had been a dispute about who should have the water-wings next and also other matters of seaside etiquette. Canon Prescott was extremely fond of children, especially small girls. He was always delighted to be summoned to act as arbiter in their disputes. He rose willingly now and accompanied the child to the water's edge. Miss Marple and Miss Prescott breathed deep sighs and turned avidly toward each other.

"Jeremy, of course rightly, is very against ill-natured gossip," said Miss Prescott, "but one cannot really ignore what people are saying. And there was, as I say, a great deal of talk at the time."

"Yes?" Miss Marple's tone urged her forward.

"This young woman, you see, Miss Greatorex, I think her name was then, I can't remember now, was a kind of cousin and she looked after Mrs. Dyson. Gave her all her medicines and things like that." There was a short, meaningful pause. "And of course there had, I understand"—Miss Prescott's voice was lowered—"been goings-on between Mr. Dyson and Miss Greatorex. A lot of people had noticed them. I mean things like that are quickly observed in a place like this. Then there was some curious story about some stuff that Edward Hillingdon got for her at a chemist."

"Oh, Edward Hillingdon came into it?"

"Oh yes, he was very much attracted. People noticed it. And Lucky—Miss Greatorex—played them off against each other. Gregory Dyson and Edward Hillingdon. One has to face it, she has always been an attractive woman."

"Though not as young as she was," Miss Marple replied.

"Exactly. But she was always very well turned out and made up. Of course not so flamboyant when she was just the poor relation. She always *seemed* very devoted to the invalid. But, well, you see how it was."

"What was this story about the chemist—how did that get known?"

"Well, it wasn't in Jamestown, I think it was when they were in Martinique. The French, I believe, are more lax than we are in the matter of drugs— This chemist talked to someone, and the story got around— Well, you know how these things happen."

Miss Marple did. None better.

"He said something about Colonel Hillingdon asking for something and not seeming to know what it was he was asking for. Consulting a piece of paper, you know, on which it was written down. Anyway, as I say, there was *talk.*"

"But I don't see quite why Colonel Hillingdon——" Miss Marple frowned in perplexity.

"I suppose he was just being used as a *cat's-paw.* Anyway, Gregory Dyson married again in an almost indecently short time. Barely a month later, I understand."

They looked at each other.

"But there was no *real* suspicion?" Miss Marple asked.

"Oh no, it was just—well, *talk*. Of course there may have been absolutely nothing in it."

"Major Palgrave thought there was."

"Did he say so to you?"

"I wasn't really listening very closely," confessed Miss Marple. "I just wondered if—er—well, if he'd said the same things to you?"

"He did point her out to me one day," said Miss Prescott.

"Really? He actually pointed her out?"

"Yes. As a matter of fact, I thought at first it was Mrs. Hillingdon he was pointing out. He wheezed and chuckled a bit and said 'Look at that woman over there. In my opinion that's a woman who's done murder and got away with it.' I was very shocked, of course. I said, 'Surely you're joking, Major Palgrave,' and he said 'Yes, yes dear lady, let's call it joking.' The Dysons and the Hillingdons were sitting at a table quite near to us, and I was afraid they'd overhear. He chuckled and said 'Wouldn't care to go to a drink party and have a certain person mix me a cocktail. Too much like supper with the Borgias.'"

"How *very* interesting," said Miss Marple. "Did he mention a—a photograph?"

"I don't remember. . . . Was it some newspaper cutting?"

Miss Marple, about to speak, shut her lips. The sun was momentarily obscured by a shadow. Evelyn Hillingdon paused beside them.

"Good morning," she said.

"I was wondering where you were," said Miss Prescott, looking up brightly.

"I've been to Jamestown, shopping."

"Oh, I see."

Miss Prescott looked round vaguely and Evelyn Hillingdon said:

"Oh, I didn't take Edward with me. Men hate shopping."

"Did you find anything of interest?"

"It wasn't that sort of shopping. I just had to go to the chemist."

With a smile and a slight nod she went on down the beach.

"Such nice people, the Hillingdons," said Miss Prescott, "though she's not really very easy to know, is she? I mean, she's always very pleasant and all that, but one never seems to get to know her any better."

Miss Marple agreed thoughtfully.

"One never knows what she is thinking," said Miss Prescott.

"Perhaps that is just as well," said Miss Marple.

"I beg your pardon?"

"Oh nothing really, only that I've always had the feeling that perhaps her thoughts might be rather disconcerting."

"Oh," said Miss Prescott, looking puzzled. "I see what you mean." She went on with a slight change of subject. "I believe they have a very charming place in Hampshire, and a boy—or is it two boys—who have just gone—or one of them—to Winchester."

"Do you know Hampshire well?"

"No. Hardly at all. I believe their house is somewhere near Alton."

"I see." Miss Marple paused and then said, "And where do the Dysons live?"

"California," said Miss Prescott. "When they are at home, that is. They are great travelers."

"One really knows so little about the people one meets when one is traveling," said Miss Marple. "I mean—how shall I put it— One only knows, doesn't one, what they choose to tell you about themselves. For instance, you don't *really* know that the Dysons live in California."

Miss Prescott looked startled.

"I'm sure Mr. Dyson mentioned it."

"Yes. Yes, exactly. That's what I mean. And the same thing perhaps with the Hillingdons. I mean when you say that they live in Hampshire, you're really repeating what *they* told *you,* aren't you?"

Miss Prescott looked slightly alarmed. "Do you mean that they don't live in Hampshire?" she asked.

"No, no, not for one moment," said Miss Marple, quickly apologetic. "I was only using them as an instance as to what one knows or doesn't know about people." She added, *"I* have told you that I live at St. Mary Mead, which is a place, no doubt, of which you have never heard. But you don't, if I may say so, know it of your *own* knowledge, do you?"

Miss Prescott forbore from saying that she really couldn't care less *where* Miss Marple lived. It was somewhere in the country and in the south of England and that is all she knew. "Oh, I do see what you mean," she agreed hastily, "and I know that one can't possibly be too careful when one is abroad."

"I didn't exactly mean *that,"* said Miss Marple.

There were some odd thoughts going through Miss Marple's mind. Did she really know, she was asking herself, that Canon Prescott and Miss Prescott were really Canon Prescott and Miss Prescott? They said so. There was no evidence to contradict them. It would really be easy, would it not, to put on a dog-collar, to wear the appropriate clothes, to make the appropriate conversation. If there was a motive . . .

Miss Marple was fairly knowledgeable about the clergy in her part of the world, but the Prescotts came from the north. Durham, wasn't it? She had no doubt they were the Prescotts, but still, it came back to the same thing— one believed what people said to one.

Perhaps one ought to be on one's guard against that. Perhaps. . . . She shook her head thoughtfully.

CHAPTER NINETEEN
Uses of a Shoe

CANON PRESCOTT CAME back from the water's edge slightly short of breath (playing with children is always exhausting).

Presently he and his sister went back to the hotel, finding the beach a little too hot.

"But," said Señora de Caspearo scornfully as they walked away— "How can a beach be too hot? It is nonsense that— And look what she wears—her arms and her neck are all covered up. Perhaps it is as well, that. Her skin it is hideous, like a plucked chicken!"

Miss Marple drew a deep breath. Now or never was the time for conversation with Señora de Caspearo. Unfortunately she did not know what to say. There seemed to be no common ground on which they could meet.

"You have children, Señora?" she inquired.

"I have three angels," said Señora de Caspearo, kissing her fingertips.

Miss Marple was rather uncertain as to whether this meant that Señora de Caspearo's offspring were in Heaven or whether it merely referred to their characters.

One of the gentlemen in attendance made a remark in Spanish and Señora de Caspearo flung back her head appreciatively and laughed loudly and melodiously.

"You understand what he said?" she inquired of Miss Marple.

"I'm afraid not," said Miss Marple apologetically.

"It is just as well. He is a wicked man."

A rapid and spirited interchange of Spanish badinage followed.

"It is infamous—infamous," said Señora de Caspearo, reverting to English with sudden gravity, "that the police do not let us go from this island. I storm, I scream, I stamp my foot—but all they say is No—No. You know how it will end—we shall all be killed."

Her bodyguard attempted to reassure her.

"But yes—I tell you it is unlucky here. I knew it from the first— That old Major, the ugly one—he had the Evil Eye—you remember? His eyes they crossed— It is bad, that! I make the Sign of the Horns every time when he looks my way." She made it in illustration. "Though since he is cross-eyed I am not always sure when he does look my way——"

"He has a glass eye," said Miss Marple in an explanatory voice. "An accident, I understand, when he was quite young. It was not his fault."

"I tell you he brought bad luck— I say it is the evil eye he had."

Her hand shot out again in the well-known Latin gesture—the first finger and the little finger sticking out, the two middle ones doubled in. "Anyway," she said cheerfully, "he is dead—I do not have to look at him any more. I do not like to look at things that are ugly."

It was, Miss Marple thought, a somewhat cruel epitaph on Major Palgrave.

Farther down the beach Gregory Dyson had come out of the sea. Lucky had turned herself over on the sand. Evelyn Hillingdon was looking at Lucky, and her expression, for some reason, made Miss Marple shiver.

"Surely I can't be cold—in this hot sun," she thought.

What was the old phrase—*"A goose walking over your grave——"*

She got up and went slowly back to her bungalow.

On the way she passed Mr. Rafiel and Esther Walters coming down the beach. Mr. Rafiel winked at her. Miss Marple did not wink back. She looked disapproving.

She went into her bungalow and lay down on her bed. She felt old and tired and worried.

She was quite certain that there was no time to be lost—no time—to—be lost. . . . It was getting late. . . . The sun was going to set—the sun—one must always look at the sun through smoked glass— Where was that piece of smoked glass that someone had given her? . . .

No, she wouldn't need it after all. A shadow had come over the sun blotting it out. A shadow. Evelyn Hillingdon's shadow— No, not Evelyn Hillingdon—The Shadow (what were the words) the *Shadow of the Valley of Death*. That was it. She must—what was it? Make the Sign of the Horns—to avert the Evil Eye—Major Palgrave's Evil Eye.

Her eyelids flickered open—she had been asleep. But there *was* a shadow—someone peering in at her window.

The shadow moved away—and Miss Marple saw who it was—It was Jackson.

'Impertinence—peering in like that,' she thought—and added parenthetically 'Just like Jonas Parry.'

The comparison reflected no credit on Jackson.

Then she wondered *why* Jackson had been peering in her bedroom. To see if she was there? Or to note that she was there, but was asleep.

She got up, went into the bathroom and peered cautiously through the window.

Arthur Jackson was standing by the door of the bungalow next door. Mr. Rafiel's bungalow. She saw him give a rapid glance round and then slip quickly inside. Interesting, thought Miss Marple. Why did he have to look round in that furtive manner. Nothing in the world could have been more natural than his going into Mr. Rafiel's bungalow since he himself had a room at the back of it. He was always going in and out of it on some errand or other. So why that quick, guilty glance round? 'Only one reason,' said Miss Marple answering her own question, 'he wanted to be sure that nobody was observing him enter at this particular moment because of something he was going to do in there.'

Everybody, of course, was on the beach at this moment, except those who had gone for expeditions. In about twenty minutes or so, Jackson himself would arrive on the beach in the course of his duties to aid Mr. Rafiel to take his sea dip. If he wanted to do anything in the bungalow unobserved, now was a very good time. He had satisfied himself that Miss Marple was asleep on her bed, he had satisfied himself that there was nobody near at hand to observe his movements. Well, she must do her best to do exactly that.

Sitting down on her bed, Miss Marple removed her neat sandal shoes and replaced them with a pair of plimsolls. Then she shook her head, removed the plimsolls, burrowed in her suitcase and took out a pair of shoes the heel on one of which she had recently caught on a hook by the door. It was now in a slightly precarious state and Miss Marple adroitly rendered it even more precarious by attention with a nail file. Then she emerged with due precaution from her door walking in stockinged feet. With all the care of a Big Game Hunter approaching up-wind of a herd of antelope, Miss Marple gently circumnavigated Mr. Rafiel's bungalow.

Cautiously she maneuvered her way around the corner of the house. She put on one of the shoes she was carrying, gave a final wrench to the heel of the other, sank gently to her knees and lay prone under the window. If

Jackson heard anything, if he came to the window to look out, an old lady would have had a fall owing to the heel coming off her shoe. But evidently Jackson had heard nothing.

Very, very gently Miss Marple raised her head. The windows of the bungalow were low. Shielding herself slightly with a festoon of creeper she peered inside. . . .

Jackson was on his knees before a suitcase. The lid of the suitcase was up and Miss Marple could see that it was a specially fitted affair containing compartments filled with various kinds of papers. Jackson was looking through the papers, occasionally drawing documents out of long envelopes. Miss Marple did not remain at her observation post for long. All she wanted was to know what Jackson was doing. She knew now. Jackson was snooping. Whether he was looking for something in particular, or whether he was just indulging his natural instincts, she had no means of judging. But it confirmed her in her belief that Arthur Jackson and Jonas Parry had strong affinities in other things than facial resemblance.

Her problem was now to withdraw. Very carefully she dropped down again and crept along the flowerbed until she was clear of the window. She returned to her bungalow and carefully put away the shoe and the heel that she had detached from it. She looked at them with affection. A good device which she could use on another day, if necessary. She resumed her own sandal shoes, and went thoughtfully down to the beach again.

Choosing a moment when Esther Walters was in the water, Miss Marple moved into the chair Esther had vacated.

Greg and Lucky were laughing and talking with Señora de Caspearo and making a good deal of noise.

Miss Marple spoke very quietly, almost under her breath, without looking at Mr. Rafiel.

"Do you know that Jackson snoops?"

"Doesn't surprise me," said Mr. Rafiel. "Caught him at it, did you?"

"I managed to observe him through a window. He had one of your suitcases open and was looking through your papers."

"Must have managed to get hold of a key to it. Resourceful fellow. He'll be disappointed though. Nothing he gets hold of in that way will do him a mite of good."

"He's coming down now," said Miss Marple, glancing up towards the hotel.

"Time for that idiotic sea dip of mine."

He spoke again—very quietly.

"As for you—don't be too enterprising. We don't want to be attending *your* funeral next. Remember your age, and be careful. There's somebody about who isn't too scrupulous, remember."

CHAPTER TWENTY
Night Alarm

I

EVENING CAME— The lights came up on the terrace— People dined and talked and laughed, albeit less loudly and merrily than they had a day or two ago— The steel band played.

But the dancing ended early. People yawned—went off to bed— The lights went out— There was darkness and stillness— The Golden Palm Tree slept. . . .

"Evelyn. Evelyn!" The whisper came sharp and urgent.

Evelyn Hillingdon stirred and turned on her pillow.

"Evelyn. Please wake up."

Evelyn Hillingdon sat up abruptly. Tim Kendal was standing in the doorway. She stared at him in surprise.

"Evelyn, *please,* could you come? It's—Molly. She's ill. I don't know what's the matter with her. I think she must have taken something."

Evelyn was quick, decisive.

"All right, Tim. I'll come. You go back to her. I'll be with you in a moment."

Tim Kendal disappeared. Evelyn slipped out of bed, threw on a dressing-gown and looked across at the other bed. Her husband, it seemed, had not been awakened. He lay there, his head turned away, breathing quietly. Evelyn hesitated for a moment, then decided not to disturb him. She went out of the door and walked rapidly to the main building and beyond it to the Kendals' bungalow. She caught up with Tim in the doorway.

Molly lay in bed. Her eyes were closed and her breathing was clearly not natural. Evelyn bent over her, rolled up an eyelid, felt her pulse and then looked at the bedside table. There was a glass there which had been used. Beside it was an empty phial of tablets. She picked it up.

"They were her sleeping pills," said Tim, "but that bottle was half full yesterday or the day before. I think she—must have taken the lot."

"Go and get Dr. Graham," said Evelyn, "and on the way knock them up and tell them to make strong coffee. Strong as possible. Hurry."

Tim dashed off. Just outside the doorway he collided with Edward Hillingdon.

"Oh, sorry, Edward."

"What's happening here?" demanded Hillingdon. "What's going on?"

"It's Molly. Evelyn's with her. I must get hold of the doctor. I suppose I ought've gone to him first but I—I wasn't sure and I thought Evelyn would know. Molly would have hated it if I'd fetched a doctor when it wasn't necessary."

He went off, running. Edward Hillingdon looked after him for a moment and then he walked into the bedroom.

"What's happening?" he said. "Is it serious?"

"Oh, there you are, Edward. I wondered if you'd woken up. This silly child has been taking things."

"Is it bad?"

"One can't tell without knowing how much she's taken. I shouldn't think it was too bad if we get going in time. I've sent for coffee. If we can get some of that down her——"

"But why should she do such a thing? You don't think——" He stopped.

"What don't I think?" asked Evelyn.

"You don't think it's because of the inquiry—the police—all that?"

"It's possible, of course. That sort of thing could be very alarming to a nervous type."

"Molly never used to seem a nervous type."

"One can't really tell," said Evelyn. "It's the most unlikely people sometimes who lose their nerve."

"Yes, I remember. . . ." Again he stopped.

"The truth is," said Evelyn, "that one doesn't really know anything about anybody." She added, "Not even the people who are nearest to you. . . ."

"Isn't that going a little too far, Evelyn—exaggerating too much?"

"I don't think it is. When you think of people, it is in the image you have made of them for yourself."

"I know you," said Edward Hillingdon quietly.

"You think you do."

"No. I'm sure." He added, "And you're sure of me."

Evelyn looked at him then turned back to the bed. She took Molly by the shoulders and shook her.

"We ought to be doing something, but I suppose it's better to wait until Dr. Graham comes— Oh, I think I hear them."

II

"She'll do now." Dr. Graham stepped back, wiped his forehead with a handkerchief and breathed a sigh of relief.

"You think she'll be all right, sir?" Tim demanded anxiously.

"Yes, yes. We got to her in good time. Anyway, she probably didn't take enough to kill her. A couple of days and she'll be as right as rain but she'll have a rather nasty day or two first." He picked up the empty bottle. "Who gave her these things anyway?"

"A doctor in New York. She wasn't sleeping well."

"Well, well. I know all we medicos hand these things out freely nowadays. Nobody tells young women who can't sleep to count sheep, or get up and eat a biscuit, or write a couple of letters and then go back to bed. Instant remedies, that's what people demand nowadays. Sometimes I think it's a pity we give them to them. You've got to learn to put up with things in life. All very well to stuff a comforter into a baby's mouth to stop it crying.

Can't go on doing that all a person's life." He gave a small chuckle. "I bet you, if you asked Miss Marple what she does if she can't sleep, she'd tell you she counted sheep going under a gate." He turned back to the bed where Molly was stirring. Her eyes were open now. She looked at them without interest or recognition. Dr. Graham took her hand.

"Well, well, my dear, and what have you been doing to yourself?"

She blinked but did not reply.

"Why did you do it, Molly, why? Tell me why?" Tim took her other hand.

Still her eyes did not move. If they rested on anyone it was on Evelyn Hillingdon. There might have been even a faint question in them, but it was hard to tell. Evelyn spoke as though there had been the question.

"Tim came and fetched me," she said.

Her eyes went to Tim, then shifted to Dr. Graham.

"You're going to be all right now," said Dr. Graham, "but don't do it again."

"She didn't mean to do it," said Tim quietly. "I'm sure she didn't mean to do it. She just wanted a good night's rest. Perhaps the pills didn't work at first and so she took more of them. Is that it, Molly?"

Her head moved very faintly in a negative motion.

"You mean—you took them on purpose?" said Tim.

Molly spoke then. "Yes," she said.

"But why, Molly, why?"

The eyelids faltered. "Afraid." The word was just heard.

"Afraid? Of what?"

But her eyelids closed down.

"Better let her be," said Dr. Graham. Tim spoke impetuously.

"Afraid of what? The police? Because they've been hounding you, asking you questions? I don't wonder. Anyone might feel frightened. But it's just their way, that's all. Nobody thinks for one moment——" he broke off.

Dr. Graham made him a decisive gesture.

"I want to go to sleep," said Molly.

"The best thing for you," said Dr. Graham.

He moved to the door and the others followed him.

"She'll sleep all right," said Graham.

"Is there anything I ought to do?" asked Tim. He had the usual, slightly apprehensive attitude of a man in illness.

"I'll stay if you like," said Evelyn kindly.

"Oh no. No, that's quite all right," said Tim.

Evelyn went back towards the bed. "Shall I stay with you, Molly?"

Molly's eyes opened again. She said, "No," and then after a pause, "just Tim."

Tim came back and sat down by the bed.

"I'm here, Molly," he said and took her hand. "Just go to sleep. I won't leave you."

She sighed faintly and her eyes closed.

The doctor paused outside the bungalow and the Hillingdons stood with him.

"You're sure there's nothing more I can do?" asked Evelyn.

"I don't think so, thank you, Mrs. Hillingdon. She'll be better with her

husband now. But possibly tomorrow—after all, he's got this hotel to run—
I think someone should be with her."

"D'you think she might—try again?" asked Hillingdon.

Graham rubbed his forehead irritably.

"One never knows in these cases. Actually, it's most unlikely. As you've
seen for yourselves, the restorative treatment is extremely unpleasant. But of
course one can never be absolutely certain. She may have more of this stuff
hidden away somewhere."

"I should never have thought of suicide in connection with a girl like
Molly," said Hillingdon.

Graham said dryly, "It's not the people who are always talking of killing
themselves, threatening to do so, who do it. They dramatize themselves that
way and let off steam."

"Molly always seemed such a happy girl. I think perhaps"—Evelyn
hesitated—"I ought to tell you, Dr. Graham."

She told him then about her interview with Molly on the beach the night
that Victoria had been killed. Graham's face was very grave when she had
finished.

"I'm glad you've told me, Mrs. Hillingdon. There are very definite
indications there of some kind of deep-rooted trouble. Yes. I'll have a word
with her husband in the morning."

III

"I want to talk to you seriously, Kendal, about your wife."

They were sitting in Tim's office. Evelyn Hillingdon had taken his place
by Molly's bedside and Lucky had promised to come and, as she expressed
it, 'spell her' later. Miss Marple had also offered her services. Poor Tim was
torn between his hotel commitments and his wife's condition.

"I can't understand it," said Tim, "I can't understand Molly any longer.
She's changed. Changed out of all seeming."

"I understand she's been having bad dreams?"

"Yes. Yes, she complained about them a good deal."

"For how long?"

"Oh, I don't know. About—oh I suppose a month—perhaps longer.
She—we—thought they were just—well, nightmares, you know."

"Yes, yes, I quite understand. But what's a much more serious sign is the
fact that she seems to have felt afraid of someone. Did she complain about
that to you?"

"Well, yes. She said once or twice that—oh, people were following her."

"Ah! Spying on her?"

"Yes, she did use that term once. She said they were her enemies and
they'd followed her here."

"Did she have enemies, Mr. Kendal?"

"No. Of course she didn't."

"No incident in England, anything you know about before you were married?"

"Oh no, nothing of that kind. She didn't get on with her family very well, that was all. Her mother was rather an eccentric woman, difficult to live with perhaps, but. . . ."

"Any signs of mental instability in her family?"

Tim opened his mouth impulsively, then shut it again. He pushed a fountain pen about on the desk in front of him.

The doctor said:

"I must stress the fact that it would be better to tell me, Tim, if that is the case."

"Well, yes, I believe so. Nothing serious, but I believe there was an aunt or something who was a bit batty. But that's nothing. I mean—well you get that in almost any family."

"Oh yes, yes, that's quite true. I'm not trying to alarm you about that, but it just might show a tendency to—well to break down or imagine things if any stress arose."

"I don't really know very much," said Tim. "After all, people don't pour out all their family histories to you, do they?"

"No, no. Quite so. She had no former friend—she was not engaged to anyone, anyone who might have threatened her or made jealous threats? That sort of thing?"

"I don't know. I don't think so. Molly *was* engaged to some other man before I came along. Her parents were very against it, I understand, and I think she really stuck to the chap more out of opposition and defiance than anything else." He gave a sudden half-grin. "You know what it is when you're young. If people cut up a fuss it makes you much keener on whoever it is."

Dr. Graham smiled too. "Ah yes, one often sees that. One should never take exception to one's children's objectionable friends. Usually they grow out of them naturally. This man, whoever he was, didn't make threats of any kind against Molly?"

"No, I'm sure he didn't. She would have told me. She said herself she just had a silly adolescent craze on him, mainly because he had such a bad reputation."

"Yes, yes. Well, that doesn't sound serious. Now there's another thing. Apparently your wife has had what she describes as blackouts. Brief passages of time during which she can't account for her actions. Did you know about that, Tim?"

"No," said Tim slowly. "No, I didn't. She never told me. I did notice, you know, now you mention it, that she seemed rather vague sometimes and . . ." He paused, thinking. "Yes, that explains it. I couldn't understand how she seemed to have forgotten the simplest things, or sometimes not to seem to know what time of day it was. I just thought she was absent-minded, I suppose."

"What it amounts to, Tim, is just this. I advise you most strongly to take your wife to see a good specialist."

Tim flushed angrily.

"You mean a mental specialist, I suppose?"

"Now, now, don't be upset by labels. A neurologist, a psychologist, someone who specializes in what the layman calls nervous breakdowns. There's a good man in Kingston. Or there's New York of course. There is something that is causing these nervous terrors of your wife's. Something perhaps for which she hardly knows the reason herself. Get advice about her, Tim. Get advice as soon as possible."

He clapped his hand on the young man's shoulder and got up.

"There's no immediate worry. Your wife has good friends and we'll all be keeping an eye on her."

"She won't—you don't think she'll try it again?"

"I think it most unlikely," said Dr. Graham.

"You can't be sure," said Tim.

"One can never be sure," said Dr. Graham, "that's one of the first things you learn in my profession." Again he laid a hand on Tim's shoulder. "Don't worry too much."

"That's easy to say," said Tim as the doctor went out of the door. "Don't worry, indeed! What does he think I'm made of?"

CHAPTER TWENTY-ONE
Jackson on Cosmetics

"YOU'RE SURE YOU don't mind, Miss Marple?" said Evelyn Hillingdon.

"No, indeed, my dear," said Miss Marple. "I'm only too delighted to be of use in any way. At my age, you know, one feels very useless in the world. Especially when I am in a place like this, just enjoying myself. No duties of any kind. No, I'll be delighted to sit with Molly. You go along on your expedition. Pelican Point, wasn't it?"

"Yes," said Evelyn. "Both Edward and I love it. I never get tired of seeing the birds diving down, catching up the fish. Tim's with Molly now. But he's got things to do and he doesn't seem to like her being left alone."

"He's quite right," said Miss Marple. "I wouldn't in his place. One never knows, does one? when anyone has attempted anything of that kind— Well, go along, my dear."

Evelyn went off to join a little group that was waiting for her. Her husband, the Dysons and three or four other people. Miss Marple checked her knitting requirements, saw that she had all she wanted with her, and walked over towards the Kendals' bungalow.

As she came up on to the loggia she heard Tim's voice through the half-open French window.

"If you'd only tell me *why* you did it, Molly. What made you? Was it anything I did? There must be some reason. If you'd only tell me."

Miss Marple paused. There was a little pause inside before Molly spoke. Her voice was flat and tired.

"I don't know, Tim, I really don't know. I suppose—something came over me."

Miss Marple tapped on the window and walked in.

"Oh there you are, Miss Marple. It is very good of you."

"Not at all," said Miss Marple. "I'm delighted to be of any help. Shall I sit here in this chair? You're looking much better, Molly. I'm so glad."

"I'm all right," said Molly. "Quite all right. Just—oh, just sleepy."

"I shan't talk," said Miss Marple. "You just lie quiet and rest. I'll get on with my knitting."

Tim Kendal threw her a grateful glance and went out. Miss Marple established herself in her chair.

Molly was lying on her left side. She had a half-stupefied, exhausted look. She said in a voice that was almost a whisper:

"It's very kind of you, Miss Marple. I—I think I'll go to sleep."

She half turned away on her pillows and closed her eyes. Her breathing grew more regular though it was still far from normal. Long experience of nursing made Miss Marple almost automatically straighten the sheet and tuck it under the mattress on her side of the bed. As she did so her hand encountered something hard and rectangular under the mattress. Rather surprised she took hold of this and pulled it out. It was a book. Miss Marple threw a quick glance at the girl in the bed, but she lay there utterly quiescent. She was evidently asleep. Miss Marple opened the book. It was, she saw, a current work on nervous diseases. It came open naturally at a certain place which gave a description of the onset of persecution mania and various other manifestations of schizophrenia and allied complaints.

It was not a highly technical book, but one that could be easily understood by a layman. Miss Marple's face grew very grave as she read. After a minute or two she closed the book and stayed thinking. Then she bent forward and with some care replaced the book where she had found it, under the mattress.

She shook her head in some perplexity. Noiselessly she rose from the chair. She walked the few steps towards the window, then turned her head sharply over her shoulder. Molly's eyes were open but even as Miss Marple turned the eyes shut again. For a minute or two, Miss Marple was not quite certain whether she might not have imagined that quick, sharp glance. Was Molly then only pretending to be asleep? That might be natural enough. She might feel that Miss Marple would start talking to her if she showed herself awake. Yes, that could be all it was.

Was she reading into that glance of Molly's a kind of slyness that was somehow innately disagreeable? One doesn't know, Miss Marple thought to herself, one really doesn't know.

She decided that she would try to manage a little talk with Dr. Graham as soon as it could be managed. She came back to her chair by the bed. She decided after about five minutes or so that Molly was really asleep. No one could have lain so still, could have breathed so evenly. Miss Marple got up again. She was wearing her plimsolls today. Not perhaps very elegant, but admirably suited to this climate and comfortable and roomy for the feet.

She moved gently round the bedroom, pausing at both of the windows, which gave out in two different directions.

The hotel grounds seemed quiet and deserted. Miss Marple came back and was standing a little uncertainly before regaining her seat, when she thought she heard a faint sound outside. Like the scrape of a shoe on the loggia? She hesitated a moment, then she went to the window, pushed it a little farther open, stepped out and turned her head back into the room as she spoke.

"I shall be gone only a very short time, dear," she said, "just back to my bungalow, to see where I could possibly have put that pattern. I was so sure I had brought it with me. You'll be quite all right till I come back, won't you?" Then turning her head back, she nodded to herself. "Asleep, poor child. A good thing."

She went quietly along the loggia, down the steps and turned sharp right to the path there. Passing along between the screen of some hibiscus bushes an observer might have been curious to see that Miss Marple veered sharply on to the flower-bed, passed round to the back of the bungalow and entered it again through the second door there. This led directly into a small room that Tim sometimes used as an unofficial office and from that into the sitting-room.

Here there were wide curtains semi-drawn to keep the room cool. Miss Marple slipped behind one of them. Then she waited. From the window here she had a good view of anyone who approached Molly's bedroom. It was some few minutes, four or five, before she saw anything.

The neat figure of Jackson in his white uniform went up the steps of the loggia. He paused for a minute at the balcony there, and then appeared to be giving a tiny discreet tap on the door of the window that was ajar. There was no response that Miss Marple could hear. Jackson looked around him, a quick furtive glance, then he slipped inside the open doors. Miss Marple moved to the door which led directly into the bedroom. She did not go through it but applied her eye to the hinge.

Jackson had walked into the room. He approached the bed and looked down for a minute on the sleeping girl. Then he turned away and walked not to the sitting-room door but to the far door which led into the adjoining bathroom. Miss Marple's eyebrows rose in slight surprise. She reflected a minute or two, then walked out into the passageway and into the bathroom by the other door.

Jackson spun round from examining the shelf over the wash-basin. He looked taken aback, which was not surprising.

"Oh," he said, "I—I didn't. . . ."

"Mr. Jackson," said Miss Marple, in great surprise.

"I thought you'd be here somewhere," said Jackson.

"Did you want anything?" inquired Miss Marple.

"Actually," said Jackson, "I was just looking at Mrs. Kendal's brand of face cream."

Miss Marple appreciated the fact that as Jackson was standing with a jar of face cream in his hand he had been adroit in mentioning that fact at once.

"Nice smell," he said, wrinkling up his nose. "Fairly good stuff, as these preparations go. The cheaper brands don't suit every skin. Bring it out in a rash as likely as not. The same thing with face powders sometimes."

"You seem to be very knowledgeable on the subject," said Miss Marple.

"Worked in the pharmaceutical line for a bit," said Jackson. "One learns to know a good deal about cosmetics there. Put stuff in a fancy jar, package it expensively, and it's astonishing what you could rook women for."

"Is that what you——?" Miss Marple broke off deliberately.

"Well no, I didn't come in here to talk about cosmetics," Jackson agreed.

'You've not had much time to think up a lie,' thought Miss Marple to herself. 'Let's see what you'll come out with.'

"Matter of fact," said Jackson, "Mrs. Walters lent her lipstick to Mrs. Kendal the other day. I came in to get it back for her. I tapped on the window and then I saw Mrs. Kendal was fast asleep, so I thought it would be quite all right if I just walked across into the bathroom and looked for it."

"I see," said Miss Marple. "And did you find it?"

Jackson shook his head. "Probably in one of her handbags," he said lightly. "I won't bother. Mrs. Walters didn't make a point of it. She only just mentioned it casually." He went on, surveying the toilet preparations: "Doesn't have very much, does she? Ah well, doesn't need it at her age. Good natural skin."

"You must look at women with quite a different eye from ordinary men," said Miss Marple, smiling pleasantly.

"Yes. I suppose various jobs do alter one's angle."

"You know a good deal about drugs?"

"Oh yes. Good working acquaintance with them. If you ask me, there are too many of them about nowadays. Too many tranquilizers and pep pills and miracle drugs and all the rest of it. All right if they're given on prescription, but there are too many of them you can get without prescription. Some of them can be dangerous."

"I suppose so," said Miss Marple. "Yes, I suppose so."

"They have a great effect, you know, on behavior. A lot of this teenage hysteria you get from time to time. It's not natural causes. The kids've been taking things. Oh, there's nothing new about it. It's been known for ages. Out in the East—not that I've ever been there—all sorts of funny things used to happen. You'd be surprised at some of the things women gave their husbands. In India, for example, in the bad old days, a young wife who married an old husband. Didn't want to get rid of him, I suppose, because she'd have been burnt on the funeral pyre, or if she wasn't burnt she'd have been treated as an outcast by the family. No catch to have been a widow in India in those days. But she could keep an elderly husband under drugs, make him semi-imbecile, give him hallucinations, drive him more or less off his head." He shook his head. "Yes, lot of dirty work."

He went on: "And witches, you know. There's a lot of interesting things known now about witches. Why did they always confess, why did they admit so readily that they *were* witches, that they had flown on broomsticks to the Witches' Sabbath."

"Torture," said Miss Marple.

"Not always," said Jackson. "Oh yes, torture accounted for a lot of it, but they came out with some of those confessions almost before torture was mentioned. They didn't so much confess as boast about it. Well, they rubbed themselves with ointments, you know. Anointing they used to call it. Some of the preparations, belladonna, atropine, all that sort of thing; if you rub them on the skin they give you hallucinations of levitation, of flying through the air. They thought it all was genuine, poor devils. And look at the Assassins—medieval people, out in Syria, the Lebanon, somewhere like that. They fed them Indian hemp, gave them hallucinations of paradise and houris, and endless time. They were told that that was what would happen to them after death, but to attain it they had to go and do a ritual killing. Oh, I'm not putting it in fancy language, but that's what it came to."

"What it came to," said Miss Marple, "is in essence the fact that people are highly credulous."

"Well yes, I suppose you could put it like that."

"They believe what they are told," said Miss Marple. "Yes indeed, we're all inclined to do that," she added. Then she said sharply, "Who told you these stories about India, about the doping of husbands with datura," and she added sharply, before he could answer, "Was it Major Palgrave?"

Jackson looked slightly surprised. "Well—yes, as a matter of fact, it was. He told me a lot of stories like that. Of course most of it must have been before his time, but he seemed to know all about it."

"Major Palgrave was under the impression that he knew a lot about everything," said Miss Marple. "He was often inaccurate in what he told people." She shook her head thoughtfully. "Major Palgrave," she said, "has a lot to answer for."

There was a slight sound from the adjoining bedroom. Miss Marple turned her head sharply. She went quickly out of the bathroom into the bedroom. Lucky Dyson was standing just inside the window.

"I—oh! I didn't think you were here, Miss Marple."

"I just stepped into the bathroom for a moment," said Miss Marple, with dignity and a faint air of Victorian reserve.

In the bathroom, Jackson grinned broadly. Victorian modesty always amused him.

"I just wondered if you'd like me to sit with Molly for a bit," said Lucky. She looked over towards the bed. "She's asleep, isn't she?"

"I think so," said Miss Marple. "But it's really quite all right. You go and amuse yourself, my dear. I thought you'd gone on that expedition?"

"I was going," said Lucky, "but I had such a filthy headache that at the last moment I cried off. So I thought I might as well make myself useful."

"That was very nice of you," said Miss Marple. She reseated herself by the bed and resumed her knitting, "but I'm *quite* happy here."

Lucky hesitated for a moment or two and then turned away and went out. Miss Marple waited a moment then tiptoed back into the bathroom, but Jackson had departed, no doubt through the other door. Miss Marple picked up the jar of face cream he had been holding, and slipped it into her pocket.

CHAPTER TWENTY-TWO
A Man in Her Life?

GETTING A LITTLE chat in a natural manner with Dr. Graham was not so easy as Miss Marple had hoped. She was particularly anxious not to approach him directly since she did not want to lend undue importance to the questions that she was going to ask him.

Tim was back, looking after Molly and Miss Marple had arranged that she should relieve him there during the time that dinner was served and he was needed in the dining-room. He had assured her that Mrs. Dyson was quite willing to take that on, or even Mrs. Hillingdon, but Miss Marple said firmly that they were both young women who liked enjoying themselves and that she herself preferred a light meal early and so that would suit everybody. Tim once again thanked her warmly. Hovering rather uncertainly round the hotel and on the pathway which connected with various bungalows, among them Dr. Graham's, Miss Marple tried to plan what she was going to do next.

She had a lot of confused and contradictory ideas in her head and if there was one thing that Miss Marple did not like, it was to have confused and contradictory ideas. This whole business had started out clearly enough. Major Palgrave with his regrettable capacity for telling stories, his indiscretion that had obviously been overheard and the corollary, his death within twenty-four hours. Nothing difficult about *that,* thought Miss Marple.

But afterwards, she was forced to admit, there was nothing *but* difficulty. Everything pointed in too many different directions at once. Once admit that you didn't believe a word that anybody had said to you, that nobody could be trusted, and that many of the persons with whom she had conversed here had had regrettable resemblances to certain persons at St. Mary Mead, and where did that lead you?

Her mind was increasingly focused on the victim. Someone was going to be killed and she had the increasing feeling that she ought to know quite well who that someone was. There had been *something.* Something she had heard? Noticed? Seen?

Something someone had told her that had a bearing on the case. Joan Prescott? Joan Prescott had said a lot of things about a lot of people. Scandal? Gossip? What exactly *had* Joan Prescott said?

Gregory Dyson, Lucky—Miss Marple's mind hovered over Lucky. Lucky, she was convinced with a certainty born of her natural suspicions, had been actively concerned in the death of Gregory Dyson's first wife. Everything pointed to it. Could it be that the predestined victim over whom she was worrying was Gregory Dyson? That Lucky intended to try her luck again with another husband, and for that reason wanted not only freedom but the handsome inheritance that she would get as Gregory Dyson's widow?

'But really,' said Miss Marple to herself, 'this is all pure conjecture. I'm being stupid. I know I'm being stupid. The truth must be quite plain, if one could just clear away the litter. Too much litter, that's what's the matter.'

"Talking to yourself?" said Mr. Rafiel.

Miss Marple jumped. She had not noticed his approach. Esther Walters was supporting him and he was coming slowly down from his bungalow to the terrace.

"I really didn't notice you, Mr. Rafiel."

"Your lips were moving. What's become of all this urgency of yours?"

"It's still urgent," said Miss Marple, "only I can't just see what must be perfectly plain——"

"I'm glad it's as simple as that— Well, if you want any help, count on me."

He turned his head as Jackson approached them along the path.

"So there you are, Jackson. Where the devil have you been? Never about when I want you."

"Sorry, Mr. Rafiel."

Dexterously he slipped his shoulder under Mr. Rafiel's. "Down to the terrace, sir?"

"You can take me to the bar," said Mr. Rafiel. "All right, Esther, you can go now and change into your evening togs. Meet me on the terrace in half an hour."

He and Jackson went off together. Mrs. Walters dropped into the chair by Miss Marple. She rubbed her arm gently.

"He *seems* a very light weight," she observed, "but at the moment my arm feels quite numb. I haven't seen you this afternoon at all, Miss Marple."

"No, I've been sitting with Molly Kendal," Miss Marple explained. "She seems really very much better."

"If you ask me there was never very much wrong with her," said Esther Walters.

Miss Marple raised her eyebrows. Esther Walters's tone had been decidedly dry.

"You mean—you think her suicide attempt . . . ."

"I don't think there *was* any suicide attempt," said Esther Walters. "I don't believe for a moment she took a real overdose and I think Dr. Graham knows that perfectly well."

"Now you interest me very much," said Miss Marple. "I wonder why you say that?"

"Because I'm almost certain that it's the case. Oh, it's a thing that happens very often. It's a way, I suppose, of calling attention to oneself," went on Esther Walters.

"'You'll be sorry when I'm dead'?" quoted Miss Marple.

"That sort of thing," agreed Esther Walters, "though I don't think that was the motive in this particular instance. That's the sort of thing you feel like when your husband's playing you up and you're terribly fond of him."

"You don't think Molly Kendal is fond of her husband?"

"Well," said Esther Walters, "do you?"

Miss Marple considered. "I have," she said, "more or less assumed it." She paused a moment before adding, "perhaps wrongly."

Esther was smiling her rather wry smile.

"I've heard a little about her, you know. About the whole business."

"From Miss Prescott?"

"Oh," said Esther, "from one or two people. There's a man in the case. Someone she was keen on. Her people were dead against him."

"Yes," said Miss Marple, "I did hear that."

"And then she married Tim. Perhaps she was fond of him in a way. But the other man didn't give up. I've wondered once or twice if he didn't actually follow her out here."

"Indeed. But—who?"

"I've no idea who," said Esther, "and I should imagine that they've been very careful."

"You think she cares for this other man?"

Esther shrugged her shoulders. "I dare say he's a bad lot," she said, "but that's very often the kind who knows how to get under a woman's skin and stay there."

"You never heard what kind of a man—what he did—anything like that?"

Esther shook her head. "No. People hazard guesses, but you can't go by that type of thing. He may have been a married man. That may have been why her people disliked it, or he may have been a real bad lot. Perhaps he drank. But she cares for him still. That I know positively."

"You've seen something, heard something?" Miss Marple hazarded.

"I know what I'm talking about," said Esther. Her voice was harsh and unfriendly.

"These murders——" began Miss Marple.

"Can't you forget murders?" said Esther. "You've got Mr. Rafiel now all tangled up in them. Can't you just—let them be? You'll never find out any more, I'm sure of that."

Miss Marple looked at her.

"You think you know, don't you?" she said.

"I think I do, yes. I'm fairly sure."

"Then oughtn't you to tell what you know—do something about it?"

"Why should I? What good would it do? I couldn't prove anything. What would happen anyway? People get let off nowadays so easily. They call it diminished responsibility and things like that. A few years in prison and you're out again, as right as rain."

"Supposing, because you don't tell what you know, somebody else gets killed—another victim?"

Esther shook her head with confidence. "That won't happen," she said.

"You can't be sure of it."

"I am sure. And in any case I don't see who——" She frowned. "Anyway," she added, almost inconsequently, "perhaps it *is*—diminished responsibility. Perhaps you can't help it—not if you are really mentally unbalanced. Oh, I don't know. By far the best thing would be if she went off with whoever it is, then we could all forget about things."

She glanced at her watch, gave an exclamation of dismay and got up.

"I must go and change."

Miss Marple sat looking after her. Pronouns, she thought, were always puzzling and women like Esther Walters were particularly prone to strew them about haphazard. Was Esther Walters for some reason convinced that a *woman* had been responsible for the deaths of Major Palgrave and Victoria? It sounded like it. Miss Marple considered.

"Ah, Miss Marple, sitting here all alone—and not even knitting?"

It was Dr. Graham for whom she had sought so long and so unsuccessfully. And here he was prepared of his own accord to sit down for a few minutes' chat. He wouldn't stay long, Miss Marple thought, because he was too bent on changing for dinner, and he usually dined fairly early. She explained that she had been sitting by Molly Kendal's bedside that afternoon.

"One can hardly believe she has made such a good recovery so quickly," she said.

"Oh well," said Dr. Graham, "it's not very surprising. She didn't take a very heavy overdose, you know."

"Oh, I understood she'd taken quite a half-bottle full of tablets."

Dr. Graham was smiling indulgently.

"No," he said, "I don't think she took that amount. I dare say she meant to take them, then probably at the last moment she threw half of them away. People, even when they think they want to commit suicide, often don't *really* want to do it. They manage not to take a full overdose. It's not always deliberate deceit, it's just the subconscious looking after itself."

"Or, I suppose it might be deliberate. I mean, wanting it to appear that . . ." Miss Marple paused.

"It's possible," said Dr. Graham.

"If she and Tim had had a row, for instance?"

"They don't have rows, you know. They seem very fond of each other. Still, I suppose it can always happen once. No, I don't think there's very much wrong with her now. She could really get up and go about as usual. Still, it's safer to keep her where she is for a day or two——"

He got up, nodded cheerfully and went off towards the hotel. Miss Marple sat where she was a little while longer.

Various thoughts passed through her mind— The book under Molly's mattress— The way Molly had feigned sleep—

Things Joan Prescott and, later, Esther Walters, had said . . .

And then she went back to the beginning of it all—to Major Palgrave—

Something struggled in her mind. Something about Major Palgrave—

Something that if she could only remember—

CHAPTER TWENTY-THREE
The Last Day

I

'AND THE EVENING and the morning were the last day,' said Miss Marple to herself.

Then, slightly confused, she sat upright again in her chair. She had dozed off, an incredible thing to do because the steel band was playing and anyone who could doze off during the steel band— Well, it showed, thought Miss Marple, that she was getting used to this place! What was it she had been saying? Some quotation that she'd got wrong. Last day? *First* day. That's what it ought to be. This wasn't the first day. Presumably it wasn't the last day either.

She sat upright again. The fact was that she was extremely tired. All this anxiety, this feeling of having been shamefully inadequate in some way. . . . She remembered unpleasantly once more that queer sly look that Molly had given her from under her half-closed eyelids. What had been going on in that girl's head? How different, thought Miss Marple, everything had seemed at first. Tim Kendal and Molly, such a natural happy young couple. The Hillingdons so pleasant, so well-bred, such what is called 'nice' people. The gay hearty extrovert, Greg Dyson, and the gay strident Lucky, talking nineteen to the dozen, pleased with herself and the world . . . A quartet of people getting on so well together. Canon Prescott, that genial kindly man. Joan Prescott, an acid streak in her, but a very nice woman, and nice women have to have their gossipy distractions. They have to know what is going on, to know when two and two make four, and when it is possible to stretch them to five! There was no harm in such women. Their tongues wagged but they were kind if you were in misfortune. Mr. Rafiel, a personality, a man of character, a man that you would never by any chance forget. But Miss Marple thought she knew something else about Mr. Rafiel.

The doctors had often given him up, so he had said, but this time, she thought, they had been more certain in their pronouncements. Mr. Rafiel knew that his days were numbered.

Knowing this with certainty, was there any action he might have been likely to take?

Miss Marple considered the question.

It might, she thought, be important.

What was it exactly he had said, his voice a little too loud, a little too sure? Miss Marple was very skilful in tones of voice. She had done so much listening in her life.

Mr. Rafiel had been telling her something that wasn't true.

Miss Marple looked round her. The night air, the soft fragrance of flowers, the tables with their little lights, the women with their pretty dresses, Evelyn in a dark indigo and white print, Lucky in a white sheath, her golden hair shining. Everybody seemed gay and full of life tonight. Even Tim Kendal was smiling. He passed her table and said:

"Can't thank you enough for all you've done. Molly's practically herself again. The doc says she can get up tomorrow."

Miss Marple smiled at him and said that that was good hearing. She found it, however, quite an effort to smile. Decidedly, she was tired . . .

She got up and walked slowly back to her bungalow. She would have liked to go on thinking, puzzling, trying to remember, trying to assemble various facts and words and glances. But she wasn't able to do it. The tired mind rebelled. It said 'Sleep! You've got to go to sleep!'

Miss Marple undressed, got into bed, read a few verses of the Thomas à Kempis which she kept by her bed, then she turned out the light. In the darkness she sent up a prayer. One couldn't do everything oneself. One had to have help. 'Nothing will happen tonight,' she murmured hopefully.

II

Miss Marple woke suddenly and sat up in bed. Her heart was beating. She switched on the light and looked at the little clock by her bedside. Two a.m. Two a.m. and outside activity of some kind was going on. She got up, put on her dressing-gown and slippers, and a woolen scarf round her head and went out to reconnoiter. There were people moving about with torches. Among them she saw Canon Prescott and went to him.

"What's happening?"

"Oh, Miss Marple? It's Mrs. Kendal. Her husband woke up, found she'd slipped out of bed and gone out. We're looking for her."

He hurried on. Miss Marple walked more slowly after him. Where had Molly gone? Why? Had she planned this deliberately, planned to slip away as soon as the guard on her was relaxed, and while her husband was deep in sleep? Miss Marple thought it was probable. But why? What was the reason? Was there, as Esther Walters had so strongly hinted, some other man? If so, who could that man be? Or was there some more sinister reason?

Miss Marple walked on, looking around her, peering under bushes. Then suddenly she heard a faint call:

"Here. . . . This way. . . ."

The cry had come from some little distance beyond the hotel grounds. It must be, thought Miss Marple, near the creek of water that ran down to the sea. She went in that direction as briskly as she could.

There were not really so many searchers as it had seemed to her at first. Most people must still be asleep in their bungalows. She saw a place on the creek bank where there were people standing. Someone pushed past her, almost knocking her down, running in that direction. It was Tim Kendal. A minute or two later she heard his voice cry out:

"Molly! My God, Molly!"

It was a minute or two before Miss Marple was able to join the little group. It consisted of one of the Cuban waiters, Evelyn Hillingdon, and two of the native girls. They had parted to let Tim through. Miss Marple arrived as he was bending over to look.

"Molly . . ." He slowly dropped on to his knees. Miss Marple saw the girl's body clearly, lying there in the creek, her face below the level of the water, her golden hair spread over the pale green embroidered shawl that covered her shoulders. With the leaves and rushes of the creek, it seemed almost like a scene from *Hamlet* with Molly as the dead Ophelia. . . .

As Tim stretched out a hand to touch her, the quiet, common-sense Miss Marple took charge and spoke sharply and authoritatively.

"Don't move her, Mr. Kendal," she said. "She mustn't be moved."

Tim turned a dazed face up to her.

"But—I must—it's Molly. I must . . ."

Evelyn Hillingdon touched his shoulder.

"She's dead, Tim. I didn't move her, but I did feel her pulse."

"Dead?" said Tim unbelievingly. "Dead? You mean she's—*drowned* herself?"

"I'm afraid so. It looks like it."

"But *why?*" A great cry burst from the young man. "*Why?* She was so happy this evening. Talking about what we'd do tomorrow. Why should this terrible death wish come over her again. Why should she steal away as she did—rush out into the night, come down here and drown herself. What despair did she have—what misery—why couldn't she *tell* me anything?"

"I don't know, my dear," said Evelyn gently. "I don't know."

Miss Marple said,

"Somebody had better get Dr. Graham. And someone will have to telephone the police."

"The police?" Tim uttered a bitter laugh. "What good will they be?"

"The police have to be notified in a case of suicide," said Miss Marple.

Tim rose slowly to his feet.

"I'll get Graham," he said heavily. "Perhaps—even now—he could—do something."

He stumbled away in the direction of the hotel.

Evelyn Hillingdon and Miss Marple stood side by side looking down at the dead girl.

Evelyn shook her head. "It's too late. She's quite cold. She must have been dead at least an hour—perhaps more. What a tragedy it all is. Those two always seemed so happy. I suppose she was always unbalanced."

"No," said Miss Marple. "I don't think she was unbalanced."

Evelyn looked at her curiously. "What do you mean?"

The moon had been behind a cloud, but now it came out into the open. It shone with a luminous silvery brightness on Molly's outspread hair . . .

Miss Marple gave a sudden ejaculation. She bent down, peering, then stretched out her hand and touched the golden head. She spoke to Evelyn Hillingdon, and her voice sounded quite different.

"I think," she said, "that we had better make sure."

Evelyn Hillingdon stared at her in astonishment.

"But you yourself told Tim we mustn't touch anything?"

"I know. But the moon wasn't out. I hadn't seen——"

Her finger pointed. Then, very gently, she touched the blonde hair and parted it so that the roots were exposed . . .

Evelyn gave a sharp ejaculation.

"Lucky!"

And then after a moment she repeated:

"Not Molly. . . . Lucky."

Miss Marple nodded. "Their hair was of much the same color—but hers, of course, was dark at the roots because it was dyed."

"But she's wearing Molly's shawl?"

"She admired it. I heard her say she was going to get one like it. Evidently she did."

"So that's why we were—deceived. . . ."

Evelyn broke off as she met Miss Marple's eyes watching her.

"Someone," said Miss Marple, "will have to tell her husband."

There was a moment's pause, then Evelyn said:

"All right. I'll do it."

She turned and walked away through the palm trees.

Miss Marple remained for a moment motionless, then she turned her head very slightly, and said:

"Yes, Colonel Hillingdon?"

Edward Hillingdon came from the trees behind her to stand by her side.

"You knew I was there?"

"You cast a shadow," said Miss Marple.

They stood a moment in silence.

He said, more as though he were speaking to himself:

"So, in the end, she played her luck too far. . . ."

"You are, I think, glad that she is dead?"

"And that shocks you? Well, I will not deny it. I am glad she is dead."

"Death is often a solution to problems."

Edward Hillingdon turned his head slowly. Miss Marple met his eyes calmly and steadfastly.

"If you think——" he took a sharp step towards her.

There was a sudden menace in his tone.

Miss Marple said quietly:

"Your wife will be back with Mr. Dyson in a moment. Or Mr. Kendal will be here with Dr. Graham."

Edward Hillingdon relaxed. He turned back to look down at the dead woman.

Miss Marple slipped away quietly. Presently her pace quickened.

Just before reaching her own bungalow, she paused. It was here that she had sat that day talking to Major Palgrave. It was here that he had fumbled in his wallet looking for the snapshot of a murderer. . . .

She remembered how he had looked up, and how his face had gone purple and red . . . "So ugly," as Señora de Caspearo had said. "He has the Evil Eye."

The Evil Eye . . . Eye . . . *Eye*. . . .

CHAPTER TWENTY-FOUR
Nemesis

I

WHATEVER THE ALARMS and excursions of the night, Mr. Rafiel had not heard them.

He was fast asleep in bed, a faint thin snore coming from his nostrils, when he was taken by the shoulders and shaken violently.

"Eh—what—what the devil's this?"

"It's me," said Miss Marple, for once ungrammatical, "though I should put it a little more strongly than that. The Greeks, I believe, had a word for it. Nemesis, if I am not wrong."

Mr. Rafiel raised himself on his pillows as far as he could. He stared at her. Miss Marple, standing there in the moonlight, her head encased in a fluffy scarf of pale pink wool, looked as unlike a figure of Nemesis as it was possible to imagine.

"So you're Nemesis, are you?" said Mr. Rafiel after a momentary pause.

"I hope to be—with your help."

"Do you mind telling me quite plainly what you're talking about like this in the middle of the night."

"I think we may have to act quickly. Very quickly. I have been foolish.

Extremely foolish. I ought to have known from the very beginning what all this was about. It was so simple."

"What was simple, and what are you talking about?"

"You slept through a good deal," said Miss Marple. "A body was found. We thought at first it was the body of Molly Kendal. It wasn't, it was Lucky Dyson. Drowned in the creek."

"Lucky, eh?" said Mr. Rafiel. "And drowned? In the creek. Did she drown herself or did somebody drown her?"

"Somebody drowned her," said Miss Marple.

"I see. At least I think I see. That's what you mean by saying it's so simple, is it? Greg Dyson was always the first possibility, and he's the right one. Is that it? Is that what you're thinking? And what you're afraid of is that he may get away with it?"

Miss Marple took a deep breath.

"Mr. Rafiel, will you trust me. We have got to stop a murder being committed."

"I thought you said it *had* been committed."

"That murder was committed in error. Another murder may be committed any moment now. There's no time to lose. We must prevent it happening. We must go at once."

"It's all very well to talk like that," said Mr. Rafiel. *"We,* you say? What do you think *I* can do about it? I can't even walk without help. How can you and I set about preventing a murder? You're about a hundred and I'm a broken up old crock."

"I was thinking of Jackson," said Miss Marple. "Jackson will do what you tell him, won't he?"

"He will indeed," said Mr. Rafiel, "especially if I add that I'll make it worth his while. Is that what you want?"

"Yes. Tell him to come with me and tell him to obey any orders I give him."

Mr. Rafiel looked at her for about six seconds. Then he said:

"Done. I expect I'm taking the biggest risk of my life. Well, it won't be the first one." He raised his voice. "Jackson." At the same time he picked up the electric bell that lay beside his hand and pressed the button.

Hardly thirty seconds passed before Jackson appeared through the connecting door to the adjoining room.

"You called and rang, sir? Anything wrong?" He broke off, staring at Miss Marple.

"Now Jackson, do as I tell you. You will go with this lady, Miss Marple. You'll go where she takes you and you'll do exactly as she says. You'll obey every order she gives you. Is that understood?"

"I——"

"Is that understood?"

"Yes, sir."

"And for doing that," said Mr. Rafiel, "you won't be the loser. I'll make it worth your while."

"Thank you, sir."

"Come along, Mr. Jackson," said Miss Marple. She spoke over her shoulder to Mr. Rafiel. "We'll tell Mrs. Walters to come to you on our way. Get her to get you out of bed and bring you along."

"Bring me along where?"

"To the Kendals' bungalow," said Miss Marple. "I think Molly will be coming back there."

II

Molly came up the path from the sea. Her eyes stared fixedly ahead of her. Occasionally, under her breath, she gave a little whimper . . .

She went up the steps of the loggia, paused a moment, then pushed open the window and walked into the bedroom. The lights were on, but the room itself was empty. Molly went across to the bed and sat down. She sat for some minutes, now and again passing her hand over her forehead and frowning.

Then, after a quick surreptitious glance round, she slipped her hand under the mattress and brought out the book that was hidden there. She bent over it, turning the pages to find what she wanted.

Then she raised her head as a sound of running footsteps came from outside. With a quick guilty movement she pushed the book behind her back.

Tim Kendal, panting and out of breath, came in, and uttered a great sigh of relief at the sight of her.

"Thank God. Where have you been, Molly? I've been searching everywhere for you."

"I went to the creek."

"You went——" he stopped.

"Yes. I went to the creek. But I couldn't wait there. I couldn't. There was someone in the water—and she was dead."

"You mean—Do you know I thought it was *you*. I've only just found out it was Lucky."

"I didn't kill her. Really, Tim, I didn't kill her. I'm sure I didn't. I mean—I'd remember if I did, wouldn't I?"

Tim sank slowly down on the end of the bed.

"You didn't— Are you sure that—? No. No, of course you didn't!" He fairly shouted the words. "Don't start thinking like that, Molly. Lucky drowned herself. Of course she drowned herself. Hillingdon was through with her. She went and lay down with her face in the water——"

"Lucky wouldn't do that. She'd never do that. But *I* didn't kill her. I swear I didn't."

"Darling, of course you didn't!" He put his arms round her but she pulled herself away.

"I hate this place. It ought to be all sunlight. It seemed to be all sunlight. But it isn't. Instead there's a shadow—a big black shadow . . . And I'm in it—and I can't get out——"

Her voice had risen to a shout.

"Hush, Molly. For God's sake, hush!" He went into the bathroom, came back with a glass.

"Look. Drink this. It'll steady you."

"I—I can't drink anything. My teeth are chattering so."

"Yes you can, darling. Sit down. Here, on the bed." He put his arm round her. He approached the glass to her lips. "There you are now. Drink it."

A voice spoke from the window.

"Jackson," said Miss Marple clearly. "Go over. Take that glass from him and hold it tightly. Be careful. He's strong and he may be pretty desperate."

There were certain points about Jackson. He was a man of training, trained to obey orders. He was a man with a great love for money, and money had been promised him by his employer, that employer being a man of stature and authority. He was also a man of extreme muscular development heightened by his training. His not to reason why, his but to do.

Swift as a flash he had crossed the room. His hand went over the glass that Tim was holding to Molly's lips, his other arm had fastened round Tim. A quick flick of the wrist and he had the glass. Tim turned on him wildly, but Jackson held him firmly.

"What the devil—let go of me. Let go of me. Have you gone mad? What are you doing?"

Tim struggled violently.

"Hold him, Jackson," said Miss Marple.

"What's going on? What's the matter here?"

Supported by Esther Walters, Mr. Rafiel came through the window.

"You ask what's the matter?" shouted Tim. "Your man's gone mad, stark, staring mad, that's what's the matter. Tell him to let go of me."

"No," said Miss Marple.

Mr. Rafiel turned to her.

"Speak up, Nemesis," he said. "We've got to have chapter and verse of some kind."

"I've been stupid and a fool," said Miss Marple, "but I'm not being a fool now. When the contents of that glass that he was trying to make his wife drink, have been analyzed, I'll wager—yes, I'll wager my immortal soul that you'll find it's got a lethal dose of narcotic in it. It's the same pattern, you see, the same pattern as in Major Palgrave's story. A wife in a depressed state, and she tries to do away with herself, husband saves her in time. Then the second time she succeeds. Yes, it's the right pattern. Major Palgrave told me the story and he took out a snapshot and then he looked up and saw——"

"Over your right shoulder——" continued Mr. Rafiel.

"No," said Miss Marple, shaking her head. *"He didn't see anything over my right shoulder."*

"What are you talking about? You told me . . ."

"I told you wrong. I was completely wrong. I was stupid beyond belief. Major Palgrave *appeared* to me to be looking over my right shoulder, glaring, in fact, at something— But he couldn't have *seen* anything, because he was looking through his left eye and his left eye was his glass eye."

"I remember—he *had* a glass eye," said Mr. Rafiel. "I'd forgotten—or I took it for granted. You mean he couldn't see anything?"

"Of course he could *see,*" said Miss Marple. "He could *see* all right, but he could only see with one eye. The eye he *could* see with was his *right* eye. And so, you see, he must have been looking at something or someone not to the right of me but to the *left* of me."

"Was there anyone on the left of you?"

"Yes," said Miss Marple. "Tim Kendal and his wife were sitting not far off. Sitting at a table just by a big hibiscus bush. They were doing accounts there. So you see the Major looked up. His glass left eye was glaring over my shoulder, but what he *saw* with his other eye was a man sitting by a hibiscus bush and the face was the same, only rather older, as the face in the snapshot. Also by a hibiscus bush. Tim Kendal had heard the story the Major had been telling and he saw that the Major had recognized him. So, of course, he had to kill him. Later, he had to kill the girl, Victoria, because she'd seen him putting a bottle of tablets in the Major's room. She didn't think anything of it at first because of course it was quite natural on various occasions for Tim Kendal to go into the guests' bungalows. He might have just been returning something to it that had been left on a restaurant table. But she thought about it and then she asked him questions and so he had to get rid of her. But this is the real murder, the murder he's been planning all along. He's a wife-killer, you see."

"What damned nonsense, what——" Tim Kendal shouted.

There was a sudden cry, a wild angry cry. Esther Walters detached herself from Mr. Rafiel, almost flinging him down and rushed across the room. She pulled vainly at Jackson.

"Let go of him—let go of him. It's not true. Not a word of it is true. Tim—Tim darling, it's not true. You could never kill anyone, I know you couldn't. I know you wouldn't. It's that horrible girl you married. She's been telling lies about you. They're not true. None of them are true. I believe in you. I love you and trust in you. I'll never believe a word anyone says. I'll——"

Then Tim Kendal lost control of himself.

"For God's sake, you damned bitch," he said, "shut up, can't you? D'you want to get me hanged? Shut up, I tell you. Shut that big, ugly mouth of yours."

"Poor silly creature," said Mr. Rafiel softly. "So that's what's been going on, is it?"

CHAPTER TWENTY-FIVE
Miss Marple Uses Her Imagination

"SO THAT'S WHAT had been going on?" said Mr. Rafiel.

He and Miss Marple were sitting together in a confidential manner.

"She'd been having an affair with Tim Kendal, had she?"

"Hardly an affair, I imagine," said Miss Marple, primly. "It was, I think, a romantic attachment with the prospect of marriage in the future."

"What—after his wife was dead?"

"I don't think poor Esther Walters knew that Molly was going to die," said Miss Marple. "I just think she believed the story Tim Kendal told her about Molly having been in love with another man, and the man having followed her here, and I think she counted on Tim's getting a divorce. I think it was all quite proper and respectable. But she was very much in love with him."

"Well, that's easily understood. He was an attractive chap. But what made *him* go for her—d'you know that too?"

"You know, don't you?" said Miss Marple.

"I dare say I've got a pretty fair idea, but I don't know how you should know about it. As far as that goes, I don't see how Tim Kendal could know about it."

"Well, I really think I could explain all that with a little imagination, though it would be simpler if you told me."

"I'm not going to tell you," said Mr. Rafiel. "You tell me, since you're being so clever."

"Well, it seems to me possible," said Miss Marple, "that as I have already hinted to you, your man Jackson was in the habit of taking a good snoop through your various business papers from time to time."

"Perfectly possible," said Mr. Rafiel, "but I shouldn't have said there was anything there that could do him much good. I took care of that."

"I imagine," said Miss Marple, "he read your will."

"Oh I see. Yes, yes, I did have a copy of my will along."

"You told me," said Miss Marple, "you told me—(as Humpty Dumpty said—very loud and clear) that you had *not* left anything to Esther Walters in your will. You had impressed that fact upon her, and also upon Jackson. It was true in Jackson's case, I should imagine. You have not left *him* anything, but you *had* left Esther Walters money, though you weren't going to let her have any inkling of the fact. Isn't that right?"

"Yes, it's quite right, but I don't know how *you* knew."

"Well, it's the way you insisted on the point," said Miss Marple. "I have a certain experience of the way people tell lies."

"I give in," said Mr. Rafiel. "All right. I left Esther £50,000. It would come as a nice surprise to her when I died. I suppose that, knowing this, Tim Kendal decided to exterminate his present wife with a nice dose of something or other and marry £50,000 and Esther Walters. Possibly to dispose of her also in good time. But how did *he* know she was going to have £50,000?"

"Jackson told him, of course," said Miss Marple. "They were very friendly, those two. Tim Kendal was nice to Jackson and, quite, I should imagine, without ulterior motive. But amongst the bits of gossip that Jackson let slip I think Jackson told him that unbeknownst to herself, Esther Walters was going to inherit a fat lot of money, and he may have said that he himself hoped to induce Esther Walters to marry him though he hadn't had much success so far in taking her fancy. Yes, I think that's how it happened."

"The things you imagine always seem perfectly plausible," said Mr. Rafiel.

"But I was stupid," said Miss Marple, "very stupid. Everything fitted in

really, you see. Tim Kendal was a very clever man as well as being a very
wicked one. He was particularly good at putting about rumors. Half the
things I've been told here came from him originally, I imagine. There were
stories going around about Molly wanting to marry an undesirable young
man, but I rather fancy that the undesirable young man was actually Tim
Kendal himself, though that wasn't the name he was using then. Her people
had heard something, perhaps that his background was rather fishy. So he
put on a high indignation act, refused to be taken by Molly to be 'shown off'
to her people and then he brewed up a little scheme with her which they
both thought great fun. She pretended to sulk and pine for him. Then a Mr.
Tim Kendal turned up, primed with the names of various old friends of
Molly's people, and they welcomed him with open arms as being the sort of
young man who would put the former delinquent one out of Molly's head. I
am afraid Molly and he must have laughed over it a good deal. Anyway, he
married her, and with her money he bought out the people who ran this
place and they came out here. I should imagine that he ran through her
money at a pretty fair rate. Then he came across Esther Walters and he saw
a nice prospect of more money."

"Why didn't he bump me off?" said Mr. Rafiel.

Miss Marple coughed.

"I expect he wanted to be fairly sure of Mrs. Walters first. Besides—I
mean . . ." She stopped, a little confused.

"Besides, he realized he wouldn't have to wait long," said Mr. Rafiel,
"and it would clearly be better for me to die a natural death. Being so rich.
Deaths of millionaires are scrutinized rather carefully, aren't they, unlike
mere wives?"

"Yes, you're quite right. Such a lot of lies as he told," said Miss Marple.
"Look at the lies he got Molly herself to believe—putting that book on
mental disorders in her way. Giving her drugs which would give her dreams
and hallucinations. You know, your Jackson was rather clever over that. I
think he recognized certain of Molly's symptoms as being the result of
drugs. And he came into the bungalow that day to potter about a bit in the
bathroom. That face cream he examined. He might have got some idea from
the old tales of witches rubbing themselves with ointments that had
belladonna in them. Belladonna in face cream could have produced just that
result. Molly would have black-outs. Times she couldn't account for,
dreams of flying through the air. No wonder she got frightened about
herself. She had all the signs of mental illness, Jackson was on the right
track. Maybe he got the idea from Major Palgrave's stories about the use of
datura by Indian women on their husbands."

"Major Palgrave!" said Mr. Rafiel. "Really, that man!"

"He brought about his own murder," said Miss Marple, "and that poor
girl Victoria's murder, and he nearly brought about Molly's murder. But he
recognized a murderer all right."

"What made you suddenly remember about his glass eye?" asked Mr.
Rafiel curiously.

"Something that Señora de Caspearo said. She talked some nonsense
about his being ugly, and having the Evil Eye; and I said it was only a glass
eye, and he couldn't help that, poor man, and she said his eyes looked
different ways, they were cross-eyes—which, of course, they were. And she

said it brought bad luck. I knew—I *knew* that I had heard something that day that was important. Last night, just after Lucky's death, it came to me what it was! And then I realized there was no time to waste . . ."

"How did Tim Kendal come to kill the wrong woman?"

"Sheer chance. I think his plan was this: Having convinced everybody—and that included Molly herself—that she was mentally unbalanced, and after giving her a sizeable dose of the drug he was using, he told her that between them they were going to clear up all these murder puzzles. But she had got to help him. After everyone was asleep, they would go separately and meet at an agreed spot by the creek.

"He said he had a very good idea who the murderer was, and they would trap him. Molly went off obediently—but she was confused and stupefied with the drug she had been given, and it slowed her up. Tim arrived there first and saw what he thought was Molly. Golden hair and pale green shawl. He came up behind her, put his hand over her mouth, and forced her down into the water and held her there."

"Nice fellow! But wouldn't it have been easier just to give her an overdose of narcotic?"

"Much easier, of course. But that *might* have given rise to suspicion. All narcotics and sedatives had been very carefully removed from Molly's reach, remember. And if she *had* got hold of a fresh supply, who more likely to have supplied it than her husband? But if, in a fit of despair, she went out and drowned herself while her innocent husband slept, the whole thing would be a romantic tragedy, and no one would be likely to suggest that she had been drowned deliberately. Besides," added Miss Marple, "murderers always find it difficult to keep things simple. They can't keep themselves from elaborating."

"You seem convinced you know all there is to be known about murderers! So you believe Tim didn't know he had killed the wrong woman?"

Miss Marple shook her head.

"He didn't even look at her face, just hurried off as quickly as he could, let an hour elapse, then started to organize a search for her, playing the part of a distracted husband."

"But what the devil was Lucky doing hanging about the creek in the middle of the night?"

Miss Marple gave an embarrassed little cough.

"It is possible, I think, that she was—er—waiting to meet someone."

"Edward Hillingdon?"

"Oh *no*," said Miss Marple. "That's all over. I wondered whether—just possibly—she might have been waiting for Jackson."

"Waiting for *Jackson?*"

"I've noticed her—look at him once or twice," murmured Miss Marple, averting her eyes.

Mr. Rafiel whistled.

"My Tom Cat Jackson! I wouldn't put it past him! Tim must have had a shock later when he found he'd killed the wrong woman."

"Yes, indeed. He must have felt quite desperate. Here was Molly alive and wandering about. And the story he'd circulated so carefully about her mental condition wouldn't stand up for a moment once she got into the hands of competent mental specialists. And once she told her damning story of his having asked her to meet him at the creek, where would Tim Kendal be? He'd only one hope—to finish off Molly as quickly as possible. Then there was a very good chance that everyone would believe that Molly, in a fit of mania, had drowned Lucky, and had then, horrified by what she had done, taken her own life."

"And it was then," said Mr. Rafiel, "that you decided to play Nemesis, eh?"

He leaned back suddenly and roared with laughter.

"It's a damned good joke," he said. "If you knew what you looked like that night with that fluffy pink wool all round your head, standing there and saying you were Nemesis! I'll never forget it!"

EPILOGUE

THE TIME HAD come and Miss Marple was waiting at the airport for her plane. Quite a lot of people had come to see her off. The Hillingdons had left already. Gregory Dyson had flown to one of the other islands and the rumor had come that he was devoting himself to an Argentinian widow. Señora de Caspearo had returned to South America.

Molly had come to see Miss Marple off. She was pale and thin but she had weathered the shock of her discovery bravely and with the help of one of Mr. Rafiel's nominees whom he had wired for to England, she was carrying on with the running of the hotel.

"Do you good to be busy," Mr. Rafiel observed. "Keep you from thinking. Got a good thing here."

"You don't think the murders——"

"People love murders when they're all cleared up," Mr. Rafiel had assured her. "You carry on, girl, and keep your heart up. Don't distrust all men because you've met one bad lot."

"You sound like Miss Marple," Molly had said, "she's always telling me Mr. Right will come along one day."

Mr. Rafiel grinned at this sentiment. So Molly was there and the two Prescotts and Mr. Rafiel, of course, and Esther—an Esther who looked older and sadder and to whom Mr. Rafiel was quite often unexpectedly kind. Jackson also was very much to the fore, pretending to be looking after Miss Marple's baggage. He was all smiles these days and let it be known that he had come into money.

There was a hum in the sky. The plane was arriving. Things were somewhat informal here. There was no 'taking your place by Channel 8' or Channel 9. You just walked out from the little flower-covered pavilion on to the tarmac.

"Good-bye, darling Miss Marple." Molly kissed her.

"Good-bye. Do try and come and visit us." Miss Prescott shook her warmly by the hand.

"It has been a great pleasure to know you," said the Canon. "I second my sister's invitation most warmly."

"All the best, Madam," said Jackson, "and remember any time you want any massage free, just you send me a line and we'll make an appointment."

Only Esther Walters turned slightly away when the time came for good-byes. Miss Marple did not force one upon her. Mr. Rafiel came last. He took her hand.

"*Ave Caesar, nos morituri te salutamus,*" he said.

"I'm afraid," said Miss Marple, "I don't know very much Latin."

"But you understand that?"

"Yes." She said no more. She knew quite well what he was telling her.

"It has been a great pleasure to know you," she said.

Then she walked across the tarmac and got into the plane.

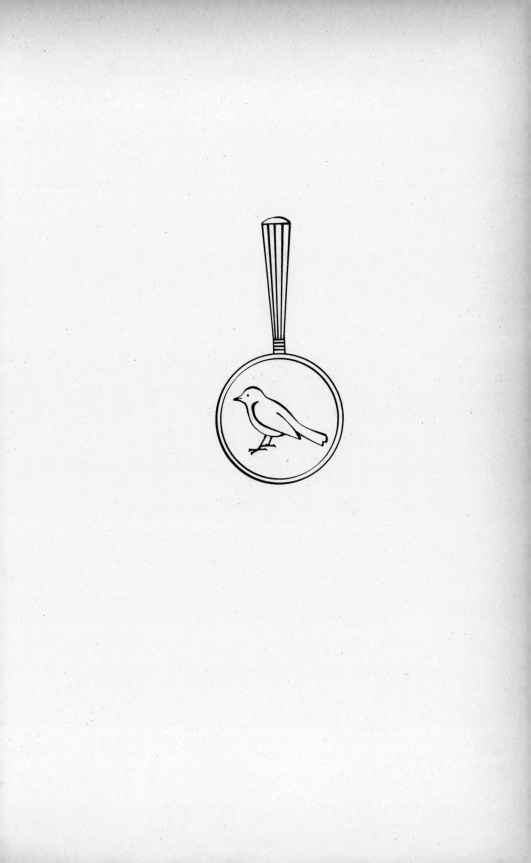

Nemesis

to daphne honeybone

CHAPTER ONE
Overture

IN THE AFTERNOONS it was the custom of Miss Jane Marple to unfold her second newspaper. Two newspapers were delivered at her house every morning. The first one Miss Marple read while sipping her early morning tea, that is, if it was delivered in time. The boy who delivered the papers was notably erratic in his management of time. Frequently, too, there was either a new boy or a boy who was acting temporarily as a stand-in for the first one. And each one would have ideas of his own as to the geographical route that he should take in delivering. Perhaps it varied monotony for him. But those customers who were used to reading their paper early so that they could snap up the more saucy items in the day's news before departing for their bus, train or other means of progress to the day's work were annoyed if the papers were late, though the middle-aged and elderly ladies who resided peacefully in St. Mary Mead often preferred to read a newspaper propped up on their breakfast table.

Today, Miss Marple had absorbed the front page and a few other items in the daily paper that she had nicknamed "The Daily All-Sorts," this being a slightly satirical allusion to the fact that her paper, the *Daily Newsgiver*, owing to a change of proprietor, to her own and to other of her friends' great annoyance, now provided articles on men's tailoring, women's dress, female heartthrobs, competitions for children, and complaining letters from women and had managed pretty well to shove any real news off any part of it but the front page, or to some obscure corner where it was impossible to find it. Miss Marple, being old-fashioned, preferred her newspapers to *be* newspapers and give you news.

In the afternoon, having finished her luncheon, treated herself to twenty minutes' nap in a specially purchased upright armchair which catered for the demands of her rheumatic back, she had opened *The Times,* which lent itself still to a more leisurely perusal. Not that *The Times* was what it used to be. The maddening thing about *The Times* was that you couldn't find anything any more. Instead of going through from the front page and knowing where everything else was so that you passed easily to any special articles on subjects in which you were interested, there were now extraordinary interruptions to this time-honored program. Two pages were suddenly devoted to travel in Capri with illustrations. Sport appeared with far more prominence than it had ever had in the old days. Court news and obituaries were a little more faithful to routine. The births, marriages and deaths which had at one time occupied Miss Marple's attention first of all owing to their prominent position had migrated to a different part of *The Times,* though of late, Miss Marple noted, they had come almost permanently to rest on the back page.

Miss Marple gave her attention first to the main news on the front page. She did not linger long on that because it was equivalent to what she had already read this morning, though possibly couched in a slightly more dignified manner. She cast her eye down the table of contents. Articles, comments, science, sport; then she pursued her usual plan, turned the paper over and had a quick run down the births, marriages and deaths, after which she proposed to turn to the page given to correspondence, where she nearly always found something to enjoy; from that she passed on to the Court Circular, on which page today's news from the sale rooms could also be found. A short article on science was often placed there, but she did not propose to read that. It seldom made sense for her.

Having turned the paper over as usual to the births, marriages and deaths, Miss Marple thought to herself, as so often before:

"It's sad really, but nowadays one is only interested in the deaths!"

People had babies, but the people who had babies were not likely to be even known by name to Miss Marple. If there had been a column dealing with babies labeled as grandchildren, there might have been some chance of a pleasurable recognition. She might have thought to herself:

"Really, Mary Prendergast has had a *third* granddaughter!" though even that perhaps might have been a bit remote.

She skimmed down Marriages, also with not a very close survey, because most of her old friends' daughters or sons had married some years ago already. She came to the Deaths column and gave that her more serious attention. Gave it enough, in fact, so as to be sure she would not miss a name. Alloway, Angopastro, Arden, Barton, Bedshaw, Burgoweisser (dear me, what a *German* name, but he seemed to be late of Leeds). Camperdown, Carpenter, Clegg. Clegg? Now was that one of the Cleggs she knew? No, it didn't seem to be. Janet Clegg. Somewhere in Yorkshire. McDonald, McKenzie, Nicholson. Nicholson? No. Again not a Nicholson she knew. Ogg, Ormerod—that must be one of the aunts, she thought. Yes, probably so. Linda Ormerod. No, she hadn't known her. Quantril? Dear me, that must be Elizabeth Quantril. Eighty-five. Well, really! She had thought Elizabeth Quantril had died some years ago. Fancy her having lived so long! So delicate she'd always been, too. Nobody had expected *her* to make old bones. Race, Radley, Rafiel. Rafiel? Something stirred. That name was familiar. Rafiel. Belford Park, Maidstone. Belford Park, Maidstone. No, she couldn't recall that address. No flowers. Jason Rafiel. Oh, well, an unusual name. She supposed she'd just heard it somewhere. Ross-Perkins. Now that might be—no, it wasn't. Ryland? Emily Ryland. No. No, she'd never known an Emily Ryland. *Deeply loved by her husband and children.* Well, very nice or very sad, whichever way you liked to look at it.

Miss Marple laid down her paper, glancing idly through the crossword while she puzzled to remember why the name Rafiel was familiar to her.

"It will come to me," said Miss Marple, knowing from long experience the way old people's memories worked.

"It'll come to me, I have no doubt."

She glanced out of the window towards the garden, withdrew her gaze and tried to put the garden out of her mind. Her garden had been the source of great pleasure and also a great deal of hard work to Miss Marple for many, many years. And now, owing to the fussiness of doctors, working in the garden was forbidden to her. She'd once tried to fight this ban, but had come to the conclusion that she had, after all, better do as she was told. She had arranged her chair at such an angle as not to be easy to look out in the garden unless she definitely and clearly wished to see something in particular. She sighed, picked up her knitting bag and took out a small child's wooly jacket in process of coming to a conclusion. The back was done and the front. Now she would have to get on with the sleeves. Sleeves were always boring. Two sleeves, both alike. Yes, very boring. Pretty colored pink wool, however. Pink wool. Now wait a minute—where did that fit in? Yes—yes—it fitted in with that name she'd just read in the paper. Pink wool. A blue sea. A Caribbean sea. A sandy beach. Sunshine. Herself knitting and—why, of course, Mr. Rafiel. That trip she had made to the Caribbean. The island of St. Honoré. A treat from her nephew Raymond. And she remembered Joan, her niece-in-law, Raymond's wife, saying.

"Don't get mixed up in any more murders, Aunt Jane. It isn't good for you."

Well, she hadn't wished to get mixed up in any murders, but it just happened. That was all. Simply because of an elderly major with a glass eye who had insisted on telling her some very long and boring stories. Poor Major—now what was *his* name? She'd forgotten that now. Mr. Rafiel and his secretary, Mrs.—Mrs. Walters, yes, Esther Walters, and his masseur-attendant, Jackson. It all came back. Well, well. Poor Mr. Rafiel. So Mr. Rafiel was dead. He had known he was going to die before very long. He had practically told her so. It seemed as though he had lasted longer than the doctors had thought. He was a strong man, an obstinate man—a very rich man.

Miss Marple remained in thought, her knitting needles working regularly, but her mind not really on her knitting. Her mind was on the late Mr. Rafiel, and remembering what she could remember about him. Not an easy man to forget, really. She could conjure his appearance up mentally quite well. Yes, a very definite personality, a difficult man, an irritable man, shockingly rude sometimes. Nobody ever resented his being rude, though. She remembered that also. They didn't resent his being rude because he was so rich. Yes, he had been very rich. He had had his secretary with him and a valet attendant, a qualified masseur. He had not been able to get about very well without help.

Rather a doubtful character that nurse-attendant had been, Miss Marple thought. Mr. Rafiel had been very rude to him sometimes. He had never seemed to mind. And that, again, of course was because Mr. Rafiel was so rich.

"Nobody else would pay him half what I do," Mr. Rafiel had said, "and he knows it. He's good at his job, though."

Miss Marple wondered whether Jackson?—Johnson?—had stayed on with Mr. Rafiel. Stayed on for what must have been—another year? A year and three or four months. She thought probably not. Mr. Rafiel was one who liked a change. He got tired of people, tired of their ways, tired of their faces, tired of their voices.

Miss Marple understood that. She had felt the same sometimes. That companion of hers, that nice, attentive, maddening woman with her cooing voice.

"Ah," said Miss Marple, "what a change for the better since—" oh, dear, she'd forgotten *her* name now—Miss—Miss Bishop?—no, not Miss Bishop; of course not. Why had she thought of the name Bishop? Oh, dear, how difficult it was.

Her mind went back to Mr. Rafiel and to—no, it wasn't Johnson, it had been Jackson, Arthur Jackson.

"Oh, dear," said Miss Marple again, "I always get *all* the names wrong. And of course it was Miss *Knight* I was thinking of. Not Miss *Bishop*. Why do I think of her as Miss Bishop?" The answer came to her. Chess, of course. A chess piece. A knight. A bishop.

"I shall be calling her Miss Castle next time I think of her, I suppose, or Miss Rook. Though, really, she's not the sort of person who would ever rook anybody. No, indeed. And now what was the name of that nice secretary that Mr. Rafiel had? Oh, yes, Esther Walters. That was right. I wonder what has happened to Esther Walters? She'd inherited money? She would probably inherit money now."

Mr. Rafiel, she remembered, had told her something about that, or she had—oh, dear, what a muddle things were when you tried to remember with any kind of exactitude. Esther Walters. It had hit her badly, that business in the Caribbean, but she would have got over it. She'd been a widow, hadn't she? Miss Marple hoped that Esther Walters had married again some nice kindly, reliable man. It seemed faintly unlikely. Esther Walters, she thought, had had rather a genius for liking the wrong kind of men to marry.

Miss Marple went back to thinking about Mr. Rafiel. No flowers, it had said. Not that she herself would have dreamed of sending flowers to Mr. Rafiel. He could buy up all the nurseries in England if he'd wanted to. And anyway, they hadn't been on those terms. They hadn't been—friends, or on terms of affection. They had been—what was the word she wanted?—allies. Yes, they had been allies for a very short time. A very exciting time. And he had been an ally worth having. She had known so. She'd known it as she had gone running through a dark, tropical night in the Caribbean and had come to him. Yes, she remembered, she'd been wearing that pink wool— what used they to call them when she was young?—a fascinator. That nice pink wool kind of shawl-scarf that she'd put round her head, and he had looked at her and laughed and later, when she had said—she smiled at the remembrance—one word she had used and he had laughed, but he hadn't laughed in the end. No, he'd done what she asked him and therefore—

"Ah!" Miss Marple sighed, it had been, she had to admit, all very exciting. And she'd never told her nephew or dear Joan about it because, after all, it was what they'd told her not to do, wasn't it? Miss Marple nodded her head. Then she murmured softly:

"Poor Mr. Rafiel, I hope he didn't—suffer."

Probably not. Probably he'd been kept by expensive doctors under sedatives, easing the end. He had suffered a great deal in those weeks in the Caribbean. He'd nearly always been in pain. A brave man.

A brave man. She was sorry he was dead because she thought that though he'd been elderly and an invalid and ill, the world had lost something through his going. She had no idea what he could have been like in business. Ruthless, she thought, and rude and overmastering and aggressive. A great attacker. But—but a good friend, she thought. And somewhere in him a deep kind of kindness that he was very careful never to show on the surface. A man she admired and respected. Well, she was sorry he was gone and she hoped he hadn't minded too much and that his passing had been easy. And now he would be cremated no doubt and put in some large, handsome marble vault. She didn't even know if he'd been married. He had never mentioned a wife, never mentioned children. A lonely man? Or had his life been so full that he hadn't needed to feel lonely? She wondered.

She sat there quite a long time that afternoon, wondering about Mr. Rafiel. She had never expected to see him again after she had returned to England and she never had seen him again. Yet in some queer way she could at any moment have felt she was in touch with him. If he had approached her or had suggested that they meet again, feeling perhaps a bond because of a life that had been saved between them, or of some other bond. A bond—

"Surely," said Miss Marple, aghast at an idea that had come into her mind, "there can't be a bond of *ruthlessness* between us?" Was she, Jane Marple—could she ever be—ruthless? "D'you know," said Miss Marple to herself, "it's extraordinary I never thought of it before. I believe, you know, I *could* be ruthless . . ."

The door opened and a dark, curly head was popped in. It was Cherry, the welcome successor to Miss Bishop—Miss Knight.

"Did you say something?" said Cherry.

"I was speaking to myself," said Miss Marple; "I just wondered if I could ever be ruthless."

"What, you?" said Cherry. "Never! You're kindness itself."

"All the same," said Miss Marple, "I believe I *could* be ruthless if there was due cause."

"What would you call due cause?"

"In the cause of justice," said Miss Marple.

"You did have it in for little Gary Hopkins, I must say," said Cherry. "When you caught him torturing his cat that day. Never knew you had it in you to go for anyone like that! Scared him stiff, you did. He's never forgotten it."

"I hope he hasn't tortured any more cats."

"Well, he's made sure you weren't about if he did," said Cherry. "In fact I'm not at all sure as there isn't other boys as got scared. Seeing you with your wool and the pretty things you knits and all that—anyone would think you were gentle as a lamb. But there's times I could say you'd behave like a lion if you was goaded into it."

Miss Marple looked a little doubtful. She could not quite see herself in the role in which Cherry was now casting her. Had she ever—she paused on the reflection, recalling various moments—there had been intense irritation

with Miss Bishop—Knight. (Really, she must *not* forget names in this way.)
But her irritation had shown itself in more or less ironical remarks. Lions,
presumably, did not use irony. There was nothing ironical about a lion. It
sprang. It roared. It used its claws; presumably it took large bites at its
prey.

"Really," said Miss Marple, "I don't think I have ever behaved quite like
that."

Walking slowly along her garden that evening with the usual feelings of
vexation rising in her, Miss Marple considered the point again. Possibly the
sight of a plant of snapdragons recalled it to her mind. Really, she had told
old George again and again that she only wanted sulfur-colored antirrhinums, not that rather ugly purple shade that gardeners always seemed so
fond of. "Sulfur yellow," said Miss Marple aloud.

Someone the other side of the railing that abutted on the lane past her
house turned her head and spoke.

"I beg your pardon? You said something?"

"I was talking to myself, I'm afraid," said Miss Marple, turning to look
over the railing.

This was someone she did not know, and she knew most people in St.
Mary Mead. Knew them by sight even if not personally. It was a thick-set
woman in a shabby but tough tweed skirt and wearing good country shoes.
She wore an emerald pullover and a knitted woolen scarf.

"I'm afraid one does at my age," added Miss Marple.

"Nice garden you've got here," said the other woman.

"Not particularly nice now," said Miss Marple. "When I could attend to
it myself—"

"Oh, I know. I understand just what you feel. I suppose you've got one of
those—I have a lot of names for them, mostly very rude—elderly chaps who
say they know all about gardening. Sometimes they do, sometimes they
don't know a thing about it. They come and have a lot of cups of tea and do
a little very mild weeding. They're quite nice, some of them, but all the
same it does make one's temper rise." She added, "I'm quite a keen
gardener myself."

"Do you live here?" asked Miss Marple with some interest.

"Well, I'm boarding with a Mrs. Hastings. I think I've heard her speak of
you. You're Miss Marple, aren't you?"

"Oh, yes."

"I've come as a sort of companion-gardener. My name is Bartlett, by the
way. Miss Bartlett. There's not really much to do there," said Miss Bartlett.
"She goes in for annuals and all that. Nothing you can really get your teeth
into." She opened her mouth and showed her teeth when making this
remark. "Of course I do a few odd jobs as well. Shopping, you know, and
things like that. Anyway, if you want any time put in here, I could put in an
hour or two for you. I'd say I might be better than any chap you've got
now."

"That would be easy," said Miss Marple. "I like flowers best. Don't care
so much for vegetables."

"I do vegetables for Mrs. Hastings. Dull but necessary. Well, I'll be
getting along." Her eyes swept over Miss Marple from head to foot, as
though memorizing her, then she nodded cheerfully and tramped off.

Mrs. Hastings? Miss Marple couldn't remember the name of any Mrs. Hastings. Certainly Mrs. Hastings was not an old friend. She had certainly never been a gardening chum. Ah, of course, it was probably those newly built houses at the end of Gibraltar Road. Several families had moved in in the last year. Miss Marple sighed, looked again with annoyance at the antirrhinums, saw several weeds which she yearned to root up, one or two exuberant suckers she would like to attack with her secateurs, and finally, sighing and manfully resisting temptation, she made a detour round by the lane and returned to her house. Her mind recurred again to Mr. Rafiel. They had been, he and she—what was the title of that book they used to quote so much when she was young? *Ships that pass in the night.* Rather apt it was, really, when she came to think of it. Ships that pass in the night . . . It was in the night that she had gone to him to ask—no, to demand—help. To insist, to say no time must be lost. And he had agreed, and put things in train at once! Perhaps she *had* been rather lionlike on that occasion? No. No, that was quite wrong. It had not been anger she had felt. It had been insistence on something that was absolutely imperative to be put in hand at once. And he'd understood.

Poor Mr. Rafiel. That ship that had passed in the night had been an interesting ship. Once you got so used to his being rude, he might have been quite an agreeable man. No! She shook her head. Mr. Rafiel could never have been an agreeable man. Well, she must put Mr. Rafiel out of her head.

Ships that pass in the night, and speak each other in passing,
Only a signal shown and a distant voice in the darkness.

She would probably never think of him again. She would look out perhaps to see if there was an obituary of him in *The Times*. But she did not think it was very likely. He was not a very well-known character, she thought. Not famous. He had just been very rich. Of course, many people did have obituaries in the paper just because they were very rich; but she thought that Mr. Rafiel's richness would possibly not have been of that kind. He had not been prominent in any great industry; he had not been a great financial genius or a noteworthy banker. He had just all his life made enormous amounts of money. . . .

CHAPTER TWO
Code Word Nemesis

I

IT WAS ABOUT a week or so after Mr. Rafiel's death that Miss Marple picked up a letter from her breakfast tray and looked at it for a moment before opening it. The other two letters that had come by this morning's post were bills, or just possibly receipts for bills. In either case they were not of any particular interest. This letter might be.

A London postmark, typewritten address, a long, good quality envelope. Miss Marple slit it neatly with the paper knife she always kept handy on her tray. It was headed Messrs. Broadribb and Schuster, Solicitors and Notaries Public, with an address in Bloomsbury. It asked her, in suitable courteous and legal phraseology, to call upon them one day in the following week, at their office, to discuss a proposition that might be to her advantage. Thursday, the twenty-fourth, was suggested. If that date was not convenient, perhaps she would let them know what date she would be likely to be in London in the near future. They added that they were solicitors to the late Mr. Rafiel, with whom they understood that she had been acquainted.

Miss Marple frowned in some slight puzzlement. She got up rather more slowly than usual thinking about the letter she had received. She was escorted downstairs by Cherry, who was meticulous in hanging about in the hall so as to make sure that Miss Marple did not come to grief walking by herself down the staircase, which was of the old-fashioned kind that turned a sharp corner in the middle of its run.

"You take very good care of me, Cherry," said Miss Marple.

"Got to," said Cherry, in her usual idiom. "Good people are scarce."

"Well, thank you for the compliment," said Miss Marple, arriving safely with her last foot on the ground floor.

"Nothing the matter, is there?" asked Cherry. "You look a bit rattled like, if you know what I mean."

"No, nothing's the matter," said Miss Marple. "I had rather an unusual letter from a firm of solicitors."

"Nobody is suing you for anything, are they?" said Cherry, who was inclined to regard solicitors' letters as invariably associated with disaster of some kind.

"Oh, no, I don't think so," said Miss Marple. "Nothing of that kind. They just asked me to call upon them next week in London."

"Perhaps you've been left a fortune," said Cherry hopefully.

"That, I think, is very unlikely," said Miss Marple.

"Well, you never know," said Cherry.

Settling herself in her chair and taking her knitting out of its embroidered knitting bag, Miss Marple considered the possibility of Mr. Rafiel having left her a fortune. It seemed even more unlikely than when Cherry had suggested it. Mr. Rafiel, she thought, was not that kind of man.

It was not possible for her to go on the date suggested. She was attending a meeting of the Women's Institute to discuss the raising of a sum for building a small additional couple of rooms. But she wrote, naming a day in the following week. In due course her letter was answered and the appointment definitely confirmed. She wondered what Messrs. Broadribb and Schuster were like. The letter had been signed by J. R. Broadribb, who was, apparently, the senior partner. It was possible, Miss Marple thought, that Mr. Rafiel might have left her some small memoir or souvenir in his will. Perhaps some book on rare flowers that had been in his library and which he thought would please an old lady who was keen on gardening. Or perhaps a cameo brooch which had belonged to some great-aunt of his. She amused herself by these fancies. They were only fancies, she thought, because in either case it would merely be a case of the executors'—if these lawyers were the executors—forwarding her by post any such object. They would not have wanted an interview.

"Oh, well," said Miss Marple, "I shall know next Tuesday."

II

"Wonder what she'll be like," said Mr. Broadribb to Mr. Schuster, glancing at the clock as he did so.

"She's due in a quarter of an hour," said Mr. Schuster. "Wonder if she'll be punctual?"

"Oh, I should think so. She's elderly, I gather, and much more punctilious than the young scatterbrains of today."

"Fat or thin, I wonder?" said Mr. Schuster.

Mr. Broadribb shook his head.

"Didn't Rafiel ever describe her to you?" asked Mr. Schuster.

"He was extraordinarily cagey in everything he said about her."

"The whole thing seems very odd to me," said Mr. Schuster. "If we only knew a bit more about what it all meant . . ."

"It might be," said Mr. Broadribb thoughtfully, "something to do with Michael."

"What? After all these years? Couldn't be. What put that into your head? Did he mention—?"

"No, he didn't mention anything. Gave me no clue at all as to what was in his mind. Just gave me instructions."

"Think he was getting a bit eccentric and all that towards the end?"

"Not in the least. Mentally he was as brilliant as ever. His physical ill-health never affected his brain, anyway. In the last two months of his life he made an extra two hundred thousand pounds. Just like that."

"He had a flair," said Mr. Schuster with due reverence. "Certainly, he always had a flair."

"A great financial brain," said Mr. Broadribb, also in a tone of reverence suitable to the sentiment. "Not many like him, more's the pity."

A buzzer went on the table. Mr. Schuster picked up the receiver. A female voice said:

"Miss Jane Marple is here to see Mr. Broadribb by appointment."

Mr. Schuster looked at his partner, raising an eyebrow for an affirmative or a negative. Mr. Broadribb nodded.

"Show her up," said Mr. Schuster. And he added, "Now we'll see."

Miss Marple entered a room where a middle-aged gentleman with a thin, spare body and a long rather melancholy face rose to greet her. This apparently was Mr. Broadribb, whose appearance somewhat contradicted his name. With him was a rather younger middle-aged gentleman of definitely more ample proportions. He had black hair, small keen eyes and a tendency to a double chin.

"My partner, Mr. Schuster," Mr. Broadribb presented.

"I hope you didn't feel the stairs too much," said Mr. Schuster. "Seventy if she is a day—nearer eighty perhaps," he was thinking in his own mind.

"I always get a little breathless going upstairs."

"An old-fashioned building this," said Mr. Broadribb apologetically. "No lift. Ah, well, we are a very long-established firm and we don't go in for as many of the modern gadgets as perhaps our clients expect of us."

"This room has very pleasant proportions," said Miss Marple politely.

She accepted the chair that Mr. Broadribb drew forward for her. Mr. Schuster, in an unobtrusive sort of way, left the room.

"I hope that chair is comfortable," said Mr. Broadribb. "I'll pull that curtain slightly, shall I? You may feel the sun a little too much in your eyes."

"Thank you," said Miss Marple gratefully.

She sat there upright, as was her habit. She wore a light tweed suit, a string of pearls and a small velvet toque. To himself Mr. Broadribb was saying, "The Provincial Lady. A good type. Fluffy old girl. May be scatty—may not. Quite a shrewd eye. I wonder where Rafiel came across her? Somebody's aunt, perhaps, up from the country?" While these thoughts passed through his head, he was making the kind of introductory small talk relating to the weather, the unfortunate effects of late frosts early in the year and such other remarks as he considered suitable.

Miss Marple made the necessary responses and sat placidly awaiting the opening of preliminaries to the meeting.

"You will be wondering what all this is about," said Mr. Broadribb, shifting a few papers in front of him and giving her a suitable smile. "You've heard, no doubt, of Mr. Rafiel's death, or perhaps you saw it in the paper."

"I saw it in the paper," said Miss Marple.

"He was, I understand, a friend of yours."

"I met him first just over a year ago," said Miss Marple. "In the West Indies," she added.

"Ah. I remember. He went out there, I believe, for his health. It did him some good, perhaps, but he was already a very ill man, badly crippled, as you know."

"Yes," said Miss Marple.

"You knew him well?"

"No," said Miss Marple, "I would not say that. We were fellow visitors in a hotel. We had occasional conversations. I never saw him again after my return to England. I live very quietly in the country, you see, and I gather that he was completely absorbed in business."

"He continued transacting business right up—well I could almost say right up to the day of his death," said Mr. Broadribb. "A very fine financial brain."

"I am sure that was so," said Miss Marple. "I realized quite soon that he was a—well, a very remarkable character altogether."

"I don't know if you have any idea—whether you've been given any idea at some time by Mr. Rafiel—as to what this proposition is that I have been instructed to put up to you?"

"I cannot imagine," said Miss Marple, "what possible kind of proposition Mr. Rafiel might have wanted to put up to me. It seems most unlikely."

"He had a very high opinion of you."

"That is kind of him, but hardly justified," said Miss Marple. "I am a very simple person."

"As you no doubt realize, he died a very rich man. The provisions of his will are on the whole fairly simple. He had already made dispositions of his fortune some time before his death. Trusts and other beneficiary arrangements."

"That is, I believe, very usual procedure nowadays," said Miss Marple, "though I am not at all cognizant of financial matters myself."

"The purpose of this appointment," said Mr. Broadribb, "is that I am instructed to tell you that a sum of money has been laid aside to become yours absolutely at the end of one year, but conditional on your accepting a certain proposition, with which I am to make you acquainted."

He took from the table in front of him a long envelope. It was sealed. He passed it across the table to her.

"It would be better, I think, that you should read for yourself of what this consists. There is no hurry. Take your time."

Miss Marple took her time. She availed herself of a small paper knife which Mr. Broadribb handed to her, slit up the envelope, took out the enclosure, one sheet of typewriting, and read it. She folded it up again, then reread it and looked at Mr. Broadribb.

"This is hardly very definite. Is there no more definite elucidation of any kind?"

"Not so far as I am concerned. I was to hand you this and tell you the amount of the legacy. The sum in question is twenty thousand pounds free of legacy duty."

Miss Marple sat looking at him. Surprise had rendered her speechless. Mr. Broadribb said no more for the moment. He was watching her closely. There was no doubt of her surprise. It was obviously the last thing Miss Marple had expected to hear. Mr. Broadribb wondered what her first words would be. She looked at him with the directness, the severity that one of his own aunts might have done. When she spoke, it was almost accusingly.

"That is a very large sum of money," said Miss Marple.

"Not quite so large as it used to be," said Mr. Broadribb (and just restrained himself from saying, "Mere chicken feed nowadays").

"I must admit," said Miss Marple, "that I am amazed. Frankly, quite amazed."

She picked up the document and read it carefully through again.

"I gather you know the terms of this?" she said.

"Yes. It was dictated to me personally by Mr. Rafiel."

"Did he not give you any explanation of it?"

"No, he did not."

"You suggested, I suppose, that it might be better if he did," said Miss Marple. There was a slight acidity in her voice now.

Mr. Broadribb smiled faintly.

"You are quite right. That is what I did. I said that you might find it difficult to—oh, to understand exactly what he was driving at."

"Very remarkable," said Miss Marple.

"There is no need, of course," said Mr. Broadribb, "for you to give me an answer now."

"No," said Miss Marple, "I should have to reflect upon this."

"It is, as you have pointed out, quite a substantial sum of money."

"I am old," said Miss Marple. "Elderly, we say, but old is a better word. Definitely old. It is both possible and indeed probable that I might not live as long as a year to earn this money, in the rather doubtful case that I *was* able to earn it?"

"Money is not to be despised at any age," said Mr. Broadribb.

"I could benefit certain charities in which I have an interest," said Miss Marple, "and there are always people. People whom one wishes one could do a little something for but one's own funds do not admit of it. And then I will not pretend that there are not pleasures and desires—things that one has not been able to indulge in or to afford—I think Mr. Rafiel knew quite well that to be able to do so quite unexpectedly would give an elderly person a great deal of pleasure."

"Yes, indeed," said Mr. Broadribb. "A cruise abroad, perhaps? One of these excellent tours as arranged nowadays. Theaters, concerts—the ability to replenish one's cellars."

"My tastes would be a little more moderate than that," said Miss Marple. "Partridges," she said thoughtfully, "it is very difficult to get partridges nowadays, and they're very expensive. I should enjoy a partridge—a whole partridge—to myself, very much. A box of *marrons glacés* are an expensive taste which I cannot often gratify. Possibly a visit to the opera. It means a car to take one to Covent Garden and back, and the expense of a night in a hotel. But I must not indulge in idle chat," she said. "I will take this back with me and reflect upon it. Really, what on earth made Mr. Rafiel—you have no idea why he should have suggested this particular proposition, and why he should think that I could be of service to him in any way? He must have known that it was over a year, nearly two years since he had seen me and that I might have got much more feeble than I have, and much more unable to exercise such small talents as I might have. He was taking a risk. There are other people surely much better qualified to undertake an investigation of this nature?"

"Frankly, one would think so," said Mr. Broadribb, "but he selected you, Miss Marple. Forgive me if this is idle curiosity, but have you had—oh, how shall I put it?—any connection with crime or the investigation of crime?"

"Strictly speaking I should say no," said Miss Marple. "Nothing professional, that is to say. I have never been a probation officer or indeed sat as a magistrate on a bench or been connected in any way with a detective agency. To explain to you, Mr. Broadribb, which I think is only fair for me to do and which I think Mr. Rafiel ought to have done, to explain it in any way all I can say is that during our stay in the West Indies, we both, Mr. Rafiel and myself, had a certain connection with a crime that took place there. A rather unlikely and perplexing murder."

"And you and Mr. Rafiel solved it?"

"I should not put it quite like that," said Miss Marple. "Mr. Rafiel, by the force of his personality, and I, by putting together one or two obvious indications that came to my notice, were successful in preventing a second murder just as it was about to take place. I could not have done it alone; I was physically far too feeble. Mr. Rafiel could not have done it alone; he was a cripple. We acted as allies, however."

"Just one other question I should like to ask you, Miss Marple. Does the word 'Nemesis' mean anything to you?"

"Nemesis," said Miss Marple. It was not a question. A very slow and unexpected smile dawned on her face. "Yes," she said, "it does mean something to me. It meant something to me and it meant something to Mr. Rafiel. I said it to him, and he was much amused by my describing myself by that name."

Whatever Mr. Broadribb had expected, it was not that. He looked at Miss Marple with something of the same astonished surprise that Mr. Rafiel had once felt in a bedroom by the Caribbean sea. A nice and quite intelligent old lady. But really—Nemesis!

"You feel the same, I am sure," said Miss Marple.

She rose to her feet.

"If you should find or receive any further instructions in this matter, you will perhaps let me know, Mr. Broadribb. It seems to me extraordinary that there should not be something of that kind. This leaves me entirely in the dark really as to what Mr. Rafiel is asking me to do or try to do."

"You are not acquainted with his family, his friends, his—"

"No. I told you. He was a fellow traveler in a foreign part of the world. We had a certain association as allies in a very mystifying matter. That is all." As she was about to go to the door, she turned suddenly and asked: "He had a secretary, Mrs. Esther Walters. Would it be infringing etiquette if I asked if Mr. Rafiel left her fifty thousand pounds?"

"His bequests will appear in the press," said Mr. Broadribb. "I can answer your question in the affirmative. Mrs. Walters' name is now Mrs. Anderson, by the way. She has remarried."

"I am glad to hear that. She was a widow with one daughter, and she was a very adequate secretary, it appears. She understood Mr. Rafiel very well. A nice woman. I am glad she has benefited."

That evening, Miss Marple, sitting in her straight-backed chair, her feet stretched out to the fireplace where a small wood fire was burining owing to the sudden cold spell which, as is its habit, can always descend on England at any moment selected by itself, took once more from the long envelope the document delivered to her that morning. Still in a state of partial unbelief, she read, murmuring the words here and there below her breath as though to impress them on her mind:

To Miss Jane Marple, resident in the village of St. Mary Mead.

This will be delivered to you after my death by the good offices of my solicitor, James Broadribb. He is the man I employ for dealing with such legal matters as fall in the field of my private affairs, not my business activities. He is a sound and trustworthy lawyer. Like the majority of the human race, he is susceptible to the sin of curiosity. I have not satisfied his curiosity. In some respects this matter will remain between you and myself. Our code word, my dear lady, is Nemesis. I don't think you will have forgotten in what place and in what circumstances you first spoke that word to me. In the course of my business activities over what is now quite a long life, I have learned one thing about a man whom I wish to employ. He has to have a flair. A flair for the particular job I want him to do. It is not knowledge, it is not experience. The only word that describes it is *flair*. A natural gift for doing a certain thing.

You, my dear, if I may call you that, have a natural flair for justice, and that has led to your having a natural flair for crime. I want you to investigate a certain crime. I have ordered a certain sum to be placed so that if you accept this request and as a result of your investigation this crime is properly elucidated, the money will become yours absolutely. I have set aside a year for you to engage on this mission. You are not young, but you are, if I may say so, tough. I think I can trust a reasonable fate to keep you alive for a year at least.

I think the work involved will not be distasteful to you. You have a natural genius, I should say, for investigation. The necessary funds for what I may describe as working capital for making this investigation will be remitted to you during that period whenever necessary. I offer this to you as an alternative to what may be your life at present.

I envisage you sitting in a chair, a chair that is agreeable and comfortable for whatever kind or form of rheumatism from which you may suffer. All persons of your age, I consider, are likely to suffer from some form of rheumatism. If this ailment affects your knees or your back, it will not be easy for you to get about much and you will spend your time mainly in knitting. I see you, as I saw you once one night as I rose from sleep disturbed by your urgency, in a cloud of pink wool.

I envisage you knitting more jackets, head scarves and a good many other things of which I do not know the name. If you prefer to continue knitting, that is your decision. If you prefer to serve the cause of justice, I hope that you may at least find it interesting.

> Let justice roll down like waters
> And righteousness like an everlasting stream.

AMOS.

CHAPTER THREE
Miss Marple Takes Action

I

MISS MARPLE READ this letter three times—then she laid it aside and sat frowning slightly while she considered the letter and its implications.

The first thought that came to her was that she was left with a surprising lack of definite information. Would there be any further information coming to her from Mr. Broadribb? Almost certainly she felt that there would be no such thing. That would not have fitted in with Mr. Rafiel's plan. Yet how on earth could Mr. Rafiel expect her to do anything, to take any course of action in a matter about which she knew nothing? It was intriguing. After a few minutes more for consideration, she decided that Mr. Rafiel had meant it to be intriguing. Her thoughts went back to him, for the brief time that she had known him. His disability, his bad temper, his flashes of brilliance, of occasional humor. He'd enjoy, she thought, teasing people. He had been enjoying, she felt, and this letter made it almost certain, baffling the natural curiosity of Mr. Broadribb.

There was nothing in the letter he had written her to give her the slightest clue as to what this business was all about. It was no help to her whatsoever. Mr. Rafiel, she thought, had very definitely not meant it to be of any help. He had had—how could she put it?—other ideas. All the same, she could not start out into the blue knowing nothing. This could almost be described as a crossword puzzle with no clues given. There would *have* to be clues. She would *have* to know what she was wanted to do, where she was wanted to go, whether she was to solve some problem sitting in her armchair and laying aside her knitting needles in order to concentrate better. Or did Mr. Rafiel intend her to take a plane or a boat to the West Indies or to South America or to some other specially directed spot? She would either have to find out for herself what it was she was meant to do, or else she would have to receive definite instructions. He might think she had sufficient ingenuity to guess at things, to ask questions, to find out that way. No, she couldn't quite believe that.

"If he does think that," said Miss Marple aloud, "he's gaga. I mean, he was gaga before he died."

But she didn't think Mr. Rafiel would have been gaga.

"I shall receive instructions," said Miss Marple. "But what instructions and when?"

It was only then that it occurred to her suddenly that without noticing it she had definitely accepted the mandate. She spoke aloud again, addressing the atmosphere.

"I believe in eternal life," said Miss Marple. "I don't know exactly where you are, Mr. Rafiel, but I have no doubt that you are *somewhere*—I will do my best to fulfill your wishes."

II

It was three days later when Miss Marple wrote to Mr. Broadribb. It was a very short letter, keeping strictly to the point.

Dear Mr. Broadribb,

    I have considered the suggestion you made to me and I am letting you know that I have decided to accept the proposal made to me by the late Mr. Rafiel. I shall do my best to comply with his wishes, though I am not at all assured of success. Indeed, I hardly see how it is possible for me to be successful. I have been given no direct instructions in his letter and have not been—I think the term is briefed—in any way. If you have any further communication you are holding for me whch sets out definite instructions, I should be glad if you will send it to me, but I imagine that as you have not done so, that is not the case.

I presume that Mr. Rafiel was of sound mind and disposition when he died? I think I am justified in asking if there has been recently in his life any criminal affair in which he might possibly have been interested, either in the course of his business or in his personal relations. Has he ever expressed to you any anger or dissatisfaction with some notable miscarriage of justice about which he felt strongly? If so, I think I should be justified in asking you to let me know about it. Has any relation or connection of his suffered some hardship, lately been the victim of some unjust dealing, or what might be considered as such?

I am sure you will understand my reasons for asking these things. Indeed, Mr. Rafiel himself may have expected me to do so.

III

Mr. Broadribb showed this to Mr. Schuster, who leaned back in his chair and whistled.

"She's going to take it on, is she? Sporting old bean," he said. Then he added, "I suppose she knows something of what it's all about, does she?"

"Apparently not," said Mr. Broadribb.

"I wish we did," said Mr. Schuster. "He was an odd cuss."

"A difficult man," said Mr. Broadribb.

"I haven't got the least idea," said Mr. Schuster, "have you?"

"No, I haven't," said Mr. Broadribb. He added, "He didn't want me to have, I suppose."

"Well, he's made things a lot more difficult by doing that. I don't see the least chance that some old girl from the country can interpret a dead man's brain and know what fantasy was plaguing him. You don't think he was leading her up the garden path? Having her on? Sort of joke, you know. Perhaps he thinks that she thinks she's the cat's whiskers at solving village problems, but he's going to teach her a sharp lesson—"

"No," said Mr. Broadribb, "I don't quite think that. Rafiel wasn't that type of man."

"He was a mischievous devil sometimes," said Mr. Schuster.

"Yes, but not—I think he was serious over this. *Something* was worrying him. In fact I'm quite sure something was worrying him."

"And he didn't tell you what it was or give you the least idea?"

"No, he didn't."

"Then how the devil can he expect—?" Schuster broke off.

"He can't really have expected anything to come of this," said Mr. Broadribb. "I mean, how is she going to set about it?"

"A practical joke, if you ask me."

"Twenty thousand pounds is a lot of money."

"Yes, but if he knows she can't do it?"

"No," said Mr. Broadribb. "He wouldn't have been as unsporting as all that. He must think she's got a chance of doing or finding out whatever it is."

"And what do we do?"

"Wait," said Mr. Broadribb. "Wait and see what happens next. After all, there has to be some development."

"Got some sealed orders somewhere, have you?"

"My dear Schuster," said Mr. Broadribb, "Mr. Rafiel had implicit trust in my discretion and in my ethical conduct as a lawyer. Those sealed instructions are to be opened only under certain circumstances, none of which has yet arisen."

"And never will," said Mr. Schuster.

That ended the subject.

IV

Mr. Broadribb and Mr. Schuster were lucky in so much as they had a full professional life to lead. Miss Marple was not so fortunate. She knitted and she reflected and she also went out for walks, occasionally remonstrated with by Cherry for so doing.

"You know what the doctor said. You weren't to take too much exercise."

"I walk very slowly," said Miss Marple, "and I am not doing anything. Digging, I mean, or weeding. I just—well, I just put one foot in front of the other and wonder about things."

"What things?" asked Cherry with some interest.

"I wish I knew," said Miss Marple, and asked Cherry to bring her an extra scarf as there was a chilly wind.

"What's fidgeting her, that's what I would like to know," said Cherry to her husband as she set before him a Chinese plate of rice and a concoction of kidneys. "Chinese dinner," she said.

Her husband nodded approval.

"You get a better cook every day," he said.

"I'm worried about her," said Cherry. "I'm worried because she's worried a bit. She had a letter and it stirred her all up."

"What she needs is to sit quiet," said Cherry's husband. "Sit quiet, take it easy, get herself new books from the library, get a friend or two to come and see her."

"She's thinking out something," said Cherry. "Sort of plan. Thinking out how to tackle something, that's how I look at it."

She broke off the conversation at this stage and took in the coffee tray and put it down by Miss Marple's side.

"Do you know a woman who lives in a new house somewhere here, she's called Mrs. Hastings?" asked Miss Marple. "And someone called Miss Bartlett, I think it is, who lives with her—?"

"What—do you mean the house that's been all done up and repainted at the end of the village? The people there haven't been there very long. I don't know what their names are. Why do you want to know? They're not very interesting. At least I shouldn't say they were."

"Are they related?" asked Miss Marple.

"No. Just friends, I think."

"I wonder why—" said Miss Marple, and broke off.

"You wondered why what?"

"Nothing," said Miss Marple. "Clear my little hand desk, will you, and give me my pen and the notepaper. I'm going to write a letter."

"Who to?" said Cherry with the natural curiosity of her kind.

"To a clergyman's sister," said Miss Marple. "His name is Canon Prescott."

"That's the one you met abroad in the West Indies, isn't it? You showed me his photo in your album."

"Yes."

"Not feeling bad, are you? Wanting to write to a clergyman and all that?"

"I'm feeling extremely well," said Miss Marple, "and I am anxious to get busy on something. It's just possible Miss Prescott might help."

Dear Miss Prescott, [wrote Miss Marple]

I hope you have not forgotten me. I met you and your brother in the West Indies, if you remember, at St. Honoré. I hope the dear Canon is well and did not suffer much with his asthma in the cold weather last winter.

I am writing to ask you if you can possibly let me have the address of Mrs. Walters—Esther Walters—whom you may remember from the Caribbean days. She was secretary to old Mr. Rafiel. She did give me her address at the time, but unfortunately I have mislaid it. I was anxious to write to her, as I have some horticultural information which she asked me about but which I was not able to tell her at the time. I heard in a roundabout way the other day that she had married again, but I don't think my informant was very certain of these facts. Perhaps you know more about her than I do.

I hope this is not troubling you too much. With kind regards to your brother and best wishes to yourself,
　　　　Yours sincerely,

JANE MARPLE.

Miss Marple felt better when she had dispatched this missive.

"At least," she said, "I've started doing something. Not that I hope much from this, but still it might help."

Miss Prescott answered the letter almost by return of post. She was a most efficient woman. She wrote a pleasant letter and enclosed the address in question.

I have not heard anything directly about Esther Walters, [she said] but like you I heard from a friend that they had seen a notice of her remarriage. Her name now is, I believe, Mrs. Alderson or Anderson. Her address is Winslow Lodge, near Alton, Hants. My brother sends his best wishes to you. It is sad that we live so far apart. We in the north of England and you south of London. I hope that we may meet on some occasion in the future.

Yours sincerely,

JOAN PRESCOTT.

"Winslow Lodge, Alton," said Miss Marple, writing it down. "Not so far away from here, really. No. Not so far away. I could—I don't know what would be the best method—possibly one of Inch's taxis. Slightly extravagant, but if anything results from it, it could be charged as expenses quite legitimately. Now do I write to her beforehand or do I leave it to chance? I think it would be better, really, to leave it to chance. Poor Esther. She could hardly remember me with any affection or kindliness."

Miss Marple lost herself in a train of thought that arose from her memories. It was quite possible that her actions in the Caribbean had saved Esther Walters from being murdered in the not-far-distant future. At any rate, that was Miss Marple's belief, but probably Esther Walters had not believed any such thing. "A nice woman," said Miss Marple, uttering the words in a soft tone aloud; "a very nice woman. The kind that would so easily marry a bad lot. In fact, the sort of woman that would marry a murderer if she were ever given half a chance. I still consider," continued Miss Marple thoughtfully, sinking her voice still lower, "that I probably saved her life. In fact, I am almost sure of it, but I don't think she would agree with that point of view. She probably dislikes me very much. Which makes it more difficult to use her as a source of information. Still, one can but try. It's better than sitting here waiting, waiting, waiting."

Was Mr. Rafiel perhaps making fun of her when he had written that letter? He was not always a particularly kindly man—he could be very careless of people's feelings.

"Anyway," said Miss Marple, glancing at the clock and deciding that she would have an early night in bed, "when one thinks of things just before going to sleep, quite often ideas come. It may work out that way."

"Sleep well?" asked Cherry as she put down an early morning tea tray on the table at Miss Marple's elbow.

"I had a curious dream," said Miss Marple.

"Nightmare?"

"No, no, nothing of that kind. I was talking to someone, not anyone I knew very well. Just talking. Then when I looked, I saw it wasn't that person at all I was talking to. It was somebody else. Very odd."

"Bit of a mixup," said Cherry helpfully.

"It just reminded me of something," said Miss Marple, "or rather of someone I once knew. Order Inch for me, will you? To come here about half-past eleven."

Inch was part of Miss Marple's past. Originally the proprietor of a cab, Mr. Inch had died, been succeeded by his son "Young Inch," then aged forty-four, who had turned the family business into a garage and acquired two aged cars. On his decease the garage acquired a new owner. There had been since then Pip's Cars, James's Taxis, and Arthur's Car Hire. Old inhabitants still spoke of Inch.

"Not going to London, are you?"

"No, I'm not going to London. I shall have lunch perhaps in Haslemere."

"Now what are you up to now?" said Cherry, looking at her suspiciously.

"Endeavoring to meet someone by accident and make it seem purely natural," said Miss Marple. "Not really very easy, but I hope that I can manage it."

At half-past eleven the taxi waited. Miss Marple instructed Cherry.

"Ring up this number, will you, Cherry? Ask if Mrs. Anderson is at home. If Mrs. Anderson answers or if she is going to come to the telephone, say a Mr. Broadribb wants to speak to her. You," said Miss Marple, "are Mr. Broadribb's secretary. If she's out, find out what time she will be in."

"And if she is in and I get her?"

"Ask what day she could arrange to meet Mr. Broadribb at his office in London next week. When she tells you, make a note of it and ring off."

"The things you think of! Why all this? Why do you want me to do it?"

"Memory is a curious thing," said Miss Marple. "Sometimes one remembers a voice even if one hasn't heard it for over a year."

"Well, Mrs. What's-a-name won't have heard mine at any time, will she?"

"No," said Miss Marple. "That is why *you* are making the call."

Cherry fulfilled her instruction. Mrs. Anderson was out shopping, she learned but would be in for lunch and all the afternoon.

"Well, that makes things easier," said Miss Marple. "Is Inch here? Ah, yes. Good morning, Edward," she said to the present driver of Arthur's taxis, whose actual name was George. "Now this is where I want you to go. It ought not to take, I think, more than an hour and a half."

The expedition set off.

CHAPTER FOUR
Esther Walters

ESTHER ANDERSON CAME out of the supermarket and went towards where she had parked her car. Parking grew more difficult every day, she thought. She collided with somebody, an elderly woman limping a little who was walking towards her. She apologized, and the other woman made an exclamation.

"Why, indeed, it's—surely—it's Mrs. Walters, isn't it? Esther Walters? You don't remember me, I expect. Jane Marple. We met in the hotel in St. Honoré oh—quite a long time ago. A year and a half."

"Miss Marple? So it is, of course. Fancy seeing you!"

"How very nice to see you. I am lunching with some friends near here, but I have to pass back through Alton later. Will you be at home this afternoon? I should so like to have a nice chat with you. It's so nice to see an old friend."

"Yes, of course. Any time after three o'clock."

The arrangement was ratified.

"Old Jane Marple," said Esther Anderson, smiling to herself. "Fancy her turning up. I thought she'd died a long time ago."

Miss Marple rang the bell of Winslow Lodge at three-thirty precisely. Esther opened the door to her and brought her in.

Miss Marple sat down in the chair indicated to her, fluttering a little in the restless manner that she adopted when slightly flustered—or at any rate, when she was seeming to be slightly flustered. In this case it was misleading, since things had happened exactly as she had hoped they would happen.

"It's so nice to see you," she said to Esther. "So very nice to see you again. You know, I do think things are so very odd in this world. You hope you'll meet people again and you're quite sure you will. And then time passes and suddenly it's all such a surprise."

"And then," said Esther, "one says it's a small world, doesn't one?"

"Yes, indeed, and I think there is something in that. I mean, it does seem a very large world and the West Indies are such a very long way from England. Well, I mean, of course I might have met you anywhere. In London or at Harrods. On a railway station or in a bus. There are so many possibilities."

"Yes, there are a lot of possibilities," said Esther. "I certainly shouldn't have expected to meet you just here, because this isn't really quite your part of the world, is it?"

"No. No, it isn't. Not that you're really so very far from St. Mary Mead where I live. Actually, I think it's only about twenty-five miles. But twenty-five miles in the country, when one hasn't got a car—and of course I couldn't afford a car, and anyway, I mean, I can't drive a car—so it wouldn't be much to the point, so one really only does see one's neighbors on the bus route, or else one goes by a taxi from the village."

"You're looking wonderfully well," said Esther.

"I was just going to say *you* were looking wonderfully well, my dear. I had no idea you lived in this part of the world."

"I have only done so for a short time. Since my marriage, actually."

"Oh, I didn't know. How interesting. I suppose I must have missed it. I always do look down the marriages."

"I've been married four or five months," said Esther. "My name is Anderson now."

"Mrs. Anderson," said Miss Marple. "Yes, I must try and remember that. And your husband?"

It would be unnatural, she thought, if she did not ask about the husband. Old maids were notoriously inquisitive.

"He is an engineer," said Esther. "He runs the Time and Motion Branch. He is"—she hesitated—" a little younger than I am."

"Much better," said Miss Marple immediately. "Oh, much better, my dear. In these days men age so much quicker than women. I know it used not to be said so, but actually it's true. I mean, they get more things the matter with them. I think, perhaps, they worry and work too much. And then they get high blood pressure or low blood pressure or sometimes a little heart trouble. They're rather prone to gastric ulcers, too. I don't think *we* worry so much, you know. I think we're a tougher sex."

"Perhaps we are," said Esther.

She smiled now at Miss Marple, and Miss Marple felt reassured. The last time she had seen Esther, Esther had looked as though she hated her, and probably she had hated her at that moment. But now, well, now perhaps she might even feel slightly grateful. She might have realized that she herself might even have been under a stone slab in a respectable churchyard instead of living a presumably happy life with Mr. Anderson.

"You look very well," she said, "and very gay."

"So do you, Miss Marple."

"Well, of course, I am rather older now. And one has so many ailments. I mean, not desperate ones, nothing of that kind, but I mean one has always some kind of rheumatism or some kind of ache and pain somewhere. One's feet are not what one would like feet to be. And there's usually one's back or a shoulder or painful hands. Oh, dear, one shouldn't talk about these things. What a very nice house you have."

"Yes, we haven't been in it very long. We moved in about four months ago."

Miss Marple looked round. She had rather thought that that was the case. She thought, too, that when they had moved in they had moved in on quite a handsome scale. The furniture was expensive, it was comfortable—comfortable and just this side of luxury. Good curtains, good covers, no particular artistic taste displayed, but then she would not have expected that. She thought she knew the reason for this appearance of prosperity. She thought it had come about on the strength of the late Mr. Rafiel's handsome legacy to Esther. She was glad to think that Mr. Rafiel had not changed his mind.

"I expect you saw the notice of Mr. Rafiel's death," said Esther, speaking almost as if she knew what was in Miss Marple's mind.

"Yes. Yes, indeed I did. It was about a month ago now, wasn't it? I was so sorry. Very distressed really, although, well, I suppose one knew—he almost admitted it himself, didn't he? He hinted several times that it wouldn't be very long. I think he was quite a brave man about it all, don't you?"

"Yes, he was a very brave man, and a very kind one really," said Esther. "He told me, you know, when I first worked for him, that he was going to give me a very good salary but that I would have to save out of it because I needn't expect to have anything more from him. Well, I certainly didn't expect to have anything more from him. He was very much a man of his word, wasn't he? But apparently he changed his mind."

"Yes," said Miss Marple. "Yes, I am very glad of that. I thought perhaps—not that he, of course, said anything—but I wondered."

"He left me a very big legacy," said Esther. "A surprisingly large sum of money. It came as a very great surprise. I could hardly believe it at first."

"I think he wanted it to be a surprise to you. I think he was perhaps that kind of man," said Miss Marple. She added: "Did he leave anything to—oh, what was his name?—the man attendant, the nurse-attendant?"

"Oh, you mean Jackson? No, he didn't leave anything to Jackson, but I believe he made him some handsome presents in the last year."

"Have you ever seen anything more of Jackson?"

"No. No, I don't think I've met him once since the time out in the islands. He didn't stay with Mr. Rafiel after they got back to England. I think he went to Lord Somebody who lives in Jersey or Guernsey."

"I would like to have seen Mr. Rafiel again," said Miss Marple. "It seems odd after we'd all been mixed up so. He and you and I and some others. And then, later, when I'd come home, when six months had passed—it occurred to me one day how closely associated we had been in our time of stress, and yet how little I really knew about Mr. Rafiel. I was thinking it only the other day, after I'd seen the notice of his death. I wished I could know a little more. Where he was born, you know, and his parents. What they were like. Whether he had any children or nephews or cousins or any family. I would so like to know."

Esther Anderson smiled slightly. She looked at Miss Marple and her expression seemed to say "Yes, I'm sure you always want to know everything of that kind about everyone you meet." But she merely said:

"No, there was really only one thing that everyone did know about him."

"That he was very rich," said Miss Marple immediately. "That's what you mean, isn't it? When you know that someone is very rich, somehow, well, you don't ask any more. I mean you don't ask to know any more. You say 'He is very rich' or you say 'He is enormously rich,' and your voice just goes down a little because it's so impressive, isn't it, when you meet someone who is immensely rich?"

Esther laughed slightly.

"He wasn't married, was he?" asked Miss Marple. "He never mentioned a wife."

"He lost his wife many years ago. About four or five years after they were married, I believe. I believe she was much younger than he was—I think she died of cancer. Very sad."

"Had he children?"

"Oh, yes, two daughters and a son. One daughter is married and lives in America. The other daughter died young, I believe. I met the American one once. She wasn't at all like her father. Rather a quiet, depressed-looking young woman." She added, "Mr. Rafiel never spoke about the son. I rather think that there had been trouble there. A scandal or something of that kind. I believe he died some years ago. Anyway, his father never mentioned him."

"Oh, dear. That was very sad."

"I think it happened quite a long time ago. I believe he took off for somewhere or other abroad and never came back—died out there, wherever it was."

"Was Mr. Rafiel very upset about it?"

"One wouldn't know with him," said Esther. "He was the kind of man who would always decide to cut his losses. If his son turned out to be unsatisfactory, a burden instead of a blessing, I think he would just shrug the whole thing off. Do what was necessary perhaps in the way of sending him money for support, but never thinking of him again."

"One wonders," said Miss Marple. "He never spoke of him or said anything?"

"If you remember, he was a man who never said anything much about personal feelings or his own life."

"No. No, of course not. But I thought perhaps, you having been—well, his secretary for so many years, that he might have confided any troubles to you."

"He was not a man for confiding troubles," said Esther. "If he had any, which I rather doubt. He was wedded to his business, one might say. He was father to his business and his business was the only kind of son or daughter that he had that mattered, I think. He enjoyed it all, investment, making money. Business coups—"

"Call no man happy until he is dead," murmured Miss Marple, repeating the words in the manner of one pronouncing them as a kind of slogan, which indeed they appeared to be in these days, or so she would have said.

"So there was nothing especially worrying him, was there, before his death?"

"No. Why should you think so?" Esther sounded surprised.

"Well, I didn't actually think so," said Miss Marple, "I just wondered because things do worry people more when they are—I won't say getting old—because he really wasn't old, but I mean things worry you more when you are laid up and can't do as much as you did and have to take things easy. Then worries just come into your mind and make themselves felt."

"Yes, I know what you mean," said Esther. "But I don't think Mr. Rafiel was like that. Anyway," she added, "I ceased being his secretary some time ago. Two or three months after I met Edmund."

"Ah, yes. Your husband. Mr. Rafiel must have been very upset at losing you."

"Oh, I don't think so," said Esther lightly. "He was not one who would be upset over that sort of thing. He'd immediately get another secretary— which he did. And then if she didn't suit him, he'd just get rid of her with a kindly golden handshake and get somebody else, till he found somebody who suited him. He was an intensely sensible man always."

"Yes. Yes, I can see that. Though he could lose his temper very easily."

"Oh, he enjoyed losing his temper," said Esther. "It made a bit of drama for him, I think."

"Drama," said Miss Marple thoughtfully. "Do you think—I have often wondered—do you think that Mr. Rafiel had any particular interest in criminology, the study of it, I mean? He—well, I don't know . . ."

"You mean because of what happened in the Caribbean?" Esther's voice had gone suddenly hard.

Miss Marple felt doubtful of going on and yet she must somehow or other try to get a little helpful knowledge.

"Well, no, not because of that, but afterwards, perhaps, he wondered about the psychology of these things. Or he got interested in the cases where justice had not been administered properly or—oh, well . . ."

She sounded more scatterbrained every minute.

"Why should he take the least interest in anything of that kind? And don't let's talk about that horrible business in St. Honoré."

"Oh, no, I think you are quite right. I'm sure I'm very sorry. I was just thinking of some of the things that Mr. Rafiel sometimes said. Queer turns of phrase, sometimes, and I just wondered if he had any theories, you know . . . about the causes of crime?"

"His interests were always entirely financial," said Esther shortly. "A really clever swindle of a criminal kind might have interested him, nothing else—"

She was looking coldly still at Miss Marple.

"I am sorry," said Miss Marple apologetically. "I—I shouldn't have talked about distressing matters that are fortunately past. And I must be getting on my way," she added. "I have got my train to catch and I shall only just have time. Oh, dear, what did I do with my bag? Oh, yes, here it is."

She collected her bag, umbrella and a few other things, fussing away until the tension had slightly abated. As she went out the door, she turned to Esther, who was urging her to stay and have a cup of tea.

"No, thank you, my dear, I'm so short of time. I'm very pleased to have seen you again and I do offer my best congratulations and hopes for a very happy life. I don't suppose you will be taking up any post again now, will you?"

"Oh, some people do. They find it interesting, they say. They get bored when they have nothing to do. But I think I shall rather enjoy living a life of leisure. I shall enjoy the legacy, too, that Mr. Rafiel left me. It was very kind of him and I think he'd want me—well, to enjoy it even if I spent it in what he'd think of perhaps as a rather silly, female way! Expensive clothes and a new hair-do and all that. He'd have thought that sort of thing very silly." She added suddenly, "I was fond of him, you know. Yes, I was quite fond of him. I think it was because he was a sort of challenge to me. He was difficult to get on with, and therefore I enjoyed managing it."

"And managing him?"

"Well, not quite managing him, but perhaps a little more than he knew I was."

Miss Marple trotted away down the road. She looked back once and waved her hand—Esther Anderson was still standing on the doorstep, and she waved back cheerfully.

"I thought this might have been something to do with her or something she knew about," said Miss Marple to herself. "I think I'm wrong. No. I don't think she's concerned in this business, whatever it is, in any way. Oh, dear, I feel Mr. Rafiel expected me to be much cleverer than I am being. I think he expected me to put things together—but what things? And what do I do next, I wonder?" She shook her head.

She had to think over things very carefully. This business had been, as it were, left to her. Left to her to refuse, to accept, to understand what it was all about? Or not to understand anything, but to go forward and hope that some kind of guidance might be given to her. Occasionally she closed her eyes and tried to picture Mr. Rafiel's face. Sitting in the garden of the hotel in the West Indies, in his tropical suit; his bad-tempered corrugated face, his flashes of occasional humor. What she really wanted to know was what had been in his mind when he worked up this scheme, when he set out to bring it about. To lure her into accepting it, to persuade her to accept it, to—well, perhaps one should say—to bully her into accepting it. The third was much the most likely, knowing Mr. Rafiel. And yet, take it that he had wanted something done and he had chosen her, settled upon her to do it. Why? Because she had suddenly come into his mind? But why should she have come into his mind?

She thought back to Mr. Rafiel and the things that had occurred at St. Honoré. Had perhaps the problem he had been considering at the time of his death sent his mind back to that visit to the West Indies? Was it in some way connected with someone who had been out there, who had taken part or been an onlooker there and was that what had put Miss Marple into his mind? Was there some link or some connection? If not, why should he suddenly think of her? What was it about her that could make her useful to him, in any way at all? She was an elderly, rather scatterbrained, quite ordinary person, physically not very strong, mentally not nearly as alert as she used to be. What had been her special qualifications, if any? She couldn't think of any. Could it possibly have been a bit of fun on Mr. Rafiel's part? Even if Mr. Rafiel had been on the point of death he might have wanted to have some kind of joke that suited his peculiar sense of humor.

She could not deny that Mr. Rafiel could quite possibly wish to have a joke, even on his deathbed. Some ironical humor of his might be satisfied.

"I must," said Miss Marple to herself firmly, "I must have some qualification for something." After all, since Mr. Rafiel was no longer in this world, he could not enjoy his joke at first hand. What qualifications had she got? "What qualities have I got that could be useful to anyone for *anything?*" said Miss Marple.

She considered herself with proper humility. She was inquisitive, she asked questions, she was the sort of age and type that could be expected to ask questions. That was one point, a possible point. You could send a private detective round to ask questions, or some psychological investigator, but it was true that you could much more easily send an elderly lady with a habit of snooping and being inquisitive, of talking too much, of wanting to find out about things, and it would seem perfectly natural.

"An old tabby," said Miss Marple to herself. "Yes, I can see I'm quite recognizable as an old tabby. There are so many old tabbies, and they're all so much alike. And, of course, yes, I'm very ordinary. An ordinary rather scatterbrained old lady. And that of course is very good camouflage. Dear me, I wonder if I'm thinking on the right lines? I do, sometimes, know what people are like. I mean, I know what people are like, because they remind me of certain other people I have known. So I know some of their faults and some of their virtues. I know what kind of people they are. There's that."

She thought again of St. Honoré and the Hotel of the Golden Palm. She had made one attempt to inquire into the possibilities of a link by her visit to Esther Walters. That had been definitely nonproductive, Miss Marple decided. There didn't seem any further link leading from there. Nothing that would tie up with his request that Miss Marple should busy herself with something, the nature of which she still had no idea!

"Dear me," said Miss Marple, "What a tiresome man you are, Mr. Rafiel!" She said it aloud and there was definite reproach in her voice.

Later, however, as she climbed into bed and applied her cozy hot water bottle to the most painful portion of her rheumatic back, she spoke again— in what might be taken as a semi-apology.

"I've done the best I could," she said.

She spoke aloud with the air of addressing one who might easily be in the room. It is true he might be anywhere, but even then there might be some telepathic or telephonic communication, and if so, she was going to speak definitely and to the point.

"I've done all I could. The best according to my limitations, and I must now leave it up to you."

With that she settled herself more comfortably, stretched out a hand, switched off the electric light, and went to sleep.

CHAPTER FIVE
Instructions from Beyond

I

IT WAS SOME three or four days later that a communication arrived by the second post. Miss Marple picked up the letter, did what she usually did to letters, turned it over, looked at the stamp, looked at the handwriting, decided that it wasn't a bill and opened it. It was typewritten.

Dear Miss Marple,
    By the time you read this, I shall be dead and also buried. Not cremated, I am glad to think. It has always seemed to me unlikely that one would manage to rise up from one's handsome bronze vase full of ashes and haunt anyone if one wanted to do so! Whereas the idea of rising from one's grave and haunting anyone is quite possible. Shall I want to do that? Who knows? I might even want to communicate with you.
    By now my solicitors will have communicated with you and will have put a certain proposition before you. I hope you will have accepted it. If you have not accepted it, don't feel in the least remorseful. It will be your choice.
    This should reach you, if my solicitors have done what they were told to do and if the posts have done the duty they are expected to perform, on the eleventh of the month. In two days from now you will receive a communication from a travel bureau in London. I hope what it proposes will not be distasteful to you. I needn't say more. I want you to have an open mind. Take care of yourself. I think you will manage to do that. You are a very shrewd person. The best of luck and may your guardian angel be at your side looking after you. You may need one.
    The best of luck.
        Your affectionate friend,
                                J. B. RAFIEL

"Two days!" said Miss Marple.

She found it difficult to pass the time. The post office did their duty and so did the Famous Houses and Gardens of Great Britain.

> Dear Miss Jane Marple,
>
> Obeying instructions given us by the late Mr. Rafiel, we send you particulars of our Tour No. 37 of the Famous Houses and Gardens of Great Britain which starts from London on Thursday next—the seventeenth.
>
> If it should be possible for you to come to our office in London, our Mrs. Sandbourne, who is to accompany the tour, will be very glad to give you all particulars and to answer all questions.
>
> Our tours last for a period of two to three weeks. This particular tour, Mr. Rafiel thinks, will be particularly acceptable to you as it will visit a part of England which as far as he knows you have not yet visited, and takes in some really very attractive scenery and gardens. He has arranged for you to have the best accommodation and all the luxury available that we can provide.
>
> Perhaps you will let us know which day would suit you to visit our office in Berkeley Street?

Miss Marple folded up the letter, put it in her bag, noted the telephone number, thought of a few friends whom she knew, rang up two of them, one of whom had been for tours with the Famous Houses and Gardens, and spoke highly of them, the other one had not been personally on a tour but had friends who had traveled with this particular firm and who said everything was very well done, though rather expensive, and not too exhausting for the elderly. She then rang up the Berkeley Street number and said she would call upon them on the following Tuesday.

The next day she spoke to Cherry on the subject.

"I may be going away, Cherry," she said. "On a tour."

"A tour?" said Cherry. "One of these travel tours? You mean a package tour abroad?"

"Not abroad. In this country," said Miss Marple. "Mainly visiting historic buildings and gardens."

"Do you think it's all right to do that at your age? These things can be very tiring, you know. You have to walk miles sometimes."

"My health is really very good," said Miss Marple, "and I have always heard that in these tours they are careful to provide restful intervals for people who are not particularly strong."

"Well, be careful of yourself, that's all," said Cherry. "We don't want you falling down with a heart attack, even if you are looking at a particularly sumptuous fountain or something. You're a bit old, you know, to do this sort of thing. Excuse me saying it, it sounds rude, but I don't like to think of you passing out because you've done too much or anything like that."

"I can take care of myself," said Miss Marple with some dignity.

"All right, but you just be careful," said Cherry.

Miss Marple packed a suitable bag, went to London, booked a room at a modest hotel. ("Ah, Bertram's Hotel," she thought in her mind, "what a wonderful hotel *that* was! Oh, dear, I must forget all those things; the St.

George is quite a pleasant place.") At the appointed time she was in Berkeley Street and was shown into the office where a pleasant woman of about thirty-five rose to meet her, explained that her name was Mrs. Sandbourne and that she would be in personal charge of this particular tour.

"Am I to understand," said Miss Marple, "that this trip is in my case—?" She hesitated.

Mrs. Sandbourne, sensing slight embarrassment, said:

"Oh, yes, I ought to have explained perhaps better in the letter we sent you. Mr. Rafiel has paid all expenses."

"You do know that he is dead?" said Miss Marple.

"Oh, yes, but this was arranged before his death. He mentioned that he was in ill-health but wanted to provide a treat for a very old friend of his who had not had the opportunity of traveling as much as she could have wished."

II

Two days later, Miss Marple, carrying her small overnight bag, her new and smart suitcase surrendered to the driver, had boarded a most comfortable and luxurious coach which was taking a northwesterly route out of London. She studied the passenger list which was attached to the inside of a handsome brochure giving details of the daily itinerary of the coach, and various information as to hotels and meals, places to be seen, and occasional alternatives on some days which, although the fact was not stressed, actually intimated that one choice of itinerary was for the young and active and that the other choice would be peculiarly suitable for the elderly, those whose feet hurt them, who suffered from arthritis or rheumatism and who would prefer to sit about and not walk long distances or up too many hills. It was all very tactful and well arranged.

Miss Marple read the passenger list and surveyed her fellow passengers. There was no difficulty about doing this because the other fellow passengers were doing much the same themselves. They were surveying her, among others, but nobody as far as Miss Marple could notice was taking any particular interest in her.

> Mrs. Riseley-Porter
> Miss Joanna Crawford
> Colonel and Mrs. Walker
> Mr. and Mrs. H. T. Butler
> Miss Elizabeth Temple
> Professor Wanstead
> Mr. Richard Jameson
> Miss Lumley
> Miss Bentham

Mr. Caspar
Miss Cooke
Miss Barrow
Mr. Emlyn Price
Miss Jane Marple

There were four elderly ladies. Miss Marple took note of them first so, as it were, to clear them out of the way. Two were traveling together. Miss Marple put them down as about seventy. They could roughly be considered as contemporaries of her own. One of them was very definitely the complaining type, one who would want to have seats at the front of the coach or else would make a point of having them at the back of the coach. Would wish to sit on the sunny side or could only bear to sit on the shady side. Who would want more fresh air or less fresh air. They had with them traveling rugs and knitted scarves and quite an assortment of guidebooks. They were slightly crippled and often in pain from feet or backs or knees, but were nevertheless of those whom age and ailments could not prevent from enjoying life while they still had it. Old girls, but definitely not stay-at-home old girls. Miss Marple made an entry in the little book she carried.

Fifteen passengers not including herself or Mrs. Sandbourne. And since she had been sent on this coach tour, one at least of those fifteen passengers must be of importance in some way. Either as a source of information or someone concerned with the law or a law case, or it might even be a murderer—a murderer who might have already killed or one who might be preparing to kill. Anything was possible, Miss Marple thought, with Mr. Rafiel! Anyway, she must make notes of these people.

On the right-hand page of her notebook she would note down who might be worthy of attention from Mr. Rafiel's point of view and on the left she would note down or cross off those who could only be of any interest if they could produce some useful information for her—information, it might be, that they did not even know they possessed. Or rather that even if they possessed it, they did not know it could possibly be useful to her or to Mr. Rafiel or to the law or to Justice with a capital "J." At the back of her little book, she might this evening make a note or two as to whether anyone had reminded her of characters she had known in the past at St. Mary Mead and other places. Any similarities might make a useful pointer. It had done so on other occasions.

The other two elderly ladies were apparently separate travelers. Both of them were about sixty. One was a well-preserved, well-dressed woman of obvious social importance in her own mind, but probably in other people's minds as well. Her voice was loud and dictatorial. She appeared to have in tow a niece, a girl of about eighteen or nineteen who addressed her as Aunt Geraldine. The niece, Miss Marple noted, was obviously well accustomed to coping with Aunt Geraldine's bossiness. She was a competent girl as well as being an attractive one.

Across the aisle from Miss Marple was a big man with square shoulders and a clumsy-looking body, looking as though he had been carelessly assembled by an ambitious child out of chunky bricks. His face looked as though nature had planned it to be round but the face had rebelled at this and decided to achieve a square effect by developing a powerful jaw. He had a thick head of grayish hair and enormous bushy eyebrows which moved up and down to give point to what he was saying. His remarks seemed mainly to come out in a series of barks as though he was a talkative sheep dog. He shared his seat with a tall dark foreigner who moved restlessly in his seat and gesticulated freely. He spoke a most peculiar English, making occasional remarks in French and German. The bulky man seemed quite capable of meeting these onslaughts of foreign language, and shifted obligingly to either French or German. Taking a quick glance at them again, Miss Marple decided that the bushy eyebrows must be Professor Wanstead and the excitable foreigner was Mr. Caspar.

She wondered what it was they were discussing with such animation, but was baffled by the rapidity and force of Mr. Caspar's delivery.

The seat in front of them was occupied by the other woman of about sixty, a tall woman, possibly over sixty, but a woman who would have stood out in a crowd anywhere. She was still a very handsome woman with dark gray hair coiled high on her head, drawn back from a fine forehead. She had a low, clear, incisive voice. A personality, Miss Marple thought. Someone! Yes, she was decidedly someone. "Reminds me," she thought to herself, "of Dame Emily Waldron." Dame Emily Waldron had been the principal of an Oxford college and a notable scientist, and Miss Marple, having once met her in her nephew's company, had never quite forgotten her.

Miss Marple resumed her survey of the passengers. There were two married couples, one American, middle-aged, amiable, a talkative wife and a placidly agreeing husband. They were obviously dedicated travelers and sightseers. There was also an English middle-aged couple whom Miss Marple noted down without hesitation as a retired military man and wife. She ticked them off from the list as Colonel and Mrs. Walker.

In the seat behind her was a tall, thin man of about thirty with a highly technical vocabulary, clearly an architect. There were also two middle-aged ladies traveling together rather further up the coach. They were discussing the brochure and deciding what the tour was going to hold for them in the way of attractions. One was dark and thin and the other was fair and sturdily built and the latter's face seemed faintly familiar to Miss Marple. She wondered where she had seen or met her before. However, she could not recall the occasion to mind. Possibly someone she had met at a cocktail party or sat opposite to in a train. There was nothing very special about her to remember.

Only one more passenger remained for her to appraise, and this was a young man, possibly of about nineteen or twenty. He wore the appropriate clothes for his age and sex: tight black jeans, a polo-necked purple sweater and his head was an outsize rich mop of nondisciplined black hair. He was looking with an air of interest at the bossy woman's niece, and the bossy woman's niece also, Miss Marple thought, was looking with some interest at him. In spite of the preponderance of old girls and middle-aged females there were, at any rate, two young people among the passengers.

They stopped for lunch at a pleasant riverside hotel, and the afternoon sightseeing was given over to Blenheim. Miss Marple had already visited Blenheim twice before, so she saved her feet by limiting the amount of sightseeing indoors and coming fairly soon to the enjoyment of the gardens and the beautiful view.

By the time they arrived at the hotel where they were to stay the night, the passengers were getting to know each other. The efficient Mrs. Sandbourne, still brisk and unwearied by her duties in directing the sightseeing, did her part very well; creating little groups by adding anyone who looked as if he or she were left out to one or other of them, murmuring, "You must make Colonel Walker describe his garden to you. Such a wonderful collection of fuchsias he has." With such little sentences she drew people together.

Miss Marple was now able to attach names to all the passengers. Bushy eyebrows turned out to be Professor Wanstead, as she had thought, and the foreigner was Mr. Caspar. The bossy woman was Mrs. Riseley-Porter and her niece was called Joanna Crawford. The young man with the hair was Emlyn Price, and he and Joanna Crawford appeared to be finding out that certain things in life, such as decided opinions, they had in common, on economics, art, general dislikes, politics and such topics.

The two eldest ladies graduated naturally to Miss Marple as a kindred old girl. They discussed happily arthritis, rheumatism, diets, new doctors, remedies both professional, patent, and reminiscences of old wives' treatments which had had success where all else failed. They discussed the many tours they had been on to foreign places in Europe; hotels, travel agencies and finally the County of Somerset where Miss Lumley and Miss Bentham lived, and where the difficulties of getting suitable gardeners could hardly be believed.

The two middle-aged ladies traveling together turned out to be Miss Cooke and Miss Barrow. Miss Marple still felt that one of these two, the fair one, Miss Cooke, was faintly familiar to her, but she still could not remember where she had seen her before. Probably it was only her fancy. It might also be just fancy, but she could not help feeling that Miss Barrow and Miss Cooke appeared to be avoiding her. They seemed rather anxious to move away if she approached. That, of course, might be entirely her imagination.

Fifteen people, one of whom at least must matter in some way. In casual conversation that evening she introduced the name of Mr. Rafiel, so as to note if anyone reacted in any way. Nobody did.

The handsome woman was identified as Miss Elizabeth Temple, who was the retired headmistress of a famous girls' school. Nobody appeared to Miss Marple likely to be a murderer, except possibly Mr. Caspar, and that was probably foreign prejudice. The thin young man was Richard Jameson, an architect.

"Perhaps I shall do better tomorrow," said Miss Marple to herself.

III

Miss Marple went to bed definitely tired out. Sightseeing was pleasant but exhausting, and trying to study fifteen or sixteen people at once and wondering as you did so which of them could possibly be connected with a murder was even more exhausting. It had a touch of such unreality about it that one could not, Miss Marple felt, take it seriously. These seemed to be all perfectly nice people, the sort of people who go on cruises and on tours and all the rest of it. However, she took another quick and cursory glance at the passenger list, making a few little entries in her notebook.

Mrs. Riseley-Porter? Not connected with crime. Too social and self-centered.

Niece, Joanna Crawford? The same? But very efficient.

Mrs. Riseley-Porter, however, might have information of some kind which Miss Marple might find had a bearing on matters. She must keep on agreeable terms with Mrs. Riseley-Porter.

Miss Elizabeth Temple? A personality. Interesting. She did not remind Miss Marple of any murderer she'd ever known. "In fact," said Miss Marple to herself, "she really radiates integrity. *If* she had committed a murder, it would be a very popular murder. Perhaps for some noble reason or for some reason that she thought noble." But that wasn't satisfactory either. Miss Temple, she thought, would always know what she was doing and why she was doing it and would not have any silly ideas about nobility when merely evil existed. "All the same," said Miss Marple, "she's *someone* and she might—she just might be a person Mr. Rafiel wanted me to meet for some reason." She jotted down these thoughts on the right-hand side of her notebook.

She shifted her point of view. She had been considering a possible murderer—what about a prospective victim? Who was a possible victim? No one very likely. Perhaps Mrs. Riseley-Porter might qualify—rich—rather disagreeable. The efficient niece might inherit. She and the anarchistic Emlyn Price might combine in the cause of anti-capitalism. Not a very credible idea, but no other feasible murderee seemed to offer.

Professor Wanstead? An interesting man, she was sure. Kindly, too. Was he a scientist or was he medical? She was not as yet sure, but she put him down on the side of science. She herself knew nothing of science, but it seemed not at all unlikely.

Mr. and Mrs. Butler? She wrote them off. Nice Americans. No connections with anyone in the West Indies or anyone she had known. No, she didn't think that the Butlers could be relevant.

Richard Jameson? That was the thin architect. Miss Marple didn't see how architecture could come into it, though it might, she supposed. A priest's hole, perhaps? One of the houses they were going to visit might have a priest's hole which would contain a skeleton. And Mr. Jameson, being an architect, would know just where the priest's hole was. He might aid her to discover it, or she might aid him to discover it and then they would find a body. "Oh, really," said Miss Marple, "what nonsense I am talking and thinking."

Miss Cooke and Miss Barrow? A perfectly ordinary pair. And yet she'd certainly seen one of them before. At least she'd seen Miss Cooke before. Oh, well, it would come to her, she supposed.

Colonel and Mrs. Walker? Nice people. Retired army folk. Served abroad mostly. Nice to talk to, but she didn't think there'd be anything for her there.

Miss Bentham and Miss Lumley? The old girls. Unlikely to be criminals, but, being elderly, they might know plenty of gossip, or have some information, or might make some illuminating remark even if it happened to come about in connection with rheumatism, arthritis or patent medicine.

Mr. Caspar? Possibly a dangerous character. Very excitable. She would keep him on the list for the present.

Emlyn Price? A student presumably. Students were very violent. Would Mr. Rafiel have sent her on the track of a student? Well, it would perhaps depend on what the student had done or wished to do or was going to do. A dedicated anarchist, perhaps.

"Oh, dear," said Miss Marple, suddenly exhausted, "I must go to bed."

Her feet ached, her back ached and her mental reactions were not, she thought, at their best. She slept at once. Her sleep was enlivened by several dreams.

One where Professor Wanstead's bushy eyebrows fell off because they were not his own eyebrows, but false ones. As she woke again, her first impression was that which so often follows dreams—a belief that the dream in question had solved everything. "Of course," she thought, "of *course!*" His eyebrows were false and that solved the whole thing. He was the criminal.

Sadly, it came to her that nothing was solved. Professor Wanstead's eyebrows coming off was of no help at all.

Unfortunately now she was no longer sleepy. She sat up in bed with some determination.

She sighed and slipped on her dressing gown, moved from her bed to an upright chair, took a slightly larger notebook from her suitcase and started work.

"The project I have undertaken," she wrote, "is connected certainly with crime of some kind. Mr. Rafiel has distinctly stated that in his letter. He said I had a flair for justice and that necessarily included a flair for crime. So crime is involved, and it is presumably not espionage or fraud or robbery, because such things have never come my way and I have no connection with such things, or knowledge of them, or special skills. What Mr. Rafiel knows of me is only what he knew during the period of time when we were both in St. Honoré. We were connected there with a murder. Murders as reported in the press have never claimed my attention. I have never read books on criminology as a subject or really been interested in such a thing. No, it has just happened that I have found myself in the vicinity of murder rather more often than would seem normal. My attention has been directed to murders involving friends or acquaintances. These curious coincidences of connections with special subjects seem to happen to people in life. One of my aunts, I remember, was on five occasions shipwrecked and a friend of mine was what I believe is officially called accident-prone. I know some of her friends refused to ride in a taxi with her. She had been in four taxi accidents and three car accidents and two railway accidents. Things like this seem to happen to certain people for no appreciable reason. I do not like to write it down, but it does appear that murders seem to happen, not to me myself, thank goodness, but seem to happen in my vicinity."

Miss Marple paused, changed her position, put a cushion in her back, and continued:

"I must try to make as logical a survey as I can of this project which I have undertaken. My instructions, or my 'briefing,' as naval friends of mine put it, are so far quite inadequate. Practically nonexistent. So I must ask myself one clear question. What is all this *about?* Answer! *I do not know.* Curious and interesting. An odd way for a man like Mr. Rafiel to go about things, especially when he was a successful business and financial operator. He wants me to guess, to employ my instinct, to observe and to obey such directions as are given to me or are hinted to me.

"So: Point 1. Direction will be given me. Direction from a dead man. Point 2. What is involved in my problem is *justice.* Either to set right an injustice or to avenge evil by bringing it to justice. This is in accord with the code word Nemesis given to me by Mr. Rafiel.

"After explanations of the principle involved, I received my first factual directive. It was arranged by Mr. Rafiel before his death that I was to go on Tour No. 37 of Famous Houses and Gardens. Why? That is what I have to ask myself. Is it for some geographical or territorial reason? A connection or a clue? Some particular famous house? Or something involving some particular garden or landscape connected? This seems unlikely. The more likely explanation lies in the *people* or one of the people on this particular coach party. None of them is known to me personally, but one of them at least must be connected with the riddle I have to solve. Somebody among our group is connected or concerned with a murder. Somebody has information or a special link with the victim of a crime, or someone personally is himself or herself a murderer—a murderer as yet un-suspected."

Miss Marple stopped here suddenly. She nodded her head. She was satisfied now with her analysis so far as it went.

And so to bed.

Miss Marple added to her notebook:

"Here endeth the First Day."

CHAPTER SIX
Love

THE FOLLOWING MORNING they visited a small Queen Anne manor house. The drive there had not been very long or tiring. It was a very charming-looking house and had an interesting history as well as a very beautiful and unusually laid-out garden.

Richard Jameson, the architect, was full of admiration for the structural beauty of the house and being the kind of young man who is fond of hearing his own voice, he slowed down in nearly every room that they went through, pointing out every special molding or fireplace, and giving historical dates and references. Some of the group, appreciative at first, began to get slightly restive, as the somewhat monotonous lecturing went on. Some of them began to edge carefully away and fall behind the party. The local caretaker, who was in charge, was not himself too pleased by having his occupation usurped by one of the sightseers. He made a few efforts to get matters back into his own hands, but Mr. Jameson was unyielding. The caretaker made a last try.

"In this room, ladies and gentlemen, the White Parlor, folks call it, is where they found a body. A young man it was, stabbed with a dagger, lying on the hearthrug. Way back in seventeen hundred and something it was. It was said that the Lady Moffatt of that day had a lover. He came through a small side door and up a steep staircase to this room through a loose panel there was to the left of the fireplace. Sir Richard Moffatt, her husband, you see, was said to be across the seas in the Low Countries. But he come home, and in he came unexpectedly and caught 'em there together."

He paused proudly. He was pleased at the response from his audience, glad of a respite from the architectural details which they had been having forced down their throats.

"Why, isn't that just too romantic, Henry?" said Mrs. Butler in her resonant trans-Atlantic tones. "Why, you know, there's quite an atmosphere in this room. I feel it. I certainly feel it."

"Mamie is very sensitive to atmospheres," said her husband proudly to those around him. "Why, once when we were in an old house down in Louisiana . . ."

The narrative of Mamie's special sensitivity got into its swing, and Miss Marple and one or two others seized their opportunity to edge gently out of the room and down the exquisitely molded staircase to the ground floor.

"A friend of mine," said Miss Marple to Miss Cooke and Miss Barrow, who were next to her, "had a most nerve-racking experience only a few years ago. A dead body on their library floor one morning."

"One of the family?" asked Miss Barrow. "An epileptic fit?"

"Oh, no, it was a murder. A strange girl in evening dress. A blonde. But her hair was dyed. She was really a brunette; and—oh . . ." Miss Marple broke off, her eyes fixed on Miss Cooke's yellow hair where it escaped from her headscarf.

It had come to her suddenly. She knew why Miss Cooke's face was familiar and she knew where she had seen her before. But when she had seen her then, Miss Cooke's hair had been dark—almost black. And now it was bright yellow.

Mrs. Riseley-Porter, coming down the stairs, spoke decisively as she pushed past them and completed the staircase and turned into the hall.

"I really cannot go up and down any more of those stairs," she declared, "and standing around in these rooms is very tiring. I believe the gardens here, although not extensive, are quite celebrated in horticultural circles. I suggest we go there without loss of time. It looks as though it might cloud over before long. I think we shall get rain before the morning is out."

The authority with which Mrs. Riseley-Porter could enforce her remarks had its usual result. All those near at hand or within hearing followed her obediently out through French doors in the dining room into the garden. The gardens had indeed all that Mrs. Riseley-Porter had claimed for them. She herself took possession firmly of Colonel Walker and set off briskly. Some of the others followed them; others took paths in the opposite direction.

Miss Marple herself made a determined beeline for a garden seat which appeared to be of comfortable proportions as well as of artistic merit. She sank down on it with relief, and a sigh matching her own was emitted by Miss Elizabeth Temple as she followed Miss Marple and came to sit beside her on the seat.

"Going over houses is always tiring," said Miss Temple. "The most tiring thing in the world. Especially if you have to listen to an exhaustive lecture in each room."

"Of course all that we were told is very interesting," said Miss Marple rather doubtfully.

"Oh, do you think so?" said Miss Temple. Her head turned slightly and her eyes met those of Miss Marple. Something passed between the two women, a kind of rapport—of understanding tinged with mirth.

"Don't you?" asked Miss Marple.

"No," said Miss Temple.

This time the understanding was definitely established between them. They sat there companionably in silence. Presently Elizabeth Temple began to talk about gardens, and this garden in particular. "It was designed by Holman," she said, "somewhere about eighteen hundred or seventeen ninety-eight. He died young. A pity. He had great genius."

"It is so sad when anyone dies young," said Miss Marple.

"I wonder," said Elizabeth Temple.

She said it in a curious, meditative way.

"But they miss so much," said Miss Marple. "So many things."

"Or escape so much," said Miss Temple.

"Being as old as I am now," said Miss Marple, "I suppose I can't help feeling that early death means missing things."

"And I," said Elizabeth Temple, "having spent nearly all my life among the young, look at life as a period in time complete in itself. What did T. S. Eliot say: *The moment of the rose and the moment of the yew tree are of equal duration.*"

Miss Marple said, "I see what you mean . . . A life of whatever length is a complete experience. But don't you"—she hesitated—"ever feel that a life could be incomplete because it has been cut unduly short?"

"Yes, that is so."

Miss Marple said, looking at the flowers near her, "How beautiful peonies are. That long border of them—so proud and yet so beautifully fragile."

Elizabeth Temple turned her head towards her.

"Did you come on this trip to see the houses or to see gardens?" she asked.

"I suppose really to see the houses," said Miss Marple. "I shall enjoy the gardens most, though, but the houses—they will be a new experience for me. Their variety and their history, and the beautiful old furniture and the pictures." She added: "A kind friend gave me this trip as a gift. I am very grateful. I have not seen very many big and famous houses in my life."

"A kind thought," said Miss Temple.

"Do you often go on these sightseeing tours?" asked Miss Marple.

"No. This is not for me exactly a sightseeing tour."

Miss Marple looked at her with interest. She half opened her lips to speak but refrained from putting a question. Miss Temple smiled at her.

"You wonder why I am here, what my motive is, my reason. Well, why don't you make a guess?"

"Oh, I wouldn't like to do that," said Miss Marple.

"Yes, do do so." Elizabeth Temple was urgent. "It would interest me. Yes, really interest me. Make a guess."

Miss Marple was silent for quite a few moments. Her eyes looked at Elizabeth Temple steadily, ranging over her thoughtfully in her appraisement. She said:

"This is not from what I know about you or what I have been told about you. I know that you are quite a famous person and that your school is a very famous one. No. I am only making my guess from what you look like. I should write you down as a pilgrim. You have the look of one who is on a pilgrimage."

There was a silence and then Elizabeth said:

"That describes it very well. Yes. I am on a pilgrimage."

Miss Marple said after a moment or two:

"The friend who sent me on this tour and paid all my expenses is now dead. He was a Mr. Rafiel, a very rich man. Did you by any chance know him?"

"Jason Rafiel? I know him by name, of course. I never knew him personally, or met him. He gave a large endowment once to an educational project in which I was interested. I was very grateful. As you say, he was a very wealthy man. I saw the notice of his death in the papers a few weeks ago. So he was an old friend of yours?"

"No," said Miss Marple. "I had met him just over a year ago abroad. In the West Indies. I never knew much about him. His life or his family or any personal friends that he had. He was a great financier but otherwise, or so people always said, he was a man who was very reserved about himself. Did you know his family or anyone . . . ?" Miss Marple paused. "I often wondered, but one does not like to ask questions and seem inquisitive."

Elizabeth was silent for a minute—then she said:

"I knew a girl once—a girl who had been a pupil of mine at Fallowfield, my school. She was no actual relation to Mr. Rafiel, but she was at one time engaged to marry Mr. Rafiel's son."

"But she didn't marry him?" Miss Marple asked.

"No."

"Why not?"

Miss Temple said:

"One might hope to say—like to say—because she had too much sense. He was not the type of a young man one would want anyone one was fond of to marry. She was a very lovely girl and a very sweet girl. I don't know why she didn't marry him. Nobody has ever told me." She sighed and then said, "Anyway, she died . . ."

"Why did she die?" said Miss Marple.

Elizabeth Temple stared at the peonies for some minutes. When she spoke she uttered one word. It echoed like the tone of a deep bell—so much so that it was startling.

"Love!" she said.

Miss Marple queried the word sharply. "Love?"

"One of the most frightening words there is in the world," said Elizabeth Temple.

Again her voice was bitter and tragic.

"Love . . ."

CHAPTER SEVEN
An Invitation

MISS MARPLE DECIDED to miss out on that afternoon's sightseeing. She admitted to being somewhat tired and would perhaps give a miss to an ancient church and its fourteenth-century glass. She would rest for a while and join them at the tearoom which had been pointed out to her on the main street. Mrs. Sandbourne agreed that she was being very sensible.

Miss Marple, resting on a comfortable bench outside the tearoom, reflected on what she planned to do next and whether it would be wise to do it or not.

When the others joined her at teatime, it was easy for her to attach herself unobtrusively to Miss Cooke and Miss Barrow and sit with them at a table for four. The fourth chair was occupied by Mr. Caspar, whom Miss Marple considered as not sufficiently conversant with the English language to matter.

Leaning across the table as she nibbled a slice of Swiss roll, Miss Marple said to Miss Cooke:

"You know, I am quite sure we have met before. I have been wondering and wondering about it—I'm not as good as I was at remembering faces, but I'm sure I have met you somewhere."

Miss Cooke looked kindly but doubtful. Her eyes went to her friend, Miss Barrow. So did Miss Marple's. Miss Barrow showed no signs of helping to probe the mystery.

"I don't know if you've ever stayed in my part of the world," went on Miss Marple. "I live in St. Mary Mead. Quite a small village, you know. At least, not so small nowadays, there is so much building going on everywhere. Not very far from Much Benham and only twelve miles from the coast at Loomouth."

"Oh," said Miss Cooke, "let me see. Well, I know Loomouth quite well and perhaps—"

Suddenly Miss Marple made a pleased exclamation.

"Why, of course! I was in my garden one day at St. Mary Mead and you spoke to me as you were passing by on the footpath. You said you were staying down there, I remember, with a friend—"

"Of course," said Miss Cooke. "How stupid of me. I do remember you now. We spoke of how difficult it was nowadays to get anyone—to do job gardening, I mean—anyone who was any *use*."

"Yes. You were not living there, I think? You were staying with someone."

"Yes, I was staying with . . . with . . ." For a moment Miss Cooke hesitated, with the air of one who hardly knows or remembers a name.

"With a Mrs. Sutherland, was it?" suggested Miss Marple.

"No, no, it was . . . er . . . Mrs.—"

"Hastings," said Miss Barrow firmly as she took a piece of chocolate cake.

"Oh, yes, in one of the new houses," said Miss Marple.

"Hastings," said Mr. Caspar unexpectedly. He beamed. "I have been to Hastings—I have been to Eastbourne, too." He beamed again. "Very nice—by the sea."

"Such a coincidence," said Miss Marple, "meeting again so soon—such a small world, isn't it?"

"Oh, well, we are all so fond of gardens," said Miss Cooke vaguely.

"Flowers very pretty," said Mr. Caspar. "I like very much—" He beamed again.

"So many rare and beautiful shrubs," said Miss Cooke.

Miss Marple went full speed ahead with a gardening conversation of some technicality—Miss Cooke responded. Miss Barrow put in an occasional remark.

Mr. Caspar relapsed into smiling silence.

Later, as Miss Marple took her usual rest before dinner, she conned over what she had collected. Miss Cooke had admitted being in St. Mary Mead. She had admitted walking past Miss Marple's house. Had agreed it was quite a coincidence. Coincidence? thought Miss Marple meditatively, turning the word over in her mouth rather as a child might do to a certain lollipop to decide its flavor. Was it a coincidence? Or had she had some reason to come there? Had she been sent there? Sent there—for what reason? Was that a ridiculous thing to imagine?

"Any coincidence," said Miss Marple to herself, "is always worth noticing. You can throw it away later if it *is* only a coincidence."

Miss Cooke and Miss Barrow appeared to be a perfectly normal pair of friends doing the kind of tour which, according to them, they did every year. They had been on an Hellenic cruise last year and a tour of bulbs in Holland the year before, and Northern Ireland the year before that. They seemed perfectly pleasant and ordinary people. But Miss Cooke, she thought, had for a moment looked as though she were about to disclaim her visit to St. Mary Mead. She had looked at her friend Miss Barrow rather as though she were seeking instruction as to what to say. Miss Barrow was presumably the senior partner.

"Of course, really, I may have been imagining all these things," thought Miss Marple. "They may have no significance whatever."

The word *danger* came unexpectedly into her mind. Used by Mr. Rafiel in his first letter—and there had been some reference to her needing a guardian angel in his second letter. Was she going into danger in this business?—and why? From whom?

Surely not from Miss Cooke and Miss Barrow. Such an ordinary-looking couple.

All the same Miss Cooke *had* dyed her hair and altered her style of hairdressing. Disguised her appearance as much as she could, in fact. Which was odd, to say the least of it! She considered once more her fellow travelers.

Mr. Caspar, now, it would have been much easier to imagine that *he* might be dangerous. Did he understand more English than he pretended to do? She began to wonder about Mr. Caspar.

Miss Marple had never quite succeeded in abandoning her Victorian view of foreigners. One never *knew* with foreigners. Quite absurd, of course, to feel like that—she had many friends from various foreign countries. All the same . . . Miss Cooke, Miss Barrow, Mr. Caspar, that young man with the wild hair—Emlyn Something—a revolutionary—a practicing anarchist? Mr. and Mrs. Butler—such nice Americans—but perhaps too good to be true?

"Really," said Miss Marple, "I must pull myself together."

She turned her attention to the itinerary of their trip. Tomorrow, she thought, was going to be rather strenuous. A morning's sightseeing drive, starting rather early; a long, rather athletic walk on a coastal path in the afternoon. Certain interesting marine flowering plants. It would be tiring. A tactful suggestion was appended. Anyone who felt like a rest could stay behind in their hotel, the Golden Boar, which had a very pleasant garden, or could do a short excursion which would only take an hour to a beauty spot nearby. She thought perhaps that she would do that.

But though she did not know it then, her plans were to be suddenly altered.

As Miss Marple came down from her room in the Golden Boar the next day after washing her hands before luncheon, a woman in a tweed coat and skirt came forward rather nervously and spoke to her.

"Excuse me, are you Miss Marple—Miss Jane Marple?"

"Yes, that is my name," said Miss Marple, slightly surprised.

"My name is Mrs. Glynne. Lavinia Glynne. I and my two sisters live near here and—well, we heard you were coming, you see—"

"You heard I was coming?" said Miss Marple with some slight surprise.

"Yes. A very old friend of ours wrote to us—oh, quite some time ago, it must have been three weeks ago, but he asked us to make a note of this date. The date of the Famous Houses and Gardens Tour. He said that a great friend of his—or a relation, I'm not quite sure which—would be on that tour."

Miss Marple continued to look surprised.

"I'm speaking of a Mr. Rafiel," said Mrs. Glynne.

"Oh! Mr. Rafiel," said Miss Marple. "You—you know that—?"

"That he died? Yes. So sad. Just after his letter came. I think it must have been certainly very soon after he wrote to us. But we felt a special urgency to try to do what he had asked. He suggested, you know, that perhaps you would like to come and stay with us for a couple of nights. This part of the tour is rather strenuous. I mean, it's all right for the young people, but it is very trying for anyone older. It involves several miles of walking and a certain amount of climbing up difficult cliff paths and places. My sisters and

I would be so very pleased if you could come and stay in our house here. It is only ten minutes' walk from the hotel and I'm sure we could show you many interesting things locally."

Miss Marple hesitated a minute. She liked the look of Mrs. Glynne, plump, good-natured, and friendly though a little shy. Besides—here again must be Mr. Rafiel's instructions—the next step for her to take? Yes, it must be so.

She wondered why she felt nervous. Perhaps because she was now at home with the people in the tour, felt part of the group although as yet she had only known them for three days.

She turned to where Mrs. Glynne was standing, looking up at her anxiously.

"Thank you—it is most kind of you. I shall be very pleased to come."

CHAPTER EIGHT
The Three Sisters

MISS MARPLE STOOD looking out of a window. Behind her, on the bed, was her suitcase. She looked out over the garden with unseeing eyes. It was not often that she failed to see a garden she was looking at in either a mood of admiration or a mood of criticism. In this case it would presumably have been criticism. It was a neglected garden, a garden on which little money had been spent possibly for some years, and on which very little work had been done. The house, too, had been neglected. It was well proportioned, the furniture in it had been good furniture once, but had had little in late years of polishing or attention. It was not a house, she thought, that had been, at any rate of late years, loved in any way. It lived up to its name: The Old Manor House—a house, built with grace and a certain amount of beauty, lived in once, cherished. The daughters and sons had married and left and now it was lived in by Mrs. Glynne who, from a word she had let fall when she showed Miss Marple up to the bedroom appointed to her, had inherited it with her sisters from an uncle and had come here to live with her sisters after her husband had died. They had all grown older, their incomes had dwindled, labor had been more difficult to get.

The other sisters, presumably, had remained unmarried, one older, one younger than Mrs. Glynne, two Miss Bradbury-Scotts.

There was no sign of anything which belonged to a child in the house. No discarded ball, no old perambulator, no little chair or a table. This was just a house with three sisters.

"Sounds very Russian," murmured Miss Marple to herself. She did mean the Three Sisters, didn't she? Chekhov, was it? or Dostoevski? Really, she couldn't remember. Three sisters. But these would certainly not be the kind of three sisters who were yearning to go to Moscow. These three sisters were presumably, she was almost sure they were, content to remain where they

were. She had been introduced to the other two who had come, one out of
the kitchen and one down a flight of stairs to welcome her. Their manners
were well bred and gracious. They were what Miss Marple would have
called in her youth by the now obsolete term "ladies"—and what she once
recalled calling "decayed ladies." Her father had said to her:

"No, dear Jane, not *decayed*. Distressed gentlewomen."

Gentlewomen nowadays were not so liable to be distressed. They were
aided by government or by societies or by a rich relation. Or, perhaps—by
someone like Mr. Rafiel. Because, after all, that was the whole point, the
whole reason for her being here, wasn't it? Mr. Rafiel had arranged all this.
He had taken, Miss Marple thought, a good deal of trouble about it. He had
known presumably, some four or five weeks before his death, just when that
death was likely to be, give and take a little, since doctors were usually
moderately optimistic, knowing from experience that patients who ought to
die within a certain period very often took an unexpected lease of life and
lingered on, still doomed, but obstinately declining to take the final step. On
the other hand, hospital nurses when in charge of patients had, Miss Marple
thought from her experience, always expected the patients to be dead the
next day, and were much surprised when they were not. But in voicing their
gloomy views to Doctor, when he came, they were apt to receive in reply as
the doctor went out of the hall door a private aside of "Linger a few weeks
yet, I shouldn't wonder." Very nice of Doctor to be so optimistic, Nurse
would think, but surely Doctor was wrong. Doctor very often wasn't wrong.
He knew that people who were in pain, helpless, crippled, even unhappy,
still liked living and wanted to live. They would take one of Doctor's pills to
help them pass the night, but they had no intention of taking a few more
than necessary of Doctor's pills just in order to pass the threshold to a world
that they did not as yet know anything about!

Mr. Rafiel. That was the person Miss Marple was thinking about as she
looked across the garden with unseeing eyes. Mr. Rafiel? She felt now that
she was getting a little closer to understanding the task laid upon her, the
project suggested to her. Mr. Rafiel was a man who made plans. Made them
in the same way that he planned financial deals and takeovers. In the words
of her servant Cherry, he had had a problem. When Cherry had a problem,
she often came and consulted Miss Marple about it.

"This was a problem that Mr. Rafiel could not deal with himself, which
must have annoyed him very much," Miss Marple thought, "because he
could usually deal with any problem himself and insisted on doing so. But
he was bedridden and dying. He could arrange his financial affairs,
communicate with his lawyers, with his employees and with such friends
and relations as he had, but there was something or someone that he had
not arranged for. A problem he had not solved, a problem he still wanted to
solve, a project he still wanted to bring about. And apparently it was not
one that could be settled by financial aid, by business dealings, by the
services of a lawyer.

"So he thought of me," said Miss Marple.

It still surprised her very much. Very much indeed. However, in the sense
she was now thinking of it, his letter had been quite explicit. He had thought
she had certain qualifications for doing something. It had to do, she thought
once again, with something in the nature of crime or affected by crime. The

only other thing he knew about Miss Marple was that she was devoted to gardens. Well, it could hardly be a gardening problem that he wanted her to solve. But he might think of her in connection with crime—crime in the West Indies and crimes in her own neighborhood at home.

A crime—where?

Mr. Rafiel had made arrangements. Arrangements, to begin with, with his lawyers. They had done their part. At the right interval of time they had forwarded to her his letter. It had been, she thought, a well-considered and well-thought-out letter. It would have been simpler, certainly, to tell her exactly what he wanted her to do and why he wanted it done. She was surprised in a way that he had not, before his death, sent for her, probably in a somewhat peremptory way and more or less lying on what he would have assured her was his deathbed, and would then have bullied her until she consented to do what he was asking her. But no, that would not really have been Mr. Rafiel's way, she thought. He could bully people, none better, but this was not a case for bullying, and he did not wish either, she was sure, to appeal to her, to beg her to do him a favor, to urge her to redress a wrong. No. That again would not have been Mr. Rafiel's way. He wanted, she thought, as he had probably wanted all his life, to pay for what he required. He wanted to pay her and therefore he wanted to interest her enough to enjoy doing certain work. The pay was offered to intrigue her, not really to tempt her. It was to arouse her interest. She did not think that he had said to himself, "Offer enough money and she'll leap at it," because, as she knew very well herself, the money sounded very agreeable but she was not in urgent need of money. She had her dear and affectionate nephew who, if she was in straits for money of any kind, if she needed repairs to her house or visits to a specialist or special treats, dear Raymond would always provide them. No. The sum he offered was to be exciting. It was to be exciting in the same way as it was exciting when you had a ticket for the Irish Sweep. It was a fine big sum of money that you could never achieve by any other means except luck.

But all the same, Miss Marple thought to herself, she would need some luck as well as hard work, she would require a lot of thought and pondering and possibly what she was doing might involve a certain amount of danger. But she'd got to find out herself what it was all about, he wasn't going to tell her, partly perhaps because he did not want to influence her? It is hard to tell anyone about something without letting slip your own point of view about it. It could be that Mr. Rafiel had thought that his own point of view might be wrong. It was not very like him to think such a thing, but it could be possible. He might suspect that his judgment, impaired by illness, was not quite as good as it used to be. So she, Miss Marple, his agent, his employee, was to make her own guesses, come to her own conclusions. Well, it was time she came to a few conclusions now. In other words, back to the old question, *What was all this about?*

She had been directed. Let her take that first. She had been directed by a man who was now dead. She had been directed away from St. Mary Mead. Therefore, the task, whatever it must be, could not be attacked from there. It was not a neighborhood problem, it was not a problem that you could solve just by looking through newspaper cuttings or making inquiries, not, that is, until you found what you had to make inquiries about. She had been directed, first to the lawyer's office, then to read a letter—two letters—in her home, then to be sent on a pleasant and well-run tour round some of the Famous Houses and Gardens of Great Britain. From that she had come to the next steppingstone—the house she was in at this moment. The Old Manor House, Jocelyn St. Mary, where lived Miss Clotilde Bradbury-Scott, Mrs. Glynne and Miss Anthea Bradbury-Scott. Mr. Rafiel had arranged that, arranged it beforehand—some weeks before he died. Probably it was the next thing he had done after instructing his lawyers and after booking a seat on the tour in her name. Therefore, she was in this house for a purpose. It might be for only two nights, it might be for longer. There might be certain things arranged which would lead her to stay longer or she would be asked to stay longer. That brought her back to where she stood now.

Mrs. Glynne and her two sisters. They must be concerned, implicated in whatever this was. She would have to find out what it was. The time was short. That was the only trouble. Miss Marple had no doubt for one moment that she had the capacity to find out things. She was one of those chatty, fluffy old ladies whom other people expect to talk, to ask questions that were, on the face of it, merely gossipy questions. She would talk about her childhood and that would lead to one of the sisters talking about theirs. She'd talk about food she had eaten, servants she had had, daughters and cousins and relations, travel, marriages, births and—yes—deaths. There must be no show of special interest in her eyes when she heard about a death. Not all. Almost automatically she was sure she could come up with the right response such as, "Oh, dear me, how *very* sad!" She would have to find out relationships, incidents, life stories, see if any suggestive incidents would pop up, so to speak. It might be some incidents in the neighborhood, not directly concerned with these three people. Something they could know about, talk about, or were pretty sure to talk about. Anyway, there would be *something* here, some clue, some pointer. The second day from now she would rejoin the tour unless she had by that time some indication that she was *not* to rejoin the tour. Her mind swept from the house to the coach and the people who had sat in it. It might be that what she was seeking had been there in the coach, and would be there again when she rejoined it. One person, several people, some innocent (some not so innocent), some long past story. She frowned a little, trying to remember something—something, that had flashed in her mind that she had thought: Really, I am sure—of what had she been sure?

Her mind went back to the three sisters. She must not be too long up here. She must unpack a few modest needs for two nights, something to change into this evening, nightclothes, sponge bag, and then go down and rejoin her hostesses and make pleasant talk. A main point had to be decided. Were the three sisters to be her allies or were the three sisters enemies? They might fall into either category. She must think about that carefully.

There was a tap on the door and Mrs. Glynne entered.

"I do hope you will be quite comfortable here. Can I help you to unpack? We have a very nice woman, Janet, who comes in, but she is only here in the morning. But she'll help you with anything."

"Oh, no, thank you," said Miss Marple. "I only took out just a few necessities."

"I thought I'd show you the way downstairs again. It's rather a rambling house, you know. There are two staircases and it does make it a little difficult. Sometimes people lose their way."

"Oh, it's very kind of you," said Miss Marple.

"I hope then you will come downstairs and we will have a glass of sherry before lunch."

Miss Marple accepted gratefully and followed her guide down the stairs. Mrs. Glynne, she judged, was a good many years younger than she herself was. Fifty, perhaps. Not much more. Miss Marple negotiated the stairs carefully; her left knee was always a little uncertain. There was, however, a banister at one side of the stairs. Very beautiful stairs they were, and she remarked on them.

"It is really a very lovely house," she said. "Built I suppose in the seventeen hundreds. Am I right?"

"Seventeen eighty," said Mrs. Glynne.

She seemed pleased with Miss Marple's appreciation. She took Miss Marple into the drawing room, a large graceful room. There were one or two rather beautiful pieces of furniture. A Queen Anne desk and a William and Mary oystershell bureau. There were also some rather cumbrous Victorian settees and cabinets. The curtains were of chintz, faded and somewhat worn, the carpet was, Miss Marple thought, Irish. Possibly a Limerick Aubusson type. The sofa was ponderous and the velvet of it much worn. The other two sisters were already sitting there. They rose as Miss Marple came in and approached her, one with a glass of sherry, the other directing her to a chair.

"I don't know whether you like sitting rather high? So many people do."

"I do," said Miss Marple. "It's so much easier. One's back, you know."

The sisters appeared to know about the difficulties of backs. The eldest of the sisters was a tall, handsome woman, dark with a black coil of hair. The other one might have been a good deal younger. She was thin, with gray hair that had once been fair hanging untidily on her shoulders and a faintly wraithlike appearance. She could be cast successfully as a mature Ophelia, Miss Marple thought.

Clotilde, Miss Marple thought, was certainly no Ophelia, but she would have made a magnificent Clytemnestra—she could have stabbed a husband in his bath with exultation. But since she had never had a husband, that solution wouldn't do. Miss Marple could not see her murdering anyone else but a husband—there had been no Agamemnon in this house.

Clotilde Bradbury-Scott, Anthea Bradbury-Scott, Lavinia Glynne. Clotilde was handsome, Lavinia was plain but pleasant-looking, Anthea had one eyelid which twitched from time to time. Her eyes were large and gray and she had an odd way of glancing round to right and then to left, and then suddenly in a rather strange manner, behind her over her shoulder. It was as though she felt someone was watching her all the time. Odd, thought Miss Marple. She wondered a little about Anthea.

They sat down and conversation ensued. Mrs. Glynne left the room apparently for the kitchen. She was, it seemed, the active domestic one of the three. The conversation took a usual course. Clotilde Bradbury-Scott explained that the house was a family one. It had belonged to her great-uncle and then to her uncle, and when he had died it was left to her and her two sisters, who had joined her there.

"He only had one son you see," explained Miss Bradbury-Scott, "and he was killed in the war. We are really the last of the family, except for some very distant cousins."

"A beautifully proportioned house," said Miss Marple. "Your sister tells me it was built about seventeen eighty."

"Yes, I believe so. One could wish, you know, it was not quite so large and rambling."

"Repairs, too," said Miss Marple, "come very heavy nowadays."

"Oh, yes, indeed," Clotilde sighed. "And in many ways we have had to let a lot of it just fall down. Sad, but there it is. A lot of the outhouses, for instance, and a greenhouse. We had a very beautiful big greenhouse."

"Lovely muscat grapevine in it," said Anthea. "And cherry pie used to grow all along the walls inside. Yes, I really regret that very much. Of course, during the war one could not get any gardeners. We had a very young gardener and then he was called up. One does not of course grudge that, but all the same it was impossible to get things repaired and so the whole greenhouse fell down."

"So did the little conservatory near the house."

Both sisters sighed with the sighing of those who have noted time passing and times changing—but not for the better.

There was a melancholy here in this house, thought Miss Marple. It was impregnated somehow with sorrow—a sorrow that could not be dispersed or removed since it had penetrated too deep. It had sunk in. . . . She shivered suddenly.

CHAPTER NINE
Polygonum Baldschuanicum

THE MEAL WAS conventional. A small joint of mutton, roast potatoes, followed by a plum tart with a small jug of cream and rather indifferent pastry. There were a few pictures round the dining-room wall, family pictures, Miss Marple presumed, Victorian portraits without any particular merit, the sideboard was large and heavy, a handsome piece of plum-colored mahogany. The curtains were of dark crimson damask and at the big mahogany table ten people could easily have been seated.

Miss Marple chatted about the incidents of the tour in so far as she had been on it. As this, however, had only been three days, there was not very much to say.

"Mr. Rafiel, I suppose, was an old friend of yours?" said the eldest Miss Bradbury-Scott.

"Not really," said Miss Marple. "I met him first when I was on a cruise to the West Indies. He was out there for his health, I imagine."

"Yes, he had been very crippled for some years," said Anthea.

"Very sad," said Miss Marple. "Very sad indeed. I really admired his fortitude. He seemed to manage to do so much work. Every day, you know, he dictated to his secretary and was continually sending off cables. He did not seem to give in at all kindly to being an invalid."

"Oh, no, he wouldn't," said Anthea.

"We have not seen much of him of late years," said Mrs. Glynne. "He was a busy man, of course. He always remembered us at Christmas very kindly."

"Do you live in London, Miss Marple?" asked Anthea.

"Oh, no," said Miss Marple. "I live in the country. A very small place halfway between Loomouth and Market Basing. About twenty-five miles from London. It used to be a very pretty Old-world village but of course like everything else, it is becoming what they call developed nowadays." She added, "Mr. Rafiel, I suppose, lived in London? At least I noticed that in the St. Honoré hotel register his address was somewhere in Eaton Square, I think, or was it Belgrave Square?"

"He had a country house in Kent," said Clotilde. "He used to entertain there, I think, sometimes. Business friends, mostly, you know, or people from abroad. I don't think any of us ever visited him there. He nearly always entertained us in London on the rare occasions when we happened to meet."

"It was very kind of him," said Miss Marple, "to suggest to you that you should invite me here during the course of this tour. Very thoughtful. One wouldn't really have expected a busy man such as he must have been to have had such kindly thoughts."

"We have invited before friends of his who have been on these tours. On the whole they are very considerate the way they arrange these things. It is impossible, of course, to suit everybody's taste. The young ones naturally wish to walk, to make long excursions, to ascend hills for a view, and all that sort of thing. And the older ones who are not up to it, remain in the hotels, but hotels round here are not really at all luxurious. I am sure you would have found today's trip and the one to St. Bonaventure tomorrow, also, very fatiguing. Tomorrow I believe there's a visit to an island, you know, in a boat, and sometimes it can be very rough."

"Even going round houses can be very tiring," said Mrs. Glynne.

"Oh, I know," said Miss Marple. "So much walking and standing about. One's feet get very tired. I suppose, really, I ought not to take these expeditions, but it is such a temptation to see beautiful buildings and fine rooms and furniture. All these things. And of course some splendid pictures."

"And the gardens," said Anthea. "You like gardens, don't you?"

"Oh, yes," said Miss Marple, "specially the gardens. From the description in the prospectus I am really looking forward very much to seeing some of the finely kept gardens of the historic houses we have still to visit." She beamed round the table.

It was all very pleasant, very natural, and yet she wondered why for some reason she had a feeling of strain—a feeling that there was something unnatural here. But what did she mean by unnatural? The conversation was ordinary enough, consisting mainly of platitudes. She herself was making conventional remarks and so were the three sisters.

The Three Sisters, thought Miss Marple, once again considering that phrase. Why did anything thought of in threes somehow seem to suggest a sinister atmosphere? The Three Sisters. The Three Witches of Macbeth. Well, one could hardly compare these three sisters to the three witches. Although Miss Marple had always thought at the back of her mind that the theatrical producers made a mistake in the way in which they produced the three witches. One production which she had seen, indeed, seemed to her quite absurd. The witches had looked more like pantomime creatures with flapping wings and ridiculously spectacular steeple hats. They had danced and slithered about. Miss Marple remembered saying to her nephew, who was standing her this Shakespearean treat, "You know, Raymond, my dear, if *I* were ever producing this splendid play, I would make the three witches *quite* different. I would have them three ordinary, normal old women. Old Scottish women. They wouldn't dance or caper. They would look at each other rather slyly and you would feel a sort of menace just behind the ordinariness of them."

Miss Marple helped herself to the last mouthful of plum tart and looked across the table at Anthea. Ordinary, untidy, very vague-looking, a bit scatterbrained. Why should she feel that Anthea was sinister?

"I am imagining things," said Miss Marple to herself. "I mustn't do that."

After luncheon she was taken on a tour of the garden. It was Anthea who was deputed to accompany her. It was, Miss Marple thought, rather a sad progress. Here, there had once been a well-kept though certainly not in any way an outstanding or remarkable garden. It had had the elements of an ordinary Victorian garden. A shrubbery, a drive of speckled laurels, no doubt there had once been a well-kept lawn and paths, a kitchen garden of about an acre and a half, too big evidently for the three sisters who lived here now. Part of it was unplanted and had gone largely to weeds. Ground elder had taken over most of the flower beds and Miss Marple's hands could hardly restrain themselves from pulling up the vagrant bindweed asserting its superiority.

Miss Anthea's long hair flapped in the wind, shedding from time to time a vague hairpin on the path or the grass. She talked rather jerkily.

"You have a very nice garden, I expect," she said.

"Oh, it's a very small one," said Miss Marple.

They had come along a grass path and were pausing in front of a kind of hillock that rested against the wall at one end of it.

"Our greenhouse," said Miss Anthea mournfully.

"Oh, yes, where you had such a delightful grapevine."

"Three vines," said Anthea. "A black Hamburg and one of those small white grapes, very sweet, you know. And a third one of beautiful muscats."

"And a heliotrope, you said."

"Cherry pie," said Anthea.

"Ah, yes, cherry pie. Such a lovely smell. Was there any bomb trouble round here? Did that—er—knock the greenhouse down?"

"Oh, no, we never suffered from anything of that kind. This neighborhood was quite free of bombs. No, I'm afraid it just fell down from decay. We hadn't been here so very long and we had no money to repair it or to build it up again. And, in fact, it wouldn't have been worth it, really, because we couldn't have kept it up even if we did. I'm afraid we just let it fall down. There was nothing else we could do. And now you see, it's all grown over."

"Ah, that, completely covered by—what is that flowering creeper just coming into bloom?"

"Oh, yes. It's quite a common one," said Anthea. "It begins with a P. Now what is the name of it," she said doubtfully. "Poly something, something like that."

"Oh, yes. I think I do know the name. Polygonum Baldschuanicum. Very quick-growing, I think, isn't it? Very useful, really, if one wants to hide any tumble-down building or anything ugly of that kind."

The mound in front of her was certainly thickly covered with the all-enveloping green and white flowering plant. It was, as Miss Marple well knew, a kind of menace to anything else that wanted to grow. Polygonum covered everything, and covered it in a remarkably short time.

"The greenhouse must have been quite a big one," she said.

"Oh, yes—we had peaches in it, too—and nectarines." Anthea looked miserable.

"It looks really very pretty now," said Miss Marple in a consoling tone. "Very pretty little white flowers, aren't they?"

"We have a very nice magnolia tree down this path to the left," said Anthea. "Once I believe there used to be a very fine border here—a herbaceous border. But that again one cannot keep up. It is too difficult. Everything is too difficult. Nothing is like it used to be—it's all spoiled—everywhere."

She led the way quickly down a path at right angles which ran along a side wall. Her pace had increased. Miss Marple could hardly keep up with her. It was, thought Miss Marple, as though she were deliberately being steered away from the polygonum mound by her hostess—steered away as from some ugly or displeasing spot. Was she ashamed perhaps that the past glories no longer remained? The polygonum certainly was growing with extraordinary abandonment. It was not even being clipped or kept to reasonable proportions. It made a kind of flowery wilderness of that bit of the garden.

She almost looks as though she was running away from it, thought Miss Marple, as she followed her hostess. Presently her attention was diverted to a broken-down pigsty which had a few rose tendrils round it.

"My great-uncle used to keep a few pigs," explained Anthea, "but of course one would never dream of doing anything of that kind nowadays, would one? Rather too noisome, I am afraid. We have a few floribunda roses near the house. I really think floribundas are such a great answer to difficulties."

"Oh, I know," said Miss Marple.

She mentioned the names of a few recent productions in the rose line. All the names, she thought, were entirely strange to Miss Anthea.

"Do you often come on these tours?"

The question came suddenly.

"You mean the tours of houses and of gardens?"

"Yes. Some people do it every year."

"Oh, I couldn't hope to do that. They're rather expensive, you see. A friend very kindly gave me a present of this to celebrate my next birthday. So kind."

"Oh. I wondered. I wondered why you came. I mean—it's bound to be rather tiring, isn't it? Still, if you usually go to the West Indies, and places like that . . ."

"Oh, the West Indies was the result of kindness, too. On the part of a nephew, that time. A dear boy. So very thoughtful for his old aunt."

"Oh, I see. Yes, I see."

"I don't know what one would do without the younger generation," said Miss Marple. "They are so kind, are they not?"

"I—I suppose so. I don't really know. I—we haven't—any young relations."

"Does your sister, Mrs. Glynne, have any children? She did not mention any. One never likes to ask."

"No. She and her husband never had any children. It's as well perhaps."

"And what do you mean by that?" Miss Marple wondered as they returned to the house.

CHAPTER TEN
"Oh! Fond, Oh! Fair, The Days That Were"

I

AT HALF-PAST EIGHT the next morning there was a smart tap on the door, and in answer to Miss Marple's "Come in" the door was opened and an elderly woman entered, bearing a tray with a teapot, a cup and a milk jug and a small plate of bread and butter.

"Early morning tea, ma'am," she said cheerfully. "It's a nice day, it is. I see you've got your curtains drawn back already. You've slept well then?"

"Very well indeed," said Miss Marple, laying aside a small devotional book which she had been reading.

"Well, it's a lovely day, it is. They'll have it nice for going to the Bonaventure Rocks. It's just as well you're not doing it. It's cruel hard on the legs, it is."

"I'm really very happy to be here," said Miss Marple. "So kind of Miss Bradbury-Scott and Mrs. Glynne to issue this invitation."

"Ah, well, it's nice for them, too. It cheers them up to have a bit of company to the house. Ah, it's a sad place nowadays, so it is."

She pulled the curtains at the window rather more fully, pushed back a chair and deposited a can of hot water in the china basin.

"There's a bathroom on the next floor," she said, "but we think it's better always for someone elderly to have their hot water here, so they don't have to climb the stairs."

"It's very kind of you, Janet, I'm sure—you know this house well?"

"I was here as a girl—I was the housemaid then. Three servants they had—a cook, a housemaid—a parlormaid—kitchenmaid, too, at one time. That was in the old Colonel's time. Horses he kept, too, and a groom. Ah, those were the days. Sad it is when things happen the way they do. He lost his wife young, the Colonel did. His son was killed in the war and his only daughter went away to live on the other side of the world. Married a New Zealander, she did. Died having a baby and the baby died, too. He was a sad man living alone here, and he let the house go—it wasn't kept up as it should have been. When he died, he left the place to his niece Miss Clotilde and her two sisters, and she and Miss Anthea came here to live—and later Miss Lavinia lost her husband and came to join them—" she sighed and shook her head. "They never did much to the house—couldn't afford it— and they let the garden go as well—"

"It all seems a great pity," said Miss Marple.

"And such nice ladies as they all are, too. Miss Anthea is the scatty one, but Miss Clotilde went to university and is very brainy—she talks three languages—and Mrs. Glynne, she's a very nice lady indeed. I thought when she came to join them as things might go better. But you never know, do you, what the future holds? I feel sometimes as though there was a doom on this house."

Miss Marple looked inquiring.

"First one thing and then another. The dreadful plane accident—in Spain it was—and everybody killed. Nasty things, airplanes—I'd never go in one of them. Miss Clotilde's friends were both killed, they were, husband and wife—the daughter was still at school luckily—and escaped, but Miss Clotilde brought her here to live and did everything for her. Took her abroad for trips—to Italy and France, treated her like a daughter. She was such a happy girl—and a very sweet nature. You'd never dream that such an awful thing could happen."

"An awful thing. What was it? Did it happen here?"

"No, not here, thank God. Though in a way you might say it *did* happen here. It was here that she met him. He was in the neighborhood—and the ladies knew his father, who was a very rich man, so he came here to visit— that was the beginning—"

"They fell in love?"

"Yes, she fell in love with him right away. He was an attractive-looking boy with a nice way of talking and passing the time of day. You'd never think—you'd never think for one moment—" She broke off.

"There was a love affair? And it went wrong? And the girl committed suicide?"

"Suicide?" The old woman stared at Miss Marple with startled eyes.

"Whoever now told you *that?* Murder it was—bare-faced murder. Strangled and her head beaten to pulp. Miss Clotilde had to go and identify her—she's never been quite the same since. They found her body a good thirty miles from here—in the scrub of a disused quarry. And it's believed that it wasn't the first murder he'd done. There had been other girls. Six months she'd been missing and the police searching far and wide. Oh! A wicked devil he was—a bad lot from the day he was born, or so it seems. They say nowadays as there are those as can't help what they do—not right in the head, and they can't be held responsible. I don't believe a word of it! Killers are killers. And they won't even hang them nowadays. I know as there's often madness as runs in old families—there was the Derwents over to Brassington—every second generation one or other of them died in the loony bin—and there was old Mrs. Paulett—walked about the lanes in her diamond tiara saying she was Marie Antoinette until they shut her up. But there wasn't anything really wrong with her—just sillylike. But this boy. Yes, he was a devil right through."

"What did they do to him?"

"They'd abolished hanging by then—or else he was too young. I can't remember it all now. They found him guilty. It may have been Bostol or Broadsand—one of those places beginning with 'B' as they sent him to."

"What was the name of the boy?"

"Michael—can't remember his last name. It's ten years ago that it happened—one forgets. Italian sort of name—like a picture. Someone who paints pictures—Raffle, that's it—"

"Michael Rafiel?"

"That's right! There was a rumor as went about that his father being so rich got him wangled out of prison. An escape like the bank robbers. But I think as that was just talk—"

So it had not been suicide. It had been murder. "Love!" Elizabeth Temple had named as the cause of a girl's death. In a way she was right. A young girl had fallen in love with a killer—and for love of him had gone unsuspecting to an ugly death.

Miss Marple gave a little shudder. On her way along the village street yesterday she had passed a newspaper placard: EPSOM DOWNS MURDER, SECOND GIRL'S BODY DISCOVERED, YOUTH ASKED TO ASSIST POLICE.

So history repeated itself. An old pattern—an ugly pattern. Some lines of forgotten verse came haltingly into her brain:

> Rose white youth, passionate, pale,
> A singing stream in a silent vale,
> A fairy prince in a prosy tale,
> Oh, there's nothing in life so finely frail
> As rose white youth.

Who was there to guard youth from pain and death—youth who could not, who had never been able to, guard itself? Did they know too little? Or was it that they knew too much, and therefore thought they knew it all?

II

Miss Marple, coming down the stairs that morning, probably rather earlier than she had been expected, found no immediate sign of her hostesses. She let herself out at the front door and wandered once round the garden. It was not because she'd really enjoyed this particular garden. It was some vague feeling that there was something here that she ought to notice, something that would give her some idea, or that had given her some idea only she had not—well, frankly, she had not been bright enough to realize just what the bright idea had been. Something she ought to take note of, something that had a bearing.

She was not at the moment anxious to see any of the three sisters. She wanted to turn a few things over in her mind—the new facts that had come to her through Janet's early tea chat.

A side gate stood open and she went through it to the village street and along a line of small shops to where a steeple poked up announcing the site of the church and its churchyard. She pushed open the lych gate and wandered about among the graves, some dating from quite a while back, some by the far wall later ones, and one or two beyond the wall in what was obviously a new enclosure. There was nothing of great interest among the older tombs. Certain names recurred as they do in villages. A good many Princes of village origin had been buried. Jasper Prince, deeply regretted. Margery Prince, Edgar and Walter Prince, Melanie Prince, 4 years old. A family record. Hiram Broad—Ellen Jane Broad, Eliza Broad, 91 years.

She was turning away from the latter when she observed an elderly man moving in slow motion among the graves, tidying up as he walked. He gave her a salute and a "good morning."

"Good morning," said Miss Marple. "A very pleasant day."

"It'll turn to rain later," said the old man.

He spoke with the utmost certainty.

"There seem to be a lot of Princes and Broads buried here," said Miss Marple.

"Ah, yes, there've always been Princes here. Used to own quite a bit of land once. There have been Broads a good many years, too."

"I see a child is buried here. Very sad when one sees a child's grave."

"Ah, that'll be little Melanie that was. Mellie, we called her. Yes, it was a sad death. Run over, she was. Ran out into the street, went to get sweets at the sweetshop. Happens a lot nowadays with cars going through at the pace they do."

"It is sad to think," said Miss Marple, "that there are so many deaths all the time. And one doesn't really notice it until one looks at the inscriptions in the churchyard. Sickness, old age, children run over, sometimes even more dreadful things. Young girls killed. Crimes, I mean."

"Ah, yes, there's a lot of that about. Silly girls, I call most of 'em. And their mums haven't got time to look after them properly nowadays—what with going out to work so much."

Miss Marple rather agreed with his criticism, but had no wish to waste time in agreement on the trend of the day.

"Staying at The Old Manor House, aren't you?" the old man asked. "Come here on the coach tour I saw. But it got too much for you, I suppose. Some of those that are gettin' on can't always take it."

"I did find it a little exhausting," confessed Miss Marple, "and a very kind friend of mine, a Mr. Rafiel, wrote to some frineds of his here and they invited me to stay for a couple of nights."

The name Rafiel clearly meant nothing to the elderly gardener.

"Mrs. Glynne and her two sisters have been very kind," said Miss Marple. "I suppose they've lived here a long time?"

"Not so long as that. Twenty years maybe. Belonged to old Colonel Bradbury-Scott, The Old Manor House did. Close on seventy he was when he died."

"Did he have any children?"

"A son what was killed in the war. That's why he left the place to his nieces. Nobody else to leave it to."

He went back to his work among the graves.

Miss Marple went into the church. It had felt the hand of a Victorian restorer, and had bright Victorian glass in the windows. One or two brasses and some tablets on the walls was all that was left of the past.

Miss Marple sat down in an uncomfortable pew and wondered about things.

Was she on the right track now? Things were connecting up—but the connections were far from clear.

A girl had been murdered (actually several girls had been murdered)—suspected young men (or "youths," as they were usually called nowadays) had been rounded up by the police, to "assist them in their inquiries." A common pattern. But this was all old history, dating back ten or twelve years. There was nothing to find out—now, no problems to solve. A tragedy labeled Finis.

What could be done by her? What could Mr. Rafiel possibly want her to do?

Elizabeth Temple . . . She must get Elizabeth Temple to tell her more. Elizabeth had spoken of a girl who had been engaged to be married to Michael Rafiel. But was that really so? That fact did not seem to be known to those in The Old Manor House.

A more familiar version came into Miss Marple's mind—the kind of story that had been reasonably frequent in her own village. Starting as always, "Boy meets girl." Developing in the usual way—

"And then the girl finds she is pregnant," said Miss Marple to herself, "and she tells the boy and she wants him to marry her. But he, perhaps, doesn't want to marry her—he has never had any idea of marrying her. But things may be made difficult for him in this case. His father, perhaps, won't hear of such a thing. Her relations will insist that he 'does the right thing.' And by now he is tired of the girl—he's got another girl perhaps. And so he takes a quick brutal way out—strangles her, beats her head to a pulp to avoid identification. It fits with his record—a brutal, sordid crime—but forgotten and done with."

She looked round the church in which she was sitting. It looked so peaceful. The reality of evil was hard to believe in. A flair for evil—that was what Mr. Rafiel had attributed to her. She rose and walked out of the church and stood looking round the churchyard again. Here, among the gravestones and their worn inscriptions no sense of evil moved in her.

Was it evil she had sensed yesterday at The Old Manor House? That deep depression of despair, that dark desperate grief? Anthea Bradbury-Scott, her eyes gazing fearfully back over one shoulder, as though fearing some presence that stood there—always stood there—behind her.

They knew something, those three sisters, but what was it that they knew?

Elizabeth Temple, she thought again. She pictured Elizabeth Temple with the rest of the coach party, striding across the downs at this moment, climbing up a steep path and gazing over the cliffs out to sea.

Tomorrow, when she rejoined the tour, she would get Elizabeth Temple to tell her more.

Miss Marple retraced her steps to The Old Manor House, walking rather slowly because she was by now tired. She could not really feel that her morning had been productive in any way. So far The Old Manor House had given her no distinctive ideas of any kind, a tale of a past tragedy told by Janet, but there were always past tragedies treasured in the memories of domestic workers and which were remembered quite as clearly as all the happy events such as spectacular weddings, big entertainments and successful operations or accidents from which people had recovered in a miraculous manner.

As she drew near the gate, she saw two female figures standing there. One of them detached itself and came to meet her. It was Mrs. Glynne.

"Oh, there you are," she said. "We wondered, you know. I thought you must have gone out for a walk somewhere and I did so hope you wouldn't overtire yourself. If I had known you had come downstairs and gone out, I would have come with you to show anything there is to show. Not that there is very much."

"Oh, I just wandered around," said Miss Marple. "The churchyard, you know, and the church. I'm always very interested in churches. Sometimes there are very curious epitaphs. Things like that. I make quite a collection of them. I suppose the church here was restored in Victorian times?"

"Yes, they did put in some rather ugly pews, I think. You know, good quality wood, and strong and all that, but not very artistic."

"I hope they didn't take away anything of particular interest."

"No, I don't think so. It's not really a very old church."

"There did not seem to be many tablets or brasses or anything of that kind," agreed Miss Marple.

"You are quite interested in ecclesiastical architecture?"

"Oh, I don't make a study of it or anything like that, but of course in my own village, St. Mary Mead, things do rather revolve round the church. I mean, they always have. In my young days, that was so. Nowadays of course it's rather different. Were you brought up in this neighborhood?"

"Oh, not really. We lived not very far away, about thirty miles or so. At Little Herdsley. My father was a retired serviceman—a major in the artillery. We came over here occasionally to see my uncle—indeed to see my great-uncle before him. No. I've not even been here very much of late years. My other two sisters moved in after my uncle's death, but at that time I was still abroad with my husband. He only died about four or five years ago."

"Oh, I see."

"They were anxious I should come and join them here and really, it seemed the best thing to do. We had lived in India for some years. My husband was still stationed there at the time of his death. It is very difficult nowadays to know where one would wish to—should I say, put one's roots down."

"Yes, indeed. I can quite see that. And you felt, of course, that you had roots here since your family had been here for a long time."

"Yes. Yes, one did feel that. Of course, I'd always kept up with my sisters, had been to visit them. But things are always very different from what one thinks they will be. I have bought a small cottage near London, near Hampton Court, where I spend a good deal of my time, and I do a little occasional work for one or two charities in London."

"So your time is fully occupied. How wise of you."

"I have felt of late that I should spend more time here perhaps. I've been a little worried about my sisters."

"Their health?" suggested Miss Marple. "One is rather worried nowadays, especially as there is not really anyone competent whom one can employ to look after people as they become rather feebler or have certain ailments. So much rheumatism and arthritis about. One is always so afraid of people falling down in the bath or an accident coming down stairs. Something of that kind."

"Clotilde has always been very strong," said Mrs. Glynne. "Tough, I should describe her. But I am rather worried sometimes about Anthea. She is vague, you know—very vague indeed. And she wanders off sometimes—and doesn't seem to know where she is."

"Yes, it is sad when people worry. There is so much to worry one."

"I don't really think there is much to worry Anthea."

"She worries about income tax, perhaps, money affairs," suggested Miss Marple.

"No, no, not that so much but—oh, she worries so much about the garden. She remembers the garden as it used to be, and she's very anxious, you know, to—well, to spend money in putting things right again. Clotilde has had to tell her that really one can't afford that nowadays. But she keeps talking of the hothouses, the peaches that used to be there. The grapes—and all that."

"And the cherry pie on the walls?" suggested Miss Marple, remembering a remark.

"Fancy your remembering that. Yes. Yes, it's one of the things one does remember. Such a charming smell, heliotrope. And such a nice name for it, cherry pie. One always remembers that. And the grapevine. The little, small, early sweet grapes. Ah, well, one must not remember the past too much."

"And the flower borders too, I suppose," said Miss Marple.

"Yes. Yes, Anthea would like to have a big well-kept herbaceous border again. Really not feasible now. It is as much as one can do to get local people who will come and mow the lawns every fortnight. Every year one seems to employ a different firm. And Anthea would like pampas grass planted again. And the Mrs. Simpkin pinks. White, you know. All long the stone edge border. And a fig tree that grew just outside the greenhouse. She remembers all these and talks about them."

"It must be difficult for you."

"Well, yes. Arguments, you see, hardly appeal in any way. Clotilde, of course, is very downright about things. She just refuses point-blank and says she doesn't want to hear another word about it."

"It is difficult," said Miss Marple, "to know how to take things. Whether one should be firm. Rather authoritative. Perhaps, even, well, just a little—a little *fierce*, you know, or whether one should be sympathetic. Listen to things and perhaps hold out hopes which one knows are not justified. Yes, it's difficult."

"But it's easier for me because you see I go away again, and then come back now and then to stay. So it's easy for me to pretend things may be easier soon and that something may be done. But really, the other day when I came home and I found that Anthea had tried to engage a most expensive firm of landscape gardeners to renovate the garden, to build up the greenhouses again—which is quite absurd because even if you put vines in they would not bear for another two or three years. Clotilde knew nothing about it and she was extremely angry when she discovered the estimate for this work on Anthea's desk. She was really quite unkind."

"So many things are difficult," said Miss Marple.

It was a useful phrase which she used often.

"I shall have to go rather early tomorrow morning, I think," said Miss Marple. "I was making inquiries at the Golden Boar where I understand the coach party assembles tomorrow morning. They are making quite an early start. Nine o'clock, I understand."

"Oh, dear. I hope you will not find it too fatiguing."

"Oh, I don't think so. I gather we are going to a place called—now wait a minute, what was it called?—Stirling St. Mary. Something like that. And it does not seem to be very far away. There's an interesting church to see on the way and a castle. In the afternoon there is a quite pleasant garden, not too many acres, but some special flowers. I feel sure that after this very nice rest that I have had here, I shall be quite all right. I understand now that I would have been very tired if I had had these two days of climbing up cliffsides and all the rest of it."

"Well, you must rest this afternoon, so as to be fresh for tomorrow," said Mrs. Glynne, as they went into the house. "Miss Marple has been to visit the church," said Mrs. Glynne to Clotilde.

"I'm afraid there is not very much to see," said Clotilde. "Victorian glass of a most hideous kind, I think myself. No expense spared. I'm afraid my uncle was partly to blame. He was very pleased with those rather crude reds and blues."

"Very crude. Very vulgar, I always think," said Lavinia Glynne.

Miss Marple settled down after lunch to have a nap, and she did not join her hostesses until nearly dinnertime. After dinner a good deal of chat went on until it was bedtime. Miss Marple set the tone in remembrances— remembrances of her own youth, her early days, places she had visited, travels or tours she had made, occasional people she had known.

She went to bed tired, with a sense of failure. She had learned nothing more, possibly because there was nothing more to learn. A fishing expedition where the fish did not rise—possibly because there were no fish there. Or it could be that she did not know the right bait to use.

CHAPTER ELEVEN
Accident

MISS MARPLE'S TEA was brought at seven-thirty the following morning so as to allow her plenty of time to get up and pack her few belongings. She was just closing her small suitcase when there was a rather hurried tap on the door and Clotilde came in, looking upset.

"Oh, dear, Miss Marple, there is a young man downstairs who has called to see you. Emlyn Price. He is on the tour with you and they sent him here."

"Of course, I remember him. Yes. Quite young?"

"Oh, yes. Very modern-looking, and a lot of hair and all that, but he has really come to—well, to break some bad news to you. There has been, I am sorry to say, an accident."

"An accident?" Miss Marple stared. "You mean—to the coach? There has been an accident on the road? Someone has been hurt?"

"No. No, it was not the coach. There was no trouble there. It was in the course of the expedition yesterday afternoon. There was a great deal of wind, you may remember, though I don't think that had anything to do with it. People strayed about a bit, I think. There is a regular path, but you can also climb up and go across the downs. Both ways lead to the Memorial Tower on the top of Bonaventure—where they were all making for. People got separated a bit and I suppose, really, there was no one actually guiding them or looking after them which, perhaps, there ought to have been. People aren't very sure-footed always and the slope overhanging the gorge is very steep. There was a bad fall of stones or rocks which came crashing down the hillside and knocked someone out on the path below."

"Oh, dear," said Miss Marple, "I am sorry. I am most terribly sorry. Who was it who was hurt?"

"A Miss Temple or Tenderdon, I understand."

"Elizabeth Temple," said Miss Marple. "Oh, dear, I am sorry. I talked to her a good deal. I sat in the next seat to her on the coach. She is, I believe, a retired schoolmistress, a very well-known one."

"Of course," said Clotilde, "I know her quite well. She was headmistress of Fallowfield, quite a famous school. I'd no idea she was on this tour. She retired as headmistress, I think a year or two ago, and there is a new, rather young headmistress there now with rather advanced progressive ideas. But Miss Temple is not very old, really; she's about sixty, I should think, and very active, fond of climbing and walking and all the rest of it. This really seems most unfortunate. I hope she's not badly hurt. I haven't heard any details yet."

"This is quite ready now," said Miss Marple, snapping down the lid of her suitcase. "I will come down at once and see Mr. Price."

Clotilde seized the case.

"Let me. I can carry this perfectly. Come down with me, and be careful of the stairs."

Miss Marple came down. Emlyn Price was waiting for her. His hair was looking even wilder than usual and he was wearing a splendid array of fancy boots and a leather jerkin and brilliant emerald green trousers.

"Such an unfortunate business," he said, seizing Miss Marple's hand. "I thought I'd come along myself and—well, break it to you about the accident. I expect Miss Bradbury-Scott has told you. It's Miss Temple. You know. The school dame. I don't know quite what she was doing or what happened, but some stones, or rather boulders, rolled down from above. It's rather a precipitous slope and it knocked her out and they had to take her off to hospital with concussion last night. I gather she's rather bad. Anyway, the tour for today is canceled and we are stopping on here tonight."

"Oh, dear," said Miss Marple, "I am sorry. I'm very sorry."

"I think they've decided not to go on today because they really have to wait and see what the medical report is, so we are proposing to spend one more night here at the Golden Boar and to rearrange the tour a little, so that perhaps we shall miss out altogether going to Grangmering, which we were going to do tomorrow, and which is not very interesting, really, or so they say. Mrs. Sandbourne has gone off early to the hospital to see how things are this morning. She's going to join us at the Golden Boar for coffee at eleven o'clock. I thought perhaps you'd like to come along and hear the latest news."

"I'll certainly come along with you," said Miss Marple. "Of course. At once."

She turned to say good-bye to Clotilde and Mrs. Glynne, who had joined her.

"I must thank you so much," she said. "You have been so kind and it has been so delightful to have these two nights here. I feel so rested and everything. Most unfortunate this has occurred."

"If you would like to spend another night," said Mrs. Glynne, "I am sure—" She looked at Clotilde.

It occurred to Miss Marple, who had as sharp a sideways glance as anyone could desire, that Clotilde had a slightly disapproving look. She almost shook her head, though it was such a small movement that it was hardly noticeable. But she was, Miss Marple thought, hushing down the suggestion that Mrs. Glynne was making.

". . . although of course I expect it would be nicer for you to be with the others and to—"

"Oh, yes, I think it would be better," said Miss Marple. "I shall know then what the plans are and what to do about things, and perhaps I could be of help in some way. One never knows. So thank you again very much. It will not be difficult, I expect, to get a room at the Golden Boar." She looked at Emlyn, who said reassuringly:

"That'll be all right. Several rooms have been vacated today. They won't be full at all. Mrs. Sandbourne, I think, has booked for all the party to stay there tonight, and tomorrow we shall see—well, we shall see how this all goes on."

Good-byes were said again and thanks. Emlyn Price took Miss Marple's belongings and started out at a good striding pace.

"It's really only just round the corner, and then the first street to the left," he said.

"Yes, I passed it yesterday, I think. Poor Miss Temple. I do hope she's not badly hurt."

"I think she is rather," said Emlyn Price. "Of course, you know what doctors are, and hospital people. They say the same thing always: 'as well as can be expected.' There's no local hospital—they had to take her to Carristown, which is about eight miles away. Anyway, Mrs. Sandbourne will be back with the news by the time we've fixed you up at the hotel."

They got there to find the tour assembled in the coffee room and coffee and morning buns and pastries were being served. Mr. and Mrs. Butler were talking at the moment.

"Oh, it's just too, too tragic this happening," said Mrs. Butler. "Just too upsetting, isn't it? Just when we were all so happy and enjoying everything so much. Poor Miss Temple. And I always thought she was very sure-footed. But there, you know, you never can tell, can you, Henry?"

"No, indeed," said Henry. "No, indeed. I am wondering really—yes, our time's very short, you know—whether we hadn't better—well, give up this tour at this point here. Not continue with it. It seems to me that there's bound to be a bit of difficulty resuming things until we know definitely. If this was—well—I mean, if this should be so serious that it could prove fatal, there might—well—I mean there might have to be an inquest or something of that kind."

"Oh, Henry, don't say dreadful things like that!"

"I'm sure," said Miss Cooke, "that you are being a little too pessimistic, Mr. Butler. I am sure that things couldn't be as serious as that."

In his foreign voice Mr. Caspar said: "But yes, they are serious. I hear yesterday. When Mrs. Sandbourne talk on telephone to doctor. It is very, very serious. They say she has concussion bad—very bad. A special doctor he is coming to look at her and see if he can operate or if impossible. Yes—it is all very bad."

"Oh, dear," said Miss Lumley. "If there's any doubt, perhaps we ought to go home, Mildred. I must look up the trains, I think." She turned to Mrs. Butler. "You see, I have made arrangements about my cats with the neighbors, and if I was delayed a day or two it might make great difficulties for everyone."

"Well, it's no good our working ourselves up too much," said Mrs. Riseley-Porter in her deep, authoritative voice. "Joanna, put this bun in the wastepaper basket, will you? It is really quite uneatable. Most unpleasant jam. But I don't want to leave it on my plate. It might make for bad feeling."

Joanna got rid of the bun. She said:

"Do you think it would be all right if Emlyn and I went out for a walk? I mean, just saw something of the town? It's not much good our sitting about here, making gloomy remarks, is it? We can't do anything."

"I think you'd be very wise to go out," said Miss Cooke.

"Yes, you go along," said Miss Barrow before Mrs. Riseley-Porter could speak.

Miss Cooke and Miss Barrow looked at each other and sighed, shaking their heads.

"The grass was very slippery," said Miss Barrow. "I slid once or twice myself, you know, on that very short turf."

"And the stones, too," said Miss Cooke. "Quite a shower of small stones fell down just as I was turning a corner on the path. Yes, one struck me on the shoulder quite sharply."

Tea, coffee, biscuits and cakes dispatched, everyone seemed somewhat dissociated and ill at ease. When a catastrophe has occurred, it is very difficult to know what is the proper way to meet it. Everyone had given their view, had expressed surprise and distress. They were now awaiting news and at the same time had a slight hankering after some form of sightseeing, some interest to carry them through the morning. Lunch would not be served until one o'clock and they really felt that to sit around and repeat their same remarks would be rather a gloomy business.

Miss Cooke and Miss Barrow rose as one woman and explained that it was necessary for them to do a little shopping. One or two things they needed, and they also wished to go to the post office and buy stamps.

"I want to send off one or two postcards. And I want to inquire about postal dues on a letter to China," said Miss Barrow.

"And I want to match some wools," said Miss Cooke. "And also it seemed to me there was rather an interesting building on the other side of the market square."

"I think it would do us all good to get out," said Miss Barrow.

Colonel and Mrs. Walker also rose and suggested to Mr. and Mrs. Butler that they, too, might go out and see what there was to see. Mrs. Butler expressed hopes of an antique shop.

"Only I don't really mean a real antique shop. More what you would call a junk shop. Sometimes you can pick up some really interesting things there."

They all trooped out. Emlyn Price had already sidled to the door and disappeared in pursuit of Joanna without troubling to use conversation to explain his departure. Mrs. Riseley-Porter, having made a belated attempt to call her niece back, said she thought that at least the lounge would be rather more pleasant to sit in. Miss Lumely agreed—Mr. Caspar escorted the ladies with the air of a foreign equerry.

Professor Wanstead and Miss Marple remained.

"I think myself," said Professor Wanstead, addressing Miss Marple, "that it would be pleasant to sit outside the hotel. There is a small terrace giving on the street. If I might persuade you?"

Miss Marple thanked him and rose to her feet. She had hardly exchanged a word so far with Professor Wanstead. He had several learned-looking books with him, one of which he was usually perusing; even in the coach he continued to try to read.

"But perhaps you, too, want to shop," he said. "For myself, I would prefer to wait somewhere peacefully for the return of Mrs. Sandbourne. It is important, I think, that we should know exactly what we are in for."

"I quite agree with you as to that," said Miss Marple. "I did a certain amount of walking round the town yesterday and I don't feel any necessity to do so again today. I'd rather wait here in case there is anything I can do to help. Not that I suppose there is, but one never knows."

They moved together through the hotel door and round the corner to where there was a little square of garden with a raised stone walk close to the wall of the hotel and on which there were various forms of basket chairs. There was no one there at the moment, so they sat down. Miss Marple looked thoughtfully at her vis-à-vis—at his corrugated and wrinkled face, his bushy brows, his luxuriant head of gray hair. He walked with a slight stoop. He had an interesting face, Miss Marple decided. His voice was dry and caustic, a professional man of some kind, she thought.

"I am not wrong, am I?" said Professor Wanstead. "You *are* Miss Jane Marple?"

"Yes, I am Jane Marple."

She was slightly surprised, though for no particular reason. They had not been long enough together for people to be identified by the other travelers. The last two nights she had not been with the rest of the party. It was quite natural.

"I thought so," said Professor Wanstead, "from a description I have had of you."

"A description of me?" Miss Marple was again slightly surprised.

"Yes, I had a description of you"—he paused for a moment; his voice was not exactly lowered, but it lost volume, although she could still hear it quite easily"from Mr. Rafiel."

"Oh," said Miss Marple, startled. "From Mr. Rafiel."

"You are surprised?"

"Well, yes, I am rather."

"I don't know that you should be."

"I didn't expect—" began Miss Marple, and then stopped.

Professor Wanstead did not speak. He was merely sitting, looking at her intently. In a minute or two, thought Miss Marple to herself, he will say to me, "What symptoms exactly, dear lady? Any discomfort in swallowing? Any lack of sleep? Digestion in good order?" She was almost sure now that he was a doctor.

"When did he describe me to you? That must have been—"

"You were going to say some time ago—some weeks ago. Before his death—that is so. He told me that you would be on this tour."

"And he knew that you would be on it, too—that you were going on it."

"You can put it that way," said Professor Wanstead. "He said," he continued, "that you would be traveling on this tour, that he had, in fact arranged for you to be traveling on this tour."

"It was very kind of him," said Miss Marple. "Very kind indeed. I was most surprised when I found he'd booked me. Such a treat. Which I could not have afforded for myself."

"Yes," said Professor Wanstead. "Very well put." He nodded his head as one who applauds a good performance by a pupil.

"It is sad that it has been interrupted in this fashion," said Miss Marple. "Very sad indeed. When I am sure we were all enjoying ourselves so much."

"Yes," said Professor Wanstead. "Yes, very sad. And unexpected, do you think, or not unexpected?"

"Now what do you mean by that, Professor Wanstead?"

His lips curled in a slight smile as he met her challenging look.

"Mr. Rafiel," he said, "spoke to me about you at some length, Miss Marple. He suggested that I should be on this tour with you. I should in due course almost certainly make your acquaintance, since members in a tour inevitably do make each other's acquaintance, though it usually takes a day or two for them to split up, as it were, into possible groupings led by similar tastes or interests. And he further suggested to me that I should, shall we say, keep an eye on you."

"Keep an eye on me?" said Miss Marple, showing some slight displeasure. "And for what reason?"

"I think reasons of protection. He wanted to be quite sure that nothing should happen to you."

"Happen to me? What should happen to me, I should like to know?"

"Possibly what happened to Miss Elizabeth Temple," said Professor Wanstead.

Joanna Crawford came round the corner of the hotel. She was carrying a shopping basket. She passed them, nodding a little, she looked towards them with slight curiosity and went on down the street. Professor Wanstead did not speak until she had gone out of sight.

"A nice girl," he said; "at least I think so. Content at present to be a beast of burden to an autocratic aunt, but I have no doubt will reach the age of rebellion fairly soon."

"What did you mean by what you said just now?" said Miss Marple, uninterested for the moment in Joanna's possible rebellion.

"That is a question which, perhaps, owing to what has happened, we shall have to discuss."

"You mean because of the accident?"

"Yes. If it was an accident."

"Do you think it wasn't an accident?"

"Well, I think it's just possible. That's all."

"I don't of course know anything about it," said Miss Marple, hesitating.

"No. You were absent from the scene. You were—shall I put it this way—were you just possibly on duty elsewhere?"

Miss Marple was silent for a moment. She looked at Professor Wanstead once or twice and then she said:

"I don't think I know exactly what you mean."

"You are being careful. You are quite right to be careful."

"I have made it a habit," said Miss Marple.

"To be careful?"

"I should not put it exactly like that, but I have made a point of being always ready to disbelieve as well as believe anything that is told to me."

"Yes, and you are quite right, too. You don't know anything about me. You know my name from the passenger list of a very agreeable tour visiting castles and historic houses and splendid gardens. Possibly the gardens are what will interest you most."

"Possibly."

"There are other people here, too, who are interested in gardens."

"Or profess to be interested in gardens."

"Ah," said Professor Wanstead. "You have noticed that."

He went on, "Well, it was my part, or at any rate to begin with, to observe you, to watch what you were doing, to be near at hand in case there was any possibility of—well, we might call it roughly—dirty work of any kind. But things are slightly altered now. You must make up your mind if I am your enemy or your ally."

"Perhaps you are right," said Miss Marple. "You put it very clearly but you have not given me any information about yourself yet on which to judge. You were a friend, I presume, of the late Mr. Rafiel?"

"No," said Professor Wanstead, "I was not a friend of Mr. Rafiel. I had met him once or twice. Once on a committee of a hospital, once at some other public event. I knew about him. He, I gather, also knew about me. If I say to you, Miss Marple, that I am a man of some eminence in my own profession, you may think me a man of bounding conceit."

"I don't think so," said Miss Marple. "I should say, if you say that about yourself, that you are probably speaking the truth. You are, perhaps, a medical man."

"Ah. You are perceptive. Miss Marple. Yes, you are quite perceptive. I have a medical degree, but I have a specialty, too. I am a pathologist and psychologist. I don't carry credentials about with me. You will probably have to take my word up to a certain point, though I can show you letters addressed to me, and possibly official documents that might convince you. I undertake mainly specialist work in connection with medical jurisprudence. To put it in perfectly plain everyday language, I am interested in the different types of criminal brain. That has been a study of mine for many years. I have written books on the subject, some of them violently disputed, some of them which have attracted adherence to my ideas. I do not do very arduous work nowadays. I spend my time mainly writing up my subject, stressing certain points that have appealed to me. From time to time I come across things that strike me as interesting—things that I want to study more closely. This I am afraid must seem rather tedious to you."

"Not at all," said Miss Marple. "I am hoping, perhaps, from what you are saying now that you will be able to explain to me certain things which Mr. Rafiel did not see fit to explain to me. He asked me to embark upon a certain project but he gave me no useful information on which to work. He left me to accept it and to proceed, as it were, completely in the dark. It seemed to me extremely foolish of him to treat the matter in that way."

"But you accepted it?"

"I accepted it. I will be quite honest with you. I had a financial incentive."

"Did that weigh with you?"

Miss Marple was silent for a moment and then she said slowly:

"You may not believe it, but my answer to that is, 'Not really.'"

"I am not surprised. But your interest was aroused. That is what you are trying to tell me."

"Yes. My interest was aroused. I had known Mr. Rafiel not well, casually, but for a certain period of time—some weeks, in fact—in the West Indies. I see you know about it, more or less."

"I know that that was where Mr. Rafiel met you and where—shall I say—you two collaborated."

Miss Marple looked at him rather doubtfully. "Oh," she said, "he said that, did he?" She shook her head.

"Yes, he did," said Professor Wanstead. "He said you had a remarkable flair for criminal matters."

Miss Marple raised her eyebrows as she looked at him.

"And I suppose that seems to you most unlikely," she said. "It surprises you."

"I seldom allow myself to be surprised at what happens," said Professor Wanstead. "Mr. Rafiel was a very shrewd and astute man, a good judge of people. He thought that you, too, were a good judge of people."

"I would not set myself up as a good judge of people," said Miss Marple. "I would only say that certain people remind me of certain other people that I have known, and that therefore I can presuppose a certain likeness between the way they would act. If you think I know all about what I am supposed to be doing here, you are wrong."

"By accident more than design," said Professor Wanstead, "we seem to have settled here in a particularly suitable spot for discussion of certain matters. We do not appear to be overlooked, we cannot easily be overheard, we are not near a window or a door and there is no balcony or window overhead. In fact, we can talk."

"I should appreciate that," said Miss Marple. "I am stressing the fact that I am myself completely in the dark as to what I am doing or supposed to be doing. I don't know why Mr. Rafiel wanted it that way."

"I think I can guess that. He wanted you to approach a certain set of facts, of happenings, unbiased by what anyone would tell you first."

"So you are not going to tell me anything either?" Miss Marple sounded irritated. "Really!" she said. "There are limits."

"Yes," said Professor Wanstead. He smiled suddenly. "I agree with you. We must do away with some of these limits. I am going to tell you certain facts that will make certain things fairly clear to you. You in turn may be able to tell me certain facts."

"I rather doubt it," said Miss Marple. "One or two rather peculiar indications, perhaps, but indications are not facts."

"Therefore—" said Professor Wanstead, and paused.

"For goodness' sake, tell me something," said Miss Marple.

CHAPTER TWELVE
A Consultation

"I'M NOT GOING to make a long story of things. I'll explain quite simply how I came into this matter. I act as confidential adviser from time to time for the Home Office. I am also in touch with certain institutions. There are certain establishments which, in the event of crime, provide board and lodging for certain types of criminals who have been found guilty of certain acts. They remain there at what is termed Her Majesty's pleasure, sometimes for a definite length of time and in direct association with their age. If they are below a certain age, they have to be received in some place of detention specially indicated. You understand that, no doubt."

"Yes, I understand quite well what you mean."

"Usually I am consulted fairly soon after whatever the—shall we call it—crime has happened, to judge such matters as treatment, possibilities in the case, prognosis favorable or unfavorable, all the various words. They do not mean much and I will not go into them. But occasionally also I am consulted by a responsible head of such an institution for a particular reason. In this matter I received a communication from a certain department which was passed to me through the Home Office. I went to visit the head of this institution—in fact, the governor responsible for the prisoners or patients or whatever you like to call them. He was by way of being a friend of mine—a friend of fairly long standing though not one with whom I was on terms of great intimacy. I went down to the institution in question and the governor laid his troubles before me. They referred to one particular inmate. He was not satisfied about this inmate. He had certain doubts. This was the case of a young man or one who had been a young man, in fact little more than a boy, when he came here. That was now several years ago. As time went on, and after the present governor had taken up his own residence there (he had not been there at the original arrival of this prisoner), he became worried. Not because he himself was a professional man, but because he was a man of experience of criminal patients and prisoners. To put it quite simply, this had been a boy who from his early youth had been completely unsatisfactory. You can call it by what term you like. A young delinquent, a young thug, a bad lot, a person of diminished responsibility. There are many terms. Some of them fit, some of them don't fit, some of them are merely puzzling. He was a criminal type. That was certain. He had joined gangs, he had beaten up people, he was a thief, he had stolen, he had embezzled, he had taken part in swindles, he had initiated certain frauds. In fact, he was a son who would be any father's despair."

"Oh, I see," said Miss Marple.

"And what do you see, Miss Marple?"

"Well, what I think I see is that you are talking of Mr. Rafiel's son."

"You are quite right. I am talking of Mr. Rafiel's son. What do you know about him?"

"Nothing," said Miss Marple. "I only heard—and that was yesterday—that Mr. Rafiel had a delinquent, or unsatisfactory, if we like to put it mildly, son. A son with a criminal record. I know very little about him. Was he Mr. Rafiel's only son?"

"Yes, he was Mr. Rafiel's only son. But Mr. Rafiel also had two daughters. One of them died when she was fourteen, the elder daughter married quite happily but had no children."

"Very sad for him."

"Possibly," said Professor Wanstead. "One never knows. His wife died young and I think it possible that her death saddened him very much, though he was never willing to show it. How much he cared for his son and daughters, I don't know. He provided for them. He did his best for them. He did his best for this son, but what his feelings were, one cannot say. He was not an easy man to read that way. I think his whole life and interest lay in his profession of making money. It was the making of it, like all great financiers, that interested him—not the actual money which he secured by it. That, as you might say, was sent out like a good servant to earn more money in more interesting and unexpected ways. He enjoyed finance. He loved finance. He thought of very little else.

"I think he did all that was possible for his son. He got him out of scrapes at school, he employed good lawyers to get him released from court proceedings whenever possible, but the final blow came, perhaps presaged by some earlier happenings. The boy was taken to court on a charge of assault against a young girl. It was said to be assault and rape and he suffered a term of imprisonment for it with some leniency shown because of his youth. But later, a second and really serious charge was brought against him."

"He killed a girl," said Miss Marple. "Is that right? That's what I heard."

"He lured a girl away from her home. It was some months before her body was found. She had been strangled. And afterwards her face and head had been disfigured by some heavy stones or rocks, presumably to prevent her identity being made known."

"Not a very nice business," said Miss Marple in her most old-ladylike tone.

Professor Wanstead looked at her for a moment or two.

"You describe it that way?"

"It is how it seems to me," said Miss Marple. "I don't like that sort of thing. I never have. If you expect me to feel sympathy, regret, urge an unhappy childhood, blame bad environment; if you expect me in fact to weep over him, this young murderer of yours, I do not feel inclined so to do. I do not like evil beings who do evil things."

"I am delighted to hear it," said Professor Wanstead. "What I suffer in the course of my profession from people weeping and gnashing their teeth and blaming everything on some happening in the past, you would hardly believe. If people knew the bad environments that people have had, the unkindness, the difficulties of their lives and the fact that nevertheless they came through unscathed, I don't think they would so often take the opposite point of view. The misfits are to be pitied, yes, they are to be pitied if I may say so for the genes with which they are born and over which they have no control themselves. I pity epileptics in the same way. If you know what genes are—"

"I know, more or less," said Miss Marple. "It's common knowledge nowadays, though naturally I have no exact chemical or technical knowledge."

"The governor, a man of experience, told me exactly why he was so anxious to have my verdict. He had felt increasingly in his experience of this particular inmate that, in plain words, the boy was not a killer. He didn't think he was the type of a killer, he was like no killer he had ever seen before, he was of the opinion that the boy was the kind of criminal type who would never go straight no matter what treatment was given to him, would never reform himself; and for whom nothing in one sense of the word could be done, but at the same time he felt increasingly certain that the verdict upon him had been a wrong one. He did not believe that the boy had killed a girl, first strangled her and then disfigured her after rolling her body into a ditch. He just couldn't bring himself to believe it. He'd looked over the facts of the case, which seemed to be fully proved. This boy had known the girl, he had been seen with her on several different occasions before the crime. They had presumably slept together and there were other points. His car had been seen in the neighborhood. He himself had been recognized and all the rest of it. A perfectly fair case. But my friend was unhappy about it, he said. He was a man who had a very strong feeling for justice. He wanted a different opinion. He wanted, in fact, not the police side which he knew, he wanted a professional medical view. That was my field, he said. My line of country entirely. He wanted me to see this young man and talk with him, visit him, make a professional appraisal of him and give him my opinion."

"Very interesting," said Miss Marple. "Yes, I call that very interesting. After all, your friend—I mean your governor—was a man of experience, a man who loved justice. He was a man whom you'd be willing to listen to. Presumably, then, you did listen to him."

"Yes," said Professor Wanstead, "I was deeply interested. I saw the subject, as I will call him. I approached him from several different attitudes. I talked to him, I discussed various changes likely to occur in the law. I told him it might be possible to bring down a lawyer, a Queen's Counsel, to see what points there might be in his favor, and other things. I approached him as a friend but also as an enemy so that I could see how he responded to different approaches, and I also made a good many physical tests, such as we use very frequently nowadays. I will not go into those with you because they are wholly technical."

"Then what did you think in the end?"

"I thought," said Professor Wanstead, "I thought my friend was likely to be right. I did not think that Michael was a murderer."

"What about the earlier case you mentioned?"

"That told against him, of course. Not in the jury's mind, because of course they did not hear about that until after the judge's summing up, but certainly in the judge's mind. It told against him, but I made a few inquiries myself afterwards. He had assaulted a girl. He had conceivably raped her, but he had not attempted to strangle her and in my opinion—I have seen a great many cases which come before the assizes—it seemed to me highly unlikely that there was a very definite case of rape. Girls, you must remember, are far more ready to be raped nowadays than they used to be. Their mothers insist, very often, that they should call it rape. The girl in question had had several boy friends who had gone further than friendship. I did not think it counted very greatly as evidence against him. The actual murder case—yes, that was undoubtedly murder—but I continued to feel by all tests—physical tests, mental tests, psychological tests—none of them accorded with this particular crime."

"Then what did you do?"

"I communicated with Mr. Rafiel. I told him that I would like an interview with him on a certain matter concerning his son. I went to him. I told him what I thought, what the governor thought, that we had no evidence, that there were no grounds of appeal at present, but that we both believed that a miscarriage of justice had been committed. I said I thought possibly an inquiry might be held, it might be an expensive business, it might bring out certain facts that could be laid before the Home Office, it might be successful, it might not. There might be something there, some evidence if you looked for it. I said it would be expensive to look for it, but I presumed that would make no difference to anyone in his position. I had realized by that time that he was a sick man, a very ill man. He told me so himself. He told me that he had been in expectation of an early death, that he'd been warned two years ago that death could not be delayed for what they first thought was about a year, but later they realized he would last rather longer because of his unusual physical strength. I asked him what he felt about his son."

"And what did he feel about his son?" said Miss Marple.

"Ah, you want to know that. So did I. He was, I think, extremely honest with me even if—"

"—even if rather ruthless?" said Miss Marple.

"Yes, Miss Marple. You are using the right word. He was a ruthless man, but he was a just man and an honest man. He said, 'I've know what my son was like for many years. I have not tried to change him because I don't believe that anyone could change him. He is made a certain way. He is crooked. He's a bad lot. He'll always be in trouble. He's dishonest. Nobody, nothing could make him go straight. I am well assured of that. I have in a sense washed my hands of him. Though not legally or outwardly; he has always had money if he required it. Help, legal or otherwise, if he gets into trouble. I have done always what I could do. Well, let us say if I had a son who was a spastic, who was sick, who was epileptic, I would do what I could for him. If I have a son who is sick morally, shall we say, and for whom there is no cure, I'd have done what I could also. No more and no less. What can I do for him now?' I told him that it depended what he wanted to do. 'There's no difficulty about that,' he said. 'I am handicapped but I can see quite clearly what I want to do. I want to get him vindicated. I want to get him released from confinement. I want to get him free to continue to lead his own life as best he can lead it. If he must lead it in further dishonesties, then he must lead it that way. I will leave provision for him, to do for him everything that can be done. I don't want him suffering, imprisoned, cut off from his life because of a perfectly natural and unfortunate mistake. If somebody else, some other man killed that girl, I want the fact brought to light and recognized. I want justice for Michael. But I am handicapped. I am a very ill man. My time is measured now not in years or months but in weeks.'

"Lawyers, I suggested—I know a firm— He cut me short. 'Your lawyers will be useless. You can employ them but they will be useless. I must arrange what I can arrange in such a limited time.' He offered me a large fee to undertake the search for the truth and to undertake everything possible with no expense spared. 'I can do next to nothing myself. Death may come at any moment. I empower you as my chief help, and to assist you at my request I will try to find a certain person.' He wrote down a name for me. Miss Jane Marple. He said, 'I don't want to give you her address. I want you to meet her in surroundings of my own choosing,' and he then told me of this tour, this charming, harmless, innocent tour of historic houses, castles and gardens. He would provide me with a reservation on it ahead for a certain date. 'Miss Jane Marple,' he said, 'will also be on that tour. You will meet her there, you will encounter her casually, and thus it will be seen clearly to be a casual meeting.'

"I was to choose my own time and moment to make myself known to you, if I thought it advisable; or not to make myself known to you if I thought that that would be the better way. You have already asked me if I or my friend the governor had any reason to suspect or know of any other person who might have been guilty of the murder. My friend the governor certainly suggested nothing of the kind, and he had already taken up the matter with the police officer who had been in charge of the case—a most reliable detective-superintendent with very good experience in these matters."

"No other man was suggested? No other friend of the girl's? No other former friend who might have been supplanted?"

"There was nothing of that kind to find. I asked Mr. Rafiel to tell me a little about you. He did not however consent to do so. He told me you were elderly. He told me that you were a person who knew about people. He told me one other thing." He paused.

"What's the other thing?" said Miss Marple. "I have some natural curiosity, you know. I really can't think of any other advantage I conceivably could have. I am slightly deaf. My eyesight is not quite as good as it used to be. I cannot really think that I have any advantages beyond the fact that I may, I suppose, seem rather foolish and simple, and am, in fact, what used to be called in rather earlier days an 'old tabby.' I *am* an old tabby. Is that the sort of thing he said?"

"No," said Professor Wanstead. "What he said was he thought you had a very fine sense of evil."

"Oh," said Miss Marple. She was taken aback.

Professor Wanstead was watching her.

"Would you say that was true?" he said.

Miss Marple was quiet for quite a long time. At last she said:

"Perhaps it is. Yes, perhaps. I have at several different times in my life been apprehensive, have recognized that there was evil in the neighborhood, the surroundings, that the environment of someone who was evil was near me, connected with what was happening."

She looked at him suddenly and smiled.

"It's rather, you know," she said, "like being born with a very keen sense of smell. You can smell a leak of gas when other people can't do so. You can distinguish one perfume from another very easily. I had an aunt once," continued Miss Marple thoughtfully, "who said she could smell when people told a lie. She said there was quite a distinctive odor came to her. Their noses twitched, she said, and then the smell came. I don't know if it was true or not, but—well, on several occasions she was quite remarkable. She said to my uncle once, 'Don't, Jack, engage that young man you were talking to this morning. He was telling you lies the whole time he was talking.' That turned out to be quite true."

"A sense of evil," said Professor Wanstead. "Well, if you do sense evil, tell me. I shall be glad to know. I don't think I have a particular sense of evil myself. Ill-health, yes, but not—not evil up here." He tapped his forehead.

"I'd better tell you briefly how I came into things now," said Miss Marple. "Mr. Rafiel, as you know, died. His lawyers asked me to come and see them, apprised me of his proposition. I received a letter from him which explained nothing. After that I heard nothing more for some little time. Then I got a letter from the company who run these tours saying that Mr. Rafiel before his death had made a reservation for me knowing that I should enjoy a trip very much, and wanting to give it to me as a surprise present. I was very astonished but took it as an indication of the first step that I was to undertake. I was to go on this tour and presumably in the course of the tour some other indication or hint or clue or direction would come to me. I think it did. Yesterday, no, the day before, I was received on my arrival here by three ladies who live at an old manor house and who very kindly extended an invitation to me. They had heard from Mr. Rafiel, they said, who had written some time before his death saying that a very old friend of his would be coming on this tour and would they be kind enough to put her up for two or three days as he thought she was not fit to attempt the particular ascent of this rather difficult climb up the headland to where there was a memorial tower which was the principal event of yesterday's tour."

"And you took that also as an indication of what you were to do?"

"Of course," said Miss Marple. "There can be no other reason for it. He was not a man to shower benefits for nothing, out of compassion for an old lady who wasn't good at walking up hills. No. He *wanted* me to go there."

"And you went there? And what then?"

"Nothing," said Miss Marple. "Three sisters."

"Three weird sisters?"

"They ought to have been," said Miss Marple, "but I don't think they were. They didn't seem to be, anyway. I don't know yet. I suppose they may have been—they may be, I mean. They seem ordinary enough. They didn't belong to this house. It had belonged to an uncle of theirs and they'd come here to live some years ago. They are in rather poor circumstances, they are amiable, not particularly interesting. All slightly different in type. They do not appear to have been well acquainted with Mr. Rafiel. Any conversation I have had with them appears to yield nothing."

"So you learned nothing during your stay?"

"I learned the facts of the case you've just told me. Not from them. From an elderly servant, who started her reminiscences dating back to the time of the uncle. She knew of Mr. Rafiel only as a name. But she was eloquent on the theme of the murder. It had all started with the visit here of a son of Mr. Rafiel's who was a bad lot, of how the girl had fallen in love with him and that he'd strangled the girl, and how sad and tragic and terrible it all was. 'With bells on, as you might say,'" said Miss Marple, using a phrase of her youth. "Plenty of exaggeration, but it was a nasty story, and she seemed to believe that the police view was that this hadn't been his only murder."

"It didn't seem to you to connect up with the three weird sisters?"

"No, only that they'd been the guardians of the girl—and had loved her dearly. No more than that."

"They might know something—something about another man?"

"Yes—that's what we want, isn't it? The other man—a man of brutality, who wouldn't hesitate to bash in a girl's head after he'd killed her. The kind of man who could be driven frantic with jealousy. There are men like that."

"No other curious things happened at The Old Manor?"

"Not really. One of the sisters, the youngest, I think, kept talking about the garden. She sounded as though she was a very keen gardener, but she couldn't be because she didn't know the names of half the things. I laid a trap or two for her, mentioning special rare shrubs and saying did she know it? and yes, she said, wasn't it a wonderful plant? I said it was not very hardy and she agreed. But she didn't know anything about plants. That reminds me—"

"Reminds you of what?"

"Well, you'll think I'm just silly about gardens and plants, but I mean one does *know* things about them. I mean, I know a few things about birds and I know some things about gardens."

"And I gather that it's not birds but gardens that are troubling you."

"Yes. Have you noticed two middle-aged women on this tour? Miss Barrow and Miss Cooke."

"Yes. I've noticed them. Pair of middle-aged spinsters traveling together."

"That's right. Well, I've found out something odd about Miss Cooke. That is her name, isn't it? I mean it's her name on the tour."

"Why—has she got another name?"

"I think so. She's the same person who visited me—I won't say visited me exactly, but she was outside my garden fence in St. Mary Mead, the village where I live. She expressed pleasure at my garden and talked about gardening with me. Told me she was living in the village and working in somebody's garden who'd moved into a new house there. I rather think," said Miss Marple, "yes, I rather think that the whole thing was lies. There again, she knew nothing about gardening. She pretended to, but it wasn't true."

"Why do you think she came there?"

"I'd no idea at the time. She said her name was Bartlett—and the name of the woman she said she was living with began with 'H,' though I can't remember it for the moment. Her hair was not only differently done but it was a different color and her clothes were of a different style. I didn't recognize her at first on this trip. Just wondered why her face was vaguely familiar. And then suddenly it came to me—because of the dyed hair. I said where I had seen her before. She admitted that she'd been there—but pretended that she, too, hadn't recognized *me*. All lies."

"And what's your opinion about all that?"

"Well, one thing certainly—Miss Cooke (to give her her present name) came to St. Mary Mead just to have a look at me—so that she'd be quite sure to be able to recognize me when we met again—"

"And why was that felt to be necessary?"

"I don't know. There are two possibilities. I'm not sure that I like one of them very much."

"I don't know," said Professor Wanstead, "that I like it very much either."

They were both silent for a minute or two, and then Professor Wanstead said:

"I don't like what happened to Elizabeth Temple. You've talked to her during this trip?"

"Yes, I have. When she's better I'd like to talk to her again—she could tell me—us—things about the girl who was murdered. She spoke to me of this girl—who had been at her school, who had been going to marry Mr. Rafiel's son—but didn't marry him. Instead she died. I asked how or why she died—and she answered with the word 'love.' I took it as meaning a suicide—but it was murder. Murder through jealousy would fit. Another man. Some other man we've got to find. Miss Temple may be able to tell us who he was."

"No other sinister possibilities?"

"I think, really, it is casual information we need. I see no reason to believe that there is any sinister suggestion in any of the coach passengers— or any sinister suggestion about the people living in The Old Manor House. But one of those three sisters may have known or remembered something that the girl or Michael once said. Clotilde used to take the girl abroad. Therefore, she may know of something that occurred on some foreign trip perhaps. Something that the girl said or mentioned or did on some trip. Some man that the girl met. Something which has nothing to do with The Old Manor House here. It is difficult because only by talking, by casual information, can you get any clue. The second sister, Mrs. Glynne, married fairly early, has spent time, I gather, in India and in Africa. She may have heard of something through her husband, or through her husband's relations, through various things that are unconnected with The Old Manor House here although she has visited it from time to time. She knew the murdered girl presumably, but I should think she knew her much less well than the other two. But that does not mean that she may not know some significant facts about the girl. The third sister is more scatterbrained, more localized, does not seem to have known the girl as well. But still, she, too, may have information about possible lovers—or boy friends—seen the girl with an unknown man. That's her, by the way, passing the hotel now."

Miss Marple, however occupied by her tête-à-tête, had not relinquished the habits of a lifetime. A public thoroughfare was always to her an observation post. All the passersby, either loitering or hurrying, had been noticed automatically.

"Anthea Bradbury-Scott—the one with the big parcel. She's going to the post office, I suppose. It's just round the corner, isn't it?"

"Looks a bit daft to me," said Professor Wanstead, "all that floating hair—gray hair, too—a kind of Ophelia of fifty."

"I thought of Ophelia, too, when I first saw her. Oh, dear, I wish I knew what I ought to do next. Stay here at the Golden Boar for a day or two, or go on with the coach tour. It's like looking for a needle in a haystack. If you stick your fingers in it long enough, you ought to come up with something— even if you do get pricked in the process."

CHAPTER THIRTEEN
Black and Red Check

I

MRS. SANDBOURNE RETURNED just as the party was sitting down to lunch. Her news was not good. Miss Temple was still unconscious. She certainly could not be moved for several days.

Having given the bulletin, Mrs. Sandbourne turned the conversation to practical matters. She produced suitable timetables of trains for those who wished to return to London and proposed suitable plans for the resumption of the tour on the morrow or the next day. She had a list of suitable short expeditions in the near neighborhood for this afternoon—small groups in hired cars.

Professor Wanstead drew Miss Marple aside as they went out of the dining room.

"You may want to rest this afternoon. If not, I will call for you here in an hour's time. There is an interesting church you might care to see—"

"That would be very nice," said Miss Marple.

II

Miss Marple sat quite still in the car that had come to fetch her. Professor Wanstead was sitting beside her. He had called for her at the time he had said.

"I thought you might enjoy seeing this particular church. And a very pretty village, too," he explained. "There's no reason, really, why one should not enjoy the local sights when one can."

"It's very kind of you, I'm sure," Miss Marple had said.

She had looked at him with that slightly fluttery gaze of hers.

"Very kind," she said. "It just seems—well, I don't want to say it seems heartless, but, well, you know what I mean."

"My dear lady, Miss Temple is not an old friend of yours or anything like that. Sad as this accident has been."

"Well," said Miss Marple again, "this is very kind of you."

The car was, she presumed, a hired one. A kindly thought to take an elderly lady to see one of the sights of the neighborhood. Professor Wanstead might have taken somebody younger, more interesting and certainly better-looking. Miss Marple looked at him thoughtfully once or twice as they drove through the village. He was not looking at her. He was gazing out of his own window.

When they had left the village behind and were on a second-class country road twisting round the hillside, he turned his head and said to her:

"We are not going to a church, I am afraid."

"No," said Miss Marple, "I thought perhaps we weren't."

"Yes, the idea would have come to you."

"Where are we going, may I ask?"

"We are going to a hospital in Carristown."

"Ah, yes, that was where Miss Temple was taken?"

It was a question, though it hardly needed to be one.

"Yes," he said. "Mrs. Sandbourne saw her and brought me back a letter from the hospital authorities. I have just finished talking to them on the telephone."

"Is she going on well?"

"No. Not going on very well."

"I see. At least—I hope I don't see," said Miss Marple.

"Her recovery is very problematical, but there is nothing that can be done. She may not recover consciousness again. On the other hand she may have a few lucid intervals."

"And you are taking me there? Why? I am not a friend of hers, you know. I only just met her for the first time on the trip."

"Yes. I realize that. I'm taking you there because in one of the lucid intervals she has had, she asked for you."

"I see," said Miss Marple. "I wonder why she should ask for me, why she should have thought that I—that I could be useful in any way to her, or do anything. She is a woman of perception. In her way, you know, a great woman. As headmistress of Fallowfield she occupied a prominent position in the educational world."

"The best girls' school there is, I suppose?"

"Yes. She was a great personality. She was herself a woman of considerable scholarship. Mathematics were her specialty, but she was an 'all-round'—what I should call an educator. Was interested in education, what girls were fitted for, how to encourage them. Oh, many other things. It is sad and very cruel if she dies," said Miss Marple. "It will seem such a waste of a life. Although she had retired from her headmistressship, she still exercised a lot of power. This accident—" She stopped. "Perhaps you do not want us to discuss the accident?"

"I think it is better that we should do so. A big boulder crashed down the hillside. It has been known to happen before, though only at very long divided intervals of time. However, somebody came and spoke to me about it," said Professor Wanstead.

"Came and spoke to you about the accident? Who was it?"

"The two young people. Joanna Crawford and Emlyn Price."

"What did they say?"

"Joanna told me that she had the impression there was someone on the hillside. Rather high up. She and Emlyn were climbing up from the lower main path, following a rough track that wound round the curve of the hill. As they turned a corner, she definitely saw, outlined against the skyline, a man or a woman who was trying to roll a big boulder forward along the ground. The boulder was rocking—and finally it started to roll, at first slowly and then gathering speed down the hillside. Miss Temple was walking along the main path below, and had come to a point just underneath it when the boulder hit her. If it was done deliberately, it might not, of course, have succeeded; it might have missed her—but it did succeed. If what was being attempted was a deliberate attack on the woman walking below, it succeeded only too well."

"Was it a man or a woman they saw?" asked Miss Marple.

"Unfortunately, Joanna Crawford could not say. Whoever it was was wearing jeans or trousers, and had on a lurid polo-neck pullover in red and black checks. The figure turned and moved out of sight almost immediately. She is inclined to think it was a man but cannot be certain."

"And she thinks, or you think, that it was a deliberate attempt on Miss Temple's life?"

"The more she mulls it over, the more she thinks that that was exactly what it was. The boy agrees."

t was very noticeable," said Miss Marple. "That is what your words
ne to infer. It was very mentionable. So much so that the girl Joanna
:ioned it specifically."

'es. And what does that suggest to you?"

'he trailing of flags," said Miss Marple thoughtfully. "Something that
)e seen, remembered, observed, recognized."

'es." Professor Wanstead looked at her with encouragement.

Vhen you describe a person you have seen—seen not close at hand but
a distance—the first thing you will describe will be their clothes. Not
faces, not their walk, not their hands, not their feet. A scarlet tam-o'-
er, a purple cloak, a bizarre leather jacket, a pullover of brilliant reds
)lacks. Something very recognizable, very noticeable. The object of it
that when that person removes that garment, gets rid of it, sends it by
n a parcel to some address, say, about a hundred miles away, or
s it in a rubbish bin in a city or burns it or tears it up or destroys it,
he will be the one person modestly and rather drably attired who will
: suspected or looked at or thought of. It must have been *meant*, that
t and black check jersey. Meant so that it will be recognized again
h actually it will never again be seen on that particular person."

very sound idea," said Professor Wanstead. "As I have told you,"
ued the professor, "Fallowfield is situated not very far from here.
1 miles, I think. So this is Elizabeth Temple's part of the world—a
ue knows well, with people in it that she also might know well."

.. It widens the possibilities," said Miss Marple. "I agree with you,"
d presently, "that the attacker is more likely to have been a man than
an. That boulder, if it was done with intent, was sent on its course
:curately. Accuracy is more a male quality than a female one. On the
and there might easily have been someone on our coach, or possibly
‹eighborhood, who saw Miss Temple in the street, a former pupil of
past years—someone whom she herself might not recognize after a
)f time. But the girl or woman would have recognized her, because a
.ster or headmistress of over sixty is not unlike the same headmaster
mistress at the age of fifty. She is recognizable. Some woman who
:ed her former headmistress and also knew that her headmistress
mething damaging about her. Someone who might in some way
danger to her." She sighed. "I myself do not know this part of the
all. Have you any particular knowledge of it?"

said Professor Wanstead. "I could not claim a personal knowledge
art of the country. I know something, however, of various things
e happened in this part of the world entirely because of what you
d me. If it had not been for my acquaintanceship with you and the
u have told me I should have been more at sea than I am.

t are you yourself actually doing here? You do not know. Yet you
: here. It was deliberately arranged by Rafiel that you should come
it you should take this coach tour, that you and I should meet.
ve been other places where we have stopped or through which we
sed, but special arrangements here were made so that you should
stay for a couple of nights here. You were put up with former
'his who would not have refused any request he made. Was there a
r that?"

"You have no idea who it might have been?"

"No idea whatever. No more have they. It migl
travelers, someone who went for a stroll that afterno
completely unknown who knew that the coach was
chose this place to make an attack on one of the pa
lover of violence for violence's sake. Or it might ha

"It seems very melodramatic if one says 'a se
Marple.

"Yes, it does. Who would want to kill a reti
mistress? That is a question we want answere
possible, that Miss Temple herself might be able
recognized the figure above her or she might m
someone who bore her ill-will for some special re:

"It still seems unlikely."

"I agree with you," said Professor Wanstea
unlikely person to be a fit victim of attack, bu
headmistress knows a great many people. A great
it this way, have passed through her hands."

"A lot of girls, you mean, have passed throug

"Yes. Yes, that is what I meant. Girls and the
must have knowledge of many things. Roman
might indulge in, unknown to their parents.
happens very often. Especially in the last ten or
to mature earlier. That is physically true, thou
word, they mature late. They remain childish lo
they like to wear, childish with their floating
represent a worship of childishness. Their baby
slips and shorts—all children's fashions. They
not to have to accept our kind of responsibili
they want to be thought grown-up and free to d
up things. And that leads sometimes to tra
aftermath of tragedy."

"Are you thinking of some particular case?'

"No. No, not really. I'm only thinking
possibilities pass through my mind? I cannot
had a *personal* enemy—an enemy ruthless
opportunity of killing her. What I do think—
"Would you like to make a suggestion?"

"Of a possibility? Well, I think I know or
You are suggesting that Miss Temple knew
had some knowledge that would be incon
somebody if it was known."

"Yes, I do feel exactly that."

"In that case," said Miss Marple, "it
someone on our coach tour who recognized
was, but who perhaps after the passage of s
or might even not have been recognized by
it back on our passengers, does it not?" S
mentioned—red and black checks, you sai

"Oh, yes? The pullover—" He looked at
struck you about that?"

"So that I could learn certain facts that I had to know," said Miss Marple.

"A series of murders that took place a good many years ago?" Professor Wanstead looked doubtful. "There is nothing unusual in that. You can say the same of many places in England and Wales. These things seem always to go in a series. First a girl found assaulted and murdered. Then another girl not very far away. Then something of the same kind perhaps twenty miles away. The same pattern of death.

"Two girls were reported missing from Jocelyn St. Mary itself, the one that we have been discussing whose body was found six months later, many miles away and who was last seen in the company of Michael Rafiel—"

"And the other?"

"A girl called Nora Broad. Not a 'quiet girl with no boy friends.' Possibly with one boy friend too many. Her body was never found. It will be—one day. There have been cases when twenty years have passed," said Wanstead. He slowed down. "We have arrived. This is Carristown, and here is the hospital."

Shepherded by Professor Wanstead, Miss Marple entered. The professor was obviously expected. He was ushered into a small room where a woman rose from a desk.

"Oh, yes," she said, "Professor Wanstead. And—er—this is—er—" She hesitated slightly.

"Miss Jane Marple," said Professor Wanstead. "I talked to Sister Barker on the telephone."

"Oh, yes. Sister Barker said that she would be accompanying you."

"How is Miss Temple?"

"Much the same, I think. I am afraid there is not much improvement to report." She rose. "I will take you to Sister Barker."

Sister Barker was a tall, thin woman. She had a low, decisive voice and dark gray eyes that had a habit of looking at you and looking away almost immediately, leaving you with the feeling that you had been inspected in a very short space of time and judgment pronounced upon you.

"I don't know what arrangements you have in mind," said Professor Wanstead.

"Well, I had better tell Miss Marple just what we have arranged. First I must make it clear to you that the patient, Miss Temple, is still in a coma with very rare lucid intervals. She appears to come to occasionally, to recognize her surroundings and to be able to say a few words. But there is nothing one can do to stimulate her. It has to be left to the utmost patience. I expect Professor Wanstead has already told you that in one of her intervals of consciousness she uttered quite distinctly the words 'Miss Jane Marple.' And then: *I want to speak to her. Miss Jane Marple.*' After that she relapsed into unconsciousness. Doctor thought it advisable to get in touch with the other occupants of the coach. Professor Wanstead came to see us and explained various matters and said he would bring you over. I am afraid that all we can ask you to do is to sit in the private ward where Miss Temple is, and perhaps be ready to make a note of any words she should say if she does regain consciousness. I am afraid the prognosis is not very hopeful. To be quite frank, which is better, I think, since you are not a near relative and are unlikely to be disturbed by this information, Doctor thinks that she is sinking fast, that she may die without recovering consciousness. There is nothing one can do to relieve the concussion. It is important that someone should hear what she says, and Doctor thinks it advisable that she should not see too many people round her if she regains consciousness. If Miss Marple is not worried at the thought of sitting there alone, there will be a nurse in the room, though not obviously so. That is, she will not be noticed from the bed, and will not move unless she's asked for. She will sit in a corner of the room shielded by a screen." She added, "We have a police official there also, ready to take down anything. The doctor thinks it advisable that he also should not be noticed by Miss Temple. One person alone, and that possibly a person she expects to see, will not alarm her or make her lose knowledge of what she wants to say to you. I hope this will not be too difficult a thing to ask you?"

"Oh, no," said Miss Marple. "I'm quite prepared to do that. I have a small notebook with me and a biro pen that will not be in evidence. I can remember things by heart for a very short time, so I need not appear to be obviously taking notes of what she says. You can trust my memory and I am not deaf—not deaf in the real sense of the word. I don't think my hearing is quite as good as it used to be, but if I am sitting near a bedside, I ought to be able to hear anything she says quite easily even if it is whispered. I am used to sick people. I have had a good deal to do with them in my time."

Again the lightning glance of Sister Barker went over Miss Marple. This time a faint inclination of the head showed satisfaction.

"It is kind of you," she said, "and I am sure that if there is any help you can give, we can rely on you to give it. If Professor Wanstead likes to sit in the waiting room downstairs, we can call him at any moment if it should be necessary. Now, Miss Marple, perhaps you will accompany me."

Miss Marple followed Sister along a passage and into a small, well-appointed single room. In the bed there, in a dimly lighted room, since the blinds were half drawn, lay Elizabeth Temple. She lay there like a statue, yet she did not give the impression of being asleep. Her breath came uncertainly in slight gasps. Sister Barker bent to examine her patient, motioned Miss Marple into a chair beside the bed. She then crossed the room to the door again. A young man with a notebook in his hand came from behind the screen there.

"Doctor's orders, Mr. Reckitt," said Sister Barker.

A nurse also appeared. She had been sitting in the opposite corner of the room.

"Call me if necessary, Nurse Edmonds," said Sister Barker, "and get Miss Marple anything she may need."

Miss Marple loosened her coat. The room was warm. The nurse approached and took it from her. Then she retired to her former position. Miss Marple sat down in the chair. She looked at Elizabeth Temple thinking, as she had thought before when looking at her in the coach, what a fine-shaped head she had. Her gray hair drawn back from it fitted her face in a perfect caplike effect. A handsome woman, and a woman of personality. Yes, a thousand pities, Miss Marple thought, a thousand pities if the world was going to lose Elizabeth Temple.

Miss Marple eased the cushion at her back, moved the chair a fraction of an inch and sat quietly to wait. Whether to wait in vain or to some point, she had no idea. Time passed. Ten minutes, twenty minutes, half an hour, thirty-five minutes. Then suddenly, quite unexpectedly, as it were, a voice came. Low, but distinct, slightly husky, with none of the resonance it had once held: "Miss Marple."

Elizabeth Temple's eyes were open now. They were looking at Miss Marple. They looked competent, perfectly sensible. She was studying the face of the woman who was sitting by her bed, studying her without any sign of emotion, of surprise—only, one would say, of scrutiny—fully conscious scrutiny. And the voice spoke again:

"Miss Marple. You are Jane Marple?"

"That is right. Yes," said Miss Marple, "Jane Marple."

"Henry often spoke of you. He said things about you."

The voice stopped. Miss Marple said with a slight query in her voice: "Henry?"

"Henry Clithering, an old friend of mine—very old friend."

"An old friend of mine, too," said Miss Marple. "Henry Clithering."

Her mind went back to the many years she had known him, Sir Henry Clithering, the things he had said to her, the assistance he had asked from her sometimes, and the assistance that she had asked from him. A very old friend.

"I remembered your name. On the passenger list. I thought it must be you. You could help. That's what he—Henry, yes—would say if he were here. You might be able to help. To find out. It's important—very important, although—it's a long time ago now—a—long—time—ago."

Her voice faltered a little, her eyes half closed. Nurse got up, came across the room, picked up a small glass and held it to Elizabeth Temple's lips. Miss Temple took a sip, nodded her head dismissively. Nurse put down the glass and went back to her chair.

"If I can help, I will," said Miss Marple. She asked no further questions.

Miss Temple said, "Good," and after a minute or two, again, "Good."

For two or three minutes she lay with her eyes closed. She might have been asleep or unconscious. Then her eyes opened again suddenly.

"Which," she said, "which of them? That's what one has got to know. Do you know what I am talking about?"

"I think so. A girl who died—Nora Broad?" A frown came quickly to Elizabeth Temple's forehead.

"No, no, no. The other girl. Verity Hunt."

There was a pause and then, "Jane Marple. You're old—older than when he talked about you. You're older, but you can still find out things, can't you?"

Her voice became slightly higher, more insistent.

"You can, can't you? Say you can. I've not much time. I know that. I know it quite well. One of them, but which? Find out. Henry would have said you can. It may be dangerous for you—but you'll find out, won't you?"

"With God's help, I will," said Miss Marple. It was a vow.

"Ah."

The eyes closed, then opened again. Something like a smile seemed to try to twitch the lips.

"The big stone from above. The stone of death."

"Who rolled that stone down?"

"Don't know. No matter—only—Verity. Find out about Verity. Truth. Another name for truth, Verity."

Miss Marple saw the faint relaxation of the body on the bed. There was a faintly whispered "Good-bye. Do your best . . ."

Her body relaxed, the eyes closed. The nurse came again to the bedside. This time she took up the pulse, felt it, and beckoned to Miss Marple. Miss Marple rose obediently and followed her out of the room.

"That's been a big effort for her," said the nurse. "She won't regain consciousness again for some time. Perhaps not at all. I hope you learned something?"

"I don't think I did," said Miss Marple, "but one never knows, does one?"

"Did you get anything?" asked Professor Wanstead as they went out to the car.

"A name," said Miss Marple. "Verity. Was that the girl's name?"

"Yes. Verity Hunt."

Elizabeth Temple died an hour and a half later. She died without regaining consciousness.

CHAPTER FOURTEEN
Mr. Broadribb Wonders

"SEE *The Times* this morning?" said Mr. Broadribb to his partner, Mr. Schuster.

Mr. Schuster said he couldn't afford *The Times*, he took the *Telegraph*.

"Well, it may be in that, too," said Mr. Broadribb. "In the deaths. Miss Elizabeth Temple, D.Sc."

Mr. Schuster looked faintly puzzled.

"Headmistress of Fallowfield. You've heard of Fallowfield, haven't you?"

"Of course," said Schuster. "Girls' school. Been going for fifty years or so. First-class, fantastically expensive. So she was the headmistress of it, was she? I thought the headmistress had resigned some time ago. Six months at least. I'm sure I read about it in the paper. That is to say there was a bit about the new headmistress. Married woman. Youngish. Thirty-five to forty. Modern ideas. Give the girls lessons in cosmetics, let 'em wear trouser suits. Something of that kind."

"Hum," said Mr. Broadribb, making the noise that solicitors of his age are likely to make when they hear something which elicits criticism based on long experience. "Don't think she'll ever make the name that Elizabeth Temple did. Quite someone, she was. Been there a long time, too."

"Yes," said Mr. Schuster, somewhat uninterested. He wondered why Broadribb was so interested in defunct schoolmistresses.

Schools were not really of particular interest to either of the two gentlemen. Their own offspring were now more or less disposed of. Mr.

Broadribb's two sons were respectively in the Civil Service and in an oil firm, and Mr. Schuster's rather younger progeny were at different universities where both of them respectively were making as much trouble for those in authority as they possibly could do. He said:

"What about her?"

"She was on a coach tour," said Mr. Broadribb.

"Those coaches," said Mr. Schuster. "I wouldn't let any of my relations go on one of those. One went off a precipice in Switzerland last week, and two months ago one had a crash and twenty were killed. Don't know who drives these things nowadays."

"It was one of those Country Houses and Gardens and Objects of Interest in Britain—or whatever they call it—tours," said Mr. Broadribb. "That's not quite the right name, but you know what I mean."

"Oh, yes, I know. Oh, the—er—yes, that's the one we sent Miss What's-a-name on. The one old Rafiel booked."

"Miss Jane Marple was on it."

"She didn't get killed too, did she?" asked Mr. Schuster.

"Not so far as I know," said Mr. Broadribb. "I just wondered a bit, though."

"Was it a road accident?"

"No. It was at one of the beauty spot places. They were walking on a path up a hill. It was a stiff walk—up a rather steep hill with boulders and things on it. Some of the boulders got loose and came rushing down the mountainside. Miss Temple was knocked out and taken to hospital with concussion and died—"

"Bad luck," said Mr. Schuster, and waited for more.

"I only wondered," said Mr. Broadribb, "because I happened to remember that—well, that Fallowfield was the school where the girl was at."

"What girl? I don't really know what you're talking about, Broadribb."

"The girl who was done in by young Michael Rafiel. I was just recalling a few things which might seem to have some slight connection with this curious Jane Marple business that old Rafiel was so keen on. Wish he'd told us more."

"What's the connection?" said Mr. Schuster.

He looked more interested now. His legal wits were in process of being sharpened, to give a sound opinion on whatever it was that Mr. Broadribb was about to confide to him.

"That girl. Can't remember her last name now. Christian name was Hope or Faith or something like that. Verity, that was her name. Verity Hunter, I think it was. She was one of that series of murdered girls. Found her body in a ditch about thirty miles away from where she'd gone missing. Been dead six months. Strangled, apparently, and her head and face had been bashed in—to delay recognition; they thought, but she was recognized all right. Clothes, handbag, jewelry nearby—some mole or scar. Oh, yes, she was identified quite easily—"

"Actually, she was the one the trial was all about, wasn't she?"

"Yes. Suspected of having done away with perhaps three other girls during the past year, Michael was. But evidence wasn't so good in the other deaths—so the police went all-out on this one—plenty of evidence—bad record. Earlier cases of assault and rape. Well, we all know what rape is nowadays. Mum tells the girl she's got to accuse the young man of rape even if the young man hasn't had much chance, with the girl at him all the time to come to the house while Mum's away at work or Dad's gone on holiday. Doesn't stop badgering him until she's forced him to sleep with her. Then, as I say, Mum tells the girl to call it rape. However, that's not the point," said Mr. Broadribb. "I wondered if things mightn't tie up a bit, you know. I thought this Jane Marple business with Rafiel might have something to do with Michael."

"Found guilty, wasn't he? And given a life sentence?"

"I can't remember now—it's so long ago. Or did they get away with a verdict of diminished responsibility?"

"And Verity Hunter or Hunt was educated at that school. Miss Temple's school. She wasn't still a schoolgirl, though, was she, when she was killed? Not that I can remember."

"Oh, no. She was eighteen or nineteen, living with relations or friends of her parents, or something like that. Nice house, nice people, nice girl, by all accounts—the sort of girl whose relations always say 'she was a very quiet girl, rather shy, didn't go about with strange people and had no boy friends.' Relations never know what boy friends a girl has. The girls take mighty good care of that. And young Rafiel was said to be very attractive to girls."

"Never been any doubt that he did it?" asked Mr. Schuster.

"Not a scrap. Told a lot of lies in the witness box, anyway. His counsel would have done better not to have let him give evidence. A lot of his friends gave him an alibi that didn't stand up, if you know what I mean. All his friends seemed to be fluent liars."

"What's your feeling about it, Broadribb?"

"Oh, I haven't got any feelings," said Mr. Broadribb, "I was just wondering if this woman's death might tie up."

"In what way?"

"Well, you know—about these boulders that fall down cliffsides and drop on top of someone. It's not always in the course of nature. Boulders usually stay where they are, in my experience."

CHAPTER FIFTEEN
Verity

"VERITY," SAID MISS Marple.

Elizabeth Margaret Temple had died the evening before. It had been a peaceful death. Miss Marple, sitting once more amid the faded chintz of the drawing room in The Old Manor House, had laid aside the baby's pink coat which she had previously been engaged in knitting and had substituted a crocheted purple scarf. This half-mourning touch went with Miss Marple's early-Victorian ideas of tactfulness in face of tragedy.

An inquest was to be held on the following day. The vicar had been approached and had agreed to hold a brief memorial service in the church as soon as arrangements could be made. Undertakers suitably attired, with proper mourning faces, took general charge of things in liaison with the police. The inquest was to take place on the following morning at 11 o'clock. Members of the coach tour had agreed to attend the inquest. And several of them had chosen to remain on so as to attend the church service also.

Mrs. Glynne had come to the Golden Boar and urged Miss Marple to return to The Old Manor House until she finally returned to the tour.

"You will get away from all the reporters."

Miss Marple had thanked all three sisters warmly and had accepted.

The coach tour would be resumed after the memorial service, driving first to South Bedestone, thirty-five miles away, where there was a good hotel which had been originally chosen for a stopping place. After that the tour would go on as usual.

There were, however, as Miss Marple had considered likely, certain persons who were disengaging themselves and returning home, or were going in other directions and not continuing on the tour. There was something to be said in favor of either decision. To leave what would become a journey of painful memories, or to continue with the sightseeing that had already been paid for and which had been interrupted only by one of those painful accidents that may happen on any sightseeing expedition. A lot would depend, Miss Marple thought, on the outcome of the inquest.

Miss Marple, after exchanging various conventional remarks proper to the occasion with her three hostesses, had devoted herself to her purple wool and had sat considering her next line of investigation. And so it was that with her fingers still busy, she had uttered the one word "Verity"— throwing it as one throws a pebble into a stream, solely to observe what the result—if any—would be. Would it mean something to her hostesses? It might or it might not. Otherwise, when she joined the members of the tour at their hotel meal this evening, which had been arranged, she would try the effect of it there. It had been, she thought to herself, the last word or almost the last word that Elizabeth Temple had spoken. So therefore, thought Miss Marple (her fingers still busy because she did not need to look at her crocheting, she could read a book or conduct a conversation while her fingers, though slightly crippled with rheumatism, would proceed correctly through their appointed movements). So therefore, "Verity."

Like a stone into a pool, causing ripples, a splash, something? Or nothing. Surely there would be a reaction of one sort or another. Yes, she had not been mistaken. Although her face registered nothing, the keen eyes behind her glasses had watched three people in a simultaneous manner as she had trained herself to do for many years now, when wishing to observe her neighbors either in church, mothers' meetings, or at other public functions in St. Mary Mead when she had been on the track of some interesting piece of news or gossip.

Mrs. Glynne had dropped the book she was holding and had looked across towards Miss Marple with slight surprise—surprise, it seemed, at that particular word coming from Miss Marple, but not surprise really to hear it.

Clotilde reacted differently. Her head shot up, she leaned forward a little, then she looked not at Miss Marple but across the room in the direction of the window. Her hands clenched themselves, she kept very still. Miss Marple, although dropping her head slightly as though she was not looking any more, noted that her eyes were filling with tears. Clotilde sat quite still and let the tears roll down her cheeks. She made no attempt to take out a handkerchief, she uttered no word. Miss Marple was impressed by the aura of grief that came from her.

Anthea's reaction was different. It was quick, excited, almost pleasurable.

"Verity? Verity, did you say? Did you know her? I'd no idea. It is Verity Hunt you mean?"

Lavinia Glynne said, "It's a Christian name?"

"*I* never knew anyone of that name," said Miss Marple, "but I did mean a Christian name. Yes. It is rather unusual, I think. Verity." She repeated it thoughtfully.

She let her purple wool ball fall and looked round with the slightly apologetic and embarrassed look of one who realizes she had made a serious faux pas, but not sure why.

"I—I am so sorry. Have I said something I shouldn't? It was only because . . ."

"No, of course not," said Mrs. Glynne. "It was just that it is—it is a name we know, a name with which we have—associations."

"It just came into my mind," said Miss Marple, still apologetic, "because, you know, it was poor Miss Temple who said it. I went to see her, you know, yesterday afternoon. Professor Wanstead took me. He seemed to think that I might be able to—to—I don't know if it's the proper word—to *rouse* her, in some way. She was in a coma and they thought—not that I was a friend of hers at any time, but we had chatted together on the tour and we often sat beside each other, as you know, on some of the days and we had talked. And he thought perhaps I might be of some use. I'm afraid I wasn't, though. Not at all. I just sat there and waited and then she did say one one or two words, but they didn't seem to mean anything. But finally, just when it was time for me to go, she did open her eyes and looked at me—I don't know if she was mistaking me for someone—but she did say that word. Verity! And, well, of course it stuck in my mind, especially with her passing away yesterday evening. It must have been someone or something that she had in her mind. But of course it might just mean—well, of course it might just mean truth. That's what verity means, doesn't it?"

She looked from Clotilde to Lavinia to Anthea.

"It was the Christian name of a girl we knew," said Lavinia Glynne. "That is why it startled us."

"Especially because of the awful way she died," said Anthea.

Clotilde said in her deep voice, "Anthea! There's no need to go into these details."

"But after all, everyone knows quite well about her," said Anthea. She looked towards Miss Marple. "I thought perhaps you might have known about her because you knew Mr. Rafiel, didn't you? Well, I mean, he wrote to us about you, so you must have known him. And I thought perhaps—well, he'd mentioned the whole thing to you."

"I'm so sorry," said Miss Marple. "I'm afraid I don't quite understand what you're talking about."

"They found her body in a ditch," said Anthea.

There was never any holding Anthea, Miss Marple thought, not once she got going. But she thought that Anthea's vociferous talk was putting additional strain on Clotilde She had taken out a handkerchief now in a quiet, noncommittal way. She brushed tears from her eyes and then sat upright, her back very straight, her eyes deep and tragic.

"Verity," she said, "was a girl we cared for very much. She lived here for a while. I was very fond of her—"

"And she was very fond of you," said Lavinia.

"Her parents were friends of mine," said Clotilde. "They were killed in a plane accident."

"She was at school at Fallowfield," explained Lavinia. "I suppose that was how Miss Temple came to remember her."

"Oh, I see," said Miss Marple. "Where Miss Temple was headmistress, is that it? I have heard of Fallowfield often, of course. It's a very fine school isn't it?"

"Yes," said Clotilde. "Verity was a pupil there. After her parents died she came to stay with us for a time while she decided what she wanted to do with her future. She was eighteen or nineteen. A very sweet girl and a very affectionate and loving one. She thought perhaps of training for nursing, but she had very good brains and Miss Temple was insistent that she ought to go to university. So she was studying and having coaching for that when— when this terrible thing happened."

She turned her face away.

"I—do you mind if we don't talk about it any more just now?"

"Oh, of course not," said Miss Marple. "I'm so sorry to have impinged on some tragedy. I didn't know. I—I haven't heard . . . I thought—well, I mean . . ." She became more and more incoherent.

That evening she heard a little more. Mrs. Glynne came to her bedroom when she was changing her dress to go out and join the others at the hotel.

"I thought I ought to come and explain a little to you," said Mrs. Glynne, "about—about the girl Verity Hunt. Of course you couldn't know that our sister Clotilde was particularly fond of her and that her really horrible death was a terrible shock. We never mention her if we can help it, but—I think it would be easier if I told you the facts completely and you will understand. Apparently Verity had, without our knowledge, made friends with an undesirable—a more than undesirable—it turned out to be a dangerous— young man who already had a criminal record. He came here to visit us when he was passing through once. We knew his father very well." She paused. "I think I'd better tell you the whole truth if you don't know, and you don't seem to. He was actually Mr. Rafiel's son Michael—"

"Oh, dear," said Miss Marple, "not—not—I can't remember his name, but I do remember hearing that there was a son—and that he hadn't been very satisfactory."

"A little more than that," said Mrs. Glynne. "He'd always given trouble. He'd been had up in court once or twice for various things. Once assaulting a teenager—other things of that type. Of course I consider myself that the magistrates are too lenient with that kind of thing. They don't want to upset a young man's university career. And so they let them off with a—I forget what they call it—a suspended sentence, something of that kind. If these boys were sent to jail at once, it would perhaps warn them off that type of life. He was a thief, too. He had forged checks, he pinched things. He was a thoroughly bad lot. We were friends of his mother's. It was lucky for her, I think, that she died young before she had time to be upset by the way her son was turning out. Mr. Rafiel did all he could, I think. Tried to find suitable jobs for the boy, paid fines for him and things like that. But I think it was a great blow to him, though he pretended to be more or less indifferent and to write it off as one of those things that happen. We had, as probably people here in the village will tell you, we had a bad outbreak of murders and violence in this district. Not only here. They were in different parts of the country, twenty miles away, sometimes fifty miles away. One or two, it's suspected by the police, were nearly a hundred miles away. But they seemed to center more or less on this part of the world. Anyway, Verity one day went out to visit a friend and—well, she didn't come back. We went to the police about it, the police sought for her, searched the whole countryside, but they couldn't find any trace of her. We advertised, they advertised, and they suggested that she'd gone off with a boy friend. Then word began to get round that she had been seen with Michael Rafiel. By now the police had their eye on Michael as a possibility for certain crimes that had occurred, although they couldn't find any direct evidence. Verity was said to have been seen, described by her clothing and other things, with a young man of Michael's appearance and in a car that corresponded to a description of his car. But there was no further evidence until her body was discovered six months later—thirty miles from here in a rather wild part of wooded country, in a ditch covered with stones and piled earth. Clotilde had to go to identify it. It was Verity, all right. She'd been strangled and her head beaten in. Clotilde has never quite got over the shock. There were certain marks, a mole and an old scar and of course her clothes and the contents of her handbag. Miss Temple was very fond of Verity. She must have thought of her just before she died."

"I'm sorry," said Miss Marple. "I'm really very, very sorry. Please tell your sister that I didn't know. I had no idea."

CHAPTER SIXTEEN
The Inquest

I

MISS MARPLE WALKED slowly along the village street on her way towards the market place where the inquest was to take place in the old-fashioned Georgian building which had been known for a hundred years as the Curfew Arms. She glanced at her watch. There was still a good twenty minutes before she need be there. She looked into the shops. She paused before the shop that sold wool and babies' jackets, and peered inside for a few moments. A girl in the shop was serving. Small woolly coats were being tried on two children. Farther along the counter there was an elderly woman.

Miss Marple went into the shop, went along the counter to a seat opposite the elderly woman, and produced a sample of pink wool. She had run out, she explained, of this particular brand of wool and had a little jacket she needed to finish. The match was soon made, some more samples of wool that Miss Marple had admired were brought out for her to look at, and soon she was in conversation, starting with the sadness of the accident which had just taken place. Mrs. Merrypit, if her name was identical with that which was written up outside the shop, was full of the importance of the accident and the general difficulties of getting local governments to do anything about the dangers of footpaths and public rights of way.

"After the rain, you see, you get all the soil washed off and then the boulders get loose and then down they comes. I remember one year they had three falls—three accidents there was. One boy nearly killed, he was, and then later that year, oh, six months later, I think, there was a man got his arm broken, and the third time it was poor old Mrs. Walker. Blind she was and pretty well deaf, too. She never heard nothing or she could have got out of the way, they say. Somebody saw it and they called out to her, but they was too far away to reach her or to run to get her. And so she was killed."

"Oh, how sad," said Miss Marple; "how tragic. The sort of thing that's not easily forgotten, is it?"

"No, indeed. I expect the coroner'll mention it today."

"I expect he will," said Miss Marple. "In a terrible way it seems quite a natural thing to happen, doesn't it, though of course there are accidents sometimes by pushing things about, you know. Just pushing, making stones rock. That sort of thing."

"Ah, well, there's boys as be up to anything. But I don't think I've ever seen them up that way fooling about."

Miss Marple went on to the subject of pullovers, bright-colored pullovers.

"It's not for myself," she said, "it's for one of my great-nephews. You know, he wants a polo-necked pullover and very bright colors he'd like."

"Yes, they do like bright colors nowadays, don't they?" agreed Mrs. Merrypit. "Not in jeans. Black jeans they like. Black or dark blue. But they like a bit of brightness up above."

Miss Marple described a pullover of check design in bright colors. There appeared to be quite a good stock of pullovers and jerseys, but anything in red and black did not seem to be on display, nor even was anything like it mentioned as having been lately in stock. After looking at a few samples, Miss Marple prepared to take her departure, chatting, first about the former murders she had heard about which had happened in this part of the world.

"They got the fellow in the end," said Mrs. Merrypit. "Nice-looking boy, hardly have thought it of him. He'd been well-brought-up, you know. Been to university and all that. Father was very rich, they say. Touched in the head, I suppose. Not that they sent him to Broadway, or whatever the place is. No, they didn't do that, but I think myself he must have been a mental case—there was five or six other girls, so they said. The police had one after another of the young men round hereabouts to help them. Geoffrey Grant they had up. They were pretty sure it was him to begin with. He was always a bit queer ever since he was a boy. Interfered with little girls going to school, you know. He used to offer them sweets and get them to come down the lanes with him and see the primroses, or something like that. Yes, they had very strong suspicions about him. But it wasn't him. And then there was another one, Bert Williams, but he'd been far away on two occasions at least—what they call an alibi, so it couldn't be him. And then at last it came to this—what's-'is-name, I can't remember him now. Luke I think his name was—no, Mike something. Very nice-looking, as I say, but he had a bad record. Yes, stealing, forging checks, all sorts of things like that. And two what you call 'em paternity cases. No, I don't mean that, but you know what I mean. When a girl's going to have a baby. You know and they make an order and make the fellow pay. He'd got two girls in the family way before this."

"Was this girl in the family way?"

"Oh, yes, she was. At first we thought when the body was found it might have been Nora Broad. That was Mrs. Broad's niece, down at the mill shop. Great one for going with the boys, she was. She'd gone away missing from home in the same way. Nobody knew where she was. So when this body turned up six months later, they thought at first it was her."

"But it wasn't?"

"No—someone quite different."

"Did her body ever turn up?"

"No. I suppose it might someday, but they think on the whole it was pushed into the river. Ah, well, you never know, do you? You never know what you may dig up off a plowed field or something like that. I was taken once to see all that treasure. Luton Loo was it—some name like that? Somewhere in the East Counties. Under a plowed field it was. Beautiful. Gold ships and Viking ships and gold plate, enormous great platters. Well, you never know. Any day you may turn up a dead body or you may turn up a gold platter. And it may be hundreds of years old like that gold plate was, or it may be a three- or four-years-old body, like Mary Lucas, who'd been missing for four years, they say. Somewhere near Reigate she was found. Ah, well, all these things! It's a sad life. Yes, it's a very sad life. You never know what's coming."

"There was another girl who'd lived here, wasn't there," said Miss Marple, "who was killed?"

"You mean the body they thought was Nora Broad's but it wasn't? Yes. I've forgotten her name now. Hope, it was, I think. Hope or Charity. One of those sort of names, if you know what I mean. Used to be used a lot in Victorian times, but you don't hear them so much nowadays. Lived at the Manor House, she did. She'd been there for some time after her parents were killed."

"Her parents died in an accident, didn't they?"

"That's right. In a plane going to Spain or Italy, one of those places."

"And you say she came to live here? Were they relations of hers?"

"I don't know if they were relations, but Mrs. Glynne, as she is now, was, I think, a great friend of her mother's or something that way. Mrs. Glynne, of course, was married and gone abroad, but Miss Clotilde—that's the eldest one, the dark one—she was very fond of the girl. She took her abroad, to Italy and France and all sorts of places, and she had her trained—a bit of typewriting and shorthand and that sort of thing, and art classes, too. She's very arty, Miss Clotilde is. Oh, she was mighty fond of the girl. Brokenhearted she was when she disappeared. Quite different to Miss Anthea—"

"Miss Anthea is the youngest one, isn't she?"

"Yes. Not quite all there, some people say. Scattylike, you know, in her mind. Sometimes you see her walking along talking to herself, you know, and tossing her head in a very queer way. Children get frightened of her sometimes. They say she's a bit queer about things. I don't know. You hear everything in a village, don't you? The great-uncle who lived here before, he was a bit peculiar, too. Used to practice revolver shooting in the garden. For no reason at all so far as anyone could see. Proud of his marksmanship, he said he was, whatever marksmanship is."

"But Miss Clotilde is not peculiar?"

"Oh, no, she's clever, she is. Knows Latin and Greek, I believe. Would have liked to go to university, but she had to look after her mother, who was an invalid for a long time. But she was very fond of Miss—now, what was her name?—Faith, perhaps. She was very fond of her and treated her like a daughter. And then along comes this young what's-his-name, Michael, I think it was—and then one day the girl just goes off without saying a word to anyone. I don't know if Miss Clotilde knew as she was in the family way."

"But you knew," said Miss Marple.

"Ah, well, I've got a lot of experience. I usually know when a girl's that way. It's plain enough to the eye. It's not only the shape, as you might say, you can tell by the look in their eyes and the way they walk and sit, and the sort of giddy fits they get and sick turns now and again. Oh, yes, I thought to myself. Here's another one of them. Miss Clotilde had to go and identify the body. Nearly broke her up, it did. She was like a different woman for weeks afterwards. Fairly loved that girl, she did."

"And the other one—Miss Anthea?"

"Funnily enough, you know, I thought she had a kind of pleased look as though she was—yes, just pleased. Not nice, eh? Farmer Plummer's daughter used to look like that. Always used to go and see pigs killed. Enjoyed it. Funny things goes on in families."

Miss Marple said good-bye, saw she had another ten minutes to go and passed on to the post office. The post office and general store of Jocelyn St. Mary was just off the Market Square.

Miss Marple went into the post office, bought some stamps, looked at some of the postcards and then turned her attention to various paperback books. A middle-aged woman with a rather vinegary face presided behind the postal counter. She assisted Miss Marple to free a book from the wire support in which the books were.

"Stick a bit sometimes, they do. People don't put them back straight, you see."

There was by now no one else in the shop. Miss Marple looked with distaste at the jacket of the book, a naked girl with bloodstained markings on her face and a sinister-looking killer bending over her with a blood-stained knife in his hand.

"Really," she said, "I don't like these horrors nowadays."

"Gone a bit too far with some of their jackets, haven't they?" said Mrs. Vinegar. "Not everyone as likes them. Too fond of violence in every way, I'd say nowadays."

Miss Marple detached a second book. *"Whatever Happened to Baby Jane?"* she read. "Oh, dear, it's a sad world one lives in."

"Oh, yes, I know. Saw in yesterday's paper, I did, some woman left her baby outside a supermarket and then someone else comes along and wheels it away. And all for no reason as far as one can see. The police found her, all right. They all seem to say the same things, whether they steal from a supermarket or take away a baby. Don't know what came over them, they say."

"Perhaps they really don't," suggested Miss Marple.

Mrs. Vinegar looked even more like vinegar.

"Take me a lot to believe that, it would."

Miss Marple looked round—the post office was still empty. She advanced to the window.

"If you are not too busy, I wonder if you could answer a question of mine," said Miss Marple. "I have done something extremely stupid. Of late years I make so many mistakes. This was a parcel addressed to a charity. I send them clothes—pullovers and children's woolies, and I did it up and addressed it and it was sent off—and only this morning it came to me suddenly that I'd made a mistake and written the wrong address. I don't suppose any list is kept of the addresses of parcels—but I thought someone might have just happened to remember it. The address I meant to put was The Dockyard and Thames Side Welfare Association."

Mrs. Vinegar was looking quite kindly now, touched by Miss Marple's patent incapacity and general state of senility and dither.

"Did you bring it yourself?"

"No, I didn't—I'm staying at The Old Manor House—and one of them—Mrs. Glynne, I think—said she or her sister would post it. Very kind of her—"

"Let me see now. It would have been on Tuesday, would it? It wasn't Mrs. Glynne who brought it in, it was the youngest one, Miss Anthea."

"Yes, yes, I think that was the day—"

"I remember it quite well. In a good-sized dress box—and moderately heavy, I think. But not what you said, Dockyard Association—I can't recall anything like that. It was the Reverend Mathews—the East Ham Women and Children's Woolen Clothing Appeal."

"Oh, yes." Miss Marple clasped her hands in an ecstasy of relief. "How clever of you—I see now how I came to do it. At Christmas I *did* send things to the East Ham Society in answer to a special appeal for knitted things, so I must have copied down the wrong address. Can you just repeat it?" She entered it carefully in a small notebook.

"I'm afraid the parcel's gone off, though—"

"Oh, yes, but I can write, explaining the mistake and ask them to forward the parcel to the Dockyard Association instead. Thank you so much."

Miss Marple trotted out.

Mrs. Vinegar produced stamps for her next customer, remarking in an aside to a colleague—"Flighty as they make them, poor old creature. Expect she's always doing that sort of thing."

Miss Marple went out of the post office and ran into Emlyn Price and Joanna Crawford.

Joanna, she noticed, was very pale and looked upset.

"I've got to give evidence," she said. "I don't know—what will they ask me? I'm so afraid. I—I don't like it. I told the police sergeant, I told him what I thought we saw."

"Don't you worry, Joanna," said Emlyn Price. "This is just a coroner's inquest, you know. He's a nice man, a doctor, I believe. He'll just ask you a few questions and you'll say what you saw."

"You saw it, too," said Joanna.

"Yes, I did," said Emlyn. "At least I saw there was someone up there. Near the boulders and things. Now come on, Joanna."

"They came and searched our rooms in the hotel," said Joanna. "They asked our permission, but they had a search warrant. They looked in our rooms and among the things in our luggage."

"I think they wanted to find that check pullover you described. Anyway, there's nothing for you to worry about. If you'd had a black and scarlet pullover yourself, you wouldn't have talked about it, would you? It was black and scarlet, wasn't it?"

"I don't know," said Emlyn Price. "I don't really know the colors of things very well. I think it was a sort of bright color. That's all I know."

"They didn't find one," said Joanna. "After all, none of us have very many things with us. You don't when you go on a coach travel. There wasn't anything like that among anybody's things. I've never seen anyone— of our lot, I mean, wearing anything like that. Not so far. Have you?"

"No, I haven't, but I suppose—I don't know that I should know if I had seen it," said Emlyn Price. "I don't always know red from green."

"No, you're a bit color-blind, aren't you?" said Joanna. "I noticed that the other day."

"What do you mean, you noticed it?"

"My red scarf. I asked if you'd seen it. You said you'd seen a green one somewhere and you brought me the red one. I'd left it in the dining room. But you didn't really know it was red."

"Well, don't go about saying I'm color-blind. I don't like it. Puts people off in some way."

"Men are more often color-blind than women," said Joanna. "It's one of those sex-link things," she added with an air of erudition. "You know, it passes through the female and comes out in the male."

"You make it sound as though it was measles," said Emlyn Price. "Well, here we are."

"You don't seem to mind," said Joanna as they walked up the steps.

"Well, I don't really. I've never been to an inquest. Things are rather interesting when you do them for the first time."

II

Dr. Stokes was a middle-aged man with graying hair and spectacles.
Police evidence was given first, then the medical evidence, with technical
details of the concussion injuries which had caused death. Mrs. Sandbourne
gave particulars of the coach tour, the expedition as arranged for that
particular afternoon, and particulars of how the fatality had occurred. Miss
Temple, she said, although not young, was a very brisk walker. The party
were going along a well-known footpath which led round the curve of a hill
which slowly mounted to the old Moorland Church, originally built in
Elizabethan times, though repaired and added to later. On an adjoining
crest was what was called the Bonaventure Memorial. It was a fairly steep
ascent and people usually climbed it at a different pace from each other. The
younger ones very often ran or walked ahead and reached their destination
much earlier than the others. The elderly ones took it slowly. She herself
usually kept at the rear of the party so that she could, if necessary, suggest
to people who were tired that they could, if they liked, go back. Miss
Temple, she said, had been talking to a Mr. and Mrs. Butler. Miss Temple,
though she was over sixty, had been slightly impatient at their slow pace
and had outdistanced them, had turned a corner and gone on ahead rather
rapidly, which she had done often before. She was inclined to get impatient
if waiting for people to catch up for too long, and preferred to make her own
pace. They had heard a cry ahead, and she and the others had run on,
turned a curve of the pathway and had found Miss Temple lying on the
ground. A large boulder detached from the hillside above where there were
several others of the same kind, must, they had thought, have rolled down
the hillside and struck Miss Temple as she was going along the path below.
A most unfortunate and tragic accident.

"You had no idea there was anything but an accident?"

"No, indeed. I can hardly see how it could have been anything but an
accident."

"You saw no one above you on the hillside?"

"No. This is the main path round the hill but of course people do wander
about over the top. I did not see anyone that particular afternoon."

Then Joanna Crawford was called. After particulars of her name and age
Dr. Stokes asked:

"You were not walking with the remainder of the party?"

"No, we had left the path. We'd gone round the hill a little higher up the
slope."

"You were walking with a companion?"

"Yes. With Mr. Emlyn Price."

"There was no one else actually walking with you?"

"No. We were talking and we were looking at one or two of the flowers.
They seemed of rather an uncommon kind. Emlyn's interested in botany."

"Were you out of sight of the rest of the party?"

"Not all the time. They were walking along the main path—some way
below us, that is."

"Did you see Miss Temple?"

"I think so. She was walking ahead of the others, and I think I saw her turn a corner of the path ahead of them. We didn't see her after this because the contour of the hill hid her."

"Did you see someone walking above you on the hillside?"

"Yes. Up among a good many boulders. There's a sort of great patch of boulders on the side of the hill."

"Yes," said Dr. Stokes, "I know exactly the place you mean. Large granite boulders. People call them the Wethers, or the Grey Wethers sometimes."

"I suppose they might look like sheep from a distance, but we weren't so very far away from them."

"And you saw someone up there?"

"Yes. Someone was more or less in the middle of the boulders, leaning over them."

"Pushing them, do you think?"

"Yes. I thought so, and wondered why. He seemed to be pushing at one on the outside of the group near the edge. They were so big and so heavy I would have thought it was impossible to push them. But the one he or she was pushing seemed to be balanced rather like a rocking stone."

"You said first *he,* now you say *he* or *she,* Miss Crawford. Which do you think it was?"

"Well, I thought—I suppose—I suppose I thought it was a man, but I wasn't actually thinking at the time. It was—he or she was—wearing trousers and a pullover, a sort of man's pullover with a polo neck."

"What color was the pullover?"

"Rather a bright red and black in checks. And there was longish hair at the back of a kind of beret, rather like a woman's hair, but then it might just as well have been a man's."

"It certainly might," said Dr. Stokes rather drily. "Identifying a male or female figure by their hair is certainly not easy these days." He went on: "What happened next?"

"Well, the stone began to roll over. It sort of toppled over the edge and then it began to gain speed. I said to Emlyn, 'Oh, it's going to go right over down the hill.' Then we heard a sort of crash as it fell. And I think I heard a cry from below, but I might have imagined it."

"And then?"

"Oh, we ran on up a bit and round the corner of the hill to see what had happened to the stone."

"And what did you see?"

"We saw the boulder below on the path with a body underneath it—and people coming running round the corner."

"Was it Miss Temple who uttered the cry?"

"I think it must have been. It might have been one of the others who was catching up and turned the corner. Oh! It was—it was horrible."

"Yes, I'm sure it was. What had happened to the figure you'd seen above? The man or woman in the red and black pullover? Was that figure still there among the stones?"

"I don't know. I never looked up there. I was—I was busy looking at the accident and running down the hill to see if one could do anything. I did just look up, I think, but there wasn't anyone in sight. Only the stones. There were a lot of contours and you could lose anyone quite easily from view."

"Could it have been one of your party?"

"Oh, no. I'm sure it wasn't one of us. I would have known because, I mean, one would have known by their clothes. I'm sure nobody was wearing a scarlet and black pullover."

"Thank you, Miss Crawford."

Emlyn Price was called next. His story was practically a replica of Joanna's.

There was a little more evidence which did not amount to much.

The coroner brought in that there was not sufficient evidence to show how Elizabeth Temple had come to her death, and adjourned the inquest for a fortnight.

CHAPTER SEVENTEEN
Miss Marple Makes a Visit

As THEY WALKED back from the inquest to the Golden Boar, hardly anyone spoke. Professor Wanstead walked beside Miss Marple, and since she was not a very fast walker, they fell slightly behind the others.

"What will happen next?" Miss Marple asked at last.

"Do you mean legally or to us?"

"I suppose both," said Miss Marple, "because one will surely affect the other."

"It will be presumably a case of the police making further inquiries arising out of the evidence given by those two young people."

"Yes."

"Further inquiry will be necessary. The inquest was bound to be adjourned. One can hardly expect the coroner to give a verdict of accidental death."

"No, I understand that." She said, "What did you think of their evidence?"

Professor Wanstead directed a sharp glance from under his beetling eyebrows.

"Have you any ideas on the subject, Miss Marple?" His voice was suggestive. "Of course," said Professor Wanstead, "we knew beforehand what they were going to say."

"Yes."

"What you mean is that you are asking what I thought about them themselves, their feelings about it."

"It was interesting," said Miss Marple. "Very interesting. The red and black check pullover. Rather important, I think, don't you? Rather striking?"

"Yes, exactly that."

He shot again that look at her under his eyebrows. "What does it suggest to you exactly?"

"I think," said Miss Marple, "I think the description of that might give us a valuable clue."

They came to the Golden Boar. It was only about half-past twelve and Mrs. Sandbourne suggested a little refreshment before going in to luncheon. As sherry and tomato juice and other liquors were being consumed, Mrs. Sandbourne proceeded to make certain announcements.

"I have taken advice," she said, "both from the coroner and Inspector Douglas. Since the medical evidence has been taken fully, there will be at the church a funeral memorial service tomorrow at eleven o'clock. I'm going to make arrangements with Mr. Courtney, the local vicar, about it. On the following day it will be best, I think, to resume our tour. The program will be slightly altered, since we have lost three days, but I think it can be reorganized on rather simpler lines. I have heard from one or two members of our party that they would prefer to return to. London, presumably by rail. I can quite understand the feelings lying behind this, and would not like to try to influence you in any way. This death has been a very sad occurrence. I still cannot help but believe that Miss Temple's death was the result of an accident. Such a thing has happened before on that particular pathway, though there do not appear in this case to have been any geological or atmospherical conditions causing it. I think a further investigation will have to be made. Of course, some hiker on a walking tour—that kind of thing— may have been pushing about boulders quite innocently, not realizing that there was a danger for someone walking below in what he or she was doing. If so, if that person comes forward, the whole thing may be cleared up quite quickly, but I agree one cannot take that for granted at present. It seems unlikely that the late Miss Temple could have had any enemy or anyone who wished her harm of any kind. What I should suggest is that we do not discuss the accident any further. Investigations will be made by the local authorities whose business it is. I think we will probably all like to attend the memorial service in the church tomorrow. And after that, on continuing the tour, I hope that it may distract our minds from the shock we have had. There are still some very interesting and famous houses to see and some very beautiful scenery also."

Luncheon being announced shortly after that, the subject was not discussed any further. That is to say, not openly. After lunch, as they took coffee in the lounge, people were prone to get together in little groups, discussing their further arrangements.

"Are you continuing on the tour?" asked Professor Wanstead of Miss Marple.

"No," said Miss Marple. She spoke thoughtfully. "No. I think—I think that what has happened inclines me to remain here a little longer."

"At the Golden Boar or at The Old Manor House?"

"That rather depends as to whether I receive any further invitation to go back to The Old Manor House. I would not like to suggest it myself, because my original invitation was for the two nights that the tour was to have stayed here originally. I think possibly it would be better for me to remain at the Golden Boar."

"You don't feel like returning to St. Mary Mead?"

"Not yet," said Miss Marple. "There are one or two things I could do here, I think. One thing I have done already." She met his inquiring gaze. "If you are going on," she said, "with the rest of the party, I will tell you what I have put in hand, and suggest a small sideline of inquiry that might be helpful. The other reason that I wish to stay here I will tell you later. There are certain inquiries—local inquiries—that I want to make. They may not lead anywhere, so I think it as well not to mention them now. And you?"

"I should like to return to London. I have work there waiting to be done. Unless, that is, I can be helpful to you here?"

"No," said Miss Marple, "I do not think so at present. I expect you have various inquiries of your own that you wish to put in hand."

"I came on the tour to meet you, Miss Marple."

"And now you have met me and know what I know, or practically all that I know, you have other inquiries to put in hand. I understand that. But before you leave here, I think there are one or two things—well, that might be helpful, might give a result."

"I see. You have ideas."

"I am remembering what you said."

"You have perhaps pinned down the smell of evil?"

"It is difficult," said Miss Marple, "to know exactly what something wrong in the atmosphere really means."

"But you do feel that there is something wrong in the atmosphere?"

"Oh, yes. Very clearly."

"And especially since Miss Temple's death which, of course, was not an accident, no matter what Mrs. Sandbourne hopes."

"No," said Miss Marple, "it was not an accident. What I don't think I have told you is that Miss Temple said to me once that she was on a pilgrimage."

"Interesting," said the Professor. "Yes, interesting. She didn't tell you what the pilgrimage was, to where or to whom?"

"No," said Miss Marple, "if she'd lived just a little longer and not been so weak, she might have told me. But unfortunately, death came a little too soon."

"So that you have not any further ideas on that subject."

"No. Only a feeling of assurance that her pilgrimage was put an end to by malign design. Someone wanted to stop her going wherever she was going, or stop her going to whomever she was going to. One can only hope that chance or Providence may throw light on that."

"That's why you're staying here?"

"Not only that," said Miss Marple. "I want to find out something more about a girl called Nora Broad."

"Nora Broad." He looked faintly puzzled.

"The other girl who disappeared about the same time as Verity Hunt did. You remember you mentioned her to me. A girl who had boy friends and was, I understand, very ready to have boy friends. A foolish girl, but attractive apparently to the male sex. I think," said Miss Marple, "that to learn a little more about her might help me in my inquiries."

"Have it your own way, Detective-Inspector Marple," said Professor Wanstead.

The service took place on the following morning. All the members of the tour were there. Miss Marple looked round the church. Several of the locals were there also—Mrs. Glynne was there and her sister Clotilde. The youngest one, Anthea, did not attend. There were one or two people from the village also, she thought. Probably not acquainted with Miss Temple but there out of a rather morbid curiosity in regard to what was now spoken of by the term "foul play." There was, too, an elderly clergyman—in gaiters, well over seventy, Miss Marple thought, a broad-shouldered old man with a noble mane of white hair. He was slightly crippled and found it difficult both to kneel and to stand. It was a fine face, Miss Marple thought, and she wondered who he was. Some old friend of Elizabeth Temple, she presumed, who might perhaps have come from quite a long distance to attend the service?

As they came out of the church, Miss Marple exchanged a few words with her fellow travelers. She knew now pretty well who was doing what. The Butlers were returning to London.

"I told Henry I just couldn't go on with it," said Mrs. Butler. "You know—I feel all the time that any minute just as we might be walking round a corner, someone, you know, might shoot us or throw a stone at us— someone who has got a down perhaps on the Famous Houses of England."

"Now then, Mamie, now then," said Mr. Butler, "don't you let your imagination go as far as that!"

"Well, you just don't know nowadays. What with hijackers about and kidnapping and all the rest of it, I don't feel really protected anywhere."

Old Miss Lumley and Miss Bentham were continuing with the tour, their anxieties allayed. "We've paid very high for this tour and it seems a pity to miss anything just because this very sad accident has happened. We rang up a very good neighbor of ours last night, and they are going to see to the cats, so we don't need to worry."

It was going to remain an accident for Miss Lumley and Miss Bentham. They had decided it was more comfortable that way.

Mrs. Riseley-Porter was also continuing on the tour. Colonel and Mrs. Walker were resolved that nothing would make them miss seeing a particularly rare collection of fuchsias in the garden due to be visited the day after tomorrow. The architect, Jameson, was also guided by his wish to see various buildings of special interest for him. Mr. Caspar, however was departing by rail, he said. Miss Cooke and Miss Barrow seemed undecided.

"Pretty good walks round here," said Miss Cooke. "I think we'll stay at the Golden Boar for a little. That's what you're going to do, isn't it, Miss Marple?"

"I really think so," said Miss Marple. "I don't feel quite equal to going on traveling and all that. I think a day or two's rest would be helpful to me after what's happened."

As the little crowd dispersed, Miss Marple took an unostentatious route of her own. From her handbag she took out a leaf torn from her notebook on which she had entered two addresses. The first, a Mrs. Blackett, lived in a neat little house and garden just by the end of the road where it sloped down towards the valley. A small neat woman opened the door.

"Mrs. Blackett?"

Yes, yes, ma'am, that's my name."

"I wonder if I might just come in and speak to you for a minute or two. I have just been to the service and I am feeling a little giddy. If I could just sit down for a minute or two?"

"Dear me, now, dear me. Oh, I'm sorry for that. Come right in, ma'am, come right in. That's right. You sit down here. Now I'll get you a glass of water—or maybe you'd like a pot of tea?"

"No, thank you," said Miss Marple, "a glass of water would put me right."

Mrs. Blackett returned with a glass of water and a pleasurable prospect of talking about ailments and giddiness and other things.

"You know, I've got a nephew like that. He oughtn't to be at his age, he's not much over fifty, but now and then he'll come over giddy all of a sudden and unless he sits down at once—why, you don't know, sometimes he'll pass out right on the floor. Terrible, it is. Terrible. And the doctors, they don't seem able to do anything about it. Here's your glass of water."

"Ah," said Miss Marple, sipping, "I feel much better."

"Been to the service, have you, for the poor lady as got done in, as some say, or accident as others. I'd say it's accident every time. But these inquests and coroners, they always want to make things look criminal, they do."

"Oh, yes," said Miss Marple. "I've been so sorry to hear of a lot of things like that in the past. I was hearing a great deal about a girl called Nora. Nora Broad, I think."

"Ah, Nora, yes. Well, she was my cousin's daughter. Yes. A long while ago, that was. Went off and never come back. These girls, there's no holding them. I said often, I did, to Nancy Broad—that's my cousin—I said to her, 'You're out working all day' and I said 'what's Nora doing? You know she's the kind that likes the boys. Well,' I said, 'there'll be trouble. You see if there isn't.' And sure enough, I was quite right."

"You mean—?"

"Ah, the usual trouble. Yes, in the family way. Mind you, I don't think as my cousin Nancy knew about it yet. But of course, I'm sixty-five and I know what's what and I know the way a girl looks and I think I know who it was, but I'm not sure. I might have been wrong because he went on living in the place and he was real cut up when Nora was missing."

"She went off, did she?"

"Well, she accepted a lift from someone—a stranger. That's the last time she was seen. I forget the make of the car now. Some funny name it had. An Audit or something like that. Anyway, she'd been seen once or twice in that car. And off she went in it. And it was said it was that same car that the poor girl what got herself murdered used to go riding in. But I don't think as that happened to Nora. If Nora'd been murdered, the body would have come to light by now. Don't you think so?"

"It certainly seems likely," said Miss Marple. "Was she a girl who did well at school and all that?"

"Ah, no, she wasn't. She was idle and she wasn't too clever at her books either. No. She was all for the boys from the time she was twelve years old onwards. I think in the end she must have gone off with someone or other for good. But she never let anyone know. She never sent as much as a postcard. Went off, I think, with someone as promised her things. You know. Another girl I knew—but that was when I was young—went off with one of them Africans. He told her as his father was a shake. Funny sort of word, but a shake, I think it was. Anyway it was somewhere in Africa or in Algiers. Yes, in Algiers it was. Somewhere there. And she was going to have all sorts of wonderful things. He had six camels, the boy's father, she said, and a whole troop of horses and she was going to live in a wonderful house, she was, with carpets hanging up all over the walls, which seems a funny place to put carpets. And off she went. She come back again three years later. Yes. Terrible time she'd had. Terrible. They lived in a nasty little house made of earth. Yes, it was. And nothing much to eat except what they call cos-cos, which I always thought was lettuce, but it seems it isn't. Something more like semolina pudding. Oh, terrible it was. And in the end he said she was no good to him and he'd divorce her. He said he'd only got to say "I divorce you,' three times, and he did and walked out and somehow or other some kind of society out there took charge of her and paid her fare home to England. And there she was. Ah, but that was about thirty to forty years ago, that was. Now Nora, that was only about seven or eight years ago. But I expect she'll be back one of these days, having learned her lesson and finding out that all these fine promises didn't come to much."

"Had she anyone to go to here except her—her mother—your cousin, I mean? Anyone who—"

"Well, there's many as was kind to her. There was the people at The Old Manor House, you know. Mrs. Glynne wasn't there then, but Miss Clotilde, she was always one to be good to the girls from school. Yes, many a nice present she's given Nora. She gave her a very nice scarf and a pretty dress once. Very nice, it was. A summer frock, a sort of foulard silk. Ah, she was very kind, Miss Clotilde was. Tried to make Nora take more interest in her schooling. Lots of things like that. Advised her against the way she was going on because, you see—well, I wouldn't like to say it, not when she's my cousin's child though, mark you, my cousin is only one who married my boy cousin, that is to say—but I mean it was something terrible the way she went on with all the boys. Anyone could pick her up. Real sad it is. I'd say she'll go on the streets in the end. I don't believe she has any future but that. I don't like to say these things, but there it is. Anyway, perhaps it's better than getting herself murdered like Miss Hunt did, what lived at The Old Manor House. Cruel, that was. They thought she'd gone off with someone, and the police, they was busy. Always asking questions and having the young men who'd been with the girl up to help them with their inquiries and all that. Geoffrey Grant there was, Billy Thompson, and the Langfords' Harry. All unemployed—with plenty of jobs going if they'd wanted to take them. Things usedn't to be like that when I was young. Girls behaved proper. And the boys knew they'd got to work if they wanted to get anywhere."

Miss Marple talked a little more, said that she was now quite restored, thanked Mrs. Blackett, and went out.

Her next visit was to a girl who was planting out lettuces.

"Nora Broad? Oh, *she* hasn't been in the village for years. Went off with someone, she did. She was a great one for boys. I always wondered where she'd end up. Did you want to see her for any particular reason?"

"I had a letter from a friend abroad," said Miss Marple untruthfully. "A very nice family and they were thinking of engaging a Miss Nora Broad. She'd been in some trouble, I think. Married someone who was rather a bad lot and had left her and gone off with another woman, and she wanted to get a job looking after children. My friend knew nothing about her, but I gathered she came from this village. So I wondered if there was anyone here who could—well, tell me something about her. You went to school with her, I understand?"

"Oh, yes, we were in the same class, we were. Mind you, I didn't approve of all Nora's goings-on. She was boy-mad, she was. Well, I had a nice boy friend myself that I was going steady with at the time, and I told her she'd do herself no good going off with every Tom, Dick and Harry that offered her a lift in a car or took her along to a pub where she told lies about her age, as likely as not. She was a good mature girl as looked a lot older than she was."

"Dark or fair?"

"Oh, she had dark hair. Pretty hair, it was. Always looselike, you know, as girls do."

"Were the police worried about her when she disappeared?"

"Yes. You see, she didn't leave no word behind. She just went out one night and didn't come back. She was seen getting into a car, and nobody saw the car again and nobody saw her. Just at that time there'd been a good many murders, you know. Not specially round here, but all over the country. The police, they were rounding up a lot of young men and boys. Thought as Nora might be a body at the time, we did. But not she. She was all right. I'd say as likely as not she's making a bit of money still in London or one of these big towns doing a striptease, something of that kind. That's the kind she was."

"I don't think," said Miss Marple, "if it's the same person that she'd be very suitable for my friend."

"She'd have to change a bit if she was to be suitable," said the girl.

CHAPTER EIGHTEEN
Archdeacon Brabazon

WHEN MISS MARPLE, slightly out of breath and rather tired, got back to the Golden Boar, the receptionist came out from her pen and across to greet her.

"Oh, Miss Marple, there is someone here who wants to speak to you. Archdeacon Brabazon."

"Archdeacon Brabazon?" Miss Marple looked puzzled.

"Yes. He's been trying to find you. He had heard you were with this tour and he wanted to talk to you before you might have left or gone to London. I told him that some of them were going back to London by the later train this afternoon, but he is very, very anxious to speak to you before you go. I have put him in the television lounge. It is quieter there. The other is very noisy just at this moment."

Slightly surprised, Miss Marple went to the room indicated. Archdeacon Brabazon turned out to be the elderly cleric whom she had noticed at the memorial service. He rose and came towards her.

"Miss Marple. Miss Jane Marple?"

"Yes, that is my name. You wanted—"

"I am Archdeacon Brabazona. I came here this morning to attend the service for a very old friend of mine, Miss Elizabeth Temple."

"Oh, yes?" said Miss Marple. "Do sit down."

"Thank you, I will. I am not quite as strong as I was." He lowered himself carefully into a chair.

"And you—"

Miss Marple sat down beside him.

"Yes," she said, "you wanted to see me?"

"Well, I must explain how that comes about. I'm quite aware that I am a complete stranger to you. As a matter of fact I made a short visit to the hospital at Carristown, talking to the matron before going on to the church here. It was she who told me that before she died Elizabeth had asked to see a fellow member of the tour. Miss Jane Marple. And that Miss Jane Marple had visited her and sat with her just a very, very short time before Elizabeth died."

He looked at her anxiously.

"Yes," said Miss Marple, "that is so. It surprised me to be sent for."

"You are an old friend of hers?"

"No," said Miss Marple. "I only met her on this tour. That's why I was surprised. We had expressed ideas to each other, occasionally sat next to each other in the coach, and had struck up quite an acquaintanceship. But I was surprised that she should have expressed a wish to see me when she was so ill."

"Yes. Yes, I can quite imagine that. She was, as I have said, a very old friend of mine. In fact, she was coming to see me, to visit me. I live in Fillminster, which is where your coach tour will be stopping the day after tomorrow. And by arrangement she was coming to visit me there, she wanted to talk to me about various matters about which she thought I could help her."

"I see," said Miss Marple. "May I ask you a question? I hope it is not too intimate a question."

"Of course, Miss Marple. Ask me anything you like."

"One of the things Miss Temple said to me was that her presence on the tour was not merely because she wished to visit historic homes and gardens. She described it by a rather unusual word to use, as a pilgrimage."

"Did she," said Archdeacon Brabazon. "Did she indeed now? Yes, that's interesting. Interesting and perhaps significant."

"So what I am asking you is, do you think that the pilgrimage she spoke of was her visit to you?"

"I think it must have been," said the Archdeacon. "Yes, I think so."

"We had been talking," said Miss Marple, "about a young girl. A girl called Verity."

"Ah, yes. Verity Hunt."

"I did not know her surname. Miss Temple, I think, mentioned her only as Verity."

"Verity Hunt is dead," said the Archdeacon. "She died quite a number of years ago. Did you know that?"

"Yes," said Miss Marple. "I knew it. Miss Temple and I were talking about her. Miss Temple told me something that I did not know. She said she had been engaged to be married to the son of a Mr. Rafiel. Mr. Rafiel is, or again I must say was, a friend of mine. Mr. Rafiel has paid the expenses of this tour out of his kindness. I think, though, that possibly he wanted—indeed, intended—me to meet Miss Temple on this tour. I think he thought she could give me certain information."

"Certain information about Verity?"

"Yes."

"That is why she was coming to me. She wanted to know certain facts."

"She wanted to know," said Miss Marple, "why Verity broke off her engagement to marry Mr. Rafiel's son."

"Verity," said Archdeacon Brabazon, "did not break off her engagement. I am certain of that. As certain as one can be of anything."

"Miss Temple did not know that, did she?"

"No. I think she was puzzled and unhappy about what happened and was coming to me to ask me why the marriage did not take place."

"And why did it not take place?" asked Miss Marple. "Please do not think that I am unduly curious. It's not idle curiosity that is driving me. I, too, am on—not a pilgrimage—but what I should call a mission. I, too, want to know why Michael Rafiel and Verity Hunt did not marry."

The Archdeacon studied her for a moment or two.

"You are involved in some way," he said. "I see that."

"I am involved," said Miss Marple, "by the dying wishes of Michael Rafiel's father. He asked me to do this for him."

"I have no reason not to tell you all I know," said the Archdeacon slowly. "You are asking me what Elizabeth Temple would have been asking me, you are asking me something I do not know myself. Those two young people, Miss Marple, intended to marry. They had made arrangements to marry. I was going to marry them. It was a marriage, I gather, which was being kept secret. I knew both these young people. I knew that dear child Verity from a long way back. I prepared her for confirmation, I used to hold services in Lent, for Easter, on other occasions, in Elizabeth Temple's school. A very fine school it was, too. A very fine woman she was. A wonderful teacher with a great sense of each girl's capabilities—for what she was best fitted for in studies. She urged careers on girls she thought would relish careers, and did not force girls that she felt were not really suited to them. She was a great woman and a very dear friend. Verity was one of the most beautiful children—girls, rather—that I have come across. Beautiful in mind, in heart, as well as in appearance. She had the great misfortune to lose her parents before she was truly adult. They were both killed in a charter plane going on a holiday to Italy. Verity went to live when she left school with a Miss Clotilde Bradbury-Scott, whom you know, probably, as living here. She had been a close friend of Verity's mother. There are three sisters, though the second one was married and living abroad, so there were only two of them living here. Clotilde, the eldest one, became extremely attached to Verity. She did everything possible to give her a happy life. She took her abroad once or twice, gave her art lessons in Italy and loved and cared for her dearly in every way. Verity, too, came to love her probably as much as she could have loved her own mother. She depended on Clotilde. Clotilde herself was an intellectual and well-educated woman. She did not urge a university career on Verity, but this I gather was really because Verity did not really yearn after one. She preferred to study art and music and such subjects. She lived at The Old Manor House and had, I think, a very happy life. She always seemed to be happy. Naturally, I did not see her after she came here, since Fillminster, where I was in the cathedral, is nearly sixty miles from here. I wrote to her at Christmas and other festivals, and she remembered me always with a Christmas card. But I saw nothing of her until the day when she suddenly turned up, a very beautiful and fully grown young woman by then, with an attractive young man whom I also happend to know slightly, Mr. Rafiel's son Michael. They came to me because they were in love with each other and wanted to get married."

"And you agreed to marry them?"

"Yes, I did. Perhaps, Miss Marple, you may think that I should not have done so. They had come to me in secret, it was obvious. Clotilde Bradbury-Scott, I should imagine, had tried to discourage the romance between them. She was well within her rights in doing so. Michael Rafiel, I will tell you frankly, was not the kind of husband you would want for any daughter or relation of yours. She was too young, really, to make up her mind, and Michael had been a source of trouble ever since his very young days. He had been had up before junior courts, he had had unsuitable friends, he had been drawn into various gangster activities, he'd sabotaged buildings and telephone boxes. He had been on intimate terms with various girls, had maintenance claims which he had had to meet. Yes, he was a bad lot with the girls as well as in other ways, yet he was extremely attractive and they fell for him and behaved in an extremely silly fashion. He had served two short jail sentences. Frankly, he had a criminal record. I was acquainted with his father, though I did not know him well, and I think that his father did all that he could—all that a man of his character could—to help his son. He came to his rescue, he got him jobs in which he might have succeeded. He paid up his debts, paid out damages. He did all this. I don't know—"

"But he could have done more, you think?"

"No," said the Archdeacon, "I've come to an age now when I know that one must accept one's fellow human beings as being the kind of people and having the kind of, shall we say in modern terms, genetic make-up which gives them the characters they have. I don't think that Mr. Rafiel had affection for his son, a great affection at any time. To say he was reasonably fond of him would be the most you could say. He gave him no love. Whether it would have been better for Michael if he had had love from his father, I do not know. Perhaps it would have made no difference. As it was, it was sad. The boy was not stupid. He had a certain amount of intellect and talent. He could have done well if he had wished to do well and had taken the trouble. But he was by nature—let us admit it frankly—a delinquent. He had certain qualities one appreciated. He had a sense of humor, he was in various ways generous and kindly. He would stand by a friend, help a friend out of a scrape. He treated his girl friends badly, got them into trouble, as the local saying is, and then more or less abandoned them and took with somebody else. So there I was faced with those two and—yes—I agreed to marry them. I told Verity, I told her quite frankly the kind of boy she wanted to marry. I found that he had not tried to deceive her in any way. He'd told her that he'd always been in trouble both with the police, and in every other way. He told her that he was going, when he married her, to turn over a new leaf. Everything would be changed. I warned her that that would not happen, he would not change. People do not change. He might mean to change. Verity, I think, knew that almost as well as I did. She admitted that she knew it. She said, 'I know what Mike is like. I know he'll probably always be like it, but I love him. I may be able to help him and I may not. But I'll take that risk.'

"And I will tell you this, Miss Marple. I know—none better, I have done a lot with young people, I have married a lot of young people and I have seen them come to grief, I have seen them unexpectedly turn out well—but I know this and recognize it. I know when a couple are really in love with each other. And by that I do not mean just sexually attracted. There is too much talk about sex, too much attention is paid to it. I do not mean that anything about sex is wrong. That is nonsense. But sex cannot take the place of love, it goes with love, but it cannot succeed by itself. To love means the words of the marriage service. For better, for worse, for richer, for poorer, in sickness and in health. That is what you take on if you love and wish to marry. Those two loved each other. To love and to cherish until death do us part. And that," said the Archdeacon, "is where my story ends. I cannot go on because I do not know what happened. I only know that I agreed to do as they asked, that I made the necessary arrangements; we settled a day, an hour, a time, a place. I think perhaps that I was to blame for agreeing to the secrecy."

"They didn't want anyone to know?" said Miss Marple.

"No. Verity did not want anyone to know, and I should say most certainly Mike did not want anyone to know. They were afraid of being stopped. To Verity, I think, besides love, there was also a feeling of escape. Natural, I think, owing to the circumstances of her life. She had lost her real guardians, her parents, she had entered on her new life after their death, at an age when a schoolgirl arrives at having a 'crush' on someone. An attractive mistress. Anything from the games mistress to the mathematics mistress, or a prefect or an older girl. A state that does not last for very long, is merely a natural part of life. Then from that you go on to the next stage when you realize that what you want in your life is what complements yourself—a relationship between a man and a woman. You start then to look about you for a mate—the mate you want in life. And if you are wise, you take your time, you have friends, but you are looking, as the old nurses used to say to children, for Mr. Right to come along. Clotilde Bradbury-Scott was exceptionally good to Verity, and Verity, I think, gave her what I should call hero-worship. She was a personality as a woman—handsome, accomplished, interesting. I think Verity adored her in an almost romantic way and I think Clotilde came to love Verity as though she were her own daughter. And so Verity grew to maturity in an atmosphere of adoration, lived an interesting life with interesting subjects to stimulate her intellect. It was a happy life, but I think little by little she was conscious—conscious without knowing she was conscious, shall we say—of a wish to escape. Escape from being loved. To escape, she didn't know into what or where. But she did know after she met Michael. She wanted to escape to a life where male and female come together to create the next stage of living in this world. But she knew that it was impossible to make Clotilde understand how she felt. She knew that Clotilde would be bitterly opposed to her taking her love for Michael seriously. And Clotilde, I fear, was right in her belief . . . I know that now. He was not a husband that Verity ought to have taken or had. The road that she started out on led not to life, not to increased living and happiness. It led to shock, pain, death. You see, Miss Marple, that I have a grave feeling of guilt. My motives were good, but I didn't know what I ought to have known. I knew Verity, but I didn't know Michael. I understood Verity's wish for secrecy because I knew what a strong personality Clotilde Bradbury-Scott had. She might have had a strong enough influence over Verity to persuade her to give up the marriage.

"You think then that that was what she did do? You think Clotilde told her enough about Michael to persuade her to give up the idea of marrying him?"

"No, I do not believe that. I still do not. Verity would have told me if so. She would have got word to me."

"What did actually happen on that day?"

"I haven't told you that yet. The day was fixed. The time, the hour and the place, and I waited. Waited for a bride and bridegroom who didn't come, who sent no word, no excuse, *nothing*. I didn't know why! I never have known why. It still seems to me unbelievable. Unbelievable, I mean, not that they did not come, that could be explicable easily enough, but that they sent no word. Some scrawled line of writing. And that is why I wondered and hoped that Elizabeth Temple, before she died, might have told you something. Given you some message perhaps for me. If she knew or had any idea that she was dying, she might have wanted to get a message to me."

"She wanted information *from* you," said Miss Marple. "That, I am sure, was the reason she was coming to you."

"Yes. Yes, that is probably true. It seemed to me, you see, that Verity would have said nothing to the people who could have stopped her. Clotilde and Anthea Bradbury-Scott, but because she had always been very devoted to Elizabeth Temple—and Elizabeth Temple had had great influence over her—it seems to me that she would have written and given her information of some kind."

"I think she did," said Miss Marple.

"Information, you think?"

"The information she gave to Elizabeth Temple," said Miss Marple, "was this. That she was going to marry Michael Rafiel. Miss Temple knew that. It was one of the things she said to me. She said: 'I knew a girl called Verity who was going to marry Michael Rafiel' and the only person who could have told her that was Verity herself. Verity must have written to her or sent some word to her. And then when I said: 'Why didn't she marry him?' she said, 'She died.'"

"Then we come to a full stop," said Archdeacon Brabazon. He sighed. "Elizabeth and I know no more than those two facts. Elizabeth, that Verity was going to marry Michael. And I that those two were going to marry, that they had arranged it and that they were coming on a settled day and time. And I waited for them, but there was no marriage. No bride, no bridegroom, no word."

"And you have no idea what happened?" said Miss Marple.

"I do not for one minute believe that Verity or Michael definitely parted, broke off."

"But *something* must have happened between them? Something that opened Verity's eyes perhaps to certain aspects of Michael's character and personality that she had not realized or known before."

"That is not a satisfying answer because still she would have let me know. She would not have left me waiting to join them together in holy matrimony. To put the most ridiculous side of it, she was a girl with beautiful manners, well-brought-up. She would have sent word. No. I'm afraid that only one thing could have happened."

"Death?" said Miss Marple. She was remembering that one word that Elizabeth Temple had said which had sounded like the deep tone of a bell.

"Yes." Archdeacon Brabazon sighed. "Death."

"Love," said Miss Marple thoughtfully.

"By that you mean—" he hesitated.

"It's what Miss Temple said to me. I said: 'What killed her?' and she said: 'Love,' and that love was the most frightening word in the world."

"I see," said the Archdeacon. "I see—or I think I see."

"What is your solution?"

"Split personality." He sighed. "Something that is not apparent to other people unless they are technically qualified to observe it. Jekyll and Hyde are real, you know. They were not Stevenson's invention as such. Michael Rafiel was a—must have been schizophrenic. He had a dual personality. I have no medical knowledge, no psychoanalytic experience. But there must have been in him the two parts of two identities. One, a well-meaning, almost lovable boy, a boy perhaps whose principal attraction was his wish for happiness. But there was also a second personality, someone who was forced by some mental deformation perhaps—something we as yet are not sure of—to kill—not an enemy, but the person he loved, and so he killed Verity. Not knowing perhaps *why* he had to or *what* it meant. There are very frightening things in this world of ours, mental quirks, mental disease or deformity of a brain. One of my parishioners was a very sad case in point. Two elderly women living together, pensioned. They had been friends in service together somewhere. They appeared to be a happy couple. And yet one day one of them killed the other. She sent for an old friend of hers, the vicar of her parish, and said: 'I have killed Louisa. It is very sad,' she said, 'but I saw the devil looking out of her eye and I knew I was being commanded to kill her.' Things like that make one sometimes despair of living. One says Why? and How? and yet one day knowledge will come. Doctors will find out or learn about some small deformity of a chromosome or gene—some gland that overworks or leaves off working."

"So you think that's what happened?" said Miss Marple.

"It did happen. The body was not found, I know, for some time afterwards. Verity just disappeared. She went away from home and was not seen again . . ."

"But it must have happened *then*—that very day—"

"But surely at the trial—"

"You mean after the body was found, when the police finally arrested Michael?"

"He had been one of the first, you know, to be asked to come and give assistance to the police. He had been seen about with the girl, she had been noticed in his car. They were sure all along that he was the man they wanted. He was their first suspect, and they never stopped suspecting him. The other young men who had known Verity were questioned, and one and all had alibis or lack of evidence. The police continued to suspect Michael, and finally the body was found. Strangled and the head and face disfigured with heavy blows. A mad frenzied attack. He wasn't sane when he struck those blows. Mr. Hyde, let us say, had taken over."

Miss Marple shivered.

The Archdeacon went on, his voice low and sad. "And yet, even now, sometimes, I hope and feel that it was some other young man who killed her—someone who was definitely mentally deranged, though no one had any idea of it. Some stranger, perhaps, whom she had met in the neighborhood. Someone whom she had met by chance, who had given her a lift in a car, and then—" He shook his head.

"I suppose that *could* have been true," said Miss Marple.

"Mike made a bad impression in court," said the Archdeacon. "Told foolish and senseless lies. Lied as to where his car had been. Got his friends to give him impossible alibis. He was frightened. He said nothing of his plan to marry. I believe his counsel was of the opinion that that would tell against him—that she might have been forcing him to marry her and that he didn't want to. It's so long ago now, I remember no details. But the evidence was dead against him. He was guilty—and he looked guilty.

"So you see, do you not, Miss Marple, that I'm a very sad and unhappy man? I made the wrong judgment, I encouraged a very sweet and lovely girl to go to her death because I did not know enough of human nature. I was ignorant of the danger she was running. I believed that if she had had any fear of him, any sudden knowledge of something evil in him, she would have broken her pledge to marry him and have come to me and told me of her fear, of her new knowledge of him. But nothing of that ever happened. Why did he kill her? Did he kill her because perhaps he knew she was going to have a child? Because by now, he had formed a tie with some other girl and did not want to be forced to marry Verity? I can't believe it. Or was it some entirely different reason? Because *she* had suddenly felt a fear of him, a knowledge of danger from him, and had broken off her association with him? Did that rouse his anger, his fury, and did that lead him to violence and to killing her? One does not know."

"You do not know," said Miss Marple, "but you do still know and believe one thing, don't you?"

"What do you mean exactly by 'believe'? Are you talking from the religious point of view?"

"Oh, no," said Miss Marple, "I didn't mean that. I mean, there seems to be in you, or so I feel it, a very strong belief that those two loved each other, that they meant to marry, but that *something* happened that prevented it—something that ended in her death, but you still really believe that they *were* coming to you to get married that day?"

"You are quite right, my dear. Yes, I cannot help still believing in two lovers who wished to get married, who were ready to take each other on for better, for worse, for richer, for poorer, in sickness and in health. She loved him and she would have taken him for better or for worse. As far as she had gone, she took him for worse. It brought about her death."

"You must go on believing as you do," said Miss Marple. "I think, you know, that *I* believe it, too."

"But then what?"

"I don't know yet," said Miss Marple. "I'm not sure, but I think Elizabeth Temple did know or was beginning to know what happened. A frightening word, she said. *Love.* I thought when she spoke that what she meant was that because of a love affair the girl had committed suicide. Because she found out something about Michael, or because something about Michael suddenly upset her and revolted her. But it couldn't have been suicide."

"No," said the Archdeacon, "that couldn't be so. The injuries were described very fully at the trial. You don't commit suicide by beating in your own head."

"Horrible!" said Miss Marple. "Horrible! And you couldn't do that to anyone you loved even if you had to kill 'for love,' could you? If he'd killed her, he couldn't have done it that way. Strangling—perhaps, but you wouldn't beat in the face and the head that you loved." She murmured, "Love, love—a frightening word."

CHAPTER NINETEEN
Good-Byes Are Said

THE COACH WAS drawn up in front of the Golden Boar on the following morning. Miss Marple had come down and was saying good-bye to various friends. She found Mrs. Riseley-Porter in a state of high indignation.

"Really, girls nowadays," she said. "No vigor. No stamina."

Miss Marple looked at her inquiringly.

"Joanna, I mean. My niece."

"Oh, dear. Is she not well?"

"Well, she says not. I can't see anything much the matter with her. She says she's got a sore throat, she feels she might have a temperature coming on. All nonsense, I think."

"Oh, I'm very sorry," said Miss Marple. "Is there anything I can do? Look after her?"

"I should leave her alone, if I were you," said Mrs. Riseley-Porter. "If you ask me, it's all an excuse."

Miss Marple looked inquiringly at her once more.

"Girls are so silly. Always falling in love."

"Emlyn Price?" said Miss Marple.

"Oh, so you've noticed it, too. Yes, they're really getting to a state of spooning about together. I don't much care for him anyway. One of these long-haired students, you know. Always going on demos or something like that. Why can't they say demonstration properly? I hate abbreviations. And how am *I* going to get along? Nobody to look after me, collect my luggage, take it in, take it out. Really. I'm paying for this complete trip and everything."

"I thought she seemed so attentive to you," said Miss Marple.

"Well, not the last day or two. Girls don't understand that people have to have a little assistance when they get to middle age. They seem to have some absurd idea—she and the Price boy—of going to visit some mountain or some landmark. About a seven- or eight-mile walk there and back."

"But surely if she has a sore throat and a temperature—?"

"You'll see, as soon as the coach is gone, the sore throat will get better and the temperature will go down," said Mrs. Riseley-Porter. "Oh, dear, we've got to get on board now. Oh, good-bye, Miss Marple. It's nice to have met you. I'm sorry you're not coming with us."

"I'm very sorry myself," said Miss Marple, "but really, you know, I'm not so young and vigorous as you are, Mrs. Riseley-Porter, and I really feel after all the—well, shock and everything else the last few days, I really must have a complete twenty-four hours' rest."

"Well, hope to see you somewhere in the future."

They shook hands. Mrs. Riseley-Porter climbed into the coach.

A voice behind Miss Marple's shoulder said:

"Bon voyage and good riddance."

She turned to see Emlyn Price. He was grinning.

"Was that addressed to Mrs. Riseley-Porter?"

"Yes. Who else?"

"I'm sorry to hear that Joanna is under the weather this morning."

Emlyn Price grinned at Miss Marple again.

"She'll be all right," he said, "as soon as that coach is gone."

"Oh, really!" said Miss Marple. "Do you mean—?"

"Yes, I do mean," said Emlyn Price. "Joanna's had enough of that aunt of hers bossing her around all the time."

"Then you are not going in the coach either?"

"No. I'm staying on here for a couple of days. I'm going to get around a bit and do a few excursions. Don't look so disapproving, Miss Marple. You're not really as disapproving as all that, are you?"

"Well," said Miss Marple, "I have known such things happen in my own youth. The excuses may have been different, and I think we had less chance of getting away with things than you do now."

Colonel and Mrs. Walker came up and shook Miss Marple warmly by the hand.

"So nice to have known you and had all those delightful horticultural talks," said the Colonel. "I believe the day after tomorrow we're going to have a real treat, if nothing else happens. Really, it's too sad, this very unfortunate accident. I must say I think myself it *is* an accident. I really think the coroner was going beyond everything in his feelings about this."

"It seems very odd," said Miss Marple, "that nobody has come forward, if they were up on top there, pushing about rocks and boulders and things, that they haven't come forward to say so."

"Think they'll be blamed, of course," said Colonel Walker. "They're going to keep jolly quiet, that's what they're going to do. Well, good-bye. I'll send you a cutting of that Magnolia highdownensis and one of the Mahonia japonica, too. Though I'm not quite sure if it would do as well where you live."

They in turn got into the coach. Miss Marple turned away. She turned to see Professor Wanstead waving to the departing coach. Mrs. Sandbourne came out, said good-bye to Miss Marple and got in the coach and Miss Marple took Professor Wanstead by the arm.

"I want you," she said. "Can we go somewhere where we can talk?"

"Yes. What about the place where we sat the other day?"

"Round here there's a very nice verandah place, I think."

They walked round the corner of the hotel. There was some gay horn blowing, and the coach departed.

"I wish, in a way, you know," said Professor Wanstead, "that you weren't staying behind. I'd rather have seen you safely on your way in the coach." He looked at her sharply. "Why are you staying here? Nervous exhaustion or something else?"

"Something else," said Miss Marple. "I'm not particularly exhausted, though it makes a perfectly natural excuse for somebody of my age."

"I feel, really, I ought to stay here and keep an eye on you."

"No," said Miss Marple, "there's no need to do that. There are other things you ought to be doing."

"What things?" He looked at her. "Have you got ideas or knowledge?"

"I think I have knowledge, but I'll have to verify it. There are certain things that I can't do myself. I think you will help to do them because you're in touch with what I refer to as the authorities."

"Meaning Scotland Yard, chief constables and the governors of Her Majesty's Prisons?"

"Yes. One or other or all of them. You might have the Home Secretary in your pocket, too."

"You certainly do have ideas! Well, what do you want me to do?"

"First of all I want to give you this address."

She took out a notebook and tore out one page and handed it to him.

"What's this? Oh, yes, well-known charity, isn't it?"

"One of the better ones, I believe. They do a lot of good. You send them clothes," said Miss Marple, "children's clothes and women's clothes. Coats. Pullovers, all those sort of things."

"Well, do you want me to contribute to this?"

"No, it's an appeal for charity, it's a bit of what belongs to what we're doing—what you and I are doing."

"In what way?"

"I want you to make inquiries there about a parcel which was sent from here two days ago, posted from this post office."

"Who posted it? Did you?"

"No," said Miss Marple. "No. But I assumed responsibility for it."

"What does that mean?"

"It means," said Miss Marple, smiling slightly, "that I went into the post office here and I explained rather incoherently and—well, like the old girl I am—that I had very foolishly asked someone to take a parcel for me and post it, and I had put the wrong address on it. I was very upset by this. The postmistress very kindly said she remembered the parcel, but the address on it was not the one I was mentioning. It was this one, the one I have just given to you. I explained that I had been very foolish and written the wrong address on it, confusing it with another one I sometimes send things to. She told me it was too late to do anything about it now because the parcel, naturally, had gone off. I said it was quite all right, that I would send a letter to the particular charity to which the parcel had been sent and explain that it had been addressed to them by mistake. Would they very kindly forward it on to the charity that I had meant to receive it."

"It seems rather a roundabout way."

"Well," said Miss Marple, "one has to say something. I'm not going to do that at all. You are going to deal with the matter. We've got to know what's inside that parcel! I have no doubt you can get means."

"Will there be anything inside the parcel to say who actually sent it?"

"I rather think not. It may have a slip of paper saying 'from friends' or it may have a fictitious name and address—something like Mrs. Pippin, Fourteen Westbourne Grove, and if anyone made inquiries there, there'd be no person of such a name living there."

"Oh. Any other alternatives?"

"It might possibly, most unlikely but possible, have a slip saying 'From Miss Anthea Bradbury-Scott'—"

"Did she—?"

"She took it to the post," said Miss Marple.

"And you had asked her to take it there?"

"Oh, no," said Miss Marple. "I hadn't asked anyone to post anything. The first I saw of the parcel was when Anthea passed the garden of the Golden Boar where you and I were sitting talking, carrying it."

"But you went to the post office and represented that the parcel was yours."

"Yes," said Miss Marple, "which was quite untrue. But post offices are careful. And, you see, I wanted to find out where it had been sent."

"You wanted to find out if such a parcel had been sent, and if it had been sent by one of the Bradbury-Scotts—or especially Miss Anthea?"

"I knew it would be Anthea," said Miss Marple, "because we'd seen her."

"Well?" He took the paper from her hand. "Yes, I can set this in motion. You think this parcel will be interesting?"

"I think the contents of it might be quite important."

"You like keeping your secrets, don't you?" said Professor Wanstead.

"Not exactly secrets," said Miss Marple; "they are only probabilities that I am exploring. One does not like to make definite assertions unless one has a little more definite knowledge."

"Anything else?"

"I think—I think that whoever's in charge of these things ought to be warned that there might be a second body to be found."

"Do you mean a second body connected with the particular crime that we have been considering? A crime that took place ten years ago?"

"Yes," said Miss Marple. "I'm quite sure of it, as a matter of fact."

"Another body. Whose body?"

"Well," said Miss Marple, "it's only my idea so far."

"Any idea where this body is?"

"Oh, yes!" said Miss Marple. "I'm quite sure I know where it is, but I have to have a little more time before I can tell you that."

"What kind of a body? Man's? Woman's? Child's? Girl's?"

"There's another girl who is missing," said Miss Marple. "A girl called Nora Broad. She disappeared from here and she's never been heard any more of. I think her body might be in a particular place."

Professor Wanstead looked at her.

"You know, the more you say, the less I like leaving you here," he said. "Having all these ideas—and possibly doing something foolish—either—" He stopped.

"Either it's all nonsense—" said Miss Marple.

"No, no, I didn't mean that. But either you know too much—which might be dangerous . . . I think I am going to stay here to keep an eye on you."

"No, you're not," said Miss Marple. "You've got to go to London and set certain things moving."

"You spoke as though you knew a good deal, Miss Marple."

"I think I do know a good deal now. But I have got to be sure."

"Yes, but if you make sure, that may be the last thing you do make sure of! We don't want a third body—yours."

"Oh, I'm not expecting anything like that," said Miss Marple.

"There might be danger, you know, if any of your ideas are right. Have you suspicions of any one particular person?"

"I think I have certain knowledge as to one person. I have got to find out—I have got to stay here. You asked me once if I felt an atmosphere of evil. Well, that atmosphere is here, all right—an atmosphere of evil, of danger, if you like—of great unhappiness, of fear . . . I've got to do something about that. The best I can do. But an old woman like me can't do very much."

Professor Wanstead counted under his breath. "One—two—three—four"

"What are you counting?" asked Miss Marple.

"The people who left in the coach. Presumably you're not interested in them, since you've let them go off and you're staying here."

"Why should I be interested in them?"

"Because you said Mr. Rafiel had sent you in the coach for a particular reason and sent you on this tour for a particular reason and sent you to The Old Manor House for a particular reason. Very well, then. The death of Elizabeth Temple ties up with someone in the coach. Your remaining here ties up with The Old Manor House."

"You're not quite right," said Miss Marple. "There are connections between the two. I want someone to tell me things."

"Do you think you can make anyone tell you things?"

"I think I might. You'll miss your train if you don't go soon."

"Take care of yourself," said Professor Wanstead.

"I mean to take care of myself."

The door into the lounge opened and two people came out—Miss Cooke and Miss Barrow.

"Hullo," said Professor Wanstead. "I thought you'd gone off with the coach."

"Well, we changed our minds at the last moment," said Miss Cooke cheerfully. "You know we've just discovered that there are some very agreeable walks near here, and there are one or two places I'm very anxious to see. A church with a very unusual Saxon font. Only four or five miles away and quite easily reached by the local bus, I think. You see, it's not only houses and gardens. I'm very interested in church architecture."

"So am I," said Miss Barrow. "There's also Finley Park, which is a very fine piece of horticultural planting not far from here. We really thought that it would be much pleasanter to stay here for a day or two."

"You're staying here at the Golden Boar?"

"Yes. We were fortunate enough to be able to get a very nice double room—really a better one than the one we have had for the last two days."

"You will miss your train," said Miss Marple again.

"I wish," said Professor Wanstead, "that you—"

"I shall be quite all right," said Miss Marple urgently. "Such a kind man," she said as he disappeared round the side of the house, "who really takes so much care of me—I might be a great-aunt of his or something like that."

"It's all been a great shock, hasn't it?" said Miss Cooke. "Perhaps you may like to come with us when we go to visit St. Martins in the Grove."

"You've very kind," said Miss Marple, "but I don't think today I feel quite strong enough for expeditions. Perhaps tomorrow if there is anything interesting to see."

"Well, we must leave you, then."

Miss Marple smiled at them both and went into the hotel.

CHAPTER TWENTY
Miss Marple Has Ideas

HAVING HAD LUNCH in the dining room, Miss Marple went out on the terrace to drink her coffee. She was just sipping her second cup when a tall, thin figure came striding up the steps and approached her, speaking rather breathlessly. She saw that it was Anthea Bradbury-Scott.

"Oh, Miss Marple, we've only just heard, you know, that you didn't go with the coach after all. We thought you were going on with the tour. We had no idea you were staying on here. Both Clotilde and Lavinia sent me here to say we do so hope you will come back to The Old Manor House and stay with us. I'm sure it will be nicer for you to be there. There are so many people coming and going here always, especially over a weekend and things like that. So we'd be very, very glad—we really would—if you would come back to us."

"Oh, that's very kind of you," said Miss Marple. "Really very kind, but I'm sure—I mean, you know it was just a two-day visit. I meant originally to go off with the coach. I mean, after the two days. If it hadn't been for this very, very tragic accident but—well, I really felt I couldn't go on any longer. I thought I must have at least, well, at least one night's rest."

"But I mean it would be so much better if you came to us. We'd try and make you comfortable."

"Oh, there's no question of that," said Miss Marple. "I was extremely comfortable staying with you. Oh, yes, I did enjoy it very much. Such a beautiful house. And all your things are so nice. You know, your china and glass and furniture. It's such a pleasure to be in a home and not a hotel."

"Then you must come with me now. Yes, you really must. I could go and pack your things for you."

"Oh—well, that's very kind of you. I can do that myself."

"Well, shall I come and help you?"

"That would be very kind," said Miss Marple.

They repaired to her bedroom where Anthea, in a somewhat slapdash manner, packed Miss Marple's belongings together. Miss Marple, who had her own ways of folding things, had to bite her lip to keep an air of complacency on her face. Really, she thought, she can't fold *anything* properly.

Anthea got hold of a porter from the hotel and he carried the suitcase round the corner and down the street to The Old Manor House. Miss Marple tipped him adequately and, still uttering fussy little speeches of thanks and pleasure, rejoined the sisters.

"The three sisters!" she was thinking. "Here we are again." She sat down in the drawing room and closed her eyes for a minute, breathing rather fast. She appeared to be somewhat out of breath. It was only natural, she felt, at her age, and after Anthea and the hotel porter had set a fast pace. But really she was trying to acquire through her closed eyes what the feeling was she had on coming into this house again. Was something in it sinister? No, not so much sinister as unhappy. Deep unhappiness. So much so it was almost frightening.

She opened her eyes again and looked at the two other occupants of the room. Mrs. Glynne had just come in from the kitchen, bearing an afternoon tea tray. She looked as she had looked all along—comfortable, no particular emotions or feelings. Perhaps almost too devoid of them, Miss Marple thought. Had she accustomed herself through perhaps a life of some stress and difficulty to show nothing to the outer world, to keep a reserve and let no one know what her inner feelings were?

She looked from her to Clotilde. She had a Clytemnestra look, as she had thought before. She had certainly not murdered her husband, for she had never had a husband to murder, and it seemed unlikely that she had murdered the girl to whom she was said to have been extremely attached. That, Miss Marple was quite sure, was true. She had seen before how the tears had welled from Clotilde's eyes when the death of Verity had been mentioned.

And what about Anthea? Anthea had taken that cardboard box to the post office. Anthea had come to fetch her. Anthea—she was very doubtful about Anthea. Scatterbrained? Too scatterbrained for her age. Eyes that wandered and came back to you. Eyes that seemed to see things that other people might not see, over your shoulder. She's frightened, thought Miss Marple. Frightened of something. What was she frightened of? Was she perhaps a mental case of some kind? Frightened perhaps of going back to some institution or establishment where she might have spent part of her life? Frightened of those two sisters of hers feeling that it was unwise for her to remain at liberty? Were they uncertain, those two, what their sister Anthea might do or say?

There was *some* atmosphere here. She wondered, as she sipped the last of her tea, what Miss Cooke and Miss Barrow were doing. Had they gone to visit that church or was that all talk, meaningless talk? It was odd. Odd the way they had come and looked at her at St. Mary Mead so as to know her again on the coach, but not to acknowledge that they had ever seen or met her before.

There were quite a lot of difficult things going on. Presently Mrs. Glynne removed the tea tray, Anthea went out into the garden and Miss Marple was left alone with Clotilde.

"I think," said Miss Marple, "that you know an Archdeacon Brabazon, do you not?"

"Oh, yes," said Clotilde, "he was in church yesterday at the service. Do you know him?"

"Oh, no," said Miss Marple, "but he did come to the Golden Boar and he came and spoke to me there. I gather he had been to the hospital and was inquiring about poor Miss Temple's death. He wondered if Miss Temple had sent any message to him. I gather she was thinking of paying him a visit. But of course I told him that although I did go there in case I could do anything, there was nothing that could be done except sit by poor Miss Temple's bed. She was unconscious, you know. I could have done nothing to help her."

"She didn't say—say anything—any explanation of what had happened?" asked Clotilde.

She asked without much interest. Miss Marple wondered if she felt more interest than she expressed, but on the whole she thought not. She thought Clotilde was busy with thoughts of something quite different.

"Do you think it was an accident?" Miss Marple asked, "or do you think there is something in that story that Mrs. Riseley-Porter's niece told about seeing someone pushing a boulder?"

"Well, I suppose if those two said so, they must have seen it."

"Yes. They both said so, didn't they," said Miss Marple, "though not quite in the same terms. But perhaps that's quite natural."

Clotilde looked at her curiously.

"You seem to be intrigued by that."

"Well, it seems so very unlikely," said Miss Marple, "an unlikely story, unless—"

"Unless what?"

"Well, I just wondered," said Miss Marple.

Mrs. Glynne came into the room again.

"You just wondered what?" she asked.

"We're talking about the accident, or the nonaccident," said Clotilde.

"But who—?"

"It seems a very odd story that they told," said Miss Marple again.

"There's something about this place," said Clotilde suddenly. "Something about this atmosphere. We never got over it here. Never. Never since—since Verity died. It's years, but it doesn't go away. A shadow's here." She looked at Miss Marple. "Don't you think so, too? Don't you feel a shadow here?"

"Well, I'm a stranger," said Miss Marple. "It's different for you and your sisters who've lived here and who knew the dead girl. She was, I gather, as Archdeacon Barbazon was saying—a very charming and beautiful girl."

"She was a lovely girl. A dear child, too," said Clotilde.

"I wish I'd known her better," said Mrs. Glynne. "Of course I was living abroad at that time. My husband and I came home on leave once, but we were mostly in London. We didn't come down here often."

Anthea came in from the garden. She was carrying in her hand a great bunch of lilies.

"Funeral flowers," she said. "Thhat's what we ought to have here today, isn't it? I'll put them in a great jar. Funeral flowers," and she laughed suddenly—a queer, hysterical little giggle.

"Anthea," said Clotilde, "don't—don't do that. It's not—it's not right."

"I'll go and put them in water," said Anthea cheerfully. She went out of the room.

"Really," said Mrs. Glynne, "Anthea! I do think she's—"

"She's getting worse," said Clotilde.

Miss Marple adopted an attitude of not listening or hearing. She picked up a small enamel box and looked at it with admiring eyes.

"She'll probably break a vase now," said Lavinia.

She went out of the room. Miss Marple said:

"You are worried about your sister, about Anthea?"

"Well, yes, she's always been rather unbalanced. She's the youngest and she was rather delicate as a girl. But lately, I think, she's got definitely worse. She hasn't got any idea, I think, of the gravity of things. She has these silly fits of hysteria—hysterical laughter at things one ought to be serious about. We don't want to—well, to send her anywhere or—you know. She ought to have treatment, I think, but I don't think she would like to go away from home. This is her home, after all. Though sometimes it's—it's very difficult."

"All life is difficult sometimes," said Miss Marple.

"Lavinia talks of going away," said Clotilde. "She talks of going to live abroad again. At Taormina, I think. She was there with her husband a lot and they were very happy. She's been at home with us now for many years, but she seems to have this longing to get away and to travel. Sometimes I think—sometimes I think she doesn't like being in the same house as Anthea."

"Oh, dear," said Miss Marple. "Yes, I have heard of cases like that where these difficulties do arise."

"She's afraid of Anthea," said Clotilde. "Definitely afraid of her. And really, I keep telling her there's nothing to be afraid of. Anthea's just rather silly at times. You know, has queer ideas and says queer things. But I don't think there's any danger of her—well, I mean of—oh, I don't know what I mean. Doing anything dangerous or strange or queer."

"There's never been any trouble of that kind?" inquired Miss Marple.

"Oh, no. There's never been anything. She gets nervous fits of temper sometimes and she takes rather sudden dislikes to people. She's very jealous, you know, over things. Very jealous of a lot of—well, fuss being made over different people. I don't know. Sometimes I think we'd better sell this house and leave it altogether."

It is sad for you, isn't it?" said Miss Marple. "I think I can understand that it must be very sad for you living here with the memory of the past."

"You understand that, do you? Yes, I can see that you do. One cannot help it. One's mind goes back to that dear, lovable child. She was like a daughter to me. She was the daughter, anyway, of one of my best friends. She was very intelligent, too. She was a clever girl. She was a good artist. She was doing very well with her art training and designing. She was taking up a good deal of designing. I was very proud of her. And then—this wretched attachment, this terrible mentally afflicted boy."

"You mean Mr. Rafiel's son, Michael Rafiel?"

"Yes. If only he'd never come here. It just happened that he was staying in this part of the world and his father suggested he might look us up and he came and had a meal with us. He could be very charming, you know. But he always had been a sad delinquent, a bad record. He'd been in prison twice, and had a very bad history with girls. But I never thought that Verity . . . just a case of infatuation. I suppose it happens to girls of that age. She was infatuated with him. Thought of nothing else, wouldn't hear a word against him. Insisted that everything that had happened to him had not been his fault. You know the things girls say. 'Everyone is against him,' that's what they always say. Everyone's against him. Nobody made allowances for him. Oh, one gets tired of hearing these things said. Can't one put a little sense into the girls?"

"They have not usually very much sense, I agree," said Miss Marple.

"She wouldn't listen. I—I tried to keep him away from the house. I told him he was not to come here any more. That, of course, was stupid. I realized that afterwards. It only meant that she went and met him outside the house. I don't know where. They had various meeting places. He used to call for her in his car at an agreed spot and bring her home late at night. Once or twice he didn't bring her home until the next day. I tried to tell them it must stop, that it must all cease, but they wouldn't listen. Verity wouldn't listen. I didn't expect him to, of course."

"She intended to marry him?" asked Miss Marple.

"Well, I don't think it ever got as far as that. I don't think he ever wanted to marry her or thought of such a thing."

"I am very sorry for you," said Miss Marple. "You must have suffered a lot."

"Yes. The worst was having to go and identify the body. That was some time after—after she'd disappeared from here. We thought, of course, that she'd run away with him and we thought that we'd get news of them some time. I knew the police seemed to be taking it rather seriously. They asked Michael to go to the police station and help them with inquiries, and his account of himself didn't seem to agree with what local people were saying.

"Then they found her. A long way from here. About thirty miles away. In a kind of ditch, a hedgy spot down an unfrequented lane where anyone hardly ever went. Yes, I had to go and view the body in the mortuary. A terrible sight. The cruelty, the force that had been used. What did he want to do that to her for? Wasn't it enough that he strangled her? He strangled her with her own scarf. I can't—I can't talk about it any more. I can't bear it, I can't bear it."

Tears rained suddenly down her face.

"I'm sorry for you," said Miss Marple. "I'm very, very sorry."

"I believe you are." Clotilde looked at her suddenly. "And even you don't know the worst of it."

"In what way?"

"I don't know—I don't know about Anthea."

"What do you mean about Anthea?"

"She was so queer at that time. She was—she was very jealous. She suddenly seemed to turn against Verity—to look at her as though she hated her. Sometimes I thought—I thought perhaps—oh, no, it's an awful thing to think, you can't think that about your own sister—she did once attack someone. You know, she used to get these storms of rage. I wondered if it *could* have been—oh, I mustn't say such things. There's no question of any such thing. Please forget what I've said. There's nothing in it, nothing at all. But—but—well, she's not quite normal. I've got to face that. When she was quite young, queer things happened once or twice—with animals. We had a parrot—a parrot that said things, silly things that parrots do say, and she wrung its neck and I've never felt the same since. I've never felt that I could trust her. I've never felt *sure*. I've never felt—oh, goodness, I'm getting hysterical, too."

"Come, come," said Miss Marple, "don't think of these things."

"No. It's bad enough to know—to know that Verity died—died in that horrible way. At any rate, other girls are safe from that boy. Life sentence he got. He's still in prison. They won't let him out to do anything to anyone else. Though why they couldn't bring it in as some mental trouble—diminished responsibility—one of these things they use nowadays. He ought to have gone to Broadmoor. I'm sure he wasn't responsible for anything that he did."

She got up and went out of the room. Mrs. Glynne had come back and passed her sister in the doorway.

"You mustn't pay any attention to Clotilde," she said. "She's never quite recovered from that ghastly business years ago. She loved Verity very much."

"She seems to be worried about your other sister."

"About Anthea? Anthea's all right. She's—er—well, she's flighty, you know. She's a bit—hysterical. Apt to get worked up about things, and she has queer fancies, imagination sometimes. But I don't think there's any need for Clotilde to worry so much. Dear me, who's that passing the window?"

Two apologetic figures suddenly showed themselves in the French window.

"Oh, do excuse us," said Miss Barrow. "We were just walking round the house to see if we could find Miss Marple. We had heard she'd come here with you and I wonder—oh, there you are, my dear Miss Marple. I wanted to tell you that we didn't get to that church after all this afternoon. Apparently it's closed for cleaning, so I think we shall have to give up any other expedition today and go on one tomorrow. I do hope you don't mind us coming in this way. I did ring at the front doorbell but it didn't seem to be ringing."

"I'm afraid it doesn't sometimes," said Mrs. Glynne. "You know, it's rather temperamental. Sometimes it rings and sometimes it doesn't. But do sit down and talk to us a little. I'd no idea that you hadn't gone with the coach."

"No, we thought we would do a little sightseeing round here, as we had got so far, and going with the coach would really be rather—well, rather painful after what has happened just a day or two ago."

"You must have some sherry," said Mrs. Glynne.

She went out of the room and presently returned. Anthea was with her, quite calm now, bringing glasses and a decanter of sherry, and they sat down together.

"I can't help wanting to know," said Mrs. Glynne, "what really is going to happen in this business. I mean of poor Miss Temple. It seems so very impossible to know what the police think. They still seem to be in charge, and I mean the inquest being adjourned, so obviously they are not satisfied. I don't know if there's anything in the nature of the wound."

"I shouldn't think so," said Miss Barrow. "I mean a blow on the head, bad concussion—well, I mean that came from the boulder. The only point is, Miss Marple, if the boulder rolled itself down or somebody rolled it."

"Oh," said Miss Cooke, "but surely you can't think that—who on earth would want to roll a boulder down, do that sort of thing? I suppose there are always hooligans about. You know, some young foreigners or students. I really wonder, you know, whether—well—"

"You mean," said Miss Marple, "you wondered if that someone was one of our fellow travelers."

"Well, I—I didn't say that," said Miss Cooke.

"But surely," said Miss Marple, "we can't help—well, thinking about that sort of thing. I mean, there must be some explanation. If the police seem sure it wasn't an accident, well, then it must have been done by somebody and—well, Miss Temple was a stranger to his place here. It doesn't seem as if anyone could have done it—anyone local, I mean. So it really comes back to—well, to all of us who were in the coach, doesn't it?"

She gave a faint rather whinnying old lady's laugh.

"Oh, surely!"

"No, I suppose I ought not to say such things. But you know, really, crimes are very interesting. Sometimes the most extraordinary things have happened."

"Have you any definite feeling yourself, Miss Marple? I should be interested to hear," said Clotilde.

"Well, one does think of possibilities."

"Mr. Caspar," said Miss Cooke. "You know, I didn't like the look of that man from the first. He looked to me—well, I thought he might have something to do with espionage or something. You know, perhaps come to this country to look for atomic secrets or something."

"I don't think we've got any atomic secrets round here," said Mrs. Glynne.

"Of course we haven't," said Anthea. "Perhaps it was someone who was following her. Perhaps it was someone who was tracking her because she was a criminal of some kind."

"Nonsense," said Clotilde. "She was the headmistress, retired, of a very well-known school, she was a very fine scholar. Why should anyone be trying to track *her* down?"

"Oh, I don't know. She might have gone peculiar or something."

"I'm sure," said Mrs. Glynne, "that Miss Marple has some ideas."

"Well, I have some ideas," said Miss Marple. "It seems to me that—well, the only people that could be . . . Oh, dear, this is so difficult to say. But I mean there are two people who just spring into one's mind as possibilities logically. I don't think that it's really so at all, because I'm sure they're both very nice people, but there's nobody else really logically who could be suspected, should I say."

"Who do you mean? This is very interesting."

"Well, I don't think I ought to say such things. It's only a—a sort of wild conjecture."

"Who do you think might have rolled the boulder down? Who do you think could have been the person that Joanna and Emlyn Price saw?"

"Well, what I did think was that—that perhaps they hadn't seen anybody."

"I don't quite understand," said Anthea. "They hadn't seen anybody?"

"Well, perhaps they might have made it all up."

"What—about seeing someone?"

"Well, it's possible, isn't it?"

"Do you mean as a sort of joke or a sort of unkind idea? What *do* you mean?"

"Well, I suppose—one does hear of young people doing very extraordinary things nowadays," said Miss Marple. "You know, putting things in horses' eyes, smashing legation windows and attacking people. Throwing stones at people, and it's usually being done by somebody young, isn't it? And they were the only young people weren't they?"

"You mean Emlyn Price and Joanna might have rolled over that boulder?"

"Well, they're the only sort of obvious people, aren't they?" said Miss Marple.

"Fancy!" said Clotilde. "Oh, I should never have thought of that. But I see—yes, I just see that there could be something in what you say. Of course, I don't know what those two were like. I haven't been traveling with them."

"Oh, they were very nice," said Miss Marple. "Joanna seemed to me a particularly—you know, capable girl."

"Capable of doing anything?" asked Anthea.

"Anthea," said Clotilde, "do be quiet."

"Yes. Quite capable," said Miss Marple. "After all, if you're going to do what may result in murder, you'd have to be rather capable so as to manage not to be seen or anything."

"They must have been in it together, though," suggested Miss Barrow.

"Oh, yes," said Miss Marple. "They were in it together and they told roughly the same story. They are the—well, they are the obvious suspects, that's all I can say. They were out of sight of the others. All the other people were on the lower path. They could have gone up to the top of the hill, they could have rocked the boulder. Perhaps they didn't mean to kill Miss Temple specially. They may have meant it just as a—well, just as a piece of anarchy or smashing something or someone—anyone, in fact. They rolled it over. And then, of course, they told the story of seeing someone there. Some rather peculiar costume or other which also sounds very unlikely and—well, I oughtn't to say these things, but I *have* been thinking about it."

"It seems to me a very interesting thought," said Mrs. Glynne. "What do you think, Clotilde?"

"I think it's a possibility. I shouldn't have thought of it myself."

"Well," said Miss Cooke, rising to her feet, "we must be going back to the Golden Boar now. Are you coming with us, Miss Marple?"

"Oh, no," said Miss Marple. "I suppose you don't know. I've forgotten to tell you. Miss Bradbury-Scott very kindly asked me to come back and stay another night—or two nights—here."

"Oh, I see. Well, I'm sure that'll be very nice for you. Much more comfortable. They seem rather a noisy lot that have arrived at the Golden Boar this evening."

"Won't you come round and have some coffee with us after dinner?" suggested Clotilde. "It's quite a warm evening. We can't offer you dinner because I'm afraid we haven't got enough in the house, but if you'll come in and have some coffee with us . . ."

"That would be very nice," said Miss Cooke. "Yes, we will certainly avail ourselves of your hospitality."

CHAPTER TWENTY-ONE
The Clock Strikes Three

I

MISS COOKE and Miss Barrow arrived very promptly at eight forty-five. One wore beige lace and the other one a shade of olive green. During dinner, Anthea had asked Miss Marple about these two ladies.

"It seems very funny of them," she said, "to want to stay behind."

"Oh, I don't think so," said Miss Marple. "I think it is really quite natural. They have a rather exact plan, I imagine."

"What do you mean by a plan?" asked Mrs. Glynne.

"Well, I should think they are always prepared for various eventualities and had a plan for dealing with them."

"Do you mean," said Anthea with some interest, "do you mean that they had a plan for dealing with murder?"

"I wish," said Mrs. Glynne, "that you wouldn't talk of poor Miss Temple's death as murder."

"But of course it's murder," said Anthea. "All I wonder is who wanted to murder her? I should think probably some pupil of hers at the school who always hated her and had it in for her."

"Do you think hate can last as long as that?" asked Miss Marple.

"Oh, I should think so. I should think you could hate anyone for years."

"No," said Miss Marple, "I think hate would die out. You could try and keep it up artificially, but I think you would fail. It's not as strong a force as love," she added.

"Don't you think that Miss Cooke or Miss Barrow or both of them might have done the murder?"

"Why should they?" said Mrs. Glynne. "Really, Anthea! They seemed very nice women to me."

"I think there's something rather mysterious about them," said Anthea. "Don't you, Clotilde?"

"I think perhaps you're right," said Clotilde. "They seemed to me to be slightly artificial, if you know what I mean."

"*I* think there's something very sinister about them," said Anthea.

"You've got such an imagination always," said Mrs. Glynne. "Anyway, they were walking along the bottom path, weren't they? You saw them there, didn't you?" she said to Miss Marple.

"I can't say that I noticed them particularly," said Miss Marple. "In fact, I had no opportunity of doing so."

"You mean—?"

"She wasn't there," said Clotilde. "She was here in our garden."

"Oh, of course. I forgot."

"A very nice, peaceful day it was," said Miss Marple. "I enjoyed it very much. Tomorrow morning I would like to go out and look again at that mass of white flowers coming into blossom at the end of the garden near that raised-up mound. It was just beginning to come out the other day. It must be a mass of bloom now. I shall always remember that as part of my visit here, you know."

"I hate it," said Anthea. "I want it taken away. I want to build up a greenhouse again there. Surely if we save enough money we can do that, Clotilde?"

"We'll leave that alone," said Clotilde. "I don't want that touched. What use is a greenhouse to us now? It would be years before grapes would bear fruit again."

"Come," said Mrs. Glynne, "we can't go on arguing over that. Let us go into the drawing room. Our guests will be coming shortly for coffee."

It was then that the guests had arrived. Clotilde brought in the tray of coffee. She poured out the cups and distributed them. She placed one before each guest and then brought one to Miss Marple. Miss Cooked leaned forward.

"Oh, do forgive me, Miss Marple, but really, do you know, I shouldn't drink that if I were you. Coffee, I mean, at this time of night. You won't sleep properly."

"Oh, do you think so?" said Miss Marple. "I am quite used to coffee in the evening."

"Yes, but this is very strong, good coffee. I should advise you not to drink it."

Miss Marple looked at Miss Cooke. Miss Cooke's face was very earnest. Her fair, unnatural-looking hair flopped over one eye. The other eye blinked slightly.

"I see what you mean," said Miss Marple. "Perhaps you are right. You know something, I gather, about diet."

"Oh, yes, I make quite a study of it. I had some training in nursing, you know, and one thing and another."

"Indeed." Miss Marple pushed the cup away slightly. "I suppose there is no photograph of this girl?" she asked. "Verity Hunt, or whatever her name was? The Archdeacon was talking about her. He seemed to have been very fond of her."

"I think he was. He was fond of all young people," said Clotilde.

She got up, went across the room and lifted the lid of a desk. From that she took a photograph and brought it over for Miss Marple to see.

"That was Verity," she said.

"A beautiful face," said Miss Marple. "Yes, a very beautiful and unusual face. Poor child."

"It's dreadful nowadays," said Anthea, "these things seem happening the whole time. Girls going out with every kind of young man. Nobody taking any trouble to look after them."

"They have to look after themselves nowadays," said Clotilde, "and they've no idea of how to do it, heaven help them!"

She stretched out a hand to take back the photograph from Miss Marple. As she did so, her sleeve caught the coffee cup and knocked it to the floor.

"Oh, dear!" said Miss Marple. "Was that my fault? Did I jog your arm?"

"No," said Clotilde, "it was my sleeve. It's rather a floating sleeve. Perhaps you would like some hot milk, if you are afraid to take coffee?"

"That would be very kind," said Miss Marple. "A glass of hot milk when I went to bed would be very soothing indeed, and always gives me a good night."

After a little more desultory conversation, Miss Cooke and Miss Barrow took their departure—a rather fussy departure in which first one and then the other came back to collect some article they'd left behind—a scarf, a handbag and a pocket handkerchief.

"Fuss, fuss, fuss," said Anthea, when they had departed.

"Somehow," said Mrs. Glynne, "I agree with Clotilde that those two don't seem real, if you know what I mean," she said to Miss Marple.

"Yes," said Miss Marple. "I do rather agree with you. They don't seem very real. I have wondered about them a good deal. Wondered, I mean, why they came on this tour and if they were really enjoying it. And what was their reason for coming."

"And have you discovered the answers to all those things?" asked Clotilde.

"I think so," said Miss Marple. She sighed. "I've discovered the answers to a lot of things," she said.

"Up to now I hope you've enjoyed yourself," said Clotilde.

"I am glad to have left the tour now," said Miss Marple. "I don't think I should have enjoyed much more of it."

"No. I can quite understand that."

Clotilde fetched a glass of hot milk from the kitchen and accompanied Miss Marple up to her room.

"Is there anything else I can get you?" she asked. "Anything at all?"

"No, thank you," said Miss Marple. "I have everything I want. I have my little night bag here, you see, so I need not do any more unpacking. Thank you," she said, "it is very kind of you and your sisters to put me up again tonight."

"Well, we couldn't do much less, having had Mr. Rafiel's letter. He was a very thoughtful man."

"Yes," said Miss Marple, "the kind of man who—well, thinks of everything. A good brain, I should think."

"I believe he was a very noted financier."

"Financially and otherwise, he thought of a lot of things," said Miss Marple. "Ah, well, I shall be glad to get to bed. Good night, Miss Bradbury-Scott."

"Shall I send you breakfast up in the morning? You'd like to have it in bed?"

"No, no, I wouldn't put you out for the world. No, no. I would rather come down. A cup of tea, perhaps, would be very nice, but I want to go out in the garden. I particularly want to see that mound all covered with white flowers, so beautiful and so triumphant—"

"Good night," said Clotilde; "sleep well."

II

In the hall of The Old Manor House the grandfather clock at the bottom of the stairs struck two o'clock. The clocks in the house did not all strike in unison and some of them, indeed, did not strike at all. To keep a house full of antique clocks in working order was not easy. At three o'clock the clock on the first floor landing struck a soft-chimed three o'clock. A faint chink of light showed through the hinge of the door.

Miss Marple sat up in bed and put her fingers on the switch of the electric lamp by her bed. The door opened very softly. There was no light outside now, but the soft footstep came through the door into the room. Miss Marple switched the light on.

"Oh," she said, "it's you. Miss Bradbury-Scott. Is there anything special?"

"I just came to see if you wanted anything," said Miss Bradbury-Scott.

Miss Marple looked at her. Clotilde had on a long purple robe. What a handsome woman she was, thought Miss Marple. Her hair framing her forehead, a tragic figure, a figure of drama. Agan Miss Marple thought of Greek plays. Clytemnestra again.

"You're sure there is nothing I can bring you?"

"No, thank you," said Miss Marple. "I'm afraid," she said apologetically, "that I have not drunk my milk."

"Oh, dear, why not?"

"I did not think it would be very good for me," said Miss Marple.

Clotilde stood there at the foot of the bed, looking at her.

"Not wholesome, you know," said Miss Marple.

"Just what do you mean by that?" Clotilde's voice was harsh now.

"I think you know what I mean," said Miss Marple. "I think you've known all the evening. Perhaps before that."

"I have no idea what you are talking about."

"No?" There was a faint satirical note to the questioning monosyllable.

"I am afraid the milk is cold now. I will take it away and get you some hot."

"Don't trouble yourself," said Miss Marple. "Even if you brought it me, I should not drink it."

"I really cannot understand the point of what you're saying. Really," said Clotilde, looking at her, "What a very extraordinary person you are. What sort of a woman are you? Why are you talking like this? Who are you?"

Miss Marple pulled down the mass of pink wool that encircled her head, a pink wool scarf of the same kind that she had once worn in the West Indies.

"One of my names," she said, "is Nemesis."

"Nemesis? And what does that mean?"

"I think you know," said Miss Marple. "You are a very well-educated woman. Nemesis is long delayed sometimes, but it comes in the end."

"What are you talking about?"

"About a very beautiful girl whom you killed," said Miss Marple.

"Whom I killed? What do you mean?"

"I mean the girl Verity."

"And why should I kill her?"

"Because you loved her," said Miss Marple.

"Of course I loved her. I was devoted to her. And she loved me."

"Somebody said to me not very long ago that love was a very frightening word. It *is* a frightening word. You loved Verity too much. She meant everything in the world to you. She was devoted to you until something else came into her life. A different kind of love came into her life. She fell in love with a boy, a young man. Not a very suitable one, not a very good specimen, not anyone with a good record, but she loved him and he loved her and she wanted to escape—to escape from the burden of the bondage of love she was living in with you. She wanted a normal woman's life. To live with the man of her choice, to have children by him. She wanted marriage and the happiness of normality."

Clotilde moved. She came to a chair and sat down in it, staring at Miss Marple.

"So," she said, "you seem to understand very well."

"Yes, I do understand."

"What you say is quite true. I shan't deny it. It doesn't matter if I do or do not deny it."

"No," said Miss Marple, "you are quite right there. It will not matter."

"Do you know at all—can you imagine—how I have suffered?"

"Yes," said Miss Marple, "I can imagine it. I've always been able to imagine things."

"Did you imagine the agony, the agony of thinking, of knowing you are going to lose the thing you love best in the world? And I was losing it to a miserable, depraved delinquent—a man unworthy of my beautiful, splendid girl. I had to stop it. I had to—I had to."

"Yes," said Miss Marple. "Sooner than let the girl go, you killed her. Because you loved her, you killed her."

"Do you think I could ever do a thing like that? Do you think I could strangle the girl I loved? Do you think I could bash her face in, crush her head to a pulp? Nothing but a vicious, depraved man would do a thing like that."

"No," said Miss Marple, "you wouldn't do that. You loved her and you would not be able to do that."

"Well, then, you see, you are talking nonsense."

"You didn't do that to her. The girl that happened to was not the girl you loved. Verity's here still, isn't she? She's here in the garden. I don't think you strangled her. I think you gave her a drink of coffee or of milk, you gave her a painless overdose of sleeping stuff. And then when she was dead, you took her out into the garden, you pulled aside the fallen bricks of the greenhouse, and you made a vault for her there, under the floor with the bricks, and covered it over. And then the polygonum was planted there and has flowered ever since, growing bigger and stronger every year. Verity has remained here with you. You never let her go."

"You fool! You crazy old fool! Do you think you are ever going to get away to tell this story?"

"I think so," said Miss Marple. "I'm not quite sure of it. You are a strong woman, a great deal stronger than I am."

"I'm glad you appreciate that."

"And you wouldn't have any scruples," said Miss Marple. "You know one doesn't stop at one murder. I have noticed that in the course of my life and in what I have observed of crime. You killed two girls, didn't you? You killed the girl you loved and you killed a different girl."

"I killed a silly little tramp, an adolescent tart, Nora Broad. How did you know about her?"

"I wondered," said Miss Marple. "I didn't think from what I saw of you that you could have borne to strangle and disfigure the girl you loved. But another girl disappeared also about that time, a girl whose body has never been found. But I thought that the body *had* been found, only they hadn't known that the body was Nora Broad's. It was dressed in Verity's clothes, it was identified as Verity by the person who would be the first applied to, the person who knew her better than anyone else. You had to go and say if the body found was the body of Verity. You recognized it. You said that that dead body was Verity's."

"And why should I do that?"

"Because you wanted the boy who had taken Verity away from you, the boy whom Verity had loved and who had loved Verity, you wanted him tried for murder. And so you hid that second body in a place where it would not be too easily discovered. When it was discovered, it would be thought to be the wrong girl. You would make sure that it was identified in the way you wanted. You dressed it in Verity's clothes, put her handbag there, a letter or two, a bangle, a little cross on a chain—you disfigured her face.

"A week ago you committed a third murder, the murder of Elizabeth Temple. You killed her because she was coming to this part of the world, and you were afraid of what she might have known, from what Verity might have written to her or told her. You thought that if Elizabeth Temple got together with Archdeacon Brabazon, they might with what they both knew come at some appraisal of the truth. Elizabeth Temple must not be allowed to meet the Archdeacon. You are a very powerful woman. You could have rolled that boulder down the hillside. It must have taken some doing, but you are very strong."

"Strong enough to deal with you," said Clotilde.

"I don't think," said Miss Marple, "that you will be allowed to do that."

"What do you mean, you miserable, shriveled-up old woman?"

"Yes," said Miss Marple, "I'm old and I have very little strength in my arms or my legs. Very little strength anywhere. But I am in my own way an emissary of justice."

Clotilde laughed. "And who'll stop me from putting an end to you?"

"I think," said Miss Marple, "my guardian angel."

"Trusting to your guardian angel, are you?" said Clotilde, and laughed again.

She advanced towards the bed.

"Possibly two guardian angels," said Miss Marple. "Mr. Rafiel always did things on a lavish scale."

Her hand slipped under the pillow and out again. In it was a whistle which she put to her lips. It was something of a sensation in whistles. It had the shrill fury that would attract a policeman from the end of a street. Two things happened almost simultaneously. The door of the room opened. Clotilde turned. Miss Barrow was standing in the doorway. At the same moment the large wardrobe hanging cupboard opened and Miss Cooke stepped out of it. There was a grim air of professionalism about them both which was very noticeable in contrast to their pleasant social behavior a little earlier in the evening.

"Two guardian angels," said Miss Marple happily. "Mr. Rafiel has done me very proud, as one used to say!"

CHAPTER TWENTY-TWO
Miss Marple Tells Her Story

"WHEN DID YOU find out," asked Professor Wanstead, "that those two women were private agents accompanying you for your protection?"

He leaned forward in his chair, looking thoughtfully at the white-haired old lady, who sat in an upright position in the chair opposite him. They were in an official government building in London, and there were four other persons present.

An official from the Public Prosecutor's Office; the Assistant Commissioner of Scotland Yard, Sir James Lloyd; the Governor of Manstone Prison, Sir Andrew McNeil. The fourth person was the Home Secretary.

"Not until the last evening," said Miss Marple. "I wasn't actually sure until then. Miss Cooke had come to St. Mary Mead and I found out fairly quickly that she was not what she represented herself to be, which was a woman knowledgeable in gardening who had come there to help a friend with her garden. So I was left with the choice of deciding what her real object had been, once she had acquainted herself with my appearance, which was obviously the only thing she could have come for. When I recognized her again on the coach, I had to make up my mind if she was accompanying the tour in the role of guardianship, or whether those two women were enemies enlisted by what I might call the other side.

"I was only really sure that last evening when Miss Cooke prevented me, by very distinct words of warning, from drinking the cup of coffee that Clotilde Bradbury-Scott had just set down in front of me. She phrased it very cleverly, but the warning was clearly there. Later, when I was wishing those two good night, one of them took my hand in both of hers, giving me a particularly friendly and affectionate handshake. And in doing so she passed something into my hand, which, when I examined it later, I found to be a high-powered whistle. I took it to bed with me, accepted the glass of milk which was urged upon me by my hostess, and wished her good night, being careful not to change my simple and friendly attitude."

"You didn't drink the milk?"

"Of course not," said Miss Marple. "What do you take me for?"

"I beg your pardon," said Professor Wanstead. "It surprises me that you didn't lock your door."

"That would have been quite the wrong thing to do," said Miss Marple. "I wanted Clotilde Bradbury-Scott to come in. I wanted to see what she would say or do. I thought it was almost certain that she *would* come in, when sufficient time had elapsed to make sure that I had drunk the milk and was in an unconscious sleep from which presumably I would not have woken up again."

"Did you help Miss Cooke to conceal herself in the wardrobe?"

"No. It was a complete surprise when she came out of that suddenly. I suppose," said Miss Marple thoughtfully, thinking it over, "I suppose she slipped in there just when I had gone down the passage to the—er—to the bathroom."

"You knew the two women were in the house?"

"I thought they would be at hand somewhere after they'd given me the whistle. I do not think it was a difficult house to which to gain access, there were no shuttered windows or burglar alarms or anything of that kind. One of them came back on the pretext of having left a handbag and a scarf. Between them they probably managed to leave a window unfastened, and I should imagine they came back into the house almost as soon as they left it, while the inhabitants inside were going up to bed."

"You took a big risk, Miss Marple."

"I hoped for the best," said Miss Marple. "One cannot go through life without attracting certain risks if they are necessary."

"Your tip about the parcel dispatched to that charity, by the way, was entirely successful. It contained a brand-new brightly colored man's polonecked pullover in scarlet and black checks. Most noticeable. What made you think of that?"

"Well," said Miss Marple, "that was really very simple. The description that Emlyn and Joanna gave of the figure they had seen made it seem almost certain that these very bright-colored and noticeable clothes were *meant* to be noticed, and that therefore it would be very important that they should not be hidden locally or kept among the person's own belongings.

They must be got out of the way as soon as could be. And really there is only one way successfully of disposing of something. That is through the general post. Anything in the nature of clothes can be very easily dispatched to charities. Think how pleased the people who collect winter garments for Unemployed Mothers, or whatever the name of the charity, would be to find a nearly brand-new woolen pullover. All I had to do was to find out the address where it had been sent."

"And you *asked* them that at the post office?" The Home Secretary looked slightly shocked.

"Not directly, of course. I mean, I had to be a little flustered and explain how I'd put the wrong address on some clothes that I was sending to a charity and could they by any chance tell me if the parcel one of my kind hostesses had brought up there had been sent off? And a very nice woman there did her best and remembered that it was *not* the address I was hoping it had been sent to, and she gave me that address that she *had* noted. She had no suspicion, I think, that I had any wish for the information apart from being—well, rather muddle-headed, elderly, and very worried about where my parcel of worn clothes had gone."

"Ah," said Professor Wanstead, "I see you are an actress, Miss Marple, as well as an avenger." Then he said, "When did you first begin to discover what had happened ten years ago?"

"To begin with," said Miss Marple, "I found things very difficult, almost impossible. In my mind I was blaming Mr. Rafiel for not having made things clear to me. But I see now that he'd been very wise not to do so. Really, you know, he was extraordinarily clever. I can see why he was such a big financier and made so much money so easily. He laid his plans so well. He gave me just enough information in small packets each time. I was, as it were, directed. First my guardian angels were alerted to note what I looked like. Then I was directed on the tour and to the people on it."

"Did you suspect, if I may use that word, anyone on the tour at first?"

"Only as possibilities."

"No feeling of evil?"

"Ah, you have remembered that. No, I did not think there was any definite atmosphere of evil. I was not told who my contact was there, but *she* made herself known to *me*."

"Elizabeth Temple?"

"Yes. It was like a searchlight," said Miss Marple, "illuminating things on a dark night. So far, you see, I had been in the dark. There were certain things that must be, must logically be. I mean, because of what Mr. Rafiel had indicated. There must be somewhere a victim and somewhere a murderer. Yes, a killer was indicated because that was the only liaison that had existed between Mr. Rafiel and myself. There had been a murder in the West Indies. Both he and I had been involved in it and all he knew of me was my connection with that. So it could not be any other type of crime. And it could not, either, be a casual crime. It must be a deliberate crime. It must be, and show itself definitely to be, the handiwork of someone who had accepted evil—evil instead of good. There seemed to be two victims indicated. There must be someone who had been killed and there must be clearly a victim of injustice—a victim who had been accused of a crime he or she had not committed. So now, while I pondered these things, I had no light upon them until I talked to Miss Temple. She was very intense, very compelling. There came the first link which I had with Mr. Rafiel. She spoke of a girl she had known, a girl who had once been engaged to Mr. Rafiel's son. Here then was my first ray of light. Presently she also told me that the girl had not married him. I asked why not and she said: 'Because she died.' I asked then how she had died, what had killed her, and she said very strongly, very compellingly—I can hear her voice still, it was like the sound of a deep bell—she said *Love*. And she said after that: 'The most frightening word there can be is love.' I did not know then exactly what she meant. In fact the first idea that came to me was that the girl had committed suicide as a result of an unhappy love affair. It can happen often enough, and a very sad tragedy it is when it does happen. That was the most I knew then—that and the fact that the journey she herself was engaged upon was no mere pleasure tour. She was going, she told me, on a pilgrimage. She was going to some place or to some person. I did not learn then who the person was; that only came later."

"Archdeacon Brabazon?"

"Yes. I had no idea then of his existence. But from then on I felt that the chief characters—the chief actors—in the drama, whichever way you like to put it, were not on the tour. They were not members of the coach party. I hesitated just for a short time, hesitated over some particular persons. I hesitated considering Joanna Crawford and Emlyn Price."

"Why fix on them?"

"Because of their youth," said Miss Marple. "Because youth is so often associated with suicide, with violence, with intense jealousy and tragic love. A man kills his girl—it happens. Yes, my mind went to them, but it did not seem to me there was any association there. No shadow of evil, of despair, of misery. I used the idea of them later as a kind of false pointer when we were drinking sherry at The Old Manor House that last evening. I pointed out how they could be the most easy suspects in the death of Elizabeth Temple. When I see them again," said Miss Marple punctiliously, "I shall apologize to them for having used them as useful characters to distract attention from my real ideas."

"And the next thing was the death of Elizabeth Temple?"

"No," said Miss Marple. "Actually the next thing was my arrival at The Old Manor House—the kindness of my reception and taking up my stay there under their hospitable roof. That again had been arranged by Mr. Rafiel. So I knew that I must go there, but not for what reason I was to go there. It might be merely a place where more information would come to me to lead me onwards in my quest. I am sorry," Miss Marple said suddenly, becoming her normal apologetic and slightly fussy self, "I am talking at much too great a length. I really must not inflict on you all that I thought and . . ."

"Please go on," said Professor Wanstead. "You may not know it, but what you are telling me is particularly interesting to me. It ties up with so much I have known and seen in the work I do. Go on giving me what you felt."

"Yes, go on," said Sir Andrew McNeil.

"It *was* feeling," said Miss Marple. "It wasn't really, you know, logical deduction. It was based on a kind of emotional reaction or susceptibility to—well, I can only call it atmosphere."

"Yes," said Wanstead, "there is atmosphere—atmosphere in houses, atmosphere in places, in the garden, in the forest, in a public house, in a cottage."

"The three sisters. That is what I thought and felt and said to myself when I went in to The Old Manor House. I was so kindly received by Lavinia Glynne. There's something about the phrase—the three sisters—that springs up in your mind as sinister. It combines with the three sisters in Russian literature, the three witches on Macbeth's heath. It seemed to me that there was an atmosphere there of sorrow, of deep-felt unhappiness, also an atmosphere of fear and a kind of struggling different atmosphere which I can only describe as an atmosphere of normality."

"Your last word interests me," said Wanstead.

"It was due, I think, to Mrs. Glynne. She was the one who came to meet me when the coach arrived and explained the invitation. She was an entirely normal and pleasant woman, a widow. She was not very happy, but when I say she was not very happy, it was nothing to do with sorrow or deep unhappiness, it was just that she had the wrong atmosphere for her own character. She took me back with her and I met the other two sisters. The next morning I was to hear from an aged housemaid who brought my early-morning tea a story of past tragedy, of a girl who had been killed by her boy friend—of several other girls in the neighborhood who'd fallen victims to violence or sexual assault. I had to make my second appraisal. I had dismissed the people in the coach as not being personally concerned in my search. Somewhere still there was a killer. I had to ask myself if one of the killers could be here—here in this house where I had been sent. Clotilde, Lavinia, Anthea. Three names of three weird sisters, three happy—unhappy—suffering—frightened—what were they? My attention was caught first by Clotilde. A tall, handsome woman. A personality. Just as Elizabeth Temple had been a personality. I felt that here where the field was limited, I must at least sum up what I could about the three sisters. Three Fates. Who could be a killer? What kind of a killer? What kind of a killing? I could feel then rising up rather slowly, like a miasma does, an atmosphere. I don't think there is any other word that expresses it except evil. Not necessarily that any one of these three was evil, but they were certainly living in an atmosphere where evil had happened, had left its shadow or was still threatening them. Clotilde, the eldest, was the first one I considered. She was handsome, she was strong, she was, I thought, a woman of intense emotional feeling. I saw her, I will admit, as a possible Clytemnestra. I had recently," Miss Marple dropped into her everyday tones, "been taken very kindly to a Greek play performed at a well-known boys' public school not far from my home. I had been very, very impressed by the acting of the Agamemnon and particularly a performance of the boy who had played Clytemnestra. A very remarkable performance. It seemed to me that in Clotilde I could imagine a woman who could plan and carry out the killing of a husband in his bath."

For a moment Professor Wanstead had all he could do to repress a laugh. It was the seriousness of Miss Marple's tone. She gave him a slight twinkle from her eyes.

"Yes, it sounds rather silly, does it not, said like that? But I could *see* her that way, playing that part, that is to say. Very unfortunately, she had no husband. She had never had a husband, and therefore did not kill a husband. Then I considered my guide to the house—Lavinia Glynne. She seemed an extremely nice, wholesome and pleasant woman. But alas, certain people who have killed have produced much that effect on the world round them. They have been charming people. Many murderers have been delightful and pleasant men, and people have been astonished. They are what I call the respectable killers—the ones who would commit murder from entirely utilitarian motives—without emotion, but to gain a required end. I didn't think it was very likely and I should be highly surprised if it was so, but I could not leave out Mrs. Glynne. She had had a husband. She was a widow and had been a widow for some years. It could be. I left it at that. And then I came to the third sister—Anthea. She was a disquieting personality—badly co-ordinated, it seemed to me, scatterbrained and in a condition of some emotion which I thought on the whole was fear. She was frightened of something. Intensely frightened of something. Well, that could fit in, too. If she had committed a crime of some kind, a crime which she had thought was finished with and past, there might have been some recrudescence, some raising up of old problems, something perhaps connected with the Elizabeth Temple inquiries; she might have felt fear that an old crime would be revived or discovered. She had a curious way of looking at you, and then looking sharply from side to side over one shoulder as though she saw something standing behind her—something that made her afraid. So she, too, was a possible answer, a possibly slightly mentally unhinged killer who could have killed because she considered herself persecuted—because she was afraid. These were only ideas. They were only a rather more pronounced assessment of possibilities that I had already gone through on the coach. But the atmosphere of the house was on me more than ever. That next day I walked in the garden with Anthea. At the end of the principal grass path was a mound—a mound created by the falling down of a former greenhouse. Owing to a lack of repairs and of gardeners at the end of the war, it had fallen into disuse, come to pieces, bricks had been piled up surmounted with earth and turf, and had been planted with a certain creeper—a creeper well known when you want to hide or cover some rather ugly piece of building in your garden. Polygonum it is called. One of the quickest flowering shrubs which swallows and kills and dries up and gets rid of everything it grows over. It grows over everything. It is in a way a rather frightening plant. It has beautiful white flowers; it can look very lovely. It was just coming into bloom. I stood there with Anthea, and she seemed to be desperately unhappy over the loss of the greenhouse. She said it had such lovely grapes, it seemed to be the thing she remembered most about the garden when she had been a child there. And she wanted, she wanted desperately to have enough money so as to dig up the mound, level the ground and rebuild the greenhouse and stock it with muscat grapes and peaches as the old greenhouse had been. It was a terrible nostalgia for the past she was feeling. It was more than that. Again, very clearly, I felt an atmosphere of fear. Something about the mound made her frightened. I couldn't then think what it was. You know the next thing that happened. It was Elizabeth Temple's death, and there was no doubt, from the story told by Emlyn Price and Joanna Crawford, that there could be only one conclusion. It was not an accident. It was deliberate murder.

"I think it was from then on," said Miss Marple, "that I knew. I came to the conclusion there had been three killings. I heard the full story of Mr. Rafiel's son, the delinquent boy, the ex-jailbird, and I thought that he was all those things, but none of them showed him as being a killer or likely to be a killer. All the evidence was against him. There was no doubt in anyone's mind that he had killed the girl whose name I had now learned as being Verity Hunt. But Archdeacon Brabazon put the final crown on the business, as it were. He had known those two young people. They had come to him with their story of wanting to get married and he had taken it upon himself to decide that they should get married. He thought that it was not perhaps a wise marriage, but it was a marriage that was justified by the fact that they both loved each other. The girl loved the boy with what he called a true love—a love as true as her name. And he thought that the boy, for all his bad sexual reputation, had truly loved the girl and had every intention of being faithful to her and trying to reform some of his evil tendencies. The Archdeacon was not optimistic. He did not, I think, believe it would be a thoroughly happy marriage, but it was to his mind what he called a necessary marriage—necessary because if you love enough you will pay the price, even if the price is disappointment and a certain amount of unhappiness. But one thing I was quite sure of. That disfigured face, that battered-in head could not have been the action of a boy who really loved the girl. This was not a story of sexual assault. In this love affair the love was rooted in tenderness. I was ready to take the Archdeacon's word for that. But I knew, too, that I'd got the right clue, the clue that was given me by Elizabeth Temple. She had said that the cause of Verity's death was love—one of the most frightening words there is.

"It was quite clear then," said Miss Marple. "I think I'd known for some time, really. It was just the small things that hadn't fitted in, but now they did. They fitted in with what Elizabeth Temple had said. The cause of Verity's death. She had said first the one word 'love' and then that 'love could be the most frightening word there was.' It was all mapped out so plainly then—the overwhelming love that Clotilde had had for this girl. The girl's hero-worship of her, dependency on her, and then as she grew a little older, her normal instincts came into play. She wanted love. She wanted to be free to love, to marry, to have children. And along came the boy that she could love. She knew that he was unreliable, she knew he was what was technically called a bad lot, but that," said Miss Marple in a more ordinary tone of voice, "is not what puts any girl off a boy. No. Young women like bad lots. They always have. They fall in love with bad lots. They are quite sure they can change them. And the nice, kind, steady, reliable husbands got the answer, in my young days, that one would be 'a sister to them,' which never satisfied them at all. Verity fell in love with Michael Rafiel, and Michael Rafiel was prepared to turn over a new leaf and marry this girl and was sure he would never wish to look at another girl again. I don't say this would have been a happy-ever-after thing, but it was, as the Archdeacon said quite surely, it *was* real love. And so they planned to get married. And I think Verity wrote to Elizabeth and told her that she was going to marry Michael Rafiel. It was arranged in secret because I think Verity did realize that what she was doing was essentially an escape. She was escaping from a life that she didn't want to live any longer, from someone whom she loved very much but not in the way she loved Michael. And she would not be allowed to do so. Permission would not be willingly given, every obstacle would be put in their way. So, like other young people, they were going to elope. There was no need for them to fly off to Gretna Green, they were of sufficiently mature age to marry. So she appealed to Archdeacon Brabazon, her old friend who had confirmed her—who was a real friend. And the wedding was arranged—the day, the time, probably even she bought secretly some garment in which to be married. They were to meet somewhere, no doubt. They were to come to the rendezvous separately. I think he came there, but she did not come. He waited, perhaps—waited and then tried to find out why she didn't come. I think then a message may have been given him, even a letter sent him, possibly in a forged handwriting, saying she had changed her mind. It was all over and she was going away for a long time to get over it. I don't know. But I don't think he ever dreamed of the real reason of why she hadn't come, of why she had sent no word. He hadn't thought for one moment that she had been deliberately, cruelly, almost madly, perhaps, destroyed. Clotilde was not going to lose the person she loved. She was not going to let her escape, she was not going to let her go to the young man whom she herself hated and loathed. She would keep Verity, keep her in her own way. But what I could not believe was—I did not believe that she'd strangled the girl and had then disfigured her face. I don't think she could have borne to do that. I think that she had rearranged the bricks of the fallen greenhouse and piled up earth and turf over most of it. The girl had already been given a drink, an overdose of sleeping draught, probably. Grecian, as it were, in tradition. One cup of hemlock—even if it wasn't hemlock. And she buried the girl there in the garden, piled the bricks over her and the earth and the turf—"

"Did neither of the other sisters suspect it?"

"Mrs. Glynne was not there then. Her husband had not died and she was still abroad. But Anthea was there. I think Anthea did know *something* of what went on. I don't know that she suspected death at first, but she knew that Clotilde had been occupying herself with the raising up of a mound at the end of the garden to be covered with flowering shrubs, to be a place of beauty. I think perhaps the truth came to her little by little. And then Clotilde, having accepted evil, done evil, surrendered to evil, had no qualms about what she would do next. I think she enjoyed planning it. She had a certain amount of influence over a sly, sexy little village girl who came to her cadging for benefits now and then. I think it was easy for her to arrange one day to take the girl on a picnic or an expedition a good long way away— thirty or forty miles. She'd chosen the place beforehand, I think. She strangled the girl, disfigured her, hid her under turned earth, leaves and branches. Why should anyone ever suspect her of doing any such thing? She put Verity's handbag there and a little chain Verity used to wear round her neck and possibly dressed her in clothes belonging to Verity. She hoped the crime would not be found out for some time, but in the meantime she spread abroad rumors of Nora Broad having been seen about in Michael's car, going about with Michael. Possibly she spread a story that Verity had broken off the engagement to be married because of his infidelity with this girl. She may have said anything and I think everything she said she enjoyed, poor lost soul."

"Why do you say 'poor lost soul,' Miss Marple?"

"Because," said Miss Marple, "I don't suppose there can be any agony so great as what Clotilde has suffered all this time—ten years now—living in eternal sorrow. Living, you see, with the thing she *had* to live with. She had kept Verity, kept her there at The Old Manor House, in the garden, kept her there forever. She didn't realize at first what that meant—her passionate longing for the girl to be alive again. I don't think she ever suffered from remorse. I don't think she had even that consolation. She just suffered— went on suffering year after year. And I know now what Elizabeth Temple meant—better perhaps than she herself did. Love *is* a very terrible thing. It is alive to evil, it can be one of the most evil things there can be. And Clotilde had to live with that day after day, year after year. I think, you know, that Anthea was frightened of that. I think she knew more clearly the whole time what Clotilde had done and she thought that Clotilde knew that she knew. And she was afraid of what Clotilde might do. Clotilde gave that parcel to Anthea to post, the one with the pullover. She said things to me about Anthea, that she was mentally disturbed, that if she suffered from persecution or jealousy, Anthea might do anything. I think—yes—that in the not-so-distant future—something might have happened to Anthea—an arranged suicide because of a guilty conscience—"

"And yet you are sorry for that woman?" asked Sir Andrew. "Malignant evil is like cancer—a malignant tumor. It brings suffering."

"Of course," said Miss Marple.

"I suppose you have been told what happened that night," said Professor Wanstead, "after your guardian angels had removed you?"

"You mean Clotilde? She had picked up my glass of milk, I remember. She was still holding it when Miss Cooke took me out of the room. I suppose she—drank it, did she?"

"Yes. Did you know that might happen?"

"I didn't think of it, no, not at the moment. I suppose I could have known it if I'd thought about it."

"Nobody could have stopped her. She was so quick about it, and nobody quite realized there was anything wrong with the milk."

"So she drank it."

"Does that surprise you?"

"No, it would have seemed to her the natural thing to do, one can't really wonder. It had come by this time that she wanted to escape—from all the things she was having to live with. Just as Verity had wanted to escape from the life that she was living there. Very odd, isn't it, that the retribution one brings on oneself fits so closely with what has caused it?"

"You sound sorrier for her than you were for the girl who died."

"No," said Miss Marple, "it's a different kind of being sorry. I'm sorry for Verity because of all that she missed, all that she was so near to obtaining—a life of love and devotion and service to the man she had chosen, and whom she truly loved—truly and in all verity. She missed all that and nothing can give that back to her. I'm sorry for her because of what she *didn't* have. But she escaped what Clotilde had to suffer—sorrow, misery, fear and a growing cultivation and imbibing of evil. Clotilde had to live with all those. Sorrow, frustrated love which she could never get back, she had to live with the two sisters who suspected, who were afraid of her, and she had to live with the girl she had kept there."

"You mean Verity?"

"Yes. Buried in the garden, buried in the tomb that Clotilde had prepared. She was *there* in The Old Manor House and I think Clotilde *knew* she was there. It might be that she even saw her or thought she saw her sometimes when she went to pick a spray of polygonum blossom. She must have felt very close to Verity then. Nothing worse could happen to her, could it, than that? Nothing worse . . ."

CHAPTER TWENTY-THREE
End Pieces

I

"THAT OLD LADY gives me the creeps," said Sir Andrew McNeil when he had said good-bye and thanks to Miss Marple.

"So gentle—and so ruthless," said the Assistant Commissioner.

Professor Wanstead took Miss Marple down to his car, which was waiting, and then returned for a few final words.

"What do you think of her, Edmund?"

"The most frightening woman I ever met," said the Home Secretary.

"Ruthless?" asked Professor Wanstead.

"No, no, I don't mean that but—well, a very frightening woman."

"Nemesis," said Professor Wanstead thoughtfully.

"Those two women," said the P.P.D. man, "you know, the security agents who were looking after her, they gave a most extraordinary description of her that night. They got into the house quite easily, hid themselves in a small downstairs room until everyone went upstairs, then one went into the bedroom and into the wardrobe and the other stayed outside the room to watch. The one in the bedroom said that when she threw open the door of the wardrobe and came out, there was the old lady sitting up in bed with a pink fluffy shawl round her neck and a perfectly placid face, twittering away and talking like an elderly schoolmarm. They said she gave them quite a turn."

"A pink fluffy shawl," said Professor Wanstead. "Yes, yes, I do remember—"

"What do you remember?"

"Old Rafiel. He told me about her, you know, and then he laughed. He said one thing he'd never forget in all his life. He said it was when one of the funniest scatterbrained old ladies he'd ever met came marching into his bedroom out in the West Indies, with a fluffy pink scarf round her neck, telling him he was to get up and do something to prevent a murder. And he said: 'What on earth do you think you're doing?' And she said she was

Nemesis. Nemesis! He could not imagine anything less like it, he said. I like the touch of the pink wooly scarf," said Professor Wanstead thoughtfully. "I like that very much."

II

"Michael," said Professor Wanstead, "I want to introduce you to Miss Jane Marple, who's been very active on your behalf."

The young man of thirty-two looked at the white-haired, rather dicky old lady with a slightly doubtful expression.

"Oh—er—" he said, "well, I guess I have heard about it. Thanks very much."

He looked at Wanstead.

"It's true, is it, they're going to give me a free pardon or something silly like that?"

"Yes. A release will be put through quite soon. You'll be a free man in a very short time."

"Oh." Michael sounded slightly doubtful.

"It will take a little getting used to, I expect," said Miss Marple kindly.

She looked at him thoughtfully, seeing him in retrospect as he might have been ten years or so ago. Still quite attractive—though he showed all the signs of strain. Attractive, yes. Very attractive, she thought he would have been once. A gaiety about him then, there would have been, and a charm. He'd lost that now, but it would come back perhaps. A weak mouth and attractively shaped eyes that could look you straight in the face, and probably had been always useful for telling lies that you really wanted to believe. Very like—who was it?—she dived into past memories—Jonathan Birkin, of course. He had sung in the choir. A really delightful baritone voice. And how fond the girls had been of him! Quite a good job he'd had as clerk in Messrs. Gabriels' firm. A pity there had been that little matter of the checks.

"Oh," said Michael. He said, with even more embarrassment: "It's been very kind of you, I'm sure, to take so much trouble."

"I've enjoyed it," said Miss Marple. "Well, I'm glad to have met you. Good-bye. I hope you've got a very good time coming to you. Our country is in rather a bad way just now, but you'll probably find some job or other that you might quite enjoy doing."

"Oh, yes. Thanks, thanks very much. I—I really am very grateful, you know."

His tone sounded still extremely unsure about it.

"It's not me you ought to be grateful to," said Miss Marple. "You ought to be grateful to your father."

"Dad? Dad never thought much of me."

"Your father when he was a dying man was determined to see that you got justice."

"Justice." Michael Rafiel considered it.

"Yes, your father thought justice was important. He was, I think, a very just man himself. In the letter he wrote me asking me to undertake this proposition, he directed me to a quotation:

"Let justice roll down like waters
And righteousness like an everlasting stream."

"Oh! What's it mean? Shakespeare?"

"No, the Bible—one has to think about it—I had to."

Miss Marple unwrapped a parcel she had been carrying.

"They gave me this," she said. "They thought I might like to have it—because I had helped to find out the truth of what had really happened. I think, though, that you are the person who should have first claim on it—that is if you really want it. But maybe you do not want it—"

She handed him the photograph of Verity Hunt that Clotilde Bradbury-Scott had shown her once in the drawing room of The Old Manor House.

He took it—and stood with it, staring down on it. His face changed, the lines of it softened, then hardened. Miss Marple watched him without speaking. The silence went on for some little time. Professor Wanstead also watched—he watched them both, the old lady and the boy.

It came to him that this was in some way a crisis—a moment that might affect a whole new way of life.

Michael Rafiel sighed—he stretched out and gave the photograph back to Miss Marple.

"No, you are right, I do not want it. All that life is gone. She's gone—I can't keep her with me. Anything I do now has got to be new—going forward. You—" he hesitated, looking at her—"you understand?"

"Yes," said Miss Marple. "I understand. I think you are right. I wish you good luck in the life you are now going to begin."

He said good-bye and went out.

"Well," said Professor Wanstead, "not an enthusiastic young man. He could have thanked you a bit more for what you did for him."

"Oh, that's quite all right," said Miss Marple. "I didn't expect him to do so. It would have embarrassed him even more. It is, you know," she added, "very embarrassing when one has to thank people and start life again and see everything from a different angle and all that. I think he might do well. He's not bitter. That's the great thing. I understand quite well why that girl loved him—"

"Well, perhaps he'll go straight this time."

"One rather doubts that," said Miss Marple. "I don't know that he'd be able to help himself unless—of course," she said, "the great thing to hope for is that he'll meet a really nice girl."

"What I like about you," said Professor Wanstead, "is your delightfully practical mind."

III

"She'll be here presently," said Mr. Broadribb to Mr. Schuster.

"Yes. The whole thing's pretty extraordinary, isn't it?"

"I couldn't believe it at first," said Broadribb. "You know, when poor old Rafiel was dying, I thought this whole thing was—well, senility or something. Not that he was old enough for that."

The buzzer went. Mr. Schuster picked up the phone.

"Oh, she's here, is she? Bring her up," he said. "She's come," he said. "I wonder now. You know, it's the oddest thing I ever heard in my life. Getting an old lady to go racketing round the countryside looking for she doesn't know what. The police think, you know, that that woman committed not just one murder but three! I ask you! Verity Hunt's body was under the mound in the garden, just as the old lady said it was. She hadn't been strangled and the face was not disfigured."

"I wonder the old lady herself didn't get done in," said Mr. Broadribb. "Far too old to be able to take care of herself."

"She had a couple of detectives, apparently, looking after her."

"What, *two* of them?"

"Yes. I didn't know that."

Miss Marple was ushered into their room.

"Congratulations, Miss Marple," said Mr. Broadribb, rising to greet her.

"Very best wishes. Splendid job," said Mr. Schuster, shaking hands.

Miss Marple sat down composedly on the other side of the desk.

"As I told you in my letter," she said, "I think I have fulfilled the terms of the proposition that was made to me. I have succeeded in what I was asked to do."

"Oh, I know. Yes, we've heard already. We've heard from Professor Wanstead and from the legal department and from the police authorities. Yes, it's been a splendid job, Miss Marple. We congratulate you."

"I was afraid," said Miss Marple, "that I would not be able to do what was required of me. It seemed so very difficult, almost impossible at first."

"Yes, indeed. It seems quite impossible to me. I don't know how you did it, Miss Marple."

"Oh, well," said Miss Marple, "it's just perseverance, isn't it, that leads to things?"

"Now about the sum of money we are holding. It's at your disposal at any time now. I don't know whether you would like us to pay it into your bank or whether you would like to consult us possibly as to the investment of it? It's quite a large sum."

"Twenty thousand pounds," said Miss Marple. "Yes, it is a very large sum by my way of thinking. Quite extraordinary," she added.

"If you would like an introduction to our brokers, they could give you possibly some ideas about investing."

"Oh, I don't want to invest any of it."

"But surely it would be—"

"There's no point in saving at my age," said Miss Marple. "I mean the point of this money—I'm sure Mr. Rafiel meant it that way—is to enjoy a few things that one thought one never would have the money to enjoy."

"Well, I see your point of view," said Mr. Broadribb. "Then your instructions would be that we pay this sum of money into your bank?"

"Middleton's Bank, One thirty-two High Street, St. Mary Mead," said Miss Marple.

"You have a deposit account, I expect. We will place it in your deposit account?"

"Certainly not," said Miss Marple. "Put it into my current account."

"You don't think—"

"I do think," said Miss Marple. "I want it in my current account."

She got up and shook hands.

"You could ask your bank manager's advice, you know, Miss Marple. It really is—one never knows when one wants something for a rainy day."

"The only thing I shall want for a rainy day will be my umbrella," said Miss Marple.

She shook hands with them both again.

"Thank you so much, Mr. Broadribb. And you, too, Mr. Schuster. You've been so kind to me, giving me all the information I needed."

"You really want that money put into your current account?"

"Yes," said Miss Marple. "I'm going to spend it, you know. I'm going to have some fun with it."

She looked back from the door and she laughed. Just for one moment Mr. Schuster, who was a man of more imagination than Mr. Broadribb had a vague impression of a young and pretty girl shaking hands with the vicar at a garden party in the country. It was, as he realized a moment later, a recollection of his own youth. But Miss Marple had, for a minute, reminded him of that particular girl, young, happy, going to enjoy herself.

"Mr. Rafiel would have liked me to have fun," said Miss Marple.

She went out of the door.

"Nemesis," said Mr. Broadribb. "That's what Rafiel called her. Nemesis! Never seen anybody less like Nemesis, have you?"

Mr. Schuster shook his head.

"It must have been another of Mr. Rafiel's little jokes," said Mr. Broadribb.

What Mrs. McGillicuddy Saw!

CAST OF CHARACTERS

CHAPTER ONE

MRS. MCGILLICUDDY PANTED along the platform in the wake of the porter carrying her suitcase. Mrs. McGillicuddy was short and stout, the porter was tall and free-striding. In addition, Mrs. McGillicuddy was burdened with a large quantity of parcels; the result of a day's Christmas shopping. The race was, therefore, an uneven one, and the porter turned the corner at the end of the platform while Mrs. McGillicuddy was still coming up the straight.

No. 1 platform was not at the moment unduly crowded, since a train had just gone out; but, in the no man's land beyond, a milling crowd was rushing in several directions at once, to and from undergrounds, left-luggage offices, tea rooms, inquiry offices, indicator boards and the two outlets, Arrival and Departure, to the outside world.

Mrs. McGillicuddy and her parcels were buffeted to and fro, but she arrived eventually at the entrance to No. 3 platform, and deposited one parcel at her feet while she searched her bag for the ticket that would enable her to pass the stern, uniformed guardian at the gate.

At that moment, a voice, raucous yet refined, burst into speech over her head.

"The train standing at Platform 3," the voice told her, "is the 4:54 for Brackhampton, Milchester, Waverton, Carvil Junction, Roxeter and stations to Chadmouth. Passengers for Brackhampton and Milchester travel at the rear of the train. Passengers for Vanequay change at Roxeter." The voice shut itself off with a click, and then reopened conversation by announcing the arrival at Platform 9 of the 4:35 from Birmingham and Wolverhampton.

Mrs. McGillicuddy found her ticket and presented it. The man clipped it, murmured: "On the right—rear portion."

Mrs. McGillicuddy padded up the platform and found her porter, looking bored and staring into space, outside the door of a third-class carriage.

"Here you are, lady."

"I'm traveling first class," said Mrs. McGillicuddy.

"You didn't say so," grumbled the porter. His eye swept her masculine-looking pepper-and-salt tweed coat disparagingly.

Mrs. McGillicuddy, who had said so, did not argue the point. She was sadly out of breath.

The porter retrieved the suitcase and marched with it to the adjoining coach where Mrs. McGillicuddy was installed in solitary splendor. The 4:54 was not much patronized, the first-class clientele preferring either the faster morning express or the 6:40 with dining cars. Mrs. McGillicuddy handed the porter his tip which he received with disappointment, clearly considering it more applicable to third-class than to first-class travel. Mrs. McGillicuddy, though prepared to spend money on comfortable travel after a night journey from the North and a day's feverish shopping, was at no time an extravagant tipper.

She settled herself back on the plush cushions with a sigh and opened a magazine. Five minutes later, whistles blew and the train started. The magazine slipped from Mrs. McGillicuddy's hand, her head dropped sideways, three minutes later she was asleep. She slept for thirty-five minutes and awoke refreshed. Resettling her hat, which had slipped askew, she sat up and looked out of the window at what she could see of the flying countryside. It was quite dark now, a dreary, misty December day— Christmas was only five days ahead. London had been dark and dreary; the country was no less so, though occasionally rendered cheerful with its constant clusters of lights as the train flashed through towns and stations.

"Serving last tea now," said an attendant, whisking open the corridor door like a jinni. Mrs. McGillicuddy had already partaken of tea at a large department store. She was for the moment amply nourished. The attendant went on down the corridor uttering his monotonous cry. With a pleased expression, Mrs. McGillicuddy looked up at the rack where her various parcels reposed. The fact towels had been excellent value and just what Margaret wanted, the space gun for Robby and the rabbit for Jean were highly satisfactory, and that evening coatee was just the thing she herself wanted, warm but dressy. The pullover for Hector, too . . . her mind dwelt with approval on the soundness of her purchases.

Her satisfied gaze returned to the window, a train traveling in the opposite direction rushed by with a screech, making the windows rattle and causing her to start. The train clattered over points and passed through a station.

Then it began suddenly to slow down, presumably in obedience to a signal. For some minutes it crawled along, then stopped, presently it began to move forward again. Another up train passed them, though with less vehemence than the first one. The train gathered speed again. At that moment another train, also on a down line, swerved inward toward them, for a moment with almost alarming effect. For a time the two trains ran parallel, now one gaining a little, now the other. Mrs. McGillicuddy looked from her window through the windows of the parallel carriages. Most of the blinds were down, but occasionally the occupants of the carriages were visible. The other train was not very full and there were many empty carriages.

At the moment when the two trains gave the illusion of being stationary, a blind in one of the carriages flew up with a snap. Mrs. McGillicuddy looked into the lighted first-class carriage that was only a few feet away.

Then she drew her breath in with a gasp and half rose to her feet.

Standing with his back to the window and to her was a man. His hands were round the throat of a woman who faced him, and he was slowly, remorselessly, strangling her. Her eyes were starting from their sockets, her face was purple and congested. As Mrs. McGillicuddy watched, fascinated, the end came, the body went limp and crumpled in the man's hands.

At the same moment, Mrs. McGillicuddy's train slowed down again and the other began to gain speed. It passed forward and a moment or two later it had vanished from sight.

Almost automatically Mrs. McGillicuddy's hand went up to the communication cord, then paused, irresolute. After all, what use would it be ringing the cord of the train in which she was traveling? The horror of what she had seen at such close quarters and the unusual circumstances made her feel paralyzed. Some immediate action was necessary—but what?

The door of her compartment was drawn back and a ticket collector said, "Ticket, please."

Mrs. McGillicuddy turned to him with vehemence.

"A woman has been strangled," she said. "In a train that has just passed. I saw it."

The ticket collector looked at her doubtfully.

"I beg your pardon, Madam?"

"A man strangled a woman! In a train. I saw it—through there." She pointed to the window.

The ticket collector looked extremely doubtful.

"Strangled?" he said disbelievingly.

"Yes, strangled! I saw it, I tell you. You must do something at once!"

The ticket collector coughed apologetically.

"You don't think, Madam, that you may have had a little nap and—er—" he broke off tactfully.

"I have had a nap, but if you think this was a dream, you're quite wrong. I saw it, I tell you."

The ticket collector's eyes dropped to the open magazine lying on the seat. On the exposed page was a girl being strangled while a man with a revolver threatened the pair from an open doorway.

He said persuasively: "Now don't you think, Madam, that you'd been reading an exciting story, and that you just dropped off, and awaking a little confused—"

Mrs. McGillicuddy interrupted him.

"I saw it," she said. "I was as wide awake as you are. And I looked out of the window into the window of the train alongside, and a man was strangling a woman. And what I want to know is, what are you going to do about it?"

"Well—Madam—"

"You're going to do something, I suppose?"

The ticket collector sighed reluctantly and glanced at his watch.

"We shall be in Brackhampton in exactly seven minutes. I'll report what you've told me. In what direction was the train you mention going?"

"This direction, of course. You don't suppose I'd have been able to see all this if a train had flashed past going in the other direction?"

The ticket collector looked as though he thought Mrs. McGillicuddy was quite capable of seeing anything anywhere as the fancy took her. But he remained polite.

"You can rely on me, Madam," he said. "I will report your statement. Perhaps I might have your name and address—just in case—"

Mrs. McGillicuddy gave him the address where she would be staying for the next few days and her permanent address in Scotland, and he wrote them down. Then he withdrew with the air of a man who has done his duty and dealt successfully with a tiresome member of the traveling public.

Mrs. McGillicuddy remained frowning and vaguely unsatisfied. Would the ticket collector really report her statement? Or had he just been soothing her down? There were, she supposed vaguely, a lot of elderly women traveling around, fully convinced that they had unmasked Communist plots, were in danger of being murdered, saw flying saucers and secret spaceships, and reported murders that had never taken place. If the man dismissed her as one of those . . .

The train was slowing down now, passing over points, and running through the bright lights of a large town.

Mrs. McGillicuddy opened her handbag, pulled out a receipted bill which was all she could find, wrote a rapid note on the back of it with her ballpoint pen, put it into a spare envelope that she fortunately happened to have, stuck the envelope down and wrote on it.

The train drew slowly into a crowded platform. The usual ubiquitous voice was intoning:

"The train now arriving at Platform 1 is the 5:38 for Milchester, Waverton, Roxeter and stations to Chadmouth. Passengers for Market Basing take the train now waiting at No. 3 platform. No. 1 Bay for stopping train to Carbury."

Mrs. McGillicuddy looked anxiously along the platform. So many passengers and so few porters. Ah, there was one! She hailed him authoritatively.

"Porter! Please take this at once to the stationmaster's office."

She handed him the envelope and with it a shilling.

Then, with a sigh, she leaned back. Well, she had done what she could. Her mind lingered with an instant's regret on the shilling. Sixpence would really have been enough . . .

Her mind went back to the scene she had witnessed. Horrible, quite horrible. She was a strong-nerved woman, but she shivered. What a strange—what a fantastic thing to happen to her, Elspeth McGillicuddy. If the blind of the carriage had not happened to fly up . . . But that, of course, was Providence.

Providence had willed that she, Elspeth McGillicuddy, should be a witness of the crime. Her lips set grimly.

Voices shouted, whistles blew, doors were banged shut. The 5:38 drew slowly out of Brackhampton Station. An hour and five minutes later it stopped at Milchester.

Mrs. McGillicuddy collected her parcels and her suitcase and got out. She peered up and down the platform. Her mind reiterated its former judgment: not enough porters. Such porters as there were seemed to be engaged with mailbags and luggage vans. Passengers nowadays seemed always expected to carry their own cases. Well, she couldn't carry her suitcase and her umbrella and all her parcels. She would have to wait. In due course she secured a porter.

"Taxi?"

"There will be something to meet me, I expect."

Outside Milchester Station, a taxi driver who had been watching the exit came forward. He spoke in a soft local voice.

"Is it Mrs. McGillicuddy? For St. Mary Mead?"

Mrs. McGillicuddy acknowledged her identity. The porter was recompensed, adequately if not handsomely. The car, with Mrs. McGillicuddy, her suitcase and her parcels, drove off into the night. It was a nine-mile drive. Sitting bolt upright in the car, Mrs. McGillicuddy was unable to relax. Her feelings yearned for expression. At last the taxi drove along the familiar village street and finally drew up at its destination; Mrs. McGillicuddy got out and walked up the brick path to the door. The driver deposited the cases inside as the door was opened by an elderly maid. Mrs. McGillicuddy passed straight through the hall to where, at the open sitting-room door, her hostess awaited her: an elderly, frail old lady.

"Elspeth!"

"Jane!"

They kissed, and without preamble or circumlocution, Mrs. McGillicuddy burst into speech.

"Oh, Jane!" she wailed. "I've just seen a murder!"

CHAPTER TWO

I

True to the precepts handed down to her by her mother and grandmother— to wit: that a true lady can neither be shocked nor surprised—Miss Marple merely raised her eyebrows and shook her head, as she said:

"Most distressing for you, Elspeth, and surely most unusual. I think you had better tell me about it at once."

That was exactly what Mrs. McGillicuddy wanted to do. Allowing her hostess to draw her nearer to the fire, she sat down, pulled off her gloves and plunged into a vivid narrative.

Miss Marple listened with close attention. When Mrs. McGillicuddy at last paused for breath, Miss Marple spoke with decision.

"The best thing, I think, my dear, is for you to go upstairs and take off your hat and have a wash. Then we will have supper—during which we will not discuss this at all. After supper we can go into the matter thoroughly and discuss it from every aspect."

Mrs. McGillicuddy concurred with this suggestion. The two ladies had supper, discussing as they ate various aspects of life as lived in the village of St. Mary Mead. Miss Marple commented on the general distrust of the new organist, related the recent scandal about the chemist's wife, and touched on the hostility between the schoolmistress and the Village Institute. They then discussed Miss Marple's and Mrs. McGillicuddy's gardens.

"Peonies," said Miss Marple as she rose from table, "are most unaccountable. Either they do—or they don't do. But if they do establish themselves, they are with you for life, so to speak, and really most beautiful varieties nowadays."

They settled themselves by the fire again, and Miss Marple brought out two old Waterford glasses from a corner cupboard, and from another cupboard produced a bottle.

"No coffee tonight for you, Elspeth," she said. "You are already overexcited—and no wonder!—and probably would not sleep. I prescribe a glass of my cowslip wine, and later, perhaps, a cup of camomile tea."

Mrs. McGillicuddy acquiescing in these arrangements, Miss Marple poured out the wine.

"Jane," said Mrs. McGillicuddy, as she took an appreciative sip, "you don't think, do you, that I dreamed it, or imagined it?"

"Certainly not," said Miss Marple with warmth.

Mrs. McGillicuddy heaved a sigh of relief.

"That ticket collector," she said, "he thought so. Quite polite, but all the same—"

"I think, Elspeth, that that was quite natural under the circumstances. It sounded—and indeed was—a most unlikely story. And you were a complete stranger to him. No, I have no doubt at all that you saw what you've told me you saw. It's very extraordinary—but not at all impossible. I recollect myself being interested, when a train ran parallel to one in which I was traveling, to notice what a vivid and intimate picture one got of what was going on in one or two of the carriages. A little girl, I remember once, was playing with a Teddy Bear and suddenly she threw it deliberately at a fat man who was asleep in the corner, and he bounced up and looked most indignant, and the other passengers looked so amused. I saw them all quite vividly. I could have described afterward exactly what they looked like and what they had on."

Mrs. McGillicuddy nodded gratefully.

"That's just how it was."

"The man had his back to you, you say. So you didn't see his face?"

"No."

"And the woman, you can describe her? Young? Old?"

"Youngish. Between thirty and thirty-five, I should think. I couldn't say closer than that."

"Good-looking?"

"That again, I couldn't say. Her face, you see, was all contorted and—"

Miss Marple said quickly:

"Yes, yes, I quite understand. How was she dressed?"

"She had on a fur coat of some kind, a palish fur. No hat. Her hair was blond."

"And there was nothing distinctive that you can remember about the man?"

Mrs. McGillicuddy took a little time to think carefully before she replied.

"He was tallish—and dark, I think. He had a heavy coat on so that I couldn't judge his build very well." She added despondently, "It's not really very much to go on, is it?"

"It's something," said Miss Marple. She paused before saying: "You feel quite sure, in your own mind, that the girl was—dead?"

"She was dead, I'm sure of it. Her tongue came out and—I'd rather not talk about it . . ."

"Of course not. Of course not," said Miss Marple quickly. "We shall know more, I expect, in the morning."

"In the morning?"

"I should imagine it will be in the morning papers. After this man had attacked and killed her, he would have a body on his hands. What would he do? Presumably he would leave the train quickly at the first station—by the way, can you remember if it was a corridor carriage?"

"No, it was not."

"That seems to point to a train that was not going far afield. It would almost certainly stop at Brackhampton. Let us say he leaves the train at Brackhampton, perhaps arranging the body in a corner seat, with the face hidden by the fur collar to delay discovery. Yes—I think that that is what he would do. But of course it will be discovered before very long—and I should imagine that the news of a murdered woman discovered on a train would be almost certain to be in the morning papers. We shall see."

II

But it was not in the morning papers.

Miss Marple and Mrs. McGillicuddy, after making sure of this, finished their breakfast in silence. Both were reflecting.

After breakfast, they took a turn round the garden. But this, usually an absorbing pastime, was today somewhat halfhearted. Miss Marple did indeed call attention to some new and rare species she had acquired for her rock garden but did so in an almost absentminded manner. And Mrs. McGillicuddy did not, as was customary, counterattack with a list of her own recent acquisitions.

"The garden is not looking at all as it should," said Miss Marple, but still speaking absentmindedly. "Doctor Haydock has absolutely forbidden me to do any stooping or kneeling—and really, what can you do if you don't stoop or kneel? There's old Edwards, of course—but so opinionated. And all this jobbing gets them into bad habits, lots of cups of tea and so much pottering—not any real work."

"Oh I know," said Mrs. McGillicuddy. "Of course there's no question of my being forbidden to stoop, but really, especially after meals—and having put on weight"—she looked down at her ample proportions—"it does bring on heartburn."

There was a silence and then Mrs. McGillicuddy planted her feet sturdily, stood still, and turned on her friend.

"Well?" she said.

It was a small, insignificant word but it acquired full significance from Mrs. McGillicuddy's tone, and Miss Marple understood its meaning perfectly.

"I know," she said.

The two ladies looked at each other.

"I think," said Miss Marple, "we might walk down to the police station and talk to Sergeant Cornish. He's intelligent and patient, and I know him very well and he knows me. I think he'll listen—and pass the information on to the proper quarter."

Accordingly some three quarters of an hour later, Miss Marple and Mrs. McGillicuddy were talking to a fresh-faced, grave man between thirty and forty who listened attentively to what they had to say.

Frank Cornish received Miss Marple with cordiality and even deference. He set chairs for the two ladies and said: "Now, what can we do for you, Miss Marple?"

Miss Marple said: "I would like you, please, to listen to my friend Mrs. McGillicuddy's story."

And Sergeant Cornish had listened. At the close of the recital he remained silent for a moment or two.

Then he said:

"That's a very extraordinary story." His eyes, without seeming to do so, had sized Mrs. McGillicuddy up while she was telling it.

On the whole, he was favorably impressed. A sensible woman, able to tell a story clearly; not, so far as he could judge, an overimaginative or a hysterical woman. Moreover, Miss Marple, so it seemed, believed in the accuracy of her friend's story and he knew all about Miss Marple. Everybody in St. Mary Mead knew Miss Marple; fluffy and dithery in appearance, but inwardly as sharp and as shrewd as they make them.

He cleared his throat and spoke.

"Of course," he said, "you may have been mistaken—I'm not saying you were, mind—but you may have been. There's a lot of horseplay goes on. It mayn't have been serious or fatal."

"I know what I saw," said Mrs. McGillicuddy grimly.

"And you won't budge from it," thought Frank Cornish, "and I'd say that likely or unlikely, you may be right."

Aloud he said: "You reported it to the railway officials, and you've come and reported it to me. That's the proper procedure and you may rely on me to have inquiries instituted."

He stopped. Miss Marple nodded her head gently, satisfied. Mrs. McGillicuddy was not quite so satisfied, but she did not say anything. Sergeant Cornish addressed Miss Marple, not so much because he wanted her ideas, as because he wanted to her what she would say.

"Granted the facts are as reported," he said. "What do you think has happened to the body?"

"There seem to be only two possibilities," said Miss Marple without hesitation. "The more likely one, of course, is that the body was left in the rain, but that seems improbable now, for it would have been found sometime last night by another traveler or by the railway staff at the train's ultimate destination."

Frank Cornish nodded.

"The only other course open to the murderer would be to push the body out of the train on to the line. It must, I suppose, be still on the track somewhere as yet undiscovered—though that does seem a little unlikely. But there would be, as far as I can see, no other way of dealing with it."

"You read about bodies being put in trunks," said Mrs. McGillicuddy, "but no one travels with trunks nowadays, only suitcases, and you couldn't get a body into a suitcase."

"Yes," said Cornish. "I agree with you both. The body, if there is a body, ought to have been discovered by now, or will be very soon. I'll let you know any developments there are—though I daresay you'll read about them in the papers. There's the possibility, of course, that the woman, though savagely attacked, was not actually dead. She may have been able to leave the train on her own feet."

"Hardly without assistance," said Miss Marple. "And if so, it will have been noticed. A man, supporting a woman who he says is ill."

"Yes, it will have been noticed," said Cornish. "Or if a woman was found unconscious or ill in a carriage and was removed to a hospital, that, too, will be on record. I think you may rest assured that you'll hear about it all in a very short time."

But that day passed and the next day. On that evening, Miss Marple received a note from Sergeant Cornish.

In regard to the matter on which you consulted me, full inquiries have been made, with no result. No woman's body has been found. No hospital has administered treatment to a woman such as you describe, and no case of a woman suffering from shock or taken ill, or leaving a station supported by a man has been observed. You may take it that the fullest inquiries have been made. I suggest that your friend may have witnessed a scene such as she described but that it was much less serious than she supposed.

CHAPTER THREE

I

"Less serious? Fiddlesticks!" said Mrs. McGillicuddy. "It was murder!"

She looked defiantly at Miss Marple and Miss Marple looked back at her.

"Go on, Jane," said Mrs. McGillicuddy. "Say it was all a mistake! Say I imagined the whole thing! That's what you think now, isn't it?"

"Anyone can be mistaken," Miss Marple pointed out gently. "Anybody, Elspeth, even you. I think we must bear that in mind. But I still think, you know, that you were most probably not mistaken. You use glasses for reading, but you've got very good far sight—and what you saw impressed you very powerfully. You were definitely suffering from shock when you arrived here."

"It's a thing I shall never forget," said Mrs. McGillicuddy with a shudder. "The trouble is, I don't see what I can do about it!"

"I don't think," said Miss Marple thoughtfully, "that there's anything more you can do about it." (If Mrs. McGillicuddy had been alert to the tones of her friend's voice, she might have noticed a very faint stress laid on the *you*). "You've reported what you saw—to the railway people and to the police. No, there's nothing more you can do."

"That's a relief, in a way," said Mrs. McGillicuddy, "because, as you

know, I'm going out to Ceylon immediately after Christmas to stay with
Roderick and I certainly do not want to put that visit off—I've been looking
forward to it so much. Though of course I would put it off if I thought it was
my duty," she added conscientiously.

"I'm sure you would, Elspeth, but as I say, I consider you've done
everything you possibly could do."

"It's up to the police," said Mrs. McGillicuddy. "And if the police choose
to be stupid—"

Miss Marple shook her head decisively.

"Oh no," she said, "the police aren't stupid. And that makes it
interesting, doesn't it?"

Mrs. McGillicuddy looked at her without comprehension and Miss
Marple reaffirmed her judgment of her friend as a woman of excellent
principles and no imagination.

"One wants to know," said Miss Marple, "what really happened."

"She was killed."

"Yes, but who killed her, and why, and what happened to her body?
Where is it now?"

"That's the business of the police to find out."

"Exactly! And they haven't found out. That means, doesn't it, that the
man was clever—very clever. I can't imagine, you know," said Miss Marple
knitting her brows, "how he disposed of it. You kill a woman in a fit of
passion—it must have been unpremeditated; you'd never choose to kill a
woman in such circumstances just a few minutes before running into a big
station. No, it must have been a quarrel—jealousy—something of that kind.
You strangle her—and there you are, as I say, with a dead body on your
hands and on the point of running into a station. What could you do except
as I said at first, prop the body up in a corner as though asleep, hiding the
face, and then yourself leave the train as quickly as possible. I don't see any
other possibility. And yet there must have been one . . ."

Miss Marple lost herself in thought.

Mrs. McGillicuddy spoke to her twice before Miss Marple answered.

"You're getting deaf, Jane."

"Just a little, perhaps. People do not seem to me to enunciate their words
as clearly as they used to do. But it wasn't that I didn't hear you. I'm afraid
I wasn't paying attention."

"I just asked about the trains to London tomorrow. Would the afternoon
be all right? I'm going to Margaret's and she isn't expecting me before
teatime."

"I wonder, Elspeth, if you would mind going up by the 12:15? We could
have an early lunch."

"Of course and—"

Miss Marple went on, drowning her friend's words:

"And I wonder, too, if Margaret would mind if you didn't arrive for tea—
if you arrived about seven, perhaps?"

Mrs. McGillicuddy looked at her friend curiously.

"What's on your mind, Jane?"

"I suggest, Elspeth, that I should travel up to London with you, and that
we should travel down again as far as Brackhampton in the train you
traveled by the other day. You would then return to London from

Brackhampton and I would come on here as you did. I, of course, would pay the fares." Miss Marple stressed this point firmly.

Mrs. McGillicuddy ignored the financial aspect.

"What on earth do you expect, Jane?" she asked. "Another murder?"

"Certainly not," said Miss Marple shocked. "But I confess I should like to see for myself, under your guidance, the—the—really it is most difficult to find the correct term—the terrain of the crime."

So accordingly on the following day Miss Marple and Mrs. McGillicuddy found themselves in two opposite corners of a first-class carriage speeding out of London by the 4:54 from Paddington. Paddington had been even more crowded than on the preceding Friday, as there were now only two days to go before Christmas, but the 4:54 was comparatively peaceful—at any rate in the rear portion.

On this occasion no train drew level with them, or they with another train. At intervals trains flashed past them toward London. On two occasions trains flashed past them the other way going at high speed. At intervals Mrs. McGillicuddy consulted her watch doubtfully.

"It's hard to tell just when— We'd passed through a station I know . . ." But they were continually passing through stations.

"We're due in Brackhampton in five minutes," said Miss Marple.

A ticket collector appeared in the doorway. Miss Marple raised her eyes interrogatively. Mrs. McGillicuddy shook her head. It was not the same ticket collector. He clipped their tickets and passed on, staggering just a little as the train swung round a long curve. It slackened speed as it did so.

"I expect we're coming into Brackhampton," said Mrs. McGillicuddy.

"We're getting into the outskirts, I think," said Miss Marple.

There were lights flashing past outside, buildings, an occasional glimpse of streets and trams. Their speed slackened further. They began crossing points.

"We'll be there in a minute," said Mrs. McGillicuddy, "and I can't really see this journey has been any good at all. Has it suggested anything to you, Jane?"

"I'm afraid not," said Miss Marple in a rather doubtful voice.

"A sad waste of good money," said Mrs. McGillicuddy but with less disapproval than she would have used had she been paying for herself. Miss Marple had been quite adamant on that point.

"All the same," said Miss Marple, "one likes to see with one's own eyes where a thing happened. This train's just a few minutes late. Was yours on time on Friday?"

"I think so. I didn't really notice."

The train drew slowly into the busy length of Brackhampton Station. The loudspeaker announced hoarsely, doors opened and shut, people got in and out, milled up and down the platform. It was a busy, crowded scene.

Easy, thought Miss Marple, for a murderer to merge into that crowd, to leave the station in the midst of that pressing mass of people, or even to select another carriage and go on in the train to wherever its ultimate destination might be. Easy to be one male passenger among many. But not so easy to make a body vanish into thin air. That body must be somewhere.

Mrs. McGillicuddy had descended. She spoke now from the platform, through the open window.

"Now take care of yourself, Jane," she said. "Don't catch a chill. It's a nasty treacherous time of year, and you're not so young as you were."

"I know," said Miss Marple.

"And don't let's worry ourselves any more over all this. We've done what we could."

Miss Marple nodded and said:

"Don't stand about in the cold, Elspeth. Or you'll be the one to catch a chill. Go and get yourself a good hot cup of tea in the refreshment room. You've got time, twelve minutes before your train back to town."

"I think perhaps I will. Good-bye, Jane."

"Good-bye, Elspeth. A happy Christmas to you. I hope you find Margaret well. Enjoy yourself in Ceylon, and give my love to dear Roderick—if he remembers me at all which I doubt."

"Of course he remembers you—very well. You helped him in some way when he was at school—something to do with money that was disappearing from a locker. He's never forgotten it."

"Oh, that!" said Miss Marple.

Mrs. McGillicuddy turned away, a whistle blew, the train began to move. Miss Marple watched the sturdy thick-set body of her friend recede. Elspeth could go to Ceylon with a clear conscience—she had done her duty and was freed from further obligation.

Miss Marple did not lean back as the train gathered speed. Instead she sat upright and devoted herself seriously to thought. Though in speech Miss Marple was woolly and diffuse, in mind she was clear and sharp. She had a problem to solve, the problem of her own future conduct; and, perhaps strangely, it presented itself to her as it had to Mrs. McGillicuddy, as a question of duty.

Mrs. McGillicuddy had said that they had both done all that they could do. It was true of Mrs. McGillicuddy, but about herself Miss Marple did not feel so sure.

It was a question, sometimes, of using one's special gifts. But perhaps that was conceited. After all, what could she do? Her friend's words came back to her, "You're not so young as you were . . ."

Dispassionately, like a general planning a campaign, or an accountant assessing a business, Miss Marple weighed up and set down in her mind the facts for and against further enterprise. On the credit side were the following:

1) *My long experience of life and human nature.*
2) *Sir Henry Clithering and his nephew (now at Scotland Yard, I believe), who was so very nice in the Little Paddocks case.*
3) *My nephew Raymond's second boy, David, who is, I am almost sure, in British Railways.*
4) *Griselda's boy Leonard who is so very knowledgeable about maps.*

Miss Marple reviewed these assets and approved them. They were all very necessary to reinforce the weaknesses on the debit side—in particular her own bodily weakness.

"It's not," thought Miss Marple, "as though I could go here, there and everywhere, making inquiries and finding out things."

Yes, that was the chief objection, her own age and weakness. Although, for her age, her health was good, yet she was old. And if Doctor Haydock had strictly forbidden her to do practical gardening he would hardly approve of her starting out to track down a murderer. For that, in effect, was what she was planning to do—and it was there that her loophole lay. For if heretofore murder had, so to speak, been forced upon her, in this case it would be that she herself set out deliberately to seek it. And she was not sure that she wanted to do so. She was old—old and tired. She felt at this moment, at the end of a tiring day, a great reluctance to enter upon any project at all. She wanted nothing at all but to reach home and sit by the fire with a nice tray of supper, and go to bed, and potter about the next day just snipping off a few things in the garden, tidying up in a very mild way, without stooping, without exerting herself.

"I'm too old for any more adventures," said Miss Marple to herself, watching absently out of the window the curving line of an embankment.

A curve.

Very faintly something stirred in her mind. Just after the ticket collector had clipped their tickets . . .

It suggested an idea. Only an idea. An entirely different idea. . . .

A little pink flush came into Miss Marple's face. Suddenly she did not feel tired at all!

"I'll write to David tomorrow morning," she said to herself.

And at the same time another valuable asset flashed through her mind.

"Of course. My faithful Florence!"

II

Miss Marple set about her plan of campaign methodically and making due allowance for the Christmas season which was a definitely retarding factor.

She wrote to her great-nephew, David West, combining Christmas wishes with an urgent request for information.

Fortunately she was invited, as on previous years, to the vicarage for Christmas dinner, and here she was able to tackle young Leonard, home for the Christmas season, about maps.

Maps of all kinds were Leonard's passion. The reason for the old lady's inquiry about a large-scale map of a particular area did not rouse his curiosity. He discoursed on maps generally with fluency, and wrote down for her exactly what would suit her purpose best. In fact, he did better. He actually found that he had such a map among his collection and he lent it to her, Miss Marple promising to take great care of it and return it in due course.

III

"Maps," said his mother Griselda who still, although she had a grown-up son, looked strangely young and blooming to be inhabiting the shabby old vicarage. "What does she want with maps? I mean, what does she want them for?"

"I don't know," said young Leonard, "I don't think she said exactly."

"I wonder now . . ." said Griselda. "It seems very fishy to me. At her age the old pet ought to give up that sort of thing."

Leonard asked what sort of thing, and Griselda said elusively:

"Oh, poking her nose into things. Why maps, I wonder?"

In due course Miss Marple received a letter from her great-nephew David West. It ran affectionately:

> Dear Aunt Jane. Now what are you up to? I've got the information you wanted. There are only two trains that can possibly apply—the 4:33 and the 5 o'clock. The former is a slow train and stops at Haling Broadway, Barwell Heath, Brackhampton and then stations to Market Basing. The 5 o'clock is the Welsh express for Cardiff, Newport and Swansea. The former might be overtaken somewhere by the 4:54, although it is due in Brackhampton five minutes earlier and the latter passes the 4:54 just before Brackhampton.
>
> In all this do I smell some scandal of a fruity character? Did you, returning from a shopping spree in town by the 4:54, observe in a passing train the mayor's wife being embraced by the sanitary inspector? But why does it matter which train it was? A weekend at Porthcawl, perhaps? Thank you for the pullover. Just what I wanted.
>
> How's the garden? Not very active this time of year, I should imagine.
>
> Yours ever,
David

Miss Marple smiled a little, then considered the information thus presented to her. Mrs. McGillicuddy had said definitely that the carriage had not been a corridor one. Therefore—not the Swansea express. The 4:33 was indicated.

Also some more traveling seemed unavoidable. Miss Marple sighed, but made her plans.

She went up to London as before on the 12:15, but this time returned not by the 4:54, but by the 4:33 as far as Brackhampton. The journey was uneventful, but she registered certain details. The train was not crowded—4:33 was before the evening rush hour. Of the first-class carriages only one had an occupant—a very old gentleman reading the *New Statesman*. Miss Marple traveled in an empty compartment and at the two stops, Haling Broadway and Barwell Heath, leaned out of the window to observe passengers entering and leaving the train. A small number of third-class passengers got in at Haling Broadway. At Barwell Heath several third-class passengers got out. Nobody entered or left a first-class carriage except the old gentleman carrying his *New Statesman.*

As the train neared Brackhampton, sweeping around a curve of line, Miss Marple rose to her feet and stood experimentally with her back to the window over which she had drawn down the blind.

Yes, she decided, the impetus of the sudden curving of the line and the slackening of speed did throw one off one's balance back against the window and the blind might, in consequence, very easily fly up. She peered out into the night. It was lighter than it had been when Mrs. McGillicuddy had made the same journey—only just dark, but there was little to see. For observation she must make a daylight journey.

On the next day she went up by the early-morning train, purchased four linen pillowcases (tut-tutting at the price!) so as to combine investigation with the provision of household necessities, and returned by a train leaving Paddington at 12:15. Again she was alone in a first-class carriage. "This taxation," thought Miss Marple, "that's what it is. No one can afford to travel first class except businessmen in the rush hours. I suppose because they can charge it to expenses."

About a quarter of an hour before the train was due at Brackhampton, Miss Marple got out the map with which Leonard had supplied her and began to observe the countryside. She had studied the map very carefully beforehand, and after noting the name of a station they passed through, she was soon able to identify where she was just as the train began to slacken for a curve. It was a very considerable curve, indeed. Miss Marple, her nose glued to the window, studied the ground beneath her (the train was running on a fairly high embankment) with close attention. She divided her attention between the country outside and her map until the train finally ran into Brackhampton.

That night she wrote and posted a letter addressed to Miss Florence Hill, 4 Madison Road, Brackhampton. On the following morning, going to the county library, she studied a *Brackhampton Directory and Gazetteer,* and a county history.

Nothing so far had contradicted the very faint and sketchy idea that had come to her. What she had imagined was possible. She would go no farther than that.

But the next step involved action—a good deal of action—the kind of action for which she, herself, was physically unfit. If her theory were to be definitely proved or disproved, she must at this point have help from some other person. The question was—who? Miss Marple reviewed various names and possibilities, rejecting them all with a vexed shake of the head. The intelligent people, on whose intelligence she could rely, were all far too busy. Not only had they all got jobs of varying importance, their leisure hours were usually apportioned long beforehand. The unintelligent who had time on their hands were simply, Miss Marple decided, no good.

She pondered in growing vexation and perplexity.

Then suddenly her forehead cleared. She ejaculated aloud a name.

"Of course!" said Miss Marple. "Lucy Eyelesbarrow!"

CHAPTER FOUR

I

The name of Lucy Eyelesbarrow had already made itself felt in certain circles.

Lucy Eyelesbarrow was thirty-two. She had taken a First in mathematics at Oxford, was acknowledged to have a brilliant mind and was confidently expected to take up a distinguished academic career.

But Lucy Eyelesbarrow, in addition to scholarly brilliance, had a core of good, sound common sense. She could not fail to observe that a life of academic distinction was singularly ill rewarded. She had no desire whatever to teach and she took pleasure in contacts with minds much less brilliant than her own. In short, she had a taste for people, all sorts of people—and not the same people the whole time. She also, quite frankly, liked money. To gain money one must exploit shortage.

Lucy Eyelesbarrow hit at once upon a very serious shortage—the shortage of any kind of skilled domestic labor. To the amazement of her friends and fellow scholars, Lucy Eyelesbarrow entered the field of domestic labor.

Her success was immediate and assured. By now, after a lapse of some years, she was known all over the British Isles. It was quite customary for wives to say joyfully to husbands, "It will be all right. I can go with you to the States. *I've got Lucy Eyelesbarrow!*" The point of Lucy Eyelesbarrow was that once she came into a house, all worry, anxiety and hard work went out of it. Lucy Eyelesbarrow did everything, saw to everything, arranged everything. She was unbelievably competent in every conceivable sphere. She looked after elderly parents, accepted the care of young children, nursed the sickly, cooked divinely, got on well with any old crusted servants there might happen to be (there usually weren't), was tactful with impossible people, soothed habitual drunkards, was wonderful with dogs. Best of all she never minded what she did. She scrubbed the kitchen floor, dug in the garden, cleaned up dog messes and carried coals!

One of her rules was never to accept an engagement for any long length of time. A fortnight was her usual period—a month at most under exceptional circumstances. For that fortnight you had to pay the earth! But, during that fortnight, your life was heaven. You could relax completely, go abroad, stay at home, do as you pleased, secure that all was going well on the home front in Lucy Eyelesbarrow's capable hands.

Naturally the demand for her services was enormous. She could have booked herself up if she chose for about three years ahead. She had been offered enormous sums to go as a permanency. But Lucy had no intention of being a permanency, nor would she book herslf for more than six months ahead. And within that period, unknown to her clamoring clients, she always kept certain free periods which enabled her either to take a short luxurious holiday (since she spent nothing otherwise and was handsomely paid and kept) or to accept any position at short notice that happened to take her fancy, either by reason of its character, or because she "liked the people." Since she was at liberty to pick and choose among the vociferous claimants for her services, she went very largely by personal liking. Mere riches would not buy you the services of Lucy Eyelesbarrow. She could pick and choose and she did pick and choose. She enjoyed her life very much and found in it a continual source of entertainment.

Lucy Eyelesbarrow read and reread the letter from Miss Marple. She had made Miss Marple's acquaintance two years ago when her services had been retained by Raymond West, the novelist, to go and look after his old aunt who was recovering from pneumonia. Lucy had accepted the job and had gone down to St. Mary Mead. She had liked Miss Marple very much. As for Miss Marple, once she had caught a glimpse out of her bedroom window of Lucy Eyelesbarrow really trenching for sweet peas in the proper way, she had leaned back on her pillows with a sigh of relief, eaten the tempting little meals that Lucy Eyelesbarrow brought to her, and listened, agreeably surprised, to the tales told by her elderly irascible maidservant of how "I taught that Miss Eyelesbarrow a crochet pattern what she'd never heard of! Proper grateful she was." And had surprised her doctor by the rapidity of her convalescence.

Miss Marple wrote asking if Miss Eyelesbarrow could undertake a certain task for her—rather an unusual one. Perhaps Miss Eyelesbarrow could arrange a meeting at which they could discuss the matter.

Lucy Eyelesbarrow frowned for a moment or two as she considered. She was in reality fully booked up. But the word unusual, and her recollection of Miss Marple's personality, carried the day and she rang up Miss Marple straightaway explaining that she could not come down to St. Mary Mead as she was at the moment working, but that she was free from two to four on the following afternoon and could meet Miss Marple anywhere in London. She suggested her own club, a rather nondescript establishment which had the advantage of having several small, dark writing rooms which were usually empty.

Miss Marple accepted the suggestion and on the following day the meeting took place.

Greetings were exchanged; Lucy Eyelesbarrow led her guest to the gloomiest of the writing rooms, and said: "I'm afraid I'm rather booked up just at present, but perhaps you'll tell me what it is you want me to undertake?"

"It's very simply, really," said Miss Marple. "Unusual, but simple. I want you to find a body."

For a moment the suspicion crossed Lucy's mind that Miss Marple was mentally unhinged, but she rejected the idea. Miss Marple was eminently sane. She meant exactly what she had said.

"What kind of a body?" asked Lucy Eyelesbarrow with admirable composure.

"A woman's body," said Miss Marple. "The body of a woman who was murdered—strangled actually—in a train."

Lucy's eyebrows rose slightly.

"Well, that's certainly unusual. Tell me about it."

Miss Marple told her. Lucy Eyelesbarrow listened attentively, without interrupting. At the end she said:

"It all depends on what your friend saw—or thought she saw—?"

She left the sentence unfinished with a question in it.

"Elspeth McGillicuddy doesn't imagine things," said Miss Marple. "That's why I'm relying on what she said. If it had been Dorothy Cartwright, now, it would have been quite a different matter. Dorothy always has a good story and quite often believes it herself, and there is usually a kind of basis of truth but certainly no more. But Elspeth is the kind of woman who finds it very hard to make herself believe that anything at all extraordinary or out of the way could happen. She's most unsuggestible, rather like granite."

"I see," said Lucy thoughtfully. "Well, let's accept it all. Where do I come in?"

"I was very much impressed by you," said Miss Marple, "and you see I haven't got the physical strength nowadays to get about and do things."

"You want me to make inquiries? That sort of thing? But won't the police have done all that? Or do you think they have been just slack?"

"Oh no," said Miss Marple. "They haven't been slack. It's just that I've got a theory about the woman's body. It's got to be somewhere. If it wasn't found in the train, then it must have been pushed or thrown out of the train—but it hasn't been discovered anywhere on the line. So I traveled down the same way to see if there was anywhere where the body could have been thrown off the train and yet wouldn't have been found on the line— and there was. The railway line makes a big curve before getting into Brackhampton, on the edge of a high embankment. If a body were thrown out there, when the train was leaning at an angle, I think it would pitch right down the embankment."

"But surely it would still be found—even there?"

"Oh yes. It would have to be taken away. But we'll come to that presently. Here's the place—on this map."

Lucy bent to study where Miss Marple's finger pointed.

"It is right in the outskirts of Brackhampton now," said Miss Marple, "but originally it was a country house with extensive park and grounds and it's still there, untouched—ringed round now with building estates and small suburban houses. It's called Rutherford Hall. It was built by a man called Crackenthorpe, a very rich manufacturer, in 1884. The original Crackenthorpe's son, an elderly man, is living there still with, I understand, a daughter. The railway encircles quite half of the property."

"And you want me to do—what?"

Miss Marple replied promptly.

"I want you to get a post there. Everyone is crying out for efficient domestic help. I should not imagine it would be difficult."

"No, I don't suppose it would be difficult."

"I understand that Mr. Crackenthorpe is said locally to be somewhat of a miser. If you accept a low salary, I will make it up to the proper figure which should, I think, be rather more than the current rate."

"Because of the difficulty?"

"Not the difficulty so much as the danger. It might, you know, be dangerous. It's only right to warn you of that."

"I don't know," said Lucy pensively, "that the idea of danger would deter me."

"I didn't think it would," said Miss Marple. "You're not that kind of person."

"I dare say you thought it might even attract me? I've encountered very little danger in my life. But do you really believe it might be dangerous?"

"Somebody," Miss Marple pointed out, "has committed a very successful crime. There has been no hue and cry, no real suspicion. Two elderly ladies have told a rather improbable story, the police have investigated it and found nothing in it. So everything is nice and quiet. I don't think that this somebody, whoever he may be, will care about the matter being raked up—especially if you are successful."

"What do I look for exactly?"

"Any signs along the embankment, a scrap of clothing, broken bushes—that kind of thing."

Lucy nodded.

"And then?"

"I shall be quite close at hand," said Miss Marple. "An old maidservant of mine, my faithful Florence, lives in Brackhampton. She has looked after her old parents for years. They are now both dead, and she takes in lodgers—all most respectable people. She has arranged for me to have rooms with her. She will look after me most devotedly, and I feel I should like to be close at hand. I would suggest that you mention you have an elderly aunt living in the neighborhood, and that you want a post within easy distance of her, and also that you stipulate for a reasonable amount of spare time so that you can go and see her often."

Again Lucy nodded.

"I was going to Taormina the day after tomorrow," she said. "The holiday can wait. But I can only promise three weeks. After that, I am booked up."

"Three weeks should be ample," said Miss Marple. "If we can't find out anything in three weeks, we might as well give up the whole thing as a mare's nest."

Miss Marple departed, and Lucy, after a moment's reflection, rang up a registry office in Brackhampton, the manageress of which she knew very well. She explained her desire for a post in the neighborhood so as to be near her "aunt." After she had turned down, with a little difficulty and a good deal of ingenuity, several more desirable places, Rutherford Hall was mentioned.

"Sounds exactly what I want," said Lucy firmly.

The registry office rang up Miss Crackenthorpe, Miss Crackenthorpe rang up Lucy.

Two days later Lucy left London en route for Rutherford Hall.

II

Driving her own small car, Lucy Eyelesbarrow turned through an imposing pair of vast iron gates. Just inside them was what had originally been a small lodge which now seemed completely derelict, whether through war damage or merely through neglect, it was difficult to be sure. A long, winding drive led through large gloomy clumps of rhododendrons up to the house. Lucy caught her breath in a slight gasp when she saw the house which was a kind of miniature Windsor Castle. The stone steps in front of the door could have done with attention and the gravel sweep was green with neglected weeds.

She pulled an old-fashioned wrought-iron bell, and its clamor sounded echoing away inside. A slatternly woman, wiping her hands on her apron, opened the door and looked at her suspiciously.

"Expected, aren't you?" she said. "Miss Somethingbarrow, she told me."

"Quite right," said Lucy.

The house was desperately cold inside. Her guide led her along a dark hall and opened a door on the right. Rather to Lucy's surprise, it was quite a pleasant sitting room, with books and chintz-covered chairs.

"I'll tell Her," said the woman, and went away shutting the door after having given Lucy a look of profound disfavor.

After a few minutes the door opened again. From the first moment Lucy decided that she liked Emma Crackenthorpe.

She was a middle-aged woman with no very outstanding characteristics, neither good looking nor plain, sensibly dressed in tweeds and pullover, with dark hair swept back from her forehead, steady hazel eyes and a very pleasant voice.

She said: "Miss Eyelesbarrow?" and held out her hand.

Then she looked doubtful.

"I wonder," she said, "if this post is really what you're looking for? I don't want a housekeeper, you know, to supervise things. I want someone to do the work."

Lucy said that that was what most people needed.

Emma Crackenthorpe said apologetically:

"So many people, you know, seem to think that just a little light dusting will answer the case, but I can do all the light dusting myself."

"I quite understand," said Lucy. "You want cooking and washing up, and housework and stoking the boiler. That's all right. That's what I do. I'm not at all afraid of work."

"It's a big house, I'm afraid, and inconvenient. Of course we only live in a portion of it—my father and myself, that is. He is rather an invalid. We live quite quietly, and there is an Aga stove. I have several brothers, but they are not here very often. Two women come in, a Mrs. Kidder in the morning and Mrs. Hart three days a week, to do brasses and things like that. You have your own car?"

"Yes. It can stand out in the open if there's nowhere to put it. It's used to it."

"Oh, there are any amount of old stables. There's no trouble about that." She frowned a moment, then said, "Eyelesbarrow—rather an unusual name. Some friends of mine were telling me about a Lucy Eyelesbarrow— the Kennedys?"

"Yes. I was with them in North Devon when Mrs. Kennedy was having a baby."

Emma Crackenthorpe smiled.

"I know they said they'd never had such a wonderful time as when you were there seeing to everything. But I had the idea that you were terribly expensive. The sum I mentioned—"

"That's quite all right," said Lucy. "I want particularly, you see, to be near Brackhampton. I have an elderly aunt in a critical state of health and I want to be within easy distance of her. That's why the salary is a secondary consideration. I can't afford to do nothing. If I could be sure of having some time off most days?"

"Oh, of course. Every afternoon, till six, if you like?"

"That seems perfect."

Miss Crackenthorpe hesitated a moment before saying: "My father is elderly and a little—difficult—sometimes. He is very keen on economy, and he says things sometimes that upset people. I wouldn't like—"

Lucy broke in quickly.

"I'm quite used to elderly people of all kinds," she said. "I always manage to get on well with them."

Emma Crackenthorpe looked relieved.

"Trouble with father!" diagnosed Lucy. "I bet he's an old tartar."

She was apportioned a large, gloomy bedroom which a small electric heater did its inadequate best to warm, and was shown round the house, a vast uncomfortable mansion. As they passed a door in the hall a voice roared out:

"That you, Emma? Got the new girl there? Bring her in. I want to look at her."

Emma flushed, glanced at Lucy apologetically.

The two women entered the room. It was richly upholstered in dark velvet, the narrow windows let in very little light, and it was full of heavy mahogany Victorian furniture.

Old Mr. Crackenthorpe was stretched out in an invalid's chair, a silverheaded stick by his side.

He was a big gaunt man, his flesh hanging in loose folds. He had a face rather like a bulldog, with a pugnacious chin. He had thick, dark hair flecked with gray, and small suspicious eyes.

"Let's have a look at you, young lady."

Lucy advanced, composed and smiling.

"There's just one thing you'd better understand straight away. Just because we live in a big house doesn't mean we're rich. We're not rich. We live simply—do you hear?—simply! No good coming here with a lot of highfalutin ideas. Cod's as good a fish as turbot any day and don't you forget it. I don't stand for waste. I live here because my father built the house and I like it. After I'm dead they can sell it up if they want to—and I expect they will want to. No sense of family. This house is well built—it's solid, and we've got our own land round us. Keeps us private. It would bring in a lot for building land but not while I'm alive. You won't get me out of here until you take me out feet first."

He glared at Lucy.

"Your house is your castle," said Lucy.

"Laughing at me?"

"Of course not. I think it's very exciting to have a real country place all surrounded by town."

"Quite so. Can't see another house from here, can you? Fields with cows in them—right in the middle of Brackhampton. You hear the traffic a bit when the wind's that way, but otherwise it's still country."

He added, without pause or change of tone, to his daughter:

"Ring up that damnfool of a doctor. Tell him that last medicine's no good at all."

Lucy and Emma retired. He shouted after them:

"And don't let that damned woman who sniffs dust in here. She's disarranged all my books."

Lucy asked:

"Has Mr. Crackenthorpe been an invalid long?"

Emma said, rather evasively:

"Oh, for years now . . . This is the kitchen."

The kitchen was enormous. A vast kitchen range stood cold and neglected. An Aga stood demurely beside it.

Lucy asked times of meals and inspected the larder. Then she said cheerfully to Emma Crackenthorpe:

"I know everything now. Don't bother. Leave it all to me."

Emma Crackenthorpe heaved a sigh of relief as she went up to bed that night.

"The Kennedys were quite right," she said. "She's wonderful."

Lucy rose at six the next morning. She did the house, prepared vegetables, assembled, cooked and served breakfast. With Mrs. Kidder she made the beds and at eleven o'clock they sat down to strong tea and biscuits in the kitchen. Mollified by the fact that Lucy "had no airs about her" and also by the strength and sweetness of the tea, Mrs. Kidder relaxed into gossip. She was a small, spare woman with a sharp eye and tight lips.

"Regular old skinflint he is. What She has to put up with! All the same, She's not what I call downtrodden. Can hold her own all right when she has to. When the gentlemen come down She's sees to it there's something decent to eat."

"The gentlemen?"

"Yes. Big family it was. The eldest, Mr. Edmund, he was killed in the war. Then there's Mr. Cedric, he lives abroad somewhere. He's not married. Paints pictures in foreign parts. Mr. Harold's in the City, lives in London—married an earl's daughter. Then there's Mr. Alfred, he's got a nice way with him, but he's a bit of a black sheep, been in trouble once or twice—and there's Miss Edith's husband, Mr. Bryan, ever so nice he is. She died some years ago, but he's always stayed one of the family. And there's Master Alexander, Miss Edith's little boy. He's at school, comes here for part of the holidays always; Miss Emma's terribly set on him."

Lucy digested all this information, continuing to press tea on her informant. Finally, reluctantly, Mrs. Kidder rose to her feet.

"Seem to have got along a treat we do, this morning," she said wonderingly. "Want me to give you a hand with the potatoes, dear?"

"They're already done."

"Well, you are a one for getting on with things! I might as well be getting along myself as there doesn't seem anything else to do."

Mrs. Kidder departed and Lucy, with time on her hands, scrubbed the kitchen table which she had been longing to do, but which she had put off so as not to offend Mrs. Kidder whose job it properly was. Then she cleaned the silver till it shone radiantly. She cooked lunch, cleared it away, washed up, and at two-thirty was ready to start exploration. She had set out the tea things ready on a tray, with sandwiches and bread and butter covered over with a damp napkin to keep them moist.

She strolled first round the gardens which would be the normal thing to do. The kitchen garden was sketchily cultivated with a few vegetables. The hothouses were in ruins. The paths everywhere were overgrown with weeds. A herbaceous border near the house was the only thing that showed free of weeds and in good condition and Lucy suspected that that had been Emma's hand. The gardener was a very old man, somewhat deaf, who was only making a show of working. Lucy spoke to him pleasantly. He lived in a cottage adjacent to the big stable yard.

Extending out from the stable yard, a back drive led through the park, which was fenced on either side of it, and under a railway arch into a small back lane.

Every few minutes a train thundered along the main line over the railway arch. Lucy watched the trains as they slackened speed going round the sharp curve that encircled the Crackenthorpe property. She passed under the railway arch and out into the lane. It seemed a little-used track. On the one side was the railway embankment, on the other was a high wall which enclosed some tall factory buildings. Lucy followed the lane until it came out into a street of small houses. She could hear a short distance away the busy hum of main-road traffic. She glanced at her watch. A woman came out of a house nearby and Lucy stopped her.

"Excuse me, can you tell me if there is a public telephone near here?"

"Post office just at the corner of the road."

Lucy thanked her and walked along until she came to the post office, which was a combination shop and post office. There was a telephone box at one side. Lucy went into it and made a call. She asked to speak to Miss Marple. A woman's voice spoke in a sharp bark.

"She's resting. And I'm not going to disturb her! She needs her rest— she's an old lady. Who shall I say called?"

"Miss Eyelesbarrow. There's no need to disturb her. Just tell her that I've arrived and everything is going on well and that I'll let her know when I've any news."

She replaced the receiver and made her way back to Rutherford Hall.

CHAPTER FIVE

I

"I suppose it will be all right if I just practice a few iron shots in the park?" asked Lucy.

"Oh yes, certainly. Are you fond of golf?"

"I'm not much good, but I like to keep in practice. It's a more agreeable form of exercise than just going for a walk."

"Nowhere to walk outside this place," growled Mr. Crackenthorpe. "Nothing but pavements and miserable little bandboxes of houses. Like to get hold of my land and build more of them. But they won't until I'm dead. And I'm not going to die to oblige anybody. I can tell you that! Not to oblige anybody!"

Emma Crackenthorpe said mildly:

"Now, Father."

"I know what they think—and what they're waiting for. All of 'em. Cedric, and that sly fox Harold with his smug face. As for Alfred I wonder he hasn't had a shot at bumping me off himself. Not sure he didn't, at Christmastime. That was a very odd turn I had. Puzzled old Quimper. He asked me a lot of discreet questions."

"Everyone gets these digestive upsets now and again, Father."

"All right, all right, say straight out that I ate too much! That's what you mean. And why did I eat too much? Because there was too much food on the table, far too much. Wasteful and extravagant. And that reminds me—you, young woman. Five potatoes you sent in for lunch—good-sized ones, too. Two potatoes are enough for anybody. So don't send in more than four in the future. The extra one was wasted today." ·

"It wasn't wasted, Mr. Crackenthorpe. I've planned to use it in a Spanish omelet tonight."

"Urgh!" As Lucy went out of the room carrying the coffee tray she heard him say, "Slick young woman, that, always got all the answers. Cooks well, though—and she's a handsome kind of girl."

Lucy Eyelesbarrow took a light iron out of the set of golf clubs she had had the forethought to bring with her and strolled out into the park, climbing over the fencing.

She began playing a series of shots. After five minutes or so, a ball, apparently sliced, pitched on the side of the railway embankment. Lucy went up and began to hunt about for it. She looked back toward the house. It was a long way off and nobody was in the least interested in what she was doing. She continued to hunt for the ball. Now and then she played shots from the embankment down into the grass. During the afternoon she searched about a third of the embankment. Nothing. She played her ball back toward the house.

Then, on the next day, she came upon something. A thornbush growing about halfway up the bank had been snapped off. Bits of it lay scattered about. Lucy examined the tree itself. Impaled on one of the thorns was a torn scrap of fur. It was almost the same color as the wood, a pale brownish color. Lucy looked at it for a moment, then she took a pair of scissors out of her pocket and snipped it carefully in half. The half she had snipped off she put in an envelope which she had in her pocket. She came down the steep slope searching about for anything else. She looked carefully at the rough grass of the field. She thought she could distinguish a kind of track which someone had made walking through the long grass. But it was very faint—not nearly so clear as her own tracks were. It must have been made some time ago and it was too sketchy for her to be sure that it was not merely imagination on her part.

She began to hunt carefully down in the grass at the foot of the embankment just below the broken thornbush. Presently her search was rewarded. She found a powder compact, a small cheap enameled affair. She wrapped it in her handkerchief and put it in her pocket. She searched on but did not find anything more.

On the following afternoon, she got into her car and went to see her invalid aunt. Emma Crackenthorpe said kindly, "Don't hurry back. We shan't want you until dinnertime."

"Thank you, but I shall be back at six by the latest."

No. 4 Madison Road was a small drab house in a small drab street. It had very clean Nottingham lace curtains, a shining white doorstep and a well-polished brass door-handle. The door was opened by a tall, grim-lookimg woman, dressed in black with a large knob of iron-gray hair.

She eyed Lucy in suspicious appraisal as she showed her in to Miss Marple.

Miss Marple was occupying the back sitting room which looked out on to a small, tidy square of garden. It was aggressively clean with a lot of mats and doilies, a great many china ornaments, a rather big Jacobean suite and two ferns in pots. Miss Marple was sitting in a big chair by the fire busily engaged in crocheting.

Lucy came in and shut the door. She sat down in the chair facing Miss Marple.

"Well!" she said, "it looks as though you were right."

She produced her findings and gave the details of their discovery.

A faint flush of achievement came into Miss Marple's cheeks.

"Perhaps one ought not to feel so," she said, "but it is rather gratifying to form a theory and get proof that it is correct!"

She fingered the small tuft of fur. "Elspeth said the woman was wearing a light-colored fur coat. I suppose the compact was in the pocket of the coat and fell out as the body rolled down the slope. It doesn't seem distinctive in any way, but it may help. You didn't take all the fur?"

"No, I left half of it on the thornbush."

Miss Marple nodded approval.

"Quite right. You are very intelligent, my dear. The police will want to check exactly."

"You are not going to the police—with these things?"

"Well—not quite yet. . . ." Miss Marple considered. "It would be better, I think, to find the body first. Don't you?"

"Yes, but isn't that rather a tall order? I mean, granting that your estimate is correct. The murderer pushed the body out of the train, then presumably got out himself at Brackhampton and at some time—probably that same night—came along and removed the body. But what happened after that? He may have taken it anywhere."

"Not anywhere," said Miss Marple. "I don't think you've followed the thing to its logical conclusion, my dear Miss Eyelesbarrow."

"Do call me Lucy. Why not anywhere?"

"Because, if so, he might much more easily have killed the girl in some lonely spot and driven the body away from there. You haven't appreciated—"

Lucy interrupted."

"Are you saying—do you mean—that this was a premeditated crime?"

"I didn't think so at first," said Miss Marple. "One wouldn't—naturally. It seemed like a quarrel and a man losing control and strangling the girl and then being faced with the problem of disposing of his victim—a problem which he had to solve within a very few minutes. But it really is too much of a coincidence that he should kill the girl in a fit of passion, and then look out of the window and find the train was going round a curve exactly at a spot where he could tip the body out, and where he could be sure of finding his way later and removing it! If he'd just thrown her out there by chance, he'd have done no more about it, and the body would, long before now, have been found."

She paused. Lucy stared at her.

"You know," said Miss Marple thoughtfully, "it's really quite a clever way to have planned a crime—and I think it was very carefully planned. There's something so anonymous about a train. If he'd killed her in the place where she lived or was staying, somebody might have noticed him come or go. Or if he'd driven her out into the country somewhere, someone might have noticed the car and its number and make. But a train is full of strangers coming and going. In a non-corridor carriage, alone with her, it was quite easy—especially if you realize that he knew exactly what he was going to do next. He knew—he must have known—all about Rutherford Hall—its geographical position, I mean, its queer isolation: an island bounded by railway lines."

"It is exactly like that," said Lucy. "It's an anachronism out of the past. Bustling urban life goes on all around it, but doesn't touch it. The tradespeople deliver in the mornings and that's all."

"So we assume, as you said, that the murderer comes to Rutherford Hall that night. It is already dark when the body falls and no one is likely to discover it before the next day."

"No, indeed."

"The murdered would come—how? In a car? Which way?"

Lucy considered.

"There's a rough lane, alongside a factory wall. He'd probably come that way, turn in under the railway arch and along the back drive. Then he could climb the fence, go along at the foot of the embankment, find the body, and carry it back to the car."

"And then," continued Miss Marple, "he took it to some place he had already chosen beforehand. This was all thought out, you know. And I don't think, as I say, that he would take it away from Rutherford Hall, or if so, not

very far. The obvious thing, I suppose, would be to bury it somewhere?''
She looked inquiringly at Lucy.

"I suppose so," said Lucy considering. "But it wouldn't be quite as easy as it sounds."

Miss Marple agreed.

"He couldn't bury it in the park. Too hard work and very noticeable. Somewhere where the earth was turned already?"

"The kitchen garden, perhaps, but that's very close to the gardener's cottage. He's old and deaf—but still it might be risky."

"Is there a dog?"

"No."

"Then in a shed, perhaps, or an outhouse?"

"That would be simpler and quicker. There are a lot of unused old buildings: broken down pigsties, harness rooms, workshops that nobody ever goes near. Or he might perhaps have thrust it into a clump of rhododendrons or shrubs somewhere."

Miss Marple nodded.

"Yes, I think that's much more probable."

There was a knock on the door and the grim Florence came in with a tray.

"Nice for you to have a visitor," she said to Miss Marple, "I've made you my special scones you used to like."

"Florence always made the most delicious teacakes," said Miss Marple.

Florence, gratified, creased her features into a totally unexpected smile and left the room.

"I think, my dear," said Miss Marple, "we won't talk any more about murder during tea. Such an unpleasant subject!"

II

After tea Lucy rose.

"I'll be getting back," she said. "As I've already told you, there's no one actually living at Rutherford Hall who could be the man we're looking for. There's only an old man and a middle-aged woman, and an old, deaf gardener."

"I didn't say he was actually living there," said Miss Marple. "All I mean is that he's someone who knows Rutherford Hall very well. But we can go into that after you've found the body."

"You seem to assume quite confidently that I shall find it," said Lucy. "I don't feel nearly so optimistic."

"I'm sure you will succeed, my dear Lucy. You are such an efficient person."

"In some ways, but I haven't had any experience in looking for bodies."

"I'm sure all it needs is a little common sense," said Miss Marple encouragingly.

Lucy looked at her, then laughed. Miss Marple smiled back at her.

Lucy set to work systematically the next afternoon.

She poked round outhouses, prodded the briars which wreathed the old pigsties, and was peering into the boiler room under the greenhouse when she heard a dry cough and turned to find old Hillman, the gardener, looking at her disapprovingly.

"You be careful you don't get a nasty fall, Miss," he warned her. "Them steps isn't safe, and you was up in the loft just now and the floor there ain't safe neither."

Lucy was careful to display no embarrassment.

"I expect you think I'm very nosy," she said cheerfully. "I was just wondering if something couldn't be made out of this place—growing mushrooms for the market, that sort of thing. Everything seems to have been let go terribly."

"That's the master, that is. Won't spend a penny. Ought to have two men and a boy here, I ought, to keep the place proper, but won't hear of it, he won't. Had all I could do to make him get a motor mower. Wanted me to mow all that front grass by hand, he did."

"But if the place could be made to pay—with some repairs?"

"Won't get a place like this to pay—too far gone. And he wouldn't care about that, anyway. Only cares about saving. Knows well enough what'll happen after he's gone—the young gentlemen'll sell up as fast as they can. Only waiting for him to pop off, they are. Going to come into a tidy lot of money when he dies, so I've heard."

"I suppose he's a very rich man?" said Lucy.

"Crackenthorpe's Fancies, that's what they are. The old gentleman started it, Mr. Crackenthorpe's father. A sharp one he was, by all accounts. Made his fortune and built this place. Hard as nails, they say, and never forgot an injury. But with all that, he was open-handed. Nothing of the miser about him. Disappointed in both his sons, so the story goes. Give 'em an education and brought 'em up to be gentlemen—Oxford and all. But they were too much of gentlemen to want to go into the business. The younger one married an actress and then smashed himself up in a car accident when he'd been drinking. The elder one, our one here, his father never fancied so much. Abroad a lot, he was, bought a lot of heathen statues and had them sent home. Wasn't so close with his money when he was young—come on him more in middle age, it did. No, they never did hit it off, him and his father, so I've heard."

Lucy digested this information with an air of polite interest. The old man leaned against the wall and prepared to go on with his saga. He much preferred talking to doing any work.

"Died afore the war, the old gentleman did. Terrible temper he had. Didn't do to give him any sauce, he wouldn't stand for it."

"And after he died, this Mr. Crackenthorpe came and lived here?"

"Him and his family, yes. Nigh to grown up they was by then."

"But surely—Oh, I see, you mean the 1914 war."

"No, I don't. Died in 1928, that's what I mean."

Lucy supposed that 1928 qualified as "before the war" though it was not the way she would have described it herself.

She said: "Well, I expect you'll be wanting to go on with your work. You mustn't let me keep you."

"Ar," said old Hillman without enthusiasm, "not much you can do this time of day. Light's too bad."

Lucy went back to the house, pausing to investigate a likely looking copse of birch and azalea on her way.

She found Emma Crackenthorpe standing in the hall reading a letter. The afternoon post had just been delivered.

"My nephew will be here tomorrow—with a school friend. Alexander's room is the one over the porch. The one next to it will do for James Stoddart-West. They'll use the bathroom just opposite."

"Yes, Miss Crackenthorpe. I'll see the rooms are prepared."

"They'll arrive in the morning before lunch." She hesitated. "I expect they'll be hungry."

"I bet they will," said Lucy. "Roast beef, do you think? And perhaps treacle tart?"

"Alexander's very fond of treacle tart."

The two boys arrived on the following morning. They both had well-brushed hair, suspiciously angelic faces, and perfect manners. Alexander Eastley had fair hair and blue eyes, Stoddart-West was dark and spectacled.

They discoursed gravely during lunch on events in the sporting world, with occasional references to the latest space fiction. Their manner was that of elderly professors discussing paleolithic implements. In comparison with them, Lucy felt quite young.

The sirloin of beef vanished in no time and every crumb of the treacle tart was consumed.

Mr. Crackenthorpe grumbled: "You two will eat me out of house and home."

Alexander gave him a blue-eyed reproving glance.

"We'll have bread and cheese if you can't afford meat, Grandfather."

"Afford it? I can afford it. I don't like waste."

"We haven't wasted any, sir," said Stoddart-West, looking down at his plate which bore clear testimony of that fact.

"You boys both eat twice as much as I do."

"We're at the body-building stage," Alexander explained. "We need a big intake of proteins."

The old man grunted.

As the two boys left the table, Lucy heard Alexander say apologetically to his friend:

"You mustn't pay any attention to my grandfather. He's on a diet or something and that makes him rather peculiar. He's terribly mean, too. I think it must be a complex of some kind."

Stoddart-West said comprehendingly:

"I had an aunt who kept thinking she was going bankrupt. Really, she had oodles of money. Pathological, the doctor said. Have you got that football, Alex?"

After she had cleared away and washed up lunch, Lucy went out. She could hear the boys calling out in the distance on the lawn. She herself went in the opposite direction, down the front drive and from there she struck across to some clumped masses of rhododendron bushes. She began to hunt carefully, holding back the leaves and peering inside. She moved from clump to clump systematically, and was raking inside with a golf club when the polite voice of Alexander Eastley made her start.

"Are you looking for something, Miss Eyelesbarrow?"

"A golf ball," said Lucy promptly. "Several golf balls, in fact. I've been practicing golf shots most afternoons and I've lost quite a lot of balls. I thought that today I really must find some of them."

"We'll help you," said Alexander obligingly.

"That's very kind of you. I thought you were playing football."

"One can't go on playing footer," explained Stoddart-West. "One gets too hot. Do you play a lot of golf?"

"I'm quite fond of it. I don't get much opportunity."

"I suppose you don't. You do the cooking here, don't you?"

"Yes."

"Did you cook the lunch today?"

"Yes. Was it all right?"

"Simply wizard," said Alexander. "We get awful meat at school, all dried up. I love beef that's pink and juicy inside. That treacle tart was pretty smashing, too."

"You must tell me what things you like best."

"Could we have apple meringue one day? It's my favorite thing."

"Of course."

Alexander sighed happily.

"There's a clock golf set under the stairs," he said. "We could fix it up on the lawn and do some putting. What about it, Stodders?"

"Good oh!" said Stoddart-West.

"He isn't really Australian," explained Alexander courteously. "But he's practicing talking that way in case his people take him out to see the Test Match next year."

Encouraged by Lucy, they went off to get the clock golf set. Later, as she returned to the house, she found them setting it out on the lawn and arguing about the position of the numbers.

"We don't want it like a clock," said Stoddart-West. "That's kid stuff. We want to make a course of it. Long holes and short ones. It's a pity the numbers are so rusty. You can hardly see them."

"They need a lick of white paint," said Lucy. "You might get some tomorrow and paint them."

"Good idea." Alexander's face lighted up. "I say, I believe there are some old pots of paint in the Long Barn—left there by the painters. Shall we see?"

"What's the Long Barn?" asked Lucy.

Alexander pointed to a long, stone building a little way from the house near the back drive.

"It's quite old," he said. "Grandfather calls it a Leak Barn and says it's Elizabethan, but that's just swank. It belonged to the farm that was here originally. My great-grandfather pulled it down and built this awful house instead."

He added: "A lot of Grandfather's collection is in the barn. Things he had sent home from abroad when he was a young man. Most of them are pretty frightful, too. The Long Barn is used sometimes for whist drives and things like that. Women's Institute stuff. And Conservative Sales of Work. Come and see it."

Lucy accompanied them willingly.

There was a big oak, nail-studded door to the barn.

Alexander raised his hand and detached a key on a nail just under some ivy to the right hand of the top of the door. He turned it in the lock, pushed the door open and they went in.

At a first glance Lucy felt that she was in a singularly bad museum. The heads of two Roman emperors in marble glared at her out of bulging eyeballs, there was a huge sarcophagus of a decadent Greco-Roman period, a simpering Venus stood on a pedestal clutching her falling draperies. Besides these works of art, there were a couple of trestle tables, some stacked-up chairs, and sundry oddments such as a rusted hand mower, two buckets, a couple of moth-eaten car seats, and a green-painted, iron garden seat that had lost a leg.

"I think I saw the paint over here," said Alexander vaguely. He went to a corner and pulled aside a tattered curtain that shut it off.

They found a couple of paint pots and brushes; the latter dry and stiff.

"You really need some turpentine," said Lucy.

They could not, however, find any. The boys suggested bicycling off to get some, and Lucy urged them to do so. Painting the clock golf numbers would keep them amused for some time, she thought.

The boys went off, leaving her in the barn.

"This really could do with a clear up," she had murmured.

"I shouldn't bother," Alexander advised her. "It gets cleaned up if it's going to be used for anything, but it's practically never used this time of year."

"Do I hang the key up outside the door again? Is that where it's kept?"

"Yes. There's nothing to pinch here, you see. Nobody would want those awful marble things and anyway they weigh a ton."

Lucy agreed with him. She could hardly admire old Mr. Crackenthorpe's taste in art. He seemed to have an unerring instinct for selecting the worst specimen of any period.

She stood looking round her after the boys had gone. Her eyes came to rest on the sarcophagus and stayed there.

That sarcophagus. . . .

The air in the barn was faintly musty as though unaired for a long time. She went over to the sarcophagus. It had a heavy, close-fitting lid. Lucy looked at it speculatively.

Then she left the barn, went to the kitchen, found a heavy crowbar, and returned.

It was not an easy task but Lucy toiled doggedly.

Slowly the lid began to rise, pried up by the crowbar.

It rose sufficiently for Lucy to see what was inside.

CHAPTER SIX

I

A few minutes later Lucy, rather pale, left the barn, locked the door and put the key back on the nail.

She went rapidly to the stables, got out her car and drove down the back drive. She stopped at the post office at the end of the road. She went into the telephone box, put in the money and dialed.

"I want to speak to Miss Marple."

"She's resting. It's Miss Eyelesbarrow, isn't it?"

"Yes."

"I'm not going to disturb her and that's flat, Miss. She's an old lady and she needs her rest."

"You must disturb her. It's urgent."

"I'm not—"

"Please do what I say at once."

When she chose, Lucy's voice could be as incisive as steel. Florence knew authority when she heard it.

Presently Miss Marple's voice spoke.

"Yes, Lucy?"

Lucy drew a deep breath.

"You were quite right," she said. "I've found it."

"A woman's body?"

"Yes. A woman in a fur coat. It's in a stone sarcophagus in a kind of Barn -*cum*-Museum near the house. What do you want me to do? I ought to inform the police, I think."

"Yes. You must inform the police. At once."

"But what about the rest of it? About you? The first thing they'll want to know is why I was prying up a lid that weighs tons for apparently no reason. Do you want me to invent a reason? I can."

"No. I think, you know," said Miss Marple in her gentle, serious voice, "that the only thing to do is to tell the exact truth."

"About you?"

"About everything."

A sudden grin split the whiteness of Lucy's face.

"That will be quite simple for me," she said. "But I imagine they'll find it quite hard to believe!"

She rang off, waited a moment, and then rang and got the police station.

"I have just discovered a dead body in a sarcophagus in the Long Barn at Rutherford Hall."

"What's that?"

Lucy repeated her statement and anticipating the next question gave her name.

She drove back, put the car away and entered the house.

She paused in the hall for a moment, thinking.

Then she gave a brief sharp nod of the head and went to the library where

Miss Crackenthorpe was sitting helping her father to do the *Times* crossword.

"Can I speak to you a moment, Miss Crackenthorpe?"

Emma looked up, a shade of apprehension on her face. The apprehension was, Lucy thought, purely domestic. In such words do useful household staff announce their imminent departure.

"Well, speak up, girl, speak up," said old Mr. Crackenthorpe irritably.

Lucy said to Emma, "I'd like to speak to you alone, please."

"Nonsense," said Mr. Crackenthorpe. "You say straight out here what you've got to say."

"Just a moment, Father." Emma rose and went toward the door.

"All nonsense. It can wait," said the old man angrily.

"I'm afraid it can't wait," said Lucy.

Mr. Crackenthorpe said, "What impertinence!"

Emma came out into the hall. Lucy followed her and shut the door behind them.

"Yes?" said Emma. "What is it? If you think there's too much to do with the boys here, I can help you and—"

"It's not that at all," said Lucy. "I didn't want to speak before your father because I understand he is an invalid and it might give him a shock. You see, I've just discovered the body of a murdered woman in that big sarcophagus in the Long Barn."

Emma Crackenthorpe stared at her.

"In the sarcophagus? A murdered woman? It's impossible!"

"I'm afraid it's quite true. I've rung up the police. They will be here at any minute."

A slight flush came into Emma's cheek.

"You should have told me first—before notifying the police."

"I'm sorry," said Lucy.

"I didn't hear you ring up—" Emma's glance went to the telephone on the hall table.

"I rang up from the post office just down the road."

"But how extraordinary—why not from here?"

Lucy thought quickly.

"I was afraid the boys might be about—might hear—if I rang up from the hall here."

"I see. . . . Yes—I see. They are coming—the police, I mean?"

"They're here now," said Lucy, as with a squeal of brakes a car drew up at the front door and the bell pealed through the house.

II

"I'm sorry, very sorry—to have asked this of you," said Inspector Bacon.

His hand under her arm, he led Emma Crackenthorpe out of the barn. Emma's face was very pale; she looked sick, but she walked firmly erect.

"I'm quite sure that I've never seen the woman before in my life."

"We're very grateful to you, Miss Crackenthorpe. That's all I wanted to know. Perhaps you'd like to lie down?"

"I must go to my father. I telephoned to Doctor Quimper as soon as I heard about this and he is with him now."

Doctor Quimper came out of the library as they crossed the hall. He was a tall, genial man, with a casual, offhand, cynical manner that his patients found very stimulating.

He and the Inspector nodded to each other.

"Miss Crackenthorpe has performed an unpleasant task very bravely," said Bacon.

"Well done, Emma," said the doctor, patting her on the shoulder. "You can take things. I've always known that. Your father's all right. Just go in and have a word with him, and then go into the dining room and get yourself a glass of brandy. That's a prescription."

Emma smiled at him gratefully and went into the library.

"That woman's the salt of the earth," said the doctor looking after her. "A thousand pities she's never married. The penalty of being the only female in a family of men. The other sister got clear, married at seventeen, I believe. This one's quite a handsome woman, really. She'd have been a success as a wife and mother."

"Too devoted to her father, I suppose," said Inspector Bacon.

"She's not really as devoted as all that—but she's got the instinct some women have to make their men folk happy. She sees that her father likes being an invalid, so she lets him be an invalid. She's the same with her brothers. Cedric feels he's a good painter, what's-his-name, Harold, knows how much she relies on his sound judgment—she lets Alfred shock her with his stories of his clever deals. Oh yes, she's a clever woman—no fool. Well, do you want me for anything? Want me to have a look at your corpse now Johnstone has done with it" (Johnstone was the police surgeon) "and see if it happens to be one of my medical mistakes?"

"I'd like you to have a look, yes, Doctor. We want to get her identified. I suppose it's impossible for old Mr. Crackenthorpe? Too much of a strain?"

"Strain? Fiddlesticks. He'd never forgive you or me if you didn't let him have a peep. He's all agog. Most exciting thing that's happened to him for fifteen years or so—and it won't cost him anything!"

"There's nothing really much wrong with him, then?"

"He's seventy-two," said the doctor. "That's all, really, that's the matter with him. He has odd rheumatic twinges—who doesn't? So he calls it arthritis. He has palpitations after meals—as well he may—he puts them down to 'heart.' But he can always do anything he wants to do! I've plenty of patients like that. The ones who are really ill usually insist desperately that they're perfectly well. Come on, let's go and see this body of yours. Unpleasant, I suppose?"

"Johnstone estimates she's been dead between a fortnight and three weeks."

"Quite unpleasant, then."

The doctor stood by the sarcophagus and looked down with frank curiosity, professionally unmoved by what he had named the "unpleasantness."

"Never seen her before. No patient of mine. I don't remember ever seeing her about in Brackhampton. She must have been quite good-looking once—hm— Somebody had it in for her all right."

They went out again into the air. Doctor Quimper glanced up at the building.

"Found in the—what do they call it?—the Long Barn—in a sarcophagus! Fantastic! Who found her?"

"Miss Lucy Eyelesbarrow."

"Oh, the latest lady help? What was she doing, poking about in sarcophagi?"

"That," said Inspector Bacon grimly, "is just what I am going to ask her. Now, about Mr. Crackenthorpe. Will you—?"

"I'll bring him along."

Mr. Crackenthorpe, muffled in scarves, came walking at a brisk pace, the doctor beside him.

"Disgraceful," he said. "Absolutely disgraceful! I brought back that sarcophagus from Florence in—let me see—it must have been in 1908—or was it 1909?"

"Steady now," the doctor warned him. "This isn't going to be nice, you know."

"No matter how ill I am, I've got to do my duty, haven't I?"

A very brief visit inside the Long Barn was, however, quite long enough. Mr. Crackenthorpe shuffled out into the air again with remarkable speed.

"Never saw her before in my life!" he said. "What's it mean? Absolutely disgraceful. It wasn't Florence—I remember now—it was Naples. A very fine specimen. And some fool of a woman has to come and get herself killed in it!"

He clutched at the folds of his overcoat on the left side.

"Too much for me . . . My heart . . . Where's Emma? Doctor. . . ."

Doctor Quimper took his arm.

"You'll be all right," he said. "I prescribe a little stimulant. Brandy."

They went back together toward the house.

"Sir. Please, sir."

Inspector Bacon turned. Two boys had arrived, breathless, on bicycles. Their faces were full of eager pleading.

"Please, sir, can we see the body?"

"No, you can't," said Inspector Bacon.

"Oh sir, please, sir. You never know. We might know who she was. Oh please, sir, do be a sport. It's not fair. Here's a murder, right in our own barn. It's the sort of chance that might never happen again. Do be a sport, sir."

"Who are you two?"

"I'm Alexander Eastley and this is my friend James Stoddart-West."

"Have you ever seen a blond woman wearing a light-colored, dyed squirrel coat anywhere about the place?"

"Well—I can't remember exactly," said Alexander astutely. "If I were to have a look—"

"Take 'em in, Sanders," said Inspector Bacon to the constable who was standing by the barn door. "One's only young once!"

"Oh sir, thank you, sir." Both boys were vociferous. "It's very kind of you, sir."

Bacon turned away toward the house.

"And now," he said to himself grimly, "for Miss Lucy Eyelesbarrow!"

III

After leading the police to the Long Barn and giving a brief account of her actions, Lucy had retired into the background, but she was under no illusion that the police had finished with her.

She was preparing potatoes for chips that evening when word was brought to her that Inspector Bacon required her presence. Putting aside the large bowl of cold water and salt in which the chips were reposing, Lucy followed the policeman to where the Inspector awaited her. She sat down and awaited his questions composedly.

She gave her name, her address in London, and added of her own accord:

"I will give you some names and addresses of reference if you want to know all about me."

The names were very good ones. An Admiral of the Fleet, the provost of an Oxford college and a Dame of the British Empire. In spite of himself Inspector Bacon was impressed.

"Now, Miss Eyelesbarrow, you went into the Long Barn to find some paint—is that right? And after having found the paint you got a crowbar, forced up the lid of this sarcophagus and found the body. What were you looking for in the sarcophagus?"

"I was looking for a body," said Lucy.

"You were looking for a body—and you found one! Doesn't that seem to you a very extraordinary story?"

"Oh yes, it is an extraordinary story. Perhaps you will let me explain it to you."

"I certainly think you had better do so."

Lucy gave him a precise recital of the events which had led up to her sensational discovery.

The Inspector summed it up in an outraged voice.

"You were engaged by an elderly lady to obtain a post here and to search the house and grounds for a dead body? Is that right?"

"Yes."

"Who is this elderly lady?"

"Miss Jane Marple. She is at present living at 4 Madison Road."

The Inspector wrote it down.

"You expect me to believe this story?"

Lucy said gently:

"Not, perhaps, until after you have interviewed Miss Marple and got her confirmation of it."

"I shall interview her all right. She must be cracked."

Lucy forbore to point out that to be proved right is not really a proof of mental incapacity. Instead she said:

"What are you proposing to tell Miss Crackenthorpe? About me, I mean?"

"Why do you ask?"

"Well, as far as Miss Marple is concerned I've done my job. I've found the body she wanted found. But I'm still engaged by Miss Crackenthorpe, and there are two hungry boys in the house and probably some more of the family will soon be coming down after all this upset. She needs domestic help. If you go and tell her that I only took this post in order to hunt for dead bodies she'll probably throw me out. Otherwise I can get on with my job and be useful."

The Inspector looked hard at her.

"I'm not saying anything to anyone at present," he said. "I haven't verified your statement yet. For all I know you may be making the whole thing up."

Lucy rose.

"Thank you. Then I'll go back to the kitchen and get on with things."

CHAPTER SEVEN

I

"We'd better have the Yard in on it; is that what you think, Bacon?"

The Chief Constable looked inquiringly at Inspector Bacon. The Inspector was a big solid man—his expression was that of one utterly disgusted with humanity.

"The woman wasn't a local, sir," he said. "There's some reason to believe—from her underclothing—that she might have been a foreigner. Of course," added Inspector Bacon hastily, "I'm not letting on about that yet awhile. We're keeping it up our sleeves until after the inquest."

The Chief Constable nodded.

"The inquest will be purely formal, I suppose?"

"Yes, sir. I've seen the coroner."

"And it's fixed for—when?"

"Tomorrow. I understand the other members of the Crackenthorpe family will be here for it. There's just a chance one of them might be able to identify her. They'll all be here."

He consulted a list he held in his hand.

"Harold Crackenthorpe, he's something in the City—quite an important figure, I understand. Alfred—don't quite know what he does. Cedric—that's the one who lives abroad. Paints!" The Inspector invested the word with its full quota of sinister significance. The Chief Constable smiled into his mustache.

"No reason, is there, to believe the Crackenthorpe family are connected with the crime in any way?" he asked.

"Not apart from the fact that the body was found on the premises," said Inspector Bacon. "And of course it's just possible that this artist member of the family might be able to identify her. What beats me is this extraordinary rigmarole about the train."

"Ah yes. You've been to see this old lady, this—er"—he glanced at the memorandum lying on his desk—"Miss Marple?"

"Yes, sir. And she's quite set and definite about the whole thing. Whether she's barmy or not, I don't know, but she sticks to her story—about what her friend saw and all the rest of it. As far as all that goes, I daresay it's just make believe—sort of thing old ladies do make up, like seeing flying saucers at the bottom of the garden, and Russian agents in the lending library. But it seems quite clear that she did engage this young woman, the lady help, and told her to look for a body—which the girl did."

"And found one," observed the Chief Constable. "Well, it's all a very remarkable story. Marple, Miss Jane Marple—the name seems familiar somehow. . . . Anyway, I'll get on to the Yard. I think you're right about its not being a local case—though we won't advertise the fact just yet. For the moment we'll tell the press as little as possible."

II

The inquest was a purely formal affair. No one came forward to identify the dead woman. Lucy was called to give evidence of finding the body and medical evidence was given as to the cause of death—strangulation. The proceedings were then adjourned.

It was a cold, blustery day when the Crackenthorpe family came out of the hall where the inquest had been held. There were five of them all told: Emma, Cedric, Harold, Alfred and Bryan Eastley, the husband of the dead daughter Edith. There was also Mr. Wimborne, the senior partner of the firm of solicitors who dealt with the Crackenthorpes' legal affairs. He had come down specially from London at great inconvenience to attend the inquest. They all stood for a moment on the pavement, shivering. Quite a crowd had assembled; the piquant details of the "Body in the Sarcophagus" had been fully reported in both the London and the local press.

A murmur went round: "That's them . . ."

Emma said sharply: "Let's get away."

The big hired Daimler drew up to the curb. Emma got in and motioned to Lucy. Mr. Wimborne, Cedric and Harold followed. Bryan Eastley said: "I'll take Alfred with me in my little bus." The chauffeur shut the door and the Daimler prepared to roll away.

"Oh, stop!" cried Emma. "There are the boys!"

The boys, in spite of aggrieved protests, had been left behind at Rutherford Hall, but they now appeared grinning from ear to ear.

"We came on our bicycles," said Stoddart-West. "The policeman was very kind and let us in at the back of the hall. I hope you don't mind, Miss Crackenthorpe," he added politely.

"She doesn't mind," said Cedric, answering for his sister. "You're only young once. Your first inquest, I expect?"

"It was rather disappointing," said Alexander. "All over so soon."

"We can't stay here talking," said Harold irritably. "There's quite a crowd. And all those men with cameras."

At a sign from him, the chauffeur pulled away from the curb. The boys waved cheerfully.

"All over so soon!" said Cedric. "That's what they think, the young innocents! It's just beginning."

"It's all very unfortunate. Most unfortunate," said Harold. "I suppose—"

He looked at Mr. Wimborne who compressed his thin lips and shook his head with distaste.

"I hope," he said sententiously, "that the whole matter will soon be cleaned up satisfactorily. The police are very efficient. However, the whole thing, as Harold says, has been most unfortunate."

He looked, as he spoke, at Lucy, and there was distinct disapproval in his glance. "If it had not been for this young woman," his eyes seemed to say, "poking about where she had no business to be, none of this would have happened."

This sentiment, or one closely resembling it, was voiced by Harold Crackenthorpe.

"By the way—er—Miss er—er Eyelesbarrow, just what made you go looking in that sarcophagus?"

Lucy had already wondered just when this thought would occur to one of the family. She had known that the police would ask it first thing: what surprised her was that it seemed to have occurred to no one else until this moment.

Cedric, Emma, Harold and Mr. Wimborne all looked at her.

Her reply, for what it was worth, had naturally been prepared for some time.

"Really," she said in a hesitating voice, "I hardly know. . . . I did feel that the whole place needed a thorough clearing out and cleaning. And there was"—she hesitated—"a very peculiar and disagreeable smell—"

She had counted accurately on the immediate shrinking of everyone from the unpleasantness of this idea.

Mr. Wimborne murmured: "Yes, yes, of course . . . about three weeks the police surgeon said. I think, you know, we must all try and not let our minds dwell on this thing." He smiled encouragingly at Emma who had turned very pale. "Remember," he said, "this wretched young woman was nothing to do with any of us."

"Ah, but you can't be so sure of that, can you?" said Cedric.

Lucy Eyelesbarrow looked at him with some interest. She had already been intrigued by the rather startling differences between the three brothers. Cedric was a big man with a weather-beaten, rugged face, unkempt dark hair and a jocund manner. He had arrived from the airport unshaven, and though he had shaved in preparation for the inquest, he was still wearing the clothes in which he had arrived and which seemed to be the only ones he had: old gray-flannel trousers and a patched and rather threadbare baggy jacket. He looked the stage Bohemian to the life and proud of it.

His brother Harold, on the contrary, was the perfect picture of a city gentleman and a director of important companies. He was tall with a neat, erect carriage, had dark hair going slightly bald on the temples, a small black mustache, and was impeccably dressed in a dark, well-cut suit and a pearl-gray tie. He looked what he was, a shrewd and successful business-man.

He now said stiffly:

"Really, Cedric, that seems a most uncalled-for remark."

"Don't see why. She was in our barn after all. What did she come there for?"

Mr. Wimborne coughed and said:

"Possibly some—er—assignation. I understand that it was a matter of local knowledge that the key was kept outside on a nail."

His tone indicated outrage at the carelessness of such procedure. So clearly marked was this that Emma spoke apologetically.

"It started during the war. For the air-raid wardens. There was a little spirit stove and they made themselves hot cocoa. And afterward, since there was really nothing there anybody could have wanted to take, we went on leaving the key hanging up. It was convenient for the Women's Institute people. If we'd kept it in the house it might have been awkward—when there was no one at home to give it them when they wanted it to get the place ready. With only daily women and no resident servants . . ."

Her voice trailed away. She had spoken mechanically, giving a wordy explanation without interest, as though her mind was elsewhere.

Cedric gave her a quick, puzzled glance.

"You're worried, Sis. What's up?"

Harold spoke with exasperation:

"Really, Cedric, can you ask?"

"Yes, I do ask. Granted a strange woman has got herself killed in the barn at Rutherford Hall (sounds like a Victorian melodrama) and granted it gave Emma a shock at the time—but Emma's always been a sensible girl—I don't see why she goes on being worried now. Dash it, one gets used to everything."

"Murder takes a little more getting used to by some people than it may in your case," said Harold acidly. "I dare say murders are two a penny in Majorca and—"

"Iviza, not Majorca."

"It's the same thing."

"Not at all—it's quite a different island."

Harold went on talking:

"My point is that though murder may be everyday commonplace to you, living among hot-blooded Latin people, nevertheless in England we take such things seriously." He added with increasing irritation, "And really, Cedric, to appear at a public inquest in those clothes—"

"What's wrong with my clothes? They're comfortable."

"They're unsuitable."

"Well, anyway, they're the only clothes I've got with me. I didn't pack my wardrobe trunk when I came rushing home to stand in with the family over this business. I'm a painter and painters like to be comfortable in their clothes."

"So you're still trying to paint?"

"Look here, Harold, when you say trying to paint—"

Mr. Wimborne cleared his throat in an authoritative manner.

"This discussion is unprofitable," he said reprovingly. "I hope, my dear Emma, that you will tell me if there is any further way in which I can be of service to you before I return to town?"

The reproof had its effect. Emma Crackenthorpe said quickly:

"It was most kind of you to come down."

"Not at all. It was advisable that someone should be at the inquest to watch the proceedings on behalf of the family. I have arranged for an interview with the Inspector at the house. I have no doubt that, distressing as all this has been, the situation will soon be clarified. In my own mind, there seems little doubt as to what occurred. As Emma has told us, the key of the Long Barn was known locally to hang outside the door. It seems highly probable that the place was used in the winter months as a place of assignation by local couples. No doubt there was a quarrel and some young man lost control of himself. Horrified at what he had done, his eye lit on the sarcophagus and he realized that it would make an excellent place of concealment."

Lucy thought to herself, "Yes, it sounds most plausible. That's just what one might think."

Cedric said, "You say a local couple—but nobody's been able to identify the girl locally."

"It's early days yet. No doubt we shall get an identification before long. And it is possible, of course, that the man in question was a local resident, but that the girl came from nowhere, perhaps from some other part of Brackhampton. Brackhampton's a big place—it's grown enormously in the last twenty years."

"If I were a girl coming to meet my young man, I'd not stand for being taken to a freezing-cold barn miles from anywhere," Cedric objected. "I'd stand out for a nice bit of cuddle in the cinema, wouldn't you, Miss Eyelesbarrow?"

"Do we need to go into all this?" Harold demanded plaintively.

And with the voicing of the question the car drew up before the front door of Rutherford Hall and they all got out.

CHAPTER EIGHT

I

On entering the library Mr. Wimborne blinked a little as his shrewd old eyes went past Inspector Bacon whom he had already met, to the fair-haired, good-looking man beyond him.

Inspector Bacon performed introductions.

"This is Detective Inspector Craddock of New Scotland Yard," he said.

"New Scotland Yard—hm." Mr. Wimborne's eyebrows rose.

Dermot Craddock, who had a pleasant manner, went easily into speech.

"We have been called in on the case, Mr. Wimborne," he said. "As you are representing the Crackenthorpe family, I feel it is only fair that we should give you a little confidential information."

Nobody could make a better show of presenting a very small portion of the truth and implying that it was the whole truth than young Inspector Craddock.

"Inspector Bacon will agree, I am sure," he added, glancing at his colleague.

Inspector Bacon agreed with all due solemnity and not at all as though the whole matter were prearranged.

"It's like this," said Craddock. "We have reason to believe, from information that has come into our possession, that the dead woman is not a native of these parts, that she actually traveled down here from London and that she had recently come from abroad. Probably—though we are not sure of that—from France."

Mr. Wimborne again raised his eyebrows.

"Indeed," he said. "Indeed?"

"That being the case," explained Inspector Bacon, "the Chief Constable felt that the Yard was better fitted to investigate the matter."

"I can only hope," said Mr. Wimborne, "that the case will be solved quickly. As you can no doubt appreciate, the whole business has been a source of much distress to the family. Although not personally concerned in any way, they are—"

He paused for a bare second, but Inspector Craddock filled the gap quickly.

"It's not a pleasant thing to find a murdered woman on your property. I couldn't agree with you more. Now I should like to have a brief interview with the various members of the family—"

"I really cannot see—"

"What they can tell me? Probably nothing of interest—but one never knows. I daresay I can get most of the information I want from you, sir. Information about this house and the family."

"And what can that possibly have to do with an unknown young woman coming from abroad and getting herself killed here?"

"Well, that's rather the point," said Craddock. "Why did she come here? Had she once had some connection with this house? Had she been, for instance, a servant here at one time? A lady's maid, for instance. Or did she come here to meet a former occupant of Rutherford Hall—"

Mr. Wimborne said coldly that Rutherford Hall had been occupied by the Crackenthorpes ever since Josiah Crackenthorpe built it in 1884.

"That's interesting in itself," said Craddock. "If you'd just give me a brief outline of the family history—"

Mr. Wimborne shrugged his shoulders.

"There is very little to tell. Josiah Crackenthorpe was a manufacturer of sweet and savory biscuits, relishes, pickles, etc. He accumulated a vast fortune. He built this house. Luther Crackenthorpe, his eldest son, lives here now."

"Any other sons?"

"One other son, Henry, who was killed in a motor accident in 1911."

"And the present Mr. Crackenthorpe has never thought of selling the house?"

"He is unable to do so," said the lawyer dryly. "By the terms of his father's will."

"Perhaps you'll tell me about the will?"

"Why should I?"

Inspector Craddock smiled.

"Because I can look it up myself if I want to at Somerset House."

Against his will, Mr. Wimborne gave a crabbed little smile.

"Quite right, Inspector. I was merely protesting that the information you ask for is quite irrelevant. As to Josiah Crackenthorpe's will, there is no mystery about it. He left his very considerable fortune in trust, the income from it to be paid to his son Luther for life, and after Luther's death the capital to be divided equally among Luther's children, Edmund, Cedric, Harold, Alfred, Emma and Edith. Edmund was killed in the war and Edith died four years ago, so that on Luther Crackenthorpe's decease the money will be divided among Cedric, Harold, Alfred, Emma and Edith's son Alexander Eastley."

"And the house?"

"That will go to Luther Crackenthorpe's eldest surviving son or his issue."

"Was Edmund Crackenthorpe married?"

"No."

"So the property will actually go—?"

"To the next son—Cedric."

"Mr. Luther Crackenthorpe himself cannot dispose of it?"

"No."

"And he has no control of the capital."

"No."

"Isn't that rather unusual? I suppose," said Inspector Craddock shrewdly, "that his father didn't like him."

"You suppose correctly," said Mr. Wimborne. "Old Josiah was disappointed that his eldest son showed no interest in the family business—or indeed in business of any kind. Luther spent his time traveling abroad and collecting *objets d'art*. Old Josiah was very unsympathetic to that kind of thing. So he left his money in trust for the next generation."

"But in the meantime the next generation have no income except what they make or what their father allows them, and their father has considerable capital but no power of disposal of it."

"Exactly. And what all this has to do with the murder of an unknown young woman of foreign origin I cannot imagine!"

"It doesn't seem to have anythng to do with it," Inspector Craddock agreed promptly. "I just wanted to ascertain all the facts."

Mr. Wimborne looked at him sharply; then, seemingly satisfied with the result of his scrutiny, rose to his feet.

"I am proposing now to return to London," he said. "Unless there is anything further you wish to know?"

He looked from one man to the other.

"No, thank you, sir."

The sound of the gong rose fortissimo from the hall outside.

"Dear me," said Mr. Wimborne. "One of the boys, I think, must be performing."

Inspector Craddock raised his voice to be heard above the clamor, as he said:

"We'll leave the family to have lunch in peace, but Inspector Bacon and I would like to return after it—say at 2:15—and have a short interview with every member of the family."

"You think that is necessary?"

"Well—" Craddock shrugged his shoulders. "It's just an off chance. Somebody might remember something that would give us a clue to the woman's identity."

"I doubt it, Inspector. I doubt it very much. But I wish you good luck. As I said just now, the sooner this distasteful business is cleared up, the better for everybody."

Shaking his head, he went slowly out of the room.

II

Lucy had gone straight to the kitchen on getting back from the inquest, and was busy with preparations for lunch when Bryan Eastley put his head in.

"Can I give you a hand in any way?" he asked. "I'm handy about the house."

Luch gave him a quick, slightly preoccupied glance. Bryan had arrived at the inquest direct in his small M.G. car and she had not as yet had much time to size him up.

What she saw was likeable enough. Eastley was an amiable-looking young man of thirty-odd with brown hair, rather plaintive blue eyes and an enormous fair mustache.

"The boys aren't back yet," he said, coming in and sitting on the end of the kitchen table. "It will take 'em another twenty minutes on their bikes."

Lucy smiled.

"They were certainly determined not to miss anything."

"Can't blame them. I mean to say—first inquest in their young lives and right in the family, so to speak."

"Do you mind getting off the table, Mr. Eastley? I want to put the baking dish down there."

Bryan obeyed.

"I say, that fat's corking hot. What are you going to put in it?"

"Yorkshire pudding."

"Good old Yorkshire. Roast beef of old England, is that the menu of today?"

"Yes."

"The funeral baked meats, in fact. Smells good," he sniffed appreciatively. "Do you mind my gassing away?"

"If you came in to help I'd rather you helped." She drew another pan from the oven. "Here—turn all these potatoes over so that they brown on the other side."

Bryan obeyed with alacrity.

"Have all these things been fizzling away in here while we've been at the inquest? Supposing they'd been all burned up."

"Most improbable. There's a regulating number on the oven."

"Kind of electric brain, eh what? Is that right?"

Lucy threw a swift look in his direction.

"Quite right. Now put the pan in the oven. Here, take the cloth. On the second shelf—I want the top one for the Yorkshire pudding."

Bryan obeyed, but not without uttering a shrill yelp.

"Burn yourself?"

"Just a bit. It doesn't matter. What a dangerous game cooking is!"

"I suppose you never do your own cooking?"

"As a matter of fact I do—quite often. But not this sort of thing. I can boil an egg, if I don't forget to look at the clock. And I can do eggs and bacon. And I can put a steak under the grill or open a tin of soup. I've got one of those little electric whatnots in my flat."

"You live in London?"

"If you call it living—yes."

His tone was despondent. He watched Lucy shoot in the dish with the Yorkshire pudding mixture.

"This is awfully jolly," he said, and sighed.

Her immediate preoccupations over, Lucy looked at him with more attention.

"What is—this kitchen?"

"Yes—reminds me of our kitchen at home—when I was a boy."

It struck Lucy that there was something strangely forlorn about Bryan Eastley. Looking closely at him, she realized that he was older than she had at first thought. He must be close on forty. It seemed difficult to think of him as Alexander's father. He reminded her of innumerable young pilots she had known during the war when she had been at the impressionable age of fourteen. She had gone on and grown up into a postwar world—but she felt as though Bryan had not gone on but had been overtaken in the passage of years. His next words confirmed this. He had subsided onto the kitchen table again.

"It's a difficult sort of world," he said, "isn't it? To get your bearings in, I mean. You see, one hasn't been trained for it."

Lucy recalled what she had heard from Emma.

"You were a fighter pilot, weren't you?" she said. "You've got a D.F.C."

"That's the sort of thing that puts you wrong. You've got a decoration and so people try to make it easy for you. Give you a job and all that. Very decent of them. But they're all white-collar jobs, and one simply isn't any good at that sort of thing. Sitting at a desk getting tangled up in figures. I've had ideas of my own, you know, tried out a wheeze or two. But you can't get the backing. Can't get the chaps to come in and put down the money. If I had a bit of capital—"

He brooded.

"You didn't know Edie, did you? My wife. No, of course you didn't. She was quite different from all this lot. Younger, for one thing. She was in the

Air Force. She always said her old man was an Ebenezer Scrooge. He is, you know. Mean as hell over money. And it's not as though he could take it with him. It's got to be divided up when he dies. Edie's share will go to Alexander, of course. He won't be able to touch the capital until he's twenty-one, though."

"I'm sorry, but will you get off the table again. I want to dish up and make gravy."

At that moment Alexander and Stoddart-West arrived with rosy faces and very much out of breath.

"Hello, Bryan," said Alexander kindly to his father. "So this is where you've got to. I say, what a smashing piece of beef. Is there Yorkshire pudding?"

"Yes, there is."

"We have awful Yorkshire pudding at school—all damp and limp."

"Get out of my way," said Lucy. "I want to make the gravy."

"Make lots of gravy. Can we have two sauceboats full?"

"Yes."

"Good oh!" said Stoddart-West, pronouncing the words carefully.

"I don't like it pale," said Alexander anxiously.

"It won't be pale."

"She's a smashing cook," said Alexander to his father.

Lucy had a momentary impression that their roles were reversed. Alexander spoke like a kindly father to his son.

"Can we help you, Miss Eyelesbarrow?" asked Stoddart-West politely.

"Yes, you can. Alexander, go and sound the gong. James, will you carry this tray into the dining room? And will you take the joint in, Mr. Eastley? I'll bring the potatoes and the Yorkshire pudding."

"There's a Scotland Yard man here," said Alexander. "Do you think he will have lunch with us?"

"That depends on what your aunt arranges."

"I don't suppose Aunt Emma would mind. She's very hospitable. But I suppose Uncle Harold wouldn't like it. He's being very sticky over this murder." Alexander went out through the door with the tray, adding a little additional information over his shoulder. "Mr. Wimborne's in the library with the Scotland Yard men now. But he isn't staying to lunch. He said he had to get back to London. Come on, Stodders. Oh, he's gone to do the gong."

At that moment the gong took charge. Stoddart-West was an artist; he gave it everything he had and all further conversation was inhibited.

Bryan carried in the joint, Lucy followed with the vegetables—returned to the kitchen to get the two brimming sauceboats of gravy.

Mr. Wimborne was standing in the hall putting on his gloves as Emma came quickly down the stairs.

"Are you really sure you won't stop for lunch, Mr. Wimborne? It's all ready."

"No. I've an important appointment in London. There is a restaurant car on the train."

"It was very good of you to come down," said Emma gratefully.

The two police officers emerged from the library.

Mr. Wimborne took Emma's hand in his.

"There's nothing to worry about, my dear," he said. "This is Detective Inspector Craddock from New Scotland Yard who has come down to take charge of the case. He is coming back at 2:15 to ask you for any facts that may assist him in his inquiry. But as I say, you have nothing to worry about." He looked toward Craddock. "I may repeat to Miss Crackenthorpe what you have told me?"

"Certainly, sir."

"Inspector Craddock has just told me that this almost certainly was not a local crime. The murdered woman is thought to have come from London and was probably a foreigner."

Emma Crackenthorpe said sharply, "A foreigner. Was she French?"

Mr. Wimborne had clearly meant his statement to be consoling. He looked slightly taken aback. Dermot Craddock's glance went quickly from him to Emma's face.

He wondered why she had leaped to the conclusion that the murdered woman was French, and why that thought disturbed her so much?

CHAPTER NINE

I

The only people who really did justice to Lucy's excellent lunch were the two boys and Cedric Crackenthorpe, who appeared completely unaffected by the circumstances which had caused him to return to England. He seemed, indeed, to regard the whole thing as a rather good joke of a macabre nature.

This attitude, Lucy noted, was most unpalatable to his brother Harold. Harold seemed to take the murder as a kind of personal insult to the Crackenthorpe family and so great was his sense of outrage that he ate hardly any lunch. Emma looked worried and unhappy and also ate very little. Alfred seemed lost in a train of thought of his own and spoke very little. He was a good-looking man with a thin, dark face and eyes set rather too close together.

After lunch the police officers returned and politely asked if they could have a few words with Mr. Cedric Crackenthorpe.

Inspector Craddock was very pleasant and friendly.

"Sit down, Mr. Crackenthorpe. I understand you have just come back from the Balearics? You live out there?"

"Have done for the last six years. In Iviza. Suits me better than this dreary country."

"You get a good deal more sunshine than we do, I expect," said Inspector Craddock agreeably. "You were home not so very long ago, I understand—for Christmas, to be exact. What made it necessary for you to come back again so soon?"

Cedric grinned.

"Got a wire from Emma—my sister. We've never had a murder on the premises before. Didn't want to miss anything—so along I came."

"You are interested in criminology?"

"Oh, we needn't put it in such highbrow terms! I just like murders. Whodunnits and all that! With a whodunnit parked right on the family doorstep, it seemed the chance of a lifetime. Besides I thought poor old Em might need a spot of help—managing the old man and the police and all the rest of it."

"I see. It appealed to your sporting instincts and also to your family feelings. I've no doubt your sister will be very grateful to you—although her two other brothers have also come to be with her."

"But not to cheer and comfort," Cedric told him. "Harold is terrifically put out. It's not at all the thing for a city magnate to be mixed up with the murder of a questionable female."

Craddock's eyebrows rose gently.

"Was she—a questionable female?"

"Well, you're the authority on that point. Going by the facts, it seemed to me likely."

"I thought perhaps you might have been able to make a guess at who she was?"

"Come now, Inspector, you already know—or your colleagues will tell you—that I haven't been able to identify her."

"I said a guess, Mr. Crackenthorpe. You might never have seen the woman before, but you might have been able to make a guess at who she was—or who she might have been?"

Cedric shook his head.

"You're barking up the wrong tree. I've absolutely no idea. You're suggesting, I suppose, that she may have come to the Long Barn to keep an assignation with one of us? But we none of us live here—the only people in the house were a woman and an old man. You don't seriously believe that she came here to keep a date with my revered Pop?"

"Our point is—Inspector Bacon agrees with me—that the woman may once have had some association with this house. It may have been a considerable number of years ago. Cast your mind back, Mr. Crackenthorpe—"

Cedric thought a moment or two, then shook his head.

"We've had foreign help from time to time, like most people, but I can't think of any likely possibility. Better ask the others. They'd know more than I would."

"We shall do that, of course."

Craddock leaned back in his chair and went on:

"As you have heard at the inquest, the medical evidence cannot fix the time of death very accurately. Longer than two weeks, less than four—which brings it somewhere around Christmastime. You have told me you came home for Christmas. When did you arrive in England and when did you leave?"

Cedric reflected.

"Let me see . . . I flew. Got here on the Saturday before Christmas—that would be the twenty-first."

"You flew straight from Majorca?"

"Yes. Left at five in the morning and got here midday."

"And you left?"

"I flew back on the following Friday, the twenty-seventh."

"Thank you."

Cedric grinned.

"Leaves me well within the limit, unfortunately. But really, Inspector, strangling young women is not my favorite form of Christmas fun."

"I hope not, Mr. Crackenthorpe."

Inspector Bacon merely looked disapproving.

"There would be a remarkable absence of peace and good will about such an action, don't you agree?"

Cedric addressed this question to Inspector Bacon who merely grunted. Inspector Craddock said politely:

"Well, thank you, Mr. Crackenthorpe. That will be all."

"And what do you think of him?" Craddock asked as Cedric shut the door behind him.

Bacon grunted again.

"Cocky enough for anything," he said. "I don't care for the type, myself. A loose living lot, these artists, and very likely to be mixed up with a disreputable class of women."

Craddock smiled.

"I don't like the way he dresses, either," went on Bacon. "No respect—going to an inquest like that. Dirtiest pair of trousers I've seen in a long while. And did you see his tie? Looked as though it was made of colored string. If you ask me, he's the kind that would easily strangle a woman and make no bones about it."

"Well, he didn't strangle this one—if he didn't leave Majorca until the twenty-first. And that's a thing we can verify easily enough."

Bacon threw him a sharp glance.

"I notice that you're not tipping your hand yet about the actual date of the crime."

"No, we'll keep that dark for the present. I always like to have something up my sleeve in the early stages."

Bacon nodded in full agreement.

"Spring it on 'em when the time comes," he said. "That's the best plan."

"And now," said Craddock, "we'll see what our correct City gentleman has to say about it all."

Harold Crackenthorpe, thin-lipped, had very little to say about it. It was most distasteful—a very unfortunate incident. The newspapers, he was afraid— Reporters, he understood, had already been asking for interviews. All that sort of thing . . . Most regrettable . . .

Harold's staccato unfinished sentences ended. He leaned back in his chair with the expression of a man confronted with a very bad smell.

The Inspector's probing produced no result. No, he had no idea who the woman was or could be. Yes, he had been at Rutherford Hall for Christmas. He had been unable to come down until Christmas Eve, but had stayed on over the following weekend.

"That's that, then," said Inspector Craddock, without pressing his questions further. He had already made up his mind that Harold Crackenthorpe was not going to be helpful.

He passed on to Alfred, who came into the room with a nonchalance that seemed just a trifle overdone.

Craddock looked at Alfred Crackenthorpe with a faint feeling of recognition. Surely he had seen this particular member of the family somewhere before. Or had it been his picture in the paper? There was something discreditable attached to the memory. He asked Alfred his occupation and Alfred's answer was vague.

"I'm in insurance at the moment. Until recently I've been interested in putting a new type of talking machine on the market. Quite revolutionary. I did very well out of that, as a matter of fact."

Inspector Craddock looked appreciative, and no one could have had the least idea that he was noticing the superficially smart appearance of Alfred's suit and gauging correctly the low price it had cost. Cedric's clothes had been disreputable, almost threadbare, but they had been originally of good cut and excellent material. Here there was a cheap smartness that told its own tale. Craddock passed pleasantly on to his routine questions. Alfred seemed interested, even slightly amused.

"It's quite an idea, that the woman might once have had a job here. Not as a lady's maid; I doubt if my sister has ever had such a thing. I don't think anyone has nowadays. But of course there is a good deal of foreign domestic labor floating about. We've had Poles, and a temperamental German or two. As Emma definitely didn't recognize the woman, I think that washes your idea out, Inspector. Emma's got a very good memory for a face. No, if the woman came from London . . . What gives you the idea she came from London, by the way?"

He slipped the question in quite casually, but his eyes were sharp and interested.

Inspector Craddock smiled and shook his head.

Alfred looked at him keenly.

"Not telling, eh? Return ticket in her coat pocket, perhaps, is that it?"

"It could be, Mr. Crackenthorpe."

"Well, granting she came from London, perhaps the chap she came to meet had the idea that the Long Barn would be a nice place to do a quiet murder. He knows the setup here, evidently. I should go looking for him if I were you, Inspector."

"We are," said Inspector Craddock, and made the two little words sound quiet and confident.

He thanked Alfred and dismissed him.

"You know," he said to Bacon, "I've seen that chap somewhere before. . . ."

Inspector Bacon gave his verdict.

"Sharp customer," he said. "So sharp that he cuts himself sometimes."

II

"I don't suppose you want to see me," said Bryan Eastley apologetically, coming into the room and hesitating by the door. "I don't exactly belong to the family."

"Let me see, you are Mr. Bryan Eastley, the husband of Miss Edith Crackenthorpe, who died four years ago?"

"That's right."

"Well, it's very kind of you, Mr. Eastley, especially if you know something that you think could assist us in some way?"

"But I don't. Wish I did. Whole thing seems so ruddy peculiar, doesn't it? Coming along and meeting some fellow in that drafty old barn in the middle of winter. Wouldn't be my cup of tea!"

"It is certainly very perplexing," Inspector Craddock agreed.

"Is it true that she was a foreigner? Word seems to have got round to that effect."

"Does that fact suggest anything to you?" The Inspector looked at him sharply, but Bryan seemed amiably vacuous.

"No, it doesn't, as a matter of fact."

"Maybe she was French," said Inspector Bacon, with dark suspicion.

Bryan was roused to slight animation. A look of interest came into his blue eyes, and he tugged at his big, fair mustache.

"Really? Gay Paree?" He shook his head. "On the whole, it seems to make it even more unlikely, doesn't it? Messing about in the barn, I mean. You haven't had any other sarcophagus murders, have you? One of these fellows with an urge—or a complex? Thinks he's Caligula or someone like that?"

Inspector Craddock did not even trouble to reject this speculation. Instead, he asked in a casual manner:

"Nobody in the family got any French connections, or—or—relationships that you know of?"

Bryan said that the Crackenthorpes weren't a very gay lot.

"Harold's respectably married," he said. "Fish-faced woman, some impoverished peer's daughter. Don't think Alfred cares about women much—spends his life going in for shady deals which usually go wrong in the end. I dare say Cedric's got a few Spanish señoritas jumping through hoops for him in Iviza. Women rather fall for Cedric. Doesn't always shave and looks as though he never washes. Don't see why that should be attractive to women, but apparently it is—I say, I'm not being very helpful, am I?"

He grinned at them.

"Better get young Alexander on the job. He and James Stoddart-West are out hunting for clues in a big way. Bet you they turn up something."

Inspector Craddock said he hoped they would. Then he thanked Bryan Eastley and said he would like to speak to Miss Emma Crackenthorpe.

III

Inspector Craddock looked with more attention at Emma Crackenthorpe than he had done previously. He was still wondering about the expression that he had surprised on her face before lunch.

A quiet woman. Not stupid. Not brilliant, either. One of those comfortable, pleasant women whom men were inclined to take for granted, and who had the art of making a house into a home, giving it an atmosphere of restfulness and quiet harmony. Such, he thought, was Emma Crackenthorpe.

Women such as this were often underrated. Behind their quiet exterior they had force of character, they were to be reckoned with. Perhaps, Craddock thought, the clue to the mystery of the dead woman in the sarcophagus was hidden away in the recesses of Emma's mind.

While these thoughts were passing through his head, Craddock was asking various unimportant questions.

"I don't suppose there is much that you haven't already told Inspector Bacon," he said. "So I needn't worry you with many questions."

"Please ask me anything you like."

"As Mr. Wimborne told you, we have reached the conclusion that the dead woman was not a native of these parts. That may be a relief to you— Mr. Wimborne seemed to think it would be—but it makes it really more difficult for us. She's less easily identified."

"But didn't she have anything? A handbag? Papers?"

Craddock shook his head.

"No handbag, nothing in her pockets."

"You've no idea of her name—of where she came from—anything at all?"

Craddock thought to himself: She wants to know—she's very anxious to know—who the woman is. Has she felt like that all along, I wonder? Bacon didn't give me that impression—and he's a shrewd man. . . .

"We know nothing about her," he said. "That's why we hoped one of you could help us. Are you sure you can't? Even if you didn't recognize her, can you think of anyone she might be?"

He thought, but perhaps he imagined it, that there was a very slight pause before she answered.

"I've absolutely no idea," she said.

Imperceptibly, Inspector Craddock's manner changed. It was hardly noticeable except as a slight hardness in his voice.

"When Mr. Wimborne told you that the woman was a foreigner, why did you assume that she was French?"

Emma was not disconcerted. Her eyebrows rose slightly.

"Did I? Yes, I believe I did. I don't really know why, except that one always tends to think foreigners are French until one finds out what nationality they really are. Most foreigners in this country are French, aren't they?"

"Oh, I really wouldn't say that was so, Miss Crackenthorpe. Not nowadays. We have so many nationalities over here. Italians, Germans, Austrians, all the Scandinavian countries."

"Yes, I suppose you're right."

"You didn't have some special reason for thinking that this woman was likely to be French?"

She didn't hurry to deny it. She just thought a moment and then shook her head almost regretfully.

"No," she said. "I really don't think so."

Her glance met his placidly, without flinching.

Craddock looked toward Inspector Bacon. The latter leaned forward and presented a small, enamel powder compact.

"Do you recognize this, Miss Crackenthorpe?"

She took it and examined it.

"No. It's certainly not mine."

"You've no idea to whom it belonged?"

"No."

"Then I don't think we need worry you any more—for the present."

"Thank you."

She smiled briefly at them, got up, and left the room. Again he may have imagined it, but Craddock thought she moved rather quickly, as though a certain relief hurried her.

"Think she knows anything?" asked Bacon.

Inspector Craddock said ruefully:

"At a certain stage one is inclined to think everyone knows a little more than they are willing to tell you."

"They usually do, too," said Bacon out of the depth of his experience. "Only," he added, "it quite often isn't anything to do with the business in hand. It's some family peccadillo or some silly scrape that people are afraid is going to be dragged into the open."

"Yes, I know. Well, at least—"

But whatever Inspector Craddock had been about to say never got said, for the door was flung open and old Mr. Crackenthorpe shuffled in, in a high state of indignation.

"A pretty pass," he said. "Things have come to a pretty pass when Scotland Yard comes down and doesn't have the courtesy to talk to the head of the family first! Who's the master of this house, I'd like to know? Answer me that. Who's master here?"

"You are, of course, Mr. Crackenthorpe," said Craddock soothingly and rising as he spoke. "But we understood that you had already told Inspector Bacon all you knew, and that your health not being good, we must not make too many demands upon it. Doctor Quimper said—"

"I daresay. I daresay. I'm not a strong man. As for Doctor Quimper, he's a regular old woman—perfectly good doctor, understands my case—but inclined to wrap me up in cotton wool. Got a bee in his bonnet about food. Went on at me Christmastime when I had a bit of a turn. What did I eat? When? Who cooked it? Who served it? Fuss, fuss fuss! But though I may have indifferent health, I'm well enough to give you all the help that's in my power. Murder in my own house, or at any rate in my own barn! Interesting building, that. Elizabethan. Local architect says not—but the fellow doesn't know what he's talking about. Not a day later than 1580—but that's not what we're talking about. What do you want to know? What's your present theory?"

"It's a little too early for theories, Mr. Crackenthorpe. We are still trying to find out who the woman was."

"Foreigner, you say?"

"We think so."

"Enemy agent?"

"Unlikely, I should say."

"You'd say! You'd say! They're everywhere, these people. Infiltrating! Why the Home Office lets them in beats me. Spying on industrial secrets, I'd bet. That's what she was doing."

"In Brackhampton?"

"Factories everywhere. One outside my own back gate."

Craddock shot an inquiring glance at Bacon, who responded:

"Metal boxes."

"How do you know that's what they're really making? Can't swallow all these fellows tell you. All right, if she wasn't a spy, who do you think she was? Think she was mixed up with one of my precious sons? It would be Alfred, if so. Not Harold, he's too careful. And Cedric doesn't condescend to live in this country. All right, then, she was Alfred's bit of skirt. And some violent fellow followed her down here, thinking she was coming to meet him, and did her in. How's that?"

Inspector Craddock said diplomatically that it was certainly a theory. But Mr. Alfred Crackenthorpe, he said, had not recognized her.

"Pah! Afraid, that's all! Alfred always was a coward. But he's a liar, remember, always was! Lie himself black in the face. None of my sons are any good. Crowd of vultures, waiting for me to die, that's their real occupation in life." He chuckled. "And they can wait. I won't die to oblige them! Well, if that's all I can do for you . . . I'm tired. Got to rest."

He shuffled out again.

"Alfred's bit of skirt?" said Bacon questioningly. "In my opinion the old man just made that up." He paused, hesitated. "I think, personally, Alfred's quite all right—perhaps a shifty customer in some ways, but not our present cup of tea. Mind you, I did just wonder about that Air Force chap."

"Bryan Eastley?"

"Yes. I've run into one or two of his type. They're what you might call adrift in the world—had danger and death and excitement too early in life. Now, they find it tame. Tame and unsatisfactory. In a way, we've given them a raw deal. Though I don't really know what we could do about it. But there they are, all past and no future, so to speak. And they're the kind that don't mind taking chances. The ordinary fellow plays safe by instinct, it's not so much morality as prudence. But these fellows aren't afraid—playing safe isn't really in their vocabulary. If Eastley were mixed up with a woman and wanted to kill her—" He stopped, threw out a hand hopelessly. "But why should he want to kill her? And if you do kill a woman, why plant her in your faer-in-law's sarcophagus? No, if you ask me, none of this lot had anything to do with the murder. If they had, they wouldn't have gone to all the trouble of planting the body on their own back doorstep, so to speak."

Craddock agreed that that hardly made sense.

"Anything more you want to do here?"

Craddock said there wasn't.

Bacon suggested coming back to Brackhampton and having a cup of tea, but Inspector Craddock said that he was going to call on an old acquaintance.

CHAPTER TEN

I

Miss Marple, sitting erect against a background of China dogs and presents from Margate, smiled approvingly at Inspector Dermot Craddock.

"I'm so glad," she said, "that you have been assigned to the case. I hoped you would be."

"When I got your letter," said Craddock, "I took it straight to the Assistant Commissioner. As it happened he had just heard from the Brackhampton people calling us in. They seemed to think it wasn't a local crime. The A.C. was very interested in what I had to tell him about you. He'd heard about you, I gather, from my uncle."

"Dear Sir Henry," murmured Miss Marple affectionately.

"He got me to tell him all about the Little Paddocks business. Do you want to hear what he said next?"

"Please tell me if it is not a breach of confidence."

"He said, 'Well, as this seems a completely cockeyed business, all thought up by a couple of old ladies who've turned out, against all probability, to be right, and since you already know one of these old ladies, I'm sending you down on the case.' So here I am! And now, my dear Miss Marple, where do we go from here? This is not, as you probably appreciate, an official visit. I haven't got my henchmen with me. I thought you and I might take down our back hair together first."

Miss Marple smiled at him.

"I'm sure," she said, "that no one who only knows you officially would ever guess that you could be so human, and better-looking than ever—don't blush. Now what, exactly, have you been told so far?"

"I've got everything, I think. Your friend Mrs. McGillicuddy's original statement to the police at St. Mary Mead, confirmation of her statement by the ticket collector and also the note to the stationmaster at Brackhampton. I may say that all the proper inquiries were made by the people concerned—the railway people and the police. But there's no doubt that you outsmarted them all by a most fantastic process of guesswork."

"Not guesswork," said Miss Marple. "And I had a great advantage. I knew Elspeth McGillicuddy. Nobody else did. There was no obvious confirmation of her story, and if there was no question of any woman being reported missing, then quite naturally they would think it was just an elderly lady imagining things—as elderly ladies often do, but not Elspeth McGillicuddy."

"Not Elspeth McGillicuddy," agreed the Inspector. "I'm looking forward to meeting her, you know. I wish she hadn't gone to Ceylon. We're arranging for her to be interviewed there by the way."

"My own process of reasoning was not really original," said Miss Marple. "It's all in Mark Twain. The boy who found the horse. I just imagined where I would go if I were a horse and I went there and there was the horse."

"You imagined what you'd do if you were a cruel and cold-blooded murderer?" said Craddock, looking thoughtfully at Miss Marple's pink and white elderly fragility. "Really, your mind—"

"Like a sink, my nephew Raymond used to say," Miss Marple agreed, nodding her head briskly. "But as I always told him, sinks are necessary domestic equipment and actually very hygienic."

"Can you go a little further still, put yourself in the murderer's place, and tell me just where he is now?"

Miss Marple sighed.

"I wish I could. I've no idea—no idea at all. But he must be someone who has lived in, or knows all about Rutherford Hall."

"I agree. But that opens up a very wide field. Quite a succession of daily women have worked there. There's the Women's Institute, and the air-raid wardens before them. They all know the Long Barn and the sarcophagus and where the key was kept. The whole setup there is widely known locally. Anybody living roundabout might hit on it as a good spot for his purpose."

"Yes, indeed. I quite understand your difficulties."

Craddock said: "We'll never get anywhere until we identify the body."

"And that, too, may be difficult?"

"Oh, we'll get there—in the end. We're checking up on all the reported disappearances of a woman of that age and appearance. There's no one outstanding who fits the bill. The Medical Officer puts her down as about thirty-five, healthy, probably a married woman, has had at least one child. Her fur coat is a cheap one, purchased at a London store. Hundreds of such coats were sold in the last three months, about sixty percent of them to blonde women. No salesgirl can recognize the photograph of the dead woman, or is likely to if the purchase were made just before Christmas. Her other clothes seem mainly of foreign manufacture, mostly purchased in Paris. There are no English laundry marks. We've communicated with Paris and they are checking up there for us. Sooner or later, of course, someone will come forward with a missing relative or lodger. It's just a matter of time."

"The compact wasn't any help?"

"Unfortunately no. It's a type sold by the hundred in the rue de Rivoli, quite cheap. By the way, you ought to have turned that over to the police at once, you know, or rather Miss Eyelesbarrow should have done so."

Miss Marple shook her head.

"But at that moment there wasn't any question of a crime having been committed," she pointed out. "If a young lady, practicing golf shots, picks up an old compact of no particular value in the long grass, surely she doesn't rush straight off to the police with it?" Miss Marple paused, and then added firmly: "I thought it much wiser to find the body first."

Inspector Craddock was tickled.

"You don't seem to have ever had any doubts but that it would be found?"

"I was sure it would. Lucy Eyelesbarrow is a most efficient and intelligent person."

"I'll say she is! She scares the life out of me, she's so devastatingly efficient. No man will ever dare marry that girl."

"Now you know, I wouldn't say that. It would have to be a special type of man, of course." Miss Marple brooded on this thought a moment. "How is she getting on at Rutherford Hall?"

"They're completely dependent upon her as far as I can see. Eating out of her hand—literally as you might say. By the way, they know nothing about her connection with you. We've kept that dark."

"She has no connection now with me. She has done what I asked her to do."

"So she could hand in her notice and go if she wanted to?"

"Yes."

"But she stays on. Why?"

"She has not mentioned her reasons to me. She is a very intelligent girl. I suspect that she has become interested."

"In the problem? Or in the family?"

"It may be," said Miss Marple, "that it is rather difficult to separate the two."

Craddock looked hard at her.

"Have you got anything particular in mind?"

"Oh no—oh, dear me, no."

"I think you have."

Miss Marple shook her head.

Dermot Craddock sighed. "So all I can do is to 'prosecute my inquiries'— to put it in jargon. A policeman's life is a dull one!"

"You'll get results, I'm sure."

"Any ideas for me? More inspired guesswork?"

"I was thinking of things like theatrical companies," said Miss Marple rather vaguely. "Touring from place to place and perhaps not many home ties. One of those young women would be much less likely to be missed."

"Yes. Perhaps you've got something there. We'll pay special attention to that angle." He added, "What are you smiling about?"

"I was thinking," said Miss Marple, "of Elspeth McGillicuddy's face when she hears we've found a body!"

II

"Well!" said Mrs. McGillicuddy. "Well!"

Words failed her. She looked across at the nicely spoken, pleasant young man who had called upon her with official credentials and then down at the photographs that he had handed her.

"That's her all right," she said. "Yes, that's her. Poor soul. Well, I must say I'm glad you've found her body. Nobody believed a word I said! The police or the railway people or anyone else. It's very galling not to be believed. At any rate, nobody could say I didn't do all I possibly could."

The nice young man made sympathetic and appreciative noises.

"Where did you say the body was found?"

"In a barn at a house called Rutherford Hall, just outside Brackhampton."

"Never heard of it. How did it get there, I wonder?"

The young man did not reply.

"Jane Marple found it, I suppose. Trust Jane."

"The body," said the young man, referring to some notes, "was found by a Miss Lucy Eyelesbarrow."

"Never heard of her either," said Mrs. McGillicuddy. "I still think Jane Marple had something to do with it."

"Anyway, Mrs. McGillicuddy, you definitely identify this picture as that of the woman whom you saw in a train?"

"Being strangled by a man. Yes, I do."

"Now, can you describe this man?"

"He was a tall man," said Mrs. McGillicuddy.

"Yes?"

"And dark."

"Yes?"

"That's all I can tell you," said Mrs. McGillicuddy. "He had his back to me. I didn't see his face."

"Would you be able to recognize him if you saw him?"

"Of course I shouldn't! He had his back to me. I never saw his face."

"You've no idea at all as to his age?"

Mrs. McGillicuddy considered.

"No—not really—I mean, I don't know. He wasn't, I'm almost sure, very young. His shoulders looked—well, set, if you know what I mean." The young man nodded. "Thirty and upward, I can't get closer than that. I wasn't really looking at him, you see. It was her—with those hands round her throat and her face—all blue. . . . You know, sometimes I dream of it even now."

"It must have been a very distressing experience," said the young man sympathetically.

He closed his notebook and said, "When are you returning to England?"

"Not for another three weeks. It isn't necessary, is it, for me?"

He quickly reassured her.

"Oh no. There's nothing you could do at present. Of course, if we make an arrest . . ."

It was left like that.

The mail brought a letter from Miss Marple to her friend. The writing was spiky and spidery and heavily underlined. Long practice made it easy for Mrs. McGillicuddy to decipher. Miss Marple wrote a very full account to her friend who devoured every word with great satisfaction.

She and Jane had shown them all right!

CHAPTER ELEVEN

I

"I simply can't make you out," said Cedric Crackenthorpe.

He eased himself down on the decaying wall of a long-derelict pigsty and stared at Lucy Eyelesbarrow.

"What can't you make out?"

"What you're doing here."

"I'm earning my living."

"As a skivvy?" he spoke disparagingly.

"You're out of date," said Lucy. "Skivvy, indeed! I'm a household help, a professional domestician, or an answer to prayer, mainly the latter."

"You can't like all the things you have to do—cooking and making beds and whirring about with a Hoover cleaner and sinking your arms up to the elbows in greasy water."

Lucy laughed.

"Not the details, perhaps, but cooking satisfies my creative instincts, and there's something in me that really revels in clearing up mess."

"I live in a permanent mess," said Cedric. "I like it," he added defiantly.

"You look as though you did."

"My cottage in Iviza is run on simple straightforward lines. Three plates, two cups and saucers, a bed, a table and a couple of chairs. There's dust everywhere and smears of paint and chips of stone—I sculpt as well as paint—and nobody's allowed to touch a thing. I won't have a woman near the place."

"Not in any capacity?"

"Just what do you mean by that?"

"I was assuming that a man of such artistic tastes presumably had some kind of love life."

"My love life, as you call it, is my own business," said Cedric with dignity. "What I won't have is a woman in her tidying-up, interfering, bossing capacity!"

"How I'd love to have a go at your cottage," said Lucy. "It would be a challenge!"

"You won't get the opportunity."

"I suppose not."

Some bricks fell out of the pigsty. Cedric turned his head and looked into its nettle-ridden depths.

"Dear old Madge," he said. "I remember her well. A sow of most endearing disposition and a prolific mother. Seventeen in the last litter, I remember. We used to come here on fine afternoons and scratch Madge's back with a stick. She loved it."

"Why has this whole place been allowed to get into the state it's in? It can't only be the war?"

"You'd like to tidy this up, too, I suppose? What an interfering female you are. I quite see now why you would be the person to discover a body! You couldn't even leave a Greco-Roman sarcophagus alone." He paused and then went on. "No, it's not only the war. It's my father. What do you think of him, by the way?"

"I haven't had much time for thinking."

"Don't evade the issue. He's as mean as hell and in my opinion a bit crazy as well. Of course he hates all of us, except perhaps Emma. That's because of my grandfather's will."

Lucy looked inquiring.

"My grandfather was the man who mada-da-monitch. With the Crunchies and the Cracker Jacks and the Cozy Crisps. All the afternoon-tea delicacies, and then, being farsighted, he switched on very early to cheesies and canapés so that now we cash in on cocktail parties in a big way. Well, the time came when father intimated that he had a soul above Crunchies. He traveled in Italy and the Balkans and Greece and dabbled in art. My grandfather was peeved. He decided my father was no man of business and a rather poor judge of art (quite right in both cases), so left all his money in trust for his grandchildren. Father had the income for life, but he couldn't touch the capital. Do you know what he did? He stopped spending money. He came here and began to save. I'd say that by now he's accumulated nearly as big a fortune as my grandfather left. And in the meantime all of us, Harold, myself, Alfred and Emma haven't got a penny of grandfather's money. I'm a stone-broke painter. Harold went into business and is now a prominent man in the City—he's the one with the money-making touch, though I've heard rumors that he's in Queer Street lately. Alfred. Well, Alfred is usually known in the privacy of the family as Flash Alf."

"Why?"

"What a lot of things you want to know! The answer is that Alf is the black sheep of the family. He's not actually been to prison yet, but he's been very near it. He was in the Ministry of Supply during the war, but left it rather abruptly under questionable circumstances. And after that there were some dubious deals in tinned fruits, and trouble over eggs. Nothing in a big way—just a few doubtful deals on the side."

"Isn't it rather unwise to tell strangers all these things?"

"Why? Are you a police spy?"

"I might be."

"I don't think so. You were here slaving away before the police began to take an interest in us. I should say—"

He broke off as his sister Emma came through the door of the kitchen garden.

"Hullo, Em? You're looking very perturbed about something."

"I am. I want to talk to you, Cedric."

"I must get back to the house," said Lucy, tactfully.

"Don't go," said Cedric. "Murder has made you practically one of the family."

"I've got a lot to do," said Lucy. "I only came out to get some parsley."

She beat a rapid retreat to the kitchen garden. Cedric's eyes followed her.

"Good-looking girl" he said. "Who is she really?"

"Oh, she's quite well known," said Emma. "She's made a specialty of this kind of thing. But never mind Lucy Eyelesbarrow, Cedric. I'm terribly worried. Apparently the police think that this girl was a foreigner, perhaps French. Cedric, you don't think that she could possibly be—Martine?"

II

For a moment or two Cedric stared at her as though uncomprehending. "Martine? But who on earth—oh, you mean Martine?"

"Yes. Do you think—"

"Why on earth should it be Martine?"

"Well, her sending that telegram was odd when you come to think of it. It must have been roughly about the same time. Do you think that she may, after all, have come down here and . . ."

"Nonsense. Why should Martine come down here and find her way into the Long Barn? What for? It seems wildly unlikely to me."

"You don't think, perhaps, that I ought to tell Inspector Bacon, or the other one?"

"Tell him what?"

"Well—about Martine. About her letter."

"Now don't you go complicating things, Sis, by bringing up a lot of irrelevant stuff that has nothing to do with all this. I was never very convinced about that letter from Martine, anyway."

"I was."

"You've always been good at believing impossible things before breakfast, old girl. My advice to you is, sit tight and keep your mouth shut. It's up to the police to identify their precious corpse. And I bet Harold would say the same."

"Oh, I know Harold would. And Alfred, also. But I'm worried, Cedric, I really am worried. I don't know what I ought to do."

"Nothing," said Cedric promptly. "You keep your mouth shut, Emma. Never go halfway to meet trouble, that's my motto."

Emma Crackenthorpe sighed. She went slowly back to the house, uneasy in her mind.

As she came into the drive, Doctor Quimper emerged from the house and opened the door of his battered Austin car. He paused when he saw her; then, leaving the car, he came toward her.

"Well, Emma," he said. "Your father's in splendid shape. Murder suits him. It's given him an interest in life. I must recommend it for more of my patients."

Emma smiled mechanically. Doctor Quimper was always quick to notice reactions.

"Anything particular the matter?" he asked.

Emma looked up at him. She had come to rely a lot on the kindliness and sympathy of the doctor. He had become a friend on whom to lean, not only a medical attendant. His calculated brusqueness did not deceive her; she knew the kindness that lay behind it.

"I am worried, yes," she admitted.

"Care to tell me? Don't, if you don't want to."

"I'd like to tell you. Some of it you know already. The point is I don't know what to do."

"I should say your judgment was usually most reliable. What's the trouble?"

"You remember—or perhaps you don't—what I once told you about my brother—the one who was killed in the war?"

"You mean about his having married, or wanting to marry, a French girl? Something of that kind?"

"Yes. Almost immediately after I got that letter, he was killed. We never heard anything of or about the girl. All we knew, actually, was her Christian name. We always expected her to write or to turn up, but she didn't. We never heard anything—until about a month ago, just before Christmas."

"I remember. You got a letter, didn't you?"

"Yes. Saying she was in England and would like to come and see us. It was all arranged and then, at the last minute, she sent a wire that she had to return unexpectedly to France."

"Well?"

"The police think that this woman who was killed—was French."

"They do, do they? She looked more of an English type to me, but one can't really judge. What's worrying you, then, is that just possibly the dead woman might be your brother's girl?"

"Yes."

"I think it's most unlikely," said Doctor Quimper, adding: "But all the same, I understand what you feel."

"I'm wondering if I ought not to tell the police about—about it all. Cedric and the others say it's quite unnecessary. What do you think?"

"Hm." Doctor Quimper pursed up his lips. He was silent for a moment or two, deep in thought. Then he said, almost unwillingly, "It's much simpler, of course, if you say nothing. I can understand what your brothers feel about it. All the same—"

"Yes."

Quimper looked at her. His eyes had an affectionate twinkle in them.

"I'd go ahead and tell 'em," he said. "You'll go on worrying if you don't. I know you."

Emma flushed a little.

"Perhaps I'm foolish."

"You do what you want to do, my dear, and let the rest of the family go hang! I'd back your judgment against the lot of them any day."

CHAPTER TWELVE

I

"Girl! You, Girl! Come in here."

Lucy turned her head, surprised. Old Mr. Crackenthorpe was beckoning to her fiercely from just inside a door.

"You want me, Mr. Crackenthorpe?"

"Don't talk so much. Come in here."

Lucy obeyed the imperative finger. Old Mr. Crackenthorpe took hold of her arm and pulled her inside the door and shut it.

"Want to show you something," he said.

Lucy looked round her. They were in a small room evidently designed to be used as a study, but equally evidently not used as such for a very long time. There were piles of dusty papers on the desk and cobwebs festooned from the corners of the ceiling. The air smelled damp and musty.

"Do you want me to clean this room?" she asked.

Old Mr. Crackenthorpe shook his head fiercely.

"No, you don't! I keep this room locked up. Emma would like to fiddle about in here, but I don't let her. It's my room. See these stones? They're geological specimens."

Lucy looked at a collection of twelve or fourteen lumps of rock, some polished and some rough.

"Lovely," she said kindly. "Most interesting."

"You're quite right. They are interesting. You're an intelligent girl. I don't show them to everybody. I'll show you some more things."

"It's very kind of you, but I ought really to get on with what I was doing. With six people in the house—"

"Eating me out of house and home. That's all they do when they come down here! Eat. They don't offer to pay for what they eat, either. Leeches! All waiting for me to die. Well, I'm not going to die just yet—I'm not going to die to please them. I'm a lot stronger than even Emma knows."

"I'm sure you are."

"I'm not so old, either. She makes out I'm an old man, treats me as an old man. You don't think I'm old, do you?"

"Of course not," said Lucy.

"Sensible girl. Take a look at this."

He indicated a large, faded chart which hung on the wall. It was, Lucy saw, a genealogical tree; some of it done so finely that one would have had to have a magnifying glass to read the names. The remote forebears, however, were written in large, proud capitals with crowns over the names.

"Descended from kings," said Mr. Crackenthorpe. "My mother's family tree, that is, not my father's. He was a vulgarian! Common old man! Didn't like me. I was a cut above him always. Took after my mother's side. Had a natural feeling for art and classical sculpture—he couldn't see anything in it, silly old fool. Don't remember my mother—died when I was two. Last of her family. They were sold up and she married my father. But you look there—Edward the Confessor—Ethelred the Unready—whole lot of them. And that was before the Normans came. Before the Normans—that's something, isn't it?"

"It is indeed."

"Now I'll show you something else." He guided her across the room to an enormous piece of dark oak furniture. Lucy was rather uneasily conscious of the strength of the fingers clutching her arm. There certainly seemed nothing feeble about old Mr. Crackenthorpe today. "See this? Came out of Lushington—that was my mother's people's place. Elizabethan, this is. Takes four men to move it. You don't know what I keep inside it, do you? Like me to show you?"

"Do show me," said Lucy politely.

"Curious, aren't you? All women are curious." He took a key from his pocket and unlocked the door of the lower cupboard. From this he took out a surprisingly new-looking cash box. This, again, he unlocked.

"Take a look here, my dear. Know what these are?"

He lifted out a small, paper-wrapped cylinder and pulled away the paper from one end. Gold coins trickled out into his palm.

"Look at these, young lady. Look at 'em, hold 'em, touch 'em. Know what they are? Bet you don't! You're too young. Sovereigns—that's what they are. Good, golden sovereigns. What we used before all these dirty bits of paper came into fashion. Worth a lot more than silly pieces of paper. Collected them a long time back. I've got other things in this box, too. Lots of things put away in here. All ready for the future. Emma doesn't know. Nobody knows. It's our secret, see, girl? D'you know why I'm telling you and showing you?"

"Why?"

"Because I don't want you to think I'm a played-out, sick old man. Lots of life in the old dog yet. My wife's been dead a long time. Always objecting to everything, she was. Didn't like the names I gave the children—good Saxon names. No interest in that family tree. I never paid any attention to what she said, though, and she was a poor-spirited creature—always gave in. Now you're a spirited filly—a very nice filly, indeed. I'll give you some advice. Don't throw yourself away on a young man. Young men are fools! You want to take care of your future. You wait—" His fingers pressed into Lucy's arm. He leaned to her ear. "I don't say more than that. Wait. Those silly fools think I'm going to die soon. I'm not. Shouldn't be surprised if I outlived the lot of them. And then we'll see! Oh yes, then we'll see. Harold's got no children. Cedric and Alfred aren't married. Emma—Emma will never marry now. She's a bit sweet on Quimper, but Quimper will never think of marrying Emma. There's Alexander, of course. Yes, there's Alexander. But, you know, I'm fond of Alexander. Yes, that's awkward. I'm fond of Alexander."

He paused for a moment, frowning, then said:

"Well, girl, what about it? What about it, eh?"

"Miss Eyelesbarrow . . ."

Emma's voice came faintly through the closed study door. Lucy seized gratefully at the opportunity.

"Miss Crackenthorpe's calling me. I must go. Thank you so much for all you have shown me."

"Don't forget . . . our secret . . ."

"I won't," said Lucy and hurried out into the hall, not quite certain as to whether she had or had not just received a conditional proposal of marriage.

II

Dermot Craddock sat at his desk in his room at New Scotland Yard. He was slumped sideways in an easy attitude and was talking into the telephone receiver which he held with one elbow propped up on the table. He was speaking in French, a language in which he was tolerably proficient.

"It was only an idea, you understand," he said.

"But decidedly it is an idea," said the voice at the other end, from the Prefecture in Paris. "Already I have set inquiries in motion in those circles. My agent reports that he has two or three promising lines of inquiry. Unless there is some family life or a lover, these women drop out of circulation very easily and no one troubles about them. They have gone on tour, or there is some new man—it is no one's business to ask. It is a pity that the photograph you sent me is so difficult for anyone to recognize. Strangulation, it does not improve the appearance. Still, that cannot be helped. I go now to study the latest reports of my agents on this matter. There will be, perhaps, something. *Au revoir, mon cher.*"

As Craddock reiterated the farewell politely, a slip of paper was placed before him on the desk. It read:

Miss Emma Crackenthorpe
To see Detective Inspector Craddock.
Rutherford Hall case.

He replaced the receiver and said to the police constable:

"Bring Miss Crackenthorpe up."

As he waited, he leaned back in his chair, thinking.

So he had not been mistaken; there was something that Emma Crackenthorpe knew—not much, perhaps, but something. And she had decided to tell him.

He rose to his feet as she was shown in, shook hands, settled her in a chair and offered her a cigarette which she refused. Then there was a momentary pause. She was trying, he decided, to find just the words she wanted. He leaned forward.

"You have come to tell me something, Miss Crackenthorpe? Can I help you? You've been worried about something, haven't you? Some little thing, perhaps, that you feel probably has nothing to do with the case, but on the other hand just might be related to it. You've come here to tell me about it, haven't you? It's to do, perhaps, with the identity of the dead woman. You think you know who she was?"

"No, no, not quite that. I think really it's most unlikely. But—"

"But there is some possibility that worries you. You'd better tell me about it, because we may be able to set your mind at rest."

Emma took a moment or two before speaking. Then she said:

"You have seen three of my brothers. I had another brother, Edmund, who was killed in the war. Shortly before he was killed, he wrote to me from France."

She opened her handbag and took out a worn and faded letter. She read from it:

"I hope this won't be a shock to you, Emmie, but I'm getting married—to a French girl. It's all been very sudden, but I know you'll be fond of Martine and look after her if anything happens to me. Will write you all the details in my next, by which time I shall be a married man! Break it gently to the old man, won't you? He'll probably go up in smoke."

Inspector Craddock held out a hand. Emma hesitated, then put the letter into it. She went on, speaking rapidly.

"Two days after receiving this letter, we had a telegram saying Edmund was missing, believed killed. Later he was definitely reported killed. It was just before Dunkirk and a time of great confusion. There was no Army record, as far as I could find out, of his having been married, but as I say, it was a confused time. I never heard anything from the girl. I tried, after the war, to make some inquiries, but I only knew her Christian name and that part of France had been occupied by the Germans and it was difficult to find out anything, without knowing the girl's surname and more about her. In the end I assumed that the marriage had never taken place and that the girl had probably married someone else before the end of the war, or might possibly herself have been killed."

Inspector Craddock nodded. Emma went on.

"Imagine my surprise to receive a letter, just about a month ago, signed *Martine Crackenthorpe*."

"You have it?"

Emma took it from her bag and handed it to him. Craddock read it with interest. It was written in a slanting French hand, an educated hand.

> Dear Mademoiselle,
>
> I hope it will not be a shock to you to get this letter. I do not even know if your brother Edmund told you that we were married. He said he was going to do so. He was killed only a few days after our marriage, and at the same time the Germans occupied our village. After the war ended, I decided that I would not write to you or approach you, though Edmund had told me to do so. But by then I had made a new life for myself, and it was not necessary. But now things have changed. For my son's sake I write this letter. He is your brother's son, you see, and I can no longer give him the advantages he ought to have. I am coming to England early next week. Will you let me know if I can come and see you? My address for letters is 126 Elvers Crescent, N. 10. I hope again this will not be the great shock to you.
>
> I remain with assurance of my excellent sentiments,
>
> MARTINE CRACKENTHORPE

Craddock was silent for a moment or two. He reread the letter carefully before handing it back.

"What did you do on receipt of this letter, Miss Crackenthorpe?"

"My brother-in-law, Bryan Eastley, happened to be staying with me at the time and I talked to him about it. Then I rang up my brother Harold in London and consulted him about it. Harold was rather skeptical about the whole thing and advised extreme caution. We must, he said, go carefully into this woman's credentials."

Emma paused and then went on:

"That, of course, was only common sense and I quite agreed. But if this girl—woman—was really the Martine about whom Edmund had written to me, I felt that we must make her welcome. I wrote to the address she gave in her letter, inviting her to come down to Rutherford Hall and meet us. A few days later I received a telegram from London— *Very sorry forced to return to France unexpectedly. Martine.* There was no further letter or news of any kind."

"All this took place, when?"

Emma frowned.

"It was shortly before Christmas. I know, becuase I wanted to suggest her spending Christmas with us. But my father would not hear of it, so I suggested she should come down the weekend after Christmas while the family would still be there. I think the wire saying she was returning to France came actually a few days before Christmas."

"And you believe that this woman whose body was found in the sarcophagus might be this Martine?"

"No, of course I don't. But when you said she was probably a foreigner, well, I couldn't help wondering . . . if perhaps—"

Her voice died away.

Craddock spoke quickly and reassuringly.

"You did quite right to tell me about this. We'll look into it. I should say there is probably little doubt that the woman who wrote to you actually did go back to France and is there now, alive and well. On the other hand, there is a certain coincidence of dates, as you yourself have been clever enough to realize. As you heard at the inquest, the woman's death, according to the police surgeon's evidence, must have occurred about three to four weeks ago. Now don't worry, Miss Crackenthorpe, just leave it to us." He added casually, "You consulted Mr. Harold Crackenthorpe. What about your father and your other brothers?"

"I had to tell my father, of course. He got very worked up," she smiled faintly. "He was convinced it was a put-up thing to get money out of us. My father gets very excited about money. He believes, or pretends to believe, that he is a very poor man and that he must save every penny he can. I believe elderly people do get obsessions of that kind sometimes. It's not true, of course; he has a very large income and doesn't actually spend a quarter of it, or used not to until these days of high income tax. Certainly he has a large amount of savings put by." She paused and then went on. "I told my other two brothers also. Alfred seemed to consider it rather a joke, though he, too, thought it was almost certainly an imposture. Cedric just wasn't interested. He's inclined to be self-centered. Our idea was that the family would receive Martine, and that our lawyer, Mr. Wimborne, should also be asked to be present."

"What did Mr. Wimborne think about the matter?"

"We hadn't got as far as discussing the matter with him. We were on the point of doing so when Martine's telegram arrived."

"You have taken no further steps?"

"Yes. I wrote to the address in London with *Please forward* on the envelope, but I have had no reply of any kind."

"Rather a curious business. Hm . . ."

He looked at her sharply.

"What do you yourself think about it?"

"I don't know what to think."

"What were your reactions at the time? Did you think the letter was genuine, or did you agree with your father and brothers? What about your brother-in-law, by the way, what did he think?"

"Oh, Bryan thought that the letter was genuine."

"And you?"

"I wasn't sure."

"And what were your feelings about it, supposing that this girl really was your brother Edmund's widow?"

Emma's face softened.

"I was very fond of Edmund. He was my favorite brother. The letter seemed to me exactly the sort of letter that a girl like Martine would write under the circumstances. The course of events she described were entirely natural. I assumed that by the time the war ended she had either married again or was with some man who was protecting her and the child. Then, perhaps, this man had died or left her, and it then seemed right to her to apply to Edmund's family, as he himself had wanted her to do. The letter seemed genuine and natural to me, but of course, Harold pointed out that if it was written by an impostor, it would be written by some woman who had known Martine and who was in possession of all the facts, and so could write a thoroughly plausible letter. I had to admit the justice of that, but all the same—"

She stopped.

"You wanted it to be true?" said Craddock gently.

She looked at him gratefully.

"Yes, I wanted it to be true. I would be so glad if Edmund had left a son."

Craddock nodded.

"As you say, the letter, on the fact of it, sounds genuine enough. What is surprising is the sequel; Martine Crackenthorpe's abrupt departure for Paris and the fact that you have never heard from her since. You had replied kindly to her, were pepared to welcome her. Why, even if she had to return to France, did she not write again? That is, presuming her to be the genuine article. If she were an impostor, of course, it's easier to explain. I thought perhaps that you might have consulted Mr. Wimborne, and that he might have instituted inquiries which alarmed the woman. That, you tell me, is not so. But it's still possible that one or other of your brothers may have done something of the kind. It's possible that this Martine may have had a background that would not stand investigation. She may have assumed that she would be dealing only with Edmund's affectionate sister, not with hardheaded, suspicious businessmen. She may have hoped to get sums of money out of you for the child—hardly a child now, a boy presumably of fifteen or sixteen—without many questions being asked. But instead she found she was going to run up against something quite different. After all, I should imagine that serious legal aspects would arise. If Edmund

Crackenthorpe left a son, born in wedlock, he would be one of the heirs to your grandfather's estate?"

Emma nodded.

"Moreover, from what I have been told, he would in due course inherit Rutherford Hall and the land round it, very valuable building land, probably, by now."

Emma looked slightly startled.

"Yes, I hadn't thought of that."

"Well, I shouldn't worry," said Inspector Craddock. "You did quite right to come and tell me. I shall make inquiries, but it seems to me highly probable that there is no connection between the woman who wrote the letter—and who was probably trying to cash in on a swindle—and the woman whose body was found in the sarcophagus."

Emma rose with a sigh of relief.

"I'm so glad I've talked with you. You've been very kind."

Craddock accompanied her to the door.

Then he rang for Detective Sergeant Wetherall.

"Bob, I've got a job for you. Go to 126 Elvers Crescent, N. 10. Take photographs of the Rutherford Hall woman with you. See what you can find out about a woman calling herself Mrs. Crackenthorpe—Mrs. Martine Crackenthorpe—who was either living there or calling for letters there, between the dates of, say the fifteenth to the end of December."

"Right, sir."

Craddock busied himself with various other matters that were waiting attention on his desk. In the afternoon he went to see a theatrical agent who was a friend of his. His inquiries were not fruitful.

Later in the day when he returned to his office he found a wire from Paris on his desk.

PARTICULARS GIVEN BY YOU MIGHT APPLY TO ANNA STRAVINSKA OF BALLET MARITSKI. SUGGEST YOU COME OVER. DESSIN, PREFEC-TURE.

Craddock heaved a big sigh of relief and his brow cleared.

At last! So much, he thought, for the Martine Crackenthorpe hare. He decided to take the night ferry to Paris.

CHAPTER THIRTEEN

I

"It's so very kind of you to have asked me to take tea with you," said Miss Marple to Emma Crackenthorpe.

Miss Marple was looking particularly woolly and fluffy, a picture of a sweet old lady. She beamed as she looked round her: at Harold Crackenthorpe in his well-cut dark suit, at Alfred handing her sandwiches with a charming smile, at Cedric standing by the mantelpiece in a ragged tweed jacket, scowling at the rest of his family.

"We are very pleased that you could come," said Emma politely.

There was no hint of the scene which had taken place after lunch that day when Emma had exclaimed: "Dear me, I quite forgot. I told Miss Eyelesbarrow that she could bring her old aunt to tea today."

"Put her off," said Harold brusquely. "We've still got a lot to talk about. We don't want strangers here."

"Let her have tea in the kitchen or somewhere with the girl," said Alfred.

"Oh no, I couldn't do that," said Emma firmly. "That would be very rude."

"Oh, let her come," said Cedric. "We can draw her out a little about the wonderful Lucy. I should like to know more about that girl, I must say. I'm not sure that I trust her. Too smart by half."

"She's very well connected and quite genuine," said Harold. "I've made it my business to find out. One wanted to be sure. Poking about and finding the body the way she did . . ."

"If we only knew who this damned woman was," said Alfred.

Harold added angrily, "I must say, Emma, that I think you were out of your senses, going and suggesting to the police that the dead woman might be Edmund's French girl friend. It will make them convinced that she came here, and that probably one or other of us killed her."

"Oh no, Harold. Don't exaggerate."

"Harold's quite right," said Alfred. "Whatever possessed you, I don't know. I've a feeling I'm being followed everywhere I go by plainclothesmen."

"I told her not to do it," said Cedric. "Then Quimper backed her up."

"It's no business of his," said Harold angrily. "Let him stick to pills and powders and national health."

"Oh, do stop quarreling," said Emma wearily. "I'm really glad this old Miss What's-her-name is coming to tea. It will do us all good to have a stranger here and be prevented from going over and over the same things again and again. I must go and tidy myself up a little."

She left the room.

"This Lucy Eyelesbarrow," said Harold and stopped. "As Cedric says, it is odd that she should nose about in the barn and go opening up a sarcophagus—really a Herculean task. Perhaps we ought to take steps. Her attitude, I thought, was rather antagonistic at lunch."

"Leave her to me," said Alfred. "I'll soon find out if she's up to anything."

"I mean, why open up that sarcophagus?"

"Perhaps she isn't really Lucy Eyelesbarrow at all," suggested Cedric.

"But what would be the point—" Harold looked thoroughly upset. "Oh damn!"

They looked at each other with worried faces.

"And here's this pestilential old woman coming to tea. Just when we want to think."

"We'll talk things over this evening," said Alfred. "In the meantime, we'll pump the old aunt about Lucy."

So Miss Marple had duly been fetched by Lucy and installed by the fire, and she was now smiling up at Alfred as he handed her sandwiches with the approval she always showed toward a good-looking man.

"Thank you so much. May I ask—? Oh, egg and sardine, yes that will be very nice. I'm afraid I'm always rather greedy over my tea. As one gets on, you know—and of course, at night only a very light meal—I have to be careful. I shall be ninety next year. Yes, indeed."

"Eighty-seven," said Lucy.

"No, dear, ninety. You young people don't know best about everything." Miss Marple spoke with a faint acidity. Then she turned to her hostess once more. "What a beautiful house you have. And so many beautiful things in it. Those bronzes, now, they remind me of some my father bought at the Paris Exhibition. Really, your grandfather did? In the classical style, aren't they? Very handsome. How delightful for you having your brothers with you. So often families are scattered—India, though I suppose that is all done with now, and Africa—the West Coast, such a bad climate."

"Two of my brothers live in London."

"That is very nice for you."

"But my brother Cedric is a painter and lives in Iviza, one of the Balearic Islands."

"Painters are so fond of islands, are they not?" said Miss Marple. "Chopin—that was Majorca, was it not? but he was a musician. It is Gauguin I am thinking of. A sad life; misspent, one feels. I myself never really care for paintings of native women, and although I know he is very much admired, I have never cared for that lurid mustard color. One really feels quite bilious looking at his pictures."

She eyed Cedric with a slightly disapproving air.

"Tell us about Lucy as a child, Miss Marple," said Cedric.

She smiled up at him delightedly.

"Lucy was always so clever," she said. "Yes, you were, dear. Now don't interrupt. Quite remarkable at arithmetic. Why I remember when the butcher overcharged me for topside of beef—"

Miss Marple launched full steam ahead into reminiscences of Lucy's childhood and from there to experiences of her own in village life.

The stream of reminiscence was interrupted by the entry of Bryan and the boys, rather wet and dirty as a result of an enthusiastic search for clues. Tea was brought in and with it came Doctor Quimper who raised his eyebrows slightly as he looked round after acknowledging his introduction to the old lady.

"Hope your father's not under the weather, Emma?"

"Oh no—that is, he was just a little tired this afternoon."

"Avoiding visitors, I expect," said Miss Marple with a roguish smile. "How well I remember my own dear father. 'Got a lot of old pussies coming?' he would say to my mother. 'Send my tea into the study.' Very naughty about it, he was."

"Please don't think—" began Emma, but Cedric cut in.

"It's always tea in the study when his dear sons come down. Psychologically to be expected, eh, Doctor?"

Doctor Quimper, who was devouring sandwiches and coffee cake with the frank appreciation of a man who has usually too little time to spend on his meals, said: "Psychology's all right if it's left to the psychologists. Trouble is, everyone is an amateur psychologist nowadays. My patients tell me exactly what complexes and neuroses they're suffering from, without giving me a chance to tell them. Thanks, Emma, I will have another cup. No time for lunch today."

"A doctor's life, I always think, is so noble and self-sacrificing," said Miss Marple.

"You can't know many doctors," said Doctor Quimper. "Leeches they used to be called and leeches they often are! At any rate we do get paid nowadays, the state sees to that. No sending in of bills that you know won't ever be met. Trouble is that all one's patients are determined to get everything they can 'out of the government,' and as a result if little Jenny coughs twice in the night, or little Tommy eats a couple of green apples, out the poor doctor has to come in the middle of the night. O well! Glorious cake, Emma. What a cook you are!"

"Not mine. Miss Eyelesbarrow's."

"You make 'em just as good," said Quimper loyally.

"Will you come and see Father?"

She rose and the doctor followed her. Miss Marple watched them leave the room.

"Miss Crackenthorpe is a very devoted daughter, I see," she said.

"Can't imagine how she sticks the old man, myself," said the outspoken Cedric.

"She has a very comfortable home here, and Father is very much attached to her," said Harold quickly.

"Em's all right," said Cedric. "Born to be an old maid."

There was a faint twinkle in Miss Marple's eyes as she said:

"Oh, do you think so?"

Harold said quickly:

"My brother didn't use the term old maid in any derogatory sense, Miss Marple."

"Oh, I wasn't offended," said Miss Marple. "I just wondered if he was right. I shouldn't say myself that Miss Crackenthorpe would be an old maid. She's the type, I think, that's quite likely to marry late in life, and make a success of it."

"Not very likely living here," said Cedric. "Never sees anybody she could marry."

Miss Marple's twinkle became more pronounced than ever.

"There are always clergymen and doctors."

Her eyes, gentle and mischievous, went from one to another.

It was clear that she had suggested to them something that they had never thought of and which they did not find overpleasing.

Miss Marple rose to her feet, dropping as she did so several little woolly scarves and her bag.

The three brothers were most attentive picking things up.

"So kind of you," fluted Miss Marple. "Oh yes, and my little blue muffler. Yes, as I say, so kind to ask me here. I've been picturing, you know, just what your home was like, so that I can visualize dear Lucy working here."

"Perfect home conditions, with murder thrown in," said Cedric.

"Cedric!" Harold's voice was angry.

Miss Marple smiled up at Cedric.

"Do you know who you remind me of? Young Thomas Eade, our bank manager's son. Always out to shock people. It didn't do in banking circles, of course, so he went to the West Indies. He came home when his father died and inherited quite a lot of money. So nice for him. He was always better at spending money than making it."

II

Lucy took Miss Marple home. On her way back a figure stepped out of the darkness and stood in the glare of the headlights just as she was about to turn into the back lane. He held up his hand and Lucy recognized Alfred Crackenthorpe.

"That's better," he observed, as he got in. "Brrr, it's cold! I fancied I'd like a nice bracing walk. I didn't. Taken the old lady home all right?"

"Yes. She enjoyed herself very much."

"One could see that. Funny what a taste old ladies have for any kind of society, however dull. And really, nothing could be duller than Rutherford Hall. Two days here is about as much as I can stand. How do you manage to stick it out, Lucy? Don't mind if I call you Lucy, do you?"

"Not at all. I don't find it dull. Of course with me it's not a permanency."

"I've been watching you. You're a smart girl, Lucy. Too smart to waste yourself cooking and cleaning."

"Thank you, but I prefer cooking and cleaning to the office desk."

"So would I. But there are other ways of living. You could be a free lance."

"I am."

"Not this way. I mean, working for yourself, pitting your wits against—"

"Against what?"

"The powers that be! All the silly pettifogging rules and regulations that hamper us all nowadays. The interesting thing is there's always a way round them if you're smart enough to find it. And you're smart. Come now, does the idea appeal to you?"

"Possibly."

Lucy maneuvered the car into the stable yard.

"Not going to commit yourself?"

"I'd have to hear more."

"Frankly, my dear girl, I could use you. You've got the sort of manner that's invaluable, creates confidence."

"Do you want me to help you sell gold bricks?"

"Nothing so risky. Just a little bypassing of the law—no more." His hand slipped up her arm. "You're a damned attractive girl, Lucy. I'd like you as a partner."

"I'm flattered."

"Meaning, nothing doing? Think about it. Think of the fun, the pleasure you'd get out of outwitting all the sobersides. The trouble is, one needs capital."

"I'm afraid I haven't got any."

"Oh, it wasn't a touch! I'll be laying my hands on some before long. My revered Papa can't live forever, mean old brute. When he pops off, I lay my hands on some real money. What about it, Lucy?"

"What are the terms?"

"Marriage if you fancy it. Women seem to, no matter how advanced and self-supporting they are. Besides, married women can't be made to give evidence against their husbands."

"Not so flattering!"

"Come off it, Lucy. Don't you realize I've fallen for you?"

Rather to her surprise Lucy was aware of a queer fascination. There was a quality of charm about Alfred, perhaps due to sheer animal magnetism. She laughed and slipped from his encircling arm.

"This is no time for dalliance. There's dinner to think about."

"So there is, Lucy, and you're a lovely cook. What's for dinner?"

"Wait and see! You're as bad as the boys!"

They entered the house and Lucy hurried to the kitchen. She was rather surprised to be interrupted in her preparations by Harold Crackenthorpe.

"Miss Eyelesbarrow, can I speak to you about something?"

"Would later do, Mr. Crackenthorpe? I'm rather behindhand."

"Certainly. Certainly. After dinner?"

"Yes, that will do."

Dinner was duly served and appreciated. Lucy finished washing up and came out into the hall to find Harold Crackenthorpe waiting for her.

"Yes, Mr. Crackenthorpe?"

"Shall we come in here?" He opened the door of the drawing room and led the way. He shut the door behind her.

"I shall be leaving early in the morning," he explained, "but I want to tell you how struck I have been by your ability."

"Thank you," said Lucy feeling a little surprised.

"I feel that your talents are wasted here—definitely wasted."

"Do you? I don't."

At any rate, he can't ask me to marry him, thought Lucy. He's got a wife already.

"I suggest that having very kindly seen us through this lamentable crisis, you call upon me in London. If you will ring up and make an appointment, I will leave instructions with my secretary. The truth is that we could use someone of your outstanding ability in the firm. We could discuss fully in what field your talents would be most ably employed. I can offer you, Miss Eyelesbarrow, a very good salary indeed with brilliant prospects. I think you will be agreeably surprised."

His smile was magnanimous.

Lucy said demurely, "Thank you, Mr. Crackenthorpe, I'll think about it."

"Don't wait too long. These opportunities should not be missed by a young woman anxious to make her way in the world."

Again his teeth flashed.

"Good night, Miss Eyelesbarrow, sleep well."

"Well," said Lucy to herself, "well. . . . This is all very interesting."

On her way up to bed, Lucy encountered Cedric on the stairs.

"Look here, Lucy, there's something I want to say to you."

"Do you want me to marry you and come to Iviza and look after you?"

Cedric looked very much taken aback and slightly alarmed.

"I never thought of such a thing."

"Sorry. My mistake."

"I just wanted to know if you've a timetable in the house?"

"Is that all? There's one on the hall table."

"You know," said Cedric, reprovingly, "you shouldn't go about thinking everyone wants to marry you. You're quite a good-looking girl but not as good-looking as all that. There's a name for that sort of thing. It grows on you and you get worse. Actually you're the last girl in the world I should care to marry. The last girl."

"Indeed?" said Lucy. "You needn't rub it in. Perhaps you'd prefer me as a stepmother?"

"What's that?" Cedric stared at her, stupefied.

"You heard me," said Lucy, and went into her room and shut the door.

CHAPTER FOURTEEN

I

Dermot Craddock was fraternizing with Armand Dessin of the Paris Prefecture. The two men had met on one or two occasions and got on well together. Since Craddock spoke French fluently, most of their conversation was conducted in that language.

"It is an idea only," Dessin warned him. "I have a picture here of the corps de ballet. That is she, the fourth from the left. It says anything to you, yes?"

Inspector Craddock said that actually it didn't. A strangled young woman is not easy to recognize, and in this picture all the young women concerned were heavily made up and were wearing extravagant bird headdresses.

"It could be," he said. "I can't go further than that. Who was she? What do you know about her?"

"Almost less than nothing," said the other cheerfully. "She was not important, you see. And the Ballet Maritski—it is not important, either. It plays in suburban theaters and goes on tour. It has no real names, no stars, no famous ballerinas. But I will take you to see Madame Joliet who runs it."

Madame Joliet was a brisk businesslike Frenchwoman with a shrewd eye, a small mustache, and a good deal of adipose tissue.

"Me, I do not like the police!" She scowled at them, without camouflaging her dislike of the visit. "Always, if they can, they make me embarrassments."

"No, no, Madame, you must not say that," said Dessin who was a tall, thin, melancholy-looking man. "When have I ever caused you embarrassments?"

"Over that little fool who drank the carbolic acid," said Madame Joliet promptly. "And all because she has fallen in love with the *chef d'orchestre*, who does not care for women and has other tastes. Over that you made the big brouhaha! Which is not good for my beautiful ballet."

"On the contrary, big box-office business," said Dessin. "And that was three years ago. You should not bear malice. Now about this girl, Anna Stravinska."

"Well, what about her?"

"Is she Russian?" asked Inspector Craddock.

"No, indeed. You mean, because of her name? But they all call themselves names like that, these girls. She was not important, she did not dance well, she was not particularly good-looking. *Elle était assez bien, c'est tout.* She danced well enough for the corps de ballet, but no solos."

"Was she French?"

"Perhaps. She had a French passport. But she told me once that she had an English husband."

"She told you that she had an English husband? Alive or dead?"

Madame Joliet shrugged her shoulders.

"Dead, or he had left her. How should I know which? These girls—there is always some trouble with men."

"When did you last see her?"

"I take my company to London for six weeks. We play at Torquay, at Bournemouth, at Eastbourne, at somewhere else I forget and at Hammersmith. Then we come back to France, but Anna, she does not come. She sends a message only that she leaves the company, that she goes to live with her husband's family, some nonsense of that kind. I did not think it is true, myself. I think it more likely that she has met a man, you understand."

Inspector Craddock nodded. He perceived that that was what Madame Joliet would invariably think.

"And it is no loss to me. I do not care. I can get girls just as good and better to come and dance, so I shrug the shoulders and do not think of it anymore. Why should I? They are all the same, these girls, mad about men."

"What date was this?"

"When we return to France? It was—yes—the Sunday before Christmas. And Anna she leaves two, or is it three, days before that? I cannot remember exactly. But the end of the week at Hammersmith we have to dance without her, and it means rearranging things. It was very naughty of her, but these girls—the moment they meet a man they are all the same. Only I say to everybody, 'Zut, I do not take her back, that one!'"

"Very annoying for you."

"Ah! me—I do not care. No doubt she passes the Christmas holiday with some man she has picked up. It is not my affair. I can find other girls—girls who will leap at the chance of dancing in the Ballet Maritski and who can dance as well or better than Anna."

Madame Joliet paused and then asked with a sudden gleam of interest,

"Why do you want to find her? Has she come into money?"

"On the contrary," said Inspector Craddock politely. "We think she may have been murdered."

Madame Joliet relapsed into indifference.

"*Ça se peut!* It happens. Ah well! She was a good Catholic. She went to Mass on Sundays, and no doubt to confession."

"Did she ever speak to you, Madame, of a son?"

"A son? Do you mean she had a child? That, now, I should consider most unlikely. These girls, all—all of them—know a useful address to which to go. M. Dessin knows that as well as I do."

"She may have had a child before she adopted a stage life," said Craddock. "During the war, for instance."

"*Ah! dans la guerre.* That is always possible. But if so, I know nothing about it."

"Who among the other girls were her closest friends?"

"I can give you two or three names, but she was not very intimate with anyone."

They could get nothing else useful from Madame Joliet.

Shown the compact, she said Anna had one of that kind, but so had most of the other girls. Anna had perhaps bought a fur coat in London, she did not know. "Me, I occupy myself with the rehearsals, with the stage lighting, with all the difficulties of my business. I have not time to notice what my artists wear."

After Madame Joliet, they interviewed the girls whose names she had given them. One or two of them had known Anna fairly well, but they all said that she had not been one to talk much about herself, and that when she did, it was, so one girl said, mostly lies.

"She liked to pretend things—stories about having been the mistress of a grand duke or of a great English financier or how she worked for the Resistance in the war, even a story about being a film star in Hollywood."

Another girl said:

"I think that really she had had a very tame bourgeois existence. She liked to be in ballet because she thought it was romantic, but she was not a good dancer. You understand that if she were to say, 'My father was a draper in Amiens,' that would not be romantic! So instead she made up things."

"Even in London," said the first girl, "she threw out hints about a very rich man who was going to take her on a cruise round the world, because she reminded him of his dead daughter who had died in a car accident. *Quelle blague!*"

"She told me she was going to stay with a rich lord in Scotland," said the second girl. "She said she would shoot the deer there."

None of this was helpful. All that seemed to emerge from it was that Anna Stravinska was a proficient liar. She was certainly not shooting deer with a peer in Scotland, and it seemed equally unlikely that she was on the sundeck of a liner cruising round the world. But neither was there any real reason to believe that her body had been found in a sarcophagus at Rutherford Hall. The identification by the girls and Madama Joliet was very uncertain and hesitating. It looked something like Anna, they all agreed. But really! All swollen up—it might be anybody!

The only fact that was established was that, on December 19, Anna

Stravinska had decided not to return to France, and that on the twentieth of December a woman resembling her in appearance had traveled to Brackhampton by the 4:54 train and had been strangled.

If the woman in the sarcophagus was not Anna Stravinska, where was Anna now?

To that, Madame Joliet's answer was simple and inevitable:

"With a man!"

And it was probably the correct answer, Craddock reflected ruefully.

One other possibility had to be considered, raised by the casual remark that Anna had once referred to having an English husband.

Had that husband been Edmund Crackenthorpe?

It seemed unlikely, considering the word picture of Anna that had been given him by those who knew her. What was much more probable was that Anna had at one time known the girl Martine sufficiently intimately to be acquainted with the necessary details. It might have been Anna who wrote that letter to Emma Crackenthorpe and, if so, Anna would have been quite likely to have taken fright at any question of an investigation. Perhaps she had even thought it prudent to sever her connection with the Ballet Maritski. Again, where was she now?

And again, inevitably, Madame Joliet's answer seemed the most likely.

With a man.

II

Before leaving Paris, Craddock discussed with Dessin the question of the woman named Martine. Dessin was inclined to agree with his English colleague that the matter had probably no connection with the woman found in the sarcophagus.

He assured Craddock that the Sûreté would do their best to discover if there actually was any record of a marriage between Lieutenant Edmund Crackenthorpe of the 4th Southshire Regiment and a French girl whose Christian name was Martine. Time: just prior to the fall of Dunkirk.

He warned Craddock, however, that a definite answer was doubtful. The area in question had not only been occupied by the Germans at almost exactly that time, but subsequently that part of France had suffered severe war damage at the time of the invasion. Many buildings and records had been destroyed.

"But rest assured, my dear colleague, we shall do our best."

With this, he and Craddock took leave of each other.

III

On Craddock's return Sergeant Wetherall was waiting to report with gloomy relish:

"Accommodation address, sir—that's what 126 Elvers Crescent is. Quite respectable and all that."

"Any identifications?"

"No. Nobody could recognize the photograph as that of a woman who had called for letters, but I don't think they would anyway. It's a month ago, very near, and a good many people use the place. It's actually a boardinghouse for students."

"She might have stayed there under another name."

"If so, they didn't recognize her as the original of the photograph."

He added:

"We circularized the hotels—nobody registering as Martine Crackenthorpe anywhere. On receipt of your call from Paris, we checked up on Anna Stravinska. She was registered with other members of the company in a cheap hotel off Brook Green—mostly theatrical there. She cleared out on the night of Thursday the nineteenth after the show. No further record."

Craddock nodded. He suggested a line of further inquiries, though he had little hope of success from them.

After some thought, he rang up Wimborne, Henderson and Carstairs and asked for an appointment with Mr. Wimborne.

In due course, he was ushered into a particularly airless room where Mr. Wimborne was sitting behind a large old-fashioned desk covered with bundles of dusty-looking papers. Various deed boxes labeled *Sir John ffouldes, dec. Lady Derrin, George Rowbotham, Esq.*, ornamented the walls; whether as relics of a bygone era or as part of present-day legal affairs, the Inspector did not know.

Mr. Wimborne eyed his visitor with the polite wariness characteristic of a family lawyer toward the police.

"What can I do for you, Inspector?"

"This letter." Craddock pushed Martine's letter across the table. Mr. Wimborne touched it with a distasteful finger but did not pick it up. His color rose very slightly and his lips tightened.

"Quite so," he said, "quite so! I received a letter from Miss Emma Crackenthorpe yesterday morning, informing me of her visit to Scotland Yard and of—ah—all the circumstances. I may say that I am at a loss to understand—quite at a loss—why I was not consulted about this letter at the time of its arrival! Most extraordinary! I should have been informed immediately."

Inspector Craddock repeated soothingly such platitudes as seemed best calculated to reduce Mr. Wimborne to an amenable frame of mind.

"I'd no idea that there was ever any question of Edmund's having married," said Mr. Wimborne in an injured voice.

Inspector Craddock said that he supposed, in wartime . . . and left it to trail away vaguely.

"Wartime!" snapped Mr. Wimborne with waspish acerbity. "Yes, indeed, we were in Lincoln's Inn Fields at the outbreak of war and there was a direct hit on the house next door, and a great number of our records were destroyed. Not the really important documents, of course; they had been removed to the country for safety. But it caused a great deal of confusion. Of course, the Crackenthorpe business was in my father's hands at that time. He died six years ago. I daresay he may have been told about this so-called marriage of Edmund's, but on the face of it, it looks as though that marriage, even if contemplated, never took place, and so, no doubt my father did not consider the story of any importance. I must say, all this sounds very fishy to me. This coming forward, after all these years, and claiming a marriage and a legitimate son. Very fishy, indeed. What proofs had she got, I'd like to know?"

"Just so," said Craddock. "What would her position or her son's position be?"

"The idea was, I suppose, that she would get the Crackenthorpes to provide for her and for the boy."

"Yes, but I meant, what would she and the son be entitled to, legally speaking, if she could prove her claim?"

"Oh, I see." Mr. Wimborne picked up his spectacles which he had laid aside in his irritation, and put them on, staring through them at Inspector Craddock with shrewd attention. "Well, at the moment, nothing. But if she could prove that the boy was the son of Edmund Crackenthorpe, born in lawful wedlock, then the boy would be entitled to his share of Josiah Crackenthorpe's trust, on the death of Luther Crackenthorpe. More than that, he'd inherit Rutherford Hall, since he's the son of the eldest son."

"Would anyone want to inherit the house?"

"To live in? I should say, certainly not. But that estate, my dear Inspector, is worth a considerable amount of money. Very considerable. Land for industrial and building purposes. Land which is now in the heart of Brackhampton. Oh yes, a very considerable inheritance."

"If Luther Crackenthorpe dies, I believe you told me that Cedric gets it?"

"He inherits the real estate, yes, as the eldest surviving son."

"Cedric Crackenthorpe, I have been given to understand, is not interested in money?"

Mr. Wimborne gave Craddock a cold stare.

"Indeed? I am inclined, myself, to take statements of such a nature with what I might term a grain of salt. There are doubtless certain unworldly people who are indifferent to money. I myself have never met one."

Mr. Wimborne obviously derived a certain satisfaction from this remark.

Inspector Craddock hastened to take advantage of this ray of sunshine.

"Harold and Alfred Crackenthorpe," he ventured, "seem to have been a good deal upset by the arrival of this letter?"

"Well they might be," said Mr. Wimborne. "Well they might be."

"It would reduce their eventual inheritance?"

"Certainly. Edmund Crackenthorpe's son—always presuming there is a son—would be entitled to a fifth share of the trust money."

"That doesn't really seem a very serious loss?"

Mr. Wimborne gave him a shrewd glance.

"It is a totally inadequate motive for murder, if that is what you mean."

"But I suppose they're both pretty hard up," Craddock murmured.

He sustained Mr. Wimborne's sharp glance with perfect impassivity.

"Oh! So the police have been making inquiries? Yes, Alfred is almost incessantly in low water. Occasionally he is very flush of money for a short time, but it soon goes. Harold, as you seem to have discovered, is at present somewhat precariously situated."

"In spite of his appearance of financial prosperity?"

"Facade. All facade! Half these City concerns don't even know if they're solvent or not. Balance sheets can be made to look all right to the inexpert eye. But when the assets that are listed aren't really assets—when those assets are trembling on the brink of a crash—where are you?"

"Where, presumably, Harold Crackenthorpe is, in bad need of money."

"Well, he wouldn't have got it by strangling his late brother's widow," said Mr. Wimborne. "And nobody's murdered Luther Crackenthorpe which is the only murder that would do the family any good. So really, Inspector, I don't quite see where your ideas are leading you."

The worst of it was, Inspector Craddock thought, that he wasn't very sure himself.

CHAPTER FIFTEEN

I

Inspector Craddock had made an appointment with Harold Crackenthorpe at his office, he and Sergeant Wetherall arrived there punctually. The office was on the fourth floor of a big block of City offices. Inside everything showed prosperity and the acme of modern business taste.

A neat young woman took his name, spoke in a discreet murmur through a telephone, and then rising, showed them into Harold Crackenthorpe's own private office.

Harold was sitting behind a large leather-topped desk and was looking as impeccable and self-confident as ever. If, as the Inspector's private knowledge led him to surmise, he was close upon Queer Street, no trace of it showed.

He looked up with a frank, welcoming interest.

"Good morning, Inspector Craddock. I hope this means that you have some definite news for us at last."

"Hardly that, I am afraid, Mr. Crackenthorpe. It's just a few more questions I'd like to ask."

"More questions? Surely by now we have answered everything imaginable."

"I daresay it feels like that to you, Mr. Crackenthorpe, but it's just a question of our regular routine."

"Well, what is it this time?" He spoke impatiently.

"I should be glad if you could tell me exactly what you were doing on the afternoon and evening of December the twentieth last, say between the hours of three p.m. and midnight."

Harold Crackenthorpe went an angry shade of plum red.

"That seems to be a most extraordinary question to ask me. What does it mean, I should like to know?"

Craddock smiled gently.

"It just means that I should like to know where you were between the hours of three p.m. and midnight on Friday, December the twentieth."

"Why?"

"It would help to narrow things down."

"Narrow them down? You have extra information, then?"

"We hope that we're getting a little closer, sir."

"I'm not at all sure that I ought to answer your question. Not, that is, without having my solicitor present."

"That, of course, is entirely up to you," said Craddock. "You are not bound to answer any questions and you have a perfect right to have a solicitor present before you do so."

"You are not—let me be quite clear—er—warning me in any way?"

"Oh no, sir." Inspector Craddock looked properly shocked. "Nothing of that kind. The questions I am asking you I am asking of several other people as well. There's nothing directly personal about this. It's just a matter of necessary eliminations."

"Well, of course, I'm anxious to assist in any way I can. Let me see now. Such a thing isn't easy to answer offhand, but we're very systematic here. Miss Ellis, I expect, can help."

He spoke briefly into one of the telephones on his desk and almost immediately a streamlined young woman in a well-cut black suit entered with a notebook.

"My secretary, Miss Ellis, Inspector Craddock. Now, Miss Ellis, the Inspector would like to know what I was doing on the afternoon and evening of—what was the date?"

"Friday, December the twentieth."

"Friday, December the twentieth. I expect you will have some record."

"Oh yes." Miss Ellis left the room, returned with an office memorandum calendar and turned the pages.

"You were in the office in the morning of December the twentieth. You had a conference with Mr. Goldie about the Cromartie merger, you lunched with Lord Forthville at the Berkeley—"

"Ah, it was that day, yes."

"You returned to the office at about three o'clock and dictated half a dozen letters. You then left to attend Sotheby's sale rooms where you were interested in some rare manuscripts which were coming up for sale that day. You did not return to the office again, but I have a note to remind you that you were attending the Catering Club dinner that evening." She looked up interrogatively.

"Thank you, Miss Ellis."

Miss Ellis glided from the room.

"That is all quite clear in my mind," said Harold. "I went to Sotheby's that afternoon but the items I wanted there went for far too high a price. I had tea in a small place in Jermyn Street—Russell's, I think it is called. I dropped into a News Theatre for about half an hour or so, then went home. I live at 43 Cardigan Gardens. The Catering Club dinner took place at seven-thirty at Caterers' Hall, and after it I returned home to bed. I think that should answer your questions?"

"That's all very clear, Mr. Crackenthorpe. What time was it when you returned home to dress?"

"I don't think I can remember exactly. Soon after six, I should think."

"And after the dinner?"

"It was, I think, half-past eleven when I got home."

"Did your manservant let you in? Or perhaps Lady Alice Crackenthorpe?"

"My wife, Lady Alice, is abroad in the South of France and has been since early in December. I let myself in with my latchkey."

"So there is no one who can vouch for your returning home when you say you did?"

Harold gave him a cold stare.

"I daresay the servants heard me come in. I have a man and wife. But really, Inspector—"

"Please, Mr. Crackenthorpe, I know these questions are annoying, but I have nearly finished. Do you own a car?"

"Yes, a Humber Hawk."

"You drive it yourself?"

"Yes. I don't use it much except at weekends. Driving in London is quite impossible nowadays."

"I presume you use it when you go down to see your father and sister at Brackhampton?"

"Not unless I am going to stay there for some length of time. If I just go down for the night, as, for instance, to the inquest the other day, I always go by train. There is an excellent train service and it is far quicker than going by car. The car my sister hires meets me at the station."

"Where do you keep your car?"

"I rent a garage in the mews behind Cardigan Gardens. Any more questions?"

"I think that's all for now," said Inspector Craddock smiling and rising. "I'm very sorry for having to bother you."

When they were outside, Sergeant Wetherall, a man who lived in a state of dark suspicion of all and sundry, remarked meaningly:

"He didn't like those questions—didn't like them at all. Put out, he was."

"If you have not committed a murder, it naturally annoys you if it seems someone thinks that you have," said Inspector Craddock mildly. "It would particularly annoy an ultrarespectable man like Harold Crackenthorpe. There's nothing in that. What we've got to find out now is if anyone actually saw Harold Crackenthorpe at the sale that afternoon, and the same applies to the teashop place. He could easily have traveled by the 4:54, pushed the woman out of the train and caught a train back to London in time to appear at the dinner. In the same way he could have driven his car down that night, moved the body to the sarcophagus and driven back again. Make inquiries in the mews."

"Yes, sir. Do you think that's what he did do?"

"How do I know?" asked Inspector Craddock. "He's a tall, dark man. He could have been on that train and he's got a connection with Rutherford Hall. He's a possible suspect in this case. Now for brother Alfred."

II

Alfred Crackenthorpe had a flat in West Hampstead, in a big modern building of slightly jerry-built type with a large courtyard in which the owners of flats parked their cars with a certain lack of consideration for others.

The flat was of the modern built-in type, evidently rented furnished. It had a long plywood table that let down from the wall, a divan bed, and various chairs of improbable proportions.

Alfred Crackenthorpe met them with engaging friendliness but was, the Inspector thought, nervous.

"I'm intrigued," he said. "Can I offer you a drink, Inspector Craddock?" He held up various bottles invitingly.

"No, thank you, Mister Crackenthorpe."

"As bad as that?" He laughed at his own little joke, then asked what it was all about.

Inspector Craddock said his little piece.

"What was I doing on the afternoon and evening of December the twentieth? How should I know? Why, that's—what?—over three weeks ago."

"Your brother Harold has been able to tell us very exactly."

"Brother Harold, perhaps. Not brother Alfred." He added with a touch of something, envious malice possibly: "Harold is the successful member of the family—busy, useful, fully employed, a time for everything and everything at that time. Even if he were to commit a murder, shall we say? it would be carefully timed and exact."

"Any particular reason for using that example?"

"Oh no—it just came into my mind as a supreme absurdity."

"Now about yourself."

Alfred spread out his hands.

"It's as I tell you, I've no memory for times or places. If you were to say Christmas Day now, then I should be able to answer you—there's a peg to hang it on. I know where I was Christmas Day. We spent that with my father at Brackhampton. I really don't know why. He grumbles at the expense of having us, and would grumble that we never came near him if we didn't come. We really do it to please my sister."

"And you did it this year?"

"Yes."

"But unfortunately your father was taken ill, was he not?"

Craddock was pursuing a side line deliberately, led by the kind of instinct that often came to him in his profession.

"He was taken ill. Living like a sparrow in the glorious cause of economy, sudden full eating and drinking had its effect."

"That was all it was, was it?"

"Of course. What else?"

"I gathered that his doctor was—worried."

"Oh, that old fool Quimper," Alfred spoke quickly and scornfully. "It's no use listening to him, Inspector. He's an alarmist of the worst kind."

"Indeed? He seemed a rather sensible kind of man to me."

"He's a complete fool. Father's not really an invalid, there's nothing wrong with his heart, but he takes in Quimper completely. Naturally, when father really felt ill, he made a terrific fuss, and had Quimper going and coming, asking questions, going into everything he'd eaten and drunk. The whole thing was ridiculous!" Alfred spoke with unusual heat.

Craddock was silent for a moment or two, rather effectively. Alfred fidgeted, shot him a quick glance, and then said petulantly:

"Well, what is all this? Why do you want to know where I was on a particular Friday, three or four weeks ago?"

"So you do remember that it was a Friday?"

"I thought you said so."

"Perhaps I did," said Inspector Craddock. "At any rate, Friday the twentieth is the day I am asking about."

"Why?"

"A routine inquiry."

"That's nonsense. Have you found out something more about this woman? About where she came from?"

"Our information is not yet complete."

Alfred gave him a sharp glance.

"I hope you're not being led aside by this wild theory of Emma's that she might have been my brother Edmund's widow. That's complete nonsense."

"This Martine did not at any time apply to you?"

"To me? Good Lord, no. That would have been a laugh."

"She would be more likely, you think, to go to your brother Harold?"

"Much more likely. His name's frequently in the papers. He's well off. Trying a touch there wouldn't surprise me. Not that she'd have got anything. Harold's as tightfisted as the old man himself. Emma, of course, is the softhearted one of the family, and she was Edmund's favorite sister. All the same, Emma isn't credulous. She was quite alive to the possibility of this woman being phony. She had it all laid on for the entire family to be there— and a hardheaded solicitor as well."

"Very wise," said Craddock. "Was there a definite date fixed for this meeting?"

"It was supposed to be soon after Christmas. The weekend of the twenty-seventh—" He stopped.

"Ah," said Craddock pleasantly. "So I see some dates have a meaning to you."

"I've told you no definite date was fixed."

"But you talked about it—when?"

"I really can't remember."

"And you can't tell me what you yourself were doing on Friday, December the twentieth?"

"Sorry, my mind's an absolute blank."

"You don't keep an engagement book?"

"Can't stand the things."

"The Friday before Christmas—it shouldn't be too difficult."

"I played golf one day with a likely prospect." Alfred shook his head. "No, that was the week before. I probably just mooched around. I spend a lot of my time doing that. I find one's business gets done in bars more than anywhere else."

"Perhaps the people here, or some of your friends, may be able to help?"

"Maybe. I'll ask them. Do what I can."

Alfred seemed more sure of himself now.

"I can't tell you what I was doing that day," he said, "but I can tell you what I wasn't doing. I wasn't murdering anyone in the Long Barn."

"Why should you say that, Mr. Crackenthorpe?"

"Come now, my dear Inspector. You're investigating this murder, aren't you? And when you begin to ask 'Where were you on such and such a day at such and such a time?' you're narrowing down things. I'd very much like to know why you've hit on Friday the twentieth between—what?—lunchtime and midnight? It couldn't be medical evidence, not after all this time. Did somebody see the deceased sneaking into the barn that afternoon? She went in and she never came out, etc? Is that it?"

The sharp, black eyes were watching him narrowly, but Inspector Craddock was far too old a hand to react to that sort of thing.

"I'm afraid we'll have to let you guess about that," he said pleasantly.

"The police are so secretive."

"Not only the police. I think, Mr. Crackenthorpe, you could remember what you were doing on that Friday if you tried. Of course, you may have reasons for not wishing to remember—"

"You won't catch me that way, Inspector. It's very suspicious, of course, very suspicious, indeed, that I can't remember, but there it is! Wait a minute now! I went to Leeds that week, stayed at a hotel close to the town hall—can't remember its name, but you'd find it easily enough. That might have been on the Friday."

"We'll check up," said the Inspector unemotionally.

He rose. "I'm sorry you couldn't have been more cooperative, Mr. Crackenthorpe."

"Most unfortunate for me! There's Cedric with a safe alibi in Iviza, and Harold, no doubt, checked with business appointments and public dinners every hour, and here am I with no alibi at all. Very sad. And all so silly. I've already told you I don't murder people. And why should I murder an unknown woman anyway? What for? Even if the corpse is the corpse of Edmund's widow, why should any of us wish to do away with her? Now if she'd been married to Harold in the war and had suddenly reappeared, then it might have been awkward for the respectable Harold—bigamy and all that. But Edmund! Why, we'd all have enjoyed making Father stump up a bit to give her an allowance and send the boy to a decent school. Father would have been wild, but he couldn't in decency refuse to do something. Won't you have a drink before you go, Inspector? Sure? Too bad I haven't been able to help you."

III

"Sir, listen, do you know what?"

Inspector Craddock looked at his excited sergeant.

"Yes, Wetherall, what is it?"

"I've placed him, sir. That chap. All the time I was trying to fix it and suddenly it came. He was mixed up in that tinned-food business with Dicky Rogers. Never got anything on him—too cagey for that. And he's been in with one or more of the Soho lot. Watches and that Italian sovereign business."

Of course! Craddock realized now why Alfred's face had seemed vaguely familiar from the first. It had all been small-time stuff, never anything that could be proved. Alfred had always been on the outskirts of the racket with a plausible, innocent reason for having been mixed up in it all. But the police had been quite sure that a small, steady profit came his way.

"That throws rather a light on things," Craddock said.

"Think he done it?"

"I shouldn't have said he was the type to do murder. But it explains other things—the reason why he couldn't come up with an alibi."

"Yes, that looks bad for him."

"Not really," said Craddock. "It's quite a clever line, just to say firmly I can't remember. Lots of people can't remember what they did and where they were even a week ago. It's especially useful if you don't particularly want to call attention to the way you spend your time—interesting rendezvous at lorry pull ups with the Dicky Rogers crowd, for instance."

"So you think he's all right?"

"I'm not prepared to think anyone's all right just yet," said Inspector Craddock. "You've got to work on it, Wetherall."

Back at his desk, Craddock sat frowning, and making little notes on the pad in front of him.

Murderer (he wrote) . . . . A tall, dark man!!!

Victim? . . .Could have been Martine, Edmund Crackenthorpe's girl
    friend or widow.

        or

        Could have been Anna Stravinska. Went out of circulation
        at appropriate time, right age and appearance, clothing,
        etc. No connection with Rutherford Hall as far as is known.
        Could be Harold's first wife! Bigamy!
            "   "   "   mistress. Blackmail?!

> If connection with Alfred, might be blackmail had knowl-
> edge that could have sent him to jail? If Cedric—might have
> had connection with him abroad—Paris? Balearics?
>   or
> Victim could be Anna S. posing as Martine
>   or
> Victim is unknown woman killed by unknown murderer!

"And most probably the latter," said Craddock aloud.

He reflected gloomily on the situation. You couldn't get far with a case until you had the motive. All the motives suggested so far seemed either inadequate or farfetched.

Now if only it had been the murder of old Mr. Crackenthorpe. Plenty of motive there.

Something stirred in his memory.

He made further notes on his pad.

> Ask Dr. Q. about Christmas illness
> Cedric—alibi.
> Consult Miss M. for latest gossip.

CHAPTER SIXTEEN

When Craddock got to 4 Madison Road he found Lucy Eyelesbarrow with Miss Marple.

He hesitated for a moment on his plan of campaign and then decided that Lucy Eyelesbarrow might prove a valuable ally.

After greetings, he solemnly drew out his notecase, extracted three pound notes, added three shillings and pushed them across the table to Miss Marple.

"What's this, Inspector?"

"Consultation fee. You're a consultant—on murder! Pulse, temperature, local reactions, possible deep-seated cause of said murder. I'm just the poor harassed local G.P."

Miss Marple looked at him and twinkled. He grinned at her. Lucy Eyelesbarrow gave a faint gasp and then laughed.

"Why, Inspector Craddock, you're human after all."

"Oh well, I'm not strictly on duty this afternoon."

"I told you we had met before," said Miss Marple to Lucy. "Sir Henry Clithering is his godfather, a very old friend of mine."

"Would you like to hear, Miss Eyelesbarrow, what my godfather said about her, the first time we met? He described her as just the finest detective God ever made—natural genius cultivated in a suitable soil. He told me never to despise the"—Dermot Craddock paused for a moment to seek for a synonym for "old pussies"—"er—elderly ladies. He said they could usually tell you what might have happened, what ought to have happened and even what actually did happen! And, he said, they can tell you why it happened! He added that this particular—er—elderly lady was at the top of the class."

"Well!" said Lucy, "that seems to be a testimonial all right."

Miss Marple was pink and confused and looked unusually dithery.

"Dear Sir Henry," she murmured. "Always so kind. Really I'm not at all clever, just, perhaps, a slight knowledge of human nature—living, you know, in a village."

She added, wtih more composure:

"Of course, I am somewhat handicapped, by not actually being on the spot. It is so helpful, I always feel, when people remind you of other people, because types are alike everywhere and that is such a valuable guide."

Lucy looked a little puzzled, but Craddock nodded comprehendingly.

"But you've been to tea there, haven't you?" he said.

"Yes, indeed. Most pleasant. I was a little disappointed that I didn't see Old Mr. Crackenthorpe, but one can't have everything."

"Do you feel that if you saw the person who had done the murder, you'd know?" asked Lucy.

"Oh, I wouldn't say that, dear. One is always inclined to guess, and guessing would be very wrong when it is a question of anything as serious as murder. All one can do is to observe the people concerned, or who might have been concerned, and see of whom they remind you."

"Like Cedric and the bank manager?"

Miss Marple corrected her.

"The bank manager's son, dear. Mr. Eade himself was far more like Mr. Harold, a very conservative man, but perhaps a little too fond of money— the sort of man, too, who would go a long way to avoid scandal."

Craddock smiled and said:

"And Alfred?"

"Jenkins at the garage," Miss Marple replied promptly. "He didn't exactly appropriate tools, but he used to exchange a broken or inferior jack for a good one. And I believe he wasn't very honest over batteries, though I don't understand these things very well. I know Raymond left off dealing with him and went to the garage on the Milchester road. As for Emma," continued Miss Marple thoughtfully, "she reminds me very much of Geraldine Webb—always very quiet, almost dowdy—and bullied a good deal by her elderly mother. Quite a surprise to everybody when the mother died unexpectedly and Geraldine came into a nice sum of money and went and had her hair cut and permed and went off on a cruise and came back married to a very nice barrister. They had two children."

The parallel was clear enough. Lucy said, rather uneasily: "Do you think you ought to have said what you did about Emma marrying? It seemed to upset the brothers."

Miss Marple nodded.

"Yes," she said. "So like men, quite unable to see what's going on under their eyes. I don't believe you noticed yourself."

"No," admitted Lucy. "I never thought of anything of that kind. They both seemed to me—"

"So old?" said Miss Marple smiling a little. "But Doctor Quimper isn't much over forty, I should say, though he's going gray on the temples, and it's obvious that he's longing for some kind of home life; and Emma Crackenthorpe is under forty, not too old to marry and have a family. The doctor's wife died quite young having a baby, so I have heard."

"I believe she did. Emma said something about it one day."

"He must be lonely," said Miss Marple. "A busy hardworking doctor needs a wife, someone sympathetic, not too young."

"Listen, darling," said Lucy. "Are we investigating crime, or are we matchmaking?"

Miss Marple twinkled.

"I'm afraid I am rather romantic. Because I am an old maid, perhaps. You know, dear Lucy, that as far as I am concerned, you have fulfilled your contract. If you really want a holiday abroad before taking up your next engagement, you would have time still for a short trip."

"And leave Rutherford Hall? Never! I'm the complete sleuth by now. Almost as bad as the boys. They spend their entire time looking for clues. They looked all through the dustbins yesterday. Most unsavory, and they hadn't really the faintest idea what they were looking for. If they come to you in triumph, Inspector Craddock, bearing a torn scrap of paper with *Martine—if you value your life keep away from the Long Barn!* on it, you'll know that I've taken pity on them and concealed it in the pigsty!"

"Why the pigsty, dear?" asked Miss Marple with interest. "Do they keep pigs?"

"Oh no, not nowadays. It's just that I go there sometimes."

For some reason Lucy blushed. Miss Marple looked at her with increased interest.

"Who's at the house now?" asked Craddock.

"Cedric's there, and Bryan's down for the weekend. Harold and Alfred are coming down tomorrow. They rang up this morning. I somehow got the impression that you had been putting the cat among the pigeons, Inspector Craddock."

Craddock smiled.

"I shook them up a little. Asked them to account for their movements on Friday, December the twentieth."

"And could they?"

"Harold could. Alfred couldn't or wouldn't."

"I think alibis must be terribly difficult," said Lucy. "Times and places and dates. They must be hard to check up on, too."

"It takes time and patience, but we manage." He glanced at his watch. "I'll be coming along to Rutherford Hall presently to have a word with Cedric, but I want to get hold of Doctor Quimper first."

"You'll be just about right. He has his surgery at six and he's usually finished about half-past. I must get back and deal with dinner."

"I'd like your opinion on one thing, Miss Eyelesbarrow. What's the family view about this Martine business, among themselves?"

Lucy replied promptly.

"They're all furious with Emma for going to you about it, and with Doctor Quimper who, it seemed, encouraged her to do so. Harold and Alfred think it was a try on and not genuine. Emma isn't sure. Cedric thinks it was phony, too, but he doesn't take it as seriously as the other two. Bryan, on the other hand, seems quite sure that it's genuine."

"Why I wonder?"

"Well, Bryan's rather like that. Just accepts things at their face value. He thinks it was Edmund's wife, or rather widow, and that she had suddenly to go back to France, but that they'll hear from her again sometime. The fact that she hasn't written or anything up to now seems to him to be quite natural because he never writes letters himself. Bryan's rather sweet. Just like a dog that wants to be taken for a walk."

"And do you take him for a walk, dear?" asked Miss Marple. "To the pigsties, perhaps?"

Lucy shot a keen glance at her.

"So many gentlemen in the house, coming and going," mused Miss Marple.

When Miss Marple uttered the word "gentlemen" she always gave it its full Victorian flavor—an echo from an era actually before her own time. You were conscious at once of dashing, full-blooded (and probably whiskered) males, sometimes wicked, but always gallant.

"You're such a handsome girl," pursued Miss Marple appraising Lucy. "I expect they pay you a good deal of attention, don't they?"

Lucy flushed slightly. Scrappy remembrances passed across her mind. Cedric leaning against the pigsty wall. Bryan sitting disconsolately on the kitchen table. Alfred's fingers touching hers as he helped her collect the coffee cups.

"Gentlemen," said Miss Marple, in the tone of one speaking of some alien and dangerous species, "are all very much alike in some ways—even if they are quite old . . ."

"Darling," cried Lucy. "A hundred years ago you would certainly have been burned as a witch!"

And she told her story of old Mr. Crackenthorpe's conditional proposal of marriage.

"In fact," said Lucy, "they've all made what you might call advances to me, in a way. Harold's was very correct; an advantageous financial position in the City. I don't think it's my attractive appearance; they must think that I know something."

She laughed.

But Inspector Craddock did not laugh.

"Be careful," he said. "They might murder you instead of making advances to you."

"I suppose it might be simpler," Lucy agreed.

Then she gave a slight shiver.

"One forgets," she said. "The boys have been having such fun that one almost thought of it all as a game. But it's not a game."

"No," said Miss Marple. "Murder isn't a game."

She was silent for a moment or two before she said:

"Don't the boys go back to school soon?"

"Yes, next week. They go tomorrow to James Stoddart-West's home for the last few days of the holidays."

"I'm glad of that," said Miss Marple gravely. "I shouldn't like anything to happen while they're there."

"You mean to old Mr. Crackenthorpe. Do you think he's going to be murdered next?"

"Oh no!" said Miss Marple. "He'll be all right. I meant to the boys."

"To the boys?"

"Well, to Alexander."

"But surely—"

"Hunting about, you know, looking for clues. Boys love that sort of thing, but it might be very dangerous."

Craddock looked at her thoughtfully.

"You're not prepared to believe, are you, Miss Marple, that it's a case of an unknown woman murdered by an unknown man? You tie it up definitely with Rutherford Hall?"

"I think there's a definite connection, yes."

"All we know about the murderer is that he's a tall, dark man. That's what your friend says and all she can say. There are three tall, dark men at Rutherford Hall. On the day of the inquest, you know, I came out to see the three brothers standing waiting on the pavement for the car to drive up. They had their backs to me and it was astonishing how, in their heavy overcoats, they looked all alike. *Three tall, dark men.* And yet, actually, they're all three quite different types." He sighed. "It makes it very difficult."

"I wonder," murmured Miss Marple. "I have been wondering whether it might perhaps be all much simpler than we suppose. Murders so often are quite simple, with an obvious rather sordid motive . . ."

"Do you believe in the mysterious Martine, Miss Marple?"

"I'm quite ready to believe that Edmund Crackenthorpe either married, or meant to marry, a girl called Martine. Emma Crackenthorpe showed you his letter, I understand, and from what I've seen of her and from what Lucy tells me, I should say Emma Crackenthorpe is quite incapable of making up a thing of that kind. Indeed, why should she?"

"So granted Martine," said Craddock thoughtfully, "there is a motive of a kind. Martine's reappearance with a son would diminish the Crackenthorpe inheritance, though hardly to a point, one would think, to activate murder. They're all very hard up."

"Even Harold?" Lucy demanded incredulously.

"Even the prosperous-looking Harold Crackenthorpe is not the sober and conservative financier he appears to be. He's been plunging heavily and mixing himself up in some rather undesirable ventures. A large sum of money, soon, might avoid a crash."

"But if so—" said Lucy and stopped.

"Yes, Miss Eyelesbarrow—"

"I know, dear," said Miss Marple. "The wrong murder, that's what you mean."

"Yes, Martine's death wouldn't do Harold, or any of the others, any good. Not until—"

"Not until Luther Crackenthorpe died. Exactly. That occurred to me. And Mr. Crackenthorpe, senior, I gather from his doctor, is in much better life than any outsider would imagine."

"He'll last for years," said Lucy. Then she frowned.

"Yes?" Craddock spoke encouragingly.

"He was rather ill at Christmastime," said Lucy. "He said the doctor made a lot of fuss about it. 'Anyone would have thought I'd been poisoned by the fuss he made.' That's what he said."

She looked inquiringly at Craddock.

"Yes," said Craddock. "That's really what I want to ask Doctor Quimper about."

"Well, I must go," said Lucy. "Heavens, it's late."

Miss Marple put down her knitting and picked up the *Times* with a half-done crossword puzzle.

"I wish I had a dictionary here," she murmured. "Tontine and Tokay—I always mix those two words up. One, I believe, is a Hungarian wine."

"That's Tokay," said Lucy looking back from the door. "But one's a five-letter word and one's a seven. What's the clue?"

"Oh, it wasn't in the crossword," said Miss Marple vaguely. "It was in my head."

Inspector Craddock looked at her very hard. Then he said good-bye and went.

CHAPTER SEVENTEEN

I

Craddock had to wait a few minutes while Quimper finished his evening surgery, and then the doctor came to him. He looked tired and depressed.

He offered Craddock a drink and when the latter accepted he mixed one for himself as well.

"Poor devils," he said as he sank down in a worn easy chair. "So scared and so stupid—no sense. Had a painful case this evening. Woman who ought to have come to me a year ago. If she'd come then, she might have been operated on successfully. Now it's too late. Makes me mad. The truth is people are an extraordinary mixture of heroism and cowardice. She's been suffering agony and borne it without a word, just because she was too scared to come and find out that what she feared might be true. At the other end of the scale are the people who come and waste my time because they've got a dangerous swelling causing them agony on their little finger which they think may be cancer and which turns out to be a common or garden chilblain! Well, don't mind me. I've blown off steam now. What did you want to see me about?"

"First, I've got you to thank, I believe, for advising Miss Crackenthorpe to come to me with the letter that purported to be from her brother's widow."

"Oh, that? Anything in it? I didn't exactly advise her to come. She wanted to. She was worried. All the dear little brothers were trying to hold her back, of course."

"Why should they?"

The doctor shrugged his shoulders.

"Afraid the lady might be proved genuine, I suppose."

"Do you think the letter was genuine?"

"No idea. Never actually saw it. I should say it was someone who knew the facts, trying to make a touch. Hoping to work on Emma's feelings. They were dead wrong, there. Emma's no fool. She wouldn't take an unknown sister-in-law to her bosom without asking a few practical questions first."

He added with some curiosity, "But why ask my views? I've got nothing to do with it."

"I really came to ask you something quite different, but I don't quite know how to put it."

Doctor Quimper looked interested.

"I understand that not long ago—at Christmastime I think it was—Mr. Crackenthorpe had rather a bad turn of illness."

He saw a change at once in the doctor's face. It hardened.

"Yes."

"I gather a gastric disturbance of some kind?"

"Yes."

"This is difficult. Mr. Crackenthorpe was boasting of his health, saying he intended to outlive most of his family. He referred to you—you'll excuse me, Doctor—"

"Oh, don't mind me. I'm not sensitive as to what my patients say about me!"

"He spoke of you as an old fuss pot." Quimper smiled. "He said you had asked him all sorts of questions not only as to what he had eaten, but as to who prepared it and served it."

The doctor was not smiling now. His face was hard again.

"Go on."

"He used some such phrase as 'talked as though he believed someone had poisoned me.'"

There was a pause.

"Had you any suspicion of that kind?"

Quimper did not answer at once. He got up and walked up and down. Finally he wheeled round on Craddock.

"What the devil do you expect me to say? Do you think a doctor can go about flinging accusations of poisoning here and there without any real evidence?"

"I'd just like to know, off the record, if that idea did enter your head?"

Doctor Quimper said evasively, "Old Crackenthorpe leads a fairly frugal life. When the family comes down, Emma steps up the food. Result—a nasty attack of gastroenteritis. The symptoms were consistent with that diagnosis."

Craddock persisted.

"I see. You were quite satisfied? You were not at all—shall we say—puzzled?"

"All right. All right. Yes, I was Yours Truly Puzzled! Does that please you?"

"It interests me," said Craddock. "What actually did you suspect, or fear?"

"Gastric cases vary, of course, but there were certain indications that would have been, shall we say, more consistent with arsenical poisoning than with plain gastroenteritis. Mind you, the two things are very much alike. Better men than myself have failed to recognize arsenical poisoning and have given a certificate in all good faith."

"And what was the result of your inquiries?"

"It seemed that what I suspected could not possibly be true. Mr. Crackenthorpe assured me that he had had similar attacks before I attended him, and from the same cause, he said. They had always taken place when there was too much rich food about."

"Which was when the house was full? With the family? Or guests?"

"Yes. That seemed reasonable enough. But frankly, Craddock, I wasn't happy. I went so far as to write to old Doctor Morris. He was my senior partner and retired soon after I joined him. Crackenthorpe was his patient originally. I asked about these earlier attacks that the old man had had."

"And what response did you get?"

Quimper grinned.

"I got a flea in the ear. I was more or less told not to be a damned fool. Well—" he shrugged his shoulders. "Presumably I was a damned fool."

"I wonder." Craddock was thoughtful.

Then he decided to speak frankly.

"Throwing discretion aside, Doctor, there are people who stand to benefit pretty considerably from Luther Crackenthorpe's death." The doctor nodded. "He's an old man and a hale and hearty one. He may live to be ninety-odd?"

"Easily. He spends his life taking care of himself, and his constitution is sound."

"And his sons and daughter are all getting on, and they are all feeling the pinch?"

"You leave Emma out of it. She's no poisoner. These attacks only happen when the others are there, not when she and he are alone."

"An elementary precaution if she's the one," the Inspector thought, but was careful not to say so aloud.

He paused, choosing his words carefully.

"Surely—I'm ignorant in these matters—but supposing just as a hypothesis that arsenic was administered, hasn't Crackenthorpe been very lucky not to succumb?"

"Now there," said the doctor, "you have got something odd. It is exactly that fact that leads me to believe that I have been, as old Morris puts it, a damned fool. You see, it's obviously not a case of small doses of arsenic administered regularly, which is what you might call the classic method of arsenic poisoning. Crackenthorpe has never had any chronic gastric trouble. In a way, that's what makes these sudden violent attacks seem unlikely. So, assuming they are not due to natural causes, it looks as though the poisoner is muffing it every time, which hardly makes sense."

"Giving an inadequate dose, you mean?"

"Yes. On the other hand, Crackenthorpe's got a strong constitution and what might do in another man doesn't do him in. There's always personal idiosyncrasy to be reckoned with. But you'd think that by now, the poisoner—unless he's unusually timid—would have stepped up the dose. Why hasn't he?

"That is," he added, "if there is a poisoner which there probably isn't! Probably all my ruddy imagination from start to finish."

"It's an odd problem," the Inspector agreed. "It doesn't seem to make sense."

II

"Inspector Craddock!"

The eager whisper made the Inspector jump.

He had been just on the point of ringing the front doorbell.

Alexander and his friend Stoddart-West emerged cautiously from the shadows.

"We heard your car and we wanted to get hold of you."

"Well, let's come inside." Craddock's hand went out to the doorbell again, but Alexander pulled at his coat with the eagerness of a pawing dog.

"We've found a clue," he breathed.

"Yes, we've found a clue," Stoddart-West echoed.

"Damn that girl," thought Craddock unamiably.

"Splendid," he said in perfunctory manner. "Let's go inside the house and look at it."

"No." Alexander was insistent. "Someone's sure to interrupt. Come to the harness room. We'll guide you."

Somewhat unwillingly, Craddock allowed himself to be guided round the corner of the house and along to the stable yard. Stoddart-West pushed open a heavy door, stretched up, and turned on a rather feeble electric light. The harness room, once the acme of Victorian spit and polish, was now the sad repository of everything that no one wanted. Broken garden chairs, rusted old garden implements, a vast decrepit mowing machine, rusted spring mattresses, hammocks and disintegrated tennis nets.

"We come here a good deal," said Alexander. "One can really be private here."

There were certain tokens of occupancy about. The decayed mattresses had been piled up to make a kind of divan, there was an old rusted table on which reposed a large tin of chocolate biscuits, there was a hoard of apples, a tin of toffee and a jigsaw puzzle.

"It really is a clue, sir," said Stoddart-West eagerly, his eyes gleaming behind his spectacles. "We found it this afternoon."

"We've been hunting for days. In the bushes—"

"And inside hollow trees."

"And we went through the ashbins."

"There were some jolly interesting things there, as a matter of fact."

"And then we went into the boiler house—"

"Old Hillman keeps a great galvanized tub there full of waste paper."

"For when the boiler goes down and he wants to start it again."

"Any odd paper that's blowing about. He picks it up and shoves it in there."

"And that's where we found it."

"Found *what?*" Craddock interrupted the duet.

"The clue. Careful, Stodders, get your gloves on."

Importantly, Stoddart-West, in the best detective-story tradition, drew on a pair of rather dirty gloves and took from his pocket a Kodak photographic folder. From this he extracted in his gloved fingers with the utmost care a soiled and crumpled envelope which he handed importantly to the Inspector.

Both boys held their breath in excitement.

Craddock took it with due solemnity. He liked the boys and he was ready to enter into the spirit of the thing.

The letter had been through the post; there was no enclosure inside, it was just a torn envelope addressed to Mrs. Martine Crackenthorpe, 126 Elvers Crescent, N. 10.

"You see?" said Alexander breathlessly. "It shows she was here—Uncle Edmund's French wife, I mean—the one there's all the fuss about. She must have actually been here and dropped it somewhere. So it looks, doesn't it?"

Stoddart-West broke in, "It looks as though she was the one who got murdered—I mean, don't you think, sir, that it simply must have been her in the sarcophagus?"

They waited anxiously.

Craddock played up. "Possible, very possible," he said.

"This is important, isn't it?"

"You'll test it for fingerprints, won't you, sir?"

"Of course," said Craddock.

Stoddart-West gave a deep sigh.

"Smashing luck for us, wasn't it?" he said. "On our last day, too."

"Last day?"

"Yes," said Alexander. "I'm going to Stodders' place tomorrow for the last few days of the holidays. Stodders' people have got a smashing house—Queen Anne, isn't it?"

"William and Mary," said Stoddart-West.

"I thought your mother said—"

"Mum's French. She doesn't really know about English architecture."

"But your father said it was built—"

Craddock was examining the envelope.

Clever of Lucy Eyelesbarrow. How had she managed to fake the postmark? He peered closely, but the light was too feeble. Great fun for the boys, of course, but rather awkward for him. Lucy, drat her, hadn't considered that angle. If this were genuine, it would enforce a course of action. There—

Beside him a learned architectural argument was being hotly pursued. He was deaf to it.

"Come on, boys," he said, "we'll go into the house. You've been very helpful."

CHAPTER EIGHTEEN

I

Craddock was escorted by the boys through the back door into the house. This was, it seemed, their common mode of entrance. The kitchen was bright and cheerful. Lucy, in a large, white apron, was rolling out pastry. Leaning against the dresser, watching her with a kind of doglike attention, was Bryan Eastley. With one hand he tugged at his large fair mustache.

"Hello, Dad," said Alexander kindly. "You out here again?"

"I like it out here," said Bryan, and added: "Miss Eyelesbarrow doesn't mind."

"Oh, I don't mind," said Lucy. "Good evening, Inspector Craddock."

"Coming to detect in the kitchen?" asked Bryan with interest.

"Not exactly. Mr. Cedric Crackenthorpe is still here, isn't he?"

"Oh yes, Cedric's here. Do you want him?"

"I'd like a word with him, yes, please."

"I'll go and see if he's in," said Bryan. "He may have gone round to the local pub."

He unpropped himself from the dresser.

"Thank you so much," said Lucy to him. "My hands are all over flour or I'd go."

"What are you making?" asked Stoddart-West anxiously.

"Peach flan."

"Good oh," said Stoddart-West.

"Is it nearly suppertime?" asked Alexander.

"No."

"Gosh! I'm terribly hungry."

"There's the end of the ginger cake in the larder."

The boys made a concerted rush and collided in the door.

"They're just like locusts," said Lucy.

"My congratulations to you," said Craddock.

"What on, exactly?"

"Your ingenuity over this!"

"Over what?"

Craddock indicated the folder containing the letter.

"Very nicely done," he said.

"What are you talking about?"

"This, my dear girl, this." He half drew it out.

She stared at him uncomprehendingly.

Craddock felt suddenly dizzy.

"Didn't you fake this clue and put it in the boiler room for the boys to find? Quick—tell me."

"I haven't the faintest idea what you're talking about," said Lucy. "Do you mean that—"

Craddock slipped the folder quickly back in his pocket as Bryan returned. "Cedric's in the library," he said. "Go on in."

He resumed his place on the dresser. Inspector Craddock went to the library.

II

Cedric Crackenthorpe seemed delighted to see the Inspector.

"Doing a spot more sleuthing down here?" he asked. "Got any farther?"

"I think I can say we are a little farther on, Mr. Crackenthorpe."

"Found out who the corpse was?"

"We've not got a definite identification, but we have a fairly shrewd idea."

"Good for you."

"Arising out of our latest information, we want to get a few statements. I'm starting with you, Mr. Crackenthorpe, as you're on the spot."

"I shan't be much longer. I'm going back to Iviza in a day or two."

"Then I seem to be just in time."

"Go ahead."

"I should like a detailed account, please, of exactly where you were and what you were doing on Friday, December the twentieth."

Cedric shot a quick glance at him. Then he leaned back, yawned, assumed an air of great nonchalance, and appeared to be lost in the effort of remembrance.

"Well, as I've already told you, I was in Iviza. Trouble is, one day there is so like another. Painting in the morning, siesta from three p.m. to five. Perhaps a spot of sketching if the light's suitable. Then an *apéritif*, sometimes with the mayor, sometimes with the doctor, at the café in the plaza. After that some kind of a scratch meal. Most of the evening in Scotty's Bar with some of my lower-class friends. Will that do you?"

"I'd rather have the truth, Mr. Crackenthorpe."

Cedric sat up.

"That's a most offensive remark, Inspector."

"Do you think so? You told me, Mr. Crackenthorpe, that you left Iviza on December the twenty-first and arrived in England that same day?"

"So I did. Em! Hi, Em!"

Emma Crackenthorpe came through the adjoining door from the small morning room. She looked inquiringly from Cedric to the Inspector.

"Look here, Em. I arrived here for Christmas on the Saturday before, didn't I? Came straight from the airport?"

"Yes," said Emma wonderingly. "You got here about lunchtime."

"There you are," said Cedric to the Inspector.

"You must think us very foolish, Mr. Crackenthorpe," said Craddock pleasantly. "We can check on these things, you know. I think, if you'll show me your passport—"

He paused expectantly.

"Can't find the damned thing," said Cedric. "Was looking for it this morning. Wanted to send it to Cook's."

"I think you could find it, Mr. Crackenthorpe. But it's not actually necessary. The records show that you actually entered this country on the evening of December the nineteenth. Perhaps you will now account to me for your movements between that time until lunchtime on December the twenty-first when you arrived here."

Cedric looked very cross indeed.

"That's the hell of life nowadays," he said angrily. "All this red tape and form filling. That's what comes of a bureaucratic state. Can't go where you like and do as you please any more! Somebody's always asking questions. What's all this fuss about the twentieth, anyway? What's special about the twentieth?"

"It happens to be the day we believe the murder was committed. You can refuse to answer, of course, but—"

"Who says I refuse to answer? Give a chap time. And you were vague enough about the date of the murder at the inquest. What's turned up new since then?"

Craddock did not reply .

Cedric said, with a sidelong glance at Emma, "Shall we go into the other room?"

Emma said quickly: "I'll leave you." At the door, she paused and turned.

"This is serious, you know, Cedric. If the twentieth was the day of the murder, then you must tell Inspector Craddock exactly what you were doing."

She went through into the next room and closed the door behind her.

"Good old Em," said Cedric. "Well, here goes! Yes, I left Iviza on the nineteenth all right. Planned to break the journey in Paris and spend a couple of days routing up some old friends on the Left Bank. But as a matter of fact, there was a very attractive woman on the plane. Quite a dish. To put it plainly, she and I got off together. She was on her way to the States, had to spend a couple of nights in London to see about some business or other. We got to London on the nineteenth. We stayed at the Kingsway Palace in case your spies haven't found that out yet! Called myself John Brown— never does to use your own name on these occasions."

"And on the twentieth?"

Cedric made a grimace.

"Morning pretty well occupied by a terrific hangover."

"And the afternoon. From three o'clock onward?"

"Let me see. Well, I mooned about, as you might say. Went into the National Gallery—that's respectable enough. Saw a film. *Rowenna of the Range*. I've always had a passion for Westerns. This was a corker. . . . Then a drink or two in the bar and a bit of a sleep in my room, and out about ten o'clock with the girl friend and a round of various hot spots. Can't even remember most of their names—Jumping Frog was one, I think. She knew 'em all. Got pretty well plastered and, to tell you the truth, don't remember much more till I woke up the next morning with an even worse hangover. Girl friend hopped off to catch her plane and I poured cold water over my head, got a chemist to give me a devil's brew, and then started off for this place, pretending I'd just arrived at Heathrow. No need to upset Emma, I thought. You know what women are, always hurt if you don't come straight home. I had to borrow money from her to pay the taxi. I was completely cleaned out. No use asking the old man. He'd never cough up. Mean old brute. Well, Inspector, satisfied?"

"Can any of this be substantiated, Mr. Crackenthorpe? Say, between three p.m. and seven p.m."

"Most unlikely, I should think," said Cedric cheerfully. "National Gallery where the attendants look at you with lackluster eyes and a crowded picture house. No, not likely."

Emma re-entered. She held a small engagement book in her hand.

"You want to know what everyone was doing on December the twentieth, is that right, Inspector Craddock?"

"Well—er—yes, Miss Crackenthorpe."

"I have just been looking in my engagement book. On the twentieth I went into Brackhampton to attend a meeting of the Church Restoration Fund. That finished about a quarter to one and I lunched with Lady Adington and Miss Bartlett, who was also on the committee, at the Cadena Café. After lunch I did some shopping, stores for Christmas and also Christmas presents. I went to Greenfold's and Lyall and Swift's, Boot's, and probably several other shops. I had tea about a quarter to five in the Shamrock Tea Rooms and then went to the station to meet Bryan who was coming by train. I got home about six o'clock and found my father in a very bad temper. I had left lunch ready for him, but Mrs. Hart who was to come in in the afternoon and give him his tea had not arrived. He was so angry that he had shut himself in his room and would not let me in or speak to me. He does not like my going out in the afternoon, but I make a point of doing so now and then."

"You're probably wise. Thank you, Miss Crackenthorpe."

He could hardly tell her that as she was a woman, height five-foot seven, her movements that afternoon were of no great importance. Instead he said: "Your other two brothers came down later, I understand?"

"Alfred came down late on Saturday evening. He tells me he tried to ring me on the telephone the afternoon I was out, but my father, if he is upset, will never answer the telephone. My brother Harold did not come down until Christmas Eve."

"Thank you, Miss Crackenthorpe."

"I suppose I mustn't ask"—she hesitated—"what has come up new that prompts these inquiries?"

Craddock took the folder from his pocket. Using the tips of his fingers, he extracted the envelope.

"Don't touch it, please, but do you recognize this?"

"But—" Emma stared at him, bewildered. "That's my handwriting. That's the letter I wrote to Martine."

"I thought it might be."

"But how did you get it? Did she—? Have you found her—?"

"It would seem possible that we have—found her. This empty envelope was found here."

"In the house?"

"In the grounds."

"Then, she did come here! She— You mean, it was Martine, there in the sarcophagus?"

"It would seem very likely, Miss Crackenthorpe," said Craddock gently.

It seemed even more likely when he got back to town. A message was awaiting him from Armand Dessin.

"One of the girl friends has had a postcard from Anna Stravinska. Apparently the cruise story was true! She has reached Jamaica and is having, in your phrase, a wonderful time!"

Craddock crumpled up the message and threw it into the wastepaper basket.

III

"I must say," said Alexander, sitting up in bed, thoughtfully consuming a chocolate bar, "that this has been the most smashing day ever. Actually finding a real clue!"

His voice was awed.

"In fact the whole holidays have been smashing," he added happily. "I don't suppose such a thing will ever happen again."

"I hope it won't happen again to me," said Lucy who was on her knees packing Alexander's clothes into a suitcase. "Do you want all this space fiction with you?"

"Not those two top ones. I've read them. The football and my football boots and the gum boots can go separately."

"What difficult things you boys do travel with."

"It won't matter. They're sending the Rolls for us. They've got a smashing Rolls. They've got one of the new Mercedes Benz, too."

"They must be rich."

"Rolling! Jolly nice, too. All the same, I rather wish we weren't leaving here. Another body might turn up."

"I sincerely hope not."

"Well, it often does in books. I mean somebody who's seen something or heard something gets done in, too. It might be you," he added, unrolling a second chocolate bar.

"Thank you!"

"I don't want it to be you," Alexander assured her. "I like you very much and so does Stodders. We think you're out of this world as a cook. Absolutely lovely grub. You're very sensible, too."

This last was clearly an expression of high approval. Lucy took it as such and said: "Thank you. But I don't intend to get killed just to please you."

"Well, you'd better be careful, then," Alexander told her.

He paused to consume more nourishment and then said in a slightly offhand voice,

"If Dad turns up from time to time, you'll look after him, won't you?"

"Yes, of course," said Lucy, a little suprised.

"The trouble with Dad is," Alexander informed her, "that London life doesn't suit him. He gets in, you know, with quite the wrong type of women." He shook his head in a worried manner.

"I'm very fond of him," he added, "but he needs someone to look after him. He drifts about and gets in with the wrong people. It's a great pity Mum died when she did. Bryan needs a proper home life."

He looked solemnly at Lucy and reached out for another chocolate bar.

"Not a fourth one, Alexander," Lucy pleaded. "You'll be sick."

"Oh, I don't think so. I ate six running once and I wasn't. I'm not the bilious type." He paused and then said, "Bryan likes you, you know."

"That's very nice of him."

"He's a bit of an ass in some ways," said Bryan's son, "but he was a jolly good fighter pilot. He's awfully brave. And he's awfully good-natured."

He paused. Then, averting his eyes to the ceiling, he said rather self-consciously:

"I think really, you know, it would be a good thing if he married again. Somebody decent. I shouldn't, myself, mind at all having a stepmother— not, I mean, if she was a decent sort. . . ."

With a sense of shock Lucy realized that there was a definite point in Alexander's conversation.

"All this stepmother bosh," went on Alexander, still addressing the ceiling, "is really quite out of date. Lots of chaps Stodders and I know have stepmothers—divorce and all that—and they get on quite well together. Depends on the stepmother, of course. And, of course, it does make a bit of confusion taking you out and on Sports Day and all that—I mean if there are two sets of parents, though again it helps if you want to cash in!" He paused, confronted with the problems of modern life. "It's nicest to have your own home and your own parents, but if your mother's dead—well, you see what I mean? If she's a decent sort," said Alexander for the third time.

Lucy felt touched.

"I think you're very sensible, Alexander," she said. "We must try and find a nice wife for your father."

"Yes," said Alexander noncommittally.

He added in an offhand manner. "I thought I'd just mention it. Bryan likes you very much. He told me so."

"Really," thought Lucy to herself. "There's too much matchmaking round here. First Miss Marple and now Alexander!"

For some reason or other, pigsties came into her mind. . . .

She stood up.

"Good night, Alexander. There will be only your washing things and pajamas to put in in the morning. Good night."

"Good night," said Alexander. He slid down in bed, laid his head on the pillow, closed his eyes, giving a perfect picture of a sleeping angel, and was immediately asleep.

CHAPTER NINETEEN

I

"Not what you'd call conclusive," said Sergeant Wetherall with his usual gloom.

Craddock was reading through the report on Harold Crackenthorpe's alibi for December 20th.

He had been noticed at Sotheby's about 3:30, but was thought to have left shortly after that. His photograph had not been recognized at Russell's teashop, but as they did a busy trade there at teatime and he was not a habitué, that was hardly surprising. His manservant confirmed that he had returned to Cardigan Gardens to dress for his dinner party at a quarter to seven—rather late, since the dinner was at 7:30, and Mr. Crackenthorpe had been somewhat irritable in consequence. Did not remember hearing him come in that evening, but as it was some time ago could not remember accurately and, in any case, he frequently did not hear Mr. Crackenthorpe come in. He and his wife liked to retire early whenever they could. The garage in the mews where Harold kept his car was a private lockup that he rented and there was no one to notice who came or went or any reason to remember one evening in particular.

"All negative," said Craddock, with a sigh.

"He was at the Caterers' dinner all night, but left rather early before the end of the speeches."

"What about the railway stations?"

But there was nothing there, either at Brackhampton or at Paddington. It was nearly four weeks ago, and it was highly unlikely that anything would have been remembered.

Craddock sighed and stretched out his hand for the data on Cedric. That again was negative, though a taxi driver had made a doubtful recognition of having taken a fare to Paddington that day sometime in the afternoon "what looked something like that bloke. Dirty trousers and a shock of hair. Cussed and swore a bit because fares had gone up since he was last in England." He identified the day because a horse called Crawler had won the 2:30 and he'd had a tidy bit on. Just after dropping the gent, he'd heard it on the radio in his cab and had gone home forthwith to celebrate.

"Thank God for racing," said Craddock, and put the report aside.

"And here's Alfred," said Sergeant Wetherall.

Some nuance in his voice made Craddock look up sharply. Wetherall had the pleased appearance of a man who has kept a tidbit until the end.

In the main the check was unsatisfactory. Alfred lived alone in his flat and came and went at unspecified times. His neighbors were not the inquisitive kind and were in any case office workers who were out all day. But toward the end of the report, Wetherall's large finger indicated the final paragraph.

Sergeant Leakie, assigned to a case of thefts from lorries, had been at the

Load of Bricks, a lorry pullup on the Waddington-Brackhampton Road, keeping certain lorry drivers under observation. He had noticed, at an adjoining table, Chick Evans, one of the Dicky Rogers mob. With him had been Alfred Crackenthorpe whom he knew by sight, having seen him give evidence in the Dicky Rogers case. He'd wondered what they were cooking up together. Time: 9:30 P.M., Friday, December 20th. Alfred Crackenthorpe had boarded a bus a few minutes later, going in the direction of Brackhampton. William Baker, ticket collector at Brackhampton Station, had clipped ticket of gentleman whom he recognized by sight as one of Miss Crackenthorpe's brothers, just before departure of 11:55 train for Paddington. Remembers day as there had been story of some batty old lady who swore she had seen somebody murdered in a train that afternoon.

"Alfred?" said Craddock as he laid the report down. "Alfred? I wonder."

"Puts him right on the spot, there," Wetherall pointed out.

Craddock nodded. Yes, Alfred could have traveled down by the 4:33 to Brackhampton, committing murder on the way. Then he could have gone out by bus to the Load of Bricks. He could have left there at 9:30 and would have had plenty of time to go to Rutherford Hall, move the body from the embankment to the sarcophagus and get into Brackhampton in time to catch the 11:55 back to London. One of the Dicky Rogers gang might even have helped him move the body, though Craddock doubted this. An unpleasant lot, but not killers.

"Alfred?" he repeated speculatively.

II

At Rutherford Hall there had been a gathering of the Crackenthorpe family. Harold and Alfred had come down from London and very soon voices were raised and tempers were running high.

On her own initiative, Lucy mixed cocktails in a jug with ice and took them toward the library. The voices sounded clearly in the hall, and indicated that a good deal of acrimony was being directed toward Emma.

"Entirely your fault, Emma." Harold's deep-bass voice rang out angrily. "How you could be so shortsighted and foolish beats me. If you hadn't taken that letter to Scotland Yard and started all this—"

Alfred's higher-pitched voice said: "You must have been out of your senses!"

"Now don't bully her," said Cedric. "What's done is done. Much more fishy if they'd identified the woman as the missing Martine and we'd all kept mum about having heard from her."

"It's all very well for you, Cedric," said Harold angrily. "You were out of the country on the twentieth which seems to be the day they are inquiring about. But it's very embarrassing for Alfred and myself. Fortunately I can remember where I was that afternoon and what I was doing."

"I bet you can," said Alfred. "If you'd arranged a murder, Harold, you'd arrange your alibi very carefully. I'm sure."

"I gather you are not so fortunate," said Harold coldly.

"That depends," said Alfred. "Anything's better than presenting a cast-iron alibi to the police if it isn't really cast iron. They're so clever at breaking these things down."

"If you are insinuating that I killed the woman—"

"Oh, do stop, all of you," cried Emma. "Of course none of you killed the woman."

"And just for your information, I wasn't out of England on the twentieth," said Cedric. "And the police are wise to it! So we're all under suspicion."

"If it hadn't been for Emma—"

"Oh, don't begin again, Harold," cried Emma.

Doctor Quimper came out of the study where he had been closeted with old Mr. Crackenthorpe. His eye fell on the jug in Lucy's hand.

"What's this? A celebration?"

"More in the nature of oil on troubled waters. They're at it hammer and tongs in there."

"Recriminations?"

"Mostly abusing Emma."

Doctor Quimper's eyebrows rose.

"Indeed?" He took the jug from Lucy's hand, opened the library door and went in.

"Good evening."

"Ah, Doctor Quimper, I should like a word with you." It was Harold's voice, raised and irritable. "I should like to know what you meant by interfering in a private and family matter, and telling my sister to go to Scotland Yard about it."

Doctor Quimper said calmly, "Miss Crackenthorpe asked my advice. I gave it to her. In my opinion she did perfectly right."

"You dare to say—"

"Girl!"

It was old Mr. Crackenthorpe's familiar salutation. He was peering out of the study door just behind Lucy.

Lucy turned rather reluctantly.

"Yes, Mr. Crackenthorpe?"

"What are you giving us for dinner tonight? I want curry. You make a very good curry. It's ages since we've had curry."

"The boys don't care much for curry, you see."

"The boys, the boys—what do the boys matter? I'm the one who matters. And anyhow, the boys have gone—good riddance. I want a nice hot curry, do you hear?"

"All right, Mr. Crackenthorpe, you shall have it."

"That's right. You're a good girl, Lucy. You look after me, and I'll look after you."

Lucy went back to the kitchen. Abandoning the fricassee of chicken which she had planned, she began to assemble the preparations for curry. The front door banged and from the window she saw Doctor Quimper stride angrily from the house to his car and drive away.

Lucy sighed. She missed the boys. And in a way she missed Bryan, too.

Oh well! She sat down and began to peel mushrooms.
At any rate she'd give the family a rattling good dinner.
Feed the brutes!

III

It was 3:00 A.M. when Doctor Quimper drove his car into the garage, closed the doors and came in pulling the front door behind him rather wearily. Well, Mrs. Josh Simpkins had a fine, healthy pair of twins to add to her present family of eight. Mr. Simpkins had expressed no elation over the arrival. "Twins," he had said gloomily. "What's the good of them? Quads now, they're good for something. All sorts of things you get sent, and the press comes round and there's pictures in the paper, and they do say as Her Majesty sends you a telegram. But what's twins except two mouths to feed instead of one? Never been twins in our family, nor in the missus's either. Don't seem fair, somehow."

Doctor Quimper walked upstairs to his bedroom and started throwing off his clothes. He glanced at his watch. Five minutes past three. It had proved an unexpectedly tricky business bringing those twins into the world, but all had gone well. He yawned. He was tired, very tired. He looked appreciatively at his bed.

Then the telephone rang.

Doctor Quimper swore and picked up the receiver.

"Doctor Quimper?"

"Speaking."

"This is Lucy Eyelesbarrow from Rutherford Hall. I think you'd better come over. Everybody seems to have been taken ill."

"Taken ill? How? What symptoms?"

Lucy detailed them.

"I'll be over straightaway. In the meantime—" He gave her short, sharp instructions.

Then he quickly resumed his clothes, flung a few extra things into his emergency bag, and hurried down to his car.

IV

It was some three hours later when the doctor and Lucy, both of them somewhat exhausted, sat down by the kitchen table to drink large cups of black coffee.

"Ha." Doctor Quimper drained his cup, set it down with a clatter on the saucer. "I needed that. Now, Miss Eyelesbarrow, let's get down to brass tacks."

Lucy looked at him. The lines of fatigue showed clearly on his face, making him look older than his forty-four years; the dark hair on his temples was flecked with gray; and there were lines under his eyes.

"As far as I can judge," said the doctor, "they'll be all right now. But how come? That's what I want to know. Who cooked the dinner?"

"I did," said Lucy.

"And what was it? In detail."

"Mushroom soup. Curried chicken and rice. Sillabubs. A savory of chicken livers in bacon."

"*Canapés Diane*," said Doctor Quimper unexpectedly.

Lucy smiled faintly.

"Yes, *Canapés Diane.*"

"All right, let's go through it. Mushroom soup, out of a tin, I suppose?"

"Certainly not. I made it."

"You made it. Out of what?"

"Half a pound of mushrooms, chicken stock, milk, a *roux* of butter and flour, and lemon juice."

"Ah. And one's supposed to say 'It must have been the mushrooms.'"

"It wasn't the mushrooms. I had some of the soup myself and I'm quite all right."

"Yes, you're quite all right. I hadn't forgotten that."

Lucy flushed.

"If you mean—"

"I don't mean. You're a highly intelligent girl. You'd be groaning upstairs, too, if I'd meant what you thought I meant. Anyway, I know all about you. I've taken the trouble to find out."

"Why on earth did you do that?"

Doctor Quimper's lips were set in a grim line.

"Because I'm making it my business to find out about the people who come here and settle themselves in. You're a bona fide young woman who does this particular job for a livelihood, and you seem never to have had any contact with the Crackenthorpe family previous to coming here. So you're not a girl friend of either Cedric, Harold or Alfred, helping them to do a bit of dirty work."

"Do you really think?"

"I think quite a lot of things," said Quimper. "But I have to be careful. That's the worst of being a doctor. Now, let's get on. Curried chicken. Did you have some of that?"

"No. When you've cooked a curry, you've dined off the smell, I find. I tasted it, of course. I had soup and some sillabub."

"How did you serve the sillabub?"

"In individual glasses."

"Now then, how much of all this is cleared up?"

"If you mean washing up, everything was washed up and put away."

Doctor Quimper groaned.

"There's such a thing as being overzealous," he said.

"Yes, I can see that as things have turned out, but there it is, I'm afraid."

"What do you have still?"

"There's some of the curry left in a bowl in the larder. I was planning to use it as a basis for mulligatawny soup this evening. There's some mushroom soup left, too. No sillabub and none of the savory."

"I'll take the curry and the soup. What about chutney? Did they have chutney with it?"

"Yes. In one of those stone jars."

"I'll have some of that, too."

He rose. "I'll go up and have a look at them again. After that, can you hold the fort until morning? Keep an eye on them all? I can have a nurse round, with full instructions, by eight o'clock."

"I wish you'd tell me straight out. Do you think it's food poisoning—or—or, well, poisoning."

"I've told you already. Doctors can't think, they have to be sure. If there's a positive result from these food specimens I can go ahead. Otherwise—"

"Otherwise?" Lucy repeated.

Doctor Quimper laid a hand on her shoulder.

"Look after two people in particular," he said. "Look after Emma. I'm not going to have anything happen to Emma . . ."

There was emotion in his voice that could not be disguised. "She's not even begun to live yet," he said. "And you know, people like Emma Crackenthorpe are the salt of the earth. Emma—well, Emma means a lot to me. I've never told her so but I shall. Look after Emma."

"You bet I will," said Lucy.

"And look after the old man. I can't say that he's ever been my favorite patient but he is my patient and I'm damned if I'm going to let him be hustled out of the world because one or other of his unpleasant sons—or all three of them, maybe—want him out of the way so that they can handle his money."

He threw her a sudden quizzical glance.

"There," he said. "I've opened my mouth too wide. But keep your eyes skinned, there's a good girl and, incidentally, keep your mouth shut."

V

Inspector Bacon was looking upset.

"Arsenic?" he said. "Arsenic?"

"Yes. It was in the curry. Here's the rest of the curry, for your fellow to have a go at. I've only done a very rough test on a little of it, but the result was quite definite."

"So there's a poisoner at work?"

"It would seem so," said Doctor Quimper dryly.

"And they're all affected, you say, except that Miss Eyelesbarrow."

"Except Miss Eyelesbarrow."

"Looks a bit fishy for her."

"What motive could she possibly have?"

"Might be barmy," suggested Bacon. "Seem all right, they do, some-times, and yet all the time they're right off their rocker, so to speak."

"Miss Eyelesbarrow isn't off her rocker. Speaking as a medical man, Miss Eyelesbarrow is as sane as you or I. If Miss Eyelesbarrow is feeding the family arsenic in their curry, she's doing it for a reason. Moreover, being a highly intelligent young woman, she'd be careful not to be the only one unaffected. What she'd do, what any intelligent poisoner would do, would be to eat a very little of the poisoned curry, and then exaggerate the symptoms."

"And then you wouldn't be able to tell?"

"That she'd had less than the others? Probably not. People don't all react alike to poisons anyway; the same amount will upset some people more than others. Of course," added Doctor Quimper cheerfully, "once the patient's dead, you can estimate fairly closely how much was taken."

"Then it might be—" Inspector Bacon paused to consolidate his ideas. "It might be that there's one of the family now who's making more fuss than he need, someone who you might say is mucking in with the rest so as to avoid arousing suspicion? How's that?"

"The idea has already occurred to me. That's why I'm reporting to you. It's in your hands now. I've got a nurse on the job that I can trust, but she can't be everywhere at once. In my opinion, nobody's had enough to cause death."

"Made a mistake, the poisoner did?"

"No. It seems to me more likely that the idea was to put enough in the curry to cause signs of food poisoning, for which probably the mushrooms would be blamed. People are always obsessed with the idea of mushroom poisoning. Then one person would probably take a turn for the worse and die."

"Because he'd been given a second dose?"

The doctor nodded.

"That's why I'm reporting to you at once, and why I've put a special nurse on the job."

"She knows about the arsenic?"

"Of course. She knows and so does Miss Eyelesbarrow. You know your own job best, of course, but if I were you, I'd get out there and make it quite clear to them all that they're suffering from arsenic poisoning. That will probably put the fear of the Lord into our murderer and he won't dare to carry out his plan. He's probably been banking on the food-poisoning theory."

The telephone rang on the Inspector's desk. He picked it up and said:

"O.K. Put her through." He said to Quimper, "It's your nurse on the phone. Yes, hullo—speaking . . . what's that? Serious relapse . . . Yes . . . Doctor Quimper's with me now . . . If you'd like a word with him—"

He handed the receiver to the doctor.

"Quimper speaking . . . I see . . . Yes . . . Quite right . . . Yes, carry on with that. We'll be along."

He put the receiver down and turned to Bacon.

"Who is it?"

"It's Alfred," said Doctor Quimper. "And he's dead."

CHAPTER TWENTY

I

Over the telephone, Craddock's voice came in sharp disbelief.

"Alfred?" he said. "Alfred?"

Inspector Bacon, shifting the telephone receiver a little, said: "You didn't expect that?"

"No, indeed. As a matter of fact, I'd just got him taped for the murderer!"

"I heard about him being spotted by the ticket collector. Looked bad for him all right. Yes, looked as though we'd got our man."

"Well," said Craddock flatly, "we were wrong."

There was a moment's silence. Then Craddock asked:

"There was a nurse in charge. How did she come to slip up?"

"Can't blame her. Miss Eyelesbarrow was all in and went to get a bit of sleep. The nurse had got five patients on her hands: the old man, Emma, Cedric, Harold and Alfred. She couldn't be everywhere at once. It seems old Mr. Crackenthorpe started creating in a big way. Said he was dying. She went in, got him soothed down, came back again and took Alfred in some tea with glucose. He drank it and that was that."

"Arsenic again?"

"Seems so. Of course it could have been a relapse, but Quimper doesn't think so and Johnson agrees."

"I suppose," said Craddock, doubtfully, "that Alfred was meant to be the victim?"

Bacon sounded interested, "You mean that whereas Alfred's death wouldn't do anyone a penn'orth of good, the old man's death would benefit the lot of them? I suppose it might have been a mistake; somebody *might* have thought the tea was intended for the old man."

"Are they sure that that's the way the stuff was administered?"

"No, of course they aren't sure. The nurse, like a good nurse, washed up the whole contraption. Cups, spoons, teapot—everything. But it seems the only feasible method."

"Meaning?" said Craddock thoughtfully, "that one of the patients wasn't as ill as the others. Saw his chance and doped the cup."

"Well, there won't be any more funny business," said Inspector Bacon grimly. "We've got two nurses on the job now, to say nothing of Miss Eyelesbarrow, and I've got a couple of men there, too. You coming down?"

"As fast as I can make it!"

II

Lucy Eyelesbarrow came across the hall to meet Inspector Craddock. She looked pale and drawn.

"You've been having a bad time of it," said Craddock.

"It's been like one long ghastly nightmare," said Lucy. "I really thought last night that they were all dying."

"About this curry—"

"It was the curry?"

"Yes, very nicely laced with arsenic. Quite the Borgia touch."

"If that's true," said Lucy. "It must—it's got to be—one of the family."

"No other possibility?"

"No, you see I only started making that damned curry quite late, after six o'clock, because Mr. Crackenthorpe specially asked for curry. And I had to open a new tin of curry powder, so that couldn't have been tampered with. I suppose curry would disguise the taste?"

"Arsenic hasn't any taste," said Craddock absently. "Now—opportunity. Which of them had the chance to tamper with the curry while it was cooking?"

Lucy considered.

"Actually," she said, "anyone could have sneaked into the kitchen while I was laying the table in the dining room."

"I see. Now who was there in the house? Old Mr. Crackenthorpe, Emma, Cedric—"

"Harold and Alfred. They'd come down from London in the afternoon. Oh, and Bryan, Bryan Eastley. But he left just before dinner. He had to meet a man in Brackhampton."

Craddock said thoughtfully, "It ties up with the old man's illness at Christmas. Quimper suspected that that was arsenic. Did they all seem equally ill last night?"

Lucy considered. "I think old Mr. Crackenthorpe seemed the worst. Doctor Quimper had to work like a maniac on him. He's a jolly good doctor, I will say. Cedric made far the most fuss. Of course, strong, healthy people always do."

"What about Emma?"

"She has been pretty bad."

"Why Alfred I wonder?" said Craddock.

"I know," said Lucy. "I suppose it was meant to be Alfred?"

"Funny, I asked that too!"

"It seems, somehow, so pointless."

"If I could only get at the motive for all this business," said Craddock. "It doesn't seem to tie up. The strangled woman in the sarcophagus was Edmund Crackenthorpe's widow, Martine. Let's assume that. It's pretty well proved by now. There must be a connection between that and the deliberate poisoning of Alfred. It's all here, in the family somewhere. Even saying one of them's mad doesn't help."

"Not really," Lucy agreed.

"Well, look after yourself," said Craddock warningly. "There's a poisoner in this house, remember, and one of your patients upstairs isn't as ill as he pretends to be."

Lucy went upstairs again slowly after Craddock's departure. An imperious voice, somewhat weakened by illness, called to her as she passed old Mr. Crackenthorpe's room.

"Girl, girl, is that you? Come here."

Lucy entered the room. Mr. Crackenthorpe was lying in bed well propped up with pillows. For a sick man he was looking, Lucy thought, remarkably cheerful.

"The house is full of damned hospital nurses," complained Mr. Crackenthorpe. "Rustling about, making themselves important, taking my temperature, not giving me what I want to eat—a pretty penny all that must be costing. Tell Emma to send 'em away. You could look after me quite well."

"Everybody's been taken ill, Mr. Crackenthorpe," said Lucy. "I can't look after everybody, you know."

"Mushrooms," said Mr. Crackenthorpe. "Damned dangerous things, mushrooms. It was that soup we had last night. You made it," he added accusingly.

"The mushrooms were quite all right, Mr. Crackenthorpe."

"I'm not blaming you, girl, I'm not blaming you. It's happened before. One blasted fungus slips in and does it. Nobody can tell. I know you're a good girl. You wouldn't do it on purpose. How's Emma?"

"Feeling rather better this afternoon."

"Ah. And Harold?"

"He's better too."

"What's this about Alfred having kicked the bucket?"

"Nobody's supposed to have told you that, Mr. Crackenthorpe."

Mr. Crackenthorpe laughed, a high, whinnying laugh of intense amusement. "I hear things," he said. "Can't keep things from the old man. They try to. So Alfred's dead, is he? He won't sponge on me any more, and he won't get any of the money either. They've all been waiting for me to die, you know; Alfred in particular. Now he's dead. I call that rather a good joke."

"That's not very kind of you, Mr. Crackenthorpe," said Lucy severely.

Mr. Crackenthorpe laughed again. "I'll outlive them all," he crowed. "You see if I don't, my girl. You see if I don't."

Lucy went to her room, took out her dictionary and looked up the word *tontine*. She closed the book thoughtfully and stared ahead of her.

III

"Don't see why you want to come to me," said Doctor Morris, irritably.

"You've known the Crackenthorpe family a long time," said Inspector Craddock.

"Yes, yes, I knew all the Crackenthorpes. I remember old Josiah Crackenthorpe. He was a hard nut—shrewd man, though. Made a lot of money." He shifted his aged form in his chair and peered under bushy eyebrows at Inspector Craddock. "So you've been listening to that young fool, Quimper," he said. "These zealous young doctors! Always getting ideas in their heads. Got it into his head that somebody was trying to poison Luther Crackenthorpe. Nonsense! Melodrama! Of course, he had gastric attacks. I treated him for them. Didn't happen very often, nothing peculiar about them."

"Doctor Quimper," said Craddock, "seemed to think there was."

"Doesn't do for a doctor to go thinking. After all, I should hope I could recognize arsenical poisoning when I saw it."

"Quite a lot of well-known doctors haven't noticed it," Craddock pointed out. "There was"—he drew upon his memory—"the Greenbarrow case, Mrs. Reney, Charles Leeds, three people in the Westbury family, all buried nicely and tidily without the doctors who attended them having the least suspicion. Those doctors were all good, reputable men."

"All right, all right," said Doctor Morris, "you're saying that I could have made a mistake. Well, I don't think I did." He paused a minute and then said, "Who did Quimper think was doing it, if it was being done?"

"He didn't know," said Craddock. "He was worried. After all, you know," he added, "there's a great deal of money there."

"Yes, yes, I know, which they'll get when Luther Crackenthorpe dies. And they want it pretty badly. That is true enough, but it doesn't follow that they'd kill the old man to get it."

"Not necessarily," agreed Inspector Craddock.

"Anyway," said Doctor Morris, "my principle is not to go about suspecting things without due cause. Due cause," he repeated. "I'll admit that what you've just told me has shaken me up a bit. Arsenic on a big scale, apparently, but I still don't see why you come to me. All I can tell you is that I didn't suspect it. Maybe I should have. Maybe I should have taken those gastric attacks of Luther Crackenthorpe's much more seriously. But you've got a long way beyond that now."

Craddock agreed. "What I really need," he said, "is to know a little more about the Crackenthorpe family. Is there any queer mental strain in them, a kink of any kind?"

The eyes under the bushy eyebrows looked at him sharply. "Yes, I can see your thoughts might run that way. Well, old Josiah was sane enough. Hard as nails, very much all there. His wife was neurotic, had a tendency to melancholia. Came of an inbred family. She died soon after Luther was born. I'd say, you know, that Luther inherited a certain—well—instability from her. He was commonplace enough as a young man, but he was always at loggerheads with his father. His father was disappointed in him and I think he resented that and brooded on it, and in the end got a kind of obsession about it. He carried that on into his own married life. You'll notice, if you talk to him at all, that he's got a hearty dislike for all his own sons. His daughters he was fond of. Both Emma and Edie, the one who died."

"Why does he dislike the sons so much?" asked Craddock.

"You'll have to go to one of these new-fashioned psychiatrists to find that out. I'd just say that Luther has never felt very adequate as a man himself, and that he bitterly resents his financial position. He has possession of an income but no power of appointment of capital. If he had the power to disinherit his sons he probably wouldn't dislike them as much. Being powerless in that respect gives him a feeling of humiliation."

"That's why he's so pleased at the idea of outliving them all?" said Inspector Craddock.

"Possibly. It is the root, too, of his parsimony, I think. I should say that he's managed to save a considerable sum out of his large income, mostly, of course, before taxation rose to its present giddy heights."

A new idea struck Inspector Craddock. "I suppose he's left his savings by will to someone? That he can do."

"Oh, yes, though God knows who he has left it to. Maybe to Emma, but I should rather doubt it. She'll get her share of the old man's money. Maybe to Alexander, the grandson."

"He's fond of him, is he?" said Craddock.

"Used to be. Of course he was his daughter's child, not a son's child. That may have made a difference. And he had quite an affection for Bryan Eastley, Edie's husband. Of course I don't know Bryan well; it's some years since I've seen any of the family. But it struck me that he was going to be very much at a loose end after the war. He's got those qualities that you need in wartime: courage, dash and a tendency to let the future take care of itself. But I don't think he's got any stability. He'll probably turn into a drifter."

"As far as you know there's no peculiar kink in any of the younger generation?"

"Cedric's an eccentric type, one of those natural rebels. I wouldn't say he was perfectly normal, but you might say, who is? Harold's fairly orthodox, not what I call a very pleasant character, coldhearted, eye to the main chance. Alfred's got a touch of the delinquent about him. He's a wrong 'un, always was. Saw him taking money out of a missionary box once that they used to keep in the hall. That type of thing. Ah well, the poor fellow's dead, I suppose I shouldn't be talking about him."

"What about—" Craddock hesitated. "Emma Crackenthorpe?"

"Nice girl, quiet, one doesn't always know what she's thinking. Has her own plans and her own ideas but she keeps them to herself. She's more character than you might think from her general manner and appearance."

"You knew Edmund, I suppose, the son who was killed in France?"

"Yes. He was the best of the bunch, I'd say. Goodhearted, gay, a nice boy."

"Did you ever hear that he was going to marry or had married a French girl just before he was killed?"

Doctor Morris frowned. "It seems as though I remember something about it," he said, "but it's a long time ago."

"Quite early on in the war, wasn't it?"

"Yes. Ah well, I daresay he'd have lived to regret it if he had married a foreign wife."

"There's some reason to believe that he did do just that," said Craddock.

In a few brief sentences he gave an account of recent happenings.

"I remember seeing something in the papers about a woman found in a sarcophagus. So it was at Rutherford Hall."

"And there's reason to believe that the woman was Edmund Crackenthorpe's widow."

"Well, well, that seems extraordinary. More like a novel than real life. But who'd want to kill the poor thing—I mean, how does it tie up with arsenical poisoning in the Crackenthorpe family?"

"In one of two ways," said Craddock, "but they are both very farfetched. Somebody perhaps is greedy and wants the whole of Josiah Crackenthorpe's fortune."

"Damn fool if he does," said Doctor Morris. "He'll only have to pay the most stupendous taxes on the income from it."

CHAPTER TWENTY-ONE

"Nasty things, mushrooms," said Mrs. Kidder.

Mrs. Kidder had made the same remark about ten times in the last few days. Lucy did not reply.

"Never touch' em myself," said Mrs. Kidder, "much too dangerous. It's a merciful Providence as there's only been one death. The whole lot might have gone and you too, Miss. A wonderful escape you've had."

"It wasn't the mushrooms," said Lucy. "They were perfectly all right."

"Don't you believe it," said Mrs. Kidder. "Dangerous they are, mushrooms. One toadstool in among the lot and you've had it.

"Funny," went on Mrs. Kidder, among the rattle of plates and dishes in the sink, "how things seem to come all together, as it were. My sister's eldest had measles and our Ernie fell down and broke 'is arm, and my 'usband came out all over with boils. All in the same week! You'd hardly believe it, would you. It's been the same thing here," went on Mrs. Kidder. "First that nasty murder and now Mr. Alfred dead with mushroom poisoning. Who'll be the next, I'd like to know?"

Lucy felt rather uncomfortably that she would like to know, too.

"My husband, he doesn't like me coming here now," said Mrs. Kidder, "thinks it's unlucky, but what I say is I've known Miss Crackenthorpe a long time now and she's a nice lady and she depends on me. And I couldn't leave poor Miss Eyelesbarrow, I said, not to do everything herself in the house. Pretty hard it is on you, Miss, all these trays."

Lucy was forced to agree that life did seem to consist very largely of trays at the moment. She was at the moment arranging trays to take to the various invalids.

"As for them nurses, they never do a hand's turn," said Mrs. Kidder. "All they want is pots and pots of tea made strong. And meals prepared. Wore out, that's what I am." She spoke in a tone of great satisfaction, though actually she had done very little more than her normal morning's work.

Lucy said solemnly, "You never spare yourself, Mrs. Kidder."

Mrs. Kidder looked pleased. Lucy picked up the first of the trays and started off up the stairs.

"What's this?" said Mr. Crackenthorpe disapprovingly.

"Beef tea and baked custard," said Lucy.

"Take it away," said Mr. Crackenthorpe. "I won't touch that sort of stuff. I told that nurse I wanted a beefsteak."

"Doctor Quimper thinks you ought not to have beefsteak just yet," said Lucy.

Mr. Crackenthorpe snorted. "I'm practically well again. I'm getting up tomorrow. How are the others?"

"Mr. Harold's much better," said Lucy. "He's going back to London tomorrow."

"Good riddance," said Mr. Crackenthorpe. "What about Cedric? Any hope that he's going back to his island tomorrow?"

"He won't be going just yet."

"Pity. What's Emma doing? Why doesn't she come to see me?"

"She's still in bed, Mr. Crackenthorpe."

"Women always coddle themselves," said Mr. Crackenthorpe, "but you're a good, strong girl," he added approvingly. "Run about all day, don't you?"

"I get plenty of exercise," said Lucy.

Old Mr. Crackenthorpe nodded his head approvingly. "You're a good strong girl," he said, "and don't think I've forgotten what I talked to you about before. One of these days you'll see what you'll see. Emma isn't always going to have things her own way. And don't listen to the others when they tell you I'm a mean old man. I'm careful of my money. I've got a nice little packet put by and I know who I'm going to spend it on when the time comes." He leered at her affectionately.

Lucy went rather quickly out of the room, avoiding his clutching hand.

The next tray was taken in to Emma.

"Oh, thank you, Lucy. I'm really feeling quite myself again by now. I'm hungry, and that's a good sign, isn't it? My dear," went on Emma as Lucy settled the tray on her knees, "I'm really feeling very upset about your aunt. You haven't had any time to go and see her, I suppose?"

"No, I haven't, as a matter of fact."

"I'm afraid she must be missing you."

"Oh, don't worry, Miss Crackenthorpe. She understands what a terrible time we've been through."

"Have you rung her up?"

"No, I haven't just lately."

"Well, do. Ring her up every day. It makes such a difference to old people to get news."

"You're very kind," said Lucy. Her conscience smote her a little as she went down to fetch the next tray. The complications of illness in the house had kept her thoroughly absorbed and she had had no time to think of anything else. She decided that she would ring Miss Marple up as soon as she had taken Cedric his meal.

There was only one nurse in the house now and she passed Lucy on the landing, exchanging greetings.

Cedric, looking incredibly tidied up and neat, was sitting up in bed writing busily on sheets of paper.

"Hullo, Lucy," he said, "what hell brew have you got for me today? I wish you'd get rid of that god-awful nurse, she's simply too arch for words. Calls me 'we' for some reason. 'And how are we this morning? Have we slept well? Oh dear, we're very naughty, throwing off the bedclothes like that.'" He imitated the refined accents of the nurse in a high falsetto voice.

"You seem very cheerful," said Lucy. "What are you busy with?"

"Plans," said Cedric. "Plans for what to do with this place when the old man pops off. It's a jolly good bit of land here, you know. I can't make up my mind whether I'd like to develop some of it myself, or whether I'll sell it in lots all in one go. Very valuable for industrial purposes. The house will do for a nursing home or a school. I'm not sure I shan't sell half the land and use the money to do something rather outrageous with the other half. What do you think?"

"You haven't got it yet," said Lucy, dryly.

"I shall have it, though," said Cedric. "It's not divided up like the other stuff. I get it outright. And if I sell it for a good fat price the money will be capital, not income, so I shan't have to pay taxes on it. Money to burn. Think of it."

"I always understood you rather despised money," said Lucy.

"Of course I despise money when I haven't got any," said Cedric. "It's the only dignified thing to do. What a lovely girl you are, Lucy, or do I just think so because I haven't seen any good-looking women for a long time?"

"I expect that's it," said Lucy.

"Still busy tidying everyone and everything up?"

"Somebody seems to have been tidying you up," said Lucy, looking at him.

"That's that damned nurse," said Cedric with feeling. "Have they had the inquest on Alfred yet? What happened?"

"It was adjourned," said Lucy.

"Police being cagey. This mass poisoning does give one a bit of a turn, doesn't it? Mentally, I mean. I'm not referring to more obvious aspects," he added. "Better look after yourself, my girl."

"I do," said Lucy.

"Has young Alexander gone back to school yet?"

"I think he's still with the Stoddart-Wests. I think it's the day after tomorrow that school begins."

Before getting her own lunch Lucy went to the telephone and rang up Miss Marple.

"I'm so terribly sorry I haven't been able to come over, but I've really been very busy."

"Of course, my dear, of course. Besides there's nothing that can be done just now. We just have to wait."

"Yes, but what are we waiting for?"

"Elspeth McGillicuddy ought to be home very soon now," said Miss Marple. "I wrote to her to fly home at once. I said it was her duty. So don't worry too much, my dear." Her voice was kindly and reassuring.

"You don't think—" Lucy began, but stopped.

"That there will be any more deaths? Oh, I hope not, my dear. But one never knows, does one? When anyone is really wicked, I mean. And I think there is great wickedness here."

"Or madness," said Lucy.

"Of course I know that is the modern way of looking at things. I don't agree myself."

Lucy rang off, went into the kitchen and picked up her tray of lunch. Mrs. Kidder had divested herself of her apron and was about to leave.

"You'll be all right, Miss, I hope?" she asked solicitously.

"Of course I shall be all right," snapped Lucy.

She took her tray not into the big, gloomy dining room but into the small study. She was just finishing the meal when the door opened and Bryan Eastley came in.

"Hello," said Lucy, "this is very unexpected."

"I suppose it is," said Bryan. "How is everybody?"

"Oh, much better. Harold's going back to London tomorrow."

"What do you think about it all? Was it really arsenic?"

"It was arsenic all right," said Lucy.

"It hasn't been in the papers yet."

"No, I think the police are keeping it up their sleeves for the moment."

"Somebody must have a pretty good down on the family," said Bryan. "Who's likely to have sneaked in and tampered with the food?"

"I suppose I'm the most likely person, really," said Lucy.

Bryan looked at her anxiously. "But you didn't, did you?" he asked. He sounded slightly shocked.

"No. I didn't," said Lucy.

Nobody could have tampered with the curry. She had made it alone in the kitchen and brought it to table, and the only person who could have tampered with it was one of the five people who sat down to the meal.

"I mean, why should you?" said Bryan. "They're nothing to you, are they? I say," he added, "I hope you don't mind my coming back here like this?"

"No, no, of course I don't. Have you come to stay?"

"Well, I'd like to, if it wouldn't be an awful bore to you."

"No. No, we can manage."

"You see, I'm out of a job at the moment and I—well, I get rather fed up. Are you really sure you don't mind?"

"Oh, I'm not the person to mind, anyway. It's Emma."

"Oh, Emma's all right," said Bryan. "Emma's always been very nice to me. In her own way, you know. She keeps things to herself a lot, in fact she's rather a dark horse, old Emma. This living here and looking after the old man would get most people down. Pity she never married. Too late now, I suppose."

"I don't think it's too late at all," said Lucy.

"Well—" Bryan considered. "A clergyman perhaps," he said hopefully. "She'd be useful in the parish and tactful with the Mothers' Union. I do mean the Mothers' Union, don't I? Not that I know what it really is, but you come across it sometimes in books. And she'd wear a hat in church on Sundays," he added.

"Doesn't sound much of a prospect to me," said Lucy, rising and picking up the tray.

"I'll do that," said Bryan, taking the tray from her. They went into the kitchen together. "Shall I help you wash up? I do like this kitchen," he added. "In fact, I know it isn't the sort of thing that people do like nowadays, but I like this whole house. Shocking taste, I suppose, but there it is. You could land a plane quite easily in the park," he added with enthusiasm.

He picked up a glass cloth and began to wipe the spoons and forks.

"Seems a waste, it coming to Cedric," he remarked. "First thing he'll do is to sell the whole thing and go beaking off abroad again. Can't see, myself, why England isn't good enough for anybody. Harold wouldn't want this house either, and of course it's much too big for Emma. Now if only it came to Alexander, he and I would be as happy together here as a couple of sandboys. Of course it would be nice to have a woman about the house." He looked thoughtfully at Lucy. "Oh, well, what's the good of talking? If Alexander were to get this place it would mean a whole lot of them would have to die first, and that's not really likely, is it? Though from what I've seen of the old boy he might easily live to be a hundred, just to annoy them all. I don't suppose he was much cut up by Alfred's death, was he?"

Lucy said shortly, "No, he wasn't."

"Cantankerous old devil," said Bryan Eastley cheerfully.

CHAPTER TWENTY-TWO

"Dreadful, the things people go about saying," said Mrs. Kidder. "I don't listen, mind you, more than I can help. But you'd hardly believe it." She waited hopefully.

"Yes, I suppose so," said Lucy.

"About that body that was found in the Long Barn," went on Mrs. Kidder, moving crablike backward on her hands and knees, as she scrubbed the kitchen floor, "saying as how she'd been Mr. Edmund's fancy piece during the war, and how she come over here and a jealous husband followed her and did her in. It is a likely thing as a foreigner would do, but it wouldn't be likely after all these years, would it?"

"It sounds most unlikely to me."

"But there's worse things than that, they say," said Mrs. Kidder. "Say anything, people will. You'd be surprised. There's those that say Mr. Harold married somewhere abroad and that she come over and found out he'd committed bigamy with that Lady Alice, and that she was going to bring 'im to court and that he met her down here and did her in and hid her body in the sarcoffus. Did you ever!"

"Shocking," said Lucy vaguely, her mind elsewhere.

"Of course I don't listen," said Mrs. Kidder virtuously, "I wouldn't put no stock in such tales myself. It beats me how people think up such things, let alone say them. All I hope is none of it gets to Miss Emma's ears. It might upset her and I shouldn't like that. She's a very nice lady, Miss Emma is, and I've not heard a word against her, not a word. And of course Mr. Alfred being dead nobody says anything against him now. Not even that it's a judgment, which they well might do. But it's awful, Miss, isn't it, the wicked talk there is."

Mrs. Kidder spoke with immense enjoyment.

"It must be quite painful for you to listen to it," said Lucy.

"Oh, it is," said Mrs. Kidder. "It is, indeed. I says to my husband, I says, 'However can they?'"

The bell rang.

"There's the doctor, Miss. Will you let 'im in, or shall I?"

"I'll go," said Lucy.

But it was not the doctor. On the doorstep stood a tall, elegant woman in a mink coat. Drawn up to the gravel sweep was a purring Rolls with a chauffeur at the wheel.

"Can I see Miss Emma Crackenthorpe, please?"

It was an attractive voice, the R' slightly blurred. The woman was attractive, too. About thirty-five, with dark hair and expensively and beautifully made up.

"I'm sorry," said Lucy, "Miss Crackenthorpe is ill in bed and can't see anyone."

"I know she has been ill, yes, but it is very important that I should see her."

"I'm afraid," Lucy began.

The visitor interrupted her. "I think you are Miss Eyelesbarrow, are you not?" She smiled, an attractive smile. "My son has spoken of you, so I know. I am Lady Stoddart-West and Alexander is staying with me now."

"Oh, I see," said Lucy.

"And it is really important that I should see Miss Crackenthorpe," continued the other. "I know all about her illness and I assure you this is not just a social call. It is because of something that the boys have said to me—that my son has said to me. It is, I think, a matter of grave importance and I would like to speak to Miss Crackenthorpe about it. Please, will you ask her?"

"Come in." Lucy ushered her visitor into the hall and into the drawing room. Then she said, "I'll go up and ask Miss Crackenthorpe."

She went upstairs, knocked on Emma's door and entered.

"Lady Stoddart-West is here," she said. "She wants to see you very particularly."

"Lady Stoddart-West?" Emma looked surprised. A look of alarm came into her face. "There's nothing wrong, is there, with the boys—with Alexander?"

"No, no," Lucy reassured her. "I'm sure the boys are all right. It seems to be something the boys have told her or said to her."

"Oh. Well—" Emma hesitated. "Perhaps I ought to see her. Do I look all right, Lucy?"

"You look very nice," said Lucy.

Emma was sitting up in bed, a soft, pink shawl was round her shoulders and brought out the faint rose-pink of her cheeks. Her dark hair had been neatly brushed and combed by the nurse. Lucy had placed a bowl of autumn leaves on the dressing table the day before. Her room looked attractive and quite unlike a sickroom.

"I'm really quite well enough to get up," said Emma. "Doctor Quimper said I could tomorrow."

"You look really quite yourself again," said Lucy. "Shall I bring Lady Stoddart-West up?"

"Yes, do."

Lucy went downstairs again. "Will you come up to Miss Crackenthorpe's room?"

She escorted the visitor upstairs, opened the door for her to pass in and then shut it. Lady Stoddart-West approached the bed with outstretched hand.

"Miss Crackenthorpe? I really do apologize for breaking in on you like this. I have seen you, I think, at the sports at the school."

"Yes," said Emma, "I remember you quite well. Do sit down."

In the chair conveniently placed by the bed, Lady Stoddart-West sat down. She said in a quiet low voice:

"You must think it very strange of me coming here like this, but I have a reason. I think it is an important reason. You see, the boys have been telling me things. You can understand that they were very excited about the murder that happened here. I confess I did not like it at the time. I was nervous. I wanted to bring James home at once. But my husband laughed. He said that obviously it was a murder that had nothing to do with the house and the family and he said that from what he remembered from his boyhood, and from James's letters, both he and Alexander were enjoying themselves so wildly that it would be sheer cruelty to bring them back. So I gave in and agreed that they should stay on until the time arranged for James to bring Alexander back with him."

Emma said: "You think we ought to have sent your son home earlier?"

"No, no, that is not what I mean at all. Oh, it is difficult for me, this! But what I have to say must be said. You see, they have picked up a good deal, the boys. They told me that this woman—the murdered woman—that the police have an idea that she may be a French girl whom your eldest brother, who was killed in the war, knew in France. That is so?"

"It is a possibility," said Emma, her voice breaking slightly, "that we are forced to consider. It may have been so."

"There is some reason for believing that the body is that of this girl, this Martine?"

"I have told you, it is a possibility."

"But why—why should they think that she was this Martine? Did she have letters on her—papers?"

"No. Nothing of that kind. But you see I had had a letter from this Martine."

"You had had a letter from *Martine?*"

"Yes. A letter telling me she was in England and would like to come and see me. I invited her down here, but got a telegram saying she was going back to France. Perhaps she did go back to France. We do not know. But since then an envelope was found here addressed to her. That seems to show that she had come down here. But I really don't see—" She broke off.

Lady Stoddart-West broke in quickly.

"You really do not see what concern it is of mine? That is very true. I should not, in your place. But when I heard this, or rather, a garbled account of this, I had to come to make sure it was really so, because, if it is—"

"Yes?" said Emma.

"Then I must tell you something that I had never intended to tell you. You see, *I am Martine*."

Emma stared at her guest as though she could hardly take in the sense of her words.

"You!" she said. "You are Martine?"

The other nodded vigorously. "But yes. It surprises you, I am sure, but it is true. I met your brother Edmund on the first days of the war. He was indeed billeted at our house. Well, you know the rest. We fell in love. We intended to be married, and then there was the retreat to Dunkirk, Edmund was reported missing. Later he was reported killed. I will not speak to you of that time. It was long ago and it is over. But I will say to you that I loved your brother very much.

"Then came the grim realities of war. The Germans occupied France. I became a worker for the Resistance. I was one of those who was assigned to pass Englishmen through France to England. It was in that way that I met my present husband. He was an Air Force officer, parachuted into France to do special work. When the war ended we were married. I considered once or twice whether I should write to you or come and see you but I decided against it. It could do no good, I thought, to rake up old memories. I had a new life and I had no wish to recall the old." She paused and then said, "But it gave me, I will tell you, a strange pleasure when I found that my son James's greatest friend at his school was a boy whom I found to be Edmund's nephew. Alexander, I may say, is very like Edmund, as I daresay you yourself appreciate. It seemed to me a very happy state of affairs that James and Alexander should be such friends."

She leaned forward and placed her hand on Emma's arm. "But you see, dear Emma, do you not, that when I heard this story about the murder, about this dead woman being suspected to be the Martine that Edmund had known, that I had to come and tell you the truth. Either you or I must inform the police of the fact. Whoever the dead woman is, she is not Martine."

"I can hardly take it in," said Emma, "that you, you should be the Martine that dear Edmund wrote to me about." She sighed, shaking her head, then she frowned perplexedly. "But I don't understand. Was it you, then, who wrote to me?"

Lady Stoddart-West shook a vigorous head. "No, no, of course I did not write to you."

"Then—" Emma stopped.

"Then there was someone pretending to be Martine who wanted perhaps to get money out of you? That is what it must have been. But who can it be?"

Emma said slowly: "I suppose there were people at the time who knew?"

The other shrugged her shoulders. "Probably, yes. But there was no one intimate with me, no one very close to me. I have never spoken of it since I came to England. And why wait all this time? It is curious, very curious."

Emma said, "I don't understand it. We will have to see what Inspector Craddock has to say." She looked with suddenly softened eyes at her visitor. "I'm so glad to know you at last, my dear."

"And I you. Edmund spoke of you very often. He was very fond of you. I am happy in my new life, but all the same, I do not quite forget."

Emma leaned back and heaved a deep sigh. "It's a terrible relief," she said. "As long as we feared that the dead woman might be Martine, it seemed to be tied up with the family. But now, oh, it's an absolute load off my back. I don't know who the poor soul was but she can't have had anything to do with us!"

CHAPTER TWENTY-THREE

The streamlined secretary brought Harold Crackenthorpe his usual afternoon cup of tea.

"Thanks, Miss Ellis, I shall be going home early today."

"I'm sure you ought really not to have come at all, Mr. Crackenthorpe," said Miss Ellis. "You look quite pulled down still."

"I'm all right," said Harold Crackenthorpe, but he did feel pulled down. No doubt about it, he'd had a very nasty turn. Ah well, that was over.

Extraordinary, he thought broodingly, that Alfred should have succumbed and the old man should have come through. After all, what was he?—seventy-three, seventy-four? Been an invalid for years. If there was one person you'd have thought would have been taken off, it would have been the old man. But no. It had to be Alfred. Alfred who, as far as Harold knew, was a healthy, wiry sort of chap. Nothing much the matter with him.

He leaned back in his chair sighing. That girl was right. He didn't feel up to things yet, but he had wanted to come down to the office. Wanted to get the hang of how affairs were going. Touch and go, that's what it was! Touch and go. All this—he looked round him—the richly appointed office, the pale gleaming wood, the expensive modern chairs, it all looked prosperous enough, and a good thing, too! That's where Alfred had always gone wrong. If you looked prosperous, people thought you were prosperous. There were no rumors going round as yet about his financial stability. All the same, the crash couldn't be delayed very long. Now if only his father had passed out instead of Alfred, as surely, surely he ought to have done. Practically seemed to thrive on arsenic! Yes, if his father had succumbed: well, there wouldn't have been anything to worry about.

Still, the great thing was not to seem worried. A prosperous appearance. Not like poor old Alfred who always looked seedy and shiftless, who looked in fact exactly what he was. One of those small-time speculators, never going all out boldly for the big money. In with a shady crowd here, doing a doubtful deal there, never quite rendering himself liable to prosecution but going very near the edge. And where had it got him? Short periods of affluence and then back to seediness and shabbiness once more. No broad outlook about Alfred. Taken all in all, you couldn't say Alfred was much loss. He'd never been particularly fond of Alfred and with Alfred out of the way the money that was coming to him from that old curmudgeon, his grandfather, would be sensibly increased, divided not into five shares but into four shares. Very much better.

Harold's face brightened a little. He rose, took his hat and coat and left the office. Better take it easy for a day or two. He wasn't feeling too strong yet. His car was waiting below and very soon he was weaving through the London traffic to his house.

Darwin, his manservant, opened the door.

"Her Ladyship has just arrived, sir," he said.

For a moment Harold stared at him. Alice! Good Heavens, was it today that Alice was coming home? He'd forgotten all about it. Good thing Darwin had warned him. It wouldn't have looked so good if he'd gone upstairs and looked too astonished at seeing her. Not that it really mattered, he supposed. Neither Alice nor he had many illusions about the feeling they had for each other. Perhaps Alice was fond of him; he didn't know.

All in all Alice was a great disappointment to him. He hadn't been in love with her, of course, but though a plain woman she was quite a pleasant one. And her family and connections had undoubtedly been useful. Not perhaps as useful as they might have been, because in marrying Alice he had been considering the position of hypothetical children. Nice relations for his boys to have. But there hadn't been any boys, or girls either, and all that had remained had been him and Alice growing older together without much to say to each other and with no particular pleasure in each other's company.

She stayed away a good deal with relations and usually went to the Riviera in the winter. It suited her and it didn't worry him.

He went upstairs now into the drawing room and greeted her punctiliously.

"So you're back, my dear. Sorry I couldn't meet you, but I was held up in the City. I got back as early as I could. How was San Raphael?"

Alice told him how San Raphael was. She was a thin woman with sandy-colored hair, a well-arched nose and vague, hazel eyes. She talked in a well-bred, monotonous and rather depressing voice. It had been a good journey back, the Channel a little rough. The customs, as usual, very trying at Dover.

"You should come by air," said Harold, as he always did. "So much simpler."

"I daresay, but I don't really like air travel. I never have. Makes me nervous."

"Saves a lot of time," said Harold.

Lady Alice Crackenthorpe did not answer. It was possible that her problem in life was not to save time but to occupy it. She inquired politely after her husband's health.

"Emma's telegram quite alarmed me," she said. "You were all taken ill, I understand."

"Yes, yes," said Harold.

"I read in the paper the other day," said Alice, "of forty people in a hotel going down with food poisoning at the same time. All this refrigeration is dangerous, I think. People keep things too long in them."

"Possibly," said Harold. Should he, or should he not mention arsenic? Somehow, looking at Alice, he felt himself quite unable to do so. In Alice's world, he felt, there was no place for poisoning by arsenic. It was a thing you read about in the papers. It didn't happen to you or your own family. But it had happened in the Crackenthorpe family. . . .

He went up to his room and lay down for an hour or two before dressing for dinner. At dinner, tête-à-tête with his wife, the conversation ran on much the same lines. Desultory, polite. The mention of acquaintances and friends at San Raphael.

"There's a parcel for you on the hall table, a small one," Alice said.

"Is there? I didn't notice it."

"It's an extraordinary thing but somebody was telling me about a murdered woman having been found in a barn or something like that. She said it was at Rutherford Hall. I suppose it must be some other Rutherford Hall."

"No," said Harold, "no, it isn't. It was in our barn, as a matter of fact."

"Really, Harold! A murdered woman in the barn at Rutherford Hall, and you never told me anything about it."

"Well, there hasn't been much time, really," said Harold, "and it was all rather unpleasant. Nothing to do with us, of course. The press milled round a good deal. Of course we had to deal with the police and all that sort of thing."

"Very unpleasant," said Alice. "Did they find out who did it?" she added, with rather perfunctory interest.

"Not yet," said Harold.

"What sort of a woman was she?"

"Nobody knows. French apparently."

"Oh, French," said Alice, and allowing for the difference in class, her tone was not unlike that of Inspector Bacon. "Very annoying for you all," she agreed.

They went out from the dining room and crossed into the small study where they usually sat when they were alone. Harold was feeling quite exhausted by now. I'll go up to be early, he thought.

He picked up the small parcel from the hall table, about which his wife had spoken to him. It was a small, neatly waxed parcel, done up with meticulous exactness. Harold ripped it open as he came to sit down in his usual chair by the fire.

Inside was a small tablet box bearing the label, *"Two to be taken nightly."* With it was a small piece of paper with the chemist's heading in Brackhampton. *"Sent by request of Doctor Quimper"* was written on it.

Harold Crackenthorpe frowned. He opened the box and looked at the tablets. Yes, they seemed to be the same tablets he had been having. But surely, surely Quimper had said that he needn't take any more? "You won't want them now." That's what Quimper had said.

"What is it, dear?" said Alice. "You look worried."

"Oh, it's just some tablets. I've been taking them at night. But I rather thought the doctor said don't take any more."

His wife said placidly, "He probably said don't forget to take them."

"He may have done, I suppose," said Harold doubtfully.

He looked across at her. She was watching him. Just for a moment or two he wondered—he didn't often wonder about Alice—exactly what she was thinking. That mild gaze of hers told him nothing. Her eyes were like windows in an empty house. What did Alice think about him, feel about him? Had she been in love with him once? He supposed she had. Or did she marry him because she thought he was doing well in the City and she was tired of her own impecunious existence? Well, on the whole, she'd done quite well out of it. She'd got a car and a house in London, she could travel abroad when she felt like it and get herself expensive clothes, though goodness knows they never looked like anything on Alice. Yes, on the whole, she'd done pretty well. He wondered if she thought so. She wasn't really fond of him, of course, but then he wasn't really fond of her. They had nothing in common, nothing to talk about, no memories to share. If there had been children, but there hadn't been any children. Odd that there were no children in the family except young Edie's boy. Young Edie. She'd been a silly girl, making that foolish, hasty wartime marriage. Well, he'd given her good advice.

He'd said, "It's all very well, these dashing young pilots, glamor, courage, all that, but he'll be no good in peacetime, you know. Probably be barely able to support you."

And Edie had said, what did it matter? She loved Bryan and Bryan loved her, and he'd probably be killed quite soon. Why shouldn't they have some happiness? What was the good of looking to the future when they might all be bombed any minute. And after all, Edie had said, the future doesn't really matter because someday there'll be all grandfather's money.

Harold squirmed uneasily in his chair. Really, that will of his grandfather's had been iniquitous! Keeping them all dangling on a string. The will hadn't pleased anybody. It didn't please the grandchildren and it made their father quite livid. The old boy was absolutely determined not to die. That's what made him take so much care of himself. But he'd have to die soon. Surely, surely, he'd have to die soon. Otherwise— All Harold's worries swept over him once more, making him feel sick and tired and giddy.

Alice was still watching him, he noticed. Those pale, thoughtful eyes, they made him uneasy somehow.

"I think I shall go to bed," he said. "It's been my first day out in the City."

"Yes," said Alice, "I think that's a good idea. I'm sure the doctor told you to take things easily at first."

"Doctors always tell you that," said Harold.

"And don't forget to take your tablets, dear," said Alice. She picked up the box and handed it to him.

He said good night and went upstairs. Yes, he needed the tablets. It would have been a mistake to leave them off too soon. He took two of them and swallowed them with a glass of water.

CHAPTER TWENTY-FOUR

"Nobody could have made more of a muck of it than I seem to have done,"
said Dermot Craddock gloomily.

He sat, his long legs stretched out, looking somehow incongruous in
faithful Florence's somewhat overfurnished parlor. He was thoroughly tired,
upset and dispirited.

Miss Marple made soft, soothing noises of dissent. "No, no, you've done
very good work, my dear boy. Very good work, indeed."

"I've done very good work, have I? I've let a whole family be poisoned,
Alfred Crackenthorpe's dead and now Harold's dead, too. What the hell's
going on there? That's what I should like to know."

"Poisoned tablets," said Miss Marple thoughtfully.

"Yes, Devilishly cunning, really. They looked just like the tablets that
he'd been having. There was a printed slip sent in with them *'by Doctor
Quimper's instructions.'* Well, Quimper never ordered them. There were
chemist's labels used. The chemist knew nothing about it, either. No. That
box of tablets came from Rutherford Hall."

"Do you actually know it came from Rutherford Hall?"

"Yes. We've had a thorough checkup. Actually it's the box that held the
sedative tablets prescribed for Emma."

"Oh, I see. For Emma . . ."

"Yes. It's got her fingerprints on it and the fingerprints of both the nurses
and the fingerprints of the chemist who made it up. Nobody else's,
naturally. The person who sent them was careful."

"And the sedative tablets were removed and something else substituted?"

"Yes. That of course is the devil with tablets. One tablet looks exactly like
another."

"You are so right," agreed Miss Marple. "I remember so very well in my
young days, the black mixture and the brown mixture—the cough mixture
that was—and the white mixture, and Doctor So-and-So's pink mixture.
People didn't mix those up nearly as much. In fact, you know, in my village
in St. Mary Mead we still like that kind of medicine. It's a bottle they
always want, not tablets. What were the tablets?" she asked.

"Aconite. They were the kind of tablets that are usually kept in a poison
bottle, diluted one in a hundred for outside application."

"And so Harold took them and died," Miss Marple said thoughtfully.
Dermot Craddock uttered something like a groan.

"You mustn't mind my letting off steam to you," he said. "Tell it all to
Aunt Jane; that's how I feel!"

"That's very, very nice of you," said Miss Marple, "and I do appreciate
it. As Sir Henry's godson I feel toward you quite differently from the way I
should feel to any ordinary detective inspector."

Dermot Craddock gave her a fleeting grin. "But the fact remains that I've
made the most ghastly mess of things all along the line," he said. "The
Chief Constable down here calls in Scotland Yard, and what do they get?
They get me making a prize ass of myself!"

"No, no," said Miss Marple.

"Yes, yes. I don't know who poisoned Alfred, I don't know who poisoned Harold, and to cap it all I haven't the least idea now who the original murdered woman was! This Martine business seemed a perfectly safe bet. The whole thing seemed to tie up. And now what happens? The real Martine shows up and turns out, most improbably, to be the wife of Sir Robert Stoddart-West. So who's the woman in the barn now? Goodness knows. First I go all out on the idea she's Anna Stravinska, and then she's out of it."

He was arrested by Miss Marple giving one of her small, peculiarly significant coughs.

"But is she?" she murmured.

Craddock stared at her. "Well, that postcard from Jamaica."

"Yes," said Miss Marple, "but that isn't really evidence, is it? I mean, anyone can get a postcard sent from almost anywhere, I suppose. I remember Mrs. Brierly, such a very bad nervous breakdown. Finally they said she ought to go to the mental hospital for observation, and she was so worried about the children knowing about it and so she wrote about fourteen postcards and arranged that they should be posted from different places abroad, and told them that Mummie was going abroad on a holiday." She added, looking at Dermot Craddock, "You see what I mean."

"Yes, of course," said Craddock, staring at her. "Naturally we'd have checked that postcard if it hadn't been for the Martine business fitting the bill so well."

"So convenient," murmured Miss Marple.

"It tied up," said Craddock. "After all there's the letter Emma received signed Martine Crackenthorpe. Lady Stoddart-West didn't send that, but somebody did. Somebody who was going to pretend to be Martine, and who was going to cash in, if possible, on being Martine. You can't deny that."

"No, no."

"And then, the envelope of the letter Emma wrote to her with the London address on it. Found at Rutherford Hall, showing she'd actually been there."

"But the murdered woman hadn't been there!" Miss Marple pointed out. "Not in the sense you mean. She only came to Rutherford Hall after she was dead. Pushed out of a train on to the railway embankment."

"Oh—yes."

"What the envelope really proves is that the murderer was there. Presumably he took that envelope off her with her other papers and things, and then dropped it by mistake—or—I wonder now, was it a mistake? Surely Inspector Bacon, and your men too, made a thorough search of the place, didn't they, and didn't find it. It only turned up later in the boiler house."

"That's understandable," said Craddock. "The old gardener chap used to spear up any odd stuff that was blowing about and shove it in there."

"Where it was very convenient for the boys to find," said Miss Marple thoughtfully.

"You think we were meant to find it?"

"Well, I just wonder. After all it would be fairly easy to know where the boys were going to look next, or even to suggest to them . . . Yes, I do wonder. It stopped you thinking about Anna Stravinska any more, didn't it?"

Craddock said, "And you think it really may be her all the time?"

"I think someone may have got alarmed when you started making inquiries about her, that's all. I think somebody didn't want those inquiries made."

"Let's hold on the basic fact that someone was going to impersonate Martine," said Craddock. "And then for some reason didn't. Why?"

"That's a very interesting question," said Miss Marple.

"Somebody sent a wire saying Martine was going back to France, then arranged to travel down with the girl and kill her on the way. You agree so far?"

"Not exactly," said Miss Marple. "I don't think, really, you're making it simple enough."

"Simple!" exclaimed Craddock. "You're mixing me up," he complained.

Miss Marple said in a distressed voice that she wouldn't think of doing anything like that.

"Come, tell me," said Craddock, "do you or do you not think you know who the murdered woman was?"

Miss Marple sighed. "It's so difficult," she said, "to put it the right way. I mean, I don't know *who* she was, but at the same time I'm fairly sure who she *was*, if you know what I mean."

Craddock threw up his head. "Know what you mean? I haven't the faintest idea." He looked out through the window. "There's your Lucy Eyelesbarrow coming to see you," he said. "Well, I'll be off. My *amour propre* is very low this afternoon and having a young woman coming in, radiant with efficiency and success, is more than I can bear."

CHAPTER TWENTY-FIVE

"I looked up tontine in the dictionary," said Lucy.

The first greetings were over and now Lucy was wandering rather aimlessly round the room, touching a china dog here, an antimacassar there, the plastic work box in the window.

"I thought you probably would," said Miss Marple equably.

Lucy spoke slowly, quoting the words. "Lorenzo Tonti, Italian banker, originator, 1653, of a form of annuity in which the shares of subscribers who die are added to the profit shares of the survivors." She paused. "That's it, isn't it? That fits well enough, and you were thinking of it even then before the last two deaths."

She took up once more her restless, almost aimless prowl round the room. Miss Marple sat watching her. This was a very different Lucy Eyelesbarrow from the one she knew.

"I suppose it was asking for it really," said Lucy. "A will of that kind, ending so that if there was only one survivor left he'd get the lot. And yet, there was quite a lot of money, wasn't there? You'd think it would be enough shared out—" She paused, the words tailing off.

"The trouble is," said Miss Marple, "that people are greedy. Some people. That's so often, you know, how things start. You don't start with murder, with wanting to do murder or even thinking of it. You just start by being greedy, by wanting more than you're going to have." She laid her knitting down on her knee and stared ahead of her into space. "That's how I came across Inspector Craddock first, you know. A case in the country. Near Medenham Spa. That began the same way, just a weak amiable character who wanted a great deal of money. Money that that person wasn't entitled to, but there seemed an easy way to get it. Not murder then. Just something so easy and simple that it hardly seemed wrong. That's how things begin. But it ended with three murders."

"Just like this," said Lucy. "We've had three murders now. The woman who impersonated Martine and who would have been able to claim a share for her son, and then Alfred, and then Harold. And now it only leaves two, doesn't it?"

"You mean," said Miss Marple, "there are only Cedric and Emma left?"

"Not Emma. Emma isn't a tall, dark man. No. I mean Cedric and Bryan Eastley. I never thought of Bryan because he's fair. He's got a great, fair mustache and blue eyes, but you—the other day—" She paused.

"Yes, go on," said Miss Marple. "Tell me. Something has upset you very badly, hasn't it?"

"It was when Lady Stoddart-West was going away. She had said good-bye and then suddenly turned to me just as she was getting into the car and asked: 'Who was that tall, dark man who was standing on the terrace as I came in?'

"I couldn't imagine who she meant at first, because Cedric was still laid up. So I said, rather puzzled, 'You don't mean Bryan Eastley?' and she said, 'Of course, that's who it was, Squadron Leader Eastley. He was hidden in our loft once in France during the Resistance. I remember the way he stood, and the set of his shoulders,' and she said, 'I should like to meet him again,' but we couldn't find him."

Miss Marple said nothing, just waited.

"And then," said Lucy, "later I looked at him . . . He was standing with his back to me and I saw what I ought to have seen before. That even when a man's fair, his hair looks dark because he plasters it down with stuff. Bryan's hair is a sort of medium brown, I suppose, but it can look dark. So, you see, it might have been Bryan that your friend saw in the train. It might. . . ."

"Yes," said Miss Marple. "I had thought of that."

"I suppose you think of everything!" said Lucy bitterly.

"Well, dear, one has to really."

"But I can't see what Bryan would get out of it. I mean, the money would come to Alexander, not to him. I suppose it would make an easier life, they could have a bit more luxury, but he wouldn't be able to tap the capital for his schemes, or anything like that."

"But if anything happened to Alexander before he was twenty-one, then Bryan would get the money as his father and next of kin," Miss Marple pointed out.

Lucy cast a look of horror at her.

"He'd never do that. No father would ever do that just—just to get the money."

Miss Marple sighed. "People do, my dear. It's very sad and very terrible, but they do.

"People do very terrible things," Miss Marple continued. "I know a woman who poisoned three of her children just for a little bit of insurance money. And then there was an old woman, quite a nice old woman apparently, who poisoned her son when he came home on leave. Then there was that old Mrs. Stanwich. That case was in the paper. I dare say you read about it. Her daughter died and her son, and then she said she was poisoned herself. There was poison in some gruel, but it came out, you know, that she'd put it there herself. She was just planning to poison the last daughter. That wasn't exactly for money. She was jealous of them for being younger than she was and alive, and she was afraid—it's a terrible thing to say but it's true—they would enjoy themselves after she was gone. She'd always kept a very tight hold on the purse strings. Yes, of course she was a little peculiar, as they say, but I never see myself that that's any real excuse. I mean you can be a little peculiar in so many different ways. Sometimes you just go about giving all your possessions away and writing checks on bank accounts that don't exist, just so as to benefit people. It shows, you see, that behind being peculiar you have quite a nice disposition. But of course if you're peculiar and behind it you have a bad disposition, well, there you are. Now, does that help you at all, my dear Lucy?"

"Does what help me?" asked Lucy bewildered.

"What I've been telling you," said Miss Marple. She added gently, "You mustn't worry, you know. You really mustn't worry. Elspeth McGillicuddy will be here any day now."

"I don't see what that has to do with it."

"No, dear, perhaps not. But I think it's important myself."

"I can't help worrying," said Lucy. "You see I've got interested in the family."

"I know, dear, it's very difficult for you because you are quite strongly attracted to both of them, aren't you, in very different ways."

"What do you mean?" said Lucy. Her tone was sharp.

"I was talking about the two sons of the house," said Miss Marple. "Or rather the son and the son-in-law. It's fortunate that the two more unpleasant members of the family died and the two more attractive ones are left. I can see that Cedric Crackenthorpe is very attractive. He is inclined to make himself out worse than he is and has a provocative way with him."

"He makes me fighting mad sometimes," said Lucy.

"Yes," said Miss Marple, "and you enjoy that, don't you? You're a girl with a lot of spirit and you enjoy a battle. Yes, I can see where that attraction lies. And then Mr. Eastley is a rather plaintive type, rather like an unhappy little boy. That of course is attractive, too."

"And one of them's a murderer," said Lucy bitterly, "and it may be either of them. There's nothing to choose between them really. There's Cedric, not caring a bit about his brother Alfred's death or about Harold's. He just sits back looking thoroughly pleased making plans for what he'll do with Rutherford Hall, and he keeps saying that it'll need a lot of money to develop it in the way he wants to do. Of course I know he's the sort of person who exaggerates his own callousness and all that. But that could be a cover, too. I mean everyone says that you're more callous than you really are. But you mightn't be. You might be even more callous than you seem!"

"Dear, dear Lucy, I'm so worried about all this."

"And then Bryan," went on Lucy. "It's extraordinary, but Bryan really seems to want to live there. He thinks he and Alexander would find it awfully jolly and he's full of schemes."

"He's always full of schemes of one kind or another, isn't he?"

"Yes, I think he is. They all sound rather wonderful, but I've got an uneasy feeling that they'd never really work. I mean, they're not practical. The idea sounds all right, but I don't think he ever considers the actual working difficulties."

"They are up in the air, so to speak?"

"Yes, in more ways than one. I mean they are usually literally up in the air. They are all air schemes. Perhaps a really good fighter pilot never does quite come down to earth again. . . ."

She added: "And he likes Rutherford Hall so much because it reminds him of the big rambling Victorian house he lived in when he was a child."

"I see," said Miss Marple thoughtfully. "Yes, I see."

Then, with a quick sideways glance at Lucy, she said with a kind of verbal pounce, "But that isn't all of it, is it, dear? There's something else."

"Oh yes, there's something else. Just something that I didn't realize until just a couple of days ago. Bryan was actually on that train."

"On the 4:33 from Paddington?"

"Yes. You see Emma thought she was required to account for her movements on December the twentieth and she went over it all very carefully—a committee meeting in the morning and then shopping in the afternoon and tea at the Green Shamrock, and then, she said, she went to meet Bryan at the station. I worked out when she'd had tea and the time, and the train she met must have been the 4:33. So I asked Bryan, quite casually, and he said, Yes, it was, and added that his car had had a bump and was being repaired and so he had to come down by train—an awful bore, he said, he hates trains. He seemed quite natural about it all. It may be quite all right, but I wish, somehow, he hadn't been on that train. . . ."

"Actually on the train," said Miss Marple thoughtfully.

"It doesn't really prove anything. The awful thing is all this suspicion. Not to know. And perhaps we never shall know!"

"Of course we shall know, dear," said Miss Marple briskly. "I mean, all this isn't going to stop just at this point. The one thing I do know about murderers is that they can never let well alone. Or perhaps one should say, ill alone. At any rate," said Miss Marple with finality, "they can't once they've done a second murder. Now don't get too upset, Lucy. The police are doing all they can, and looking after everybody, and the great thing is that Elspeth McGillicuddy will be here very soon now!"

CHAPTER TWENTY-SIX

I

"Now, Elspeth, you're quite clear as to what I want you to do?"

"I'm clear enough," said Mrs. McGillicuddy, "but what I say to you is, Jane, that it seems very odd."

"It's not odd at all," said Miss Marple.

"Well, I think so. To arrive at the house and to ask almost immediately whether I can—er—go upstairs."

"It's very cold weather," Miss Marple pointed out, "and after all, you might have eaten something that disagreed with you and—er—have to ask to go upstairs. I mean, these things happen. I remember poor Louisa Felby came to see me once and she had to ask to go upstairs five times during one little half hour. That," added Miss Marple parenthetically, "was a bad Cornish pasty."

"If you'd just tell me what you're driving at, Jane," said Mrs. McGillicuddy.

"That's just what I don't want to do," said Miss Marple.

"How irritating you are, Jane. First you make me come all the way back to England before I need—"

"I'm sorry about that," said Miss Marple, "but I couldn't do anything else. Someone, you see, may be killed at any moment. Oh, I know they're all on their guard and the police are taking all the precautions they can, but there's always the outside chance that the murderer might be too clever for them. So you see, Elspeth, it was your duty to come back. After all, you and I were brought up to do our duty, weren't we?"

"We certainly were," said Mrs. McGillicuddy, "no laxness in our young days."

"So that's quite all right," said Miss Marple. "And that's the taxi now," she added, as a faint hoot was heard outside the house.

Mrs. McGillicuddy donned her heavy pepper-and-salt coat and Miss Marple wrapped herself up with a good many shawls and scarves. Then the two ladies got into the taxi and were driven to Rutherford Hall.

II

"Who can this be driving up?" Emma asked, looking out of the window, as the taxi swept past it. "I do believe it's Lucy's old aunt."

"What a bore," said Cedric.

He was lying back in a long chair looking at *Country Life* with his feet reposing on the side of the mantelpiece.

"Tell her you're not at home."

"When you say tell her I'm not at home, do you mean that I should go out and say so? Or that I should tell Lucy to tell her aunt so?"

"Hadn't thought of that," said Cedric. "I suppose I was thinking of our butler-and-footman days, if we ever had them. I seem to remember a footman before the war. He had an affair with the kitchen maid and there was a terrific rumpus about it. Isn't there one of those old hags about the place cleaning?"

But at that moment the door was opened by Mrs. Hart, whose afternoon it was for cleaning the brasses, and Miss Marple came in, very fluttery, in a whirl of shawls and scarves, with a tall, uncompromising figure behind her.

"I do hope," said Miss Marple, taking Emma's hand, "that we are not intruding. But you see, I'm going home the day after tomorrow, and I couldn't bear not to come over and see you and say good-bye and thank you again for your goodness to Lucy. Oh, I forgot. May I introduce my friend, Mrs. McGillicuddy, who is staying with me?"

"How d'you do," said Mrs. McGillicuddy, looking at Emma with complete attention and then shifting her gaze to Cedric, who had now risen to his feet. Lucy entered the room at this moment.

"Aunt Jane, I had no idea . . ."

"I had to come and say good-bye to Miss Crackenthorpe," said Miss Marple, turning to her, "who has been so very, very kind to you, Lucy."

"It's Lucy who's been very kind to us," said Emma.

"Yes, indeed," said Cedric. "We've worked her like a galley slave. Waiting on the sickroom, running up and down the stairs, cooking little invalid messes . . ."

Miss Marple broke in. "I was so very, very sorry to hear of your illness. I do hope you're quite recovered now, Miss Crackenthorpe?"

"Oh, we're quite well again now," said Emma.

"Lucy told me you were all very ill. So dangerous, isn't it, food poisoning? Mushrooms, I understand."

"The cause remains rather mysterious," said Emma.

"Don't you believe it," said Cedric. "I bet you've heard the rumors that are flying round, Miss—er—"

"Marple," said Miss Marple.

"Well, as I say, I bet you've heard the rumors that are flying round. Nothing like arsenic for raising a little flutter in the neighborhood."

"Cedric," said Emma, "I wish you wouldn't. You know Inspector Craddock said . . ."

"Bah," said Cedric, "everybody knows. Even you've heard something, haven't you?" He turned to Miss Marple and Mrs. McGillicuddy.

"I myself," said Mrs. McGillicuddy, "have only just returned from abroad. The day before yesterday," she added.

"Ah, well, you're not up in our local scandal then," said Cedric. "Arsenic in the curry, that's what it was. Lucy's aunt knows all about it, I bet."

"Well," said Miss Marple, "I did just hear—I mean, it was just a hint, but of course I didn't want to embarrass you in any way, Miss Crackenthorpe."

"You must pay no attention to my brother," said Emma. "He just likes making people uncomfortable." She gave him an affectionate smile as she spoke.

The door opened and Mr. Crackenthorpe came in, tapping angrily with his stick.

"Where's tea?" he said. "Why isn't tea ready? You! Girl!" he addressed Lucy, "why haven't you brought tea in?"

"It's just ready, Mr. Crackenthorpe. I'm bringing it in now. I was just getting the table ready."

Lucy went out of the room again and Mr. Crackenthorpe was introduced to Miss Marple and Mrs. McGillicuddy.

"Like my meals on time," said Mr. Crackenthorpe. "Punctuality and economy. Those are my watchwords."

"Very necessary, I'm sure," said Miss Marple, "especially in these times with taxation and everything."

Mr. Crackenthorpe snorted. "Taxation! Don't talk to me of those robbers. A miserable pauper, that's what I am. And it's going to get worse, not better. You wait, my boy," he addressed Cedric, "when you get this place ten to one the Socialists will have it off you and turn it into a Welfare Center or something. And take all your income to keep it up with!"

Lucy reappeared with a tea tray, Bryan Eastley following her carrying a tray of sandwiches, bread and butter and cake.

"What's this? What's this?" Mr. Crackenthorpe inspected the tray. "Frosted cake? We having a party today? Nobody told me about it."

A faint flush came into Emma's face.

"Doctor Quimper's coming to tea, Father. It's his birthday today and—"

"Birthday?" snorted the old man, "what's he doing with a birthday? Birthdays are only for children. I never count my birthdays and I won't let anyone else celebrate them either."

"Much cheaper," agreed Cedric. "You save the price of candles on your cake."

"That's enough from you, boy," said Mr. Crackenthorpe.

Miss Marple was shaking hands with Bryan Eastley. "I've heard about you, of course," she said, "from Lucy. Dear me, you remind me so much of someone I used to know at St. Mary Mead. That's the village where I've lived for so many years, you know. Ronnie Wells, the solicitor's son. Couldn't seem to settle somehow when he went into his father's business. He went out to East Africa and started a series of cargo boats on the lakes out there. Victoria Nyanza, or is it Albert I mean? Anyway, I'm sorry to say that it wasn't a success, and he lost all his capital. Most unfortunate! Not any relation of yours, I suppose? The likeness is so great."

"No," said Bryan, "I don't think I've any relations called Wells."

"He was engaged to a very nice girl," said Miss Marple. "Very sensible. She tried to dissuade him, but he wouldn't listen to her. He was wrong of course. Women have a lot of sense, you know, when it comes to money matters. Not high finance, of course. No woman can hope to understand that, my dear father said. But everyday matters. . . . What a delightful view you have from this window," she added, making her way across and looking out.

Emma joined her.

"Such an expanse of parkland! How picturesque the cattle look against the trees. One would never dream that one was in the middle of a town."

"We're rather an anachronism, I think," said Emma. "If the windows were open now you'd hear far off the noise of the traffic."

"Oh, of course," said Miss Marple, "there's noise everywhere, isn't there? Even in St. Mary Mead. We're now quite close to an airfield, you know, and really the way those jet planes fly over. Most frightening. Two panes in my little greenhouse broken the other day. Going through the sound barrier, or so I understand, though what it means I never have known."

"It's quite simple, really," said Bryan, approaching amiably. "You see, it's like this."

Miss Marple dropped her handbag and Bryan politely picked it up. At the same moment Mrs. McGillicuddy approached Emma and murmured, in an anguished voice, and the anguish was quite genuine, since Mr. McGillicuddy deeply disliked the task which she was now performing:

"I wonder, could I go upstairs for a moment?"

"Of course," said Emma.

"I'll take you," said Lucy.

Lucy and Mrs. McGillicuddy left the room together.

"Very cold driving today," said Miss Marple in a vaguely explanatory manner.

"About the sound barrier," said Bryan, "you see, it's like this—Oh, hello, there's Quimper."

The doctor drove up in his car. He came in rubbing his hands and looking very cold.

"Going to snow," he said, "that's my guess. Hello, Emma, how are you? Good lord, what's all this?"

"We made you a birthday cake," said Emma. "D'you remember? You told me today was your birthday."

"I didn't expect all this," said Quimper. "You know it's years—why, it must be, yes, sixteen years—since anyone's remembered my birthday." He looked almost uncomfortably touched.

"Do you know Miss Marple?" Emma introduced him.

"Oh yes," said Miss Marple, "I met Doctor Quimper here before and he came and saw me when I had a very nasty chill the other day and he was most kind."

"All right again now, I hope?" said the doctor.

Miss Marple assured him that she was quite all right now.

"You haven't been to see me lately, Quimper," said Mr. Crackenthorpe. "I might be dying for all the notice you take of me!"

"I don't see you dying yet awhile," said Doctor Quimper.

"I don't mean to," said Mr. Crackenthorpe. "Come on, let's have tea. What're we waiting for?"

"Oh, please," said Miss Marple, "don't wait for my friend. She would be most upset if you did."

They sat down and started tea. Miss Marple accepted a piece of bread and butter first, and then went on to a sandwich.

"Are they—?" She hesitated.

"Fish," said Bryan. "I helped make 'em."

Mr. Crackenthorpe gave a cackle of laughter.

"Poisoned fishpaste," he said. "That's what they are. Eat 'em at your peril."

"Please, Father!"

"You've got to be careful what you eat in this house," said Mr. Crackenthorpe to Miss Marple. "Two of my sons have been murdered like flies. Who's doing it—that's what I want to know."

"Don't let him put you off," said Cedric, handing the plate once more to Miss Marple. "A touch of arsenic improves the complexion, they say, so long as you don't have too much."

"Eat one yourself, boy," said old Mr. Crackenthorpe.

"Want me to be official taster?" said Cedric. "Here goes."

He took a sandwich and put it whole into his mouth. Miss Marple gave a gentle, ladylike little laugh and took a sandwich. She took a bite and said:

"I do think it's so brave of you all to make these jokes. Yes, really, I think it's very brave indeed. I do admire bravery so much."

She gave a sudden gasp and began to choke. "A fish bone," she gasped out, "in my throat."

Quimper rose quickly. He went across to her, moved her backwards toward the window and told her to open her mouth. He pulled out a case from his pocket, selecting some forceps from it. With quick professional skill he peered down the old lady's throat. At that moment the door opened and Mrs. McGillicuddy, followed by Lucy, came in. Mrs. McGillicuddy gave a sudden gasp as her eyes fell on the tableau in front of her: Miss Marple leaning back and the doctor holding her throat and tilting up her head.

"But that's him," cried Mrs. McGillicuddy. "That's the man in the train. . . ."

With incredible swiftness Miss Marple slipped from the doctor's grasp and came toward her friend.

"I thought you'd recognize him, Elspeth!" she said. "No. Don't say another word." She turned triumphantly round to Doctor Quimper. "You didn't know, did you, Doctor, when you strangled that woman in the train, that somebody actually saw you do it? It was my friend here. Mrs. McGillicuddy. She saw you. Do you understand? *Saw you with her own eyes.* She was in another train that was running parallel with yours."

"What the hell—" Doctor Quimper made a quick step toward Mrs. McGillicuddy but again, swiftly, Miss Marple was between him and her.

"Yes," said Miss Marple. "She saw you, and she recognizes you, and she'll swear to it in court. It's not often, I believe," went on Miss Marple in her gentle plaintive voice, "that anyone actually sees a murder committed. It's usually circumstantial evidence of course. But in this case the conditions were very unusual. There was actually an eye witness to murder."

"You devilish old hag," said Doctor Quimper. He lunged forward at Miss Marple but this time it was Cedric who caught him by the shoulder.

"So you're the murdering devil, are you?" said Cedric as he swung him round. "I never liked you and I always thought you were a wrong 'un, but Lord knows, I never suspected you."

Bryan Eastley came quickly to Cedric's assistance. Inspector Craddock and Inspector Bacon entered the room from the farther door.

"Doctor Quimper," said Bacon, "I must caution you that . . ."

"You can take your caution to hell," said Doctor Quimper. "Do you think anyone's going to believe what a couple of batty old women say? Who's ever heard of all this rigmarole about a train!"

Miss Marple said, "Elspeth McGillicuddy reported the murder to the police at once on the twentieth of December and gave a description of the man."

Doctor Quimper gave a sudden heave of the shoulders. "If ever a man had the devil's own luck," said Doctor Quimper.

"But—" said Mrs. McGillicuddy.

"Be quiet, Elspeth," said Miss Marple.

"Why should I want to murder a perfectly strange woman?" said Doctor Quimper.

"She wasn't a strange woman," said Inspector Craddock. "She was your wife."

CHAPTER TWENTY-SEVEN

"So you see," said Miss Marple, "it really turned out to be, as I began to suspect, very, very simple. The simplest kind of crime. So many men seem to murder their wives."

Mrs. McGillicuddy looked at Miss Marple and Inspector Craddock. "I'd be obliged," she said, "if you'd put me a little more up to date."

"He saw a chance, you see," said Miss Marple, "of marrying a rich wife, Emma Crackenthorpe. Only he couldn't marry her because he had a wife already. They'd been separated for years but she wouldn't divorce him. That fitted in very well with what Inspector Craddock told me of this girl who called herself Anna Stravinska. She had an English husband, so she told one of her friends, and it was also said she was a very devout Catholic. Doctor Quimper couldn't risk marrying Emma bigamously, so he decided, being a very ruthless and cold-blooded man, that he would get rid of his wife. The idea of murdering her in the train and later putting her body in the sarcophagus in the barn was really rather a clever one. He meant it to tie up, you see, with the Crackenthorpe family. Before that he'd written a letter to Emma which purported to be from the girl Martine whom Edmund Crackenthorpe had talked of marrying. Emma had told Doctor Quimper all about her brother, you see. Then, when the moment arose he encouraged her to go to the police with the story. He wanted the dead woman identified as Martine. I think he may have heard that inquiries were being made by the Paris police about Anna Stravinska, and so he arranged to have a postcard come from her from Jamaica.

"It was easy for him to arrange to meet his wife in London, to tell her that he hoped to be reconciled with her and that he would like her to come down and 'meet his family.' We won't talk about the next part of it, which is very unpleasant to think about. Of course he was a greedy man. When he thought about taxation, and how much it cuts into income, he began thinking that it would be nice to have a good deal more capital. Perhaps he'd already thought of that before he decided to murder his wife. Anyway he started spreading rumors that someone was trying to poison old Mr. Crackenthorpe so as to get the ground prepared, and then he ended by administering arsenic to the family. Not too much, of course, for he didn't want old Mr. Crackenthorpe to die."

"But I still don't see how he managed," said Craddock. "He wasn't in the house when the curry was being prepared."

"Oh, but there wasn't any arsenic in the curry then," said Miss Marple. "He added it to the curry afterward when he took it away to be tested. He probably put the arsenic in the cocktail jug earlier. Then of course it was quite easy for him in his role of medical attendant, to poison off Alfred Crackenthorpe and also to send the tablets to Harold in London, having safeguarded himself by telling Harold that he wouldn't need any more tablets. Everything he did was bold and audacious and cruel and greedy, and I am really very, very glad," finished Miss Marple, looking as fierce as a fluffy old lady can look, "that they haven't abolished capital punishment yet because I do feel that if there is anyone who ought to hang, it's Doctor Quimper."

"Hear, hear," said Inspector Craddock.

"It occurred to me, you know," continued Miss Marple, "that even if you only see anybody from the back view, so to speak, nevertheless a back view is characteristic. I thought that if Elspeth were to see Doctor Quimper in exactly the same position as she'd seen the man in the train, that is, with his back to her bent over a woman whom he was holding by the throat, then I was almost sure she would recognize him, or would make some kind of startled exclamation. That is why I had to lay my little plan with Lucy's kind assistance."

"I must say," said Mrs. McGillicuddy, "it gave me quite a turn. I said 'That's him' before I could stop myself. And yet, you know, I hadn't actually seen the man's face and . . ."

"I was terribly afraid that you were going to say so, Elspeth," said Miss Marple.

"I was," said Mrs. McGillicuddy. "I was going to say that of course I hadn't seen his face."

"That," said Miss Marple, "would have been quite fatal! You see, dear, he thought you really did recognize him. I mean, he couldn't know that you hadn't seen his face."

"A good thing I held my tongue then," said Mrs. McGillicuddy.

"I wasn't going to let you say another word," said Miss Marple.

Craddock laughed suddenly. "You two!" he said. "You're a marvelous pair. What next, Miss Marple? What's the happy ending? What happens to poor Emma Crackenthorpe, for instance?"

"She'll get over the doctor, of course," said Miss Marple, "and I dare say if her father were to die—and I don't think he's quite so robust as he thinks he is—that she'd go on a cruise or perhaps stay abroad like Geraldine Webb, and I dare say something might some of it. A nicer man than Doctor Quimper, I hope."

"What about Lucy Eyelesbarrow? Wedding bells there, too?"

"Perhaps," said Miss Marple. "I shouldn't wonder."

"Which of 'em is she going to choose?" said Dermot Craddock.

"Don't you know?" said Miss Marple.

"No, I don't," said Craddock. "Do you?"

"Oh yes, I think so," said Miss Marple.

And she twinkled at him.

The Body in the Library

CAST OF CHARACTERS

CHAPTER ONE

MRS. BANTRY WAS dreaming. Her sweet peas had just taken a First at the flower show. The vicar, dressed in cassock and surplice, was giving out the prizes in church. His wife wandered past, dressed in a bathing suit, but, as is the blessed habit of dreams, this fact did not arouse the disapproval of the parish in the way it would assuredly have done in real life. Mrs. Bantry was enjoying her dream a good deal. She usually did enjoy those early-morning dreams that were terminated by the arrival of early-morning tea. Somewhere in her inner consciousness was an awareness of the usual early-morning noises of the household. The rattle of the curtain rings on the stairs as the housemaid drew them, the noises of the second housemaid's dustpan and brush in the passage outside. In the distance the heavy noise of the front-door bolt being drawn back.

Another day was beginning. In the meantime she must extract as much pleasure as possible from the flower show, for already its dreamlike quality was becoming apparent.

Below her was the noise of the big wooden shutters in the drawing room being opened. She heard it, yet did not hear it. For quite half an hour longer the usual household noises would go on, discreet, subdued, not disturbing because they were so familiar. They would culminate in a swift, controlled sound of footsteps along the passage, the rustle of a print dress, the subdued chink of tea things as the tray was deposited on the table outside, then the soft knock and the entry of Mary to draw the curtains. In her sleep Mrs. Bantry frowned. Something disturbing was penetrating through the dream state, something out of its time. Footsteps along the passage, footsteps that were too hurried and too soon. Her ears listened unconsciously for the chink of china, but there was no chink of china. The knock came at the door. Automatically, from the depths of her dream, Mrs. Bantry said, "Come in." The door opened; now there would be the chink of curtain ring as the curtains were drawn back.

But there was no chink of curtain rings. Out of the dim green light Mary's voice came, breathless, hysterical. "Oh, ma'am, oh, ma'am, there's a body in the library!" And then, with a hysterical burst of sobs, she rushed out of the room again.

Mrs. Bantry sat up in bed. Either her dream had taken a very odd turn or else—or else Mary had really rushed into the room and had said—incredibly fantastic!—that there was a body in the library. "Impossible," said Mrs. Bantry to herself. "I must have been dreaming." But even as she said it, she felt more and more certain that she had not been dreaming; that Mary, her superior self-controlled Mary, had actually uttered those fantastic words.

Mrs. Bantry reflected a minute and then applied an urgent conjugal elbow to her sleeping spouse. "Arthur, Arthur, wake up." Colonel Bantry grunted, muttered and rolled over on his side. "Wake up, Arthur. Did you hear what she said?"

"Very likely," said Colonel Bantry indistinctly. "I quite agree with you, Dolly," and promptly went to sleep again.

Mrs. Bantry shook him. "You've got to listen. Mary came in and said that there was a body in the library."

"Eh, what?"

"A body in the library."

"Who said so?"

"Mary."

Colonel Bantry collected his scattered faculties and proceeded to deal with the situation. He said, "Nonsense, old girl! You've been dreaming."

"No, I haven't. I thought so, too, at first. But I haven't. She really came in and said so."

"Mary came in and said there was a body in the library?"

"Yes."

"But there couldn't be," said Colonel Bantry.

"No—no, I suppose not," said Mrs. Bantry doubtfully. Rallying, she went on, "But then why did Mary say there was?"

"She can't have."

"She did."

"You must have imagined it."

"I didn't imagine it."

Colonel Bantry was by now thoroughly awake and prepared to deal with the situation on its merits. He said kindly, "You've been dreaming, Dolly. It's that detective story you were reading—*The Clue of the Broken Match*. You know, Lord Edgbaston finds a beautiful blonde dead on the library hearthrug. Bodies are always being found in libraries in books. I've never known a case in real life."

"Perhaps you will now," said Mrs. Bantry. "Anyway, Arthur, you've got to get up and see."

"But really, Dolly, it must have been a dream. Dreams often do seem wonderfully vivid when you first wake up. You feel quite sure they're true."

"I was having quite a different sort of dream—about a flower show and the vicar's wife in a bathing dress—something like that." Mrs. Bantry jumped out of bed and pulled back the curtains. The light of a fine autumn day flooded the room. "I did not dream it," said Mrs. Bantry firmly. "Get up at once, Arthur, and go downstairs and see about it."

"You want me to go downstairs and ask if there's a body in the library? I shall look a fool."

"You needn't ask anything," said Mrs. Bantry. "If there is a body—and of course it's just possible that Mary's gone mad and thinks she sees things that aren't there—well, somebody will tell you soon enough. You won't have to say a word."

Grumbling, Colonel Bantry wrapped himself in his dressing gown and left the room. He went along the passage and down the staircase. At the foot of it was a little knot of huddled servants; some of them were sobbing. The butler stepped forward impressively. "I'm glad you have come, sir. I have directed that nothing should be done until you came. Will it be in order for me to ring up the police, sir?"

"Ring 'em up about what?"

The butler cast a reproachful glance over his shoulder at the tall young woman who was weeping hysterically on the cook's shoulder. "I understood, sir, that Mary had already informed you. She said she had done so."

Mary gasped out, "I was so upset, I don't know what I said! It all came over me again and my legs gave way and my insides turned over! Finding it like that—Oh, oh, oh!"

She subsided again onto Mrs. Eccles, who said, "There, there, my dear," with some relish.

"Mary is naturally somewhat upset, sir, having been the one to make the gruesome discovery," explained the butler. "She went into the library, as usual, to draw the curtains, and—and almost stumbled over the body."

"Do you mean to tell me," demanded Colonel Bantry, "that there's a dead body in my library—my library?"

The butler coughed. "Perhaps, sir, you would like to see for yourself."

"Hullo, 'ullo, 'ullo. Police station here. Yes, who's speaking?" Police Constable Palk was buttoning up his tunic with one hand while the other held the telephone receiver. "Yes, yes, Gossington Hall. Yes? . . . Oh, good morning, sir." Police Constable Palk's tone underwent a slight modification. It became less impatiently official, recognizing the generous patron of the police sports and the principal magistrate of the district. "Yes, sir? What can I do for you? . . . I'm sorry, sir, I didn't quite catch—A body, did you say? . . . Yes? . . . Yes, if you please, sir. . . . That's right, sir. . . . Young woman not known to you, you say? . . . Quite, sir. . . . Yes, you can leave it all to me."

Police Constable Palk replaced the receiver, uttered a long-drawn whistle and proceeded to dial his superior officer's number. Mrs. Palk looked in from the kitchen, whence proceeded an appetizing smell of frying bacon. "What is it?"

"Rummiest thing you ever heard of," replied her husband. "Body of a young woman found up at the Hall. In the colonel's library."

"Murdered?"

"Strangled, so he says."

"Who was she?"

"The colonel says he doesn't know her from Adam."

"Then what was she doing in 'is library?"

Police Constable Palk silenced her with a reproachful glance and spoke officially into the telephone. "Inspector Slack? Police Constable Palk here. A report has just come in that the body of a young woman was discovered this morning at seven-fifteen—"

Miss Marple's telephone rang when she was dressing. The sound of it flurried her a little. It was an unusual hour for her telephone to ring. So well ordered was her prim spinster's life that unforeseen telephone calls were a source of vivid conjecture. "Dear me," said Miss Marple, surveying the ringing instrument with perplexity. "I wonder who that can be?"

Nine o'clock to nine-thirty was the recognized time for the village to make friendly calls to neighbors. Plans for the day, invitations, and so on, were always issued then. The butcher had been known to ring up just before nine if some crisis in the meat trade had occurred. At intervals during the day spasmodic calls might occur, though it was considered bad form to ring up after nine-thirty at night.

It was true that Miss Marple's nephew, a writer, and therefore erratic, had been known to ring up at the most peculiar times; once as late as ten minutes to midnight. But whatever Raymond West's eccentricities, early rising was not one of them. Neither he nor anyone of Miss Marple's acquaintance would be likely to ring up before eight in the morning. Actually a quarter to eight. Too early even for a telegram, since the post office did not open until eight. "It must be," Miss Marple decided, "a wrong number." Having decided this, she advanced to the impatient instrument and quelled its clamor by picking up the receiver. "Yes?" she said.

"Is that you, Jane?"

Miss Marple was much surprised. "Yes, it's Jane. You're up very early, Dolly."

Mrs. Bantry's voice came, breathless and agitated, over the wire. "The most awful thing has happened."

"Oh, my dear!"

"We've just found a body in the library."

For a moment Miss Marple thought her friend had gone mad. "You've found a what?"

"I know. One doesn't believe it, does one? I mean I thought they only happened in books. I had to argue for hours with Arthur this morning before he'd even go down and see."

Miss Marple tried to collect herself. She demanded breathlessly, "But whose body is it?"

"It's a blonde."

"A what?"

"A blonde. A beautiful blonde—like books again. None of us have ever seen her before. She's just lying there in the library, dead. That's why you've got to come up at once."

"You want me to come up?"

"Yes, I'm sending the car down for you."

Miss Marple said doubtfully, "Of course, dear, if you think I can be of any comfort to you—"

"Oh, I don't want comfort. But you're so good at bodies."

"Oh, no, indeed. My little successes have been mostly theoretical."

"But you're very good at murders. She's been murdered, you see; strangled. What I feel is that if one has got to have a murder actually happening in one's house, one might as well enjoy it, if you know what I mean. That's why I want you to come and help me find out who did it and unravel the mystery, and all that. It really is rather thrilling, isn't it?"

"Well, of course, my dear, if I can be of any help."

"Splendid! Arthur's being rather difficult. He seems to think I shouldn't enjoy myself about it at all. Of course, I do know it's very sad and all that, but then I don't know the girl—and when you've seen her you'll understand what I mean when I say she doesn't look real at all."

A little breathless, Miss Marple alighted from the Bantry's car, the door of which was held open for her by the chauffeur. Colonel Bantry came out on the steps and looked a little surprised. "Miss Marple? Er—very pleased to see you."

"Your wife telephoned to me," explained Miss Marple.

"Capital, capital. She ought to have someone with her. She'll crack up otherwise. She's putting a good face on things at the moment, but you know what it is—"

At this moment Mrs. Bantry appeared and exclaimed, "Do go back and eat your breakfast, Arthur. Your bacon will get cold."

"I thought it might be the inspector arriving," explained Colonel Bantry.

"He'll be here soon enough," said Mrs. Bantry. "That's why it's important to get your breakfast first. You need it."

"So do you. Much better come and eat something, Dolly."

"I'll come in a minute," said Mrs. Bantry. "Go on, Arthur." Colonel Bantry was shooed back into the dining room rather like a recalcitrant hen. "Now!" said Mrs. Bantry with an intonation of triumph. "Come on."

She led the way rapidly along the long corridor to the east of the house. Outside the library door Constable Palk stood on guard. He intercepted Mrs. Bantry with a show of authority. "I'm afraid nobody is allowed in, madam. Inspector's orders."

"Nonsense, Palk," said Mrs. Bantry. "You know Miss Marple perfectly well." Constable Palk admitted to knowing Miss Marple. "It's very important that she should see the body," said Mrs. Bantry. "Don't be stupid, Palk. After all, it's my library, isn't it?"

Constable Palk gave way. His habit of giving in to the gentry was lifelong. The inspector, he reflected, need never know about it. "Nothing must be touched or handled in any way," he warned the ladies.

"Of course not," said Mrs. Bantry impatiently. "We know that. You can come in and watch, if you like." Constable Palk availed himself of this permission. It had been his intention anyway. Mrs. Bantry bore her friend triumphantly across the library to the big old-fashioned fireplace. She said, with a dramatic sense of climax, "There!"

Miss Marple understood then just what her friend had meant when she said the dead girl wasn't real. The library was a room very typical of its owners. It was large and shabby and untidy. It had big, sagging armchairs, and pipes and books and estate papers laid out on the big table. There were one or two good old family portraits on the walls, and some bad Victorian water colors, and some would-be-funny hunting scenes. There was a big vase of flowers in the corner. The whole room was dim and mellow and casual. It spoke of long occupation and familiar use and of links with tradition.

And across the old bearskin hearthrug there was sprawled something new and crude and melodramatic. The flamboyant figure of a girl. A girl with unnaturally fair hair dressed up off her face in elaborate curls and rings. Her thin body was dressed in a backless evening dress of white spangled satin; the face was heavily made up, the powder standing out grotesquely on its blue, swollen surface, the mascara of the lashes lying thickly on the distorted cheeks, the scarlet of the lips looking like a gash. The fingernails were enameled a deep blood red, and so were the toenails in their cheap silver sandal shoes. It was a cheap, tawdry, flamboyant figure, most incongruous in the solid, old-fashioned comfort of Colonel Bantry's library. Mrs. Bantry said in a low voice, "You see what I mean? It just isn't true?"

The old lady by her side nodded her head. She looked down long and thoughtfully at the huddled figure. She said at last in a gentle voice, "She's very young."

"Yes; yes, I suppose she is." Mrs. Bantry seemed almost surprised, like one making a discovery.

There was the sound of a car crunching on the gravel outside. Constable Palk said with urgency, "That'll be the inspector."

True to his ingrained belief that the gentry didn't let you down, Mrs. Bantry immediately moved to the door. Miss Marple followed her. Mrs. Bantry said, "That'll be all right, Palk." Constable Palk was immensely relieved.

Hastily downing the last fragments of toast and marmalade with a drink of coffee, Colonel Bantry hurried out into the hall and was relieved to see Colonel Melchett, the chief constable of the county, descending from a car, with Inspector Slack in attendance. Melchett was a friend of the colonel's; Slack he had never very much taken to—an energetic man who belied his name and who accompanied his bustling manner with a good deal of disregard for the feelings of anyone he did not consider important.

"Morning, Bantry," said the chief constable. "Thought I'd better come along myself. This seems an extraordinary business."

"It's—it's"—Colonel Bantry struggled to express himself—"it's incredible—fantastic!"

"No idea who the woman is?"

"Not in the slightest. Never set eyes on her in my life."

"Butler know anything?" asked Inspector Slack.

"Lorrimer is just as taken aback as I am."

"Ah," said Inspector Slack. "I wonder."

Colonel Bantry said, "There's breakfast in the dining room, Melchett, if you'd like anything."

"No, no, better get on with the job. Haydock ought to be here any minute now. . . . Ah, here he is." Another car drew up and big, broad-shouldered Doctor Haydock, who was also the police surgeon, got out. A second police car had disgorged two plain-clothes men, one with a camera.

"All set, eh?" said the chief constable. "Right. We'll go along. In the library, Slack tells me."

Colonel Bantry groaned. "It's incredible! You know, when my wife insisted this morning that the housemaid had come in and said there was a body in the library, I just wouldn't believe her."

"No, no, I can quite understand that. Hope your missus isn't too badly upset by it all."

"She's been wonderful—really wonderful. She's got old Miss Marple up here with her—from the village, you know."

"Miss Marple?" The chief constable stiffened. "Why did she send for her?"

"Oh, a woman wants another woman—don't you think so?"

Colonel Melchett said with a slight chuckle, "If you ask me, your wife's going to try her hand at a little amateur detecting. Miss Marple's quite the local sleuth. Put it over us properly once, didn't she, Slack?"

Inspector Slack said, "That was different."

"Different from what?"

"That was a local case, that was, sir. The old lady knows everything that goes on in the village, that's true enough. But she'll be out of her depth here."

Melchett said dryly, "You don't know very much about it yourself yet, Slack."

"Ah, you wait, sir. It won't take me long to get down to it."

In the dining room Mrs. Bantry and Miss Marple, in their turn, were partaking of breakfast. After waiting on her guest, Mrs. Bantry said urgently, "Well, Jane?" Miss Marple looked up at her slightly bewildered. Mrs. Bantry said hopefully, "Doesn't it remind you of anything?"

For Miss Marple had attained fame by her ability to link up trivial village happenings with graver problems in such a way as to throw light upon the latter.

"No," said Miss Marple thoughtfully. "I can't say that it does—not at the moment. I was reminded a little of Mrs. Chetty's youngest—Edie, you know—but I think that was just because this poor girl bit her nails and her front teeth stuck out a little. Nothing more than that. And of course," went on Miss Marple, pursuing the parallel further, "Edie was fond of what I call cheap finery too."

"You mean her dress?" said Mrs. Bantry.

"Yes, very tawdry satin, poor quality."

Mrs. Bantry said, "I know. One of those nasty little shops where everything is a guinea." She went on hopefully, "Let me see. What happened to Mrs. Chetty's Edie?"

"She's just gone into her second place, and doing very well, I believe," said Miss Marple.

Mrs. Bantry felt slightly disappointed. The village parallel didn't seem to be exactly hopeful.

"What I can't make out," said Mrs. Bantry, "is what she could possibly be doing in Arthur's study. The window was forced, Palk tells me. She might have come down here with a burglar, and then they quarreled— But that seems such nonsense, doesn't it?"

"She was hardly dressed for burglary," said Miss Marple thoughtfully.

"No, she was dressed for dancing or a party of some kind. But there's nothing of that kind down here or anywhere near."

"N-no," said Miss Marple doubtfully.

Mrs. Bantry pounced. "Something's in your mind, Jane."

"Well, I was just wondering—"

"Yes?"

"Basil Blake."

Mrs. Bantry cried impulsively, "Oh, no!" and added as though in explanation, "I know his mother."

The two women looked at each other. Miss Marple sighed and shook her head. "I quite understand how you feel about it."

"Selina Blake is the nicest woman imaginable. Her herbaceous borders are simply marvelous; they make me green with envy. And she's frightfully generous with cuttings."

Miss Marple passing over these claims to consideration on the part of Mrs. Blake, said, "All the same, you know, there has been a lot of talk."

"Oh, I know, I know. And of course Arthur goes simply livid when he hears him mentioned. He was really very rude to Arthur, and since then Arthur won't hear a good word for him. He's got that silly slighting way of talking that these boys have nowadays—sneering at people sticking up for their school or the Empire or that sort of thing. And then, of course, the clothes he wears! People say," continued Mrs. Bantry, "that it doesn't matter what you wear in the country. I never heard such nonsense. It's just in the country that everyone notices." She paused and added wistfully, "He was an adorable baby in his bath."

"There was a lovely picture of the Cheviot murderer as a baby in the paper last Sunday," said Miss Marple.

"Oh, but, Jane, you don't think he—"

"No, no, dear, I didn't mean that at all. That would indeed be jumping to conclusions. I was just trying to account for the young woman's presence down here. St. Mary Mead is such an unlikely place. And then it seemed to me that the only possible explanation was Basil Blake. He does have parties. People come down from London and from the studios—you remember last July? Shouting and singing—the most terrible noise—everyone very drunk, I'm afraid—and the mess and the broken glass next morning simply unbelievable—so old Mrs. Berry told me—and a young woman asleep in the bath with practically nothing on!"

Mrs. Bantry said indulgently, "I suppose they were film people."

"Very likely. And then—what I expect you've heard—several weekends lately he's brought down a young woman with him—a platinum blonde."

Mrs. Bantry exclaimed, "You don't think it's this one?"

"Well, I wondered. Of course, I've never seen her close to—only just getting in and out of the car, and once in the cottage garden when she was sunbathing with just some shorts and a brassière. I never really saw her face. And all these girls, with their makeup and their hair and their nails, look so alike."

"Yes. Still, it might be. It's an idea, Jane."

CHAPTER TWO

It was an idea that was being at that moment discussed by Colonel Melchett and Colonel Bantry. The chief constable, after viewing the body and seeing his subordinates set to work on their routine tasks, had adjourned with the master of the house to the study in the other wing. Colonel Melchett was an irascible-looking man with a habit of tugging at his short red mustache. He did so now, shooting a perplexed sideways glance at the other man. Finally he rapped out, "Look here, Bantry; got to get this off my chest. Is it a fact that you don't know from Adam who this woman is?"

The other's answer was explosive, but the chief constable interrupted him, "Yes, yes, old man, but look at it like this: Might be deuced awkward for you. Married man—fond of your missus and all that. But just between ourselves, if you were tied up with this girl in any way, better say so now. Quite natural to want to suppress the fact; should feel the same myself. But it won't do. Murder case. Facts bound to come out. Dash it all, I'm not suggesting you strangled the girl—not the sort of thing you'd do. I know that! But, after all, she came here—to this house. Put it, she broke in and was waiting to see you, and some bloke or other followed her down and did her in. Possible, you know. See what I mean?"

"I've never set eyes on that girl in my life! I'm not that sort of man!"

"That's all right then. Shouldn't blame you, you know. Man of the world. Still, if you say so—Question is, what was she doing down here? She doesn't come from these parts, that's quite certain."

"That whole thing's a nightmare," fumed the angry master of the house.

"The point is, old man, what was she doing in your library?"

"How should I know? I didn't ask her here."

"No, no. But she came here all the same. Looks as though she wanted to see you. You haven't had any odd letters or anything?"

"No, I haven't."

Colonel Melchett inquired delicately, "What were you doing yourself last night?"

"I went to the meeting of the Conservative Association. Nine o'clock, at Much Benham."

"And you got home when?"

"I left Much Benham just after ten. Had a bit of trouble on the way home, had to change a wheel. I got back at a quarter to twelve."

"You didn't go into the library?"

"No."

"Pity."

"I was tired. I went straight up to bed."

"Anyone waiting up for you?"

"No. I always take the latchkey. Lorrimer goes to bed at eleven, unless I give orders to the contrary."

"Who shuts up the library?"

"Lorrimer. Usually about seven-thirty this time of year."

"Would he go in there again during the evening?"

"Not with my being out. He left the tray with whisky and glasses in the hall."

"I see. What about your wife?"

"She was in bed when I got home, and fast asleep. She may have sat in the library yesterday evening, or in the drawing room. I didn't ask her."

"Oh, well, we shall soon know all the details. Of course it's possible one of the servants may be concerned, eh?"

Colonel Bantry shook his head. "I don't believe it. They're all a most respectable lot. We've had 'em for years."

Melchett agreed. "Yes, it doesn't seem likely that they're mixed up in it. Looks more as though the girl came down from town—perhaps with some young fellow. Though why they wanted to break into this house—"

Bantry interrupted. "London. That's more like it. We don't have goings on down here—at least—"

"Well, what is it?"

"Upon my word!" exploded Colonel Bantry. "Basil Blake!"

"Who's he?"

"Young fellow connected with the film industry. Poisonous young brute. My wife sticks up for him because she was at school with his mother, but of all the decadent useless young jackanapes— Wants his behind kicked. He's taken that cottage on the Lansham Road—you know, ghastly modern bit of building. He has parties there—shrieking, noisy crowds—and he has girls down for the weekend."

"Girls?"

"Yes, there was one last week—one of these platinum blondes." The colonel's jaw dropped.

"A platinum blonde, eh?" said Melchett reflectively.

"Yes. I say, Melchett, you don't think—"

The chief constable said briskly, "It's a possibility. It accounts for a girl of this type being in St. Mary Mead. I think I'll run along and have a word with this young fellow Braid—Blake—what did you say his name was?"

"Blake. Basil Blake."

"Will he be at home, do you know?" asked Melchett.

"Let me see, what's today? Saturday? Usually gets here some time Saturday morning."

Melchett said grimly, "We'll see if we can find him."

Basil Blake's cottage, which consisted of all modern conveniences enclosed in a hideous shell of half timbering and sham Tudor, was known to the postal authorities and to William Booker, Builder, as "Chatsworth"; to Basil and his friends as "The Period Piece"; and to the village of St. Mary Mead at large as "Mr. Booker's new house." It was little more than a quarter of a mile from the village proper, being situated on a new building estate that had been bought by the enterprising Mr. Booker just beyond the Blue Boar, with frontage on what had been a particularly unspoiled country lane. Gossington Hall was about a mile farther on along the same road.

Lively interest had been aroused in St. Mary Mead when the news went round that "Mr. Booker's new house" had been bought by a film star. Eager watch was kept for the first appearance of the legendary creature in the village, and it may be said that as far as appearances went Basil Blake was all that could be asked for. Little by little, however, the real facts leaked out. Basil Blake was not a film star, not even a film actor. He was a very junior person, rejoicing in the position of about fifteenth in the list of those responsible for set decorations at Lenville Studios, headquarters of British New Era Films. The village maidens lost interest and the ruling class of censorious spinsters took exception to Basil Blake's way of life. Only the landlord of the Blue Boar continued to be enthusiastic about Basil and Basil's friends. The revenues of the Blue Boar had increased since the young man's arrival in the place.

The police car stopped outside the distorted rustic gate of Mr. Booker's fancy, and Colonel Melchett, with a glance of distaste at the excessive half timbering of Chatsworth, strode up to the front door and attacked it briskly with the knocker. It was opened much more promptly than he had expected. A young man with straight, somewhat long black hair, wearing orange corduroy trousers and a royal-blue shirt, snapped out, "Well, what do you want?"

"Are you Mr. Basil Blake?"

"Of course I am."

"I should be glad to have a few words with you if I may, Mr. Blake."

"Who are you?"

"I am Colonel Melchett, the chief constable of the county."

Mr. Blake said insolently, "You don't say so. How amusing."

And Colonel Melchett, following the other in, understood precisely what Colonel Bantry's reactions had been. The toe of his own boot itched. Containing himself, however, he said, with an attempt to speak pleasantly, "You're an early riser, Mr. Blake."

"Not at all. I haven't been to bed yet."

"Indeed?"

"But I don't suppose you've come here to inquire into my hours of bed-going, or if you have it's rather a waste of the county's time and money. What is it you want to speak to me about?"

Colonel Melchett cleared his throat. "I understand, Mr. Blake, that last weekend you had a visitor—a—er—fair-haired young lady."

Basil Blake stared, threw back his head and roared with laughter. "Have the old cats been on to you from the village? About my morals? Damn it all, morals aren't a police matter. You know that."

"As you say," said Melchett dryly, "your morals are no concern of mine. I have come to you because the body of a fair-haired young woman of slightly—er—exotic appearance has been found—murdered."

"'Struth!" Blake stared at him. "Where?"

"In the library at Gossington Hall."

"At Gossington? At old Bantry's? I say, that's pretty rich—old Bantry! The dirty old man!"

Colonel Melchett went very red in the face. He said sharply through the renewed mirth of the young man opposite him, "Kindly control your tongue, sir. I came to ask you if you can throw any light on this business."

"You've come round to ask me if I've missed a blonde? Is that it? Why should—Hullo, 'ullo, 'ullo! What's this?"

A car had drawn up outside with a scream of brakes. Out of it tumbled a young woman dressed in flapping black-and-white pajamas. She had scarlet lips, blackened eyelashes and a platinum-blond head. She strode up to the door, flung it open, and exclaimed angrily, "Why did you run out on me?"

Basil Blake had risen. "So there you are. Why shouldn't I leave you? I told you to clear out, and you wouldn't."

"Why should I because you told me? I was enjoying myself."

"Yes, with that filthy brute, Rosenberg. You know what he's like."

"You were jealous, that's all."

"Don't flatter yourself. I hate to see a girl I like who can't hold her drink and lets a disgusting Central European paw her about."

"That's a lie. You were drinking pretty hard yourself and going on with the black-haired Spanish girl."

"If I take you to a party, I expect you to be able to behave yourself."

"And I refuse to be dictated to, and that's that. You said we'd go to the party and come on down here afterwards. I'm not going to leave a party before I'm ready to leave it."

"No, and that's why I left you flat. I was ready to come down here and I came. I don't hang round waiting for any fool of a woman."

"Sweet, polite person you are."

"You seem to have followed me down, all right."

"I wanted to tell you what I thought of you."

"If you think you can boss me, my girl, you're wrong."

"And if you think you can order me about, you can think again."

They glared at each other. It was at this moment that Colonel Melchett seized his opportunity and cleared his throat loudly. Basil Blake swung round on him. "Hullo, I forgot you were here. About time you took yourself off, isn't it? Let me introduce you—Dinah Lee—Colonel Blimp, of the county police. . . . And now, colonel, that you've seen that my blonde is alive and in good condition, perhaps you'll get on with the good work concerning old Bantry's little bit of fluff. Good morning!"

Colonel Melchett said, "I advise you to keep a civil tongue in your head, young man, or you'll let yourself in for trouble," and stumped out, his face red and wrathful.

CHAPTER THREE

In his office at Much Benham, Colonel Melchett received and scrutinized the reports of his subordinates. ". . . so it all seems clear enough, sir," Inspector Slack was concluding. "Mrs. Bantry sat in the library after dinner and went to bed just before ten. She turned out the lights when she left the room, and presumably no one entered the room afterward. The servants went to bed at half past ten, and Lorrimer, after putting the drinks in the hall, went to bed at a quarter to eleven. Nobody heard anything out of the usual, except the third housemaid, and she heard too much! Groans and a bloodcurdling yell and sinister footsteps and I don't know what. The second housemaid, who shares a room with her, says the other girl slept all night through without a sound. It's those ones that make up things that cause us all the trouble."

"What about the forced window?"

"Amateur job. Simmons says, done with a common chisel, ordinary pattern; wouldn't have made much noise. Ought to be a chisel about the house, but nobody can find it. Still, that's common enough where tools are concerned."

"Think any of the servants know anything?"

Rather unwillingly Inspector Slack replied, "No, sir. I don't think they do. They all seemed very shocked and upset. I had my suspicions of Lorrimer—reticent, he was, if you know what I mean—but I don't think there's anything in it."

Melchett nodded. He attached no importance to Lorrimer's reticence. The energetic Inspector Slack often produced that effect on the people he interrogated. The door opened and Doctor Haydock came in. "Thought I'd look in and give you the rough gist of things."

"Yes, yes, glad to see you. Well?"

"Nothing much. Just what you'd think. Death was due to strangulation. Satin waistband of her own dress, which was passed round the neck and crossed at the back. Quite easy and simple to do. Wouldn't have needed great strength—that is, if the girl was taken by surprise. There are no signs of a struggle."

"What about time of death?"

"Say between ten o'clock and midnight."

"You can't get nearer than that?"

Haydock shook his head with a slight grin. "I won't risk my professional reputation. Not earlier than ten and not later than midnight."

"And your own fancy inclines to which time?"

"Depends. There was a fire in the grate, the room was warm—all that would delay rigor and cadaveric stiffening."

"Anything more you can say about her?"

"Nothing much. She was young—about seventeen or eighteen, I should say. Rather immature in some ways but well developed muscularly. Quite a healthy specimen. She was *virgo intacta*, by the way." And with a nod of his head the doctor left the room.

Melchett said to the inspector, "You're quite sure she'd never been seen before at Gossington?"

"The servants are positive of that. Quite indignant about it. They'd have remembered if they'd ever seen her about in the neighborhood, they say."

"I expect the would," said Melchett. "Anyone of that type sticks out a mile round here. Look at that young woman of Blake's."

"Pity it wasn't her," said Slack. "Then we should be able to get on a bit."

"It seems to me this girl must have come down from London," said the chief constable thoughtfully. "Don't believe there will be any local leads. In that case, I suppose, we should do well to call in the Yard. It's a case for them, not for us."

"Something must have brought her down here, though," said Slack. He added tentatively, "Seems to me, Colonel and Mrs. Bantry must know something. Of course I know they're friends of yours, sir—"

Colonel Melchett treated him to a cold stare. He said stiffly, "You may rest assured that I'm taking every possibility into account. Every possibility." He went on, "You've looked through the list of persons reported missing, I suppose?"

Slack nodded. He produced a typed sheet. "Got 'em here. Mrs. Saunders, reported missing a week ago, dark-haired, blue-eyed, thirty-six. 'Tisn't her. And anyway, everyone knows, except her husband, that she's gone off with a fellow from Leeds—commercial. Mrs. Barnard—she's sixty-five. Pamela Reeves, sixteen, missing from her home last night, had attended Girl Guide rally, dark brown hair in pig-tails, five feet five—"

Melchett said irritably, "Don't go on reading idiotic details, Slack. This wasn't a schoolgirl. In my opinion—" He broke off as the telephone rang. "Hullo. . . . Yes, yes, Much Benham police headquarters. . . . What? . . .

Just a minute." He listened and wrote rapidly. Then he spoke again, a new tone in his voice. "Ruby Keene, eighteen, occupation, professional dancer, five feet four inches, slender, platinum-blond hair, blue eyes, retroussé nose, believed to be wearing white diamanté evening dress, silver sandal shoes. Is that right? . . . What? . . . Yes, not a doubt of it, I should say. I'll send Slack over at once." He rang off and looked at his subordinate with rising excitement. "We've got it, I think. That was the Glenshire police." Glenshire was the adjoining county. "Girl reported missing from the Majestic Hotel, Danemouth."

"Danemouth," said Inspector Slack. "That's more like it." Danemouth was a large and fashionable watering place on the coast not far away.

"It's only a matter of eighteen miles or so from here." said the chief constable. "The girl was a dance hostess or something at the Majestic. Didn't come on to do her turn last night and the management was very fed up about it. When she was still missing this morning, one of the other girls got the wind up about her, or someone else did. It sounds a bit obscure. You'd better go over to Danemouth at once, Slack. Report there to Superintendent Harper and cooperate with him."

CHAPTER FOUR

Activity was always to Inspector Slack's taste. To rush in a car, to silence rudely those people who were anxious to tell him things, to cut short conversations on the plea of urgent necessity—all this was the breath of life to Inspector Slack. In an incredibly short time, therefore, he had arrived at Danemouth, reported at police headquarters, had a brief interview with a distracted and apprehensive hotel manager, and, leaving the latter with the doubtful comfort of "Got to make sure it is the girl first, before we start raising the wind," was driving back to Much Benham in company with Ruby Keene's nearest relative. He had put through a short call to Much Benham before leaving Danemouth, so the chief constable was prepared for his arrival, though not perhaps for the brief introduction of "This is Josie, sir."

Colonel Melchett stared at his subordinate coldly. His feeling was that Slack had taken leave of his senses. The young woman who had just got out of the car came to the rescue. "That's what I'm known as professionally," she explained with a momentary flash of large, handsome white teeth. "Raymond and Josie, my partner and I call ourselves, and of course all the hotel know me as Josie. Josephine Turner's my real name."

Colonel Melchett adjusted himself to the situation and invited Miss Turner to sit down, meanwhile casting a swift professional glance over her. She was a good-looking young woman of perhaps nearer thirty than twenty; her looks depending more on skillful grooming than actual features. She looked competent and good-tempered, with plenty of common sense. She was not the type that would ever be described as glamorous, but she had, nevertheless, plenty of attraction. She was discreetly made up and wore a dark tailor-made suit. She looked anxious and upset, but not, the colonel decided, particularly grief-stricken. As she sat down she said, "It seems too awful to be true. Do you really think it's Ruby?"

"That, I'm afraid, is what we've got to ask you to tell us. I'm afraid it may be rather unpleasant for you."

Miss Turner said apprehensively, "Does she—does she look very terrible?"

"Well, I'm afraid it may be rather a shock to you."

"Do—do you want me to look at her right away?"

"It would be best, I think, Miss Turner. You see, it's not much good asking you questions until we're sure. Best get it over, don't you think?"

"All right."

They drove down to the mortuary. When Josie came out after a brief visit she looked rather sick. "It's Ruby, all right," she said shakily. "Poor kid! Goodness, I do feel queer! There isn't"—she looked round wistfully—"any gin?"

Gin was not available, but brandy was and, after gulping a little down, Miss Turner regained her composure. She said frankly, "It gives you a turn, doesn't it, seeing anything like that? Poor little Ruby! What swine men are, aren't they?"

"You believe it was a man?"

Josie looked slightly taken aback. "Wasn't it? Well, I mean—I naturally thought—"

"Any special man you were thinking of?"

She shook her head vigorously. "No, not me. I haven't the least idea. Naturally, Ruby wouldn't have let on to me if—"

"If what?"

Josie hesitated. "Well, if she'd been—going about with anyone."

Melchett shot her a keen glance. He said no more until they were back at his office. Then he began, "Now, Miss Turner, I want all the information you can give me."

"Yes, of course. Where shall I begin?"

"I'd like the girl's full name and address, her relationship to you and all that you know about her."

Josephine Turner nodded. Melchett was confirmed in his opinion that she felt no particular grief. She was shocked and distressed, but no more. She spoke readily enough. "Her name was Ruby Keene—her professional name, that is. Her real name was Rosy Legge. Her mother was my mother's cousin. I've known her all my life, but not particularly well, if you know what I mean. I've got a lot of cousins; some in business, some on the stage. Ruby was more or less training for a dancer. She had some good engagements last year in panto and that sort of thing. Not really classy, but good provincial companies. Since then she's been engaged as one of the dancing partners at the Palais de Danse in Brixwell, South London. It's a nice, respectable place and they look after the girls well, but there isn't a great deal of money in it." She paused. Colonel Melchett nodded.

"Now this is where I come in. I've been dance and bridge hostess at the Majestic in Danemouth for three years. It's a good job, well paid and pleasant to do. You look after people when they arrive. Size them up, of course—some like to be left alone and others are lonely and want to get into the swing of things. You try and get the right people together for bridge and all that, and get the young people dancing with one another. It needs a bit of tact and experience."

Again Melchett nodded. He thought that this girl would be good at her job. She had a pleasant, friendly way with her and was, he thought, shrewd without being in the least intellectual.

"Besides that," continued Josie, "I do a couple of exhibition dances every evening with Raymond. Raymond Starr—he's the tennis and dancing pro. Well, as it happens, this summer I slipped on the rocks bathing one day and gave my ankle a nasty turn." Melchett had noticed that she walked with a slight limp.

"Naturally, that put the stop to dancing for a bit and it was rather awkward. I didn't want the hotel to get someone else in my place. There's always a danger"—for a minute her good-natured blue eyes were hard and sharp; she was the female fighting for existence—"that they may queer your pitch, you see. So I thought of Ruby and suggested to the manager that I should get her down. I'd carry on with the hostess business and the bridge and all that. Ruby would just take on the dancing. Keep it in the family, if you see what I mean." Melchett said he saw.

"Well, they agreed, and I wired to Ruby and she came down. Rather a chance for her. Much better class than anything she'd ever done before. That was about a month ago."

Colonel Melchett said, "I understand. And she was a success?"

"Oh, yes," Josie said carelessly. "She went down quite well. She doesn't dance as well as I do, but Raymond's clever and carried her through, and she was quite nice-looking, you know—slim and fair and baby-looking. Overdid the makeup a bit—I was always at her about that. But you know what girls are. She was only eighteen, and at that age they always go and overdo it. It doesn't do for a good-class place like the Majestic. I was always ticking her off about it and getting her to tone it down."

Melchett asked, "People liked her?"

"Oh, yes. Mind you, Ruby hadn't got much come-back. She was a bit dumb. She went down better with the older men than with the young ones."

"Had she got any special friend?"

The girl's eyes met his with complete understanding. "Not in the way you mean. Or, at any rate, not that I knew about. But then, you see, she wouldn't tell me."

Just for a moment Melchett wondered why not. Josie did not give the impression of being a strict disciplinarian. But he only said, "Will you describe to me now when you last saw your cousin."

"Last night. She and Raymond do two exhibition dances. One at ten-thirty and the other at midnight. They finished the first one. After it, I noticed Ruby dancing with one of the young men staying at the hotel. I was playing bridge with some people in the lounge. There's a glass panel between the lounge and the ballroom. That's the last time I saw her. Just after midnight Raymond came up in a terrible taking; said where was Ruby; she hadn't turned up and it was time to begin. I was vexed, I can tell you! That's the sort of silly things girls do and get the management's back up, and then they get the sack! I went up with him to her room, but she wasn't there. I noticed that she'd changed; the dress she'd been dancing in—a sort of pink, foamy thing with full skirts—was lying over a chair. Usually she kept the same dress on, unless it was the special dance night—Wednesdays, that is.

"I'd no idea where she'd got to. We got the band to play one more fox trot. Still no Ruby, so I said to Raymond I'd do the exhibition dance with him. We chose one that was easy on my ankle and made it short, but it played up my ankle pretty badly all the same. It's all swollen this morning. Still Ruby didn't show up. We sat about waiting up for her until two o'clock. Furious with her, I was."

Her voice vibrated slightly. Melchett caught the note of real anger in it. Just for a moment, he wondered. He had a feeling of something deliberately left unsaid. He said, "And this morning, when Ruby Keene had not returned and her bed had not been slept in, you went to the police?" He knew, from Slack's brief telephone message from Danemouth, that that was not the case. But he wanted to hear what Josephine Turner would say.

She did not hesitate. She said, "No, I didn't."

"Why not, Miss Turner?"

Her eyes met his frankly. She said, "You wouldn't—in my place!"

"You think not?"

Josie said, "I've got my job to think about! The one thing a hotel doesn't want is scandal—especially anything that brings in the police. I didn't think anything had happened to Ruby. Not for a minute! I thought she'd just made a fool of herself about some young man. I thought she'd turn up all right, and I was going to give her a good dressing down when she did! Girls of eighteen are such fools."

Melchett pretended to glance through his notes. "Ah, yes, I see it was a Mr. Jefferson who went to the police. One of the guests staying at the hotel?"

Josephine Turner said shortly, "Yes."

Colonel Melchett asked, "What made this Mr. Jefferson do that?"

Josie was stroking the cuff of her jacket. There was a constraint in her manner. Again Colonel Melchett had a feeling that something was being withheld.

She said rather sullenly, "He's an invalid. He—he gets all het up rather easily. Being an invalid, I mean."

Melchett passed from that. He asked, "Who was the young man with whom you last saw your cousin dancing?"

"His name's Bartlett. He's been there about ten days."

"Were they on very friendly terms?"

"Not specially, I should say. Not that I knew, anyway." Again a curious note of anger in her voice.

"What does he have to say?"

"Said that after their dance Ruby went upstairs to powder her nose."

"That was when she changed her dress?"

"I suppose so."

"And that is the last thing you know? After that, she just—"

"Vanished," said Josie. "That's right."

"Did Miss Keene know anybody in St. Mary Mead? Or in this neighborhood?"

"I don't know. She may have. You see, quite a lot of young men come in to Danemouth to the Majestic, from all round about. I wouldn't know where they lived unless they happened to mention it."

"Did you ever hear your cousin mention Gossington?"

"Gossington?" Josie looked patently puzzled.

"Gossington Hall."

She shook her head. "Never heard of it." Her tone carried conviction. There was curiosity in it too.

"Gossington Hall," explained Colonel Melchett, "is where her body was found."

"Gossington Hall?" She stared. "How extraordinary!"

Melchett thought to himself, *Extraordinary's the word.* Aloud he said, "Do you know a Colonel or Mrs. Bantry?"

Again Josie shook her head.

"Or a Mr. Basil Blake?"

She frowned slightly. "I think I've heard that name. Yes, I'm sure I have, but I don't remember anything about him."

The diligent Inspector Slack slid across to his superior officer a page torn from his notebook. On it was penciled: "Col. Bantry dined at Majestic last week." Melchett looked up and met the inspector's eye. The chief constable flushed. Slack was an industrious and zealous officer and Melchett disliked him a good deal, but he could not disregard the challenge. The inspector was tacitly accusing him of favoring his own class—of shielding an "old school tie." He turned to Josie. "Miss Turner, I should like you, if you do not mind, to accompany me to Gossington Hall." Coldly, defiantly, almost ignoring Josie's murmur of assent, Melchett's eyes met Slack's.

CHAPTER FIVE

St. Mary Mead was having the most exciting morning it had known for a long time. Miss Wetherby, a long-nosed, acidulated spinster, was the first to spread the intoxicating information. She dropped in upon her friend and neighbor, Miss Hartnell. "Forgive me coming so early, dear, but I thought perhaps you mightn't have heard the news."

"What news?" demanded Miss Hartnell. She had a deep bass voice and visited the poor indefatigably, however hard they tried to avoid her ministrations.

"About the body of a young woman that was found this morning in Colonel Bantry's library."

"In Colonel Bantry's library?"

"Yes. Isnt' it terrible?"

"His poor wife!" Miss Hartnell tried to disguise her deep and ardent pleasure.

"Yes, indeed. I don't suppose she had any idea."

Miss Hartnell observed censoriously, "She thought too much about her garden and not enough about her husband. You've got to keep an eye on a man all the time—all the time," repeated Miss Hartnell fiercely.

"I know. I know. It's really too dreadful."

"I wonder what Jane Marple will say? Do you think she knew anything about it? She's so sharp about these things."

"Jane Marple has gone up to Gossington."

"What? This morning?"

"Very early. Before breakfast."

"But really! I do think—well, I mean, I think that is carrying things too far. We all know Jane likes to poke her nose into things, but I call this indecent!"

"Oh, but Mrs. Bantry sent for her."

"Mrs. Bantry sent for her?"

"Well, the car came. With Muswell driving it."

"Dear me. How very peculiar."

They were silent a minute or two, digesting the news. "Whose body?" demanded Miss Hartnell.

"You know that dreadful woman who comes down with Basil Blake?"

"That terrible peroxide blonde?" Miss Hartnell was slightly behind the times. She had not yet advanced from peroxide to platinum. "The one who lies about in the garden with practically nothing on?"

"Yes, my dear. There she was on the hearthrug, strangled!"

"But what do you mean—at Gossington?" Miss Wetherby nodded with infinite meaning. "Then Colonel Bantry too—" Again Miss Wetherby nodded. "Oh!"

There was a pause as the ladies savored this new addition to village scandal. "What a wicked woman!" trumpeted Miss Hartnell with righteous wrath.

"Quite, quite abandoned, I'm afraid!"

"And Colonel Bantry—such a nice quiet man—"

Miss Wetherby said zestfully, "Those quiet ones are often the worst. Jane Marple always says so."

Mrs. Price Ridley was among the last to hear the news. A rich and dictatorial widow, she lived in a large house next door to the vicarage. Her informant was her little maid, Clara. "A woman, you say, Clara? Found dead on Colonel Bantry's hearthrug?"

"Yes, mum. And they say, mum, as she hadn't anything on at all, mum—not a stitch!"

"That will do, Clara. It is not necessary to go into details."

"No, mum, and they say, mum, that at first they thought it was Mr. Blake's young lady what comes down for the weekends with 'im to Mr. Booker's new 'ouse. But now they say it's quite a different young lady. And the fishmonger's young man, he says he'd never have believed it of Colonel Bantry—not with him handing round the plate on Sundays and all."

"There is a lot of wickedness in the world, Clara," said Mrs. Price Ridley. "Let this be a warning to you."

"Yes, mum. Mother, she never will let me take a place where there's a gentleman in the 'ouse."

"That will do, Clara," said Mrs. Price Ridley.

It was only a step from Mrs. Price Ridley's house to the vicarage. Mrs. Price Ridley was fortunate enough to find the vicar in his study. The vicar, a gentle, middle-aged man, was always the last to hear anything.

"Such a terrible thing," said Mrs. Price Ridley, panting a little because she had come rather fast. "I felt I must have your advice, your counsel about it, dear vicar."

Mr. Clement looked mildly alarmed. He said, "Has anything happened?"

"Has anything happened!" Mrs. Price Ridley repeated the question dramatically. "The most terrible scandal! None of us had any idea of it. An abandoned woman, completely unclothed, strangled on Colonel Bantry's hearthrug."

The vicar stared. He said, "You—you are feeling quite well?"

"No wonder you can't believe it! I couldn't at first! The hypocrisy of the man! All these years."

"Please tell me exactly what all this is about."

Mrs. Price Ridley plunged into a full-swing narrative. When she had finished, the Reverend Mr. Clement said mildly, "But there is nothing, is there, to point to Colonel Bantry's being involved in this?"

"Oh, dear vicar, you are so unworldly! But I must tell you a little story. Last Thursday—or was it the Thursday before—well, it doesn't matter—I was going up to London by the cheap day train. Colonel Bantry was in the same carriage. He looked, I thought, very abstracted. And nearly the whole way he buried himself behind *The Times*. As though, you know, he didn't want to talk." The vicar nodded his head with complete comprehension and possible sympathy.

"At Paddington I said good-by. He had offered to get me a taxi, but I was taking the bus down to Oxford Street; but he got into one, and I distinctly heard him tell the driver to go to—Where do you think?" Mr. Clement looked inquiring.

"An address in St. John's Wood!" Mrs. Price Ridley paused triumphantly. The vicar remained completely unenlightened. "That, I consider, proves it," said Mrs. Price Ridley.

At Gossington, Mrs. Bantry and Miss Marple were sitting in the drawing room. "You know," said Mrs. Bantry, "I can't help feeling glad they've taken the body away. It's not nice to have a body in one's house."

Miss Marple nodded. "I know, dear. I know just how you feel."

"You can't," said Mrs. Bantry. "Not until you've had one. I know you had one next door once, but that's not the same thing. I only hope," she went on, "that Arthur won't take a dislike to the library. We sit there so much. What are you doing, Jane?" For Miss Marple, with a glance at her watch, was rising to her feet.

"Well, I was thinking I'd go home, if there's nothing more I can do for you."

"Don't go yet," said Mrs. Bantry. "The fingerprint men and the photographers and most of the police have gone, I know, but I still feel something might happen. You don't want to miss anything."

The telephone rang and she went off to answer. She returned with a beaming face. "I told you more things would happen. That was Colonel Melchett. He's bringing the poor girl's cousin along."

"I wonder why?" said Miss Marple.

"Oh, I suppose to see where it happened, and all that."

"More than that, I expect," said Miss Marple.

"What do you mean, Jane?"

"Well, I think, perhaps, he might want her to meet Colonel Bantry."

Mrs. Bantry said sharply, "To see if she recognizes him? I suppose—oh, yes, I suppose they're bound to suspect Arthur."

"I'm afraid so."

"As though Arthur could have anything to do with it!"

Miss Marple was silent. Mrs. Bantry turned on her accusingly. "And don't tell me about some frightful old man who kept his housemaid. Arthur isn't like that."

"No, no, of course not."

"No, but he really isn't. He's just, sometimes, a little bit silly about pretty girls who come to tennis. You know, rather fatuous and avuncular. There's no harm in it. And why shouldn't he? After all," finished Mrs. Bantry rather obscurely, "I've got the garden."

Miss Marple smiled. "You must not worry, Dolly," she said.

"No, I don't mean to. But all the same I do, a little. So does Arthur. It's upset him. All these policemen looking about. He's gone down to the farm. Looking at pigs and things always soothes him if he's been upset. . . . Hullo, here they are."

The chief constable's car drew up outside. Colonel Melchett came in, accompanied by a smartly dressed young woman. "This is Miss Turner, Mrs. Bantry. The cousin of the—er—victim."

"How do you do," said Mrs. Bantry, advancing with outstretched hand. "All this must be rather awful for you."

Josephine Turner said frankly, "Oh, it is. None of it seems real, somehow. It's like a bad dream."

Mrs. Bantry introduced Miss Marple. Melchett said casually, "Your good man about?"

"He had to go down to one of the farms. He'll be back soon."

"Oh." Melchett seemed rather at a loss.

Mrs. Bantry said to Josie, "Would you like to see where—where it happened? Or would you rather not?"

Josephine said, after a moment's pause, "I think I'd like to see."

Mrs. Bantry led her to the library, with Miss Marple and Melchett following behind. "She was there," said Mrs. Bantry, pointing dramatically. "On the hearthrug."

"Oh!" Josie shuddered. But she also looked perplexed. She said, her brow creased, "I just can't understand it! I can't!"

"Well, we certainly can't," said Mrs. Bantry.

Josie said slowly, "It isn't the sort of place—" and broke off.

Miss Marple nodded her head gently in agreement with the unfinished sentiment. "That," she murmured, "is what makes it so very interesting."

"Come now, Miss Marple," said Colonel Melchett good-humoredly, "haven't you got an explanation?"

"Oh, yes, I've got an explanation," said Miss Marple. "Quite a feasible one. But of course it's only my own idea. Tommy Bond," she continued, "and Mrs. Martin, our new schoolmistress. She went to wind up the clock and a frog jumped out."

Josephine Turner looked puzzled. As they all went out of the room she murmured to Mrs. Bantry, "Is the old lady a bit funny in the head?"

"Not at all," said Mrs. Bantry indignantly.

Josie said, "Sorry. I thought perhaps she thought she was a frog or something."

Colonel Bantry was just coming in through the side door. Melchett hailed him and watched Josephine Turner as he introduced them. But there was no sign of interest or recognition in her face. Melchett breathed a sigh of relief. Curse Slack and his insinuations. In answer to Mrs. Bantry's questions, Josie was pouring out the story of Ruby Keene's disappearance. "Frightfully worrying for you, my dear," said Mrs. Bantry.

"I was more angry than worried," said Josie. "You see, I didn't know then."

"And yet," said Miss Marple, "you went to the police. Wasn't that—excuse me—rather premature?"

Josie said eagerly, "Oh, but I didn't. That was Mr. Jefferson."

Mrs. Bantry said, "Jefferson?"

"Yes, he's an invalid."

"Not Conway Jefferson? But I know him well. He's an old friend of ours. . . . Arthur, listen. Conway Jefferson, he's staying at the Majestic, and it was he who notified the police! Isn't that a coincidence?"

Josephine Turner said, "Mr. Jefferson was there last summer too."

"Fancy! And we never knew. I haven't seen him for a long time." She turned to Josie. "How—how is he nowadays?"

Josie considered. "I think he's wonderful, really—quite wonderful. Considering, I mean. He's always cheerful—always got a joke."

"Are the family there with him?"

"Mr. Gaskell, you mean? And young Mrs. Jefferson? And Peter? Oh, yes."

There was something inhibiting in Josephine Turner's rather attractive frankness of manner. When she spoke of the Jeffersons there was something not quite natural in her voice. Mrs. Bantry said, "They're both very nice, aren't they? The young ones, I mean."

Josie said rather uncertainly, "Oh, yes; yes, they are. I—we—yes, they are really."

"And what," demanded Mrs. Bantry as she looked through the window at the retreating car of the chief constable, "did she mean by that? 'They are really.' Don't you think, Jane, that there's something—"

Miss Marple fell upon the words eagerly. "Oh, I do; indeed I do. It's quite unmistakable! Her manner changed at once when the Jeffersons were mentioned. She had seemed quite natural up to then."

"But what do you think it is, Jane?"

"Well, my dear, you know them. All I feel is that there is something, as you say, about them which is worrying that young woman. Another thing. Did you notice that when you asked her if she wasn't anxious about the girl being missing, she said that she was angry? And she looked angry—really angry! That strikes me as interesting, you know. I have a feeling—perhaps I'm wrong—that that's her main reaction to the fact of the girl's death. She didn't care for her, I'm sure. She's not grieving in any way. But I do think, very definitely, that the thought of that girl, Ruby Keene, makes her angry. And the interesting point is: Why?"

"We'll find out!" said Mrs. Bantry. "We'll go over to Danemouth and stay at the Majestic—yes, Jane, you too. I need a change for my nerves after what has happened here. A few days at the Majestic—that's what we need. And you'll meet Conway Jefferson. He's a dear—a perfect dear. It's the saddest story imaginable. He had a son and a daughter, both of whom he loved dearly. They were both married, but they still spent a lot of time at home. His wife, too, was the sweetest woman, and he was devoted to her. They were flying home one year from France and there was an accident. They were all killed. The pilot, Mrs. Jefferson, Rosamund and Frank. Conway had both legs so badly injured they had to be amputated. And he's been wonderful—his courage, his pluck. He was a very active man, and now he's a helpless cripple, but he never complains. His daughter-in-law lives with him; she was a widow when Frank Jefferson married her, and she had a son by her first marriage—Peter Carmody. They both live with Conway. And Mark Gaskell, Rosamund's husband, is there, too, most of the time. The whole thing was the most awful tragedy."

"And now," said Miss Marple, "there's another tragedy."

Mrs. Bantry said, "Oh, yes, yes, but it's nothing to do with the Jeffersons."

"Isn't it? said Miss Marple. "It was Mr. Jefferson who reported to the police."

"So he did. You know, Jane, that is curious."

CHAPTER SIX

Colonel Melchett was facing a much annoyed hotel manager. With him was Superintendent Harper, of the Glenshire police, and the inevitable Inspector Slack—the latter rather disgruntled at the chief constable's willful usurpation of the case. Superintendent Harper was inclined to be soothing with the almost tearful Mr. Prestcott; Colonel Melchett tended toward a blunt brutality. "No good crying over spilt milk," he said sharply. "The girl's dead—strangled. You're lucky that she wasn't strangled in your hotel. This puts the inquiry in a different county and lets your establishment down extremely lightly. But certain inquiries have got to be made, and the sooner we get on with it the better. You can trust us to be discreet and tactful. So I

suggest you cut the cackle and come to the horses. Just what, exactly, do
you know about the girl?"

"I know nothing of her—nothing at all. Josie brought her here."

"Josie's been here some time?"

"Two years—no, three."

"And you like her?"

"Yes, Josie's a good girl—a nice girl. Competent. She gets on with people
and smooths over differences. Bridge, you know, is a touchy sort of game."
Colonel Melchett nodded feelingly. His wife was a keen but an extremely
bad bridge player. Mr. Prestcott went on, "Josie was very good at calming
down unpleasantness. She could handle people well—sort of bright and
firm, if you know what I mean."

Again Melchett nodded. He knew now what it was that Miss Josephine
Turner had reminded him of. In spite of the makeup and the smart turnout,
there was a distinct touch of the nursery governess about her.

"I depend upon her," went on Mrs. Prestcott. His manner became
aggrieved. "What does she want to go playing about on slippery rocks in
that damn-fool way for? We've got a nice beach here. Why couldn't she
bathe from that? Slipping and falling and breaking her ankle! It wasn't fair
to me! I pay her to dance and play bridge and keep people happy and
amused, not to go bathing off rocks and breaking her ankle. Dancers ought
to be careful of their ankles, not take risks. I was very annoyed about it. It
wasn't fair to the hotel."

Melchett cut the recital short. "And then she suggested that this girl—her
cousin—come down?"

Prestcott assented grudgingly. "That's right. It sounded quite a good
idea. Mind you, I wasn't going to pay anything extra. The girl could have
her keep, but as for salary, that would have to be fixed up between her and
Josie. That's the way it was arranged. I didn't know anything about the
girl."

"But she turned out all right?"

"Oh, yes, there wasn't anything wrong with her—not to look at, anyway.
She was very young, of course; rather cheap in style, perhaps, for a place of
this kind, but nice manners—quiet and well-behaved. Danced well. People
liked her."

"Pretty?"

It had been a question hard to answer from a view of the blue, swollen
face. Mr. Prestcott considered. "Fair to middling. Bit weaselly, if you know
what I mean. Wouldn't have been much without makeup. As it was, she
managed to look quite attractive."

"Many young men hanging about after her?"

"I know what you're trying to get at, sir." Mr. Prestcott became excited.
"I never saw anything! Nothing special. One or two of the boys hung
around a bit, but all in the day's work, so to speak. Nothing in the
strangling line, I'd say. She got on well with the older people, too; had a
kind of prattling way with her. Seemed quite a kid, if you know what I
mean. It amused them."

Superintendent Harper said in a deep, melancholy voice, "Mr. Jefferson,
for instance?"

The manager agreed. "Yes, Mr. Jefferson was the one I had in mind. She
used to sit with him and his family a lot. He used to take her out for drives

sometimes. Mr. Jefferson's very fond of young people and very good to them. I don't want to have any misunderstanding. Mr. Jefferson's a cripple. He can't get about much—only where his wheelchair will take him. But he's always keen on seeing young people enjoy themselves; watches the tennis and the bathing, and all that, and gives parties for young people here. He likes youth, and there's nothing bitter about him, as there well might be. A very popular gentleman and, I'd say, a very fine character."

Melchett asked, "And he took an interest in Ruby Keene?"

"Her talk amused him, I think."

"Did his family share his liking for her?"

"They were always very pleasant to her."

Harper said, "And it was he who reported the fact of her being missing to the police?"

He contrived to put into the words a significance and a reproach to which the manager instantly responded, "Put yourself in my place, Mr. Harper. I didn't dream for a minute anything was wrong. Mr. Jefferson came along to my office, storming and all worked up. The girl hadn't slept in her room. She hadn't appeared in her dance last night. She must have gone for a drive and had an accident, perhaps. The police must be informed at once. Inquiries made. In a state, he was, and quite highhanded. He rang up the police station then and there."

"Without consulting Miss Turner?"

"Josie didn't like it much. I could see that. She was very annoyed about the whole thing—annoyed with Ruby, I mean. But what could she say?"

"I think," said Melchett, "we'd better see Mr. Jefferson. . . . Eh, Harper?"

Superintendent Harper agreed. Mr. Prestcott went up with them to Conway Jefferson's suite. It was on the first floor, overlooking the sea. Melchett said carelessly, "Does himself pretty well, eh? Rich man?"

"Very well off indeed, I believe. Nothing's ever stinted when he comes here. Best rooms reserved, food usually à la carte, expensive wines—best of everything."

Melchett nodded. Mr. Prestcott tapped on the outer door and a woman's voice said, "Come in."

The manager entered, the others behind him. Mr. Prestcott's manner was apologetic as he spoke to the woman who turned her head, at their entrance, from her seat by the window. "I am so sorry to disturb you, Mrs. Jefferson, but these gentlemen are from the police. They are very anxious to have a word with Mr. Jefferson. Er—Colonel Melchett, Superintendent Harper, Inspector—er—Slack, Mrs. Jefferson!" Mrs. Jefferson acknowledged the introduction by bending her head.

A plain woman, was Melchett's first impression. Then, as a slight smile came to her lips and she spoke, he changed his opinion. She had a singularly charming and sympathetic voice, and her eyes—clear hazel eyes—were beautiful. She was quietly but not unbecomingly dressed and was, he judged, about thirty-five years of age. She said, "My father-in-law is asleep. He is not strong at all, and this affair has been a terrible shock to him. We had to have the doctor, and the doctor gave him a sedative. As soon as he wakes he will, I know, want to see you. In the meantime, perhaps I can help you? Won't you sit down?"

Mr. Prestcott, anxious to escape, said to Colonel Melchett, "Well—er—if that's all I can do for you—" and thankfully received permission to depart.

With his closing of the door behind him, the atmosphere took on a mellow and more social quality. Adelaide Jefferson had the power of creating a restful atmosphere. She was a woman who never seemed to say anything remarkable, but who succeeded in stimulating other people to talk and in setting them at their ease. She struck, now, the right note when she said, "This business has shocked us all very much. We saw quite a lot of the poor girl, you know. It seems quite unbelievable. My father-in-law is terribly upset. He was very fond of Ruby."

Colonel Melchett said, "It was Mr. Jefferson, I understand, who reported her disappearance to the police."

He wanted to see exactly how she would react to that. There was a flicker—just a flicker—of—annoyance?—concern?—he could not say what exactly, but there was something, and it seemed to him that she had definitely to brace herself, as though to an unpleasant task, before going on. She said, "Yes, that is so. Being an invalid, he gets easily upset and worried. We tried to persuade him that it was all right, that there was some natural explanation, and that the girl herself would not like the police being notified. He insisted. Well"—she made a slight gesture—"he was right and we were wrong!"

Melchett asked, "Exactly how well did you know Ruby Keene, Mrs. Jefferson?"

She considered. "It's difficult to say. My father-in-law is very fond if young people and likes to have them round him. Ruby was a new type to him; he was amused and interested by her chatter. She sat with us a good deal in the hotel and my father-in-law took her out for drives in the car."

Her voice was quite noncommittal. Melchett thought: *She could say more if she chose.* He said, "Will you tell me what you can of the course of events last night?"

"Certainly, but there is very little that will be useful, I'm afraid. After dinner Ruby came and sat with us in the lounge. She remained even after the dancing had started. We had arranged to play bridge later, but we were waiting for Mark—that is, Mark Gaskell, my brother-in-law—he married Mr. Jefferson's daughter, you know—who had some important letters to write, and also for Josie. She was going to make a fourth with us."

"Did that often happen?"

"Quite frequently. She's a first-class player, of course, and very nice. My father-in-law is a keen bridge player and, whenever possible, liked to get hold of Josie to make the fourth, instead of an outsider. Naturally, as she has to arrange the fours, she can't always play with us, but she does whenever she can, and as"—her eyes smiled a little—"my father-in-law spends a lot of money in the hotel, the management is quite pleased for Josie to favor us."

Melchett asked, "You like Josie?"

"Yes, I do. She's always good-humored and cheerful, works hard and seems to enjoy her job. She's shrewd without being at all intellectual and—well, never pretends about anything. She's natural and unaffected."

"Please go on, Mrs. Jefferson."

"As I say, Josie had to get her bridge fours arranged and Mark was writing, so Ruby sat and talked with us a little longer than usual. Then Josie came along, and Ruby went off to do her first solo dance with Raymond—

he's the dance and tennis professional. She came back to us afterward, just as Mark joined us. Then she went off to dance with a young man and we four started our bridge." She stopped and made a slight, significant gesture of helplessness. "And that's all I know! I just caught a glimpse of her once, dancing, but bridge is an absorbing game and I hardly glanced through the glass partition at the ballroom. Then, at midnight, Raymond came along to Josie very upset and asked where Ruby was. Josie, naturally, tried to shut him up, but—"

Superintendent Harper interrupted. He said in his quiet voice, "Why 'naturally,' Mrs. Jefferson?"

"Well—" She hesitated; looked, Melchett thought, a little put out. "Josie didn't want the girl's absence made too much of. She considered herself responsible for her in a way. She said Ruby was probably up in her bedroom, said the girl had talked about having a headache earlier. I don't think that was true, by the way; Josie said it by way of excuse. Raymond went off and telephoned up to Ruby's room, but apparently there was no answer, and he came back in rather a state—temperamental, you know. Josie went off with him and tried to soothe him down, and in the end she danced with him instead of Ruby. Rather plucky of her, because you could see afterward it had hurt her ankle. She came back to us when the dance was over and tried to calm down Mr. Jefferson. He had got worked up by then. We persuaded him, in the end, to go to bed; told him Ruby had probably gone for a spin in a car and that they'd had a puncture. He went to bed worried and this morning he began to agitate at once." She paused. "The rest you know."

"Thank you, Mrs. Jefferson. Now I'm going to ask you if you've any idea who could have done this thing?"

She said immediately, "No idea whatever. I'm afraid I can't help you in the slightest."

He pressed her. "The girl never said anything? Nothing about jealousy? About some man she was afraid of? Or intimate with?"

Adelaide Jefferson shook her head to each query. There seemed nothing more that she could tell them. The superintendent suggested that they should interview young George Bartlett and return to see Mr. Jefferson later. Colonel Melchett agreed and the three men went out, Mrs. Jefferson promising to send word as soon as Mr. Jefferson was awake. "Nice woman," said the colonel, as they closed the door behind them.

"A very nice lady indeed," said Superintendent Harper.

CHAPTER SEVEN

George Bartlett was a thin, lanky youth with a prominent Adam's apple and an immense difficulty in saying what he meant. He was in such a state of dither that it was hard to get a calm statement from him. "I say, it is awful, isn't it? Sort of thing one reads about in the Sunday papers, but one doesn't feel it really happens, don't you know?"

"Unfortunately there is no doubt about it, Mr. Bartlett," said the superintendent.

"No, no, of course not. But it seems so rum somehow. And miles from here and everything—in some country house, wasn't it? Awfully county and all that. Created a bit of a stir in the neighborhood, what?"

Colonel Melchett took charge. "How well did you know the dead girl, Mr. Bartlett?"

George Bartlett looked alarmed. "Oh, n-n-not well at all, s-s-sir. No, hardly, if you know what I mean. Danced with her once or twice, passed the time of day, bit of tennis—you know!"

"You were, I think, the last person to see her alive last night?"

"I suppose I was. Doesn't it sound awful? I mean she was perfectly all right when I saw her—absolutely."

"What time was that, Mr. Bartlett?"

"Well, you know, I never know about time. Wasn't very late, if you know what I mean."

"You danced with her?"

"Yes, as a matter of fact—well, yes, I did. Early on in the evening, though. Tell you what. It was just after her exhibition dance with the pro fellow. Must have been ten, half past, eleven—I don't know."

"Never mind the time. We can fix that. Please tell us exactly what happened."

"Well, we danced, don't you know. Not that I'm much of a dancer."

"How you dance is not really relevant, Mr. Bartlett."

George Bartlett cast an alarmed eye on the colonel and stammered, "No—er—n-n-no, I suppose it isn't. Well, as I say, we danced round and round, and I talked, but Ruby didn't say very much, and she yawned a bit. As I say, I don't dance awfully well, and so girls—well, inclined to give it a miss, if you know what I mean too. I know where I get off, so I said 'righty ho,' and that was that."

"What was the last you saw of her?"

"She went off upstairs."

"She said nothing about meeting anyone? Or going for a drive? Or—or having a date?" The colonel used the colloquial expression with a slight effort.

Bartlett shook his head. "Not to me." He looked rather mournful. "Just gave me the push."

"What was her manner? Did she seem anxious, abstracted, anything on her mind?"

George Bartlett considered. Then he shook his head. "Seemed a bit bored. Yawned, as I said. Nothing more."

Colonel Melchett said, "And what did you do, Mr. Bartlett?"

"Eh?"

"What did you do when Ruby Keene left you?"

George Bartlett gaped at him. "Let's see now. What did I do?"

"We're waiting for you to tell us."

"Yes, yes, of course. Jolly difficult, remembering things, what? Let me see, Shouldn't be surprised if I went into the bar and had a drink."

"Did you go into the bar and have a drink?"

"That's just it. I did have a drink. Don't think it was just then. Have an idea I wandered out, don't you know. Bit of air. Rather stuffy for September. Very nice outside. Yes, that's it. I strolled around a bit, then I came in and had a drink, and then I strolled back to the ballroom. Wasn't much doing. Noticed what's-er-name—Josie—was dancing again. With the tennis fellow. She'd been on the sick list—twisted ankle or something."

"That fixes the time of your return at midnight. Do you intend us to understand that you spent over an hour walking about outside?"

"Well, I had a drink, you know. I was—well, I was thinking of things."

This statement received more incredulity than any other. Colonel Melchett said sharply, "What were you thinking about?"

"Oh, I don't know. Things," said Mr. Bartlett vaguely.

"You have a car, Mr. Bartlett?"

"Oh, yes, I've got a car."

"Where was it—in the hotel garage?"

"No, it was in the courtyard, as a matter of fact. Thought I might go for a spin, you see."

"Perhaps you did go for a spin?"

"No, no, I didn't. Swear I didn't."

"You didn't, for instance, take Miss Keene for a spin?"

"Oh, I say, look here. What are you getting at? I didn't, I swear I didn't. Really, now."

"Thank you, Mr. Bartlett. I don't think there is anything more at the present. At present," repeated Colonel Melchett, with a good deal of emphasis on the words.

They left Mr. Bartlett looking after them with a ludicrous expression of alarm on his unintellectual face. "Brainless young ass," said Colonel Melchett. "Or isn't he?"

Superintendent Harper shook his head. "We've got a long way to go," he said.

CHAPTER EIGHT

Neither the night porter nor the barman proved helpful. The night porter remembered ringing up Miss Keene's room just after midnight and getting no reply. He had not noticed Mr. Bartlett leaving or entering the hotel. A lot of gentlemen and ladies were strolling in and out, the night being fine. And there were side doors off the corridor as well as the one in the main hall. He was fairly certain Miss Keene had not gone out by the main door, but if she had come down from her room, which was on the first floor, there was a staircase next to it and a door out at the end of the corridor leading onto the side terrace. She could have gone out of that, unseen, easily enough. It was not locked until the dancing was over at two o'clock.

The barman remembered Mr. Bartlett being in the bar the preceding evening, but could not say when. Somewhere about the middle of the evening, he thought. Mr. Bartlett had sat against the wall and was looking rather melancholy. He did not know how long he was in there. There were a lot of outside guests coming and going in the bar. He had noticed Mr. Bartlett, but he couldn't fix the time in any way.

As they left the bar they were accosted by a small boy about nine years old. He burst immediately into excited speech. "I say, are you the detectives? I'm Peter Carmody. It was my grandfather, Mr. Jefferson, who rang up the police about Ruby. Are you from Scotland Yard? You don't mind my speaking to you, do you?"

Colonel Melchett looked as though he were about to return a short answer, but Superintendent Harper intervened. He spoke benignly and heartily. "That's all right, my son. Naturally interests you, I expect?"

"You bet it does. Do you like detective stories? I do. I read them all and I've got autographs from Dorothy Sayers and Agatha Christie and Dickson Carr and H. C. Bailey. Will the murder be in the papers?"

"It'll be in the papers all right," said Superintendent Harper grimly.

"You see, I'm going back to school next week and I shall tell them all that I knew her—really knew her well."

"What did you think of her, eh?"

Peter considered. "Well, I didn't like her very much. I think she was rather a stupid sort of girl. Mum and Uncle Mark didn't like her much, either. Only grandfather. Grandfather wants to see you, by the way. Edwards is looking for you."

Superintendent Harper murmured encouragingly, "So your mother and your Uncle Mark didn't like Ruby Keene much? Why was that?"

"Oh, I don't know. She was always butting in. And they didn't like grandfather making such a fuss of her. I expect," said Peter cheerfully, "that they're glad she's dead."

Superintendent Harper looked at him thoughtfully. He said, "Did you hear them—er—say so?"

"Well, not exactly. Uncle Mark said, 'Well, it's one way out anyway,' and mum said, 'Yes, but such a horrible one,' and Uncle Mark said it was no good being hypocritical."

The men exchanged glances. At that moment a clean-shaven man neatly dressed in blue serge came up to them. "Excuse me, gentlemen. I am Mr. Jefferson's valet. He is awake now and sent me to find you, as he is very anxious to see you."

Once more they went up to Conway Jefferson's suite. In the sitting room Adelaide Jefferson was talking to a tall, restless man who was prowling nervously about the room. He swung around sharply to view the new-comers. "Oh, yes. Glad you've come. My father-in-law's been asking for you. He's awake now. Keep him as calm as you can, won't you? His health's not too good. It's a wonder, really, that this shock didn't do for him."

Harper said, "I'd no idea his health was as bad as that."

"He doesn't know it himself," said Mark Gaskell. "It's his heart, you see. The doctor warned Addie that he mustn't be overexcited or startled. He more or less hinted that the end might come any time, didn't he, Addie?"

Mrs. Jefferson nodded. She said, "It's incredible that he's rallied the way he has."

Melchett said dryly, "Murder isn't exactly a soothing incident. We'll be as careful as we can." He was sizing up Mark Gaskell as he spoke. He didn't much care for the fellow. A bold, unscrupulous, hawklike face. One of those men who usually get their own way and whom women frequently admire. *But not the sort of fellow I'd trust,* the colonel thought to himself. Unscrupulous—that was the word for him. The sort of fellow who wouldn't stick at anything.

In the big bedroom overlooking the sea, Conway Jefferson was sitting in his wheelchair by the window. No sooner were you in the room with him than you felt the power and magnetism of the man. It was as though the injuries which had left him a cripple had resulted in concentrating the vitality of his shattered body into a narrower and more intense focus. He had a fine head, the red of the hair slightly grizzled. The face was rugged and powerful, deeply sun-tanned, and the eyes were a startling blue. There was no sign of illness or feebleness about him. The deep lines on his face were the lines of suffering, not the lines of weakness. Here was a man who would never rail against fate, but accept it and pass on to victory. He said, "I'm glad you've come." His quick eyes took them in. He said to Melchett, "You're the chief constable of Radfordshire? Right. And you're Superintendent Harper? Sit down. Cigarettes on the table beside you."

They thanked him and sat down. Melchett said, "I understand, Mr. Jefferson, that you were interested in the dead girl?"

A quick, twisted smile flashed across the lined face. "Yes, they'll all have told you that! Well, it's no secret. How much has my family said to you?" He looked quickly from one to the other as he asked the question.

It was Melchett who answered. "Mrs. Jefferson told us very little beyond the fact that the girl's chatter amused you and that she was by way of being a protégée. We have only exchanged half a dozen words with Mr. Gaskell."

Conway Jefferson smiled. "Addie's a discreet creature, bless her. Mark would probably have been more outspoken. I think, Melchett, that I'd better tell you some facts rather fully. It's necessary, in order that you should understand my attitude. And, to begin with, it's necessary that I go back to the big tragedy of my life. Eight years ago I lost my wife, my son and my daughter in an airplane accident. Since then I've been like a man who's lost half himself—and I'm not speaking of my physical plight! I was a family man. My daughter-in-law and my son-in-law have been very good to me. They've done all they can to take the place of my flesh and blood. But I've realized—especially of late—that they have, after all, their own lives to live. So you must understand that, essentially, I'm a lonely man. I like young people. I enjoy them. Once or twice I've played with the idea of adopting some girl or boy. During this last month I got very friendly with the child who's been killed. She was absolutely natural—completely naïve. She chattered on about her life and her experiences—in pantomime, with touring companies, with mum and dad as a child in cheap lodgings. Such a different life from any I've known! Never complaining, never seeing it as sordid. Just a natural, uncomplaining, hard-working child, unspoiled and charming. Not a lady, perhaps, but thank God neither vulgar nor— abominable word—ladylike. I got more and more fond of Ruby. I decided, gentlemen, to adopt her legally. She would become, by law, my daughter.

That, I hope, explains my concern for her and the steps I took when I heard of her unaccountable disappearance."

There was a pause. Then Superintendent Harper, his unemotional voice robbing the question of any offense, asked, "May I ask what your son-in-law and daughter-in-law said to that?"

Jefferson's answer came back quickly. "What could they say? They didn't, perhaps, like it very much. It's the sort of thing that arouses prejudice. But they behaved very well—yes, very well. It's not as though, you see, they were dependent on me. When my son Frank married, I turned over half my worldly goods to him then and there. I believe in that. Don't let your children wait until you're dead. They want the money when they're young, not when they're middle-aged. In the same way, when my daughter Rosamund insisted on marrying a poor man, I settled a big sum of money on her. That sum passed to him at her death. So, you see, that simplified the matter from the financial angle."

"I see, Mr. Jefferson," said Superintendent Harper.

But there was a certain reserve in his tone. Conway Jefferson pounced upon it. "But you don't agree, eh?"

"It's not for me to say, sir, but families, in my experience, don't always act reasonable."

"I daresay you're right, superintendent, but you must remember that Mr. Gaskell and Mrs. Jefferson aren't, strictly speaking, my family. They're not blood relations."

"That, of course, makes a difference," admitted the superintendent.

For a moment Conway Jefferson's eyes twinkled. He said, "That's not to say that they didn't think me an old fool! That would be the average person's reaction. But I wasn't being a fool! I know character. With education and polishing, Ruby Keene could have taken her place anywhere."

Melchett said, "I'm afraid we're being rather impertinent and inquisitive, but it's important that we should get at all the facts. You proposed to make full provision for the girl—that is, settle money upon her—but you hadn't already done so?"

Jefferson said, "I understand what you're driving at—the possibility of someone's benefiting by the girl's death. But nobody could. The necessary formalities for legal adoption were under way, but they hadn't yet been completed."

Melchett said slowly, "Then, if anything happened to you?" He left the sentence unfinished, as a query.

Conway Jefferson was quick to respond, "Nothing's likely to happen to me! I'm a cripple, but I'm not an invalid. Although doctors do like to pull long faces and give advice about not overdoing things. Not overdoing things! I'm as strong as a horse! Still, I'm quite aware of the fatalities of life. I've good reason to be! Sudden death comes to the strongest man—especially in these days of road casualties. But I'd provided for that. I made a new will about ten days ago."

"Yes?" Superintendent Harper leaned forward.

"I left the sum of fifty thousand pounds to be held in trust for Ruby Keene until she was twenty-five, when she would come into the principal."

Superintendent Harper's eyes opened. So did Colonel Melchett's. Harper said in an almost awed voice, "That's a very large sum of money, Mr. Jefferson."

"In these days, yes, it is."

"And you were leaving it to a girl you had only known a few weeks?"

Anger flashed into the vivid blue eyes. "Must I go on repeating the same thing over and over again? I've no flesh and blood of my own—no nieces or nephews or distant cousins, even! I might have left it to charity. I prefer to leave it to an individual." He laughed. "Cinderella turned into a princess overnight! A fairy godfather instead of a fairy godmother. Why not? It's my money. I made it."

Colonel Melchett asked, "Any other bequests?"

"A small legacy to Edwards, my valet, and the remainder to Mark and Addie in equal shares."

"Would—excuse me—the residue amount to a large sum?"

"Probably not. It's difficult to say exactly; investments fluctuate all the time. The sum involved, after death duties and expenses had been paid, would probably have come to something between five and ten thousand pounds net."

"I see."

"And you needn't think I was treating them shabbily. As I said, I divided up my estate at the time my children married. I left myself, actually, a very small sum. But after—after the tragedy I wanted something to occupy my mind. I flung myself into business. At my house in London I had a private line put in, connecting my bedroom with my office. I worked hard; it helped me not to think, and it made me feel that my—my mutilation had not vanquished me. I threw myself into work"—his voice took on a deeper note; he spoke more to himself than to his audience—"and by some subtle irony, everything I did prospered! My wildest speculations succeeded. If I gambled, I won. Everything I touched turned to gold. Fate's ironic way of righting the balance, I suppose."

The lines of suffering stood out on his face again. Recollecting himself, he smiled wryly at them.

"So, you see, the sum of money I left Ruby was indisputably mine, to do with as my fancy dictated."

Melchett said quickly, "Undoubtedly, my dear fellow. We are not questioning that for a moment."

Conway Jefferson said, "Good. Now I want to ask some questions in my turn, if I may. I want to hear more about this terrible business. All I know is that she—that little Ruby was found strangled in a house some twenty miles from here."

"That is correct. At Gossington Hall."

Jefferson frowned. "Gossington? But that's—"

"Colonel Bantry's house."

"Bantry! Arthur Bantry? But I know him. Know him and his wife! Met them abroad some years ago. I didn't realize they lived in this part of the world. Why, it's—" He broke off.

Superintendent Harper slipped in smoothly, "Colonel Bantry was dining in the hotel here Tuesday of last week. You didn't see him?"

"Tuesday? Tuesday? No, we were back late. Went over to Harden Head and had dinner on the way back."

Melchett said, "Ruby Keene never mentioned the Bantrys to you?"

Jefferson shook his head. "Never. Don't believe she knew them. Sure she didn't. She didn't know anybody but theatrical folk and that sort of thing." He paused, and then asked abruptly, "What's Bantry got to say about it?"

"He can't account for it in the least. He was out at a Conservative meeting last night. The body was discovered this morning. He says he's never seen the girl in his life."

Jefferson nodded. He said, "It certainly seems fantastic."

Superintendent Harper cleared his throat. He said, "Have you any idea at all, sir, who can have done this?"

"Good God, I wish I had!" The veins stood out on his forehead. "It's incredible, unimaginable! I'd say it couldn't have happened, if it hadn't happened!"

"There's no friend of hers from her past life, no man hanging about or threatening her?"

"I'm sure there isn't. She'd have told me if so. She's never had a regular boyfriend. She told me so herself." Superintendent Harper thought, *Yes, I daresay that's what she told you. But that's as may be.* Conway Jefferson went on, "Josie would know better than anyone if there had been some man hanging about Ruby or pestering her. Can't she help?"

"She says not."

Jefferson said, frowning, "I can't help feeling it must be the work of some maniac—the brutality of the method, breaking into a country house, the whole thing so unconnected and senseless. There are men of that type, men outwardly sane, but who decoy girls, sometimes children, away and kill them."

Harper said, "Oh, yes, there are such cases, but we've no knowledge of anyone of that kind operating in this neighborhood."

Jefferson went on, "I've thought over all the various men I've seen with Ruby. Guests here and outsiders—men she'd danced with. They all seem harmless enough—the usual type. She had no special friend of any kind."

Superintendent Harper's face remained quite impassive, but, unseen by Conway Jefferson, there was still a speculative glint in his eye. It was quite possible, he thought, that Ruby Keene might have had a special friend, even though Conway Jefferson did not know about it. He said nothing, however.

The chief constable gave him a glance of inquiry and then rose to his feet. He said, "Thank you, Mr. Jefferson. That's all we need for the present."

Jefferson said, "You'll keep me informed of your progress?"

"Yes, yes, we'll keep in touch with you."

The two men went out. Conway Jefferson leaned back in his chair. His eyelids came down and veiled the fierce blue of his eyes. He looked, suddenly, a very tired man. Then, after a minute or two, the lids flickered. He called, "Edwards?"

From the next room the valet appeared promptly. Edwards knew his master as no one else did. Others, even his nearest, knew only his strength; Edwards knew his weakness. He had seen Conway Jefferson tired, discouraged, weary of life, momentarily defeated by infirmity and loneliness.

"Yes, sir?"

Jefferson said, "Get on to Sir Henry Clithering. He's at Melborne Abbas.

Ask him, from me, to get here today if he can, instead of tomorrow. Tell him it's very urgent."

CHAPTER NINE

When they were outside Jefferson's door, Superintendent Harper said, "Well, for what it's worth, we've got a motive, sir."

"H'm," said Melchett. "Fifty thousand pounds, eh?"

"Yes, sir. Murder's been done for a good deal less than that."

"Yes, but—"

Colonel Melchett left the sentence unfinished. Harper, however, understood him. "You don't think it's likely in his case? Well, I don't either, as far as that goes. But it's got to be gone into, all the same."

"Oh, of course."

Harper went on, "If, as Mr. Jefferson says, Mr. Gaskell and Mrs. Jefferson are already well provided for and in receipt of a comfortable income, well, it's not likely they'd set out to do a brutal murder."

"Quite so. Their financial standing will have to be investigated, of course. Can't say I like the appearance of Gaskell much—looks a sharp, unscrupulous sort of fellow—but that's a long way from making him out a murderer."

"Oh, yes, sir, as I say, I don't think it's likely to be either of them, and from what Josie said I don't see how it would have been humanly possible. They were both playing bridge from twenty minutes to eleven until midnight. No, to my mind, there's another possibility much more likely."

Melchett said, "Boyfriend of Ruby Keene's?"

"That's it, sir. Some disgruntled young fellow; not too strong in the head perhaps. Someone, I'd say, she knew before she came here. This adoption scheme, if he got wise to it, may just have put the lid on things. He saw himself losing her, saw her being removed to a different sphere of life altogether, and he went mad and blind with rage. He got her to come out and meet him last night, had a row with her over it, lost his head completely and did her in."

"And how did she come to be in Bantry's library?"

"I think that's feasible. They were out, say, in his car at the time. He came to himself, realized what he'd done, and his first thought was how to get rid of the body. Say they were near the gates of a big house at the time. The idea comes to him that if she's found there the hue and cry will center round the house and its occupants and will leave him comfortably out of it. She's a little bit of a thing. He could easily carry her. He's got a chisel in the car. He forces a window and plops her down on the hearthrug. Being a strangling case, there's no blood or mess to give him away in the car. See what I mean, sir?"

"Oh, yes, Harper, it's all perfectly possible. But there's still one thing to be done. *Cherchez l'homme.*"

"What? Oh, very good, sir." Superintendent Harper tactfully applauded Melchett's joke, although, owing to the excellence of the colonel's French accent, he almost missed the sense of the words.

"Oh—er—I say—er—c-c-could I speak to you a minute?" It was George Bartlett who thus waylaid the two men.

Colonel Melchett, who was not attracted to Mr. Bartlett, and who was eager to see how Slack had got on with the investigation of the girl's room and the questioning of the chambermaids, barked sharply, "Well, what is it—what is it?"

Young Mr. Bartlett retreated a step or two, opening and shutting his mouth and giving an unconscious imitation of a fish in a tank. "Well—er— probably isn't important, don't you know. Thought I ought to tell you. Matter of fact, can't find my car."

"What do you mean, can't find your car?" Stammering a good deal, Mr. Bartlett explained that what he meant was that he couldn't find his car.

Superintendent Harper said, "Do you mean it's been stolen?"

George Bartlett turned gratefully to the more placid voice. "Well, that's just it, you know. I mean, one can't tell, can one? I mean someone may just have buzzed off in it, not meaning any harm, if you know what I mean."

"When did you last see it, Mr. Bartlett?"

"Well, I was tryin' to remember. Funny how difficult it is to remember anything, isn't it?"

Colonel Melchett said coldly, "Not, I should think, to a normal intelligence. I understood you to say that it was in the courtyard of the hotel last night."

Mr. Bartlett was bold enough to interrupt. He said, "That's just it—was it?"

"What do you mean by 'was it'? You said it was."

"Well, I mean I thought it was. I mean—well, I didn't go out and look, don't you see?"

Colonel Melchett sighed. He summoned all his patience. He said, "Let's get this quite clear. When was the last time you saw—actually saw—your car? What make is it, by the way?"

"Minoan Fourteen."

"And you last saw it when?"

George Bartlett's Adam's apple jerked convulsively up and down. "Been trying to think. Had it before lunch yesterday. Was going for a spin in the afternoon. But somehow—you know how it is—went to sleep instead. Then, after tea, had a game of squash and all that, and a bath afterward."

"And the car was then in the courtyard of the hotel?"

"Suppose so. I mean, that's where I'd put it. Thought, you see, I'd take someone for a spin. After dinner, I mean. But it wasn't my lucky evening. Nothing doing. Never took the old bus out after all."

Harper said, "But as far as you knew, the car was still in the courtyard?"

"Well, naturally. I mean, I'd put it there, what?"

"Would you have noticed if it had not been there?"

Mr. Bartlett shook his head. "Don't think so, you know. Lot of cars going and coming and all that. Plenty of Minoans."

Superintendent Harper nodded. He had just cast a casual glance out of the window. There were at that moment no fewer than eight Minoan 14's in the courtyard—it was the popular cheap car of the year.

"Aren't you in the habit of putting your car away at night?" asked Colonel Melchett.

"Don't usually bother," said Mr. Bartlett. "Fine weather and all that, you know. Such a fag putting a car away in a garage."

Glancing at Colonel Melchett, Superintendent Harper said, "I'll join you upstairs, sir. I'll just get hold of Sergeant Higgins and he can take down particulars from Mr. Bartlett."

"Right, Harper."

Mr. Bartlett murmured wistfully, "Thought I ought to let you know, you know. Might be important, what?"

Mr. Prestcott had supplied his additional dancer with board and lodging. Whatever the board, the lodging was the poorest the hotel possessed. Josephine Turner and Ruby Keene had occupied rooms at the extreme end of a mean and dingy little corridor. The rooms were small, faced north onto a portion of the cliff that backed the hotel, and were furnished with the odds and ends of suites that had once represented luxury and magnificence in the best suites. Now, when the hotel had been modernized and the bedrooms supplied with built-in receptacles for clothes, these large Victorian oak and mahogany wardrobes were relegated to those rooms occupied by the hotel's resident staff, or given to guests in the height of the season when all the rest of the hotel was full.

As Melchett and Harper saw at once, the position of Ruby Keene's room was ideal for the purpose of leaving the hotel without being observed, and was particularly unfortunate from the point of view of throwing light on the circumstances of that departure. At the end of the corridor was a small staircase which led down to an equally obscure corridor on the ground floor. Here there was a glass door which led out on the side terrace of the hotel, an unfrequented terrace with no view. You could go from it to the main terrace in front, or you could go down a winding path and come out in a lane that eventually rejoined the cliff road. Its surface being bad, it was seldom used.

Inspector Slack had been busy harrying chambermaids and examining Ruby's room for clues. They had been lucky enough to find the room exactly as it had been left the night before. Ruby Keene had not been in the habit of rising early. Her usual procedure, Slack discovered, was to sleep until about ten or half past and then ring for breakfast. Consequently, since Conway Jefferson had begun his representations to the manager very early, the police had taken charge of things before the chambermaids had touched the room. They had actually not been down that corridor at all. The other rooms there, at this season of the year, were opened and dusted only once a week. "That's all to the good, as far as it goes," Slack explained. "It means that if there were anything to find, we'd find it, but there isn't anything."

The Glenshire police had already been over the room for fingerprints, but there were none unaccounted for. Ruby's own, Josie's, and the two chambermaids'—one on the morning and one on the evening shift. There were also a couple of prints made by Raymond Starr, but these were accounted for by his story that he had come up with Josie to look for Ruby when she did not appear for the midnight exhibition dance.

There had been a heap of letters and general rubbish in the pigeonholes of the massive mahogany desk in the corner. Slack had just been carefully sorting through them, but he had found nothing of a suggestive nature. Bills, receipts, theater programs, cinema stubs, newspaper cuttings, beauty hints torn from magazines. Of the letters, there were some from Lil, apparently a friend from the Palais de Danse, recounting various affairs and gossip, saying they "missed Rube a lot. Mr. Findeison asked after you ever so often! Quite put out, he is! Young Reg has taken up with May now you've gone. Barney asks after you now and then. Things going much as usual. Old Grouser still as mean as ever with us girls. He ticked off Ada for going about with a fellow."

Slack had carefully noted all the names mentioned. Inquiries would be made, and it was possible some useful information might come to light. Otherwise the room had little to yield in the way of information.

Across a chair in the middle of the room was the foamy pink dance frock Ruby had worn early in the evening, with a pair of satin high-heeled shoes kicked off carelessly on the floor. Two sheer silk stockings were rolled into a ball and flung down. One had a ladder in it. Melchett recalled that the dead girl had had bare legs. This, Slack learned, was her custom. She used makeup on her legs instead of stockings, and only sometimes wore stockings for dancing; by this means saving expense. The wardrobe door was open and showed a variety of rather flashy evening dresses and a row of shoes below. There was some soiled underwear in the clothes basket; some nail parings, soiled face-cleaning tissue and bits of cotton wool stained with rouge and nail polish in the wastepaper basket—in fact, nothing out of the ordinary. The facts seemed plain to read. Ruby had hurried upstairs, changed her clothes and hurried off again—where?

Josephine Turner, who might be supposed to know most about Ruby's life and friends, had proved unable to help. But this, as Inspector Slack pointed out, might be natural. "If what you tell me is true, sir—about this adoption business, I mean—well, Josie would be all for Ruby breaking with any old friends she might have, and who might queer the pitch, so to speak. As I see it, this invalid gentleman gets all worked up about Ruby Keene being such a sweet, innocent, childish little piece of goods. Now supposing Ruby's got a tough boyfriend—that won't go down so well with the old boy. So it's Ruby's business to keep that dark. Josie doesn't know much about the girl, anyway—not about her friends and all that. But one thing she wouldn't stand for—Ruby's messing up things by carrying on with some undesirable fellow. So it stands to reason that Ruby—who, as I see it, was a sly little piece!—would keep very dark about seeing any old friend. She wouldn't let on to Josie anything about it; otherwise Josie would say, 'No, you don't, my girl.' But you know what girls are—especially young ones—always ready to make a fool of themselves over a tough guy. Ruby wants to see him. He comes down here, cuts up rough about the whole business and wrings her neck."

"I expect you're right, Slack," said Colonel Melchett, disguising his usual repugnance for the unpleasant way Slack had of putting things. "If so, we ought to be able to discover this tough friend's identity fairly easily."

"You leave it to me, sir," said Slack with his usual confidence. "I'll get hold of this Lil girl at that Palais de Danse place and turn her right inside out. We'll soon get at the truth." Colonel Melchett wondered if they would.

Slack's energy and activity always made him feel tired. "There's one other person you might be able to get a tip from, sir," went on Slack. "And that's the dance-and-tennis-pro fellow. He must have seen a lot of her, and he'd know more than Josie would. Likely enough she'd loosen her tongue a bit to him."

"I have already discussed that point with Superintendent Harper."

"Good, sir. I've done the chambermaids pretty thoroughly. They don't know a thing. Looked down on these two, as far as I can make out. Scamped the service as much as they dared. Chambermaid was in here last at seven o'clock last night, when she turned down the bed and drew the curtains and cleared up a bit. There's a bathroom next door, if you'd like to see it."

The bathroom was situated between Ruby's room and the slightly larger room occupied by Josie. It was unilluminating. Colonel Melchett silently marveled at the amount of aids to beauty that women could use. Rows of jars of face cream, cleansing cream, vanishing cream, skin-feeding cream. Boxes of different shades of powder. An untidy heap of every variety of lipstick. Hair lotions and brightening applications. Eyelash black, mascara, blue stain for under the eyes, at least twelve different shades of nail varnish, face tissues, bits of cotton wool, dirty powder puffs. Bottles of lotions— astringent, tonic, soothing, and so on. "Do you mean to say," he murmured feebly, "that women use all these things?"

Inspector Slack, who always knew everything, kindly enlightened him. "In private life, sir, so to speak, a lady keeps to one or two distinct shades— one for evening, one for day. They know what suits them and they keep to it. But these professional girls, they have to ring a change, so to speak. They do exhibition dances, and one night it's a tango, and the next a crinoline Victorian dance, and then a kind of Apache dance, and then just ordinary ballroom, and of course the makeup varies a good bit."

"Good Lord," said the colonel. "No wonder the people who turn out these creams and messes make a fortune."

"Easy money, that's what it is," said Slack. "Easy money. Got to spend a bit in advertisement, of course."

Colonel Melchett jerked his mind away from the fascinating and age-long problem of woman's adornments. He said, "There's still this dancing fellow. Your pigeon, superintendent."

"I suppose so, sir."

As they went downstairs Harper asked, "What did you think of Mr. Bartlett's story, sir?"

"About his car? I think, Harper, that that young man wants watching. It's a fishy story. Supposing that he did take Ruby Keene out in that car last night, after all?"

CHAPTER TEN

Superintendent Harper's manner was slow and pleasant and absolutely noncommittal. These cases where the police of two counties had to collaborate were always difficult. He liked Colonel Melchett and considered him an able chief constable, but he was nevertheless glad to be tackling the present interview by himself. Never do too much at once, was Superintendent Harper's rule. Bare routine inquiry for the first time. That left the persons you were interviewing relieved, and predisposed them to be more unguarded in the next interview you had with them.

Harper already knew Raymond Starr by sight. A fine-looking specimen, tall, lithe and good-looking, with very white teeth in a deeply bronzed face. He was dark and graceful. He had a pleasant, friendly manner and was very popular in the hotel. "I'm afraid I can't help you much, superintendent. I knew Ruby quite well, of course. She'd been here over a month and we had practiced our dances together, and all that. But there's really very little to say. She was quite a pleasant and rather stupid girl."

"It's her friendships we're particularly anxious to know about. Her friendships with men."

"So I suppose. Well, I don't know anything. She'd got a few young men in tow in the hotel, but nothing special. You see, she was nearly always monopolized by the Jefferson family."

"Yes, the Jefferson family." Harper paused meditatively. He shot a shrewd glance at the young man. "What did you think of that business, Mr. Starr?"

Raymond Starr said coolly, "What business?"

Harper said, "Did you know that Mr. Jefferson was proposing to adopt Ruby Keene legally?"

This appeared to be news to Starr. He pursed up his lips and whistled. He said, "The clever little devil! Oh, well, there's no fool like an old fool."

"That's how it strikes you, is it?"

"Well, what else can one say? If the old boy wanted to adopt someone, why didn't he pick upon a girl of his own class?"

"Ruby never mentioned the matter to you?"

"No, she didn't. I knew she was elated about something, but I didn't know what it was."

"And Josie?"

"Oh, I think Josie must have known what was in the wind. Probably she was the one who planned the whole thing. Josie's no fool. She's got a head on her, that girl."

Harper nodded. It was Josie who had sent for Ruby Keene. Josie, no doubt, who had encouraged the intimacy. No wonder she had been upset when Ruby had failed to show up for her dance that night and Conway Jefferson had begun to panic. She was envisaging her plans going awry. He asked, "Could Ruby keep a secret, do you think?"

"As well as most. She didn't talk about her own affairs much."

"Did she ever say anything—anything at all—about some friend of hers—someone from her former life—who was coming to see her here or whom she had had difficulty with? You know the sort of thing I mean, no doubt."

"I know perfectly. Well, as far as I'm aware, there was no one of the kind. Not by anything she ever said."

"Thank you. Now will you just tell me in your own words exactly what happened last night?"

"Certainly. Ruby and I did our ten-thirty dance together."

"No signs of anything unusual about her then?"

Raymond considered. "I don't think so. I didn't notice what happened afterward. I had my own partners to look after. I do remember noticing she was not in the ballroom. At midnight she hadn't turned up. I was very annoyed and went to Josie about it. Josie was playing bridge with the Jeffersons. She hadn't any idea where Ruby was, and I think she got a bit of a jolt. I noticed her shoot a quick, anxious glance at Mr. Jefferson. I persuaded the band to play another dance and I went to the office and got them to ring up Ruby's room. There wasn't any answer. I went back to Josie. She suggested that Ruby was perhaps asleep in her room. Idiotic suggestion really, but it was meant for the Jeffersons, of course! She came away with me and said we'd go up together."

"Yes, Mr. Starr. And what did she say when she was alone with you?"

"As far as I can remember, she looked very angry and said, 'Damned little fool. She can't do this sort of thing. It will ruin all her chances. Who's she with? Do you know?'

"I said that I hadn't the least idea. The last I'd seen of her was dancing with young Bartlett. Josie said, 'She wouldn't be with him. What can she be up to? She isn't with that film man, is she?'"

Harper said sharply, "Film man? Who was he?"

Raymond said, "I don't know his name. He's never stayed here. Rather an unusual-looking chap—black hair and theatrical-looking. He has something to do with the film industry, I believe—or so he told Ruby. He came over to dine here once or twice and danced with Ruby afterward, but I don't think she knew him at all well. That's why I was surprised when Josie mentioned him. I said I didn't think he'd been here tonight. Josie said, 'Well, she must be out with someone. What on earth am I going to say to the Jeffersons?' I said what did it matter to the Jeffersons? And Josie said it did matter. And she said, too, that she'd never forgive Ruby if she went and messed things up.

"We'd got to Ruby's room by then. She wasn't there, of course, but she'd been there, because the dress she had been wearing was lying across a chair. Josie looked in the wardrobe and said she thought she'd put on her old white dress. Normally she'd have changed into a black velvet dress for our Spanish dance. I was pretty angry by this time at the way Ruby had let me down. Josie did her best to soothe me and said she'd dance herself, so that old Prestcott shouldn't get after us all. She went away and changed her dress, and we went down and did a tango—exaggerated style and quite showy, but not really too exhausting upon the ankles. Josie was very plucky about it, for it hurt her, I could see. After that, she asked me to help her soothe the Jeffersons down. She said it was important. So, of course, I did what I could."

Superintendent Harper nodded. He said, "Thank you, Mr. Starr." To himself he thought, *It was important all right. Fifty thousand pounds.* He watched Raymond Starr as the latter moved gracefully away. He went down the steps of the terrace, picking up a bag of tennis balls and a racket on the way. Mrs. Jefferson, also carrying a racket, joined him, and they went toward the tennis courts.

"Excuse me, sir." Sergeant Higgins, rather breathless, was standing at Superintendent Harper's side. The superintendent, jerked from the train of thought he was following, looked startled. "Message just come through for you from headquarters, sir. Laborer reported this morning saw glare as of fire. Half an hour ago they found a burnt-out car near a quarry—Venn's Quarry—about two miles from here. Traces of a charred body inside."

A flush came over Harper's heavy features. He said, "What's come to Glenshire? An epidemic of violence?" He asked, "Could they get the number of the car?"

"No, sir. But we'll be able to identify it, of course, by the engine number. A Minoan Fourteen, they think it is."

CHAPTER ELEVEN

Sir Henry Clithering, as he passed through the lounge of the Majestic, hardly glanced at its occupants. His mind was preoccupied. Nevertheless, as is the way of life, something registered in his subconscious. It waited its time patiently.

Sir Henry was wondering, as he went upstairs, just what had induced the sudden urgency of his friend's message. Conway Jefferson was not the type of man who sent urgent summonses to anyone. Something quite out of the usual must have occurred, decided Sir Henry.

Jefferson wasted no time in beating about the bush. He said, "Glad you've come. . . . Edwards, get Sir Henry a drink. . . . Sit down, man. You've not heard anything, I suppose? Nothing in the papers yet?"

Sir Henry shook his head, his curiosity aroused. "What's the matter?"

"Murder's the matter. I'm concerned in it, and so are your friends, the Bantrys."

"Arthur and Dolly Bantry?" Clithering sounded incredulous.

"Yes; you see, the body was found in their house."

Clearly and succinctly, Conway Jefferson ran through the facts. Sir Henry listened without interrupting. Both men were accustomed to grasping the gist of a matter. Sir Henry, during his term as commissioner of the Metropolitan Police, had been renowned for his quick grip on essentials. "It's an extraordinary business," he commented when the other had finished. "How do the Bantrys come into it, do you think?"

"That's what worries me. You see, Henry, it looks to me as though possibly the fact that I know them might have a bearing on the case. That's the only connection I can find. Neither of them, I gather, ever saw the girl before. That's what they say, and there's no reason to disbelieve them. It's most unlikely they should know her. Then isn't it possible that she was decoyed away and her body deliberately left in the house of friends of mine?"

Clithering said, "I think that's far-fetched."

"It's possible, though," persisted the other.

"Yes, but unlikely. What do you want me to do?"

Conway Jefferson said bitterly, "I'm an invalid. I disguise the fact—

refuse to face it—but now it comes home to me. I can't go about as I'd like to, asking questions, looking into things. I've got to stay here meekly grateful for such scraps of information as the police are kind enough to dole out to me. Do you happen to know Melchett, by the way, the chief constable of Radfordshire?''

"Yes, I've met him." Something stirred in Sir Henry's brain. A face and figure noted unseeingly as he passed through the lounge. A straight-backed old lady whose face was familiar. It linked up with the last time he had seen Melchett. He said, "Do you mean you want me to be a kind of amateur sleuth? That's not my line."

Jefferson said, "You're not an amateur, that's just it."

"I'm not a professional any more. I'm on the retired list now."

Jefferson said, "That simplifies matters."

"You mean that if I were still at Scotland Yard I couldn't butt in? That's perfectly true."

"As it is," said Jefferson, "your experience qualifies you to take an interest in the case, and any cooperation you offer will be welcomed."

Clithering said slowly, "Etiquette permits, I agree. But what do you really want, Conway? To find out who killed this girl?"

"Just that."

"You've no idea yourself?"

"None whatever."

Sir Henry said slowly, "You probably won't believe me, but you've got an expert at solving mysteries sitting downstairs in the lounge at this minute. Someone who's better than I am at it, and who, in all probability, may have some local dope."

"What are you talking about?"

"Downstairs in the lounge, by the third pillar from the left, there sits an old lady with a sweet, placid, spinsterish face and a mind that has plumbed the depths of human iniquity and taken it as all in the day's work. Her name's Miss Marple. She comes from the village of St. Mary Mead, which is a mile and a half from Gossington; she's a friend of the Bantrys and, where crime is concerned, she's the goods, Conway."

Jefferson stared at him with thick puckered brows. He said heavily, "You're joking."

"No, I'm not. You spoke of Melchett just now. The last time I saw Melchett there was a village tragedy. Girl supposed to have drowned herself. Police, quite rightly, suspected that it wasn't suicide but murder. They thought they knew who did it. Along to me comes old Miss Marple, fluttering and dithering. She's afraid, she says, they'll hang the wrong person. She's got no evidence, but she knows who did do it. Hands me a piece of paper with a name written on it. And, Jefferson, she was right!"

Conway Jefferson's brows came down lower than ever. He grunted disbelievingly.

"Woman's intuition, I suppose," he said skeptically.

"No, she doesn't call it that. Specialized knowledge is her claim."

"And what does that mean?"

"Well, you know, Jefferson, we use it in police work. We get a burglary and we usually know pretty well who did it—of the regular crowd, that is.

We know the sort of burglar who acts in a particular sort of way. Miss Marple has an interesting, though occasionally trivial, series of parallels from village life."

Jefferson said skeptically, "What is she likely to know about a girl who's been brought up in a theatrical milieu and probably never been in a village in her life?"

"I think," said Sir Henry Clithering firmly, "that she might have ideas."

Miss Marple flushed with pleasure as Sir Henry bore down upon her. "Oh, Sir Henry, this is indeed a great piece of luck, meeting you here."

Sir Henry was gallant. He said, "To me, it is a great pleasure."

Miss Marple murmured, flushing. "So kind of you."

"Are you staying here?"

"Well, as a matter of fact we are."

"We?"

"Mrs. Bantry's here too." She looked at him sharply. "Have you heard yet— Yes, I can see you have. It is terrible, is it not?"

"What's Dolly Bantry doing here? Is her husband here too?"

"No. Naturally, they both reacted quite differently. Colonel Bantry, poor man, just shuts himself up in his study or goes down to one of the farms when anything like this happens. Like tortoises, you know; they draw their heads in and hope nobody will notice them. Dolly, of course, is quite different."

"Dolly, in fact," said Sir Henry, who knew his old friend fairly well, "is almost enjoying herself, eh?"

"Well—er—yes. Poor dear."

"And she's brought you along to produce the rabbits out of the hat for her?"

Miss Marple said composedly, "Dolly thought that a change of scene would be a good thing and she didn't want to come alone." She met his eye and her own gently twinkled. "But of course your way of describing it is quite true. It's rather embarrassing for me, because, of course, I am no use at all."

"No ideas? No village parallels?"

"I don't know much about it all yet."

"I can remedy that, I think. I'm going to call you into consultation, Miss Marple."

He gave a brief recital of the course of events. Miss Marple listened with keen interest. "Poor Mr. Jefferson," she said. "What a very sad story. These terrible accidents. To leave him alive, crippled, seems more cruel than if he had been killed too."

"Yes, indeed. That's why all his friends admire him so much for the resolute way he's gone on, conquering pain and grief and physical disabilities."

"Yes, it is splendid."

"The only thing I can't understand is this sudden outpouring of affection for this girl. She may, of course, have had some remarkable qualities."

"Probably not," said Miss Marple placidly.

"You don't think so?"

"I don't think her qualities entered into it."

Sir Henry said, "He isn't just a nasty old man, you know."

"Oh, no, no!" Miss Marple got quite pink. "I wasn't implying that for a minute. What I was trying to say was—very badly, I know—that he was just looking for a nice bright girl to take his dead daughter's place, and then this girl saw her opportunity and played it for all she was worth! That sounds rather uncharitable, I know, but I have seen so many cases of the kind. The young maidservant at Mr. Harbottle's, for instance. A very ordinary girl, but quiet, with nice manners. His sister was called away to nurse a dying relative, and when she got back she found the girl completely above herself, sitting down in the drawing room laughing and talking and not wearing her cap or apron. Miss Harbottle spoke to her very sharply, and the girl was impertinent, and then old Mr. Harbottle left her quite dumbfounded by saying that he thought she had kept house for him long enough and that he was making other arrangements.

"Such a scandal as it created in the village, but poor Miss Harbottle had to go and live most uncomfortably in rooms in Eastbourne. People said things, of course, but I believe there was no familiarity of any kind. It was simply that the old man found it much pleasanter to have a young, cheerful girl telling him how clever and amusing he was than to have his sister continually pointing out his faults to him, even if she was a good, economical manager."

There was a moment's pause and then Miss Marple resumed, "And there was Mr. Badger, who had the chemist's shop. Made a lot of fuss over the young lady who worked in his cosmetics section. Told his wife they must look on her as a daughter and have her to live in the house. Mrs. Badger didn't see it that way at all."

Sir Henry said, "If she'd only been a girl in his own rank of life—a friend's child—"

Miss Marple interrupted him. "Oh, but that wouldn't have been nearly as satisfactory from his point of view. It's like King Cophetua and the beggar maid. If you're really rather a lonely tired old man, and if, perhaps, your own family have been neglecting you"—she paused for a second—"well, to befriend someone who will be overwhelmed with your magnificence—to put it rather melodramatically, but I hope you see what I mean—well, that's much more interesting. It makes you feel a much greater person—a beneficent monarch! The recipient is more likely to be dazzled, and that, of course, is a pleasant feeling for you." She paused and said, "Mr. Badger, you know, bought the girl in his shop some really fantastic presents—a diamond bracelet and a most expensive radio-gramophone. Took out a lot of his savings to do it. However, Mrs. Badger, who was a much more astute woman than poor Miss Harbottle—marriage, of course, helps—took the trouble to find out a few things. And when Mr. Badger discovered that the girl was carrying on with a very undesirable young man connected with the race-courses, and had actually pawned the bracelet to give him the money—well, he was completely disgusted and the affair passed over quite safely. And he gave Mrs. Badger a diamond ring the following Christmas."

Her pleasant, shrewd eyes met Sir Henry's. He wondered if what she had been saying was intended as a hint. He said, "Are you suggesting that if there had been a young man in Ruby Keene's life, my friend's attitude towards her might have altered?"

"It probably would, you know. I daresay in a year or two he might have liked to arrange for her marriage himself; though more likely he wouldn't— gentlemen are usually rather selfish. But I certainly think that if Ruby Keene had had a young man she'd have been careful to keep very quiet about it."

"And the young man might have resented that?"

"I suppose that is the most plausible solution. It struck me, you know, that her cousin, the young woman who was at Gossington this morning, looked definitely angry with the dead girl. What you've told me explains why. No doubt she was looking forward to doing very well out of the business."

"Rather a cold-blooded character, in fact?"

"That's too harsh a judgment, perhaps. The poor thing has had to earn her living, and you can't expect her to sentimentalize because a well-to-do man and woman—as you have described Mr. Gaskell and Mrs. Jefferson— are going to be done out of a further large sum of money to which they have really no particular moral right. I should say Miss Turner was a hard-headed, ambitious young woman with a good temper and considerable *joie de vivre*. A little," added Miss Marple, "like Jessie Golden, the baker's daughter."

"What happened to her?" asked Sir Henry.

"She trained as a nursery governess and married the son of the house, who was home on leave from India. Made him a very good wife, I believe."

Sir Henry pulled himself clear of these fascinating side issues. He said, "Is there any reason, do you think, why my friend Conway Jefferson should suddenly have developed this 'Cophetua complex,' if you like to call it that?"

"There might have been."

"In what way?"

Miss Marple said, hesitating a little, "I should think—it's only a suggestion, of course—that perhaps his son-in-law and daughter-in-law might have wanted to get married again."

"Surely he couldn't have objected to that?"

"Oh, no, not objected. But, you see, you must look at it from his point of view. He has a terrible shock and loss; so have they. The three bereaved people live together and the link between them is the loss they have all sustained. But Time, as my dear mother used to say, is a great healer. Mr. Gaskell and Mrs. Jefferson are young. Without knowing it themselves, they may have begun to feel restless, to resent the bonds that tied them to their past sorrow. And so, feeling like that, old Mr. Jefferson would have become conscious of a sudden lack of sympathy without knowing its cause. It's usually that. Gentlemen so easily feel neglected. With Mr. Harbottle it was Miss Harbottle going away. And with the Badgers it was Mrs. Badger taking such an interest in spiritualism and always going out to séances."

"I must say," said Sir Henry ruefully, "that I do dislike the way you reduce us all to a general common denominator."

Miss Marple shook her head sadly. "Human nature is very much the same anywhere, Sir Henry."

Sir Henry said distastefully, "Mr. Harbottle! Mr. Badger! And poor Conway! I hate to intrude the personal note, but have you any parallel for my humble self in your village?"

"Well, of course, there is Briggs."

"Who's Briggs?"

"He was the head gardener up at Old Hall. Quite the best man they ever had. Knew exactly when the under-gardeners were slacking off—quite uncanny it was! He managed with only three men and a boy, and the place was kept better than it had been with six. And took several Firsts with his sweet peas. He's retired now."

"Like me," said Sir Henry.

"But he still does a little jobbing, if he likes the people."

"Ah," said Sir Henry. "Again like me. That's what I'm doing now. Jobbing. To help an old friend."

"Two old friends."

"Two?" Sir Henry looked a little puzzled.

Miss Marple said, "I suppose you meant Mr. Jefferson. But I wasn't thinking of him. I was thinking of Colonel and Mrs. Bantry."

"Yes, yes, I see." He asked sharply, "Was that why you alluded to Dolly Bantry as 'poor dear' at the beginning of our conversation?"

"Yes. She hasn't begun to realize things yet. I know, because I've had more experience. You see, Sir Henry, it seems to me that there's a great possibility of this crime being the kind of crime that never does get solved. Like the Brighton trunk murders. But if that happens it will be absolutely disastrous for the Bantrys. Colonel Bantry, like nearly all retired military men, is really abnormally sensitive. He reacts very quickly to public opinion. He won't notice it for some time, and then it will begin to go home to him. A slight here, and a snub there, and invitations that are refused, and excuses that are made, and then, little by little, it will dawn upon him, and he'll retire into his shell and get terribly morbid and miserable."

"Let me be sure I understand you rightly, Miss Marple. You mean that, because the body was found in his house, people will think that he had something to do with it?"

"Of course they will! I've no doubt they're saying so already. They'll say so more and more. And people will cold-shoulder the Bantrys and avoid them. That's why the truth has got to be found out and why I was willing to come here with Mrs. Bantry. An open accusation is one thing and quite easy for a soldier to meet. He's indignant and he has a chance of fighting. But this other whispering business will break him—will break them both. So, you see, Sir Henry, we've got to find out the truth."

Sir Henry said, "Any ideas as to why the body should have been found in his house? There must be an explanation of that. Some connection."

"Oh, of course."

"The girl was last seen here about twenty minutes to eleven. By midnight, according to the medical evidence, she was dead. Gossington's about twenty miles from here. Good road for sixteen of those miles, until one turns off the main road. A powerful car could do it in well under half an hour. Practically any car could average thirty-five. But why anyone should either kill her here and take her body out to Gossington or should take her out to Gossington and strangle her there, I don't know."

"Of course you don't, because it didn't happen."

"Do you mean that she was strangled by some fellow who took her out in a car, and he then decided to push her into the first likely house in the neighborhood?"

"I don't think anything of the kind. I think there was a very careful plan made. What happened was that the plan went wrong."

Sir Henry stared at her. "Why did the plan go wrong?"

Miss Marple said rather apologetically, "Such curious things happen, don't they? If I were to say that this particular plan went wrong because human beings are so much more vulnerable and sensitive than anyone thinks, it wouldn't sound sensible, would it? But that's what I believe and—" She broke off. "Here's Mrs. Bantry now."

CHAPTER TWELVE

Mrs. Bantry was with Adelaide Jefferson. The former came up to Sir Henry and exclaimed, "You!"

"I, myself." He took both her hands and pressed them warmly. "I can't tell you how distressed I am at all this, Mrs. B."

Mrs Bantry said mechanically, "Don't call me Mrs. B!" and went on, "Arthur isn't here. He's taking it all rather seriously. Miss Marple and I have come here to sleuth. Do you know Mrs. Jefferson?"

"Yes, of course."

He shook hands. Adelaide Jefferson said, "Have you seen my father-in-law?"

"Yes. I have."

"I'm glad. We're anxious about him. It was a terrible shock."

Mrs. Bantry said, "Let's go out on the terrace and have drinks and talk about it all." The four of them went out and joined Mark Gaskell, who was sitting at the extreme end of the terrace by himself. After a few desultory remarks and the arrival of the drinks, Mrs. Bantry plunged straight into the subject with her usual zest for direct action. "We can talk about it, can't we?" she said. "I mean we're all old friends—except Miss Marple, and she knows all about crime. And she wants to help."

Mark Gaskell looked at Miss Marple in a somewhat puzzled fashion. He said doubtfully, "Do you—er—write detective stories?" The most unlikely people, he knew, wrote detective stories. And Miss Marple, in her old-fashioned spinster's clothes, looked a singularly unlikely person.

"Oh, no, I'm not clever enough for that."

"She's wonderful," said Mrs. Bantry impatiently. "I can't explain now, but she is. . . . Now, Addie, I want to know all about things. What was she really like, this girl?"

"Well—" Adelaide Jefferson paused, glanced across at Mark and half laughed. She said, "You're so direct."

"Did you like her?"

"No, of course I didn't."

"What was she really like?" Mrs. Bantry shifted her inquiry to Mark Gaskell.

Mark said deliberately, "Common or garden gold digger. And she knew her stuff. She's got her hooks into Jeff all right." Both of them called their father-in-law "Jeff."

Sir Henry thought, looking disapprovingly at Mark, *Indiscreet fellow. Shouldn't be so outspoken.* He had always disapproved a little of Mark Gaskell. The man had charm, but he was unreliable—talked too much, was occasionally boastful—not quite to be trusted, Sir Henry thought. He had sometimes wondered if Conway Jefferson thought so too.

"But couldn't you do something about it?" demanded Mrs. Bantry.

Mark said dryly, "We might have, if we'd realized it in time."

He shot a glance at Adelaide and she colored faintly. There had been reproach in that glance.

She said, "Mark thinks I ought to have seen what was coming."

"You left the old boy alone too much, Addie. Tennis lessons and all the rest of it."

"Well, I had to have some exercise." She spoke apologetically. "Anyway, I never dreamed—"

"No," said Mark, "neither of us ever dreamed. Jeff has always been such a sensible, levelheaded old boy."

Miss Marple made a contribution to the conversation. "Gentlemen," she said with her old maid's way of referring to the opposite sex as though it were a species of wild animal, "are frequently not so levelheaded as they seem."

"I'll say you're right," said Mark. "Unfortunately, Miss Marple, we didn't realize that. We wondered what the old boy saw in that rather insipid and meretricious little bag of tricks. But we were pleased for him to be kept happy and amused. We thought there was no harm in her. No harm in her! I wish I'd wrung her neck."

"Mark," said Addie, "you really must be careful what you say."

He grinned at her engagingly. "I suppose I must. Otherwise people will think I actually did wring her neck. Oh, well, I suppose I'm under suspicion anyway. If anyone had an interest in seeing that girl dead, it was Addie and myself."

"Mark," cried Mrs. Jefferson, half laughing and half angry, "you really mustn't!"

"All right, all right," said Mark Gaskell pacifically. "But I do like speaking my mind. Fifty thousand pounds our esteemed father-in-law was proposing to settle upon that half-baked, nitwitted little slypuss."

"Mark, you mustn't! She's dead!"

"Yes, she's dead, poor little devil. And after all, why shouldn't she use the weapons that Nature gave her? Who am I to judge? Done plenty of rotten things myself in my life. No, let's say Ruby was entitled to plot and scheme, and we were mugs not to have tumbled to her game sooner."

Sir Henry said, "What did you say when Conway told you he proposed to adopt the girl?"

Mark thrust out his hands. "What could we say? Addie, always the little lady, retained her self-control admirably. Put a brave face upon it. I endeavored to follow her example."

"I should have made a fuss!" said Mrs. Bantry.

"Well, frankly speaking, we weren't entitled to make a fuss. It was Jeff's money. We weren't his flesh and blood. He'd always been damned good to us. There was nothing for it but to bite on the bullet." He added reflectively, "but we didn't love little Ruby."

Adelaide Jefferson said, "If only it had been some other kind of girl. Jeff had two godchildren, you know. If it had been one of them—well, one would have understood it." She added with a shade of resentment, "And Jeff's always seemed so fond of Peter."

"Of course," said Mrs. Bantry. "I always have known Peter was your first husband's child, but I'd quite forgotten it. I've always thought of him as Mr. Jefferson's grandson."

"So have I," said Adelaide. Her voice held a note that made Miss Marple turn in her chair and look at her.

"It was Josie's fault," said Mark. "Josie brought her here."

Adelaide said, "Oh, but surely you don't think it was deliberate, do you? Why, you've always liked Josie so much."

"Yes, I did like her. I thought she was good sport."

"It was sheer accident, her bringing the girl down."

"Josie's got a good head on her shoulders, my girl."

"Yes, but she couldn't foresee—"

Mark said, "No, she couldn't. I admit it. I'm not really accusing her of planning the whole thing. But I've no doubt she saw which way the wind was blowing long before we did, and kept very quiet about it."

Adelaide said with a sigh, "I suppose one can't blame her for that."

Mark said, "Oh, we can't blame anyone for anything!"

Mrs. Bantry asked, "Was Ruby Keene very pretty?"

Mark stared at her. "I thought you'd seen—"

Mrs. Bantry said hastily, "Oh, yes, I saw her—her body. But she'd been strangled, you know, and one couldn't tell—" She shivered.

Mark said thoughtfully, "I don't think she was really pretty at all. She certainly wouldn't have been without any makeup. A thin ferrety little face, not much chin, teeth running down her throat, nondescript sort of nose—"

"It sounds revolting," said Mrs. Bantry.

"Oh, no, she wasn't. As I say, with makeup she managed to give quite an effect of good looks. . . . Don't you think so, Addie?"

"Yes, rather chocolate-box, pink-and-white business. She had nice blue eyes."

"Yes, innocent-baby stare, and the heavily blacked lashes brought out the blueness. Her hair was bleached, of course. It's true, when I come to think of it, that in coloring—artificial coloring, anyway—she had a kind of spurious resemblance to Rosamund—my wife, you know. I daresay that's what attracted the old man's attention to her." He sighed. "Well, it's a bad business. The awful thing is that Addie and I can't help being glad, really, that she's dead." He quelled a protest from his sister-in-law, "It's no good, Addie. I know what you feel. I feel the same. And I'm not going to pretend! But at the same time, if you know what I mean, I really am most awfully concerned for Jeff about the whole business. It's hit him very hard. I—" He stopped and stared toward the doors leading out of the lounge onto the terrace. "Well, well. See who's here. . . . What an unscrupulous woman you are, Addie."

Mrs. Jefferson looked over her shoulder, uttered an exclamation and got up, a slight color rising in her face. She walked quickly along the terrace and went up to a tall, middle-aged man with a thin brown face who was looking uncertainly about him.

Mrs. Bantry said, "Isn't that Hugo McLean?"

Mark Gaskell said, "Hugo McLean it is. Alias William Dobbin."

Mrs. Bantry murmured, "He's very faithful, isn't he?"

"Doglike devotion," said Mark. "Addie's only got to whistle and Hugo comes trotting along from any odd corner of the globe. Always hopes that someday she'll marry him. I daresay she will."

Miss Marple looked beamingly after them. She said, "I see. A romance?"

"One of the good old-fashioned kind," Mark assured her. "It's been going on for years. Addie's that kind of woman." He added meditatively, "I suppose Addie telephoned him this morning. She didn't tell me she had."

Edwards came discreetly along the terrace and paused at Mark's elbow. "Excuse me, sir. Mr. Jefferson would like you to come up."

"I'll come at once." Mark sprang up. He nodded to them, said, "See you later," and went off.

Sir Henry leaned forward to Miss Marple. He said, "Well, what do you think of the principal beneficiaries of the crime?"

Miss Marple said thoughtfully, looking at Adelaide Jefferson as she stood talking to her old friend, "I should think, you know, that she was a very devoted mother."

"Oh, she is," said Mrs. Bantry. "She's simply devoted to Peter."

"She's the kind of woman," said Miss Marple, "that everyone likes. The kind of woman that could go on getting married again and again. I don't mean a man's woman—that's quite different."

"I know what you mean," said Sir Henry.

"What you both mean," said Mrs. Bantry, "is that she's a good listener."

Sir Henry laughed. He said, "And Mark Gaskell?"

"Ah," said Miss Marple. "He's a downy fellow."

"Village parallel, please?"

"Mr. Cargill, the builder. He bluffed a lot of people into having things done to their houses they never meant to do. And how he charged them for it! But he could always explain his bill away plausibly. A downy fellow. He married money. So did Mr. Gaskell, I understand."

"You don't like him."

"Yes, I do. Most women would. But he can't take me in. He's a very attractive person, I think. But a little unwise, perhaps, to talk as much as he does."

"'Unwise' is the word," said Sir Henry. "Mark will get himself into trouble if he doesn't look out." A tall dark young man in white flannels came up the steps to the terrace and paused just for a minute, watching Adelaide Jefferson and Hugo McLean. "And that," said Sir Henry obligingly, "is X, whom we might describe as an interested party. He is the tennis and dancing pro, Raymond Starr, Ruby Keene's partner."

Miss Marple looked at him with interest. She said, "He's very nice-looking, isn't he?"

"I suppose so."

"Don't be absurd, Sir Henry," said Mrs. Bantry. "There's no supposing about it. He is good-looking."

Miss Marple murmured, "Mrs. Jefferson has been taking tennis lessons, I think she said."

"Do you mean anything by that, Jane, or don't you?"

Miss Marple had no chance of replying to this downright question. Young Peter Carmody came across the terrace and joined them. He addressed himself to Sir Henry. "I say, are you a detective too? I saw you talking to the superintendent—the fat one is a superintendent, isn't he?"

"Quite right, my son."

"And somebody told me you were a frightfully important detective from London. The head of Scotland Yard or something like that."

"The head of Scotland Yard is usually a complete dud in books, isn't he?"

"Oh, no; not nowadays. Making fun of the people is very old-fashioned. Do you know who did the murder yet?"

"Not yet, I'm afraid."

"Are you enjoying this very much, Peter?" asked Mrs. Bantry.

"Well, I am rather. It makes a change, doesn't it? I've been hunting round to see if I could find any clues, but I haven't been lucky. I've got a souvenir though. Would you like to see it? Fancy, mother wanted me to throw it away. I do think one's parents are rather trying sometimes." He produced from his pocket a small match box. Pushing it open, he disclosed the precious contents. "See, it's a fingernail. Her fingernail! I'm going to label it Fingernail of the Murdered Woman and take it back to school. It's a good souvenir, don't you think?"

"Where did you get it?" asked Miss Marple.

"Well, it was a bit of luck, really. Because of course I didn't know she was going to be murdered then. It was before dinner last night. Ruby caught her nail in Josie's shawl and it tore it. Mums cut it off for her and gave it to me and said put it in the wastepaper basket, and I meant to, but I put it in my pocket instead, and this morning I remembered and looked to see if it was still there, and it was, so now I've got it as a souvenir."

"Disgusting," said Mrs. Bantry.

Peter said politely, "Oh, do you think so?"

"Got any other souvenirs?" asked Sir Henry.

"Well, I don't know. I've got something that might be."

"Explain yourself, young man."

Peter looked at him thoughtfully. Then he pulled out an envelope. From the inside of it he extracted a piece of brown tape-like substance. "It's a bit of that chap George Bartlett's shoelace," he explained. "I saw his shoes outside the door this morning and I bagged a bit just in case."

"In case what?"

"In case he should be the murderer, of course. He was the last person to see her, and that's always frightfully suspicious, you know. . . . Is it nearly dinnertime, do you think? I'm frightfully hungry. It always seems such a long time between tea and dinner. . . . Hullo, there's Uncle Hugo. I didn't know mums had asked him to come down. I suppose she sent for him. She always does if she's in a jam. Here's Josie coming. . . . Hi, Josie!"

Josephine Turner, coming along the terrace, stopped and looked rather startled to see Mrs. Bantry and Miss Marple. Mrs. Bantry said pleasantly, "How d'you do, Miss Turner. We've come to do a bit of sleuthing."

Josie cast a guilty glance round. She said, lowering her voice, "It's awful. Nobody knows yet. I mean it isn't in the papers yet. I suppose everyone will be asking me questions, and it's so awkward. I don't know what I ought to say."

Her glance went rather wistfully toward Miss Marple, who said, "Yes, it will be a very difficult situation for you, I'm afraid."

Josie warmed to this sympathy. "You see, Mr. Prestcott said to me, 'Don't talk about it.' And that's all very well, but everyone is sure to ask me and you can't offend people, can you? Mr. Prestcott said he hoped I'd feel able to carry on as usual, and he wasn't very nice about it, so, of course, I want to do my best. And I really don't see why it should all be blamed on me."

Sir Henry said, "Do you mind me asking you a frank question?"

"Oh, do ask me anything you like," said Josie a little insincerely.

"Has there been any unpleasantness between you and Mrs. Jefferson and Mr. Gaskell over all this?"

"Over the murder, do you mean?"

"No, I don't mean the murder."

Josie stood twisting her fingers together. She said rather sullenly, "Well, there has and there hasn't, if you know what I mean. Neither of them has said anything. But I think they blame it on me—Mr. Jefferson taking such a fancy to Ruby, I mean. It wasn't my fault, though, was it? These things happen, and I never dreamt of such a thing happening beforehand, not for a moment. I—I was quite dumbfounded." Her words rang out with what seemed undeniable sincerity.

Sir Henry said kindly, "I'm sure you were. But once it had happened?"

Josie's chin went up. "Well, it was a piece of luck, wasn't it? Everyone's got the right to have a piece of luck sometimes." She looked from one to the other of them in a slightly defiant, questioning manner, and then went on across the terrace and into the hotel.

Peter said judicially, "I don't think she did it."

Miss Marple murmured, "It's interesting, that piece of fingernail. It had been worrying me, you know—how to account for her nails."

"Nails?" asked Sir Henry.

"The dead girl's nails," explained Mrs. Bantry. "They were quite short and, now that Jane says so, of course it was a little unlikely. A girl like that usually has absolute talons!"

Miss Marple said, "But of course if she tore one off, then she might clip the others close so as to match. Did they find nail parings in her room, I wonder?"

Sir Henry looked at her curiously. He said, "I'll ask Superintendent Harper when he gets back."

"Back from where?" asked Mrs. Bantry. "He hasn't gone over to Gossington, has he?"

Sir Henry said gravely, "No. There's been another tragedy. Blazing car in a quarry."

Miss Marple caught her breath. "Was there someone in the car?"

"I'm afraid so, yes."

Miss Marple said thoughtfully, "I expect that will be the Girl Guide who's missing—Patience—no, Pamela Reeves."

Sir Henry stared at her. "Now why on earth do you think that?"

Miss Marple got rather pink. "Well, it was given out on the wireless that she was missing from her home since last night. And her home was Daneleigh Vale—that's not very far from here—and she was last seen at the Girl Guide rally up on Danebury Downs. That's very close indeed. In fact, she'd have to pass through Danemouth to get home. So it does rather fit in, doesn't it? I mean it looks as though she might have seen—or perhaps heard—something that no one was supposed to see and hear. If so, of course, she'd be a source of danger to the murderer and she'd have to be removed. Two things like that must be connected, don't you think?"

Sir Henry said, his voice dropping a little, "You think a second murder?"

"Why not?" Her quiet, placid gaze met his. "When anyone has committed one murder he doesn't shrink from another, does he? Nor even from a third."

"A third? You don't think there will be a third murder?"

"I think it's just possible. Yes, I think it's highly possible."

"Miss Marple," said Sir Henry, "you frighten me. Do you know who is going to be murdered?"

Miss Marple said, "I've a very good idea."

CHAPTER THIRTEEN

Colonel Melchett and Superintendent Harper looked at each other. Harper had come over to Much Benham for a consultation. Melchett said gloomily, "Well, we know where we are—or rather where we aren't!"

"Where we aren't expresses it better, sir."

"We've got two deaths to take into account," said Melchett. "Two murders. Ruby Keene and the child, Pamela Reeves. Not much to identify her by, poor kid, but enough. One shoe escaped burning and has been identified as hers, and a button from her Girl Guide uniform. A fiendish business, superintendent."

Superintendent Harper said very quietly, "I'll say you're right, sir."

"I'm glad to say Haydock is quite certain she was dead before the car was set on fire. The way she was lying thrown across the seat shows that. Probably knocked on the head, poor kid."

"Or strangled, perhaps."

"You think so?"

"Well, sir, there are murderers like that."

"I know. I've seen the parents—the poor girl's mother's beside herself. Damned painful, the whole thing. The point for us to settle is: are the two murders connected?"

The superintendent ticked off the points on his fingers. "Attended rally of Girl Guides on Danebury Downs. Stated by companion to be normal and cheerful. Did not return with three companions by the bus to Medchester. Said to them that she was going to Danemouth to Woolworth's and would take the bus home from there. That's likely enough—Woolworth's in Danemouth is a big affair—the girl lived in the back country and didn't get many chances of going into town. The main road into Danemouth from the downs does a big round inland; Pamela Reeves took a short cut over two fields and a footpath and lane which would bring her into Danemouth near the Majestic Hotel. The lane, in fact, actually passes the hotel on the west side. It's possible, therefore, that she overheard or saw something— something concerning Ruby Keene—which would have proved dangerous to the murderer—say, for instance, that she heard him arranging to meet Ruby Keene at eleven that evening. He realizes that this schoolgirl has overheard and he has to silence her."

Colonel Melchett said, "That's presuming, Harper, that the Ruby Keene crime was premeditated, not spontaneous."

Superintendent Harper agreed. "I believe it was, sir. It looks as though it would be the other way—sudden violence, a fit of passion or jealousy—but I'm beginning to think that that's not so. I don't see, otherwise, how you can account for the death of the child. If she was a witness of the actual crime it would be late at night, round about eleven P.M., and what would she be doing round about the Majestic Hotel at that time of night? Why, at nine o'clock her parents were getting anxious because she hadn't returned."

"The alternative is that she went to meet someone in Danemouth unknown to her family and friends, and that her death is quite unconnected with the other death."

"Yes, sir, and I don't believe that's so. Look how even the old lady, old Miss Marple, tumbled to it at once that there was a connection. She asked at once if the body in the burnt car was the body of the Girl Guide. Very smart old lady, that. These old ladies are, sometimes. Shrewd, you know. Put their fingers on the vital spot."

"Miss Marple has done that more than once," said Colonel Melchett dryly.

"And besides, sir, there's the car. That seems to me to link up her death definitely with the Majestic Hotel. It was Mr. George Bartlett's car."

Again the eyes of the two men met. Melchett said, "George Bartlett? Could be! What do you think?"

Again Harper methodically recited various points. "Ruby Keene was last seen with George Bartlett. He says she went to her room—borne out by the dress she was wearing being found there—but did she go to her room and change in order to go out with him? Had they made a date to go out together earlier—discussed it, say, before dinner—and did Pamela Reeves happen to overhear?"

Colonel Melchett said, "He didn't report the loss of his car until the following morning, and he was extremely vague about it then; pretended that he couldn't remember exactly when he had last noticed it."

"That might be cleverness, sir. As I see it, he's either a very clever gentleman pretending to be a silly ass, or else—well, he is a silly ass."

"What we want," said Melchett, "is motive. As it stands, he had no motive whatever for killing Ruby Keene."

"Yes, that's where we're stuck every time. Motive. All the reports from the Palais de Danse at Brixwell are negative, I understand."

"Absolutely! Ruby Keene had no special boyfriend. Slack's been into the matter thoroughly. Give Slack his due; he is thorough."

"That's right, sir. 'Thorough' is the word."

"If there was anything to ferret out he'd have ferreted it out. But there's nothing there. He got a list of her most frequent dancing partners—all vetted and found correct. Harmless fellows, and all able to produce alibis for that night."

"Ah," said Superintendent Harper. "Alibis. That's what we're up against."

Melchett looked at him sharply. "Think so? I've left that side of the investigation to you."

"Yes, sir. It's been gone into—very thoroughly. We applied to London for help over it."

"Well?"

"Mr. Conway Jefferson may think that Mr. Gaskell and young Mrs. Jefferson are comfortably off, but that is not the case. They're both extremely hard up."

"Is that true?"

"Quite true, sir. It's as Mr. Conway Jefferson said; he made over considerable sums of money to his son and daughter when they married. That was a number of years ago though. Mr. Frank Jefferson fancied himself as knowing good investments. He didn't invest in anything absolutely wildcat, but he was unlucky and showed poor judgment more than once. His holdings have gone steadily down. I should say that Mrs. Jefferson found it very difficult to make both ends meet and send her son to a good school."

"But she hasn't applied to her father-in-law for help?"

"No, sir. As far as I can make out she lives with him and, consequently, has no household expenses."

"And his health is such that he wasn't expected to live long?"

"That's right, sir. Now for Mr. Mark Gaskell. He's a gambler, pure and simple. Got through his wife's money very soon. Has got himself tangled up rather badly just at present. He needs money badly, and a good deal of it."

"Can't say I liked the looks of him much," said Colonel Melchett. "Wild-looking sort of fellow, what? And he's got a motive, all right. Twenty-five thousand pounds it meant to him, getting that girl out of the way. Yes, it's a motive all right."

"They both had a motive."

"I'm not considering Mrs. Jefferson."

"No, sir, I know you're not. And, anyway, the alibi holds for both of them. They couldn't have done it. Just that."

"You've got a detailed statement of their movements that evening?"

"Yes, I have. Take Mr. Gaskell first. He dined with his father-in-law and Mrs. Jefferson, had coffee with them afterward when Ruby Keene joined them. Then said he had to write letters and left them. Actually, he took his car and went for a spin down to the front. He told me quite frankly he couldn't stick playing bridge for a whole evening. The old boy's mad on it. So he made letters an excuse. Ruby Keene remained with the others. Mark Gaskell returned when she was dancing with Raymond. After the dance Ruby came and had a drink with them, then she went off with young Bartlett, and Gaskell and the others cut for partners and started their bridge. That was at twenty minutes to eleven, and he didn't leave the table until after midnight. That's quite certain, sir. Everyone says so—the family, the waiters, everyone. Therefore, he couldn't have done it. And Mrs. Jefferson's alibi is the same. She, too, didn't leave the table. They're out, both of them—out." Colonel Melchett leaned back, tapping the table with a paper cutter.

Superintendent Harper said, "That is, assuming the girl was killed before midnight."

"Haydock said she was. He's a very sound fellow in police work. If he says a thing, it's so."

"There might be reasons—health, physical idiosyncrasy or something."

"I'll put it to him." Melchett glanced at his watch, picked up the telephone receiver and asked for a number. He said, "Haydock ought to be in now. Now, assuming that she was killed after midnight—"

Harper said, "Then there might be a chance. There was some coming and going afterward. Let's assume that Gaskell had asked the girl to meet him outside somewhere—say at twenty past twelve. He slips away for a minute or two, strangles her, comes back, and disposes of the body later—in the early hours of the morning."

Melchett said, "Takes her by car twenty miles to put her in Bantry's library? Dash it all, it's not a likely story."

"No, it isn't," the superintendent admitted at once.

The telephone rang. Melchett picked up the receiver. "Hullo, Haydock, is that you? Ruby Keene. Would it be possible for her to have been killed after midnight?"

"I told you she was killed between ten and midnight."

"Yes, I know, but one could stretch it a bit, what?"

"No, you couldn't stretch it. When I say she was killed before midnight I mean before midnight, and don't try and tamper with the medical evidence."

"Yes, but couldn't there be some physiological what not? You know what I mean?"

"I know that you don't know what you're talking about. The girl was perfectly healthy and not abnormal in any way, and I'm not going to say she was just to help you fit a rope round the neck of some wretched fellow whom you police wallahs have got your knife into. Now, don't protest. I know your ways. And, by the way, the girl wasn't strangled willingly—that is to say, she was drugged first. Powerful narcotic. She died of strangulation, but she was drugged first." Haydock rang off.

Melchett said gloomily, "Well, that's that."

Harper said, "Thought I'd found another likely starter, but it petered out."

"What's that? Who?"

"Strictly speaking, he's your pigeon, sir. Name of Basil Blake. Lives near Gossington Hall."

"Impudent young jackanapes!" The colonel's brow darkened as he remembered Basil Blake's outrageous rudeness. "How's he mixed up in it?"

"Seems he knew Ruby Keene. Dined over at the Majestic quite often, danced with the girl. Do you remember what Josie said to Raymond when Ruby was discovered to be missing, 'She isn't with that film man, is she?' I've found out it was Blake she meant. He's employed with the Lenville Studios, you know. Josie has nothing to go upon except a belief that Ruby was rather keen on him."

"Very promising, Harper, very promising."

"Not so good as it sounds, sir. Basil Blake was at a party at the studios that night. You know the sort of thing. Starts at eight with cocktails and goes on and on until the air's too thick to see through and everyone passes out. According to Inspector Slack, who's questioned him, he left the show round about midnight. At midnight Ruby Keene was dead."

"Anyone bear out his statement?"

"Most of them, I gather, sir, were rather—er—far gone. The—er—young woman now at the bungalow, Miss Dinah Lee, says that statement is correct."

"Doesn't mean a thing."

"No, sir, probably not. Statements taken from other members of the party bear Mr. Blake's statement out, on the whole, though ideas as to time are somewhat vague."

"Where are these studios?"

"Lenville, sir, thirty miles southwest of London."

"H'm—about the same distance from here?"

"Yes, sir."

Colonel Melchett rubbed his nose. He said in a rather dissatisfied tone, "Well, it looks as though we could wash him out."

"I think so, sir. There is no evidence that he was seriously attracted by Ruby Keene. In fact"—Superintendent Harper coughed primly—"he seems fully occupied with his own young lady."

Melchett said, "Well, we are left with X, an unknown murderer—so unknown Slack can't find a trace of him. Or Jefferson's son-in-law, who might have wanted to kill the girl, but didn't have a chance to do so. Daughter-in-law ditto. Or George Bartlett, who has an alibi, but, unfortunately, no motive either. Or with young Blake, who has an alibi and no motive. And that's the lot! No, stop. I suppose we ought to consider the dancing fellow, Raymond Starr. After all, he saw a lot of the girl."

Harper said slowly, "Can't believe he took much interest in her—or else he's a thundering good actor. And, for all practical purposes, he's got an alibi too. He was more or less in view from twenty minutes to eleven until midnight, dancing with various partners. I don't see that we can make a case against him."

"In fact, said Colonel Melchett, "we can't make a case against anybody."

"George Bartlett's our best hope," Harper said. "If we could only hit on a motive."

"You've had him looked up?"

"Yes, sir. Only child. Coddled by his mother. Came into a good deal of money on her death a year ago. Getting through it fast. Weak rather than vicious."

"May be mental," said Melchett hopefully.

Superintendent Harper nodded. He said, "Has it struck you, sir, that that may be the explanation of the whole case?"

"Criminal lunatic, you mean?"

"Yes, sir. One of those fellows who go about strangling young girls. Doctors have a long name for it."

"That would solve all our difficulties," said Melchett.

"There's only one thing I don't like about it," said Superintendent Harper.

"What?"

"It's too easy."

"H'm—yes, perhaps. So, as I said at the beginning, where are we?"

"Nowhere, sir," said Superintendent Harper.

CHAPTER FOURTEEN

Conway Jefferson stirred in his sleep and stretched. His arms were flung out, long, powerful arms into which all the strength of his body seemed to be concentrated since his accident. Through the curtains the morning light glowed softly. Conway Jefferson smiled to himself. Always, after a night of rest, he woke like this, happy, refreshed, his deep vitality renewed. Another day! So, for a minute, he lay. Then he pressed the special bell by his hand. And suddenly a wave of remembrance swept over him. Even as Edwards, deft and quiet-footed, entered the room a groan was wrung from his master. Edwards paused with his hand on the curtains. He said, "You're not in pain, sir?"

Conway Jefferson said harshly, "No. Go on, pull 'em." The clear light flooded the room. Edwards, understanding, did not glance at his master.

His face grim, Conway Jefferson lay remembering and thinking. Before his eyes he saw again the pretty, vapid face of Ruby. Only in his mind he did not use the adjective "vapid." Last night he would have said "innocent." A naïve, innocent child! And now? A great weariness came over Conway Jefferson. He closed his eyes. He murmured below his breath, "Margaret." It was the name of his dead wife.

"I like your friend," said Adelaide Jefferson to Mrs. Bantry. The two women were sitting on the terrace.

"Jane Marple's a very remarkable woman," said Mrs. Bantry.

"She's nice too," said Addie, smiling.

"People call her a scandalmonger," said Mrs. Bantry, "but she isn't really."

"Just a low opinion of human nature?"

"You could call it that."

"It's rather refreshing," said Adelaide Jefferson, "after having had too much of the other thing." Mrs. Bantry looked at her sharply. Addie explained herself. "So much high thinking—idealization of an unworthy object!"

"You mean Ruby Keene?"

Addie nodded. "I don't want to be horrid about her. There wasn't any harm in her. Poor little rat, she had to fight for what she wanted. She wasn't bad. Common and rather silly and quite good-natured, but a decided little gold digger. I don't think she schemed or planned. It was just that she was quick to take advantage of a possibility. And she knew just how to appeal to an elderly man who was lonely."

"I suppose," said Mrs. Bantry thoughtfully, "that Conway was lonely."

Addie moved restlessly. She said, "He was this summer." She paused and then burst out, "Mark will have it that it was all my fault! Perhaps it was; I don't know." She was silent for a minute, then, impelled by some need to talk, she went on speaking in a difficult, almost reluctant way. "I—I've had such an odd sort of life. Mike Carmody, my first husband, died so soon after we were married it—it knocked me out. Peter, as you know, was born after his death. Frank Jefferson was Mike's great friend. So I came to see a lot of him. He was Peter's godfather—Mike had wanted that. I got very fond of him and—oh, sorry for him too."

"Sorry?" queried Mrs. Bantry with interest.

"Yes, just that. It sounds odd. Frank had always had everything he wanted. His father and his mother couldn't have been nicer to him. And yet—how can I say it?—you see, old Mr. Jefferson's personality is so strong. If you live with it you can't somehow have a personality of your own. Frank felt that.

"When we were married he was very happy—wonderfully so. Mr. Jefferson was very generous. He settled a large sum of money on Frank; said he wanted his children to be independent and not have to wait for his death. It was so nice of him—so generous. But it was much too sudden. He ought really to have accustomed Frank to independence little by little.

"It went to Frank's head. He wanted to be as good a man as his father, as clever about money and business, as farseeing and successful. And of course he wasn't. He didn't exactly speculate with the money, but he invested in the wrong things at the wrong time. It's frightening, you know, how soon money goes if you're not clever about it. The more Frank dropped, the more eager he was to get it back by some clever deal. So things went from bad to worse."

"But, my dear," said Mrs. Bantry, "couldn't Conway have advised him?"

"He didn't want to be advised. The one thing he wanted was to do well on his own. That's why we never let Mr. Jefferson know. When Frank died there was very little left; only a tiny income for me. And I—I didn't let his father know either. You see"—she turned abruptly—"it would have seemed like betraying Frank to him. Frank would have hated it so. Mr. Jefferson was ill for a long time. When he got well he assumed that I was a very-well-off widow. I've never undeceived him. It's been a point of honor. He knows I'm very careful about money, but he just approves of that, thinks I'm a thrifty sort of woman. And of course Peter and I have lived with him practically ever since, and he's paid for all our living expenses. So I've never had to worry." She said slowly, "We've been like a family all these years, only—only, you see—or don't you see?—I've never been Frank's widow to him; I've been Frank's wife."

Mrs. Bantry grasped the implication. "You mean he's never accepted their deaths?"

"No. He's been wonderful. But he's conquered his own terrible tragedy by refusing to recognize death. Mark is Rosamund's husband and I'm Frank's wife, and though Frank and Rosamund aren't exactly here with us they are still existent."

Mrs. Bantry said softly, "It's a wonderful triumph of faith."

"I know. We've gone on, year after year. But suddenly, this summer, something went wrong in me. I felt—felt rebellious. It's an awful thing to say, but I didn't want to think of Frank any more! All that was over—my love and companionship with him, and my grief when he died. It was something that had been and wasn't any longer.

"It's awfully hard to describe. It's like wanting to wipe the slate clean and start again. I wanted to be me—Addie, still reasonably young and strong and able to play games and swim and dance—just a person. Even Hugo—you know Hugo McLean?—he's a dear and wants to marry me, but of course I've never really thought of it, but this summer I did begin to think of it—not seriously, only vaguely." She stopped and shook her head. "And so I suppose it's true. I neglected Jeff. I don't mean really neglected him, but my mind and thoughts weren't with him. When Ruby, as I saw, amused him, I was rather glad. It left me freer to go and do my own things. I never dreamed—of course I never dreamed—that he would be so—so infatuated with her!"

Mrs. Bantry asked, "And when did you find out?"

"I was dumbfounded—absolutely dumbfounded! And, I'm afraid, angry too."

"I'd have been angry," said Mrs. Bantry.

"There was Peter, you see. Peter's whole future depends on Jeff. Jeff practically looked on him as a grandson, or so I thought, but of course he wasn't a grandson. He was no relation at all. And to think that he was going to be disinherited!" Her firm, well-shaped hands shook a little where they lay in her lap. "For that's what it felt like. And for a vulgar golddigging little simpleton! Oh, I could have killed her!"

She stopped, stricken. Her beautiful hazel eyes met Mrs. Bantry's in a pleading horror. She said, "What an awful thing to say!"

Hugo McLean, coming quietly up behind them, asked, "What's an awful thing to say?"

"Sit down, Hugo. You know Mrs. Bantry, don't you?"

McLean had already greeted the older lady. He said, now, in a slow, persevering way, "What was an awful thing to say?"

Addie Jefferson said, "That I'd like to have killed Ruby Keene."

Hugo McLean reflected a minute or two. Then he said, "No, wouldn't say that if I were you. Might be misunderstood." His eyes, steady, reflective gray eyes, looked at her meaningly. He said, "You've got to watch your step, Addie." There was a warning in his voice.

When Miss Marple came out of the hotel and joined Mrs. Bantry a few minutes later, Hugo McLean and Adelaide Jefferson were walking down the path to the sea together. Seating herself, Miss Marple remarked, "He seems very devoted."

"He's been devoted for years! One of those men."

"I know. Like Major Bury. He hung round an Ango-Indian widow for quite ten years. A joke among her friends! In the end she gave in, but, unfortunately, ten days before they were to have been married she ran away with the chauffeur. Such a nice woman, too, and usually so well balanced."

"People do do very odd things," agreed Mrs. Bantry. "I wish you'd been here just now, Jane. Addie Jefferson was telling me all about herself—how her husband went through all his money, but they never let Mr. Jefferson know. And then, this summer, things felt different to her—"

Miss Marple nodded. "Yes. She rebelled, I suppose, against being made to live in the past. After all, there's a time for everything. You can't sit in the house with the blinds down forever. I suppose Mrs. Jefferson just pulled them up and took off her widow's weeds, and her father-in-law, of course, didn't like it. Felt left out in the cold, though I don't suppose for a minute he realized who put her up to it. Still, he certainly wouldn't like it. And so, of course, like old Mr. Badger when his wife took up spiritualism, he was just ripe for what happened. Any fairly nice-looking young girl who listened prettily would have done."

"Do you think," said Mrs. Bantry, "that that cousin, Josie, got her down deliberately—that it was a family plot?"

Miss Marple shook her head. "No, I don't think so at all. I don't think Josie has the kind of mind that could foresee people's reactions. She's rather dense in that way. She's got one of those shrewd, limited, practical minds that never do foresee the future and are usually astonished by it."

"It seems to have taken everyone by surprise," said Mrs. Bantry. "Addie—and Mark Gaskell, too, apparently."

Miss Marple smiled. "I daresay he had his own fish to fry. A bold fellow with a roving eye! Not the man to go on being a sorrowing widower for years, no matter how fond he may have been of his wife. I should think they were both restless under old Mr. Jefferson's yoke of perpetual remembrance. Only," added Miss Marple cynically, "it's easier for gentlemen, of course."

At that very moment Mark was confirming this judgment on himself in a talk with Sir Henry Clithering. With characteristic candor Mark had gone straight to the heart of things. "It's just dawned on me," he said, "that I'm Favorite Suspect Number One to the police! They've been delving into my financial troubles. I'm broke, you know; or very nearly. If dear old Jeff dies according to schedule in a month or two, and Addie and I divide the dibs also according to schedule, all will be well. Matter of fact, I owe rather a lot. If the crash comes, it will be a big one! If I can stave it off, it will be the other way round; I shall come out on top and be very rich."

Sir Henry Clithering said, "You're a gambler, Mark."

"Always have been. Risk everything, that's my motto! Yes, it's a lucky thing for me that somebody strangled that poor kid. I didn't do it. I'm not a strangler. I don't really think I could ever murder anybody. I'm too easygoing. But I don't suppose I can ask the police to believe that! I must look to them like the answer to the criminal investigator's prayer! Motive, on the spot, not burdened with high moral scruples! I can't imagine why I'm not in the jug already. That superintendent's got a very nasty eye."

"You've got that useful thing, an alibi."

"An alibi is the fishiest thing on God's earth! No innocent person ever has an alibi! Besides, it all depends on the time of death, or something like that, and you may be sure if three doctors say the girl was killed at midnight, at least six will be found who will swear positively that she was killed at five in the morning—and where's my alibi then?"

"Well, you are able to joke about it."

"Damned bad taste, isn't it?" said Mark cheerfully. "Actually, I'm rather scared. One is, with murder! And don't think I'm not sorry for old Jeff. I am. But it's better this way—bad as the shock was—than if he'd found her out."

"What do you mean, found her out?"

Mark winked. "Where did she go off to last night? I'll lay you any odds you like she went to meet a man. Jeff wouldn't have liked that. He wouldn't have liked it at all. If he'd found she was deceiving him—that she wasn't the prattling little innocent she seemed—well, my father-in-law is an odd man. He's a man of great self-control, but that self-control can snap. And then, look out!"

Sir Henry glanced at him curiously. "Are you fond of him or not?"

"I'm very fond of him, and at the same time I resent him. I'll try and explain. Conway Jefferson is a man who likes to control his surroundings. He's a benevolent despot, kind, generous and affectionate, but his is the tune and the others dance to his piping."

Mark Gaskell paused.

"I loved my wife. I shall never feel the same for anyone else. Rosamund was sunshine and laughter and flowers, and when she was killed I felt just like a man in the ring who's had a knockout blow. But the referee's been counting a good long time now. I'm a man, after all. I like women. I don't want to marry again—not in the least. Well, that's all right. I've had to be discreet, but I've had my good times all right. Poor Addie hasn't. Addie's a really nice woman. She's the kind of woman men want to marry. Give her half a chance and she would marry again, and be very happy and make the chap happy too.

"But old Jeff saw her always as Frank's wife and hypnotized her into seeing herself like that. He doesn't know it, but we've been in prison. I broke out, on the quiet, a long time ago. Addie broke out this summer, and it gave him a shock. It broke up his world. Result, Ruby Keene." Irrepressibly he sang:

> "But she is in her grave, and oh!
> The difference to me!

"Come and have a drink, Clithering."

It was hardly surprising, Sir Henry reflected, that Mark Gaskell should be an object of suspicion to the police.

CHAPTER FIFTEEN

Doctor Metcalf was one of the best-known physicians in Danemouth. He had no aggressive bedside manner, but his presence in the sickroom had an invariably cheering effect. He was middle-aged, with a quiet pleasant voice. He listened carefully to Superintendent Harper and replied to his questions with gentle precision. Harper said, "Then I can take it, Doctor Metcalf, that what I was told by Mrs. Jefferson was substantially correct?"

"Yes, Mr. Jefferson's health is in a precarious state. For several years now the man has been driving himself ruthlessly. In his determination to live like other men he has lived at a far greater pace than the normal man of his age. He has refused to rest, to take things easy, to go slow, or any of the other phrases with which I and his other medical advisers have tendered our opinion. The result is that the man is an overworked engine. Heart, lungs, blood pressure—they're all overstrained."

"You say Mr. Jefferson has resolutely refused to listen?"

"Yes. I don't know that I blame him. It's not what I say to my patients, superintendent, but a man may as well wear out as rust out. A lot of my colleagues do that, and take it from me, it's not a bad way. In a place like Danemouth one sees most of the other thing. Invalids clinging to life, terrified of overexerting themselves, terrified of a breath of drafty air, of a stray germ, of an injudicious meal."

"I expect that's true enough," said Superintendent Harper. "What it amounts to, then, is this: Conway Jefferson is strong enough, physically speaking—or I suppose I mean muscularly speaking. Just what can he do in the active line, by the way?"

"He has immense strength in his arms and shoulders. He was a very powerful man before his accident. He is extremely dexterous in his handling of his wheelchair, and with the aid of crutches he can move himself about a room—from his bed to the chair, for instance."

"Isn't it possible for a man injured as Mr. Jefferson was to have artificial legs?"

"Not in his case. There was a spine injury."

"I see. Let me sum up again. Jefferson is strong and fit in the muscular sense. He feels well and all that?"

Metcalf nodded.

"But his heart is in a bad condition; any overstrain or exertion, or a shock or a sudden fright, and he might pop off. Is that it?"

"More or less. Overexertion is killing him slowly because he won't give in when he feels tired. That aggravates the cardiac condition. It is unlikely that exertion would kill him suddenly. But a sudden shock or fright might easily do so. That is why I expressly warned his family."

Superintendent Harper said slowly, "But in actual fact a shock didn't kill him. I mean, doctor, that there couldn't have been a much worse shock than this business, and he's still alive."

Doctor Metcalf shrugged his shoulders. "I know. But if you'd had my experience, superintendent, you'd know that case history shows the impossibility of prognosticating accurately. People who ought to die of shock and exposure don't die of shock and exposure, et cetera, et cetera. The human frame is tougher than one can imagine possible. Moreover, in my experience, a physical shock is more often fatal than a mental shock. In plain language, a door banging suddenly would be more likely to kill Mr. Jefferson than the discovery that a girl he was fond of had died in a particularly horrible manner."

"Why is that, I wonder?"

"The breaking of a piece of bad news nearly always sets up a defense reaction. It numbs the recipient. They are unable, at first, to take it in. Full realization takes a little time. But the banged door, someone jumping out of a cupboard, the sudden onslaught of a motor as you cross a road—all those things are immediate in their action. The heart gives a terrified leap—to put it in layman's language."

Superintendent Harper said slowly, "But as far as anyone would know, Mr. Jefferson's death might easily have been caused by the shock of the girl's death?"

"Oh, easily." The doctor looked curiously at the other. "You don't think—"

"I don't know what I think," said Superintendent Harper vexedly.

"But you'll admit, sir, that the two things would fit in very prettily together," he said a little later to Sir Henry Clithering. "Kill two birds with one stone. First the girl, and the fact of her death takes off Mr. Jefferson, too, before he's had any opportunity of altering his will."

"Do you think he will alter it?"

"You'd be more likely to know that, sir, than I would. What do you say?"

"I don't know. Before Ruby Keene came on the scene I happen to know that he had left his money between Mark Gaskell and Mrs. Jefferson. I don't see why he should now change his mind about that. But of course he might do so."

Superintendent Harper agreed.

"You never know what bee a man is going to get in his bonnet; especially when he doesn't feel there's any moral obligation in the disposal of his fortune. No blood relations in this case."

Sir Henry said, "He is fond of the boy—of young Peter."

"D'you think he regards him as a grandson? You'd know that better than I would, sir."

Sir Henry said slowly, "No, I don't think so."

"There's another thing I'd like to ask you, sir. It's a thing I can't judge for myself. But they're friends of yours, and so you'd know. I'd like very much to know just how fond Mr. Jefferson is of Mr. Gaskell and young Mrs. Jefferson. Nobody doubts that he was much attached to them both, but he was attached to them, as I see it, because they were, respectively, the husband and the wife of his daughter and his son. But supposing, for instance, one of them had married again?"

Sir Henry reflected. He said, "It's an interesting point you raise there. I don't know. I'm inclined to suspect—this is a mere opinion—that it would have altered his attitude a good deal. He would have wished them well, borne no rancor, but I think—yes, I rather think that he would have taken very little more interest in them."

Superintendent Harper nodded. "In both cases, sir?"

"I think so, yes. In Mr. Gaskell's almost certainly, and I rather think in Mrs. Jefferson's also, but that's not nearly so certain. I think he was fond of her for her own sake."

"Sex would have something to do with that," said Superintendent Harper sapiently. "Easier for him to look on her as a daughter than to look on Mr. Gaskell as a son. It works both ways. Women accept a son-in-law as one of the family easily enough, but there aren't many times when a woman looks on her son's wife as a daughter." Superintendent Harper went on, "Mind if we walk along this path, sir, to the tennis court? I see Miss Marple's sitting there. I want to ask her to do something for me. As a matter of fact, I want to rope you both in."

"In what way, superintendent?"

"To get at stuff that I can't get at myself. I want you to tackle Edwards for me, sir."

"Edwards? What do you want from him?"

"Everything you can think of. Everything he knows and what he thinks. About the relations between the various members of the family, his angle on the Ruby Keene business. Inside stuff. He knows better than anyone the state of affairs. And he wouldn't tell me. But he'll tell you. Because you're a gentleman and a friend of Mr. Jefferson's."

Sir Henry said grimly, "I've been sent for, urgently, to get at the truth. I mean to do my utmost." He added, "Where do you want Miss Marple to help you?"

"With some girls. Some of those Girl Guides. We've rounded up half a dozen or so—the ones who were most friendly with Pamela Reeves. It's possible that they may know something. You see, I've been thinking. It seems to me that if that girl was going to Woolworth's she would have tried to persuade one of the other girls to go with her. So I think it's possible that Woolworth's was only an excuse. If so, I'd like to know where the girl was really going. She may have let slip something. If so, I feel Miss Marple's the person to get it out of these girls. I'd say she knows a thing or two about girls."

"It sounds to me the kind of village domestic problem that is right up Miss Marple's street. She's very sharp, you know."

The superintendent smiled. He said, "I'll say you're right. Nothing much gets past her."

Miss Marple looked up at their approach and welcomed them eagerly. She listened to the superintendent's request and at once acquiesced. "I should like to help you very much, superintendent, and I think that perhaps I could be of some use. What with the Sunday school, you know, and Brownies and our Guides, and the orphanage quite near—I'm on the committee, you know, and often run in to have a little talk with the matron—and then servants—I usually have very young maids. Oh, yes, I've quite a lot of experience in when a girl is speaking the truth and when she's holding something back."

"In fact, you're an expert," said Sir Henry.

Miss Marple flashed him a reproachful glance and said, "Oh, please don't laugh at me, Sir Henry."

"I shouldn't dream of laughing at you. You've had the laugh on me too many times."

"One does see so much evil in a village," murmured Miss Marple in an explanatory voice.

"By the way," said Sir Henry, "I've cleared up one point you asked me about. The superintendent tells me that there were nail clippings in Ruby's wastepaper basket."

Miss Marple said thoughtfully, "There were? Then that's that—"

"Why did you want to know, Miss Marple?" asked the superintendent.

Miss Marple said, "It was one of the things that—well, that seemed wrong when I looked at the body. The hands were wrong somehow, and I couldn't at first think why. Then I realized that girls who are very much made up, and all that, usually have very long fingernails. Of course, I know that girls everywhere do bite their nails; it's one of those habits that are very hard to break oneself of. But vanity often does a lot to help. Still, I presumed that this girl hadn't cured herself. And then the little boy—Peter, you know—he said something which showed that her nails had been long, only she caught one and broke it. So then, of course, she might have trimmed off the rest to make an even appearance, and I asked about clippings and Sir Henry said he'd find out."

Sir Henry remarked, "You said just now 'one of the things that seemed wrong when I looked at the body.' Was there something else?"

Miss Marple nodded vigorously. "Oh, yes!" she said. "There was the dress. The dress was all wrong."

Both men looked at her curiously. "Now, why?" said Sir Henry.

"Well, you see, it was an old dress. Josie said so, definitely, and I could see for myself that it was shabby and rather worn. Now, that's all wrong."

"I don't see why."

Miss Marple got a little pink. "Well, the idea is, isn't it, that Ruby Keene changed her dress and went off to meet someone on whom she presumably had what my young nephews call a 'crush'?"

The superintendent's eyes twinkled a little. "That's the theory. She'd got a date with someone—a boyfriend, as the saying goes."

"Then why," demanded Miss Marple, "was she wearing an old dress?"

The superintendent scratched his head thoughtfully. He said, "I see your point. You think she'd wear a new one?"

"I think she'd wear her best dress. Girls do."

Sir Henry interposed, "Yes, but look here, Miss Marple. Suppose she was going outside to this rendezvous. Going in an open car, perhaps, or walking in some rough going. Then she'd not want to risk messing a new frock and she'd put on an old one."

"That would be the sensible thing to do," agreed the superintendent.

Miss Marple turned on him. She spoke with animation, "The sensible thing to do would be to change into trousers and a pullover, or into tweeds. That, of course—I don't want to be snobbish, but I'm afraid it's unavoidable—that's what a girl of—of our class would do.

"A wellbred girl," continued Miss Marple, warming to her subject, "is always very particular to wear the right clothes for the right occasion. I mean, however hot the day was, a wellbred girl would never turn up at a point-to-point in a silk flowered frock."

"And the correct wear to meet a lover?" demanded Sir Henry.

"If she were meeting him inside the hotel or somewhere where evening dress was worn, she'd wear her best evening frock, of course, but outside she'd feel she'd look ridiculous in evening dress and she'd wear her most attractive sports wear."

"Granted, Fashion Queen, but the girl Ruby—"

Miss Marple said, "Ruby, of course, wasn't—well, to put it bluntly, Ruby wasn't a lady. She belonged to the class that wear their best clothes, however unsuitable to the occasion. Last year, you know, we had a picnic outing at Scrantor Rocks. You'd be surprised at the unsuitable clothes the girls wore. Foulard dresses and patent-leather shoes and quite elaborate hats, some of them. For climbing about over rocks and in gorse and heather. And the young men in their best suits. Of course, hiking's different again. That's practically a uniform, and girls don't seem to realize that shorts are very unbecoming unless they are very slender."

The superintendent said slowly, "And you think that Ruby Keene—"

"I think that she'd have kept on the frock she was wearing—her best pink one. She'd only have changed it if she'd had something newer still."

Superintendent Harper said, "And what's your explanation, Miss Marple?"

Miss Marple said, "I haven't got one—yet. But I can't help feeling that it's important."

CHAPTER SIXTEEN

Inside the wire cage, the tennis lesson that Raymond Starr was giving had come to an end. A stout middle-aged woman uttered a few appreciative squeaks, picked up a sky-blue cardigan and went off toward the hotel. Raymond called out a few gay words after her. Then he turned toward the bench where the three onlookers were sitting. The balls dangled in a net in his hand, his racket was under one arm. The gay, laughing expression on his face was wiped off as though by a sponge from a slate. He looked tired and worried. Coming toward them he said, "That's over." Then the smile broke out again, that charming, boyish, expressive smile that went so harmoniously with his suntanned face and dark, lithe grace. Sir Henry found himself wondering how old the man was. Twenty-five, thirty, thirty-five? It was impossible to say. Raymond said, shaking his head a little, "She'll never be able to play, you know."

"All this must," said Miss Marple, "be very boring for you."

Raymond said simply, "It is sometimes. Especially at the end of the summer. For a time the thought of the pay buoys one up, but even that fails to stimulate imagination in the end."

Superintendent Harper got up. He said abruptly, "I'll call for you in half an hour's time, Miss Marple, if that will be all right?"

"Perfectly, thank you. I shall be ready."

Harper went off. Raymond stood looking after him. Then he said, "Mind if I sit for a bit?"

"Do," said Sir Henry. "Have a cigarette?" He offered his case, wondering as he did so why he had a slight feeling of prejudice against Raymond Starr. Was it simply because he was a professional tennis coach and dancer? If so, it wasn't the tennis, it was the dancing. The English, Sir Henry decided, had a distrust for any man who danced too well. This fellow moved with too much grace. Ramon—Raymond—which was his name? Abruptly, he asked the question.

The other seemed amused. "Ramon was my original professional name. Ramon and Josie—Spanish effect, you know. Then there was rather a prejudice against foreigners, so I became Raymond—very British."

Miss Marple said, "And is your real name something quite different?"

He smiled at her. "Actually my real name is Ramon. I had an Argentine grandmother, you see." *And that accounts for that swing from the hips,* thought Sir Henry parenthetically. "But my first name is Thomas. Painfully prosaic." He turned to Sir Henry. "You come from Devonshire, don't you, sir? From Stane? My people lived down that way. At Alsmonston."

Sir Henry's face lit up. "Are you one of the Alsmonston Starrs? I didn't realize that."

"No, I don't suppose you would." There was a slight bitterness in his voice.

Sir Henry said, "Bad luck—er—all that."

"The place being sold up after it had been in the family for three hundred years? Yes, it was rather! Still, our kind have to go, I suppose! We've outlived our usefulness. My elder brother went to New York. He's in publishing—doing well. The rest of us are scattered up and down the earth. I'll say it's hard to get a job nowadays when you've nothing to say for yourself except that you've had a public school education. Sometimes, if you're lucky, you get taken on as a reception clerk at a hotel. The tie and the manner are an asset there. The only job I could get was showman in a plumbing establishment. Selling superb peach and lemon colored porcelain baths. Enormous showrooms, but as I never knew the price of the damned things or how soon we could deliver them, I got fired.

"The only things I could do were dance and play tennis. I got taken on at a hotel on the Riviera. Good pickings there. I suppose I was doing well. Then I overheard an old colonel—real old colonel, incredibly ancient, British to the backbone and always talking about Poona. He went up to the manager and said at the top of his voice: 'Where's the gigolo? I want to get hold of the gigolo. My wife and daughter want to dance, yer know. Where is the feller? What does he sting yer for? It's the gigolo I want.'" Raymond said, "Silly to mind. But I did. I chucked it. Came here. Less pay, but pleasanter. Mostly teaching tennis to rotund women who will never, never be able to play. That and dancing with the wallflower daughters of rich clients! Oh, well, it's life, I suppose. Excuse today's hardluck story." He laughed. His teeth flashed out white, his eyes crinkled up at the corners. He looked suddenly healthy and happy and very much alive.

Sir Henry said, "I'm glad to have a chat with you. I've been wanting to talk with you."

"About Ruby Keene? I can't help you, you know. I don't know who killed her. I knew very little about her. She didn't confide in me."

Miss Marple said, "Did you like her?"

"Not particularly. I didn't dislike her." His voice was careless, uninterested.

Sir Henry said, "So you've no suggestions?"

"I'm afraid not. I'd have told Harper if I had. It just seems to me one of those things! Petty, sordid little crime, no clues, no motive."

"Two people had a motive," said Miss Marple.

Sir Henry looked at her sharply.

"Really?" Raymond looked surprised.

Miss Marple looked insistently at Sir Henry, and he said rather unwillingly, "Her death probably benefits Mrs. Jefferson and Mr. Gaskell to the amount of fifty thousand pounds."

"What?" Raymond looked really startled—more than startled, upset. "Oh, but that's absurd—absolutely absurd. Mrs. Jefferson—neither of them—could have had anything to do with it. It would be incredible to think of such a thing."

Miss Marple coughed. She said gently, "I'm afraid, you know, you're rather an idealist."

"I?" He laughed. "Not me! I'm a hardboiled cynic."

"Money," said Miss Marple, "is a very powerful motive."

"Perhaps," Raymond said hotly. "But that either of those two would strangle a girl in cold blood—" He shook his head. Then he got up. "Here's Mrs. Jefferson now. Come for her lesson. She's late." His voice sounded amused. "Ten minutes late!"

Adelaide Jefferson and Hugo McLean were walking rapidly down the path toward them. With a smiling apology for her lateness, Addie Jefferson went onto the court. McLean sat down on the bench. After a polite inquiry whether Miss Marple minded a pipe, he lit it and puffed for some minutes in silence, watching critically the two white figures about the tennis court. He said at last, "Can't see what Addie wants to have lessons for. Have a game, yes. No one enjoys it better than I do. But why lessons?"

"Wants to improve her game," said Sir Henry.

"She's not a bad player," said Hugo. "Good enough, at all events. Dash it all, she isn't aiming to play at Wimbledon." He was silent for a minute or two. Then he said, "Who is this Raymond fellow? Where do they come from, these pros? Fellow looks like a Dago to me."

"He's one of the Devonshire Starrs," said Sir Henry.

"What? Not really?"

Sir Henry nodded. It was clear that this news was unpleasing to Hugo McLean. He scowled more than ever. He said, "Don't know why Addie sent for me. She seems not to have turned a hair over this business. Never looked better. Why send for me?"

Sir Henry asked with some curiosity, "When did she send for you?"

"Oh—er—when all this happened."

"How did you hear? Telephone or telegram?"

"Telegram."

"As a matter of curiosity, when was it sent off?"

"Well, I don't know exactly."

"What time did you receive it?"

"I didn't exactly receive it. It was telephoned on to me, as a matter of fact."

"Why, where were you?"

"Fact is, I'd left London the afternoon before. I was staying at Danebury Head."

"What? Quite near here?"

"Yes, rather funny, wasn't it? Got the message when I got in from a round of golf and came over here at once."

Miss Marple gazed at him thoughtfully. He looked hot and uncomfortable. She said, "I've heard it's very pleasant at Danebury Head and not very expensive."

"No, it's not expensive. I couldn't afford it if it was. It's a nice little place."

"We must drive over there one day," said Miss Marple.

"Eh? What? Oh—er—yes, I should." He got up. "Better take some exercise, get an appetite." He walked away stiffly.

"Women," said Sir Henry, "treat their devoted admirers very badly." Miss Marple smiled, but made no answer. "Does he strike you as rather a dull dog?" asked Sir Henry. "I'd be interested to know."

"A little limited in his ideas, perhaps," said Miss Marple. "But with possibilities, I think—oh, definitely possibilities."

Sir Henry, in his turn, got up. "It's time for me to go and do my stuff. I see Mrs. Bantry is on her way to keep you company."

Mrs. Bantry arrived breathless and sat down with a gasp. She said, "I've been talking to chambermaids. But it isn't any good. I haven't found out a thing more! Do you think that girl can really have been carrying on with someone without everybody in the hotel knowing all about it?"

"That's a very interesting point, dear. I should say definitely not. Somebody knows, depend upon it, if it's true. But she must have been very clever about it."

Mrs. Bantry's attention had strayed to the tennis court. She said approvingly, "Addie's tennis is coming on a lot. Attractive young man, that tennis pro. Addie's quite nice-looking. She's still an attractive woman. I shouldn't be at all surprised if she married again."

"She'll be quite a rich woman, too, when Mr. Jefferson dies," said Miss Marple.

"Oh, don't always have such a nasty mind, Jane. Why haven't you solved this mystery yet? We don't seem to be getting on at all. I thought you'd know at once." Mrs. Bantry's tone held reproach.

"No, no, dear, I didn't know at once—not for some time."

Mrs. Bantry turned startled and incredulous eyes on her. "You mean you know now who killed Ruby Keene?"

"Oh, yes," said Miss Marple. "I know that!"

"But, Jane, who is it? Tell me at once."

Miss Marple shook her head very firmly and pursed up her lips. "I'm sorry, Dolly, but that wouldn't do at all."

"Why wouldn't it do?"

"Because you're so indiscreet. You would go round telling everyone—or if you didn't tell, you'd hint."

"No, indeed, I wouldn't. I wouldn't tell a soul."

"People who use that phrase are always the last to live up to it. It's no good, dear. There's a long way to go yet. A great many things that are quite obscure. You remember when I was so against letting Mrs. Partridge collect for the Red Cross and I couldn't say why. The reason was that her nose had twitched in just the same way that that maid of mine, Alice, twitched her nose when I sent her out to pay the accounts. Always paid them a shilling or so short and said it could go on to next week, which, of course, was exactly what Mrs. Partridge did, only on a much larger scale. Seventy-five pounds it was she embezzled."

"Never mind Mrs. Partridge," said Mrs. Bantry.

"But I had to explain to you. And if you care, I'll give you a hint. The trouble in this case is that everybody has been much too credulous and believing. You simply cannot afford to believe everything that people tell you. When there's anything fishy about, I never believe anyone at all. You see, I know human nature so well."

Mrs. Bantry was silent for a minute or two. Then she said in a different tone of voice, "I told you, didn't I, that I didn't see why I shouldn't enjoy myself over this case? A real murder in my own house! The sort of thing that will never happen again."

"I hope not," said Miss Marple.

"Well, so do I really. Once is enough. But it's my murder, Jane. I want to enjoy myself over it."

Miss Marple shot a glance at her Mrs. Bantry said belligerently, "Don't you believe that?"

Miss Marple said sweetly, "Of course, Dolly, if you tell me so."

"Yes, but you never believe what people tell you, do you? You've just said so. Well, you're quite right." Mrs. Bantry's voice took on a sudden bitter note. She said, "I'm not altogether a fool. You may think, Jane, that I don't know what they're saying all over St. Mary Mead—all over the county! They're saying, one and all, that there's no smoke without fire; that if the girl was found in Arthur's library, then Arthur must know something about it. They're saying that the girl was Arthur's mistress; that she was his illegitimate daughter; that she was blackmailing him; they're saying anything that comes into their heads. And it will go on like that! Arthur won't realize it at first; he won't know what's wrong. He's such a dear old stupid that he'd never believe people would think things like that about him. He'll be cold-shouldered and looked at askance—whatever that means!— and it will dawn on him little by little, and suddenly he'll be horrified and cut to the soul, and he'll fasten up like a clam and just endure, day after day. It's because of all that's going to happen to him that I've come here to ferret out every single thing about it that I can! This murder's got to be solved! If it isn't, then Arthur's whole life will be wrecked, and I won't have that happen. I won't! I won't! I won't!" She paused for a minute and said, "I won't have the dear old boy go through hell for something he didn't do. That's the only reason I came to Danemouth and left him alone at home— to find out the truth."

"I know, dear," said Miss Marple. "That's why I'm here too."

CHAPTER SEVENTEEN

In a quiet hotel room Edwards was listening deferentially to Sir Henry Clithering. "There are certain questions I would like to ask you, Edwards, but I want you first to understand quite clearly my position here. I was at one time commissioner of the police at Scotland Yard. I am now retired into private life. Your master sent for me when this tragedy occurred. He begged me to use my skill and experience in order to find out the truth." Sir Henry paused. Edwards, his pale, intelligent eyes on the other's face, inclined his head. He said, "Quite so, Sir Henry."

Clithering went on slowly and deliberately, "In all police cases there is necessarily a lot of information that is held back. It is held back for various reasons—because it touches on a family skeleton, because it is considered to have no bearing on the case, because it would entail awkwardness and embarrassment to the parties concerned."

Again Edwards said, "Quite so, Sir Henry."

"I expect, Edwards, that by now you appreciate quite clearly the main points of this business. The dead girl was on the point of becoming Mr. Jefferson's adopted daughter. Two people had a motive in seeing that this should not happen. Those two people are Mr. Gaskell and Mrs. Jefferson."

The valet's eyes displayed a momentary gleam. He said, "May I ask if they are under suspicion, sir?"

"They are in no danger of arrest, if that is what you mean. But the police are bound to be suspicious of them and will continue to be so until the matter is cleared up."

"An unpleasant position for them, sir."

"Very unpleasant. Now to get at the truth, one must have all the facts of the case. A lot depends, must depend, on the reactions, the words and gestures, of Mr. Jefferson and his family. How did they feel, what did they show, what things were said? I am asking you, Edwards, for inside information—the kind of inside information that only you are likely to have. You know your master's moods. From observation of them you probably know what caused them. I am asking this, not as a policeman but as a friend of Mr. Jefferson's. That is to say, if anything you tell me is not, in my opinion, relevant to the case, I shall not pass it on to the police." He paused.

Edwards said quietly, "I understand you, sir. You want me to speak quite frankly; to say things that, in the ordinary course of events, I should not say, and that—excuse me, sir—you wouldn't dream of listening to."

Sir Henry said, "You're a very intelligent fellow, Edwards. That's exactly what I do mean."

Edwards was silent for a minute or two, then he began to speak. "Of course I know Mr. Jefferson fairly well by now. I've been with him quite a number of years. And I see him in his 'off' moments, not only in his 'on' ones. Sometimes, sir, I've questioned in my own mind whether it's good for anyone to fight fate in the way Mr. Jefferson has fought. It's taken a terrible toll on him, sir. If, sometimes, he could have given way, been an unhappy, lonely, broken old man—well, it might have been better for him in the end.

But he's too proud for that. He'll go down fighting—that's his motto. But that sort of thing leads, Sir Henry, to a lot of nervous reaction. He looks a good-tempered gentleman. I've seen him in violent rages when he could hardly speak for passion. And the one thing that roused him, sir, was deceit."

"Are you saying that for any particular reason, Edwards?"

"Yes, sir. I am. You asked me, sir, to speak quite frankly."

"That is the idea."

"Well, then, Sir Henry, in my opinion the young woman that Mr. Jefferson was so taken up with wasn't worth it. She was, to put it bluntly, a common little piece. And she didn't care tuppence for Mr. Jefferson. All that play of affection and gratitude was so much poppycock. I don't say there was any harm in her, but she wasn't, by a long way, what Mr. Jefferson thought her. It was funny, that, sir, for Mr. Jefferson was a shrewd gentleman; he wasn't often deceived over people. But there, a gentleman isn't himself in his judgment when it comes to a young woman being in question. Young Mrs. Jefferson, you see, whom he'd always depended upon a lot for sympathy, had changed a good deal this summer. He noticed it and he felt it badly. He was fond of her, you see. Mr. Mark he never liked much."

Sir Henry interjected. "And yet he had him with him constantly?"

"Yes, but that was for Miss Rosamund's sake. Mrs. Gaskell, that was. She was the apple of his eye. He adored her. Mr. Mark was Miss Rosamund's husband. He always thought of him like that."

"Supposing Mr. Mark had married someone else?"

"Mr. Jefferson, sir, would have been furious."

Sir Henry raised his eyebrows. "As much as that?"

"He wouldn't have shown it, but that's what it would have been."

"And if Mrs. Jefferson had married again?"

"Mr. Jefferson wouldn't have liked that either, sir."

"Please go on, Edwards."

"I was saying, sir, that Mr. Jefferson fell for this young woman. I've often seen it happen with the gentlemen I've been with. Comes over them like a kind of disease. They want to protect the girl, and shield her, and shower benefits upon her, and nine times out of ten the girl is very well able to look after herself and has a good eye to the main chance."

"So you think Ruby Keene was a schemer?"

"Well, Sir Henry, she was quite inexperienced, being so young, but she had the makings of a very fine schemer indeed when she'd once got well into her swing, so to speak. In another five years she'd have been an expert at the game."

Sir Henry said, "I'm glad to have your opinion of her. It's valuable. Now, do you recall any incidents in which this matter was discussed between Mr. Jefferson and the members of his family?"

"There was very little discussion, sir. Mr. Jefferson announced what he had in mind and stifled any protests. That is, he shut up Mr. Mark, who was a bit outspoken. Mrs. Jefferson didn't say much—she's a quiet lady— only urged him not to do anything in a great hurry."

Sir Henry nodded. "Anything else? What was the girl's attitude?"

With marked distaste the valet said, "I should describe it, Sir Henry, as jubilant."

"Ah, jubilant, you say? You had no reason to believe, Edwards, that"—he sought about for a phrase suitable to Edwards—"that—er—her affections were engaged elsewhere?"

"Mr. Jefferson was not proposing marriage, sir. He was going to adopt her."

"Cut out the 'elsewhere' and let the question stand."

The valet said slowly, "There was one incident, sir. I happened to be a witness of it."

"That is gratifying. Tell me."

"There is probably nothing in it, sir. It was just that one day, the young woman chancing to open her handbag, a small snapshot fell out. Mr. Jefferson pounced on it and said, 'Hullo, kitten, who's this, eh?'

"It was a snapshot, sir, of a young man, a dark young man with rather untidy hair, and his tie very badly arranged. Miss Keene pretended that she didn't know anything about it. She said, 'I've no idea, Jeffie. No idea at all. I don't know how it could have got into my bag. I didn't put it there.'

"Now, Mr. Jefferson, sir, wasn't quite a fool. That story wasn't good enough. He looked angry, his brows came down heavy, and his voice was gruff when he said, 'Now then, kitten, now then. You know who it is right enough.' She changed her tactics quick, sir. Looked frightened. She said, 'I do recognize him now. He comes here sometimes and I've danced with him. I don't know his name. The silly idiot must have stuffed his photo into my bag one day. These boys are too silly for anything!' She tossed her head and giggled and passed it off. But it wasn't a likely story, was it? And I don't think Mr. Jefferson quite believed it. He looked at her once or twice after that in a sharp way, and sometimes, if she'd been out, he asked her where she'd been."

Sir Henry said, "Have you ever seen the original of the photo about the hotel?"

"Not to my knowledge, sir. Of course I am not much downstairs in the public apartments."

Sir Henry nodded. He asked a few more questions, but Edwards could tell him nothing more.

In the police station at Danemouth Superintendent Harper was interviewing Jessie Davis, Florence Small, Beatrice Henniker, Mary Price and Lilian Ridgeway. They were girls much of an age, differing slightly in mentality. They ranged from "county" to farmers' and shopkeepers' daughters. One and all, they told the same story. Pamela Reeves had been just the same as usual; she had said nothing to any of them except that she was going to Woolworth's and would go home by a later bus.

In the corner of Superintendent Harper's office sat an elderly lady. The girls hardly noticed her. If they did they may have wondered who she was. She was certainly no police matron. Possibly they assumed that she, like them, was a witness to be questioned. The last girl was shown out. Superintendent Harper wiped his forehead and turned round to look at Miss

Marple. His glance was inquiring, but not hopeful. Miss Marple, however, spoke crisply, "I'd like to speak to Florence Small."

The superintendent's eyebrows rose, but he nodded and touched a bell. A constable appeared. Harper said, "Florence Small."

The girl reappeared, ushered in by the constable. She was the daughter of a well-to-do farmer—a tall girl with fair hair, a rather foolish mouth and frightened brown eyes. She was twisting her hands and looked nervous. Superintendent Harper looked at Miss Marple, who nodded. The superintendent got up. He said, "This lady will ask you some questions." He went out, closing the door behind him.

Florence looked uneasily at Miss Marple. Her eyes looked rather like those of one of her father's calves.

Miss Marple said, "Sit down, Florence."

Florence Small sat down obediently. Unrecognized by herself, she felt suddenly more at home, less uneasy. The unfamiliar and terrorizing atmosphere of a police station was replaced by something more familiar—the accustomed tone of command of somebody whose business it was to give orders.

Miss Marple said, "You understand, Florence, that it's of the utmost importance that everything about poor Pamela's doings on the day of her death should be known?"

Florence murmured that she quite understood.

"And I'm sure you want to do your best to help?" Florence's eyes were wary as she said of course she did. "To keep back any piece of information is a very serious offense," said Miss Marple.

The girl's fingers twisted nervously in her lap. She swallowed once or twice. "I can make allowances," went on Miss Marple, "for the fact that you are naturally alarmed at being brought into contact with the police. You are afraid, too, that you may be blamed for not having spoken sooner. Possibly you are afraid that you may also be blamed for not stopping Pamela at the time. But you've got to be a brave girl and make a clean breast of things. If you refuse to tell what you know now, it will be a very serious matter indeed—very serious—practically perjury—and for that, as you know, you can be sent to prison."

"I—I don't—"

Miss Marple said sharply, "Now don't prevaricate, Florence! Tell me all about it at once! Pamela wasn't going to Woolworth's, was she?" Florence licked her lips with a dry tongue and gazed imploringly at Miss Marple, like a beast about to be slaughtered. "Something to do with the films, wasn't it?" asked Miss Marple.

A look of intense relief mingled with awe passed over Florence's face. Her inhibitions left her. She gasped, "Oh, yes!"

"I thought so," said Miss Marple. "Now I want you to tell me all the details, please."

Words poured from Florence in a gush. "Oh, I've been ever so worried. I promised Pam, you see, I'd never say a word to a soul. And then, when she was found, all burned up in that car—oh, it was horrible and I thought I should die—I felt it was all my fault. I ought to have stopped her. Only I never thought, not for a minute, that it wasn't all right. And then I was asked if she'd been quite as usual that day and I said 'Yes' before I'd had time to think. And not having said anything then, I didn't see how I could say anything later. And after all, I didn't know anything—not really—only what Pam told me."

"What did Pam tell you?"

"It was as we were walking up the lane to the bus on the way to the rally. She asked me if I could keep a secret, and I said yes, and she made me swear not to tell. She was going into Danemouth for a film test after the rally! She'd met a film producer—just back from Hollywood, he was. He wanted a certain type, and he told Pam she was just what he was looking for. He warned her, though, not to build on it. You couldn't tell, he said, not until you saw how a person photographed. It might be no good at all. It was a kind of Bergner part, he said. You had to have someone quite young for it. A schoolgirl, it was, who changes places with a revue artist and has a wonderful career. Pam's acted in plays at school and she's awfully good. He said he could see she could act, but she'd have to have some intensive training. It wouldn't be all beer and skittles, he told her; it would be hard work. Did she think she could stick it?"

Florence Small stopped for breath. Miss Marple felt rather sick as she listened to the glib rehash of countless novels and screen stories. Pamela Reeves, like most other girls, would have been warned against talking to strangers, but the glamour of the films would have obliterated all that.

"He was absolutely businesslike about it all," continued Florence. "Said if the test was successful she'd have a contract, and he said that as she was young and inexperienced she ought to let a lawyer look at it before she signed it. But she wasn't to pass on that he'd said that. He asked her if she'd have trouble with her parents, and Pam said she probably would, and he said, 'Well, of course that's always a difficulty with anyone as young as you are, but I think if it was put to them that this was a wonderful chance that wouldn't happen once in a million times, they'd see reason.' But anyway, he said, it wasn't any good going into that until they knew the result of the test. She mustn't be disappointed if it failed. He told her about Hollywood and about Vivien Leigh—how she'd suddenly taken London by storm, and how these sensational leaps into fame did happen. He himself had come back from America to work with the Lenville Studios and put some pep into the English film companies."

Miss Marple nodded.

Florence went on, "So it was all arranged. Pam was to go into Danemouth after the rally and meet him at his hotel and he'd take her along to the studios—they'd got a small testing studio in Danemouth, he told her. She'd have her test and she could catch the bus home afterward. She could say she'd been shopping, and he'd let her know the result of the test in a few days, and if it was favorable Mr. Harmsteiter, the boss, would come along and talk to her parents.

"Well, of course, it sounded too wonderful! I was green with envy! Pam got through the rally without turning a hair—we always call her a regular poker face. Then, when she said that she was going into Danemouth to Woolworth's, she just winked at me.

"I saw her start off down the footpath." Florence began to cry. "I ought to have stopped her! I ought to have stopped her! I ought to have known a thing like that couldn't be true! I ought to have told someone. Oh, dear, I wish I was dead!"

"There, there." Miss Marple patted her on the shoulder. "It's quite all right. No one will blame you, Florence. You've done the right thing in telling me."

She devoted some minutes to cheering the child up.

Five minutes later she was telling the girl's story to Superintendent Harper. The latter looked very grim. "The clever devil!" he said. "I'll cook his goose for him! This puts rather a different aspect on things."

"Yes, it does."

Harper looked at her sideways. "It doesn't surprise you?"

"I expected something of the kind," Miss Marple said.

Superintendent Harper said curiously, "What put you on to this particular girl? They all looked scared to death and there wasn't a pin to choose between them, as far as I could see."

Miss Marple said gently, "You haven't had as much experience with girls telling lies as I have. Florence looked at you very straight, if you remember, and stood very rigid and just fidgeted with her feet like the others. But you didn't watch her as she went out of the door. I knew at once then that she'd got something to hide. They nearly always relax too soon. My little maid Janet always did. She'd explain quite convincingly that the mice had eaten the end of a cake and give herself away by smirking as she left the room."

"I'm very grateful to you," said Harper. He added thoughtfully, "Lenville Studios, eh?"

Miss Marple said nothing. She rose to her feet.

"I'm afraid," she said, "I must hurry away. So glad to have been able to help you."

"Are you going back to the hotel?"

"Yes, to pack up. I must go back to St. Mary Mead as soon as possible. There's a lot for me to do there."

CHAPTER EIGHTEEN

Miss Marple passed out through the French windows of her drawing room, tripped down her neat garden path, through a garden gate, in through the vicarage garden gate, across the vicarage garden and up to the drawing-room window, where she tapped gently on the pane. The vicar was busy in his study composing his Sunday sermon, but the vicar's wife, who was young and pretty, was admiring the progress of her offspring across the hearthrug. "Can I come in, Griselda?"

"Oh, do, Miss Marple. Just look at David! He gets so angry because he can only crawl in reverse. He wants to get to something, and the more he tries the more he goes backwards into the coalbox!"

"He's looking very bonny, Griselda."

"He's not bad, is he?" said the young mother, endeavoring to assume an indifferent manner. "Of course I don't bother with him much. All the books say a child should be left alone as much as possible."

"Very wise, dear," said Miss Marple. "Ahem—I came to ask if there was anything special you are collecting for at the moment?"

The vicar's wife turned somewhat astonished eyes upon her. "Oh, heaps of things," she said cheerfully. "There always are." She ticked them off on her fingers. "There's the Nave Restoration Fund, and St. Giles' Mission, and our Sale of Work next Wednesday, and the Unmarried Mothers, and a Boy Scouts Outing, and the Needlework Guild, and the Bishop's Appeal for Deep-Sea Fishermen."

"Any of them will do," said Miss Marple. "I thought I might make a little round—with a book, you know—if you would authorize me to do so."

"Are you up to something? I believe you are. Of course I authorize you. Make it the Sale of Work; it would be lovely to get some real money instead of those awful sachets and comic penwipers and depressing children's frocks and dusters all done up to look like dolls. . . . I suppose," continued Griselda, accompanying her guest to the window, "that you wouldn't like to tell me what it's all about?"

"Later, my dear," said Miss Marple, hurrying off.

With a sigh the young mother returned to the hearthrug and, by way of carrying out her principles of stern neglect, butted her son three times in the stomach, so that he caught hold of her hair and pulled it with gleeful yells. They then rolled over and over in a grand rough and tumble until the door opened and the vicarage maid announced to the most influential parishioner, who didn't like children, "Missus is in here."

Whereupon Griselda sat up and tried to look dignified and more what a vicar's wife should be.

Miss Marple, clasping a small black book with penciled entries in it, walked briskly along the village street until she came to the crossroads. Here she turned to the left and walked past the Blue Boar until she came to Chatsworth, alias "Mr. Booker's new house." She turned in at the gate, walked up to the front door and knocked on it briskly. The door was opened by the blond young woman named Dinah Lee. She was less carefully made up than usual and, in fact, looked slightly dirty. She was wearing gray slacks and an emerald jumper.

"Good morning," said Miss Marple briskly and cheerfully. "May I just come in for a minute?" She pressed forward as she spoke, so that Dinah Lee, who was somewhat taken aback at the call, had no time to make up her mind. "Thank you so much," said Miss Marple, beaming amiably at her and sitting down rather gingerly on a period bamboo chair. "Quite warm for the time of year, is it not?" went on Miss Marple, still exuding geniality.

"Yes, rather. Oh, quite," said Miss Lee. At a loss how to deal with the situation, she opened a box and offered it to her guest. "Er—have a cigarette?"

"Thank you so much, but I don't smoke. I just called, you know, to see if I could enlist your help for our Sale of Work next week."

"Sale of Work?" said Dinah Lee, as one who repeats a phrase in a foreign language.

"At the vicarage," said Miss Marple. "Next Wednesday."

"Oh!" Miss Lee's mouth fell open. "I'm afraid I couldn't—"

"Not even a small subscription—half a crown perhaps?" Miss Marple exhibited her little book.

"Oh—er—well, yes. I daresay I could manage that." The girl looked relieved and turned to hunt in her handbag.

Miss Marple's sharp eyes were looking round the room. She said, "I see you've no hearthrug in front of the fire." Dinah Lee turned round and stared at her. She could not but be aware of the very keen scrutiny the old lady was giving her, but it aroused in her no other emotion than slight annoyance. Miss Marple recognized that. She said, "It's rather dangerous, you know. Sparks fly out and mark the carpet."

Funny old tabby, thought Dinah, but she said quite amiably, if somewhat vaguely, "There used to be one. I don't know where it's got to."

"I suppose," said Miss Marple, "it was the fluffy woolly kind?"

"Sheep," said Dinah. "That's what it looked like." She was amused now. An eccentric old bean, this. She held out a half crown. "Here you are," she said.

"Oh, thank you, my dear." Miss Marple took it and opened the little book. "Er—what name shall I write down?"

Dinah's eyes grew suddenly hard and contemptuous. *Nosy old cat,* she thought. *That's all she came for—prying around for scandal.* She said clearly and with malicious pleasure. "Miss Dinah Lee."

Miss Marple looked at her steadily. She said, "This is Mr. Basil Blake's cottage, isn't it?"

"Yes, and I'm Miss Dinah Lee!" Her voice rang out challengingly, her head went back, her blue eyes flashed.

Very steadily Miss Marple looked at her. She said, "Will you allow me to give you some advice, even though you may consider it impertinent?"

"I shall consider it impertinent. You had better say nothing."

"Nevertheless," said Miss Marple, "I am going to speak. I want to advise you, very strongly, not to continue using your maiden name in the village."

Dinah stared at her. She said, "What—what do you mean?"

Miss Marple said earnestly, "In a very short time you may need all the sympathy and good will you can find. It will be important to your husband, too, that he shall be thought well of. There is a prejudice in old-fashioned country districts against people living together who are not married. It has amused you both, I dare say, to pretend that that is what you are doing. It kept people away, so that you weren't bothered with what I expect you would call 'old frumps.' Nevertheless, old frumps have their uses."

Dinah demanded, "How did you know we are married?"

Miss Marple smiled a deprecating smile. "Oh, my dear," she said.

Dinah persisted, "No, but how did you know? You didn't—you didn't go to Somerset House?"

A momentary flicker showed in Miss Marple's eyes. "Somerset House? Oh, no. But it was quite easy to guess. Everything, you know, gets round in a village. The—er—the kind of quarrels you have—typical of early days of marriage. Quite—quite unlike an illicit relationship. It has been said, you know—and I think quite truly—that you can only really get under anybody's skin if you are married to them. When there is no—no legal bond, people are much more careful; they have to keep assuring themselves how happy and halcyon everything is. They have, you see, to justify themselves. They dare not quarrel! Married people, I have noticed, quite enjoy their battles and the —er—appropriate reconcilations." She paused, twinkling benignly.

"Well, I—" Dinah stopped and laughed. She sat down and lit a cigarette. "You're absolutely marvelous!" she said. Then she went on, "But why do you want us to own up and admit to respectability?"

Miss Marple's face was grave now. She said, "Because any minute now your husband may be arrested for murder."

CHAPTER NINETEEN

For an interval Dinah stared at Miss Marple. Then she said incredulously, "Basil? Murder? Are you joking?"

"No, indeed. Haven't you seen the papers?"

Dinah caught her breath. "You mean that girl at the Majestic Hotel. Do you mean they suspect Basil of killing her?"

"Yes."

"But it's nonsense!"

There was the whir of a car outside, the bang of a gate. Basil Blake flung open the door and came in, carrying some bottles. He said, "Got the gin and the vermouth. Did you—" He stopped and turned incredulous eyes on the prim, erect visitor.

Dinah burst out breathlessly, "Is she mad? She says you're going to be arrested for the murder of that girl Ruby Keene."

"Oh, God!" said Basil Blake. The bottles dropped from his arms onto the sofa. He reeled to a chair and dropped down in it and buried his face in his hands. He repeated, "Oh, my God! Oh, my God!"

Dinah darted over to him. She caught his shoulders. "Basil, look at me! It isn't true! I know it isn't true! I don't believe it for a moment!"

His hand went up and gripped hers. "Bless you, darling."

"But why should they think— You didn't even know her, did you?"

"Oh, yes, he knew her," said Miss Marple.

Basil said fiercely, "Be quiet, you old hag! . . . Listen, Dinah, darling. I hardly knew her at all. Just ran across her once or twice at the Majestic. That's all—I swear that's all!"

Dinah said, bewildered, "I don't understand. Why should anyone suspect you, then?"

Basil groaned. He put his hands over his eyes and rocked to and fro.

Miss Marple said, "What did you do with the hearthrug?"

His reply came mechanically, "I put it in the dustbin."

Miss Marple clucked her tongue vexedly. "That was stupid—very stupid. People don't put good hearthrugs in dustbins. It had spangles in it from her dress, I suppose?"

"Yes, I couldn't get them out."

Dinah cried, "What are you talking about?"

Basil said sullenly, "Ask her. She seems to know all about it."

"I'll tell you what I think happened, if you like," said Miss Marple. "You can correct me, Mr. Blake, if I go wrong. I think that after having had a violent quarrel with your wife at a party and after having had, perhaps, rather too much—er—to drink, you drove down here. I don't know what time you arrived."

Basil Blake said sullenly, "About two in the morning. I meant to go up to town first; then, when I got to the suburbs, I changed my mind. I thought Dinah might come down here after me. So I drove down here. The place was all dark. I opened the door and turned on the light and I saw—and I saw—" He gulped and stopped.

Miss Marple went on, "You saw a girl lying on the hearthrug. A girl in a white evening dress, strangled. I don't know whether you recognized her then—"

Basil Blake shook his head violently. "I couldn't look at her after the first glance; her face was all blue, swollen; she'd been dead some time and she was there—in my living room!" He shuddered.

Miss Marple said gently, "You weren't, of course, quite yourself. You were in a fuddled state and your nerves are not good. You were, I think, panic-stricken. You didn't know what to do—"

"I thought Dinah might turn up any minute. And she'd find me there with a dead body—a girl's dead body—and she'd think I'd killed her. Then I got an idea. It seemed—I don't know why—a good idea at the time. I thought: 'I'll put her in old Bantry's library. Damned pompous old stick, always looking down his nose, sneering at me as artistic and effeminate. Serve the pompous old brute right,' I thought. 'He'll look a fool when a dead lovely is found on his hearthrug.'" He added with a pathetic eagerness to explain, "I was a bit drunk, you know, at the time. It really seemed positively amusing to me. Old Bantry with a dead blonde."

"Yes, yes," said Miss Marple. "Little Tommy Bond had very much the same idea. Rather a sensitive boy, with an inferiority complex, he said teacher was always picking on him. He put a frog in the clock and it jumped out at her. You were just the same," went on Miss Marple, "only, of course, bodies are more serious matters than frogs."

Basil groaned again. "By the morning I'd sobered up. I realized what I'd done. I was scared stiff. And then the police came here—another damned pompous ass of a chief constable. I was scared of him, and the only way I could hide it was by being abominably rude. In the middle of it all, Dinah drove up."

Dinah looked out of the window. She said, "There's a car driving up now. There are men in it."

"The police, I think," said Miss Marple.

Basil Blake got up. Suddenly he became quite calm and resolute. He even smiled. He said, "So I'm in for it, am I? All right, Dinah, sweet, keep your head. Get onto old Sims—he's the family lawyer—and go to mother and tell her about our marriage. She won't bite. And don't worry. I didn't do it. So it's bound to be all right, see, sweetheart?"

There was a tap on the cottage door. Basil called, "Come in."

Inspector Slack entered with another man. He said, "Mr. Basil Blake?"

"Yes."

"I have a warrant here for your arrest on the charge of murdering Ruby Keene on the night of September twentieth last. I warn you that anything you say may be used at your trial. You will please accompany me now. Full facilities will be given you for communicating with your solicitor."

Basil nodded. He looked at Dinah, but did not touch her. He said, "So long, Dinah."

Cool customer, thought Inspector Slack. He acknowledged the presence of Miss Marple with a half bow and a "Good morning," and thought to himself, *Smart old pussy; she's on to it. Good job we've got that hearthrug. That and finding out from the car-park man at the studio that he left that party at eleven instead of midnight. Don't think those friends of his meant to commit perjury. They were bottled, and Blake told 'em firmly the next day it was twelve o'clock when he left, and they believed him. Well, his goose is cooked good and proper. Mental, I expect. Broadmoor, not hanging. First the Reeves kid, probably strangled her, drove her out to the quarry, walked back into Danemouth, picked up his own car in some side lane, drove to this party, then back to Danemouth, brought Ruby Keene out here, strangled her, put her in old Bantry's library, then probably got the wind up about the car in the quarry, drove there, set it on fire and got back here. Mad—sex and blood lust—lucky this girl's escaped. What they call recurring mania, I expect.*

Alone with Miss Marple, Dinah Blake turned to her. She said, "I don't know who you are, but you've got to understand this: Basil didn't do it."

Miss Marple said, "I know he didn't. I know who did do it. But it's not going to be easy to prove. I've an idea that something you said just now may help. It gave me an idea—the connection I'd been trying to find. Now, what was it?"

CHAPTER TWENTY

"I'm home, Arthur!" declared Mrs. Bantry, announcing the fact like a royal proclamation as she flung open the study door.

Colonel Bantry immediately jumped up, kissed his wife and declared heartily, "Well, well, that's splendid!"

The colonel's words were unimpeachable, the manner very well done, but an affectionate wife of as many years' standing as Mrs. Bantry was not deceived. She said immediately, "Is anything the matter?"

"No, of course not, Dolly. What should be the matter?"

"Oh, I don't know," said Mrs. Bantry vaguely. "Things are so queer, aren't they?"

She threw off her coat as she spoke, and Colonel Bantry picked it up carefully and laid it across the back of the sofa. All exactly as usual, yet not as usual. Her husband, Mrs. Bantry thought, seemed to have shrunk. He looked thinner, stooped more, there were pouches under his eyes, and those eyes were not ready to meet hers. He went on to say, still with that affection of cheerfulness, "Well, how did you enjoy your time at Danemouth?"

"Oh, it was great fun. You ought to have come, Arthur."

"Couldn't get away, my dear. Lot of things to attend to here."

"Still, I think the change would have done you good. And you like the Jeffersons?"

"Yes, yes, poor fellow. Nice chap. All very sad."

"What have you been doing with yourself since I've been away?"

"Oh, nothing much; been over the farms, you know. Agreed that Anderson shall have a new roof. Can't patch it up any longer."

"How did the Radfordshire Council meeting go?"

"I—well, as a matter of fact, I didn't go."

"Didn't go? But you were taking the chair."

"Well, as a matter of fact, Dolly, seems there was some mistake about that. Asked me if I'd mind if Thompson took it instead."

"I see," said Mrs. Bantry. She peeled off a glove and threw it deliberately into the wastepaper basket. Her husband went to retrieve it and she stopped him, saying sharply, "Leave it. I hate gloves." Colonel Bentry glanced at her uneasily. Mrs. Bantry said sternly, "Did you go to dinner with the Duffs on Thursday?"

"Oh, that? It was put off. Their cook was ill."

"Stupid people," said Mrs. Bantry. She went on, "Did you go to the Naylors' yesterday?"

"I rang up and said I didn't feel up to it; hoped they'd excuse me. They quite understood."

"They did, did they?" said Mrs. Bantry grimly. She sat down by the desk and absent-mindedly picked up a pair of gardening scissors. With them she cut off the fingers, one by one, of her second glove.

"What are you doing, Dolly?"

"Feeling destructive," said Mrs. Bantry. She got up. "Where shall we sit after dinner, Arthur? In the library?"

"Well—er—I don't think so—eh? Very nice in here—or the drawing room."

"I think," said Mrs. Bantry, "that we'll sit in the library."

Her steady eyes met his. Colonel Bantry drew himself up to his full height. A sparkle came into his eye. He said, "You're right, my dear. We'll sit in the library!"

Mrs. Bantry put down the telephone receiver with a sigh of annoyance. She had rung up twice, and each time the answer had been the same. Miss Marple was out. Of a naturally impatient nature, Mrs. Bantry was never one to acquiesce in defeat. She rang up, in rapid succession, the vicarage, Mrs. Price Ridley, Miss Hartnell, Miss Wetherby and, as a last resort, the fishmonger, who, by reason of his advantageous geographical position, usually knew where everybody was in the village. The fishmonger was sorry, but he had not seen Miss Marple at all in the village that morning. She had not been on her usual round. "Where can the woman be?" demanded Mrs. Bantry impatiently, aloud.

There was a deferential cough behind her. The discreet Lorrimer murmured, "You were requiring Miss Marple, madam? I have just observed her approaching the house."

Mrs. Bantry rushed to the front door, flung it open and greeted Miss Marple breathlessly, "I've been trying to get you everywhere. Where have you been?" She glanced over her shoulder. Lorrimer had discreetly vanished. "Everything's too awful! People are beginning to cold-shoulder Arthur. He looks years older. We must do something, Jane. You must do something!"

Miss Marple said, "You needn't worry, Dolly," in a rather peculiar voice.

Colonel Bantry appeared from the study door. "Ah, Miss Marple. Good morning. Glad you've come. My wife's been ringing you up like a lunatic."

"I thought I'd better bring you the news," said Miss Marple as she followed Mrs. Bantry into the study.

"News?"

"Basil Blake has just been arrested for the murder of Ruby Keene."

"Basil Blake?" cried the colonel.

"But he didn't do it," said Miss Marple.

Colonel Bantry took no notice of this statement. It is doubtful if he even heard it. "Do you mean to say he strangled that girl and then brought her along and put her in my library?"

"He put her in your library," said Miss Marple, "but he didn't kill her."

"Nonsense. If he put her in my library, of course he killed her! The two things go together!"

"Not necessarily. He found her dead in his own cottage."

"A likely story," said the colonel derisively. "If you find a body—why, you ring up the police, naturally, if you're an honest man."

"Ah," said Miss Marple, "but we haven't all got such iron nerves as you have, Colonel Bantry. You belong to the old school. This younger generation is different."

"Got no stamina," said the colonel, repeating a well-worn opinion of his.

"Some of them," said Miss Marple, "have been through a bad time. I've heard a good deal about Basil. He did ARP work, you know, when he was only eighteen. He went into a burning house and brought out four children, one after another. He went back for a dog, although they told him it wasn't safe. The building fell in on him. They got him out, but his chest was badly crushed and he had to lie in plaster for a long time after that. That's when he got interested in designing."

"Oh!" The colonel coughed and blew his nose. "I—er—never knew that."

"He doesn't talk about it," said Miss Marple.

"Er—quite right. Proper spirit. Must be more in the young chap than I thought. Shows you ought to be careful in jumping to conclusions." Colonel Bantry looked ashamed. "But all the same"—his indignation revived—"what did he mean, trying to fasten a murder on me?"

"I don't think he saw it like that," said Miss Marple. "He thought of it more as a—as a joke. You see, he was rather under the influence of alcohol at the time."

"Bottled, was he?" said Colonel Bantry, with an Englishman's sympathy for alcoholic excess. "Oh, well, can't judge a fellow by what he does when he's drunk. When I was at Cambridge, I remember I put a certain utensil—well—well, never mind. Deuce of a row there was about it." He chuckled, then checked himself sternly. He looked at Miss Marple with eyes that were shrewd and appraising. He said, "You don't think he did the murder, eh?"

"I'm sure he didn't."

"And you think you know who did?"

Miss Marple nodded.

Mrs. Bantry, like an ecstatic Greek chorus, said, "Isn't she wonderful?" to an unhearing world.

"Well, who was it?"

Miss Marple said, "I was going to ask you to help me. I think if we went up to Somerset House we should have a very good idea."

CHAPTER TWENTY-ONE

Sir Henry's face was very grave. He said, "I don't like it."

"I am aware," said Miss Marple, "that it isn't what you call orthodox. But it is so important, isn't it, to be quite sure—to 'make assurance doubly sure,' as Shakespeare has it? I think, if Mr. Jefferson would agree—"

"What about Harper? Is he to be in on this?"

"It might be awkward for him to know too much. But there might be a hint from you. To watch certain persons—have them trailed, you know."

Sir Henry said slowly, "Yes, that would meet the case."

Superintendent Harper looked piercingly at Sir Henry Clithering. "Let's get this quite clear, sir. You're giving me a hint?"

Sir Henry said, "I'm informing you of what my friend has just informed me—he didn't tell me in confidence—that he purposes to visit a solicitor in Danemouth tomorrow for the purpose of making a new will."

The superintendent's bushy eyebrows drew downward over his steady eyes. He said, "Does Mr. Conway Jefferson propose to inform his son-in-law and daughter-in-law of that fact?"

"He intends to tell them about it this evening."

"I see." The superintendent tapped his desk with a penholder. He repeated again, "I see." Then the piercing eyes bored once more into the eyes of the other man. Harper said, "So you're not satisfied with the case against Basil Blake?"

"Are you?"

The superintendent's mustaches quivered. He said, "Is Miss Marple?"

The two men looked at each other. Then Harper said, "You can leave it to me. I'll have men detailed. There will be no funny business, I can promise you that."

Sir Henry said, "There is one more thing. You'd better see this." He unfolded a slip of paper and pushed it across the table.

This time the superintendent's calm deserted him. He whistled. "So that's it, is it? That puts an entirely different complexion on the matter. How did you come to dig up this?"

"Women," said Sir Henry, "are eternally interested in marriages."

"Especially," said the superintendent, "elderly single women."

Conway Jefferson looked up as his friend entered. His grim face relaxed into a smile. He said, "Well, I told 'em. They took it very well."

"What did you say?"

"Told 'em that, as Ruby was dead, I felt that the fifty thousand I'd originally left her should go to something that I could associate with her memory. It was to endow a hostel for young girls working as professional dancers in London. Damned silly way to leave your money—surprised they swallowed it—as though I'd do a thing like that." He added meditatively, "You know, I made a fool of myself over that girl. Must be turning into a silly old man. I can see it now. She was a pretty kid, but most of what I saw in her I put there myself. I pretended she was another Rosamund. Same coloring, you know. But not the same heart or mind. Hand me that paper; rather an interesting bridge problem."

Sir Henry went downstairs. He asked a question of the porter.

"Mr. Gaskell, sir? He's just gone off in his car. Had to go to London."

"Oh, I see. Is Mrs. Jefferson about?"

"Mrs. Jefferson, sir, has just gone up to bed."

Sir Henry looked into the lounge and through to the ballroom. In the lounge Hugo McLean was doing a crossword puzzle and frowning a good deal over it. In the ballroom, Josie was smiling valiantly into the face of a stout, perspiring man as her nimble feet avoided his destructive tread. The stout man was clearly enjoying his dance. Raymond, graceful and weary, was dancing with an anemic-looking girl with adenoids, dull brown hair and an expensive and exceedingly unbecoming dress. Sir Henry said under his breath, "And so to bed," and went upstairs.

It was three o'clock. The wind had fallen, the moon was shining over the quiet sea. In Conway Jefferson's room there was no sound except his own heavy breathing as he lay half propped up on pillows. There was no breeze to stir the curtains at the window, but they stirred. For a moment they parted and a figure was silhouetted against the moonlight. Then they fell back into place. Everything was quiet again, but there was someone else inside the room. Nearer and nearer to the bed the intruder stole. The deep breathing on the pillow did not relax. There was no sound, or hardly any sound. A finger and thumb were ready to pick up a fold of skin; in the other hand the hypodermic was ready. And then, suddenly, out of the shadows a hand came and closed over the hand that held the needle; the other arm held the figure in an iron grasp. An unemotional voice, the voice of the law, said, "No, you don't! I want that needle!" The light switched on, and from his pillows Conway Jefferson looked grimly at the murderer of Ruby Keene.

CHAPTER TWENTY-TWO

Sir Henry Clithering said, "Speaking as Watson, I want to know your methods, Miss Marple."

Superintendent Harper said, "I'd like to know what put you on to it first."

Colonel Melchett said, "You've done it again, by Jove, Miss Marple. I want to hear all about it from the beginning."

Miss Marple smoothed the pure silk of her best evening gown. She flushed and smiled and looked very selfconscious. She said, "I'm afraid you'll think my 'methods,' as Sir Henry calls them, are terribly amateurish. The truth is, you see, that most people—and I don't exclude policemen— are far too trusting for this wicked world. They believe what is told them. I never do. I'm afraid I always like to prove a thing for myself."

"That is the scientific attitude," said Sir Henry.

"In this case," continued Miss Marple, "certain things were taken for granted from the first, instead of just confining oneself to the facts. The facts, as I noted them, were that the victim was quite young and that she bit her nails and that her teeth stuck out a little—as young girls' so often do if not corrected in time with a plate—and children are very naughty about their plates and take them out when their elders aren't looking.

"But that is wandering from the point. Where was I? Oh, yes, looking down at the dead girl and feeling sorry, because it is always sad to see a young life cut short, and thinking that whoever had done it was a very wicked person. Of course it was all very confusing, her being found in Colonel Bantry's library, altogether too like a book to be true. In fact, it made the wrong pattern. It wasn't, you see, meant, which confused us a lot. The real idea had been to plant the body on poor young Basil Blake—a much more likely person—and his action in putting it in the colonel's library delayed things considerably and must have been a source of great annoyance to the real murderer. Originally, you see, Mr. Blake would have been the first object of suspicion. They'd have made inquiries at Danemouth, found he knew the girl, then found he had tied himself up with another girl, and they'd have assumed that Ruby came to blackmail him or something like that, and that he'd strangled her in a fit of rage. Just an ordinary, sordid, what I call nightclub type of crime!

"But that, of course, all went wrong, and interest became focused much too soon on the Jefferson family—to the great annoyance of a certain person.

"As I've told you, I've got a very suspicious mind. My nephew Raymond tells me, in fun, of course—that I have a mind like a sink. He says that most Victorians have. All I can say is that the Victorians knew a good deal about human nature. As I say, having this rather insanitary—or surely sanitary?—mind, I looked at once at the money angle of it. Two people stood to benefit by this girl's death—you couldn't get away from that. Fifty thousand pounds is a lot of money; especially when you are in financial difficulties, as both these people were. Of course they both seemed very nice, agreeable people; they didn't seem likely people, but one never can tell, can one?

"Mrs. Jefferson, for instance—everyone liked her. But it did seem clear that she had become very restless that summer and that she was tired of the life she led, completely dependent on her father-in-law. She knew, because the doctor had told her, that he couldn't live long, so that was all right—to put it callously—or it would have been all right if Ruby Keene hadn't come along. Mrs. Jefferson was passionately devoted to her son, and some women have a curious idea that crimes committed for the sake of their offspring are almost morally justified. I have come across that attitude once or twice in the village. 'Well, 'twas all for Daisy, you see, miss,' they say, and seem to think that that makes doubtful conduct quite all right. Very lax thinking.

"Mr. Mark Gaskell, of course, was a much more likely starter, if I may use such a sporting expression. He was a gambler and had not, I fancied, a very high moral code. But for certain reasons I was of the opinion that a woman was concerned in this crime.

"As I say, with my eye on motive the money angle seemed very suggestive. It was annoying, therefore, to find that both these people had alibis for the time when Ruby Keene, according to the medical evidence, had met her death. But soon afterward there came the discovery of the burnt-out car with Pamela Reeves' body in it, and then the whole thing leaped to the eye. The alibis, of course, were worthless.

"I now had two halves of the case, and both quite convincing, but they did not fit. There must be a connection, but I could not find it. The one person whom I knew to be concerned in the crime hadn't got a motive. It was stupid of me," said Miss Marple meditatively. "If it hadn't been for Dinah Lee I shouldn't have thought of it—the most obvious thing in the world. Somerset House! Marriage! It wasn't a question of only Mr. Gaskell or Mrs. Jefferson; there was the further possibility of marriage. If either of those two was married, or even was likely to marry, then the other party to the marriage contract was involved too. Raymond, for instance, might think he had a pretty good chance of marrying a rich wife. He had been very assiduous to Mrs. Jefferson, and it was his charm, I think, that awoke her from her long widowhood. She had been quite content just being a daughter to Mr. Jefferson. Like Ruth and Naomi—only Naomi, if you remember, took a lot of trouble to arrange a suitable marriage for Ruth.

"Besides Raymond, there was Mr. McLean. She liked him very much, and it seemed highly possible that she would marry him in the end. He wasn't well off and he was not far from Danemouth on the night in question. So, it seemed, didn't it," said Miss Marple, "as though anyone might have done it? But, of course, really, in my own mind, I knew. You couldn't get away, could you, from those bitten nails?"

"Nails?" said Sir Henry. "But she tore her nail and cut the others."

"Nonsense," said Miss Marple. "Bitten nails and closecut nails are quite different! Nobody could mistake them who knew anything about girls' nails—very ugly, bitten nails, as I always tell the girls in my class. Those nails, you see, were a fact. And they could only mean one thing. The body in Colonel Bantry's library wasn't Ruby Keene at all.

"And that brings you straight to the one person who must be concerned. Josie! Josie identified the body. She knew—she must have known—that it wasn't Ruby Keene's body. She said it was. She was puzzled—completely puzzled—at finding that body where it was. She practically betrayed that fact. Why? Because she knew—none better—where it ought to have been found! In Basil Blake's cottage. Who directed our attention to Basil? Josie, by saying to Raymond that Ruby might have been with the film man. And before that, by slipping a snapshot of him into Ruby's handbag. Josie! Josie, who was shrewd, practical, hard as nails and all out for money.

"Since the body wasn't the body of Ruby Keene, it must be the body of someone else. Of whom? Of the other girl who was also missing. Pamela Reeves! Ruby was eighteen, Pamela sixteen. They were both healthy, rather immature, but muscular girls. But why, I asked myself, all this hocus-pocus? There could be only one reason—to give certain persons an alibi. Who had alibis for the supposed time of Ruby Keene's death? Mark Gaskell, Mrs. Jefferson and Josie.

"It was really quite interesting, you know, tracing out the course of events, seeing exactly how the plan had worked out. Complicated and yet simple. First of all, the selection of the poor child, Pamela; the approach to her from the film angle. A screen test; of course the poor child couldn't resist it. Not when it was put up to her as plausibly as Mark Gaskell put it. She comes to the hotel, he is waiting for her, he takes her in by the side door and introduces her to Josie—one of their makeup experts! That poor child—it makes me quite sick to think of it! Sitting in Josie's bathroom while Josie bleaches her hair and makes up her face and varnishes her fingernails and toenails. During all this the drug was given. In an ice-cream soda, very likely. She goes off into a coma. I imagine that they put her into one of the empty rooms opposite. They were only cleaned once a week, remember.

"After dinner Mark Gaskell went out in his car—to the sea front, he said. That is when he took Pamela's body to the cottage, arranged it, dressed in one of Ruby's old dresses, on the hearthrug. She was still unconscious, but not dead, when he strangled her with the belt of the frock. Not nice, no, but I hope and pray she knew nothing about it. Really, I feel quite pleased to think of him hanging. . . . That must have been just after ten o'clock. Then back at top speed and into the lounge where Ruby Keene, still alive, was dancing her exhibition dance with Raymond. I should imagine that Josie had given Ruby instructions beforehand. Ruby was accustomed to doing what Josie told her. She was to change, go into Josie's room and wait. She, too, was drugged; probably in the after-dinner coffee. She was yawning, remember, when she talked to young Bartlett.

"Josie came up later with Raymond to 'look for her,' but nobody but Josie went into Josie's room. She probably finished the girl off then—with an injection, perhaps, or a blow on the back of the head. She went down, danced with Raymond, debated with the Jeffersons where Ruby could be and finally went up to bed. In the early hours of the morning she dressed the girl in Pamela's clothes, carried the body down the side stairs and out—she was a strong, muscular young woman—fetched George Bartlett's car, drove two miles to the quarry, poured petrol over the car and set it alight. Then she walked back to the hotel, probably timing her arrival there for eight or nine o'clock—up early in her anxiety about Ruby!"

"An intricate plot," said Colonel Melchett.

"Not more intricate than the steps of a dance," said Miss Marple.

"I suppose not."

"She was very thorough," said Miss Marple. "She even foresaw the discrepancy of the nails. That's why she managed to break one of Ruby's nails on her shawl. It made an excuse for pretending that Ruby had clipped her nails close."

Harper said, "Yes, she thought of everything. And the only real proof you had was a schoolgirl's bitten nails."

"More than that," said Miss Marple. "People will talk too much. Mark Gaskell talked too much. He was speaking of Ruby and he said, 'her teeth ran down her throat.' But the dead girl in Colonel Bantry's library had teeth that stuck out."

Conway Jefferson said rather grimly, "And was the last dramatic finale your idea, Miss Marple?"

"Well, it was, as a matter of fact. It's so nice to be sure, isn't it?"

"Sure is the word," said Conway Jefferson grimly.

"You see," said Miss Marple, "once those two knew that you were going to make a new will, they'd have to do something. They'd already committed two murders on account of the money. So they might as well commit a third. Mark, of course, must be absolutely clear, so he went off to London and established an alibi by dining at a restaurant with friends and going on to a nightclub. Josie was to do the work. They still wanted Ruby's death to be put down to Basil's account, so Mr. Jefferson's death must be thought due to his heart failing. There was digitalis, so the superintendent tells me, in the syringe. Any doctor would think death from heart trouble quite natural in the circumstances. Josie had loosened one of the stone balls on the balcony and she was going to let it crash down afterward. His death would be put down to the shock of the noise."

Melchett said, "Ingenious devil."

Sir Henry said, "So the third death you spoke of was to be Conway Jefferson?"

Miss Marple shook her head. "Oh, no, I meant Basil Blake. They'd have got him hanged if they could."

"Or shut up in Broadmoor," said Sir Henry.

Through the doorway floated Adelaide Jefferson. Hugo McLean followed her. The latter said, "I seem to have missed most of this! Haven't got the hang of it yet. What was Josie to Mark Gaskell?"

Miss Marple said, "His wife. They were married a year ago. They were keeping it dark until Mr. Jefferson died."

Conway Jefferson grunted. He said, "Always knew Rosamund had married a rotter. Tried not to admit it to myself. She was fond of him. Fond of a murderer! Well, he'll hang, as well as the woman. I'm glad he went to pieces and gave the show away."

Miss Marple said, "She was always the strong character. It was her plan throughout. The irony of it is that she got the girl down here herself, never dreaming that she would take Mr. Jefferson's fancy and ruin all her own prospects."

Jefferson said, "Poor lass. Poor little Ruby."

Adelaide laid her hand on his shoulder and pressed it gently. She looked almost beautiful tonight. She said, with a little catch in her breath, "I want to tell you something, Jeff. At once. I'm going to marry Hugo."

Conway Jefferson looked up at her for a moment. He said gruffly, "About time you married again. Congratulations to you both. By the way, Addie, I'm making a new will tomorrow."

She nodded. "Oh, yes. I know."

Jefferson said, "No, you don't. I'm settling ten thousand pounds on you. Everything else goes to Peter when I die. How does that suit you, my girl?"

"Oh, Jeff!" Her voice broke. "You're wonderful!"

"He's a nice lad. I'd like to see a good deal of him in—in the time I've got left."

"Oh, you shall!"

"Got a great feeling for crime, Peter has," said Conway Jefferson meditatively. "Not only has he got the fingernail of the murdered girl—one of the murdered girls, anyway—but he was lucky enough to have a bit of Josie's shawl caught in with the nail. So he's got a souvenir of the murderess too! That makes him very happy!"

Hugo and Adelaide passed by the ballroom. Raymond came up to them. Adelaide said rather quickly, "I must tell you my news. We're going to be married."

The smile on Raymond's face was perfect—a brave, pensive smile. "I hope," he said, ignoring Hugo and gazing into her eyes, "that you will be very, very happy."

They passed on and Raymond stood looking after them. "A nice woman," he said to himself. "A very nice woman. And she would have had money too. The trouble I took to mug up that bit about the Devonshire Starrs. Oh, well, my luck's out. Dance, dance, little gentleman!"

And Raymond returned to the ballroom.